Sappho, Clemence Dane, Sheridan Le Fanu

Sapphic Violets: Lesbian Classics Boxed Set

e-artnow 2022

Sappho, Clemence Dane, Sheridan Le Fanu

Sapphic Violets: Lesbian Classics Boxed Set

Sappho, Regiment of Women, Mrs. Dalloway & Carmilla

Translator: Bliss Carman

e-artnow, 2022
Contact: info@e-artnow.org

ISBN 978-80-273-4265-5

Contents

Sappho: One Hundred Lyrics	15
INTRODUCTION	16
I	18
II	19
III	20
IV	21
V	23
VI	24
VII	25
VIII	26
IX	27
X	28
XI	29
XII	30
XIII	31
XIV	32
XV	33
XVI	34
XVII	35
XVIII	36
XIX	37
XX	38
XXI	39
XXII	40
XXIII	41
XXIV	42
XXV	43
XXVI	44
XXVII	45
XXVIII	46
XXIX	47
XXX	48
XXXI	49
XXXII	51
XXXIII	52
XXXIV	53
XXXV	54
XXXVI	55

XXXVII	56
XXXVIII	57
XXXIX	58
XL	59
XLI	60
XLII	61
XLIII	62
XLIV	63
XLV	64
XLVI	65
XLVII	66
XLVIII	67
XLIX	68
L	69
LI	70
LII	71
LIII	72
LIV	73
LV	74
LVI	75
LVII	76
LVIII	77
LIX	78
LX	79
LXI	80
LXII	81
LXIII	82
LXIV	83
LXV	84
LXVI	85
LXVII	86
LXVIII	87
LXIX	88
LXX	89
LXXI	90
LXXII	91
LXXIII	92
LXXIV	93
LXXV	94
LXXVI	95

LXXVII	96
LXXVIII	97
LXXIX	98
LXXX	99
LXXXI	100
LXXXII	101
LXXXIII	102
LXXXIV	103
LXXXV	104
LXXXVI	105
LXXXVII	106
LXXXVIII	107
LXXXIX	108
XC	110
XCI	111
XCII	112
XCIII	113
XCIV	114
XCV	115
XCVI	117
XCVII	119
XCVIII	120
XCIX	121
C	122
EPILOGUE	124
Regiment of Women	127
CHAPTER I	128
CHAPTER II	132
CHAPTER III	135
CHAPTER IV	140
CHAPTER V	142
CHAPTER VI	150
CHAPTER VII	154
CHAPTER VIII	158
CHAPTER IX	163
CHAPTER X	168
CHAPTER XI	172
CHAPTER XII	174
CHAPTER XIII	183
CHAPTER XIV	189

CHAPTER XV	192
CHAPTER XVI	200
CHAPTER XVII	204
CHAPTER XVIII	210
CHAPTER XIX	213
CHAPTER XX	217
CHAPTER XXI	221
CHAPTER XXII	224
CHAPTER XXIII	230
CHAPTER XXIV	233
CHAPTER XXV	236
CHAPTER XXVI	240
CHAPTER XXVII	246
CHAPTER XXVIII	251
CHAPTER XXIX	253
CHAPTER XXX	256
CHAPTER XXXI	260
CHAPTER XXXII	266
CHAPTER XXXIII	269
CHAPTER XXXIV	275
CHAPTER XXXV	280
CHAPTER XXXVI	285
CHAPTER XXXVII	288
CHAPTER XXXVIII	293
CHAPTER XXXIX	296
CHAPTER XL	301
CHAPTER XLI	307
CHAPTER XLII	311
CHAPTER XLIII	317
CHAPTER XLIV	321
CHAPTER XLV	325
CHAPTER XLVI	326
CHAPTER XLVII	330
Carmilla	335
Prologue	336
Chapter 1. An Early Fright	337
Chapter 2. A Guest	340
Chapter 3. We Compare Notes	344
Chapter 4. Her Habits — A Saunter	348

Chapter 5. A Wonderful Likeness	353
Chapter 6. A Very Strange Agony	355
Chapter 7. Descending	357
Chapter 8. Search	360
Chapter 9. The Doctor	362
Chapter 10. Bereaved	365
Chapter 11. The Story	367
Chapter 12. A Petition	370
Chapter 13. The Woodman	373
Chapter 14. The Meeting	376
Chapter 15. Ordeal and Execution	379
Conclusion	381
Mrs. Dalloway	383

Sappho: One Hundred Lyrics

by Bliss Carman

INTRODUCTION

The Poetry Of Sappho. —If all the poets and all the lovers of poetry should be asked to name the most precious of the priceless things which time has wrung in tribute from the triumphs of human genius, the answer which would rush to every tongue would be "The Lost Poems of Sappho." These we know to have been jewels of a radiance so imperishable that the broken gleams of them still dazzle men's eyes, whether shining from the two small brilliants and the handful of star-dust which alone remain to us, or reflected merely from the adoration of those poets of old time who were so fortunate as to witness their full glory.

For about two thousand five hundred years Sappho has held her place as not only the supreme poet of her sex, but the chief lyrist of all lyrists. Every one who reads acknowledges her fame, concedes her supremacy; but to all except poets and Hellenists her name is a vague and uncomprehended splendour, rising secure above a persistent mist of misconception. Beyond her poetry, she is well known as a symbol of love and desire between women, with the English words sapphic and lesbian being derived from her own name and the name of her home island respectively.

Sappho was at the height of her career about six centuries before Christ, at a period when lyric poetry was peculiarly esteemed and cultivated at the centres of Greek life. Among the *Molic* peoples of the Isles, in particular, it had been carried to a high pitch of perfection, and its forms had become the subject of assiduous study. Its technique was exact, complex, extremely elaborate, minutely regulated; yet the essential fires of sincerity, spontaneity, imagination and passion were flaming with undiminished heat behind the fixed forms and restricted measures. The very metropolis of this lyric realm was Mitylene of Lesbos, where, amid the myrtle groves and temples, the sunlit silver of the fountains, the hyacinth gardens by a soft blue sea, Beauty and Love in their young warmth could fuse the most rigid forms to fluency. Here Sappho was the acknowledged queen of song-revered, studied, imitated, served, adored by a little court of attendants and disciples, loved and hymned by Alcaeus, and acclaimed by her fellow craftsmen throughout Greece as the wonder of her age. That all the tributes of her contemporaries show reverence not less for her personality than for her genius is sufficient answer to the calumnies with which the ribald jesters of that later period, the corrupt and shameless writers of Athenian comedy, strove to defile her fame. It is sufficient, also, to warrant our regarding the picturesque but scarcely dignified story of her vain pursuit of Phaon and her frenzied leap from the Cliff of Leucas as nothing more than a poetic myth, reminiscent, perhaps, of the myth of Aphrodite and Adonis-who is, indeed, called Phaon in some versions. The story is further discredited by the fact that we find no mention of it in Greek literature-even among those Attic comedians who would have clutched at it so eagerly and given it so gross a turn-till a date more than two hundred years after Sappho's death. It is a myth which has begotten some exquisite literature, both in prose and verse, from Ovid's famous epistle to Addison's gracious fantasy and some impassioned and imperishable dithyrambs of Mr. Swinburne; but one need not accept the story as a fact in order to appreciate the beauties which flowered out from its coloured unreality.

The applause of contemporaries, however, is not always justified by the verdict of after-times, and does not always secure an immortality of renown. The fame of Sappho has a more stable basis. Her work was in the world's possession for not far short of a thousand years —a thousand years of changing tastes, searching criticism, and familiar use. It had to endure the wear and tear of quotation, the commonizing touch of the school and the market-place. And under this test its glory grew ever more and more conspicuous. Through those thousand years poets and critics vied with one another in proclaiming her verse the one unmatched exemplar of lyric art. Such testimony, even though not a single fragment remained to us from which to judge her poetry for ourselves, might well convince us that the supremacy acknowledged by those who knew all the triumphs of the genius of old Greece was beyond the assault of any modern rival. We might safely accept the sustained judgment of a thousand years of Greece.

Fortunately for us, however, two small but incomparable odes and a few scintillating fragments have survived, quoted and handed down in the eulogies of critics and expositors. In these the wisest minds, the greatest poets, and the most inspired teachers of modern days have found justification for the unanimous verdict of antiquity. The tributes of Addison, Tennyson, and others, the throbbing paraphrases and ecstatic interpretations of Swinburne, are too well known to call for special comment in this brief note; but the concise summing up of her genius by Mr. Watts-Dunton in his remarkable essay on poetry is so convincing and illuminating that it seems to demand quotation here: "Never before these songs were sung, and never since did the human soul, in the grip of a fiery passion, utter a cry like hers; and, from the executive point of view, in directness, in lucidity, in that high, imperious verbal economy which only nature can teach the artist, she has no equal, and none worthy to take the place of second."

The poems of Sappho so mysteriously lost to us seem to have consisted of at least nine books of odes, together with *epithalamia*, epigrams, elegies, and monodies. Of the several theories which have been advanced to account for their disappearance, the most plausible seems to be that which represents them as having been burned at Byzantium in the year 380 Anno Domini, by command of Gregory Nazianzen, in order that his own poems might be studied in their stead and the morals of the people thereby improved. Of the efficacy of this act no means of judging has come down to us.

In recent years there has arisen a great body of literature upon the subject of Sappho, most of it the abstruse work of scholars writing for scholars. But the gist of it all, together with the minutest surviving fragment of her verse, has been made available to the general reader in English by Mr. Henry T. Wharton, in whose altogether admirable little volume we find all that is known and the most apposite of all that has been said up to the present day about

> "Love's priestess, mad with pain and joy of song,
> Song's priestess, mad with joy and pain of love."

Perhaps the most perilous and the most alluring venture in the whole field of poetry is that which Mr. Carman has undertaken in attempting to give us in English verse those lost poems of Sappho of which fragments have survived. The task is obviously not one of translation or of paraphrasing, but of imaginative and, at the same time, interpretive construction. It is as if a sculptor of to-day were to set himself, with reverence, and trained craftsmanship, and studious familiarity with the spirit, technique, and atmosphere of his subject, to restore some statues of Polyclitus or Praxiteles of which he had but a broken arm, a foot, a knee, a finger upon which to build. Mr. Carman's method, apparently, has been to imagine each lost lyric as discovered, and then to translate it; for the indefinable flavour of the translation is maintained throughout, though accompanied by the fluidity and freedom of purely original work.

C.G.D. ROBERTS.

> Now to please my little friend
> I must make these notes of spring,
> With the soft south-west wind in them
> And the marsh notes of the frogs.

> I must take a gold-bound pipe,
> And outmatch the bubbling call
> From the beechwoods in the sunlight,
> From the meadows in the rain.

I

Cyprus, Paphos, or Panormus
May detain thee with their splendour
Of oblations on thine altars,
O imperial Aphrodite.

Yet do thou regard, with pity   5
For a nameless child of passion,
This small unfrequented valley
By the sea, O sea-born mother.

II

What shall we do, Cytherea?
Lovely Adonis is dying.
Ah, but we mourn him!

Will he return when the Autumn
Purples the earth, and the sunlight 5
Sleeps in the vineyard?

Will he return when the Winter
Huddles the sheep, and Orion
Goes to his hunting?

Ah, but thy beauty, Adonis, 10
With the soft spring and the south wind,
Love and desire!

III

Power and beauty and knowledge —
Pan, Aphrodite, or Hermes —
Whom shall we life-loving mortals
Serve and be happy?

Lo now, your garlanded altars, 5
Are they not goodly with flowers?
Have ye not honour and pleasure
In lovely Lesbos?

Will ye not, therefore, a little
Hearten, impel, and inspire 10
One who adores, with a favour
Threefold in wonder?

IV

O Pan of the evergreen forest,
Protector of herds in the meadows,
Helper of men at their toiling —
Tillage and harvest and herding —
How many times to frail mortals 5
Hast thou not hearkened!

Now even I come before thee
With oil and honey and wheat-bread,
Praying for strength and fulfilment
Of human longing, with purpose 10
Ever to keep thy great worship
Pure and undarkened.

* * * * *

O Hermes, master of knowledge,
Measure and number and rhythm,
Worker of wonders in metal, 15
Moulder of malleable music,
So often the giver of secret
Learning to mortals!

Now even I, a fond woman,
Frail and of small understanding, 20
Yet with unslakable yearning
Greatly desiring wisdom,
Come to the threshold of reason
And the bright portals.

* * * * *

And thou, sea-born Aphrodite, 25
In whose beneficent keeping
Earth, with her infinite beauty,
Colour and fashion and fragrance,
Glows like a flower with fervour
Where woods are vernal! 30

Touch with thy lips and enkindle
This moon-white delicate body,
Drench with the dew of enchantment
This mortal one, that I also
Grow to the measure of beauty 35
Fleet yet eternal.

V

O Aphrodite,
God-born and deathless,
Break not my spirit
With bitter anguish:
Thou wilful empress, 5
I pray thee, hither!

As once aforetime
Well thou didst hearken
To my voice far off—
Listen, and leaving 10
Thy father's golden
House in yoked chariot,

Come, thy fleet sparrows
Beating the mid-air
Over the dark earth. 15
Suddenly near me,
Smiling, immortal,
Thy bright regard asked

What had befallen—
Why I had called thee —20
What my mad heart then
Most was desiring.
"What fair thing wouldst thou
Lure now to love thee?

"Who wrongs thee, Sappho? 25
If now she flies thee,
Soon shall she follow; —
Scorning thy gifts now,
Soon be the giver; —
And a loth loved one 30

"Soon be the lover."
So even now, too,
Come and release me
From mordant love pain,
And all my heart's will 35
Help me accomplish!

VI

Peer of the gods he seems,
Who in thy presence
Sits and hears close to him
Thy silver speech-tones
And lovely laughter. 5

Ah, but the heart flutters
Under my bosom,
When I behold thee
Even a moment;
Utterance leaves me; 10

My tongue is useless;
A subtle fire
Runs through my body;
My eyes are sightless,
And my ears ringing; 15

I flush with fever,
And a strong trembling
Lays hold upon me;
Paler than grass am I,
Half dead for madness. 20

Yet must I, greatly
Daring, adore thee,
As the adventurous
Sailor makes seaward
For the lost sky-line 25

And undiscovered
Fabulous islands,
Drawn by the lure of
Beauty and summer
And the sea's secret. 30

VII

The Cyprian came to thy cradle,
When thou wast little and small,
And said to the nurse who rocked thee
"Fear not thou for the child:

"She shall be kindly favoured, 5
And fair and fashioned well,
As befits the Lesbian maidens
And those who are fated to love."

Hermes came to thy cradle,
Resourceful, sagacious, serene, 10
And said, "The girl must have knowledge,
To lend her freedom and poise.

Naught will avail her beauty,
If she have not wit beside.
She shall be Hermes' daughter, 15
Passing wise in her day."

Great Pan came to thy cradle,
With calm of the deepest hills,
And smiled, "They have forgotten
The veriest power of life. 20

"To kindle her shapely beauty,
And illumine her mind withal,
I give to the little person
The glowing and craving soul."

VIII

Aphrodite of the foam,
Who hast given all good gifts,
And made Sappho at thy will
Love so greatly and so much,

Ah, how comes it my frail heart 5
Is so fond of all things fair,
I can never choose between
Gorgo and Andromeda?

IX

Nay, but always and forever
Like the bending yellow grain,
Or quick water in a channel,
Is the heart of man.

Comes the unseen breath in power 5
Like a great wind from the sea,
And we bow before his coming,
Though we know not why.

X

Let there be garlands, Dica,
Around thy lovely hair.
And supple sprays of blossom
Twined by thy soft hands.

Whoso is crowned with flowers 5
Has favour with the gods,
Who have no kindly eyes
For the ungarlanded.

XI

When the Cretan maidens
Dancing up the full moon
Round some fair new altar,
Trample the soft blossoms of fine grass,

There is mirth among them. 5
Aphrodite's children
Ask her benediction
On their bridals in the summer night.

XII

In a dream I spoke with the Cyprus-born,
And said to her,
"Mother of beauty, mother of joy,
Why hast thou given to men

"This thing called love, like the ache of a wound 5
In beauty's, side,
To burn and throb and be quelled for an hour
And never wholly depart?"

And the daughter of Cyprus said to me,
"Child of the earth, 10
Behold, all things are born and attain,
But only as they desire —

"The sun that is strong, the gods that are wise,
The loving heart,
Deeds and knowledge and beauty and joy — 15
But before all else was desire."

XIII

Sleep thou in the bosom
Of the tender comrade,
While the living water
Whispers in the well-run,
And the oleanders 5
Glimmer in the moonlight.

Soon, ah, soon the shy birds
Will be at their fluting,
And the morning planet
Rise above the garden; 10
For there is a measure
Set to all things mortal.

XIV

Hesperus, bringing together
All that the morning star scattered —

Sheep to be folded in twilight,

   Children for mothers to fondle —

Me too will bring to the dearest, 5
Tenderest breast in all Lesbos.

XV

In the grey olive-grove a small brown bird
Had built her nest and waited for the spring.
But who could tell the happy thought that came
To lodge beneath my scarlet tunic's fold?

All day long now is the green earth renewed 5
With the bright sea-wind and the yellow blossoms.
From the cool shade I hear the silver plash
Of the blown fountain at the garden's end.

XVI

In the apple boughs the coolness
Murmurs, and the grey leaves flicker
Where sleep wanders.

In this garden all the hot noon
I await thy fluttering footfall 5
Through the twilight.

XVII

Pale rose leaves have fallen
In the fountain water;
And soft reedy flute-notes
Pierce the sultry quiet.

But I wait and listen, 5
Till the trodden gravel
Tells me, all impatience,
It is Phaon's footstep.

XVIII

The courtyard of her house is wide
And cool and still when day departs.
Only the rustle of leaves is there
And running water.

And then her mouth, more delicate 5
Than the frail wood-anemone,
Brushes my cheek, and deeper grow
The purple shadows.

XIX

There is a medlar-tree
Growing in front of my lover's house,
And there all day
The wind makes a pleasant sound.

And when the evening comes, 5
We sit there together in the dusk,
And watch the stars
Appear in the quiet blue.

XX

I behold Arcturus going westward
Down the crowded slope of night-dark azure,
While the Scorpion with red Antares
Trails along the sea-line to the southward.

From the ilex grove there comes soft laughter —5
My companions at their glad love-making —
While that curly-headed boy from Naxos
With his jade flute marks the purple quiet.

XXI

Softly the first step of twilight
Falls on the darkening dial,
One by one kindle the lights
In Mitylene.

Noises are hushed in the courtyard, 5
The busy day is departing,
Children are called from their games —
Herds from their grazing.

And from the deep-shadowed angles
Comes the soft murmur of lovers, 10
Then through the quiet of dusk
Bright sudden laughter.

From the hushed street, through the portal,
Where soon my lover will enter,
Comes the pure strain of a flute 15
Tender with passion.

XXII

Once you lay upon my bosom,
While the long blue-silver moonlight
Walked the plain, with that pure passion
All your own.

Now the moon is gone, the Pleiads 5
Gone, the dead of night is going;
Slips the hour, and on my bed
I lie alone.

XXIII

I loved thee, Atthis, in the long ago,
When the great oleanders were in flower
In the broad herded meadows full of sun.
And we would often at the fall of dusk
Wander together by the silver stream, 5
When the soft grass-heads were all wet with dew,
And purple-misted in the fading light.
And joy I knew and sorrow at thy voice,
And the superb magnificence of love —
The loneliness that saddens solitude, 10
And the sweet speech that makes it durable —
The bitter longing and the keen desire,
The sweet companionship through quiet days
In the slow ample beauty of the world,
And the unutterable glad release 15
Within the temple of the holy night.
O Atthis, how I loved thee long ago
In that fair perished summer by the sea!

XXIV

I shall be ever maiden,
If thou be not my lover,
And no man shall possess me
Henceforth and forever.

But thou alone shalt gather 5
This fragile flower of beauty —
To crush and keep the fragrance
Like a holy incense.

Thou only shalt remember
This love of mine, or hallow 10
The coming years with gladness,
Calm and pride and passion.

XXV

It was summer when I found you
In the meadow long ago —
And the golden vetch was growing
By the shore.

Did we falter when love took us 5
With a gust of great desire?
Does the barley bid the wind wait
In his course?

XXVI

I recall thy white gown, cinctured
With a linen belt, whereon
Violets were wrought, and scented
With strange perfumes out of Egypt.

And I know thy foot was covered 5
With fair Lydian broidered straps;
And the petals from a rose-tree
Fell within the marble basin.

XXVII

Lover, art thou of a surety
Not a learner of the wood-god?
Has the madness of his music
Never touched thee?

Ah, thou dear and godlike mortal,   5
If Pan takes thee for his pupil,
Make me but another Syrinx
For that piping.

XXVIII

With your head thrown backward
In my arm's safe hollow,
And your face all rosy
With the mounting fervour;

While the grave eyes greaten 5
With the wise new wonder,
Swimming in a love-mist
Like the haze of Autumn;

From that throat, the throbbing
Nightingale's for pleading, 10
Wayward, soft, and welling
Inarticulate love-notes,

Come the words that bubble
Up through broken laughter,
Sweeter than spring-water, 15
"Gods, I am so happy!"

XXIX

Ah, what am I but a torrent,
Headstrong, impetuous, broken,
Like the spent clamour of waters
In the blue canyon?

Ah, what art thou but a fern-frond, 5
Wet with blown spray from the river,
Diffident, lovely, sequestered,
Frail on the rock-ledge?

Yet, are we not for one brief day,
While the sun sleeps on the mountain, 10
Wild-hearted lover and loved one,
Safe in Pan's keeping?

XXX

Love shakes my soul, like a mountain wind
Falling upon the trees,
When they are swayed and whitened and bowed
As the great gusts will.

I know why Daphne sped through the grove 5
When the bright god came by,
And shut herself in the laurel's heart
For her silent doom.

Love fills my heart, like my lover's breath
Filling the hollow flute, 10
Till the magic wood awakes and cries
With remembrance and joy.

Ah, timid Syrinx, do I not know
Thy tremor of sweet fear?
For a beautiful and imperious player 15
Is the lord of life.

XXXI

Love, let the wind cry
On the dark mountain,
Bending the ash-trees
And the tall hemlocks,
With the great voice of 5
Thunderous legions,
How I adore thee.

Let the hoarse torrent
In the blue canyon,
Murmuring mightily 10
Out of the grey mist
Of primal chaos,
Cease not proclaiming
How I adore thee.

Let the long rhythm 15
Of crunching rollers,
Breaking and bellowing
On the white seaboard,
Titan and tireless,
Tell, while the world stands, 20
How I adore thee.

Love, let the clear call
Of the tree-cricket,
Frailest of creatures,
Green as the young grass, 25
Mark with his trilling
Resonant bell-note,
How I adore thee.

Let the glad lark-song
Over the meadow, 30
That melting lyric
Of molten silver,
Be for a signal
To listening mortals,
How I adore thee. 35

But more than all sounds,
Surer, serener,

Fuller with passion
And exultation,
Let the hushed whisper 40
In thine own heart say,
How I adore thee.

XXXII

Heart of mine, if all the altars
Of the ages stood before me,
Not one pure enough nor sacred
Could I find to lay this white, white
Rose of love upon. 5

I who am not great enough to
Love thee with this mortal body
So impassionate with ardour,
But oh, not too small to worship
While the sun shall shine —10

I would build a fragrant temple
To thee, in the dark green forest,
Of red cedar and fine sandal,
And there love thee with sweet service
All my whole life long. 15

I would freshen it with flowers,
And the piney hill-wind through it
Should be sweetened with soft fervours
Of small prayers in gentle language
Thou wouldst smile to hear. 20

And a tinkling Eastern wind-bell,
With its fluttering inscription,
From the rafters with bronze music
Should retard the quiet fleeting
Of uncounted hours. 25

And my hero, while so human,
Should be even as the gods are,
In that shrine of utter gladness,
With the tranquil stars above it
And the sea below. 30

XXXIII

Never yet, love, in earth's lifetime,
Hath any cunningest minstrel
Told the one seventh of wisdom,
Ravishment, ecstasy, transport,
Hid in the hue of the hyacinth's 5
Purple in springtime.

Not in the lyre of Orpheus,
Not in the songs of Musaeus,
Lurked the unfathomed bewitchment
Wrought by the wind in the grasses, 10
Held by the rote of the sea-surf,
In early summer.

Only to exquisite lovers,
Fashioned for beauty's fulfilment,
Mated as rhythm to reed-stop 15
Whence the wild music is moulded,
Ever appears the full measure
Of the world's wonder.

XXXIV

"Who was Atthis?" men shall ask,
When the world is old, and time
Has accomplished without haste
The strange destiny of men.

Haply in that far-off age 5
One shall find these silver songs,
With their human freight, and guess
What a lover Sappho was.

XXXV

When the great pink mallow
Blossoms in the marshland,
Full of lazy summer
And soft hours,

Then I hear the summons 5
Not a mortal lover
Ever yet resisted,
Strange and far.

In the faint blue foothills,
Making magic music, 10
Pan is at his love-work
On the reeds.

I can guess the heart-stop,
Fall and lull and sequence,
Full of grief for Syrinx 15
Long ago.

Then the crowding madness,
Wild and keen and tender,
Trembles with the burden
Of great joy. 20

Nay, but well I follow,
All unskilled, that fluting.
Never yet was reed-nymph
Like to thee.

XXXVI

When I pass thy door at night
I a benediction breathe:
"Ye who have the sleeping world
In your care,

"Guard the linen sweet and cool, 5
Where a lovely golden head
With its dreams of mortal bliss
Slumbers now!"

XXXVII

Well I found you in the twilit garden,
Laid a lover's hand upon your shoulder,
And we both were made aware of loving
Past the reach of reason to unravel,
Or the much desiring heart to follow. 5

There we heard the breath among the grasses
And the gurgle of soft-running water,
Well contented with the spacious starlight,
The cool wind's touch and the deep blue distance,
Till the dawn came in with golden sandals. 10

XXXVIII

Will not men remember us
In the days to come hereafter —
Thy warm-coloured loving beauty
And my love for thee?

Thou, the hyacinth that grows 5
By a quiet-running river;
I, the watery reflection
And the broken gleam.

XXXIX

I grow weary of the foreign cities,
The sea travel and the stranger peoples.
Even the clear voice of hardy fortune
Dares me not as once on brave adventure.

For the heart of man must seek and wander, 5
Ask and question and discover knowledge;
Yet above all goodly things is wisdom,
And love greater than all understanding.

So, a mariner, I long for land-fall —
When a darker purple on the sea-rim, 10
O'er the prow uplifted, shall be Lesbos
And the gleaming towers of Mitylene.

XL

Ah, what detains thee, Phaon,
So long from Mitylene,
Where now thy restless lover
Wearies for thy coming?

A fever burns me, Phaon; 5
My knees quake on the threshold,
And all my strength is loosened,
Slack with disappointment.

But thou wilt come, my Phaon,
Back from the sea like morning, 10
To quench in golden gladness
The ache of parted lovers.

XLI

Phaon, O my lover,
What should so detain thee,

Now the wind comes walking
Through the leafy twilight?

All the plum-leaves quiver 5
With the coolth and darkness,

After their long patience
In consuming ardour.

And the moving grasses
Have relief; the dew-drench 10

Comes to quell the parching
Ache of noon they suffered.

I alone of all things
Fret with unsluiced fire.

And there is no quenching 15

In the night for Sappho,

Since her lover Phaon
Leaves her unrequited.

XLII

O heart of insatiable longing,
What spell, what enchantment allures thee
Over the rim of the world
With the sails of the sea-going ships?

And when the rose-petals are scattered 5
At dead of still noon on the grass-plot,
What means this passionate grief—
This infinite ache of regret?

XLIII

Surely somehow, in some measure,
There will be joy and fulfilment —
Cease from this throb of desire —
Even for Sappho!

Surely some fortunate hour 5
Phaon will come, and his beauty
Be spent like water to plenish
Need of that beauty!

Where is the breath of Poseidon,
Cool from the sea-floor with evening? 10
Why are Selene's white horses
So long arriving?

XLIV

O but my delicate lover,
Is she not fair as the moonlight?
Is she not supple and strong
For hurried passion?

Has not the god of the green world, 5
In his large tolerant wisdom,
Filled with the ardours of earth
Her twenty summers?

Well did he make her for loving;
Well did he mould her for beauty; 10
Gave her the wish that is brave
With understanding.

"O Pan, avert from this maiden
Sorrow, misfortune, bereavement,
Harm, and unhappy regret," 15
Prays one fond mortal.

XLV

Softer than the hill-fog to the forest
Are the loving hands of my dear lover,
When she sleeps beside me in the starlight
And her beauty drenches me with rest.

As the quiet mist enfolds the beech-trees, 5
Even as she dreams her arms enfold me,
Half awaking with a hundred kisses
On the scarlet lily of her mouth.

XLVI

I seek and desire,
Even as the wind
That travels the plain
And stirs in the bloom
Of the apple-tree. 5

I wander through life,
With the searching mind
That is never at rest,
Till I reach the shade
Of my lover's door. 10

XLVII

Like torn sea-kelp in the drift
Of the great tides of the sea,
Carried past the harbour-mouth
To the deep beyond return,

I am buoyed and borne away
On the loveliness of earth,
Little caring, save for thee,
Past the portals of the night.

XLVIII

Fine woven purple linen
I bring thee from Phocaea,
That, beauty upon beauty,
A precious gift may cover
The lap where I have lain. 5

And a gold comb, and girdle,
And trinkets of white silver,
And gems are in my sea-chest,
Lest poor and empty-handed
Thy lover should return. 10

And I have brought from Tyre
A Pan-flute stained vermilion,
Wherein the gods have hidden
Love and desire and longing,
Which I shall loose for thee. 15

XLIX

When I am home from travel,
My eager foot will stay not
Until I reach the threshold
Where I went forth from thee.

And there, as darkness gathers 5
In the rose-scented garden,
The god who prospers music
Shall give me skill to play.

And thou shalt hear, all startled,
A flute blown in the twilight, 10
With the soft pleading magic
The green wood heard of old.

Then, lamp in hand, thy beauty
In the rose-marble entry!
And unreluctant Hermes 15
Shall give me words to say.

L

When I behold the pharos shine
And lay a path along the sea,
How gladly I shall feel the spray,
Standing upon the swinging prow;

And question of my pilot old, 5
How many watery leagues to sail
Ere we shall round the harbour reef
And anchor off the wharves of home!

LI

Is the day long,
O Lesbian maiden,
And the night endless
In thy lone chamber
In Mitylene? 5

All the bright day,
Until welcome evening
When the stars kindle
Over the harbour,
What tasks employ thee? 10

Passing the fountain
At golden sundown,
One of the home-going
Traffickers, hast thou
Thought of thy lover? 15

Nay, but how far
Too brief will the night be,
When I returning
To the dear portal
Hear my own heart beat! 20

LII

Lo, on the distance a dark blue ravine,
A fold in the mountainous forests of fir,
Cleft from the sky-line sheer down to the shore!

Above are the clouds and the white, pealing gulls,
At its foot is the rough broken foam of the sea, 5
With ever anon the long deep muffled roar —
A sigh from the fitful great heart of the world.

Then inland just where the small meadow begins,
Well bulwarked with boulders that jut in the tide,
Lies safe beyond storm-beat the harbour in sun. 10

See where the black fishing-boats, each at its buoy,
Ride up on the swell with their dare-danger prows,
To sight o'er the sea-rim what venture may come!

And look, where the narrow white streets of the town
Leap up from the blue water's edge to the wood, 15
Scant room for man's range between mountain and sea,
And the market where woodsmen from over the hill
May traffic, and sailors from far foreign ports
With treasure brought in from the ends of the earth.

And see the third house on the left, with that gleam 20
Of red burnished copper-the hinge of the door
Whereat I shall enter, expected so oft
(Let love be your sea-star!), to voyage no more.

LIII

Art thou the top-most apple
The gatherers could not reach,
Reddening on the bough?
Shall not I take thee?

Art thou a hyacinth blossom 5
The shepherds upon the hills
Have trodden into the ground?
Shall not I lift thee?

Free is the young god Eros,
Paying no tribute to power, 10
Seeing no evil in beauty,
Full of compassion.

Once having found the beloved,
However sorry or woeful,
However scornful of loving, 15
Little it matters.

LIV

How soon will all my lovely days be over,
And I no more be found beneath the sun —
Neither beside the many-murmuring sea,
Nor where the plain-winds whisper to the reeds,
Nor in the tall beech-woods among the hills 5
Where roam the bright-lipped Oreads, nor along
The pasture-sides where berry-pickers stray
And harmless shepherds pipe their sheep to fold!

For I am eager, and the flame of life
Burns quickly in the fragile lamp of clay. 10
Passion and love and longing and hot tears
Consume this mortal Sappho, and too soon
A great wind from the dark will blow upon me,
And I be no more found in the fair world,
For all the search of the revolving moon 15
And patient shine of everlasting stars.

LV

Soul of sorrow, why this weeping?
What immortal grief hath touched thee
With the poignancy of sadness —
Testament of tears?

Have the high gods deigned to show thee 5
Destiny, and disillusion
Fills thy heart at all things human,
Fleeting and desired?

Nay, the gods themselves are fettered
By one law which links together 10
Truth and nobleness and beauty,
Man and stars and sea.

And they only shall find freedom
Who with courage rise and follow
Where love leads beyond all peril, 15
Wise beyond all words.

LVI

It never can be mine
To sit in the door in the sun
And watch the world go by,
A pageant and a dream;

For I was born for love, 5
And fashioned for desire,
Beauty, passion, and joy,
And sorrow and unrest;

And with all things of earth
Eternally must go, 10
Daring the perilous bourn
Of joyance and of death,

A strain of song by night,
A shadow on the hill,
A hint of odorous grass, 15
A murmur of the sea.

LVII

Others shall behold the sun
Through the long uncounted years —
Not a maid in after time
Wise as thou!

For the gods have given thee
Their best gift, an equal mind 5
That can only love, be glad,
And fear not.

LVIII

Let thy strong spirit never fear,
Nor in thy virgin soul be thou afraid.
The gods themselves and the almightier fates
Cannot avail to harm

With outward and misfortunate chance 5
The radiant unshaken mind of him
Who at his being's centre will abide,
Secure from doubt and fear.

His wise and patient heart shall share
The strong sweet loveliness of all things made, 10
And the serenity of inward joy
Beyond the storm of tears.

LIX

Will none say of Sappho,
Speaking of her lovers,
And the love they gave her —
Joy and days and beauty,
Flute-playing and roses,   5
Song and wine and laughter —

Will none, musing, murmur,
"Yet, for all the roses,
All the flutes and lovers,
Doubt not she was lonely   10
As the sea, whose cadence
Haunts the world for ever."

LX

When I have departed,
Say but this behind me,
"Love was all her wisdom,
All her care.

"Well she kept love's secret —
Dared and never faltered —
Laughed and never doubted
Love would win.

"Let the world's rough triumph
Trample by above her,
She is safe forever
From all harm.

"In a land that knows not
Bitterness nor sorrow,
She has found out all
Of truth at last."

LXI

There is no more to say now thou art still,
There is no more to do now thou art dead,
There is no more to know now thy clear mind
Is back returned unto the gods who gave it.

Now thou art gone the use of life is past, 5
The meaning and the glory and the pride,
There is no joyous friend to share the day,
And on the threshold no awaited shadow.

LXII

Play up, play up thy silver flute;
The crickets all are brave;
Glad is the red autumnal earth
And the blue sea.

Play up thy flawless silver flute; 5
Dead ripe are fruit and grain.
When love puts on his scarlet coat,
Put off thy care.

LXIII

A beautiful child is mine,
Formed like a golden flower,
Cleis the loved one.
And above her I value
Not all the Lydian land, 5
Nor lovely Hellas.

LXIV

Ah, but now henceforth
Only one meaning
Has life for me.

Only one purport,
Measure and beauty, 5
Has the bright world.

What mean the wood-winds,
Colour and morning,

   Bird, stream, and hill?

And the brave city 10
With its enchantment?
Thee, only thee!

LXV

Softly the wind moves through the radiant morning,
And the warm sunlight sinks into the valley,
Filling the green earth with a quiet joyance,
Strength, and fulfilment.

Even so, gentle, strong and wise and happy, 5
Through the soul and substance of my being,
Comes the breath of thy great love to me-ward,
O thou dear mortal.

LXVI

What the west wind whispers
At the end of summer,
When the barley harvest
Ripens to the sickle,
Who can tell? 5

What means the fine music
Of the dry cicada,
Through the long noon hours
Of the autumn stillness,
Who can say? 10

How the grape ungathered
With its bloom of blueness
Greatens on the trellis
Of the brick-walled garden,
Who can know? 15

Yet I, too, am greatened,
Keep the note of gladness,
Travel by the wind's road,
Through this autumn leisure —
By thy love. 20

LXVII

Indoors the fire is kindled;
Beechwood is piled on the hearthstone;
Cold are the chattering oak-leaves;
And the ponds frost-bitten.

Softer than rainfall at twilight, 5
Bringing the fields benediction
And the hills quiet and greyness,
Are my long thoughts of thee.

How should thy friend fear the seasons?
They only perish of winter 10
Whom Love, audacious and tender,
Never hath visited.

LXVIII

You ask how love can keep the mortal soul
Strong to the pitch of joy throughout the years.

Ask how your brave cicada on the bough
Keeps the long sweet insistence of his cry;

Ask how the Pleiads steer across the night 5
In their serene unswerving mighty course;

Ask how the wood-flowers waken to the sun,
Unsummoned save by some mysterious word;

Ask how the wandering swallows find your eaves
Upon the rain-wind with returning spring; 10

Ask who commands the ever-punctual tide
To keep the pendulous rhythm of the sea;

And you shall know what leads the heart of man
To the far haven of his hopes and fears.

LXIX

Like a tall forest were their spears,
Their banners like a silken sea,
When the great host in splendour passed
Across the crimson sinking sun.

And then the bray of brazen horns 5
Arose above their clanking march,
As the long waving column filed
Into the odorous purple dusk.

O lover, in this radiant world
Whence is the race of mortal men, 10
So frail, so mighty, and so fond,
That fleets into the vast unknown?

LXX

My lover smiled, "O friend, ask not
The journey's end, nor whence we are.
That whistling boy who minds his goats
So idly in the grey ravine,

"The brown-backed rower drenched with spray, 5
The lemon-seller in the street,
And the young girl who keeps her first
Wild love-tryst at the rising moon —

"Lo, these are wiser than the wise.
And not for all our questioning 10
Shall we discover more than joy,
Nor find a better thing than love!

"Let pass the banners and the spears,
The hate, the battle, and the greed;
For greater than all gifts is peace, 15
And strength is in the tranquil mind."

LXXI

Ye who have the stable world
In the keeping of your hands.
Flocks and men, the lasting hills,
And the ever-wheeling stars;

Ye who freight with wondrous things 5
The wide-wandering heart of man
And the galleon of the moon,
On those silent seas of foam;

Oh, if ever ye shall grant
Time and place and room enough 10
To this fond and fragile heart
Stifled with the throb of love,

On that day one grave-eyed Fate,
Pausing in her toil, shall say,
"Lo, one mortal has achieved 15
Immortality of love!"

LXXII

I heard the gods reply:
"Trust not the future with its perilous chance;
The fortunate hour is on the dial now.

"To-day be wise and great,
And put off hesitation and go forth 5
With cheerful courage for the diurnal need.

"Stout be the heart, nor slow
The foot to follow the impetuous will,
Nor the hand slack upon the loom of deeds.

"Then may the Fates look up 10
And smile a little in their tolerant way,
Being full of infinite regard for men."

LXXIII

The sun on the tide, the peach on the bough,
The blue smoke over the hill,
And the shadows trailing the valley-side,
Make up the autumn day.

Ah, no, not half! Thou art not here 5
Under the bronze beech-leaves,
And thy lover's soul like a lonely child
Roams through an empty room.

LXXIV

If death be good,
Why do the gods not die?
If life be ill,
Why do the gods still live?

If love be naught, 5
Why do the gods still love?
If love be all,
What should men do but love?

LXXV

Tell me what this life means,
O my prince and lover,
With the autumn sunlight
On thy bronze-gold head?

With thy clear voice sounding 5
Through the silver twilight —
What is the lost secret
Of the tacit earth?

LXXVI

Ye have heard how Marsyas,
In the folly of his pride,
Boasted of a matchless skill —
When the great god's back was turned;

How his fond imagining 5
Fell to ashes cold and grey,
When the flawless player came
In serenity and light.

So it was with those I loved
In the years ere I loved thee. 10
Many a saying sounds like truth,
Until Truth itself is heard.

Many a beauty only lives
Until Beauty passes by,
And the mortal is forgot 15
In the shadow of the god.

LXXVII

Hour by hour I sit,
Watching the silent door.
Shadows go by on the wall,
And steps in the street.

Expectation and doubt 5
Flutter my timorous heart.
So many hurrying home —
And thou still away.

LXXVIII

Once in the shining street,
In the heart of a seaboard town,
As I waited, behold, there came
The woman I loved.

As when, in the early spring, 5
A daffodil blooms in the grass,
Golden and gracious and glad,
The solitude smiled.

LXXIX

How strange is love, O my lover!
With what enchantment and power
Does it not come upon mortals,
Learned or heedless!

How far away and unreal, 5
Faint as blue isles in a sunset
Haze-golden, all else of life seems,
Since I have known thee!

LXXX

How to say I love you:
What, if I but live it,
Were the use in that, love?
Small, indeed.

Only, every moment 5
Of this waking lifetime
Let me be your lover
And your friend!

Ah, but then, as sure as
Blossom breaks from bud-sheath, 10
When along the hillside
Spring returns,

Golden speech should flower
From the soul so cherished,
And the mouth your kisses 15
Filled with fire.

LXXXI

Hark, love, to the tambourines
Of the minstrels in the street,
And one voice that throbs and soars
Clear above the clashing time!

Some Egyptian royal love-lilt, 5
Some Sidonian refrain,
Vows of Paphos or of Tyre,
Mount against the silver sun.

Pleading, piercing, yet serene,
Vagrant in a foreign town, 10
From what passion was it born,
In what lost land over sea?

LXXXII

Over the roofs the honey-coloured moon,
With purple shadows on the silver grass,

And the warm south-wind on the curving sea,
While we two, lovers past all turmoil now,

Watch from the window the white sails come in, 5
Bearing what unknown ventures safe to port!

So falls the hour of twilight and of love
With wizardry to loose the hearts of men,

And there is nothing more in this great world
Than thou and I, and the blue dome of dusk. 10

LXXXIII

In the quiet garden world,
Gold sunlight and shadow leaves
Flicker on the wall.

And the wind, a moment since,
With rose-petals strewed the path 5
And the open door.

Now the moon-white butterflies
Float across the liquid air,
Glad as in a dream;

And, across thy lover's heart, 10
Visions of one scarlet mouth
With its maddening smile.

LXXXIV

Soft was the wind in the beech-trees;
Low was the surf on the shore;
In the blue dusk one planet
Like a great sea-pharos shone.

But nothing to me were the sea-sounds, 5
The wind and the yellow star,
When over my breast the banner
Of your golden hair was spread.

LXXXV

Have you heard the news of Sappho's garden,
And the Golden Rose of Mitylene,
Which the bending brown-armed rowers lately
Brought from over sea, from lonely Pontus?

In a meadow by the river Halys, 5
Where some wood-god hath the world in keeping,
On a burning summer noon they found her,
Lovely as a Dryad, and more tender.

Her these eyes have seen, and not another
Shall behold, till time takes all things goodly, 10
So surpassing fair and fond and wondrous —
Such a slave as, worth a great king's ransom,

No man yet of all the sons of mortals
But would lose his soul for and regret not;
So hath Beauty compassed all her children 15
With the cords of longing and desire.

Only Hermes, master of word music,
Ever yet in glory of gold language
Could ensphere the magical remembrance
Of her melting, half sad, wayward beauty, 20

Or devise the silver phrase to frame her,
The inevitable name to call her,
Half a sigh and half a kiss when whispered,
Like pure air that feeds a forge's hunger.

Not a painter in the Isles of Hellas 25
Could portray her, mix the golden tawny
With bright stain of poppies, or ensanguine
Like the life her darling mouth's vermilion,

So that, in the ages long hereafter,
When we shall be dust of perished summers, 30
Any man could say who found that likeness,
Smiling gently on it, "This was Gorgo!"

LXXXVI

Love is so strong a thing,
The very gods must yield,
When it is welded fast
With the unflinching truth.

Love is so frail a thing, 5
A word, a look, will kill.
Oh lovers, have a care
How ye do deal with love.

LXXXVII

Hadst thou, with all thy loveliness, been true,
Had I, with all my tenderness, been strong,
We had not made this ruin out of life,
This desolation in a world of joy,
My poor Gorgo. 5

Yet even the high gods at times do err;
Be therefore thou not overcome with woe,
But dedicate anew to greater love
An equal heart, and be thy radiant self
Once more, Gorgo. 10

LXXXVIII

As, on a morn, a traveller might emerge
From the deep green seclusion of the hills,
By a cool road through forest and through fern,
Little frequented, winding, followed long
With joyous expectation and day-dreams, 5
And on a sudden, turning a great rock
Covered with frondage, dark with dripping water,
Behold the seaboard full of surf and sound,
With all the space and glory of the world
Above the burnished silver of the sea —10

Even so it was upon that first spring day
When time, that is a devious path for men,
Led me all lonely to thy door at last;
And all thy splendid beauty, gracious and glad,
(Glad as bright colour, free as wind or air, 15
And lovelier than racing seas of foam)
Bore sense and soul and mind at once away
To a pure region where the gods might dwell,
Making of me, a vagrant child before,
A servant of joy at Aphrodite's will. 20

LXXXIX

Where shall I look for thee,
Where find thee now,
O my lost Atthis?

Storm bars the harbour,
And snow keeps the pass 5
In the blue mountains.

Bitter the wind whistles,
Pale is the sun,
And the days shorten.

Close to the hearthstone, 10
With long thoughts of thee,
Thy lonely lover

Sits now, remembering
All the spent hours
And thy fair beauty. 15

Ah, when the hyacinth
Wakens with spring,
And buds the laurel,

Doubt not, some morning
When all earth revives, 20
Hearing Pan's flute-call

Over the river-beds,
Over the hills,
Sounding the summons,

I shall look up and behold 25
In the door,

Smiling, expectant,

Loving as ever
And glad as of old,
My own lost Atthis! 30

XC

A sad, sad face, and saddest eyes that ever
Beheld the sun,
Whence came the grief that makes of all thy beauty
One sad sweet smile?

In this bright portrait, where the painter fixed them, 5
I still behold
The eyes that gladdened, and the lips that loved me,
And, gold on rose,

The cloud of hair that settles on one shoulder
Slipped from its vest. 10
I almost hear thy Mitylenean love-song
In the spring night,

When the still air was odorous with blossoms,
And in the hour
Thy first wild girl's-love trembled into being, 15
Glad, glad and fond.

Ah, where is all that wonder? What god's malice
Undid that joy
And set the seal of patient woe upon thee,
O my lost love? 20

XCI

Why have the gods in derision
Severed us, heart of my being?
Where have they lured thee to wander,
O my lost lover?

While now I sojourn with sorrow, 5
Having remorse for my comrade,
What town is blessed with thy beauty,
Gladdened and prospered?

Nay, who could love as I loved thee,
With whom thy beauty was mingled 10
In those spring days when the swallows
Came with the south wind?

Then I became as that shepherd
Loved by Selene on Latmus,
Once when her own summer magic 15
Took hold upon her

With a sweet madness, and thenceforth
Her mortal lover must wander
Over the wide world for ever,
Like one enchanted. 20

XCII

Like a red lily in the meadow grasses,
Swayed by the wind and burning in the sunlight,
I saw you, where the city chokes with traffic,
Bearing among the passers-by your beauty,
Unsullied, wild, and delicate as a flower. 5
And then I knew, past doubt or peradventure,
Our loved and mighty Eleusinian mother
Had taken thought of me for her pure worship,
And of her favour had assigned my comrade
For the Great Mysteries-knew I should find you 10
When the dusk murmured with its new-made lovers,
And we be no more foolish but wise children,
And well content partake of joy together,
As she ordains and human hearts desire.

XCIII

When in the spring the swallows all return,
And the bleak bitter sea grows mild once more,
With all its thunders softened to a sigh;

When to the meadows the young green comes back,
And swelling buds put forth on every bough, 5
With wild-wood odours on the delicate air;

Ah, then, in that so lovely earth wilt thou
With all thy beauty love me all one way,
And make me all thy lover as before?

Lo, where the white-maned horses of the surge, 10
Plunging in thunderous onset to the shore,
Trample and break and charge along the sand!

XCIV

Cold is the wind where Daphne sleeps,
That was so tender and so warm
With loving-with a loveliness
Than her own laurel lovelier.

Now pipes the bitter wind for her, 5
And the snow sifts about her door,
While far below her frosty hill
The racing billows plunge and boom.

XCV

Hark, where Poseidon's
White racing horses
Trample with tumult
The shelving seaboard!

Older than Saturn, 5
Older than Rhea,
That mournful music,
Falling and surging

With the vast rhythm
Ceaseless, eternal, 10
Keeps the long tally
Of all things mortal.

How many lovers
Hath not its lulling
Cradled to slumber
With the ripe flowers, 15

Ere for our pleasure
This golden summer
Walked through the corn-lands
In gracious splendour! 20

How many loved ones
Will it not croon to,
In the long spring-days
Through coming ages,

When all our day-dreams 25
Have been forgotten,
And none remembers

   Even thy beauty!

They too shall slumber
In quiet places, 30
And mighty sea-sounds
Call them unheeded.

XCVI

Hark, my lover, it is spring!
On the wind a faint far call
Wakes a pang within my heart,
Unmistakable and keen.

At the harbour mouth a sail 5
Glimmers in the morning sun,
And the ripples at her prow
Whiten into crumbling foam,

As she forges outward bound
For the teeming foreign ports. 10
Through the open window now,
Hear the sailors lift a song!

In the meadow ground the frogs
With their deafening flutes begin —
The old madness of the world 15
In their golden throats again.

Little fifers of live bronze,
Who hath taught you with wise lore
To unloose the strains of joy,
When Orion seeks the west? 20

And you feathered flute-players,
Who instructed you to fill
All the blossomy orchards now
With melodious desire?

I doubt not our father Pan 25
Hath a care of all these things.
In some valley of the hills
Far away and misty-blue,

By quick water he hath cut
A new pipe, and set the wood 30
To his smiling lips, and blown,
That earth's rapture be restored.

And those wild Pandean stops
Mark the cadence life must keep.
O my lover, be thou glad; 35
It is spring in Hellas now.

XCVII

When the early soft spring wind comes blowing
Over Rhodes and Samos and Miletus,
From the seven mouths of Nile to Lesbos,
Freighted with sea-odours and gold sunshine,

What news spreads among the island people 5
In the market-place of Mitylene,
Lending that unwonted stir of gladness
To the busy streets and thronging doorways?

Is it word from Ninus or Arbela,
Babylon the great, or Northern Imbros? 10
Have the laden galleons been sighted
Stoutly labouring up the sea from Tyre?

Nay, 'tis older news that foreign sailor
With the cheek of sea-tan stops to prattle
To the young fig-seller with her basket 15
And the breasts that bud beneath her tunic,

And I hear it in the rustling tree-tops.
All this passionate bright tender body
Quivers like a leaf the wind has shaken,
Now love wanders through the aisles of springtime. 20

XCVIII

I am more tremulous than shaken reeds,
And love has made me like the river water.

Thy voice is as the hill-wind over me,
And all my changing heart gives heed, my lover.

Before thy least lost murmur I must sigh, 5
Or gladden with thee as the sun-path glitters.

XCIX

Over the wheat-field,
Over the hill-crest,
Swoops and is gone
The beat of a wild wing,
Brushing the pine-tops, 5
Bending the poppies,
Hurrying Northward
With golden summer.

What premonition,
O purple swallow, 10
Told thee the happy
Hour of migration?
Hark! On the threshold
(Hush, flurried heart in me!),
Was there a footfall? 15
Did no one enter?

Soon will a shepherd
In rugged Dacia,
Folding his gentle
Ewes in the twilight, 20
Lifting a level
Gaze from the sheepfold,
Say to his fellows,
"Lo, it is springtime."

This very hour 25
In Mitylene,
Will not a young girl
Say to her lover,
Lifting her moon-white
Arms to enlace him, 30
Ere the glad sigh comes,
"Lo, it is lovetime!"

C

Once more the rain on the mountain,
Once more the wind in the valley,
With the soft odours of springtime
And the long breath of remembrance,
O Lityerses! 5

Warm is the sun in the city.
On the street corners with laughter
Traffic the flower-girls. Beauty
Blossoms once more for thy pleasure
In many places. 10

Gentlier now falls the twilight,
With the slim moon in the pear-trees;
And the green frogs in the meadows
Blow on shrill pipes to awaken
Thee, Lityerses. 15

Gladlier now crimson morning
Flushes fair-built Mitylene —
Portico, temple, and column —
Where the young garlanded women
Praise thee with singing. 20

Ah, but what burden of sorrow
Tinges their slow stately chorus,
Though spring revisits the glad earth?
Wilt thou not wake to their summons,
O Lityerses? 25

Shall they then never behold thee —
Nevermore see thee returning
Down the blue cleft of the mountains,
Nor in the purple of evening
Welcome thy coming? 30

Nevermore answer thy glowing
Youth with their ardour, nor cherish
With lovely longing thy spirit,
Nor with soft laughter beguile thee,
O Lityerses? 35

Heedless, assuaged, art thou sleeping
Where the spring sun cannot find thee,
Nor the wind waken, nor woodlands
Bloom for thy innocent rapture
Through golden hours? 40

Hast thou no passion nor pity
For thy deserted companions?
Never again will thy beauty
Quell their desire nor rekindle,
O Lityerses? 45

Nay, but in vain their clear voices
Call thee. Thy sensitive beauty
Is become part of the fleeting
Loveliness, merged in the pathos
Of all things mortal. 50

In the faint fragrance of flowers,
On the sweet draft of the sea-wind,
Linger strange hints now that loosen
Tears for thy gay gentle spirit,
O Lityerses! 55

EPILOGUE

Now the hundred songs are made,
And the pause comes. Loving Heart,
There must be an end to summer,
And the flute be laid aside.

On a day the frost will come, 5
Walking through the autumn world,
Hushing all the brave endeavour
Of the crickets in the grass.

On a day (Oh, far from now!)
Earth will hear this voice no more; 10
For it shall be with thy lover
As with Linus long ago.

All the happy songs he wrought
From remembrance soon must fade,
As the wash of silver moonlight 15
From a purple-dark ravine.

Frail as dew upon the grass
Or the spindrift of the sea,
Out of nothing they were fashioned
And to nothing must return. 20

Nay, but something of thy love,
Passion, tenderness, and joy,
Some strange magic of thy beauty,
Some sweet pathos of thy tears,

Must imperishably cling 25
To the cadence of the words,
Like a spell of lost enchantments
Laid upon the hearts of men.

Wild and fleeting as the notes
Blown upon a woodland pipe, 30
They must haunt the earth with gladness
And a tinge of old regret.

For the transport in their rhythm
Was the throb of thy desire,
And thy lyric moods shall quicken 35
Souls of lovers yet unborn.

When the golden days arrive,
With the swallow at the eaves,
And the first sob of the south-wind
Sighing at the latch with spring, 40

Long hereafter shall thy name
Be recalled through foreign lands,
And thou be a part of sorrow
When the Linus songs are sung.

Regiment of Women

by Clemence Dane

'The monstrous empire of a cruell woman we knowe to be the onlie occasion of all these miseries: and yet with silence we passe the time as thogh the mater did nothinge appertein to us.'
    JOHN KNOX, *First Blast of the Trumpet against the Monstrous Regiment of Women.*

To E. A.

Here's Our Book
As it grew.
But it's Your Book!
For, but for you,
Who'd look
At My Book?

C. D.

CHAPTER I

The school secretary pattered down the long corridor and turned into a class-room.

The room was a big one. There were old-fashioned casement windows and distempered walls; the modern desks, ranged in double rows, were small and shallow, scarred, and incredibly inky. In the window-seats stood an over-populous fish-bowl, two trays of silkworms, and a row of experimental jam-pots. There were pictures on the walls—*The Infant Samuel* was paired with *Cherry Ripe*, and Alfred, in the costume of Robin Hood, conscientiously ignored a neat row of halfpenny buns. The form was obviously a low one.

Through the opening door came the hive-like hum of a school at work, but the room was empty, save for a mistress sitting at the raised desk, idle, hands folded, ominously patient. A thin woman, undeveloped, sallow-skinned, with a sensitive mouth, and eyes that were bold and shining.

They narrowed curiously at sight of the new-comer, but she was greeted with sufficient courtesy.

"Yes, Miss Vigers?"

Henrietta Vigers was spare, precise, with pale, twitching eyes and a high voice. Her manner was self-sufficient, her speech deliberate and unnecessarily correct: her effect was the colourless obstinacy of an elderly mule. She stared about her inquisitively.

"Miss Hartill, I am looking for Milly Fiske. Her mother has telephoned——Where is the class? I can't be mistaken. It's a quarter to one. You take the Lower Third from twelve-fifteen, don't you?"

"Yes," said Clare Hartill.

"Well, but-where is it?" The secretary frowned suspiciously. She was instinctively hostile to what she did not understand.

"I don't know," said Clare sweetly.

Henrietta gaped. Clare, justly annoyed as she was, could not but be grateful to the occasion for providing her with amusement. She enjoyed baiting Henrietta.

"I should have thought you could tell me. Don't you control the time-table? I only know"—her anger rose again—"that I have been waiting here since a quarter past twelve. I have waited quite long enough, I think. I am going home. Perhaps you will be good enough to enquire into the matter."

"But haven't you been to look for them?" began Henrietta perplexedly.

"No," said Clare. "I don't, you know. I expect people to come to me. And I don't like wasting my time." Then, with a change of tone, "Really, Miss Vigers, I don't know whose fault it is, but it has no business to happen. The class knows perfectly well that it is due here. You must see that I can't run about looking for it."

"Of course, of course!" Henrietta was taken aback. "But I assure you that it's nothing to do with me. I have rearranged nothing. Let me see-who takes them before you?"

Clare shrugged her shoulders.

"How should I know? I hardly have time for my own classes——"

Henrietta broke in excitedly.

"It's Miss Durand! I might have known. Miss Durand, naturally. Miss Hartill, I will see to the matter at once. It shall not happen again. I will speak to Miss Marsham. I might have known."

"Miss Durand?" Clare's annoyance vanished. She looked interested and a trifle amused. "That tall girl with the yellow hair? I've heard about her. I haven't spoken to her yet, but the children approve, don't they?" She laughed pointedly and Henrietta flushed. "I rather like the look of her."

"Do you?" Henrietta smiled sourly. "I can't agree. A most unsuitable person. Miss Marsham engaged her without consulting me-or you either, I suppose? The niece or daughter or something, of an old mistress. I wonder you didn't hear-but of course you were away the first fortnight. A terrible young woman-boisterous-undignified—a bad influence on the children!"

Clare's eyes narrowed again.

"Are you sure? The junior classes are working quite as well as usual-better indeed. I've been surprised. Of course, to-day— —"

"To-day is an example. She has detained them, I suppose. It has happened before-five minutes here-ten there-every one is complaining. Really—I shall speak to Miss Marsham."

"Of course, if that's the case, you had better," said Clare, rather impatiently, as she moved towards the door. She regretted the impulse that had induced her to explain matters to Miss Vigers. If it did not suit her dignity to go in search of her errant pupils, still less did it accord with a complaint to the fidgety secretary. She should have managed the affair for herself. However-it could not be helped....Henrietta Vigers was looking important....Henrietta Vigers would enjoy baiting the new-comer—what was her name-Durand? Miss Durand would submit, she supposed. Henrietta was a petty tyrant to the younger mistresses, and Clare Hartill was very much aware of the fact. But the younger mistresses did not interest her; she was no more than idly contemptuous of their flabbiness. Why on earth had none of them appealed to the head mistress? But the new assistant was a spirited-looking creature....Clare had noticed her keen nostrils-nothing sheepish there....And Henrietta disliked her-distinctly a point in her favour....Clare suspected that trouble might yet arise....She paused uncertainly. Even now she might herself interfere....But Miss Durand had certainly had no right to detain Clare's class....It was gross carelessness, if not impertinence....Let her fight it out with Miss Vigers.... Nevertheless-she wished her luck....

With another glance at her watch, and a cool little nod to her colleague, she left the classroom, and was shortly setting out for her walk home.

Henrietta looked after her with an angry shrug.

For the hundredth time she assured herself that she was submitting positively for the last time to the dictates of Clare Hartill; that such usurpation was not to be borne....Who, after all, had been Authority's right hand for the last twenty years? Certainly not Clare Hartill....Why, she could recall Clare's first term, a bare eight years ago! She had disliked her less in those days; had respected her as a woman who knew her business....The school had been going through a lean year, with Miss Marsham, the head mistress, seriously ill; with a weak staff, and girls growing riotous and indolent. So lean a year, indeed, that Henrietta, left in charge, had one day taken a train and her troubles to Bournemouth, and poured them out to Authority's bath-chair. And Edith Marsham, the old warhorse, had frowned and nodded and chuckled, and sent her home again, no wiser than she came. But a letter had come for her later, and the bearer had been a quiet, any-aged woman with disquieting eyes. They had summed Henrietta up, and Henrietta had resented it. The new assistant, given, according to instructions, a free hand, had gone about her business, asking no advice. But there had certainly followed a peaceful six months. Then had come speech-day and Henrietta's world had turned upside down. She had not known such a speech-day for years. Complacent parents had listened to amazingly efficient performances-the guest of honour had enjoyed herself with obvious, naïve surprise: there had been the bomb-shell of the lists. Henrietta had nothing to do with the examinations, but she knew such a standard had not been reached for many a long term. And the head mistress, restored and rubicund, had alluded to her, Henrietta's, vice-regency in a neat little speech. She had received felicitations, and was beginning, albeit confusedly, to persuade herself that the stirring of the pie had been indeed due to her own forefinger, when the guests left, and she had that disturbing little interview with her principal.

Edith Marsham had greeted her vigorously. She was still in her prime then, old as she was. She had another six years before senility, striking late, struck heavily.

"Well-what do you think of her, eh? I hope you were a good girl-did as she told you?"

Henrietta had flushed, resenting it that Miss Marsham, certainly a head mistress of forty years' standing, should, as she aged, treat her staff more and more as if it were but a degree removed from the Upper Sixth. The younger women might like it, but it did not accord with Henrietta's notions of her own dignity. She was devoutly thankful that Miss Marsham reserved her freedom for private interviews; had, in public at least, the grand manner. Yet she had a respect for her; knew her dimly for a notable dame, who could have coerced a recalcitrant cabinet as easily as she bullied the school staff.

She had rubbed her hands together, shrewd eyes a-twinkle.

"I knew what I was doing! How long have you been with me, Henrietta? Twelve years ago, eh? Ah, well, it's longer ago than that. Let me see-she's twenty-eight now, Clare Hartill-and she left me at sixteen. A responsibility, a great responsibility. An orphan-too much money. A difficult child—I spent a lot of time on her, and prayer, too, my dear. Well, I don't regret it now. When I met her at Bournemouth that day-oh, I wasn't pleased with you, Henrietta! It has taken me forty years to build up my school, and I can't be ill two months, but——Well, I made up my mind. I found her at a loose end. I talked to her. She'll take plain speaking from me. I told her she'd had enough of operas and art schools, and literary societies (she's been running round Europe for the last ten years). I told her my difficulty—I told her to come back to me and do a little honest work. Of course she wouldn't hear of it."

"Then how did you persuade Miss Hartill?"

But Henrietta, raising prim brows, had but drawn back a chuckle from the old woman.

"How many types of schoolgirl have you met, Henrietta? Here, under me?"

Henrietta fidgeted. The question was an offence. It was not in her department. She had no note of it in her memorandum books.

"Really—I can hardly tell you-blondes and brunettes, do you mean? No two girls are quite the same, are they?"

But Miss Marsham had not attended.

"Just two-that's my experience. The girl from whom you get work by telling her you are sure she can do it-and the girl from whom you get work by telling her you are sure she can't. You'll soon find out which I told Clare Hartill. And now, understand this, Henrietta. There are to be no dissensions. I want Clare Hartill to stay. If she gets engrossed in the work, she will. She won't interfere with you, you'll find. She's too lazy. Get on with her if you can."

But Henrietta had not got on with her, had resented fiercely Miss Marsham's preferential treatment of the new-comer. That Miss Marsham was obviously wise in her generation did not appease her *amour propre*. She knew that where she had failed, Clare had been uncannily successful. Yet Clare was not aggressively efficient: indeed it was a grievance that she was so apparently casual, so gracefully indifferent. But, as if it were a matter of course, she did whatever she set out to do so much better, so much more graphically than it had ever been done before, that inevitably she attracted disciples. But Henrietta's grievance went deeper. She denied her any vestige of personal charm, and at the same time insisted fiercely that she was an unscrupulous woman, in that she used her personal charm to accomplish her aims: her aims, in Henrietta's eyes, being the ousting of the secretary from her position of trust and possible succession to the headship. Henrietta did not realise that it was herself, far more than Clare, who was jeopardising that position. Though there was no system of prefecture among the staff, she had come to consider herself responsible for the junior mistresses, encouraging them to bring complaints to her, rather than to the head of the school. Old Miss Marsham, little as she liked relaxing her hold on the reins, dreaded, as old age must, the tussle that would inevitably follow any insistence on her prerogatives, and had acquiesced; yet with reservations. Had one of the younger mistresses rebelled and carried her grievance to the higher court, Miss Vigers' eyes might have been opened; but as yet no one had challenged her self-assumed supremacy. Clare, who might have done so, cared little who supervised the boarders or was supreme in the matter of time-table and commissariat. Her interest lay in the actual work, in the characters and possibilities of the workers. There she brooked no interference, and Henrietta attempted little, for when she did she was neatly and completely routed.

But the more chary Henrietta grew of interfering with Clare's activities, the more she realised that it was her duty (she would not have said pleasure) to supervise the younger women. She had a gift that was almost genius of appearing among them at awkward moments. If a child were proving refractory and victory hanging in the balance, Miss Vigers would surely choose that moment to knock at the class-room door, and, politely refusing to inconvenience the embarrassed novice, wait, all-observant, until the scene ended, before explaining her errand. Later in the day the young mistress would be button-holed, and the i's and t's of her errors of judgment dotted and crossed. Those who would not submit to tutelage she contrived to render so uncomfortable that, sooner or later, they retired in favour of temperaments more sheeplike or more thick-skinned.

To Alwynne Durand, at present under grave suspicion of tampering with Clare Hartill's literature class, she had been from the first inimical. She had been engaged without Henrietta's sanction; she was young, and pretty, and already ridiculously popular. And there was the affair of the nickname. Alwynne had certainly looked out of place at the mistresses' table, on the day of her arrival, with her yellow hair and green gown —"like a daffodil stuck into a bunch of everlastings," as an early adorer had described her. The phrase had appealed and spread, and within a week she was "Daffy" to the school; but her popularity among her colleagues had not been heightened by rumours of the collective nickname the contrast with their junior had evoked. Her obvious shyness and desire to please were, however, sufficiently disarming, and her first days had not been made too difficult for her by any save Henrietta. But Henrietta was sure she was incompetent-called to witness her joyous, casual manner, her unorthodox methods, her way of submerging the mistress in the fellow-creature. She had labelled her undisciplined-which Alwynne certainly was-lax and undignified; had prophesied that she would be unable to maintain order; had been annoyed to find that, inspiring neither fear nor awe, she was yet quite capable of making herself respected. Alwynne's jolliness never seemed to expose her to familiarities, ready as she was to join in the laugh against herself when, new to the ways of the school, she outraged Media, or reduced Persia to hysterical giggles. She was soon reckoned up by the shrewd children as "mad, but a perfect dear," and she managed to make her governance so enjoyable that it would have been considered bad form, as well as bad policy, to make her unconventionality an excuse for ragging. She had, indeed, easily assimilated the school atmosphere. She was humble and anxious to learn, had no notions of her own importance. But she was quick-tempered, and though she could be meek and grateful to experience backed by good manners, she reared at patronage. Inevitably she made mistakes, the mistakes of her age and temperament, but common sense and good humour saved her from any serious blunders.

Miss Vigers had, nevertheless, noted each insignificant slip, and carried the tale, less insignificant in bulk, in her mind, ready to produce at a favourable opportunity.

And now the opportunity had arisen. Miss Hartill had delivered Miss Durand into her hand. Miss Hartill, she was glad to note, had not shown any interest in the new-comer....Miss Hartill had a way of taking any one young and attractive under her protection....That it was with Miss Hartill that the girl had come into conflict, however, did away with any need of caution....Miss Durand needed putting in her place....Henrietta, in all speed, would reconduct her thither.

CHAPTER II

Miss Vigers hurried along to the Upper Third class-room. She straightened her jersey, and patted her netted hair as she went, much in the manner of a countryman squaring for a fight, opened the door, after a tap so rudimentary as to be inaudible to those within, and entered aggressively, the light of battle in her eye.

To her amazement and annoyance her entry was entirely unnoticed. The entire class had deserted its desks and was clustered round the rostrum, where Alwynne Durand, looking flushed and excited and prettier than a school-mistress had any business to be, was talking fast and eagerly. She had a little stick in her hand which she was using as a conductor's baton, emphasising with it the points of the story she was evidently telling. A map and some portraits were pinned to the blackboard beside her, and the children's heads were grouped, three and four together, over pictures apparently taken from the open portfolio lying before her on the desk. But their eyes were on Miss Durand, and the varying yet intent attitudes gave the collective effect of an audience at a melodrama. They were obviously and breathlessly interested, and the occasional quick crackle of question and answer merely accentuated the tension. Once, as Alwynne paused a moment, her stick hovering uncertainly over the map, a child, with a little wriggle of impatience, piped up—

"We'll find it afterwards. Oh, go on, Miss Durand! Please, go on!"

And Alwynne, equally absorbed, went on and the class hung upon her words.

The listener was outraged. Children were to be allowed to give orders-to leave their places-to be obviously and hugely enjoying themselves-in school hours-and the whole pack of them due elsewhere! She had never witnessed so disgraceful a scene.

Her dry precision shivered at Alwynne's coruscating adjectives. (It is not to be denied that Alwynne, at that period of her career, was lax and lavish in speech, altogether too fond of conceits and superlatives.) She cut aridly into the lecture.

"Miss Durand! Are you aware of the time?"

Alwynne jumped, and the class jumped with her.

It was curious to watch that which but a moment before had been one absorbed, collective personality suddenly disintegrating into Lotties and Maries and Sylvias, shy, curious, impish or indifferent, after their kind. Miss Vigers's presence intimidated: each peeping personality retired, snail-like, into its schoolgirl shell. With a curious yet distinct consciousness of guilt, they edged away from the two women, huddling sheepishly together, watching and waiting, inimical to the disturber of their enjoyment, but distinctly doubtful as to whether "Daffy," in the encounter that they knew quite well was imminent, would be able to hold her own.

But Miss Durand was self-possessed. She looked down at Miss Vigers from her high seat and gave a natural little laugh.

"Oh, Miss Vigers! How you startled me!"

"I'm sorry. I have been endeavouring to attract your attention for some moments. Are you aware of the time?"

Alwynne glanced at the clock. The hands stood at an impossible hour.

"There!" she remarked penitently, "it's stopped again!"

She smiled at the class, all ears and interest.

"One of you children will just have to remind me. Helen? No, you do the chalks already. Millicent!" She singled out a dreamy child, who was taking surreptitious advantage of the interruption to pore over the pictures that had slid from the desk to the floor of the rostrum.

"Milly! Your head's a sieve too! Will you undertake to remind me? Each time I have to be reminded-in goes a penny to the mission-and each time you forget to remind me, you do the same. It'll do us both good! And if we both forget-the rest of the class must pull us up."

The little girl nodded, serious and important.

Alwynne turned to Henrietta.

"Excuse me, Miss Vigers, were you wanting to speak to me? I'm afraid we're in rather a muddle. Children-pick up those pictures: at least-Helen and Milly! Go back to your desks, the rest of you." And then, to Henrietta again, "I suppose the gong will go in a minute?"

She was being courteous, but she was implying quite clearly that she considered the interruption of her lesson unnecessary.

Henrietta's eyes snapped.

"The twelve-fifteen gong went a long time ago, Miss Durand. It's nearly one. Miss Hartill wishes to know what has happened to her class."

"My hat!" murmured Alwynne, appalled.

It was the most rudimentary murmur—a mere movement of the lips; but Henrietta caught it. Justifiably, she detested slang. She stiffened yet more, but Alwynne was continuing with deprecating gestures.

"This is dreadful! I'm awfully sorry, Miss Vigers, but, you know, we never heard the gong! Not a sound! Are you sure it rang?" (This to Henrietta, who never slackened her supervision of the relays of prefects responsible for the ever-punctual gong. But Alwynne had no eye for detail.) She continued agitatedly, unconscious of offence —

"But of course I must go and explain to Miss Hartill at once. Children-get your things together, and go straight to the Lower Second. I'll come with you. Miss Vigers, I am so sorry-it was entirely my fault, of course, but we none of us heard the gong."

But as she spoke, and the girls, attentive and curious, obediently gathered up their belongings and filed into the passage, the gong, audible enough to any one less absorbed than Alwynne and her class had been, boomed for its last time that morning, the prolonged boom that was the signal for the day-girls to go home. The children dispersed hurriedly, and Alwynne was left alone with Henrietta.

Alwynne was grave-distinctly distressed.

"I must go and explain to Miss Hartill at once," she repeated, making for the door.

"You needn't trouble yourself," Henrietta called after her. "Miss Hartill went home half-an-hour-ago."

The irrepressible note of gratification in her voice startled Alwynne. She turned and faced her.

"I don't understand! You said she was waiting."

"When I left her, she had been waiting over half-an-hour. She told me that she should do so no longer. Miss Hartill is not accustomed to be kept waiting while the junior mistresses amuse themselves."

Alwynne raised her eyebrows and regarded her carefully.

"Did Miss Hartill ask you to tell me that? Are you her messenger?" she asked blandly.

The last sentence had enlightened her, at any rate, as to Miss Vigers's personal attitude to herself. She was perfectly aware that she had been guilty of gross carelessness; that, if Miss Hartill chose, she could make it a serious matter for her; but for the moment her apprehensive regrets, as well as her profound sense of the apology due to the formidable Miss Hartill, were shrivelled in the white heat of her anger at the tone Henrietta Vigers was permitting herself. She was as much hurt as horrified by the revelation of an antipathy she had been unconscious of exciting; it was her first experience of gratuitous ill-will. She rebelled hotly, incapable of analysing her emotion, indifferent to the probable consequences of a defiance of the older woman, but passionately resolved that she would not allow any one alive to be rude to her.

And Henrietta, amazed at the veiled rebuke of her manner, also lost her temper.

"Miss Hartill and I were overwhelmed by such an occurrence. Do you realise what you are doing, Miss Durand? You keep the children away from their lesson-you alter the school timetable to suit your convenience-without a remark, or warning, or apology."

"I've told you already that I didn't hear the gong," interrupted Alwynne, between courtesy and impatience. She was trying hard to control herself.

133

"That is nonsense. Everybody hears the gong. You didn't choose to hear it, I suppose. Anyhow, I feel it my duty to tell you that such behaviour will not be tolerated, Miss Durand, in this, or any school. It is not your place to make innovations. I was horrified just now when I came in. The class-room littered about with pictures and papers-the children not in their places-allowed to interrupt and argue. I never heard of such a thing."

Alwynne's chin went up.

"Excuse me, Miss Vigers, but I hardly see that it is your business to criticise my way of teaching."

"I am speaking to you for your own good," said Henrietta.

"That is kind of you; but if you speak to me in such a tone, you cannot expect me to listen."

Henrietta hesitated.

"Miss Durand, you are new to the school——"

"That gives you no right to be rude to me!"

Henrietta took a step towards her.

"Rude? And you? I consider you insolent. Ever since you came to the school you have been impossible. You go your own way, teach in your own way——"

"I do as I'm told," said Alwynne sharply.

"In your own way. You neither ask nor take advice——"

"At any rate, Miss Marsham is satisfied with me-she told me so last week." She felt it undignified to be justifying herself, but she feared that silent contempt would be lost on Miss Vigers. Also, such an attitude was not easy to Alwynne; she had a tongue; when she was angry, the brutal effectiveness of Billingsgate must always tempt her.

Henrietta countered coldly —

"I am sorry that I shall be obliged to undeceive her; that is, unless you apologise——"

"To Miss Hartill? Certainly! I intend to. I hope I know when I'm in the wrong."

"To me——"

"To you?" cried Alwynne, with a little high-pitched laugh. "If you tell me what for?"

"In Miss Marsham's absence I take her place," began Henrietta.

"Miss Hartill, I was told, did that."

"You are mistaken. The younger mistresses come to me for orders."

"I shall be the exception, then. I am not a housemaid. Will you let me get to my desk, please, Miss Vigers? I want my books."

She brushed past Henrietta, cheeks flaming, chin in air, and opened her desk.

The secretary, for all her anger, hesitated uncertainly. She was unused to opposition, and had been accustomed to allow herself a greater licence of speech than she knew. Alwynne's instant resentment, for all its crude young insolence, was, she realised, to some extent justified. She had, she knew, exceeded her powers, but she had not stopped to consider whether Alwynne would know that she had done so, or, knowing, have the courage to act upon that knowledge. She had been staggered by the girl's swift counter-attack and was soon wishing that she had left her alone; but she had gone too far to retreat with dignity; also, she had by no means regained control of her temper.

"I can only report you to Miss Marsham," she remarked lamely, to Alwynne's back.

Alwynne turned.

"You needn't trouble. If Miss Hartill doesn't, I shall go to her myself."

"You?" said Henrietta uneasily.

"Why," cried Alwynne, flaming out at her, "d'you think I'm afraid of you? D'you think I am going to stand this sort of thing? I know I was careless, and I'm sorry. I'm going straight down to Miss Hartill to tell her so. And if she slangs me-it's all right. And if Miss Marsham slangs me-it's all right. She's the head of the school. But I won't be slanged by you. You are rude and interfering and I shall tell Miss Marsham so."

Shaking with indignation she slammed down the lid of her desk: and with her head held high, and a dignity that a friendly word would have dissolved into tears, walked out of the class-room.

CHAPTER III

Alwynne Durand was quite aware that she was an arrant coward. The cronies of her not remote schooldays would have exclaimed at the label, have cited this or that memorable audacity in confutation, but Alwynne herself knew better. When her impulsiveness had jockeyed her into an uncomfortable situation, pure pride could always be trusted to sustain her, strengthen her shoulders and sharpen her wits; but she triumphed with shaking knees. Alwynne, touchy with the touchiness of eighteen, was bound to fling down her glove before Henrietta Vigers, and be ostentatiously ready to face cornet, flute, harp, sackbut, psaltery, and all kinds of music. But Alwynne, half-an-hour later, on her way to Miss Hartill and her overdue apology, was bound also to be feeling more like a naughty schoolgirl than a mistress of six weeks' standing has any business to feel, to be uneasily wondering what she should say, how she should say it, and why on earth she had been fool enough to get herself into the mess.

If it had been any one but Miss Hartill, with whom she had not exchanged five words, but whom she had heard discussed, nevertheless, from every conceivable and inconceivable point of view, with that accompanying profusion of anecdote of which only schoolgirl memory, so traditional as well as personal, is capable.

Miss Marsham, she had been given to understand might be head mistress, but Miss Hartill was Miss Hartill. Alwynne, accustomed as she was to the cults of a boarding-school, had ended by growing exceedingly curious. Yet when Miss Hartill had returned, a week or two late, to her post, Alwynne could not, as she phrased it, for the life of her see what all the fuss was about. Miss Hartill was ordinary enough. Alwynne had looked up one morning, from an obscure corner of the Common-room, at the sound of a clicking latch, had had an impression of a tall woman, harshly outlined by the white panelled door, against which she leaned lazily as she quizzed the roomful of women. Alwynne told herself that she was not at all impressed.... This the Miss Hartill of a hundred legends? This the Olympian to whom three-fourths of the school said its prayers? Who had split the staff into an enthusiastic majority and a minority that concealed its dislike? Queer! Alwynne, shrugging her shoulders over the intricacies of a school's enthusiasms, had leaned back in her chair to watch, between amusement and contempt, the commotion that had broken out. There was a babble of welcome, a cross-fire of question and answer. And then, over the heads of the little group that had gathered about the door, a pair of keen, roving eyes had settled on herself, coolly appraising. Alwynne had been annoyed with herself for flushing under the stare. She had a swift impression of being summed up, all raw and youthful and ambitious as she was, her attitude of unwilling curiosity detected, expected even. There had been a flicker of a smile, amused, faintly insolent....

But it had all been merest impression. Miss Hartill, who had been, indeed, surrounded, inaccessible, from the instant of her entrance until the prayer bell rang, did not look her way a second time. But the impression had remained, and Alwynne, obscure in her newness and her corner, found herself reconsidering this Miss Hartill, more roused than she would confess. If she were not the Hypatia-Helen of the class-rooms, she was none the less a personality! Whether Alwynne would like her was another matter.

Alwynne, in the next few days, had not come into direct contact with Miss Hartill. She had noticed, however, a certain stirring of the school atmosphere, a something of briskness and tension that affected her pleasantly. The children, she supposed, were getting into their stride.... But she began to see that the classes chiefly affected were the classes with which Miss Hartill had most to do, that the mistresses, too, were working with unusual energy, and that Miss Vigers was less in evidence than heretofore; that, in short, Miss Hartill's return was making a difference. Insensibly she slipped into the fashion of being slightly in awe of her-was daily and undeniably relieved that her work had as yet escaped the swift eyes and lazy criticism. But she was also aware that she would be distinctly gratified if Miss Hartill should at any time express satisfaction with her and her efforts. Miss Hartill was certainly interesting. She had wondered if she should ever get to know her; had hoped so.

And now Napoleon Buonaparte and a stopped clock had between them managed the business for her effectually. She was going to know Miss Hartill—a justifiably, and, according to Miss Vigers, excessively indignant Miss Hartill. She looked forward without enthusiasm to that acquaintance. She did not know what she should say to Miss Hartill.... But Miss Hartill would do the talking, she imagined.... She was extremely sorry for herself as she knocked at Miss Hartill's door.

The maid left her stranded in the hall, and she waited, uncomfortably conscious of voices in the next room.

"Brand? But I don't know any——Drand! Oh, Durand! What an extraordinary time to———All right Bagot. No. Lunch as usual."

The maid slipped across the hall again to her kitchen as Miss Hartill came forward, polite, unsmiling. She did not offer her hand, but stood waiting for Alwynne to deliver herself of her errand.

But Alwynne was embarrassed. The exordium she had so carefully prepared during her walk was eluding her. It had been easy to arrange the conversation beforehand, but Miss Hartill in the flesh was disconcerting. She jumbled her opening sentences, flushed, floundered, and was silent. Ensued a pause.

Clare surveyed her visitor quizzically, enjoying her discomfort. Alwynne was at her prettiest at a disadvantage. She had an air of shedding eight of her eighteen years, of recognising in her opponent a long-lost nurse.

Clare repressed a chuckle.

"Try again, Miss Durand," she said solemnly.

"I came," said Alwynne blankly. "You see, I came——" She paused again.

"Yes, I think I see that," said Clare, as one enlightened.

Alwynne eyed her dubiously. There might or might not have been a twinkle in her colleague's eye. She took heart of grace and began again.

"Miss Hartill, I'm awfully sorry! It was me—I, I mean, I kept the girls. I didn't hear the gong. Really and truly I didn't. Honestly, it was an accident. I thought I ought to come and apologise. Truly, I'm most awfully sorry, quite apart from avoiding getting into a row. Because I've got into that already."

Clare's lips twitched. Alwynne was built on generous lines. She had a good carriage, could enter a room effectively. Clare had not been unaware of her secure manner. Her present collapse was the more amusing. Clare was beginning to guess that what Miss Durand did, she did wholeheartedly.

"I expect you're simply wild with me. Miss Vigers said you would be," said Alwynne hopelessly.

"Miss Vigers ought to know," said Clare.

There was another pause.

"I'm frightfully sorry," said Alwynne suggestively.

"Are you, Miss Durand?"

"I mean, apart from upsetting you, I'm so savage with myself. One doesn't exactly enjoy making a fool of oneself, does one, Miss Hartill? You know how it feels. And it's my first post, and I did mean to do it well, and I've only been here six weeks, and I'm in a row with three people already."

"How-three?" said Clare with interest.

"Well-there's you——"

"I think we're settling that," said Clare, with her sudden smile.

"Are we?" Alwynne looked up so warily that Clare laughed outright.

"But the other two, Miss Durand-the other two? This grows interesting."

"Well, you see," Alwynne expanded, "I had an awful row with Miss Vigers-and she's sure to tell Miss Marsham. I suppose I was rude, but she did make me so mad. I don't see that it was her business to come and slang me before my class."

"My class," corrected Clare.

"I wouldn't have minded you," said Alwynne, lifting ingenuous eyes.

"I'm flattered," murmured Clare.

"Well-you would have understood," said Alwynne with conviction. "But Miss Vigers——I ask you, Miss Hartill, what would be the use of talking about Napoleon to Miss Vigers?"

"I give it up," said Clare promptly.

"There you are!" Alwynne waved her hand triumphantly.

"But, excuse me"—Clare was elaborately respectful—"has Napoleon any traceable connection with the kidnapping of my class?"

"Oh, I thought I explained." Alwynne plunged into her story. "You see, I was giving them Elocution-they're learning the *Incident in the French Camp* —you know?"

Clare nodded.

"Well, I thought they were rather more wooden than usual, and I found out that they knew practically nothing about Napoleon! Marengo-Talleyrand-never heard of 'em! Waterloo, and that he behaved badly to his wife-that's all they knew!"

"The English in a nutshell!" murmured Clare.

"So, of course, I told them all about him, and his life, and tit-bits like the Sèvres tea-things, and Madame Sans-gêne. They loved it. And I was showing them pictures and I suppose we got absorbed. You can't help it with Napoleon, somehow. Oh, Miss Hartill, doesn't it seem crazy, though, to keep those children at Latin exercises, and the exports of Lower Tooting, and Bills of Attainder in the reign of Queen Anne, before they know about things like Napoleon, and Homer, and the Panama Canal? Wouldn't you rather know about the life of Buddha than the war of Jenkins's ear? Not that I ever got to the Georges myself! Oh, it makes me so wild! It's like stuffing them with pea-nuts, when one has got a basket of peaches on one's arm. It isn't education! It's goose-cramming! I can't explain properly what I mean. I expect you think I'm a fool!"

"An enthusiast. It's much the same," said Clare absently. "You'll get over it." Then, with a twinkle: "Reform's an excellent thing, of course-but why annex my class to experiment with?"

Alwynne defervesced.

There was an unhappy pause.

"You know, I'm most awfully sorry," said Alwynne at last, as one making a brilliant and original contribution to the discussion.

A piercing shriek from the kitchen interrupted them. Alwynne jumped, but Clare was undisturbed.

"It's only Bagot. She's always having accidents. But she's an excellent cook. After all, what's a shilling's worth of crockery a week compared with a good cook? But to return to Napoleon and the Lower Third——"

"You don't think she's hurt herself?" Alwynne ventured to interrupt. "She did squeal."

Clare looked suddenly concerned.

"I hope not. I haven't had lunch yet."

She went to the kitchen door, reappearing with a slightly harried air.

"Miss Durand, I wish you'd come here a minute. She's cut her hand. Oh, lavishly! Most careless! What is one to do? I suppose one must bandage it?"

Her tone of helpless disgust was so genuine that Alwynne was inclined to laugh. So there were circumstances that could be too much even for Miss Hartill! How reassuring! And how it warmed the cockles of one's heart to her! Her lips twitched mischievously as she looked from the disconcerted mistress to the sniffing maid, but she lost no time in stripping off her gloves and setting to work, issuing orders the while that Clare obeyed with a meekness that surprised herself.

"Linen, please, Miss Hartill, or old rags! It's rather a bad cut." Then, to the maid, "How on earth did you do it? A tin-opener? No, no, Miss Hartill! a duster's no good. An old handkerchief or something." She was achieving complicated effects with a fork and a knotted scarf as she spoke, and Clare, obediently tearing linen into strips, considered her critically. The girl was capable then, as well as amusing.... That tourniquet might not be professional, but it was at least effective.... The bleeding was stopping.... Very good of her to toil over Bagot's unappetising hand.... Clare marvelled at her unconcern, for she was dainty enough in her own person to please even Clare's fastidious eye. Clare supposed that it was a good thing that some people had the nursing instinct.... She thanked her stars that she herself had not....

Alwynne, unconscious of scrutiny, put in her final safety-pin, settled the sling and stepped back at last, surveying her handiwork with some pride.

"It'll want a stitch, though. She'd better go to the doctor, I think," she said decisively. "Shall I come with you?" This to the maid, complacently the centre of attention.

But the maid preferred to fetch her mother. "Her mother lived quite close, miss. If Miss 'Artill could get on ——"

"She can't do any cooking with that hand," said Alwynne to Clare, more in decision than appeal, and Clare acquiescing, she fetched hat and coat, manipulated hatpins, and bundled the girl forth.

She returned to the kitchen to find Miss Hartill, skirts clutched high, eyeing the crowded table with distaste, and prodding with a toasting-fork at the half-prepared meal.

"Isn't it disgusting? How these people bleed! I can't stand a mess! Really, I'm very much obliged to you, Miss Durand for seeing to Bagot. I'm no good at that sort of thing. I hate touching people. You don't think it was a bad cut, though?"

"It must have hurt! She won't be able to use her hand for a day or two."

Clare rubbed her nose peevishly. She had a comical air of resenting the necessity for concerning herself with her own domestic arrangements.

"Well, what am I to do? And I loathe charwomen. She might at least have got lunch first!"

"The meat's cooked, anyhow," said Alwynne hopefully, drawing forth a congealing dishful.

Clare shivered.

"Take it away! It's all over Bagot."

"I don't think it is." Alwynne examined it cautiously.

Clare gave her a short laugh.

"Anyhow, it doesn't appeal any more. Never mind, Miss Durand, I shall manage —I mustn't keep you."

Alwynne disregarded the hint. She seemed preoccupied.

"There aren't any eggs, I suppose," she ventured diffidently.

Clare flung out vague hands.

"Heaven knows! It's Bagot's business. Why?"

"Because," Alwynne had crossed the room and was struggling with a stiff cupboard door, "Elsbeth says I'm a fool at cooking (Elsbeth's my aunt, you know), but I can make omelets ——" The door gave suddenly and Alwynne fell forward into the dark pantry. There was a clatter as of scattered bread-pans. She soon emerged, however, floury but serene.

"Yes! There are some! It wouldn't take ten minutes, Miss Hartill. That is-if——" she sought delicately for a tactful phrase: "if you would perhaps like to go away and read. If any one stands about and watches-you know what I mean ——"

"Are you proposing to cook my lunch?" Clare demanded.

"Of course, if you don't like omelets," said Alwynne demurely.

Clare laughed outright.

"I do —I do. All right, Miss Durand, I'm too hungry to refuse. But I see through it, you know. It's to cry quits!"

Alwynne broke in indignantly —

"It isn't! It's the *amende honorable* —at least, if it doesn't scorch."

"All right, I accept it!" Clare pacified her; then, as she left the kitchen, "Miss Durand?"

"Yes, Miss Hartill?"

"Are you going to make one for Miss Vigers?"

Alwynne's face fell.

"I'd forgotten Miss Vigers."

Clare twinkled.

"Perhaps-if it doesn't scorch—I'll see what I can do," she promised her.

The lunch was a success. Alwynne, dishing up, had her hat ordered off her head, and was soon sharing the omelet and marvelling at herself for being where she was, and Clare, for her part, found herself enjoying her visitor as much as her meal.

Clare Hartill led a sufficiently solitary life. She was a woman of feverish friendships and sudden ruptures. Always the cleverest and most restless of her circle, she usually found her affinities as unable to satisfy her demands on their intellect as on their emotions. Disillusionment would be swift and final: Clare never forgave a bore. Gradually it came to pass that intercourse she so carefully fostered with her elder pupils became her absorbing and satisfying interest. She plumed herself on her independence of social amenities, did not guess, would not have admitted, that her pleasure in a chance table companion had its flavour of pathos. It was enough to acknowledge to herself that Alwynne Durand, with her enthusiasms, her incoherencies, and her capacities had certainly caught her difficult fancy. She liked the girl's manner; its compound of shyness and audacity, deference and independence pleased her sophisticated taste. She found her racy and original, and, in the exertion of drawing her out, was herself at her best. A brilliant talker, she chose to listen, and soon heard all there was to hear of Alwynne's short history; of her mother's sister, Elsbeth Loveday (Clare pricked up her ears at the name), who had reared her from babyhood; of her schooldays; her crude young likes and dislikes; her hero-worships and passionate, vague ambitions. Clare knew it all by heart, had heard the tale from more pairs of lips than she could remember, for more years than she cared to count. But Alwynne, nevertheless, told it in a way of her own that appealed to Clare and interested her anew. She told herself that the girl was worth cultivating; and what with apt comments, apter silences, and the half-finished phrases and abrupt noddings of perfect comprehension, contrived to make Alwynne think her the most sympathetic person she had ever had the fortune to meet. Indeed, they pleased each other so well that when Alwynne, towards tea-time, made an unwilling move, Clare was as unwilling, for her part, to let her go.

"It was certainly a most excellent omelet," she said, as she sped her from the door. "I suppose you won't come and cook me another to-night?"

Alwynne took her at her word.

"I will! Of course I will! Would you like me to, really? I will! I'd love to!"

Clare laughed.

"Oh, I was only in fun. Whatever would your aunt say?"

"She wouldn't mind," began Alwynne eagerly.

Clare temporised.

"But your work? Haven't you any work?"

Alwynne overwhelmed her.

"That's all right! It isn't much! I'll sit up. I wish you'd let me. I would love to. You must have some one to cook your supper for you, mustn't you?"

"Well, of course, if you'd really like to——" Clare hesitated between jest and earnest.

But Alwynne was wholly in earnest.

"I'll come. Thank you very much indeed," said Alwynne, eyes sparkling.

CHAPTER IV

In the months that followed the eating of the omelet, Alwynne would have agreed that the cynic who said that "an entirely successful love-affair can only be achieved by foundlings" should have included friendship in his dictum. For relations ... well, everybody knew what everybody meant when relations were mentioned in that particular tone; and Elsbeth, dearest of maiden aunts, was nevertheless at times aggressively a relation: privileged to wet-blanket enthusiasms.

Elsbeth made, indeed, no stand against the alliance that had sprung mushroom-like into existence; was courteous, in her sweet silent fashion, to Clare Hartill at their occasional meetings; but she remained subtly uninterested. But when, again, had that suppressed and self-effacing personality shown interest in any living thing save Alwynne herself?

Alwynne, shrugging her shoulders, and ignoring, as youth must, the affectionate prevision that had lapped her all her life, supposed that she must not expect too much of poor, dear Elsbeth.... (It was characteristic of their relationship that she never called her guardian "Aunt.") Elsbeth, darling Elsbeth-but a little limited, perhaps? Hardly to be expected that she should appreciate a Miss Hartill....

Elsbeth, though Alwynne never guessed it, quite understood what went on in her niece's mind: was resigned to it. She knew that she was not a clever woman. She had been too much occupied, all her life, in smoothing the way for other people, to have had leisure for her own cultivation, physical or mental. Her two years of teaching, in the uncertificated 'eighties, had but served to reveal to herself her ingrained incapacity for government. She had never forgotten the humiliation of those months when Clare Hartill, a pitiless fourteen-year-old girl, had headed one successful revolt after another against her. It had been an episode; with the advent of Alwynne she had returned to domesticity; but the experience had intensified her innate lack of self-esteem. There were times when she seriously debated whether, in bringing up her orphaned niece, she were indulging herself at the expense of her duty. She knew quite well, and rejoiced shamefacedly in the knowledge, that Alwynne, her beautiful, brilliant, headstrong girl, could twist the old aunt round her little finger. And that, of course, could not be good for Alwynne.

Alwynne was, to do her justice, extremely fond of her aunt. Till the advent of Clare Hartill, Elsbeth had been the pole-star of her world. All the more disconcerting of Elsbeth, receiver of confidences, therefore, to be so entirely uninterested in the comet that was deflecting Alwynne from her accustomed orbit.

She wondered occasionally what her aunt's history had been. Elsbeth was reticent: never a woman of reminiscences. Her relations were distant ones, whom she rarely mentioned and apparently more rarely missed. Alwynne was the more surprised one breakfast, when, retailing the school's latest scandal, she was interrupted by an exclamation of pleasure.

"Alwynne! The Lumsdens are coming back!" Elsbeth rustled foreign paper delightedly.

Alwynne wrinkled her brows.

"The Lumsdens? Oh-those cousins of yours?"

"Yes. The youngest, Rosemary, only died last year. Don't you remember? They've lived abroad for years on account of her health, and her son Roger always went out to her for his holidays."

"Roger? Is that the velveteen boy in the big album?"

Elsbeth laughed.

"He must be thirty by now. The estate went to him. It was let, you know, and the Great House at Dene-to a school, I believe. They had lost money. And Rosemary was always extravagant. Roger went to America for a time. But still he's well enough off. He came home when his mother died last year, and now, it seems, he's taken a house close to their old home, and settled down as a market-gardener. The Lumsdens are to come and keep house for him. He's very fond of his aunts, I know. Well! To think of seeing Jean and Alicia again after all these years. They want us to come and stay when they've settled down."

140

"You'll enjoy that?" Alwynne eyed her aunt curiously. Elsbeth's pale cheeks were pink, her faded eyes dreamy. Her unconscious hand was rapping out its tune upon the tablecloth—the only symptom of excitement that Elsbeth ever showed. "Were you fond of them? Why haven't you ever been to see them, Elsbeth?"

"Time flies. And I certainly can't afford to gad about the Riviera. And there was you, you know. Besides——" she hesitated.

"Besides what?"

Elsbeth did not seem to hear.

"You'll like Dene, Alwynne. Oh, yes, I know it well. I used to stay with them-before the Great House was let. Years ago. And Roger—I hope you'll get on with Roger. I haven't seen him since he was five. A jolly little fellow. And from what Alicia says——"

But Alwynne would not take any interest in Roger. He had a snub nose in the photograph; and besides, she hated men. So dull. As Clare said—— Indeed, she wasn't always quoting Clare! She didn't always set up Clare's judgment against Elsbeth's! Elsbeth needn't get huffy! She would like to go down to Dene very much, if Elsbeth wanted to, some time or other.

But when the holidays came and the formal invitation, Alwynne was less amenable.

Why couldn't Elsbeth go alone? Elsbeth couldn't expect her to go and stay with utter strangers. She hated strangers. Besides, there was Clare. (It was "Clare" and "Alwynne" by that time.) She and Clare had planned out every day of the holidays. Everything fixed. She really couldn't ask Clare to upset all her arrangements. It wouldn't be fair. Awfully sorry, of course, but why couldn't Alwynne's dear Elsbeth go by herself? She, Alwynne, could keep house. Oh, perfectly well! She wasn't a fool! She wouldn't dream of spoiling Elsbeth's holiday, but Elsbeth must see that there was no need for Alwynne to share it.

But Elsbeth was unusually obstinate. Elsbeth, it appeared, wanted Alwynne with her; wanted to show Alwynne to these old friends; wanted to show these old friends to Alwynne; wouldn't enjoy the visit without Alwynne at her elbow; refused utterly to be convinced of unreasonableness. Alwynne would enjoy the change, the country-didn't Alwynne love the country? —and if she herself, and Alicia, and Jean, were not of Alwynne's generation, there was always Roger! By all accounts Roger was very nice; witness the aunts who adored him.

Alwynne snorted.

She argued the matter mercilessly, length, breadth, depth and back again, and ended, as Elsbeth knew she would, by getting her own way. But Elsbeth did not go to Dene by herself. There she was mulish. Go visiting and leave the housekeeping to Alwynne's tender mercies? Heaven forbid! There was more in housekeeping than dusting a bedroom, making peppermint creams, or wasting four eggs on an omelet.

So Alwynne spent her pleasant holidays in and out of Clare Hartill's pocket and Elsbeth stayed at home. But Elsbeth had learned her lesson. It was many a long day before she again suggested a visit to Dene.

CHAPTER V

One of Alwynne's duties was the conduct of a small "extra" class, consisting of girls, who, for reasons of stupidity, ill-health or defective grounding, fell too far below the average of knowledge in their respective classes. She devoted certain afternoons in the week to coaching them, and was considered to be unusually successful in her methods. She could be extremely patient, and had quaint and unorthodox ways of insinuating facts into her pupils' minds. As she told Elsbeth, she invented their memories for them. She was sufficiently imaginative to realise their difficulties, yet sufficiently young to dream of developing, in due course, all her lame ducks into swans. She was intensely interested in hearing how her coaching had succeeded; her pleasure at an amended place in class was so genuine, her disappointment at a collapse so comically real, yet so devoid of contempt, so tinged with conviction that it was anybody's fault but the culprit's, that either attitude was an incentive to real effort. Like Clare, she did not suffer fools gladly, but unlike Clare, she had not the moral courage to be ruthless. Stupidity seemed as terrible to her as physical deformity; she treated it with the same touch of motherliness, the same instinctive desire to spare it realisation of its own unsightliness.

Her rather lovable cowardice brought a mixed reward; she stifled in sick-rooms, yet invalids liked her well; she was frankly envious of Clare's circle of brilliant girls and as inevitably surrounded by inarticulate adorers, who bored her mightily, but whose clumsy affection she was too kindhearted to suppress.

It had been well for Alwynne, however, that her following was of the duller portion of the school. This Clare could endure, could countenance; such boy-bishopry could not affect her own sovereignty, and her subject's consequence increased her own. But to see Alwynne swaying, however unconsciously, minds of a finer type, would not have been easy for Clare. She had grown very fond of Alwynne; but the sentiment was proprietary; she could derive no pleasure from her that was not personal, and, in its most literal sense, selfish. She was unmaternal to the core. She could not see human property admired by others with any sensation but that of a double jealousy; she was subtly angered that Alwynne could attract, yet was caught herself in the net of those attractions, and unable to endure to watch them spread for any but herself.

Alwynne, quite unconscious of the trait, had at first done herself harm by her unfeigned interest in Clare's circle. It took the elder woman some suspicious weeks to realise that Alwynne lacked completely her own *dompteuse* instinct, her craving for power; that she was as innocent of knowledge of her own charm as unwedded Eve; that her impulse to Clare was an impulse of the freshest, sweetest hero-worship; but the realisation came at last, and Clare opened her hungry heart to her, and, warmed by Alwynne's affection, wondered that she had hesitated so long.

Alwynne never guessed that she had been doubted. Clare was proud of her genuine skill as a character reader-had been a little pleased to give Alwynne proof of her penetration when occasion arose; and Alwynne, less trained, less critical, thought her omniscient, and never dreamed that the motives of her obscurest actions, the sources of her most veiled references were not plain to Clare. Secure of comprehension, she went her way: any one in whom Clare was interested must needs attract her: so she took pains to become intimate with Clare's adorers, from a very real sympathy with their appreciation of Clare, whom she no more grudged to them than a priestess would grudge the unveiling of her goddess to the initiate. She received their confidences, learned their secrets, fanned the flame of their enthusiasms. Too lately a schoolgirl herself, too innocent and ignorant to dream of danger, she did her loyal utmost in furtherance of the cult, measuring the artificial and unbalanced emotions she encountered by the rule of her own saner affection, and, in her desire to see her friend appreciated, in all good faith utilised her degree of authority to encourage what an older woman would have recognised and combated as incipient hysteria.

Gradually she became, through her frank sympathy, combined with her slightly indeterminate official position, the intermediary, the interpreter of Clare to the feverish school. Clare herself, her initial distrust over, found this useful. She could afford to be moody, erratic, whimsical; to be extravagant in her praises and reproofs; to deteriorate, at times, into a caricature of her own bizarre personality, with the comfortable assurance that there was ever a magician in her wake to steady her tottering shrines, mix oil with her vitriol, and prove her pinchbeck gold.

Fatal, this relaxation of effort, to a woman of Clare's type. Love of some sort was vital to her. Of this her surface personality was dimly, ashamedly aware, and would, if challenged, have frigidly denied; but the whole of her larger self knew its need, and saw to it that that need was satisfied. Clare, unconscious, had taught Clare, conscious, that there must be effort-constant, straining effort at cultivation of all her alluring qualities, at concealment of all in her that could repulse-effort that all appearances of complete success must never allow her to relax. She knew well the evanescent character of a schoolgirl's affection; so well that when her pupils left the school she seldom tried to retain her hold upon them. Their letters would come thick as autumn leaves at first; she rarely answered, or after long intervals; and the letters dwindled and ceased. She knew that, in the nature of things, it must be so, and had no wish to prolong the farewells.

Also, her interest in her correspondents usually died first; to sustain it required their physical nearness. But every new year filled the gaps left by the old, stimulated Clare to fresh exertion.

So the lean years went by. Then came vehement Alwynne-no schoolgirl-yet more youthful and ingenuous than any mistress had right to be, loving with all the discrimination of a fine mind, and all the ardour of an affectionate child. Here was no question of a fleeting devotion that must end as the schooldays ended. Here was love for Clare at last, a widow's cruse to last her for all time. Clare thanked the gods of her unbelief, and, relaxing all effort, settled herself to enjoy to the full the cushioning sense of security; the mock despot of their pleasant, earlier intercourse becoming, as she bound Alwynne ever more closely to her, albeit unconsciously, a very real tyrant indeed.

Yet she had no intention of weakening her hold on any lesser member of her chosen coterie. Alwynne was too ingenuous, too obviously subject through her own free impulse, to entirely satisfy: Clare's love of power had its morbid moments, when a struggling victim, head averted, pleased her. There was never, among the new-comers, a child, self-absorbed, nonchalant or rebellious, who passed a term unmolested by Miss Hartill. Egoism aroused her curiosity, her suspicion of hidden lands, virgin, ripe for exploration; indifference piqued her; a flung gauntlet she welcomed with frank amusement. She had been a rebel in her own time, and had ever a thrill of sympathy for the mutinies she relentlessly crushed. War, personal war, delighted her; she was a mistress of tactics, and the certainty of eventual victory gave zest to her campaigns. She did not realise that the strain upon her childish opponents was very great. The finer, the more sensitive the character, the more complete the eventual defeat, the more permanent its effects. Clare was pitiless after victory: not till then did she examine into the nature thus enslaved, seldom did she find it worth the trouble of the skirmish. In most cases she gave semi-liberty; enough of smiles to keep the children feverishly at work to please her (the average of achievement in her classes was astounding), and enough of indifference to prevent them from becoming a nuisance. To the few that pleased her fastidious taste, she gave of her best, lavishly, as she had given to Alwynne. There are women to-day, old girls of the school, who owe Clare Hartill the best things of their lives, their wide knowledge, their original ideas, their hopeful futures and happy memories: to whom she was an inspiration incarnate. The Clare they remember is not the Clare that Elsbeth knew, that Alwynne learned to know, that Clare herself, one bitter night, faced and blanched at. But which of them had knowledge of the true Clare, who shall say?

* * * * *

In Clare's favourite class was a certain Louise Denny. She was thirteen-nearly three years below the average of the class in age. How far beyond it in all else, not even Clare realised.

Clare had discovered her, as she phrased it, in the limbo of the Lower Third. She had been paying one of her surprise visits to the afternoon extra needlework classes —(the possibility of her occasional appearance, book in hand, was responsible for the school's un-English proficiency in hemming, darning and kindred mysteries), to read aloud to the children carefully edited excerpts from Poe's *Tales*, had forgotten her copy and had been shyly offered another, private property from Louise Denny's desk. Thereon must Alwynne, for a week or two, resign perforce her Lower Third literature classes to Clare, intent on her blue rose. Louise's compositions had been read-Clare and Alwynne spent a long evening over them, weighing, comparing, discussing. Clare could be exquisitely tender, could keep all-patient vigil over an unfolding mind, provided that the calyx concealed a rare enough blossom. Louise was encouraged, her shyness swept aside, her ideas developed, her knowledge tested; she was fed, too, cautiously, on richer and richer food-stray evening lectures, picture galleries with Alwynne, headiest of cicerones; the freedom of the library and long talks with Clare. Finally Clare, bearing down all opposition, transplanted her to the Lower Fifth, containing at that time some brilliantly clever girls. Louise justified her by speedily capturing, and doggedly retaining, the highest place in the class.

Clare was delighted. Her critics-there were some mistresses who vaguely disapproved of the experiment-were refuted, and the class, already needing no spur, outdoing itself in its efforts to compete with the intruder, swept the board at an important public examination.

On the morning of the announcement of results, Clare entered her form-room radiant. It was a low, many-windowed room, with desks ranged single-file along the walls. The class being a small one, the girls were accustomed to sit for their lessons at a large oval table at the upper end of the room. Beside the passage doorway, there was a smaller one, that led into the studio, and was never used by the children. Clare, however, would sometimes enter by it, but so seldom that they invariably forgot to keep watch. Clare enjoyed the occasional view she thus obtained of her unconscious and relaxed subjects, and the piquancy of their uncensored conversation; she enjoyed still more the sudden hush, the crisp thrill, that ran through their groups, when they became aware of her, observant in the doorway.

On the morning in question she had watched them for some little while. Before each girl lay her open exercise-book and school edition of Browning. They were deep in discussion of their work, very eager upon some question. By the empty chair at the head of the table sat Marion Hughes, blonde and placid, a rounded elbow on her neatly written theme, that her neighbour was trying to pull away, to compare with her own well-inked manuscript. This neighbour, one Agatha Middleton, was dark, gaunt, with restless eyes and restless tongue. She was old for her fifteen years, and had been original until she discovered that her originality appealed to Miss Hartill. Since then she had imitated her own mannerisms, and was rapidly degenerating into an eccentric. The law of opposites had decreed that the sedate Marion should be her bosom friend. They went up the school together, an incongruous, yet well-suited pair, for they were so unlike that there could be no rivalry. Marion was alternately amused and dazzled by the pyrotechnic Agatha. Agatha's respect for Marion's common sense was pleasantly tempered by a conviction of superior mental agility. Finally, they were united by their common devotion to their form-mistress. Whether it would have occurred to Marion, unprompted, to admire Miss Hartill, is uncertain. Her affections were domestic and calm. But adoration was in the air, and she had not sufficient originality to be unfashionable. She was caught, too, in Agatha's whirlwind emotions, and ended by worshipping Clare conscientiously and sincerely. Clare, on her side, respected her, as she told Alwynne, for her "painstaking and intelligent stupidity," and, recognising a nature too worthy for neglect, yet too lymphatic to be suitable for experiments, was uniformly kind to her. Agatha, she had revelled in for six weeks, and had since more or less ignored as a bore. Below the pair sat a spectacled student, predestined to scholarships and a junior mistress-ship; opposite, between giggling twins, a vivid little Jewess, whose showy work was due to the same vanity that tied her curls with giant bows, and over-corsetted her matured figure. At the foot of the oval, directly opposite Clare's vacant chair, stood Louise, flushed and excited, chanting low-voicedly a snatch of verse.

During a lull in the hubbub Marion called to her down the table—

"How many pages?"

Louise flushed. She was still a little in awe of these elders whom she had outstripped. She rapidly counted the leaves of her essay, and held up both hands, smiling shyly.

Marion exclaimed.

"Ten? You marvel! I only got to seven. I simply didn't understand it. Whatever did you find to say?"

Agatha fell upon the query.

"That's nothing! I've done twenty-two!" she cried triumphantly, and turned to face the shower of comments.

"Miss Hartill will bless you. She said last time that you thought ink and ideas were synonyms."

"Agatha only writes three words to a line anyway."

They liked her, but she was of the type whose imperiousness provokes snubs.

"Well, I thought I shouldn't get it done under forty-an essay on *The Dark Tower*. It's the beastliest yet. *The Ancient Mariner* was nothing to it. I've made an awful hash-didn't you?"

"I understood all right when she read it, and explained. It's so absurd not to let one take notes. I've been years at it. Fortunately she said we needn't learn it-Louise and I —with all our extra work." An unimaginative hockey captain fluttered her pages distractedly.

"Oh, but I have!" Louise looked up quickly.

"Why?" The hockey captain opened her eyes and mouth.

"Oh, I rather wanted to."

The little Jewess giggled.

"'*Déjà?*'" she murmured. She did not love Clare.

Marion returned to the subject with her usual perseverance.

"Did you understand it, kid?"

Louise stammered a little.

"When she reads it, and when I say it aloud, I think I do. It was impossible to write it down."

"Let's see what you have put." Agatha, by a quick movement, possessed herself of Louise's exercise-book. Louise, shy and desperate, strove silently with her neighbours, who, curious, held her back, while Agatha, holding the book at arm's length, recited from it in a high mocking voice.

"*Childe Roland to the Dark Tower came.* Description! Description! Description! for three-five-seven pages! You've let yourself go, Louise! Ah, here we are —*The meaning of the poem.* Now we're getting to it. *Shakespeare and Browning may have known all the real history of Childe Roland; the reason of his quest, the secret of the horror of the Tower; but we are left in ignorance. That does not matter, for, as we read, the inner meaning of the terrible poem kills all curiosity. Shuddering we close the book, and pray to God that Childe Roland's journey may never be ours; that for our adventurous souls, knight-erranting through this queer life, there may never come a choice of ways, a turning from the pleasant high-road, to go upon a hideous journey; till, crossing the Plains of Loneliness, Fear and Sorrow, we face the Hills of Madness, and enter the Dark Tower of that Despair which is our soul's death.* With capital letters galore! What a sentence! Here, shut up, you spit-fire!" Louise had wrenched herself free and flung herself upon Agatha, in a white heat of anger.

"Give it me! You've no right! You've no right!" she gasped. Her shyness had gone, she was blazing with indignation.

Agatha, the book held teasingly out of reach, affected to search for her place. Louise raised her clenched fist desperately.

A cool hand caught her wrist in a firm yet kindly grip. A hush fell on the voluble group and Agatha collapsed into an apologetic nonentity.

Clare, who had entered in her usual noiseless fashion, stood a moment between the combatants, watching the effect of her appearance. Her hand shifted to Louise's bony little shoulder; through the thin blouse she could feel the driven blood pulsing. She did not move till she felt the child regaining comparative calm, when, giving her a gentle push towards her place, she walked slowly to the head of the table and seated herself. The class watched her furtively. It was quite aware that all rules of decorum had been transgressed-that pains and penalties would be in order with any other mistress. But with Miss Hartill there was always glorious uncertainty-and Miss Hartill did not look annoyed. Little gestures began to break the tension and Agatha, relieved, smiled a shade too broadly. Instantly Clare closed with her.

She began blandly —

"Agatha, I thought you could read aloud better than that. You are not doing your work justice. Pass me your essay."

"It's Louise's," said Agatha helplessly.

"Ah, I see. And you kindly read it to us for her? It's a pity you didn't understand what you read-but an excuse, of course. Louise must not expect too much."

Agatha flung up her head angrily.

"Oh, I understood it all right. I thought it was silly."

"You did? Read me your own."

"Now?"

"Certainly."

Now Clare, as she corrected and commented upon the weekly essays, did occasionally, if the mood took her, read extracts, humorous chiefly, therefrom; but it had never been customary for a pupil to read her own work aloud. Agatha had the pioneer spirit-but she was no fool. She comprehended that, with Clare inimical, she could climb no higher than the pillory. She fell back upon the tradition of the school.

"Oh, Miss Hartill—I can't!"

"Why not?"

"No one ever does ——"

Clare waited.

Agatha protested redly, her fear of ridicule outweighing her fear of Clare.

"Miss Hartill, I simply couldn't. Before everybody-all this tosh —I mean all this stuff I wrote. It's a written essay. I couldn't make it sound right aloud."

Clare waited.

"It's not good enough, Miss Hartill. Honestly! And we never have. You've never made us. I couldn't."

Clare waited.

Agatha twisted her hands uneasily. The schoolgirl shyness that is physical misery was upon her.

"I —don't want to, Miss Hartill. I can't. It's not fair to have one's stuff-to be laughed at-to be ——" she subsided just in time.

The class sat, breathless, all eyes on Clare.

And Clare waited; waited till defiance faded to unease-unease to helplessness, till the girl, overborne by the utter silence, gave way, and dropping her eyes to her exercise, fluttering its pages in angry embarrassment, finally, with a giggle of pure nervousness, embarked on the opening sentence.

Clare cut through the clustering adjectives.

"Stand up, please."

Resistance was over. She rose sullenly.

She had been proud of her essay, had worked at it sincerely, knew its periods by heart. But her pleasure in it was destroyed, as completely, she realised, as she had destroyed that of little Louise. More-for Louise had found a champion. That, she recognised jealously. Unjust! Her essay was no worse, read soberly-yet she was forced to render it ridiculous. She read a couple of pages in hurried jerks, stumbling over the illegibilities of her own handwriting, baulked by Clare's interpolations. She heard her own voice, high-pitched and out of control, perverting her meaning, felt the laden sentences breaking up into chaos on her lips. In her flurry she pronounced familiar words amiss, Clare's calm voice carefully correcting. Once she heard a chuckle. Two pages ... three ... only that ... she remembered that she had boasted of twenty ... seventeen to be read yet and they were all laughing. To have to stand there ... three pages....

"But as Childe Roland turned round ——"

"Louder, please," said Clare.

"But as Childe Roland turned round ——" and even Marion was laughing...."*Turned round to look once more back to the high road ——"*

"And slower."

"To the high road ——" She stopped suddenly, a lump in her throat.

"Go on, Agatha."

"To the high road ——" The letters danced up and down mistily. *"To the high road where the cripple-where the cripple ——*Oh, Miss Hartill," she cried imploringly, "isn't it enough?"

It was surrender. Clare nodded.

"Yes, you may sit down now. Your essay, please: thank you. And now I'll read you, once more, what Louise has to say on the same subject. I dare say you'll find, Agatha, that you were almost as unfair to her essay, as you were to-your own." And she smiled her sudden dazzling smile. Agatha, against her will, smiled tremulously back.

Clare, with a glance at the little figure, huddling at the foot of the table, began to read. The essay, for all its schoolgirl slips and extravagances, was unusual. The thought embodied in it, though tinged with morbidity, striking and matured. Clare did it more than justice. Her beautiful voice made music of the crude sentences, revealed, embellished, glorified. Her own interest growing as she read, infected the class; she swept them along with her, mutually enthusiastic. She ended abruptly, her voice like the echoes of a deep bell.

Marion broke the little pause.

"I liked that," she said, as if surprised at herself.

"So did I," Clare was pleased.

She dipped her pen in red ink and initialled the foot of the essay.

"That was good work, Louise. Now, the others."

But Louise, shy and glowing, broke in —

"But it wasn't all mine, Miss Hartill, not a bit."

Clare looked at her, half frowning.

"Not yours? Your handwriting ——?"

"Oh, I wrote it. But you've made it different. I hadn't meant it like that."

Clare raised a quizzical eyebrow.

"I have misinterpreted ——?"

Louise was too much in earnest to be fluttered.

"I only mean-you made it sound so beautiful that it was like listening to-to an organ. I didn't bother about the words while you read. It was all colours and gold-like the things in the Venetian room. You know. The meaning didn't matter. But I did mean something, not half so good, of course, only quite different. Horrid and grizzly like the plain he travelled through, Childe Roland. It ought to have sounded harsh and starved, like rats pattering-what I meant-not beautiful."

"I see." Clare was interested. She was quite aware that she had used her magnificent voice to impress arbitrarily her opinion of Louise's work upon the class. That Louise, impressionable as she knew her to be, should have yet detected the trick, amused her greatly.

"So you think I didn't understand your essay?"

Louise's shy laugh was very pleasant.

"Oh, Miss Hartill. I'm not so stupid. It's only that I can't have got the-the ——"

"Atmosphere!" The girl in spectacles helped her.

"The atmosphere that I meant to; so you put in a different one to help it. And it did. But it wasn't what I meant."

Clare glanced at her inscrutably, and began to score the other essays. She would get at Louise's meaning in her own way. She skimmed a couple, Agatha, be it recorded, receiving the coveted initials, before she spoke again.

*"*Didn't I tell you to learn *Childe Roland*, too? Ah, I thought so. Begin, Marion, while I finish these. Two verses."

147

Her pen scratched on, as Marion's expressionless voice rose, fell and finished. Agatha continued, jarringly dramatic. Two more followed her. Then Clare put down her pen.

"'For mark!'..."

There was a warning undertone in Louise's colourless voice, that crept across the room like a shadow. Clare lifted her head and stared at her.

> "For mark! no sooner was I fairly found
> Pledged to the plain, after a pace or two,
> Than, pausing to throw backward a last view
> O'er the safe road, 'twas gone; grey plain all round:
> Nothing but plain to the horizon's bound.
> I might go on; nought else remained to do."

There was horror in the whispering voice: the accents of one bowed beneath intolerable burdens, sick with the knowledge of nearing doom, gay with the flippancy of despair. Louise was looking straight before her, vacant as a medium, her hands lying laxly in her lap. Clare made a quick sign to her neighbour to be silent, and the strained voice rose anew.

Clare listened perplexedly. She told herself that this was sheer technique-some trick had been played, she was harbouring some child actress of parts-only to be convinced of folly. She knew all about Louise. Besides, she had heard the child read aloud before. Good, clean, intelligent delivery. But nothing like this-this was uncanny. Uncanny, yet magnificent. The artist in her settled down to enjoyment; yet she was uneasy, too.

"And just as far as ever from the end!"

The creeping voice toiled on across the haunted plain, growing louder, clearer, nearer.

Vision was forced upon Clare, serene in her form-room, swift and sudden vision. She not only heard, every sense responded. At her feet lay the waste land of the poem, she smelt the dank air, shrank from the clammy undergrowth, watched the bowed figure of the wandering knight, stumbling forwards doggedly. It was coming towards her, the outline blurred in the evening mist, the face hidden. The voice was surely his?

> "Not hear? when noise was everywhere! it tolled
> Increasing like a bell."

She heard it alive with warning.

Nearer, ever nearer; the bowed form was at her very feet, as the voice rose anew in despairing defiance.

"To view the last of me — —"

The helmeted head was flung back; the voice echoed from hill to hill —

> "I saw them and I knew them all. And yet
> Dauntless the slug-horn to my lips I set,
> And blew. Childe Roland to the Dark Tower came."

The figure fell, face upwards, at her feet. Clare tore at the visor with desperate hands, for at the last line, the strong voice had broken, quavering into the pitiful treble of a frightened child. The bars melted under her touch, as dream things will, and she was staring down at no bearded face, but at Louise. Louise herself, with blank, dead eyes in a broken, blood-flecked face. The dead mouth smiled.

"You see, that was what I meant, Miss Hartill. That atmosphere."

Clare roused herself with a start. Louise, rosily alive, and quivering with eagerness, was waiting for her comments. She got none.

"Begin again," said Clare mechanically, to the next girl.

The brightness died out of Louise's face, as she subsided in her seat. Clare, dazed as she was, saw it, and was touched. The child deserved praise-should not be punished for the vagaries of Clare's own phantasy. And the monkey could recite! She shook off the impression of that recital as best she could. Curious, the freaks of the imagination! She must tell Alwynne of the adventure-Alwynne, dreamer of dreams....And Alwynne was interested in Louise; was coaching her....Perhaps she was responsible ... had coached her in that very poem? She hoped not ... it would be interference....She did not like interference. But no-that performance was entirely original, she felt sure. There was genius in the child-sheer genius ... and but for Clare herself, she would yet be rotting undeveloped in the Lower Third. She was pleased with herself, pleased with Louise too; ready to tell her so, to see the child's face light up again delightedly; she was less attractive in repose....

Clare's chance came.

It was the turn of the hockey captain to recite. She appealed to Clare.

"Oh, Miss Hartill! You said I needn't, Louise and I—because of all our extra work. Not the poem."

Clare considered.

"I remember. Very well. But Louise?" She looked at her questioningly, half smiling. "When did you find the time?"

Louise laughed.

"I don't know, Miss Hartill. It found itself."

"Ah! And how much extra work have you, Louise?"

Louise reflected.

"All the afternoons, I think. And three evenings when I go to lectures. And, of course, gallery days, when I make up in the evenings."

"And homework?"

"Oh, there's heaps of time at night always."

Clare smiled upon her class.

"Well, Lower Fifth-what do you think of it?"

The class opened its mouth.

"Louise is moved up four forms. She's thirteen. She's top of the class and first in to-day's results. You hear what her extra work is. And she finds time to learn *Childe Roland* —optional. What do you think of it?"

Agatha bit down her envy.

"It's pretty good," she said.

Clare's glance approved her.

"Yes. So I think. It's so good that I'm more than pleased. I'm—impressed. Rather proud of my youngest pupil. For next time you will learn———" And with one of her quick transitions, she began to dictate her homework.

The gong clanged as she finished. Alwynne's voice was heard in the passage, inquiring for Miss Hartill, and Clare hurried out. Followed a confused banging of books and desk-lids, a tangle of fragmentary remarks, and much trampling of boots on uncarpeted boards, as one after another followed her. Within five minutes the room was bare, save for Clare's forgotten satchel at the upper end of the big table, and Louise, motionless in her chair at the foot.

CHAPTER VI

Louise was tasting happiness.

Happiness was a new and absorbing experience to Louise. The only child of a former marriage, she had grown up among boisterous half-brothers with whom she had little fellowship. Her father, a driving, thriving merchant, was prouder of his second brood of apple-cheeked youngsters than of his first-born, who fitted into the scheme of life as ill as her mother had done. He had imagined himself in love with his first wife, had married her, piqued by her elusive ways, charmed by her pale, wood-sorrel beauty; and she, shy and unawakened, had taken his six feet of bone and muscle for outward and visible sign of the matured spiritual strength her nature needed. The disappointment was mutual as swift; it had taken no longer than the honeymoon to convince the one that he had burdened himself with a phantast, the other that she was tied to a philistine. For a year they shared bed and board, severed and inseparable as earth and moon; then the wife having passed on to a daughter the heritage of a nature rare and impracticable as a sensitive plant, died and was forgotten.

The widower's speedy re-marriage proved an unqualified success. Indeed, the worthy man's after life was so uniformly and deservedly prosperous (he was as shrewd and industrious in his business as he was genial and domesticated in his home), that he might be forgiven if his affection for his eldest child were tepid; for, apart from her likeness to his first wife, she was, in existing, a constant reminder of the one mistake of a prosperous career. He was kind to her, however, in his fashion; gave her plenty of pocket-money (he was fond of giving); saw to it that she had a sufficiency of toys and sweets, though it piqued him that she had never been known to ask for any. Otherwise was content to leave her to his wife.

The second Mrs. Denny, kindly, capable and unimaginative as her husband, had her sense of duty to her step-daughter; but she was too much occupied in bearing and rearing her own family, whose numbers were augmented with Victorian regularity, to consider more than the physical well-being of the child. Louise was well fed and warmly clad, her share was accorded her in the pleasures of the nursery. What more could a busy woman do!

Louise, docile and reserved, was not unhappy. Until she went to school, however, her mental outlook resembled that of a person suffering from myopia. Her elders, her half-brothers, all the persons of her small world, were indefinite figures among whom she moved, confused and blundering. She knew of their existence, but to focus them seemed as impossible as to establish communication. She did not try over hard; she was sensitive to ridicule; it was easier to retire within her childish self, be her own confidante and questioner.

She had an intricate imagination and before she learned to read had created for herself a fantastically complete inner world, in which she moved, absorbed and satisfied. Indeed, her outward surroundings became at last so dangerously shadowy that her manner began to show how entire was her abstraction, and Mrs. Denny, sworn foe to "sulks" and "moping," saw fit to engage a governess as an antidote.

The governess, a colourless lady, achieved little, though she was useful in taking the little boys for walks. But she taught Louise to read, and thereafter the child assumed entire charge of her own education.

The mother's books, velvety with dust that had sifted down upon them since the day, six years back, when they had been tumbled in piles on an attic floor by busy maids preparing for the advent of the second Mrs. Denny, were discovered, one rainy day, by a pinafored Siegfried, alert for treasure. Contented years were passed in consuming the trove.

Her mother's choice of books was so completely to her taste that they gave the lonely child her first experience of mental companionship; suggesting to her that there might be other intelligences in the world about her than the kindly, stolid folk who cherished her growing body and ignored her growing mind. She was almost startled at times to realise how completely this vague mother of hers would have understood her. Each new volume, fanciful or quizzical or gracious, seemed a direct gift from an invisible yet human personality, that concerned itself with her as no other had ever done; that was never occupied with the dustiness of the attic, or a forgotten tea-hour, but was astonishingly sensitive to the needs of a little soul, struggling unaided to birth. The pile of books, to her hungry affections, became the temple, the veritable dwelling-place of her mother's spirit.

Seated on the sun-baked floor, book on knee, the noises of the high road floating up to her, distance-dulled and soothing, she would shake her thick hair across her face, and see through its veil a melting, shifting shadow of a hand that helped to turn her pages. The warm floor was a soft lap; the battered trunk a shoulder that supported; the faint breeze a kiss upon her lips. The fantastic qualities the mother had bequeathed, recreated her in the mind of her child, bringing vague comfort (who knows?) alike to the dead and the living Louise.

Yet the impalpable intercourse, compact of make-believe and yearnings, was, at its sweetest, no safe substitute for the human companionships that were lacking in the life of Louise. Half consciously she desired an elder sister, a friend, on whom to lavish the stores of her ardent, reticent nature.

At twelve she was sent to school. At first it did little for her. She was unaccustomed to companions of her own age and sex and, quite simply, did not know how to make friends with many who would have been willing enough, if she could have contributed her share, the small change of joke and quarrel and confidence, towards intimacy. But Louise was too inured to the solitude of crowds to be troubled by her continued loneliness. She met the complaints of Mrs. Denny, that she made no friends like other children, with a shrug of resignation. What could she do? She supposed that she was not nice enough; people didn't like her.

Secretly her step-mother agreed. She was kind to Louise, but she, too, did not like her. She found her irritating. Her dreamy, absent manner, her very docility and absence of self-assertion were annoying to a hearty woman who was braced rather than distressed by an occasional battle of wills. She thought her shyness foolish, doubted the insincerity of her humility, and looked upon her shrinking from publicity, noise and rough caresses, her love of books and solitude, as a morbid pose. Yet she was just a woman and did not let the child guess at her dislike, though she made no pretence of actual affection. She knew perfectly well that Louise's mother (they had been schoolgirls together), had irritated her in exactly the same way.

Educationally, too, the first year at school affected Louise but slightly. Her brothers' governesses had done their best for the shy, intelligent girl, and her wide reading had trained, her awkwardness and childish appearance obscured, a personality in some respects dangerously matured. But her dreaminess and total ignorance of the routine of lesson-learning hampered her curiously; she learnt mechanically, using her brain but little for her easy tasks, and she was not considered particularly promising.

With Clare's intervention the world was changed for Louise; she had her first taste of active pleasure.

It is difficult to realise what an effect a woman of Clare's temperament must have had on the impressionable child. In her knowledge, her enthusiasms, her delicate intuition and her keen intellectual sympathy, she must have seemed the embodiment of all dreams, the fulfilment of every longing, the ideal made flesh. A wanderer in an alien land, homesick, hungry, for whom, after weary days, a queen descends from her throne, speaking his language, supplying his unvoiced wants, might feel something of the adoring gratitude that possessed Louise. She rejoiced in Clare as a vault-bred flower in sunlight.

On all human beings, child or adult, emotional adventure entails, sooner or later, physical exhaustion; the deeper, the more novel the experience, the greater the drain on the bodily strength. To Louise, involved in the first passionate experience of her short life, in an affection as violent and undisciplined as a child's must be, an affection in itself completely occupying her mind and exhausting her energies, the amount of work made necessary by the position to which Clare and her own ambition had assigned her, was more of a burden than either realised. Only Alwynne, sympathetic coach (for Louise had two years' back work to condense and assimilate), guessed how great were the efforts the child was making. Clare, who always affected unconsciousness of her own effect on the ambitions of the children, had persuaded herself that Louise was entirely in her right place; and Louise herself was too young, and too feverishly happy, to consider the occasional headaches, fits of lassitude and nights cinematographed with dreams, as anything but irritating pebbles in her path to success-and Clare.

The weeks in her new class had been spread with happiness—a happiness that had grown like Elijah's cloud, till, on the day of the Browning lesson, as she listened to the beloved voice making music of her halting sentences, to the words of praise, of affection even, that followed, it stretched from horizon to horizon.

As she sat in the deserted class-room, her neat packet of sandwiches untasted in the satchel at her elbow, she re-lived that golden hour, dwelling on its incidents as a miser counts money. There was the stormy beginning; Agatha's mockery; her own raging helplessness; Clare's entrance; the exquisite thrill she had felt at her touch, that was not only gratitude for championship.... Never before had Clare been so near to her, so gentle, so protecting.... And afterwards, facing Louise at the foot of the table, how beautiful she had been.... Yet some of the girls could not see it.... They were fools.... Her head had been framed in the small, square window, so darkened and cobwebbed by crimson vines that only the merest blur of white clouds and blue hills was visible.... She had worn a gown of duller blue that lay in stiff folds: the bowl of Christmas roses, that mirrored themselves on the dark, polished table, had hidden the papers and the smeared ink-pot. Suddenly Louise remembered some austere Dutch Madonnas over whom delightful, but erratic Miss Durand had lingered, on their last visit to a picture gallery. She called them beautiful. Louise, with fascinated eyes sidling past a wallful of riotous Rubens, to fix on the soap and gentian of a Sasseferato, had wondered if Miss Durand were trying to be funny. She remembered, too, how some of the younger girls, comparing favourites, had called Miss Hartill ugly. She had raged loyally-yet, secretly, all but agreed. With her child's love of pink and white prettiness she had had no eyes for Clare's irregular features. But to-day something in Clare's pose had recalled the Dutch pictures, and in a flash she had understood, and wondered at her blindness. Miss Durand was right: the drawn, grey faces and rigid outlines had beauty, had charm-the charm of her stern smile.... The saints were hedged with lilies, and she, too, had had white flowers before her, that filled the air with the smell of the marvellous Roman church at Westminster.... The painted ladies were Madonnas-mothers-and Miss Hartill, too, had worn for a moment their protective look, half fierce, half tender....

Why was it? What has made her so kind? Not only to-day, but always? The girls feared her, some of them; those that she did not like talked of her temper and her tongue; Rose Levy hated her; even Agatha and Marion, and all of them, were a little frightened, though they adored.... Louise was never frightened.... How could one be frightened of one so kind and wonderful? She could say what she liked to Miss Hartill, and be sure that she would understand.... It was like being in the attic, talking aloud.... Mother would have been like that.... If it could be....

Louise, her chin in her doubled fists, launched out upon her sea of make-believe.

If it could be.... If it were possible, that Mother-not Mamma, cheery, obtuse Mamma of nursery and parlour-but Mother, the shadow of the attic-had come back? All things are possible to him that believeth: and Mr. Chesterton had said there was no real reason why tulips should not grow on oaks.... Heaps of people-all India-believed in reincarnation, and there was *The Gateless Barrier* and *The Dead Leman* for proof.... Might it not be?

The idea was intoxicating. She did not actually believe in it, but she played with it, wistfully, letting her imagination run riot. She wove fantastic variations on the themes "why not," "perhaps," "who knows."

She was but thirteen and very lonely.

She was in far too exalted a mood to have an appetite for her sandwiches, or time for the books beside her. She was due for extra work with Alwynne at three, and the intervening hour should have been used for preparation. Wasting her time meant sitting up at night, as Louise was well aware, and a tussle with Mrs. Denny, concerned for the waste of gas. But for all that, she would not and could not rouse herself from the trance of pleasure that was upon her.

Her mind was contemplating Clare as a mystic contemplates his divinity; rapt in an ecstasy of adoration, oblivious alike of place and time. She did not hear the luncheon gong, or the gong for afternoon school, or a door, opening and shutting behind her. Yet it did not startle her, when, turning dreamily to tap on her shoulder, she found herself facing Miss Hartill herself. Miss Hartill should have left the school before lunch, she knew, but it was all in order. What could surprise one on this miraculous day? She did not even rise, as etiquette demanded; but she smiled up at Clare with an expression of welcoming delight that disarmed comment.

Clare, too, could ignore conventions. She was merely touched and amused by the child's expression.

"Well, Louise? Very busy?"

Louise glanced vaguely at her books.

"Yes. I ought to be, I mean. I don't believe I've touched anything. I was thinking——"

"Two hours on end? Do you know the time? I heard Miss Durand clamouring for you just now." Clare looked mischievous. She could forgive forgetfulness of other people's classes.

Louise was serene.

"I'm sorry. I'm very sorry. I'd forgotten. I must go."

But she made no movement. She sat looking at Miss Hartill as if nothing else existed for her. The intent, fearless adoration in her eyes was very pleasant to Clare; novel, too, after the more sophisticated glances of the older girls.

With an odd little impulse of motherliness she picked up Louise's books, stacked them neatly and fitted them into the satchel. Louise watched her. Miss Hartill buckled the strap and handed her the bundle.

"There you are, Louise! Run along, my child, I'm afraid you'll get a scolding." She stooped to her, bright-eyed, laughing. "And what were you thinking of, Louise, for two long hours?"

"You," said Louise simply.

A touch of colour stole into Clare's thin cheeks. She took the small face between her hands and kissed it lightly.

"Silly child!" said Miss Hartill.

CHAPTER VII

Alwynne, drumming with her fingers on the window-sill, as she stood by Louise's desk, was distinctly annoyed. Louise, for the first time since she had known her, was late. It was, indeed, not one of her assigned classes; but she and Louise had found their hours together so insufficient for all the work that they were trying to make good, that Alwynne had good-naturedly arranged to give her a daily extra lesson. It bit into Alwynne's meagre free time; but she was fond of Louise; proud of her, too; and there was Clare! Clare was so anxious for Louise's success. Clare had been so pleased with the plan....

Perhaps it was natural that Alwynne, as she made the arrangement, forgot to consult Elsbeth. She told her about it afterwards, and Elsbeth praised her for her unselfishness, and was anxious lest she should be overtired. She did not remind Alwynne that she was alone all day; that she had been accustomed to look forward to the gay tea-hour, when Alwynne returned, full of news and nonsense. She resigned herself cheerfully to a solitary meal, and to keeping the muffins hot against Alwynne's uncertain home-coming.

The extra lessons had been a real boon to Louise, and she had grown attached to Alwynne and intimate with her. Alwynne's elder-sisterly attitude to the children she taught, although it horrified the older women, was seldom abused; it merely made her the recipient of quaint confidences, and gave her an insight into the characters of her pupils that was invaluable to girls and governess alike. To developing girls a confidante is a necessity. The present boarding-school system of education ousts the mother from that, her natural position; renders her, to the daughter steeped in an alien atmosphere, an outsider, lacking all understanding. Invaluable years pass before the artificial gulf that boarding-school creates between them, is spanned. And the substitute for the only form of sympathy and interest that is entirely untainted by selfish impulses is usually the chance acquaintance, the neighbour of desk and bedroom; occasionally, very occasionally, for the girl's feverish admiration usually precludes sane acquaintanceship, a mistress of more than average insight. Such a mistress, Alwynne, in spite of, or perhaps because of, her youthful indiscretions of manner, was in a fair way to become.

And of all the children who had opened their affairs to her, none had experienced more completely the tonic effect of a kind heart and a sense of humour, than Louise.

She would come to her lesson, overtired from the strain of the morning classes, over-stimulated from the contact with Clare, over-hopeful or utterly depressed, as the mood took her. Alwynne's cheerful interest was balm to the child's overwrought nerves. Alwynne let her spend a quarter of an hour or more in confiding the worries and excitements of the day, after which, Louise, curiously revived, contrived to get through an amazing amount of work. There was no doubt as to Louise's capacity for advanced work, but her state of mind affected her output; she was, as Alwynne once phrased it to Clare, "like a violin—you had to tune her up before she was fit for use." And Alwynne's "tuning" had done more than she or Clare or even Louise herself had guessed, towards her success in her new class.

Bit by bit, Alwynne had heard all about Louise; the details of her meagre home-life; her attitude to the busy world of school, that frightened while it attracted her; her difficulties with her fellows; her delight in her work. Finally, there was Clare. Louise was very shy about Clare; inclined to scent mockery, to be on the defensive; but Alwynne's own matter-of-fact enthusiasm had its effect. Also Alwynne's interest, though it invited, never demanded confidences. It took Louise some time to realise that it arose from simple friendliness of soul; that there was neither curiosity nor pedagogic zeal behind it; that, though she was teased and laughed at, she was respected, and, out of school hours, treated as an equal; that she and her schoolgirl secrets were safe with Miss Durand. It was, indeed, in the light of after events, pathetic that Louise, dazzled by Clare's will-o'-the-wisp brilliance, never realised how close to her for a season the friend, the elder sister she had longed for, really stood. With the egoism of a child, and a child in love, she was humbly and passionately grateful for Clare's least sign of interest, yet accepted all the many little kindnesses that Alwynne showed her, as a matter of course. She scarcely realised, absorbed as she was in Clare, that she was even fond of Miss Durand, yet she relied on her implicitly: and Alwynne, innocent of the jealous, acquisitive impulse that tainted Clare's intercourse with any girl who caught her fancy, was not at all disturbed or hurt by Louise's attitude. She looked after the child as she would have looked after a starving cat or a fugitive emperor, if they had come her way, as a matter of course, and as instinctively as she ate her dinner.

She was thinking of Louise, as she sat waiting, and a little curious as to what the child would say to her. She had heard all about the Browning lesson, at lunch, from Rose Levy, whose veiled, epigrammatic malice was usually amusing. Agatha had been on her other side, and she had anticipated equally amusing protests and contradictions and a highly coloured and totally different version. But Agatha had been unusually subdued that morning. Both had made it apparent, however, that Clare had been more than a little pleased with Louise.

But, however triumphant Louise's morning might have been, she had no business to be late now. What did she mean by keeping her waiting? Twice had Alwynne been down to the preparation room, searching for her: she did not mean to be impertinent of course, but it was, at least, casual. Alwynne, with easy, evanescent indignation, resolved to give Louise a taste of her tongue.

Here the child herself burst in upon her meditations, flushed to her glowing eyes, that were bright as if with drugs, excited as Alwynne had never yet guessed that she could be, charged with some indefinable quality as a live wire is charged with electricity. She stammered her apologies mechanically, sure of pardon, and, the formality complied with, was eager, touchingly eager for questions and the relief of communication.

But Alwynne, at nineteen, could not be expected to forego a legitimate grievance.

She read Louise a little lecture on punctuality and politeness, and settled at once to the work in hand. She said, with intention, that they must not waste any more time.

Louise submitted with her usual meekness, and did, Alwynne could see, do her utmost to apply herself to her work. But her answers were ludicrously vague and *mal à propos*, and she met Alwynne's comments, momentarily sharper, with an abstracted smile.

Suddenly Alwynne lost patience with her.

"I don't know what's the matter with you to-day, Louise," she said sharply. "I don't believe you've taken in a word of what I've said. If you can't take a little more trouble, I'd better go home."

Louise, obviously and pathetically jerked back to consciousness from some dreamer's Paradise, looked up at her with scared, apologetic eyes. The radiance dimmed slowly from her face. She made no answer, only to put up her hand to her head, with a queer little gesture of helplessness.

"What's the matter with you?" demanded Alwynne, but already more gently. Her anger was always fleeting as a puff of smoke.

But Louise merely shrugged her shoulders and looked vaguely at her again. Then she returned to her work.

Alwynne, walking up and down the room watched her intently as she bent over the Latin grammar. She was wrinkling her brows over a piece of prose that she had already construed at the previous lesson, and with an ease that had astonished Alwynne. She looked bewildered and put her hand to her head again. Her efforts to recall her wandering thoughts were patent and almost physical in their intensity; her small hand hovered, contracting and relaxing, like a baby catching at butterflies.

Alwynne was puzzled by her. The child was sincere: but obviously something momentous had happened, and was still occupying her, to the exclusion of all else. Alwynne wished that she had been less hasty: she felt that she should not have checked her.

She stood a moment beside her, reading what she had written. It was scarcely legible, and made no sense. She put a hand on her shoulder —

"Louise, you are writing nonsense. What is it? Tell me what the matter is?"

Louise laid down her pen, gave her a quick, shy smile, hesitated uncertainly, then, to Alwynne's dismay, collapsed on the low desk in a fit of wild, hysterical crying.

Alwynne always shed the mistress in emergency.

She whipped her arms about the child, and, sitting down, gathered her into her lap. She felt how the little, thin body was wrenched and shaken by the sobs it did not attempt to control, but she said nothing, only held it comfortingly tight.

Slowly the paroxysm subsided, and the words came, jerky, fragmentary, faint. Alwynne bent close to catch them.

Louise was so sorry...she was all right now...Miss Durand must think her crazy. No-no-nothing wrong...it was the other way round...she was so happy that it frightened her...she was madly happy...she had been in heaven all day...it was too wonderful to tell any one about...even Miss Durand....Miss Hartill-no one could ever know what Miss Hartill was....She had been so good to her-so wonderful....She had made Louise so happy that she was frightened... she couldn't believe it was possible to be so madly happy....That was all....Yes, it had made her cry-the pure happiness....Wasn't it silly? Only she was so dreadfully tired....It had hurt her head trying to do the Latin-because she was so tired....Yes, she had had headaches lately.... But she didn't care-it was worth it, to please Miss Hartill....It was queer that being so happy should make her want to cry; it was comical, wasn't it?

She began to laugh as she spoke, with tears brimming over her lashes, and for a few moments was inclined to be hysterical again.

But Alwynne's firm grasp and calm voice was too much for Louise's will, weakened by emotion and fatigue; she was soon coaxed and hushed into quiet again, and after lying passively for a while in Alwynne's arms, fell into the sudden light sleep of utter exhaustion.

Alwynne, rocking her gently, sat on in the darkening room, without a thought of the passage of time; puzzling over the problem in her arms.

She was too ignorant and inexperienced to understand Louise's outburst, or to realise the dangerous strain that the child's sensibilities were undergoing but the touch of the little figure, clinging, nestling to her, stirred her. She was vaguely aware that something-somehow-was amiss. Innocently she rejoiced that Clare was being kind to Louise, that the child was so happy and content; but the complaint of fatigue, the frequent headaches, troubled her. She would speak to Elsbeth....Perhaps the child needed a tonic? Elsbeth would know....

She glanced down. How different people looked asleep....She had never before realised how young Louise was. What was she? Thirteen? But what a baby she looked, with her thin, child's shape and small, clutching hands....It was the long-lashed lids that did it, hiding the beautiful eyes that were so much older, as she saw now, than the rest of Louise. With her soul asleep, Louise looked ten, and a frail little ghost of ten, at that.

Alwynne frowned. She supposed Clare Hartill realised how young Louise was, was right in allowing her to work so hard? But Clare knew all about girls, and what did she, Alwynne, know? After all Louise had never flagged before....It was probably the usual end of term fatigue-and of course it was necessarily an unusually stiff three months for her....She needed a holiday.... Next term would come more easily to her, poor little impetuous Louise....Alwynne realised that she was growing fond of the child.

Suddenly she heard footsteps in the corridor, and her own name in Clare's impatient accents. Louise, too, roused at the sound, and, jerking herself upright, slid from Alwynne's lap to her feet, as the door opened and the light was switched on with a snap. Clare stood in the doorway.

Serenely Alwynne rose, smoothing the creases in her dress, while with the other hand she steadied Louise, swaying and blinking in the strong light. Clare's sharp eyes appreciated her calm no less than the tear-stains on Louise's cheek; she guessed distortedly at the situation. She bit her lip. She found nothing to be annoyed at, yet she was not pleased.

"Alwynne! I've been hunting for you high and low. I thought you were coming home to tea with me."

Alwynne beamed at her.

"Of course! And do you know, I forgot to tell Elsbeth. Isn't it disgraceful? But I'm coming." She turned to Louise.

"My dear, run along home, and get to bed early; you look dreadfully tired. Doesn't she, Miss Hartill?"

But Clare was already in the passage.

Alwynne hurried after her, with a last cheerful nod, and Louise heard the echo of their footsteps die away in the distance.

Still dazed and heavy with sleep, her thoughts obscured and chaotic, she sat down again stupidly at her desk in the alcove of the window. She leaned her forehead against the cold pane and looked out.

It was a wild night. The wind soughed and shrieked in the bare trees: the rain tore past in gusts; the lamp-post at the corner was mirrored in the wet pavement, like a moon on an oily sea.

Louise pushed open the casement. The wind lulled as she did so, and she lent out. The air, at least, was mild, and a faint back-wash of rain sprayed soothingly upon her hot cheeks and swollen eyes.

Slowly her thoughts shaped themselves. So the day was over-the happiest day she had ever had.... She thought God was very wonderful to have made such a woman as Miss Hartill. She sent Him a hasty little prayer of thanks. But she had been very foolish that afternoon.... She could not understand it now.... She hoped Miss Durand would not tell Miss Hartill.... Miss Hartill had been in a great hurry! Was that why she had not said good-night to her? But such a little word. She wondered why Miss Hartill had not said good-night to her....

The front door below the window creaked and opened. Louise peered downwards. Miss Durand and Miss Hartill came down the steps sheltering under one umbrella, talking. Their voices floated up.

"I hope you don't spoil her, Alwynne? Yes, I know——" Alwynne was murmuring friendly adjectives. "But a mistress is in a peculiar position. You should not let yourself be too familiar——" A gust of wind and rain whirling down the road bore away the rest of the sentence.

Louise shut the window. She shivered a little as she gathered up her books.

Her happiest day was over.

CHAPTER VIII

A week before Christmas Alwynne began to wonder how the day itself should be spent, or rather, if her plans for the spending would ever pass Elsbeth's censorship. She was doubtful. For the last two or three years Christmas had been to them a rock of collision.

"The pity of it!" thought Alwynne. Once it had been the event, the crowning glory, the very reason of the ending year. A year, indeed, had always presented itself to her in advance as a wide country through which she must make her way, to reach the hostel, Christmas, hidden in the mists of time, on its further border. She had the whole map of the land in her mind, curiously vivid and distinct. She had never consciously devised the picture; it had, from the first, presented itself complete and unalterable. She stood, on New Year's Day, at the entrance of a country lane which ran between uneven hedges through a varying countryside of fields and woods and heatherland. Each change in the surroundings represented a month, the smaller differences the weeks and days. She went down this winding lane as the days went by, in slow content. January was a silent expanse of high tableland, snow-bound to the horizon. Winding down hill through the sodden grassland of the bare February country, where she lighted on nothing but early parsnip fronds and sleepy celandine buds in the dripping wickery hedges, she passed at last into the wood of March, a wood of pollard hazels and greening oaks and bramble-guarded dingles, where the anemones grew, and the first primroses. She slipped and slithered in and out of mossy leaf-pits, and the briars clawed her hair and pinafore, as she robbed the primrose clumps with wet, reddened fingers. The wind shrieked overhead and wrestled wildly with the bare branches, but beyond there was blue sky and a drift of cloud. But, unawares, she would always head through the wood to where the trees grew thinner and dash out at last, through a mist of pale cuckoo-pint, into the cowslip field that was April.

The path ran on through May and June between fields of ox-eye daisies and garden roses, always down hill, till she tumbled into August, the deep hot valley. There she found the sea.

With September the road lifted steadily, growing stony and ever steeper. It wound on ahead of her like a silver thread through a brocade of red and gold and purple, that was heather and bracken and beech. But the beech blossoms could never be gathered; they fell apart into a shower of dull leaves, and left her with a branch of bare twigs in her hand. The briony berries that she twisted into wreaths stained her straw hat with their black, evil juice; even the manna-like old-man's-beard smelled sour and rotten. The decaying, witchlike beauty of the season tricked and frightened her; autumn was a hard hill to climb.

But far away, on the summit of that difficult hill, stood a house. An old house, gaily bricked, dressed in ivy, with a belfry from which carols rang out unceasingly. It was always night-time where it stood and cheerful lights were set in every window. Alwynne never saw the house till she had turned the bend of the road into November; then it faced her suddenly and she would wave to the distant windows with a thrill of excitement, and quicken her steps, with the goal of the journey in sight at last. There was yet a weary climb before it was reached; every day of December was a boulder, painfully beclambered. But she would come to the gates at last, and tear up the frosty drive, from the shadow of whose shrubberies Jacob Marley peered and clanked at her and ghosts of Christmas turkeys gobbled horribly, to the open holly-hung doorway where Santa Claus, authentic in beard and dressing-gown, welcomed her with Elsbeth's voice. Followed stay-at-home days of delirious merry-making, from which she awoke a week later, to find herself, her back to a closed door, a spent cracker in her hand, looking out again, eager and a little wistful, across the white untrodden plain of yet another January.

But ever the next Christmas beckoned her anew.

To Elsbeth, too, Christmas was the day of delights, and Alwynne the queen of it. To Elsbeth, too, the pleasure of it began many weeks earlier in the secret fashioning of quaint gifts and surprises, and the anticipation of the small niece's delight in them. Elsbeth would have cheerfully cut off one of her slim fingers if Alwynne had happened to covet it. The childless woman loved Alwynne-the child in Alwynne she worshipped.

But though the delight of actual motherhood was denied Elsbeth, she was spared none of its chagrins.

Stooping for years to a child's level, she was cruelly shaken when Alwynne, suddenly and inexplicably, as it always seems, grew up. It took Elsbeth almost as many years to straighten herself again. Years when Alwynne, in the arrogance of her enterprising youth, thought that Elsbeth was sometimes awfully childish. She supposed that she was growing old; she used not to be like that....

Thereafter, each Christmas, challenging comparison as it did with the memory-mellowed charm of its forerunners, emphasised the change that had taken place. Yearly the ideal Christmas lured them to the old observances; yearly the reality satisfied them less.

Elsbeth still sat up half the night on Christmas Eve, at work upon the little tree. Alwynne still planned gorgeous and laborious presents for her aunt. Elsbeth still filled a stocking (outsize) with tip-toe secrecy, and Alwynne, at sixteen, still ran across in her dressing-gown, and curled up on Elsbeth's bed to unpack it.

But at sixteen one is too old and too young to be a child any more. The tree was a fir-tree, pure and simple; the fairy lights stank of tallow; and not even for the sake of a new bright sixpence, would Alwynne, in the thick of a vegetarian fad, devour a slice of the evil-coloured Christmas pudding.

Elsbeth, as she saw her old-time jokes and small surprises that could no longer surprise, fall utterly flat, thought that school had altered Alwynne altogether; that she was assuming airs of maturity ridiculous in a child of her age, ("Sixteen? She's a mere baby still," affirmed poor Elsbeth,) that she was growing indifferent, superior, heartless. And Alwynne, trying to appear amused, wondered why Christmas was so different from what it used to be and wished heartily that Elsbeth would not try to be skittish. It didn't suit her-made her seem undignified. Each, longing for the old days, when the other had conjured up so easily the true spirit of the festival, tried her affectionate best to do so still; each, failing inevitably, inevitably blamed the other. Neither realised, that Dan Christmas is the god of very little children, and that where they are not, he, too, does not linger.

But the last restless, unsatisfactory day had settled the matter for them finally. Alwynne had fidgeted through morning service, and pained her aunt, on the walk home, with her sceptical young comments; had omitted to kiss her under the mistletoe; had sat through the ceremonious meal, answering Elsbeth's cheerful pleasantries in monosyllables; and finally, after an unguarded remark, and the inevitable reproving comment, had flung out of the room in a fever of irritation. She came near thinking Elsbeth a foolish and intolerable old maid. And Elsbeth, sitting sadly over the fire all the lonely afternoon, puzzled meekly over Alwynne's hardness of heart, and cried a little, in pure longing, for the baby of a few years back, to whom she had been as God.

They were reconciled, of course, by tea-time. Alwynne, quieted by solitude, was soon bewildered at her own ill-humour, shocked at the sentiments she had been able to entertain, remorseful at hurting Elsbeth's feelings and spoiling her Christmas Day. They were able to send each other to bed happy again.

But they had no more snap-dragons and early stockings. The next Christmas, shorn of its splendours, was a strange day to them both, but, at least, a peaceful one, with Alwynne at her gentlest, and Elsbeth, forgiving her as best she could, for her long skirts and her seventeen years.

With the passing of yet another year, however, Alwynne's last scruple as to the sacrosanct privacy of Christmas celebrations vanished utterly. The ideal day, she saw at last, and clearly, should be neither a children's carnival, nor a symposium of relatives. (Alwynne knew of none but Elsbeth, but she dearly loved a phrase.) Christmas should be a time of social intercourse, of peace and goodwill towards men-the human race-neighbours and friends-not merely relations.... One should not shut oneself up....It would be a sound idea, for instance, to ask some one to dinner....A friend of Elsbeth's —or there was Clare! It would be very jolly if Clare could come to dinner....Clare was delightful when she was in holiday mood; she could keep the table in a roar....A little fun would do Elsbeth good....Surely Elsbeth would enjoy having Clare to dinner?

159

She found herself, however, experiencing considerable difficulty in opening up the project to her aunt. Elsbeth, to whom the possibility of such a request had long ago presented itself, who could have told you by sheer intuition at what exact moment the idea occurred to her niece, gave her no help. Alwynne had contrived to put her in the position of appearing to approve Clare Hartill. Clare, she felt, had had something to do with that. She knew that it would be unwise to lose the advantage of her apparent tolerance; knew that Clare expected her to lose it by some impulsive expression of mistrust or dislike, and intended to utilise the lapse for her own ends. It would be easy for Clare to pose as the generous victim of unreasoning hostility. But Clare should not, she resolved, have the opportunity. She, Elsbeth, would never be so far lacking in cordiality as to give her any sort of handle. But Clare Hartill should not eat her Christmas dinner with them, vowed Elsbeth, for all that.

So for a couple of days, Alwynne, approaching Elsbeth from all possible angles, found no crack in her armour, and somewhat puzzled, but entirely unsuspicious, thought it hard that Elsbeth should be, at times, so curiously unresponsive. She would not have scrupled to ask her aunt outright to invite Clare, but she quite genuinely wished to find out first if Elsbeth would mind, and never guessed that the difficulty she found in opening the matter was the answer to that question.

The arrival of the turkey was her opportunity.

Sailing into the kitchen in search of raisins (the more maturely dignified Alwynne's deportment, the more likely her detection in some absurd child's habit or predilection), she found Elsbeth raging low-voiced, and the small maid gaping admiration over the brobdingnagian proportions of their Christmas dinner.

"Look at it, Alwynne! What am I to do? Twenty pounds! And we shan't get through ten! Really, it's too bad —I wrote so distinctly. It's impossible to return it-to Devonshire! No time. It's the twenty-second already. How shall we ever get through it?"

"We might get some one in to help us," began Alwynne delightedly. But Elsbeth, very busy all of a sudden, with basin and egg-beater, whisked and bustled her out of the kitchen.

Alwynne returned to the matter, however, later in the day.

"Elsbeth, we shall never manage that turkey alone."

"Of course, I must send some over to Mrs. Marpler," began Elsbeth hastily.

Mrs. Marpler was a charwoman. Alwynne contrived to make their succession of little maids adore her, but she and Mrs. Marpler detested one another cordially. Mrs. Marpler's offences, according to Alwynne, were that she was torpid, inefficient, breathed heavily, smelled of cats, and, by the complicated and judicious recital of the authentic calamities which regularly befell her, lured from Elsbeth more than her share of the broken meats and old clothes of the establishment, perquisites which Alwynne, entirely incredulous, coveted for pet dependents of her own. Alwynne's offences, according to Mrs. Marpler, were, the aforementioned incredulity, her hostile influence on Miss Loveday, a certain crispness of manner and a tendency to open all windows in Mrs. Marpler's neighbourhood. The feud distressed Elsbeth, and Alwynne's diagnosis of Mrs. Marpler's character; for she liked to believe the best of every one. Alwynne forced her to agree, but secretly she sympathised with her feckless char-lady.

"Marpler has been out of work three weeks, and as poor Mrs. Marpler says, where their Christmas dinner is to come from ——"

"How much extra did you pay her this week?" demanded Alwynne remorselessly. "And last week-and the week before-and the week before that? Of course he's out of work. Who wouldn't be?"

"My dear Alwynne, if you think they can buy a Christmas dinner on what I gave them —" retorted Elsbeth heatedly. "But it's absurd to argue with you. What do you know of what food costs?"

"Anyhow, Mrs. Baker, with six children ——" began Alwynne, who also had been primed by a protégée. But she recollected that she did not wish to annoy Elsbeth at this juncture. Clare must take precedence of Mrs. Baker. "Well, you can send them the legs and the carcase," she conceded; "even then there will be more than we can possibly manage. Couldn't we ask some one to spend the day with us?"

"I hardly think," said Elsbeth, with a touch of severity, "that you would find any one. Most people like to keep Christmas with their Relations."

"Well, I haven't got any. But by all accounts I think I should hate 'em in the plural as much as I love 'em in the singular." She blew Elsbeth a kiss. "But if we could find some one-to help us eat up the turkey-and spend the evening-it would be rather jolly, don't you think? It was dullish last year, wasn't it?"

"Was it?" said Elsbeth, with careful brightness. "I'm sorry. I had thought you enjoyed it."

"Oh, why is she so touchy? I didn't mean anything," cried Alwynne within herself. And aloud —

"Oh, I only meant without a tree or anything specially Christmassy — —"

"Alwynne," said Elsbeth, with scrupulous patience, "it was you who suggested not having one."

"I know, I know, I know, I know!" cried Alwynne, in a fever.

Elsbeth sighed.

Alwynne repented.

"Elsbeth darling, I didn't mean to be rude; I'm a beast. And I didn't mean it wasn't nice last year. I only meant-it would be-be a change to have some one-because of the turkey-and I thought, perhaps Clare — —"

"Can't you exist for a day without seeing Clare Hartill?" asked Elsbeth, with a wry smile.

Alwynne dimpled.

"Not very well," she said.

Elsbeth stared at her plate. Alwynne edged her chair along the table, till she sat at Elsbeth's elbow. She slid an arm round her neck.

"Elsbeth! Elsbeth, dear! You're not cross, Elsbeth? It's a very big turkey. Do, Elsbeth!"

"Do what?"

"Ask Clare. You like her, don't you?"

No answer.

"Don't you, Elsbeth?" Alwynne's tone was a little anxious.

"Would you care if I didn't?" The pattern of her plate still interested Elsbeth. She was tracing its windings with her fork.

"You silly-it would just spoil everything. That's just it —I would like to get you two fond of each other, only with Clare so busy there's never a chance of your really getting acquainted."

"I knew Clare Hartill long before you did, Alwynne. I knew her as a schoolgirl."

"But not well-not as I know her."

"No, not as you know her."

"There you are," said Alwynne, with satisfaction. "That's why-you don't know her properly. Oh, Elsbeth, you must share all my good things, and Clare's the very best of them. Do let her come."

"She may be engaged; she probably is."

"Oh, no-Clare will be alone —I know, because — —" she stopped herself.

Elsbeth questioned her with her eyes.

"Oh, nothing-only I happen to know," said Alwynne.

"Because?"

Alwynne shook her head mischievously.

"Oh, well, if you won't tell me — —" began Elsbeth.

"Oh, I will, I will," cried Alwynne hastily.

"My dear, I don't want to know Miss Hartill's secrets, or yours either," said Elsbeth huffily. But to herself, "Why am I losing my temper over these silly trifles?"

"Elsbeth dear, it was nothing. Only Clare did ask me to spend Christmas Day with her."

"Well?" said Elsbeth jealously.

161

"What?" asked Alwynne's ingenuous eyes.

"Are you going?"

Alwynne nestled up to her, humming with careful flatness the final bars of *Home, sweet home*.

"Elsbeth, you old darling—I do believe you're jealous! Are you, Elsbeth? Are you?"

"Are you going?" repeated Elsbeth.

Alwynne was sobered by her tone.

"I'm going to spend my Christmas Day in my own home, with my own Elsbeth," she said, "and I think you needn't have asked me."

Elsbeth melted.

"My dear, I'm a silly old woman——"

"Yes, you tell me that once a week."

"One day you'll believe it.—All right-you can ask your Miss Hartill-or shall I write?"

Alwynne hugged her.

"Elsbeth, you're an angel! I'll go round at once. Oh, it will be jolly."

"If she comes."

Alwynne turned, on the way to her bedroom. Elsbeth's intonation was peculiar.

"What do you mean?"

"I don't think she'll come, Alwynne."

"But I know she'll be alone——"

"Well, you go and ask her."

"But why do you say that-in that tone?"

"I may be wrong. But I've known her longer than you have. But run along and ask her."

"But why? Why?"

"Oh, don't bother me, child," cried Elsbeth impatiently. "Run along and ask her."

CHAPTER IX

"I had a letter from Louise yesterday," announced Clare.

She was curled up in a saddle-bag before the roaring golden fire, and was busy with paper and pencil. Alwynne, big with her as yet unissued invitation, sat cross-legged on the white bearskin at her feet. The floor was littered with papers and book-catalogues. At Christmas-time Clare ordered books as a housewife orders groceries, and she and Alwynne had spent a luxurious evening over her lists. The vivid flames lit up Clare's thin, lazy length, and turned the hand she held up against their heat into transparent carnelian. Her face was in shadow, but there were dancing specks of light in her sombre eyes that kept time with the leaping blaze. Clare was a sybarite over her fires. She would not endure coal or gas or stove-wood, and wood only, must be used; and she would pay any price for apple-wood, ostensibly for the quality of its flame, secretly for the mere pleasure of burning fuel with so pleasant a name; for she liked beautiful words as a child likes chocolate —a sober, acquisitive liking. She had, too, though she would not own it, a delight in destruction, costly destruction; she enjoyed the sensation of reckless power that it gave her. The trait might be morbid, but there was not a trace of pose in it; she could have enjoyed a Whittington bonfire, without needing a king to gasp applause. Yet she shivered nightly as she undressed in her cold bedroom, rather than commit the extravagance of an extra fire. She never realised the comicality of her contradictoriness, or even its existence in her character, though it qualified every act and impulse of her daily life. Her soul was, indeed, a hybrid, combining the temper of a Calvinist with the tastes of a Renascence bishop.

At the moment she was in gala mood. The autumn term was but four days dead, she had not had time to tire of holidays, though, within a week, she would be bored again, and restless for the heavy work under which she affected to groan. Her chafing mind seldom allowed her indolent body much of the peace it delighted in-was ever the American in lotus-land. It was fidgeted at the moment by Alwynne's absorption in a lavishly illustrated catalogue.

"Did you hear, Alwynne? A letter from Louise."

Alwynne's "Oh?" was absent. It was in the years of the Rackham craze, and she had just discovered a reproduction of the *Midsummer* Helen.

"Any message?" Clare knew how to prod Alwynne.

The girl glanced up amused but a little indignant.

"You've answered it already? Well! And the weeks I've had to wait sometimes."

"This was such a charming letter," said Clare smoothly. "It deserved an answer. She really has the quaintest style. And Alwynne-never a blot or a flourish! It's a pleasure to read."

Alwynne laughed ruefully. She would always squirm good-humouredly under Clare's pin-pricks, with such amusement at her own discomfiture that Clare never knew whether to fling away her needle for good, or, for the mere experiment's sake, to stab hard and savagely. At that stage of their intimacy, Alwynne's guilelessness invariably charmed and disarmed her-she knew that it would take a very crude display of cruelty to make Alwynne believe that she was being hurt intentionally. Clare was amused by the novel pedestal upon which she had been placed; she was accustomed to the panoply of Minerva, or the bow of Diana Huntress, but she had never before been hailed as Bona Dea. It tickled her to be endowed with every domestic virtue, to be loved, as Alwynne loved her, with the secure and fearless affection of a daughter for a newly-discovered and adorable young mother. She appreciated Alwynne's determination of their relationship, her nice sense of the difference in age, her modesty in reserving any claim to an equality in their friendship, her frank and affectionate admiration-yet, while it pleased her, it could pique. Calm comradeship or surrendering adoration she could cope with, but the subtle admixture of such alien states of mind was puzzling. She had acquired a lover with a sense of humour and she felt that she had her hands full. Her imperious will would, in time, she knew, eliminate either the lover or the humour-it annoyed her that she was not as yet quite convinced that it would be the humour. She intended to master Alwynne, but she realised that it would be a question of time, that she would give her more trouble than the children to whom she was accustomed. Alwynne's utter unrealisation of the fact that a trial of strength was in progress, was disconcerting: yet Clare, jaded and super-subtle, found her innocence endearing. Without relaxing in her purpose, she yet caught herself wondering if an ally were not better than a slave. But the desire for domination was never entirely shaken off, and Alwynne's free bearing was in itself an ever-present challenge. Clare loved her for it, but her pride was in arms. It was her misfortune not to realise that, for all her Olympian poses, she had come to love Alwynne deeply and enduringly.

Alwynne, meanwhile, laughing and pouting on the hearth, the firelight revealing every change of expression in her piquant face, was declining to be classed with Agatha Middleton; her handwriting may be bad, but it wasn't a beetle-track; anyhow, Queen Elizabeth had a vile fist-Clare admired Queen Elizabeth, didn't she? She had always so much to say to Clare, that if she stopped to bother about handwriting——! Had Clare never got into a row for untidiness in her own young days? Elsbeth had hinted....But of course she reserved judgment till she had heard Clare's version! She settled to attention and Clare, inveigled into reminiscences, found herself recounting quaint and forgotten incidents to her own credit and discredit, till, before the evening was over, Alwynne knew almost as much of Clare's schooldays as Clare did herself. She could never resist telling Alwynne stories, Alwynne was always so genuinely breathless with interest.

They returned to Louise at last, and Alwynne read the letter, chuckling over the odd phrases, and dainty marginal drawings. She would have dearly liked to see Clare's answer. She was glad, for all her protests, that Clare had been moved to answer; she knew so well the delight it would give Louise. The child would need cheering up. For, quite resignedly and by the way, Louise had mentioned that the Denny family had developed whooping-cough, and emigrated to Torquay, and she, in quarantine, though it was hoped she had escaped infection, was preparing for a solitary Christmas.

Alwynne looked up at Clare with wrinkled brows.

"Poor child! But what can I do? I haven't had whooping-cough, and Elsbeth is always so afraid of infection; or else she could have come to us. I know Elsbeth wouldn't have minded."

"You are going to leave me to myself then? You've quite made up your mind?"

Alwynne's eyes lighted up.

"Oh, Clare, it's all right. You are coming! At least—I mean-Elsbeth sends her kindest regards, and she would be so pleased if you will come to dinner with us on Christmas Day," she finished politely.

Clare laughed.

"It's very kind of your aunt."

"Yes, isn't it?" said Alwynne, with ingenuous enthusiasm.

"I'm afraid I can't come, Alwynne."

Alwynne's face lengthened.

"Oh, Clare! Why ever not?"

Clare hesitated. She had no valid reason, save that she preferred the comfort of her own fireside and that she had intended Alwynne to come to her. Alwynne's regretful refusal when she first mooted the arrangement, she had not considered final, but this invitation upset her plans. Elsbeth's influence was opposing her. She hated opposition. Also she did not care for Elsbeth. It would not be amiss to make Elsbeth (not her dislike of Elsbeth) the reason for her refusal. It would have its effect on Alwynne sooner or later.

She considered Alwynne narrowly, as she answered—

"My dear, I had arranged to be at home, for one thing."

Alwynne looked hurt.

"Of course, if you don't care about it—" she began.

Clare rallied her.

"Be sensible, my child. It is most kind of Miss Loveday; but-wasn't it chiefly your doing, Alwynne? Imagine her dismay if I accepted. A stranger in the gate! On Christmas Day! One must make allowances for little prejudices, you know."

"She'll be awfully disappointed," cried Alwynne, so eager for Clare that she believed it.

"Will she?" Clare laughed pleasantly. "Every one doesn't wear your spectacles. What would she do with me, for a whole day?"

"We shouldn't see her much," began Alwynne. "She spends most of her time in church. I go in the morning—(yes, I'm very good!) but I've drawn the line at turning out after lunch."

"Then why shouldn't you come to me instead? It would be so much better. I shall be alone, you know." Clare's wistful intonation was not entirely artificial.

Alwynne was distressed.

"Oh, Clare, I'd love to-you know I'd love to-but how could I? Elsbeth would be dreadfully hurt. I couldn't leave her alone on Christmas Day."

"But you can me?"

"Clare, don't put it like that. You know I shall want to be with you all the time. But Elsbeth's like my mother. It would be beastly of me. You must put relations first at Christmas-time, even if they're not first really."

She smiled at Clare, but she felt disloyal as she said it, and hated herself. Yet wasn't it true? Clare came first, though Elsbeth must never guess it. Dear old Elsbeth was pretty dense, thank goodness! Where ignorance is bliss, etcetera! Yet she, Alwynne, felt extraordinarily mean....

Clare watched her jealously. She had set her heart on securing Alwynne for Christmas Day, and had thought, ten minutes since, with a secret, confident smile, that there would not be much difficulty. And here was Alwynne holding out-refusing categorically! It was incredible! Yet she could not be angry: Alwynne so obviously was longing to be with her.... Equally obviously prepared to risk her displeasure (a heavy penalty already, Clare guessed, to Alwynne), rather than ignore the older claim. Clare thought that an affection that could be so loyal to a tedious old maid was better worth deflecting than many a more ardent, unscrupulous enthusiasm. Alwynne was showing strength of character.

She persisted nevertheless—

"Well, it's a pity. I must eat my Christmas dinner alone, I suppose."

"Oh, Clare, you might come to us," cried Alwynne. "I can't see why you won't."

Clare shrugged her shoulders.

"If you can't see why, my dear Alwynne, there's no more to be said."

Alwynne most certainly did not see; but Clare's delicately reproachful tone convicted her, and incidentally Elsbeth, of some failure in tact. She supposed she had blundered ... she often did.... But Elsbeth, at least, must be exonerated ... she did so want Clare to think well of Elsbeth....

She perjured herself in hasty propitiation.

"Yes. Yes—I do see. I ought to have known, of course. Elsbeth was quite right. She said you wouldn't, all along."

"Oh?" Clare sat up. "Oh? Your aunt said that, did she?" She spoke with detachment, but inwardly she was alert, on guard. Elsbeth had suddenly become worth attention.

"Oh, yes." Alwynne's voice was rueful. "She was quite sure of it. She said I might ask you, with pleasure, if I didn't believe her-you see, she'd love you to come-but she didn't think you would."

"I wonder," said Clare, laughing naturally, "what made her say that?"

"She said she knew you better than I did," confided Alwynne, with one of her spurts of indignation. "As if——"

"Yes, it's rather unlikely, isn't it?" said Clare, with an intimate smile. "But you're not going?"

"I must. Look at the time! Elsbeth will be having fits!" Alwynne called from the hall where she was hastily slipping on her coat and hat.

Clare stood a moment-thinking.

165

So the duel had been with Elsbeth! So that negligible and mouse-like woman had been aware-all along ... had prepared, with a thoroughness worthy of Clare herself, for the inevitable encounter ... had worsted Clare completely.... It was amazing.... Clare was compelled to admiration. It was clear to her now that Elsbeth must have distrusted her from the beginning. It had been Elsbeth's doing, not hers, that their intercourse had been so slight.... Yet she had never restrained Alwynne; she had risked giving her her head.... She was subtle! This affair of the Christmas dinner for instance-Clare appreciated its cleverness. Elsbeth had not wanted her, Clare now saw clearly; had been anxious to avoid the intimacy that such an invitation would imply; equally anxious, surely, that Alwynne should not guess her uneasy jealousy: so she had risked the invitation, counting on her knowledge of Clare's character (Clare stamped with vexation-that the woman should have such a memory!) secure that Clare, unsuspicious of her motives, would, by refusing, do exactly as Elsbeth wished. It had been the neatest of gossamer traps-and Clare had walked straight into it.... She was furious. If Alwynne, maddeningly unsuspicious Alwynne, had but enlightened her earlier in the evening! Now she was caught, committed by her own decision of manner to the course of action she most would have wished to avoid.... She could not change her mind now without appearing foolishly vacillating.... It would not do.... She had been bluffed, successfully, gorgeously bluffed.... And Elsbeth was sitting at home enjoying the situation ... too sure of herself and Clare even to be curious as to the outcome of it all. She knew. Clare stamped again. Oh, but she would pay Elsbeth for this.... The *casus belli* was infinitely trivial, but the campaign should be Homeric.... And this preliminary engagement could not affect the final issues.... She always won in the end.... But, after all, Elsbeth could not be blamed, though she must be crushed; Alwynne was worth fighting for! Elsbeth was a fool.... If she had treated Clare decently, Clare might-possibly-have shared Alwynne with her.... She believed she would have had scruples.... Now they were dispelled.... Alwynne, by fair means or foul, should be detached ... should become Clare's property ... should be given up to no living woman or man.

She followed Alwynne into the hall and lit the staircase candle. She would see Alwynne out. She would have liked to keep Alwynne with her for a month. She was a delightful companion; it was extraordinary how indispensable she made herself. Clare knew that her flat would strike her as a dreary place to return to, when she had shut the door on Alwynne. She would sit and read and feel restless and lonely. Yet she did not allow herself to feel lonely as a rule; she scouted the weakness. But Alwynne wound herself about you, thought Clare, and you never knew, till she had gone, what a difference she made to you.

She wished she could keep Alwynne another couple of hours.... But it was eleven already ... her hold was not yet strong enough to warrant innovations to which Elsbeth could object.... Her time would come later.... How much later would depend on whether it were affection that swayed Alwynne, or only a sense of duty.... She believed, because she hoped, that it was duty —a sense of duty was more easily suborned than an affection.... For the present, however, Alwynne must be allowed to do as she thought right. Clare knew when she was beaten, and, with her capacity for wry admiration of virtues that she had not the faintest intention of incorporating in her own character, she was able to applaud Alwynne heartily. Yet she did not intend to make victory easy to her.

They went down the flights of stairs silently, side by side. Alwynne opened the entrance doors and stood a moment, fascinated.

"Look, Clare! What a night!"

The moon was full and flooded earth and sky with bright, cold light. The garden, roadway, roofs, trees and fences glittered like powdered diamonds, white with frost and moonshine. The silence was exquisite.

They stood awhile, enjoying it.

Suddenly Clare shivered. Alwynne became instantly and anxiously practical.

"Clare, what am I thinking of? Go in at once-you'll catch a dreadful cold."

With unusual passivity Clare allowed herself to be hurried in. At the staircase Alwynne said good-bye, handing her her candle, and waiting till she should have passed out of sight. On the fourth step Clare hesitated, and turned —

"Alwynne-come to me for Christmas?"

Alwynne flung out her hands.

"Clare! I mustn't."

"Alwynne-come to me for Christmas?"

"You know I mustn't! You know you'd think me a pig if I did, now wouldn't you?"

"I expect so."

"But I'll come in for a peep at you," cried Alwynne, brightening, "while Elsbeth's at afternoon service. I could do that. And to say Merry Christmas!"

"Come to dinner?"

"I can't."

"Then you needn't come at all." Clare turned away.

Alwynne caught her hand, as it leaned on the balustrade. In the other the candle shook a little.

"Lady Macbeth! Dear Lady Macbeth! Miss Hartill of the Upper Sixth, whom I'm scared to death of, really-you're behaving like a very naughty small child. Now, aren't you? Honestly? Oh, do turn round and crush me with a look for being impudent, and then tell me that I'm only doing what you really approve. I don't want to, Clare, but you know you hate selfishness."

Clare looked down at her.

"All right, Alwynne. You must do as you like."

"Say good-night to me," demanded Alwynne. "Nicely, Clare, very nicely! It's Christmas-time."

Carefully Clare deposited her candlestick on the stair above. Leaning over the banisters, she put her arms round Alwynne and kissed her passionately and repeatedly.

"Good-night, my darling," said Clare.

Then, recoiling, she caught up her candlestick, and without another word or look, hurried up the stairs.

Alwynne walked home on air.

CHAPTER X

Elsbeth bore the news of Clare's defection with stoicism; but her motherly soul was disturbed by Alwynne's disappointment, though she could not stifle her pleasure in its cause. She felt, indeed, somewhat guilty, and was eager to atone by acquiescing in Alwynne's plan of visiting Clare while she went to church; and met her more than half way over the question of an altered tea-hour.

Alwynne, who from the first had been fretted, though but half consciously, by the faintly repellent manner assumed by each of the two women at mention of the other, was soothed by Elsbeth's advances. Elsbeth was a dear, after all: there was no one quite like Elsbeth.... For all her obstinacies and unreasonableness, she never really failed you.... She could be depended on to love you at your worst; you could quarrel with her with never a fear of real alienation.... Elsbeth might not be exciting, but she was as indispensable as food.... She was, after all, the starting-point and ultimate goal of all one's adventures.... Clare would lose some of her delightfulness, if there were no Elsbeth to whom to en-sky on her.... Alwynne did not see what she wanted with a mother, so long as she had Elsbeth.... She had said so once to her aunt and had never guessed, as she was chidden for sacrilege against the picture over her bed, at the exquisite pleasure she had given.

After the little coolness of the past few days (her aunt's fault entirely, Alwynne knew, and so could be unruffled) Elsbeth's renewal of sympathetic interest was very soothing. Alwynne was glad to foster it by talking of Clare, and Clare, and nothing but Clare, for the rest of the week. In church on Christmas morning, poor Elsbeth, settling her spiritual accounts, begging forgiveness for uncharitable thoughts, and assuring her Maker that she wished Clare no evil, could yet sigh for the useful age of miracles, and patron saints, and devils, when a prayer in the right quarter could transport your enemy to inaccessible islands of the Antipodes. She would have been magnanimous, have bargained for every comfort-Eden's climate and hot and cold water laid on-but the island must be definitely inaccessible and Antipodean.

Clare, too, had spent her morning, if not in prayer, at least in profound meditation. She felt stranded, and was wishing for Alwynne, and anathematising the superfluous and intriguing aunt.

Clare made the mistake of all tortuous intelligences in being unable to credit appearances. She was being, as usual, unjust to Elsbeth, Alwynne, and the world at large. She could not believe in simplicity combined with brains: a simple soul was necessarily a simpleton in her eyes. Because her own words were ever two edged, her meaning flavoured by reservations and implications, she literally could not accept a speech as expressing no more and no less than its plain dictionary meaning. With any one of her own type of mind she was at her ease; her mistake lay in not recognising how rare that type was; in detecting subtleties where none existed, and wasting hint, suggestion and innuendo on minds that drove as heartily through them as an ox walks through a spider thread stretched from post to gatepost of the meadow he means to enter.

Elsbeth, whom she had considered a negligible fool, had yesterday startled her into respect-not for the kindly and selfless pleasure in Alwynne's pleasure, that had, for all her little jealous anxieties, prompted the invitation to Clare, but for the totally imaginary cunning with which, in Clare's eyes, it had invested her. Alwynne's repetition of Elsbeth's remark had enlightened Clare: enlightened her to qualities in Elsbeth which Elsbeth herself would have been horrified to possess.

Clare saw, in the manner of the invitation, a gauntlet flung down, the preliminaries to a conflict, with Alwynne herself for the prize; and the first warning of an antagonist sufficiently like herself to be considered dangerous, the more dangerous, indeed, for the apparently uninteresting harmlessness that could mask a mind in reality so scheming and so complex. She did not realise that if she did finally close with Elsbeth, with the intention of robbing her of Alwynne, she would have far more to fear from her simple, affectionate goodness of heart than from any subtlety of intellect with which Clare was choosing to invest her.

She wondered, as she frittered away the morning, how she should best counter Elsbeth's attack. She would call, of course-in state; it would be due; she would not be judged deficient in courtesies. Alwynne should be there (she would ensure that), and she, Clare, would be exceedingly charming, and very delicately emphasise the contrast between Elsbeth and herself. It would be quite easy, with Alwynne already biassed. Her eyes sparkled with anticipation. It would be amusing. She should enjoy routing Elsbeth.

And there was the case of Alwynne to be considered. She had been excessively nice to Alwynne lately, had, in fact, allowed her, for a moment, to see how necessary she was becoming to Clare.... That was a mistake.... One must never let people feel secure of their hold upon one.... That little speech of Alwynne's last night, mocking and tender-she had thrilled to it at the time-did it not, ever so faintly, shadow forth a readjustment of attitudes, sound a note of equality? That, though it had pleased her at the moment, must not be....Alwynne must be checked.... It would not hurt her....She was subdued as easily as a child, and as easily revived....She never bore malice. Clare, who never forgot or forgave a pinprick, had often marvelled at her, could even now scarcely believe in the spontaneity of her good temper. But Alwynne, certainly, had been going too far lately; was absurdly popular in the school; could, Clare guessed, have annexed more than one of her own special worshippers, if she had chosen. Louise, she knew, confided in her: she thought with a double stab of jealousy of the scene she had witnessed but a few days since; of Louise, fresh from her commendations, from her kiss even (that rare impulse, regretted as soon as gratified), at rest in Alwynne's arms. She recalled Louise's startled look and Alwynne's contrasting serenity. She had not enquired what it all meant-that was not her way. But she had not forgotten it. Alwynne was hers. Louise was hers. But they had nothing to seek from one another! Alwynne, undoubtedly, as the elder, the dearer, required the check; not little Louise. Louise's letter had genuinely touched her-she thought she would go and see the child, spend her Christmas Day charitably, in amusing her. And if (in after-thought) Alwynne came round in the afternoon, and found her gone-it couldn't be helped! It wouldn't hurt Alwynne to be disappointed....It wouldn't hurt Alwynne to spend a day of undiluted Elsbeth....And Louise would be amusingly charmed to see Clare....It was pleasant to please a child —a clever, appreciative child....She would go round directly after lunch....The maid should go home for the afternoon....She laughed mischievously as she imagined the blankness of Alwynne's face, when she should be confronted by silence and a closed door. Poor, dear Alwynne! Well, it wouldn't hurt her.

But Alwynne set out gaily on Christmas afternoon, and, first escorting Elsbeth to the lychgate of her favourite church, walked on as quickly as her narrow fur-edged skirt would let her.

The clocks were striking three as she turned into Friar's Lane.

It was a cold, still day, and Alwynne shivered a little, and drew her furs closely about her, as she stood outside the door of Clare's flat. She had rung, but the maid was usually slow in answering.

The passage was damply cold. It would be all the jollier to toast oneself before one of Clare's imperial fires....She wished the maid would hurry up. She waited a moment and then rang again.

There was no answer.

It struck her that the maid might have been given the afternoon off; but it was funny that Clare did not hear.

She rang again. She could hear the bell tinging shrilly within, but there was no other sound save the tick of the solemn little grandmother on the inner side of the wall.

Suddenly it occurred to her that Clare might be dozing. Clare never slept in the afternoons, but she did occasionally doze in her chair for a few minutes. She denied that she did so as strenuously as people always and unaccountably do; but Alwynne knew better. It always delighted her when Clare succumbed to drowsiness; a good sleeper herself, she had been appalled by Clare's acquiescence in four wakeful nights out of seven, and after a casual description that

Clare had once given her of the arid miseries of insomnia, ten minutes' unexpected slumber did not give Clare herself more ease than it gave Alwynne.

The possibility of such an explanation of the silence, therefore, had to be considered respectfully: if Clare slept, far be it from Alwynne to wake her! Yet she could not go away.... Clare, after that unlucky clash of wills, would be doubly hurt if Alwynne left without seeing her first....But if Clare were asleep....

Resignedly Alwynne sat herself down on Clare's doorstep to wait until a movement within should be the signal to ring again.

She was not annoyed; she always had plenty to think about; and it would be very pleasant, when Clare did at last open the door, to be received with open arms, and pitied, and scolded, and warmed....It was certainly very cold....All the draughts of the town seemed to have their home on the staircase, and to come sliding and slithering and undulating past, like a brood of invisible snakes.

She shifted her position. The doorstep was icy. She got up, and placed her muff, her chinchilla muff (shades of Elsbeth! her beautiful, new chinchilla muff) on the whitened doorstep. Then she sat on it.

"Ah! That's better," murmured Alwynne appreciatively. She was grateful to Elsbeth for reminding her to wear her muff.

But it did not get any warmer, and the daylight was beginning to fade. She glanced at her watch-twenty minutes past three. Surely Clare was awake again now. But she would wait another five minutes. She watched the hands-marvelled at the interminable length of a minute, and was drifting off on her favourite speculation as to the essential unreality of time, when simultaneously the grandmother struck the half-hour and she sneezed. She jumped up horrified. A cold would mean a week's absence from Clare, and a restatement of Elsbeth's thesis "of the advisability of wearing flannel petticoats and long-sleeved bodices."

Also, half of her hoarded hour was gone. She rang again impatiently. No answer. Clare must be out....Gone to the post? No, Alwynne had been waiting half-an-hour, she would have returned by now....Impossible that Clare should be out on Christmas afternoon, when she had refused an invitation and was expecting Alwynne herself....She rang; and waited; and rang again and again and yet again.

"If Clare has gone out ———" cried Alwynne indignantly; and subjected the handle to a final series of vicious tugs. The bell within pealed and rocked and jarred, gave a last hysterical gurgle and was dumb. She had broken the bell. She had broken Clare Hartill's bell!

Alwynne looked round about her guiltily; she felt more like nine than nineteen. The flight of stairs was still empty and silent. No one had seen her come; no one would see her go....If she went quietly away, and said nothing about it? For Clare would be annoyed....She always got so annoyed over little things....What a pity to have a fuss with Clare over such a little thing as a broken bell!

She crept on tip-toe down the stairs and out into the road. Then she paused.

Was she being mean? After all-there was no earthly use in telling Clare....Clare would never let her pay for the mending....Yet naturally she would be annoyed to come back and find her bell broken....She would think it was the milkman or the paper-boy....Alwynne hoped they would not get into trouble....Perhaps, after all, she had better tell Clare. Such an absurd thing to confess to, though-that she had been in such a temper that she had broken the bell! Clare would be sarcastic....Yet it was Clare's fault for being out....That was unkind....She would tell Clare so ...she would write and tell her....She would write a note now, and tell her about the bell at the same time....She retraced her steps, pulled out her note-book and pencil, and began to scribble —

> *Dear Clare* —*I'm awfully sorry but I'm afraid I've broken the bell. I couldn't make you hear. I thought you were asleep, but I suppose you are out. I must have rung too hard, but I didn't think you would be out.* Heavily underlined. *I'm dreadfully sorry about the bell.*

She hesitated. If Clare would let her pay for a new one, she wouldn't feel so bad....Yet how could she suggest it? It would sound so crude....If only Clare would not be angry....Absurd to be feeling afraid of Clare-but then she had never done anything so stupid before....Angry or not, Clare would never let her pay....Yet should she suggest it? She bit her pencil in distracted indecision, till the lead broke off between her teeth.

That settled it. The damp stump was barely capable of scoring an *Alwynne*.

She pinned the paper to the door with her only hatpin (a present of the forenoon) and reluctantly departed.

It was a pity that her best hat blew off twice into the mud.

Elsbeth was glad to get Alwynne back so early. Had Alwynne enjoyed herself?

Alwynne sneezed as she answered.

Before the evening was over Alwynne reeked of eucalyptus.

CHAPTER XI

Louise was at the nursery window, staring out into the brown, bare garden. The sky was smooth and a dark yellow, the naked trees barred it like a tiger's hide. The gathering dusk had swallowed up the wind. Not a twig stirred, not a sparrow's chirp broke the thick stillness. Spellbound, the world awaited the imminent snow.

Louise, sitting motionless in the window-seat, with her little pink nose flattening itself against the panes in dreary expectation of a stray unlikely postman, looked, with her peaked, ivory face and dark, unwinking eyes, her colourless clothes, and the sprig of holly with never a scarlet berry pinned to her flat little chest, like the mood of the December day made flesh.

Clare, at least, thought so. Dispensing with the indifferent maid, she had found her own way to the nursery, and pushing open the unlatched door, stood an instant, appraising the child and her surroundings. She noted with distaste the remains of the barely tasted lunch, still encumbering the table, and impingeing on the little pile of austere Christmas presents, so carefully arranged: the gloves and stockings and the prim Prayer Book a mere background for a dainty calendar that she recognised. She smiled, with a touch of irritation-did Alwynne ever forget any one, she wondered? But it was not suitable for a mistress to send her pupils presents.... She wished she had thought of sending Louise something herself...something more original than that obviously over-prized calendar....It was not much of a Christmas table, she thought ...not much of a Christmas Day for a child....

She marvelled that a well-furnished room could look so dreary. Louise's huddled pose, the neglected fire, the book crushed face downwards on the floor, combined to touch her. With her incurable feeling for the effective attitude, she remained straight and stiff in the shadows of the doorway, but her gesture was beautiful in its awkward tenderness as she stretched out her hand to the window.

"Merry Christmas, Louise!"

For an instant the child was silent, rigid, incredulous: then came a whirl of petticoats and a flash of black legs. Louise, wild with excitement, dropped to the floor and dashed across the room.

"Oh, Miss Hartill! Oh, Miss Hartill! You?"

"Well, are you pleased to see me?"

"Please, won't you sit down?" Louise, between delight and embarrassment, did curious things with the big arm-chair. "I can't believe it's you. And on Christmas Day! Won't you please sit down? Is the room too warm for you? Will you take off your furs? Would you like some tea? I'll make up the fire-it's cold in here. Will you take this chair? Oh, Miss Hartill! It's like the Queen calling on one. I don't know what to do." She looked up at Clare, blushing. Her pleasure and excitement were pretty enough.

Clare laughed.

"I'll tell you what to do. Run and put on your coat and hat. Would you like to come and spend the rest of the day with me?"

"With you?" Louise's eyes opened. "But it's Christmas Day?"

"Well?"

"I shan't be in the way?"

"I don't think so," said Clare coolly. "I'll send you home if you are."

She twinkled, but Louise was serious.

"You could do that, couldn't you?" she remarked with relief. "Oh, Miss Hartill, you are good! And I was hating my Christmas Day so. Won't you sit down while I get my things on?"

"Hurry up!" said Clare. And Louise fled to her bedroom.

Their walk back to Friar's Lane was a silent one. The snow was at last beginning to fall. Clare, half hypnotised by the steady silent motion, tramped forward, keeping time to some fragment of tune within her head. She was warmed by the pleasant consciousness of a kindly action performed, but its object, trotting beside her, was half forgotten.

Louise, very shy at encountering Miss Hartill unofficially, was far too timid to speak unless she were addressed. But she was perfectly happy; marvelling and rejoicing at her situation (Miss Hartill's guest, bound for her home!), overflowing with dog-like devotion to the Olympian who had actually remembered her existence. She was glad of the silent walk. It gave her time to realise her own happiness; to learn by heart that picture of Clare, against the background of the empty nursery, to get her every sentence by rote, and store all safely in her memory before turning to the contemplation of the incredible adventure upon which she was now embarking.

Clare, preceding Louise up the staircase, found Alwynne's note awaiting her. She frowned as she read it and felt for her latch-key. It was just like Alwynne to leave a note like that for any one to read....And the hatpin for any one to steal....She wished it had been stolen before it had scratched her paint....And the bell! It was really annoying of Alwynne! It would cost her five shillings to put right....She, Clare, was not mean, but she did begrudge money for that sort of thing....Really, Alwynne might offer to pay for it....But that, of course, would never occur to Alwynne....She was altogether too reckless about other people's belongings....Her own were her own affair....But to break Clare's bell....She must have been quite comprehensively annoyed to have actually broken it....Clare laughed. She had had a sudden vision of Alwynne's blank face and indignant pealings. Poor old Alwynne! Well-it wouldn't hurt her....If she were careful to let Alwynne know to whom she had been sacrificed, Alwynne might not be quite so partisan over Louise next term....That wouldn't be a bad thing....She did not approve of intimacies between the girls and the mistresses....But she, Clare, would make it up to both of them.... She would begin now, with Louise....She would devote herself to amusing Louise....She would give Louise the time of her life....Louise would be sure to tell Alwynne about it afterwards....

CHAPTER XII

"What are you going to do with yourself all the holidays?" asked Clare, with a touch of curiosity. Louise had slipped off her chair on to the soft hearthrug, and sat, hugging her knees and staring up at Clare.

"Read," she said briefly, and gave a little gurgle of anticipation.

"All day long?"

"Oh, yes, Miss Hartill. I never get a chance in term time. There's such heaps to read. I'd like to live in a library."

"Yet a peep at the world outside beats all the books that were ever written."

"I wonder." Louise rubbed her chin meditatively against her knees before she delivered herself. "You know —I think the way things strike people is much more interesting than the things themselves. I like exploring people's minds. Do you know?"

"I know," said Clare. She laughed mischievously. "You mean-that what you think I am, for instance, is much more interesting than what I really am."

Louise protested mutely. Her black eyes glowed.

"I daresay you're right, Louise. You wear pink spectacles, you see. I'm quite sure you would be appalled if any one took them off. I'm a horrid person really."

Louise looked puzzled; then the twinkle in Miss Hartill's eyes enlightened her. Miss Hartill was teasing. She laughed merrily.

Clare shook her head.

"It's quite true. I'm an egoist, Louise!"

"It's not true," said Louise passionately. She was on guard in an instant, ready to justify Miss Hartill to herself and the world.

It amused Clare to excite her.

"My good child-what do you know about it?"

"Lots," said Louise, with a catch in her voice. "You're not! You're not!"

"I am." Clare leaned forward, much tickled. She could afford to attempt to disillusion Louise.... Louise would not believe her, but she could not say later that she had not been warned. But at the same time, Clare warmed her cold and cynical self in the pure flame of affection her self-criticism was fanning. "I am," she repeated. "Why do you think I came round to see you to-day?"

Louise looked up at her shyly, dwelling on her answer as if it gave her exquisite pleasure.

"Because-because you knew I was alone, and you hated me to be miserable on Christmas Day."

"You?" Clare's eyebrows lifted for a second, but a glance into the child's candid eyes dispelled the vague suspicion.... Louise and conceit were incompatible. She listened with a touch of compunction to the innocent answer.

"Not me specially, of course. Any one who was down. Only it happened to be me. I think you can't help being good to people: you're made that way." Her eyes were full of wondering admiration.

Clare was touched. She sighed as she answered —

"I wish I were. You shouldn't believe in people, Louise. I came round because-yes, you were a lonely scrap of a schoolgirl, certainly-but there were lots of other reasons. I wanted a walk and I wanted to be amused, and I wanted-and I wanted ——" she moved restlessly in her chair, "All pure egoism, anyhow."

"But you came," said Louise.

"To please you, or to punish some one else? I don't know!"

Louise enjoyed her incomprehensibility. She stored up her remarks to puzzle over later. Yet she would ask questions if Miss Hartill were in a talking mood.

"Do I know them?" (She had an odd habit of using the plural when she wished to be discreet.) She wondered who had been punished, and why, and thrilled deliciously, as she did to a ghost story. She thought that it would be terrible to have offended Miss Hartill: yet immensely exciting.... She wondered if all her courage would go if Miss Hartill were angry? She had always despised poor Jeanne du Barrie: but Miss Hartill raging would be harder to face than a mob....

"What have they done?" asked Louise eagerly.

"They? It's your dear Miss Durand," said Clare, with a grim smile. "I'm very angry with her, Louise. She's been behaving badly."

Louise's eyes widened: she looked alarmed and distressed.

"Oh, but Miss Hartill-she hasn't! She couldn't! What has she done?"

"Shall I tell you?" Clare leaned forward mysteriously.

Louise nodded breathlessly.

"She wouldn't copy me and be an egoist. And I wanted her to, rather badly, Louise. There, that's all! You're none the wiser, are you? Never mind, you will be, some day. Don't look so worried, you funny child."

"Why do you call yourself such names? You're not an egoist? You can't be," cried Louise desperately.

Clare laughed.

"Can't I? Most people are. It's not a synonym for murderess! Stop frowning, child. Why, I don't believe you know what it means even. Do you know what an egoist is, Louise?"

"Sir Willoughby Patterne!" said Louise promptly.

Clare threw up her hands.

"What next? I wish I'd had charge of you earlier. You shouldn't try so hard to say 'Humph,' little pig."

"I don't." Louise was indignant.

"Then what possesses you to steer your cockle-boat on to Meredith? Well-what do you think of him? What have you read?"

"About all. He's queer. He's not Dickens or Scott, of course ——" Her tone deprecated.

"Of course not," said Clare, with grave sympathy.

"But I like him. I like Chloe. I like the sisters-you know —'Fine Shades and Nice Feeling' ——"

"Why?" Clare shot it at her.

"I don't know. They made me laugh. They're awfully real people. And I liked that book where the two gentlemen drink wine. 'Veuve' something."

"What on earth did you see in that?" Clare was amused.

"I don't know. I just liked them. Of course, I adore Shagpat."

"That I understand. It's a fairy tale to you, isn't it?"

"Not a proper one-only Arabian Nightsy."

"What's a proper one, Louise?"

Louise hesitated.

"Well, heaps that one loves aren't. Grimm's and Hans Andersen's aren't, or even *The Wondrous Isles*. And, of course, none of the Lang books. I hate those. You know, proper fairy stories aren't easy to get. You have to dig. You get bits out of the notes in the Waverley Novels, and there's *Kilmeny*, and *The Celtic Twilight*, and *The Lore of Proserpine*, and Lemprière. Do you believe in fairies, Miss Hartill?"

"It depends on the mood I'm in," said Clare seriously, "and the place. Elves and electric railways are incompatible."

Louise flung herself upon the axiom.

"Do you think so? Now I don't, Miss Hartill—I don't. If they are-they can stand railways. But you just believe in them literarily ——"

"Literally," Clare corrected.

"No, no-literaturily-just as a pretty piece of writing. You'll never see them if you think of them like that, Miss Hartill. The Greeks didn't —they just believed in Pan, and the Oreads, and the Dryads, and all those delicious people; and the consequence was that the country was

175

simply crammed with them. You just read Lemprière! I wish I'd lived then. Miss Hartill, did you ever see a Good Person?"

"I'm afraid not, Louise. But I had a nurse who used to tell me about her grand-aunt: she was supposed to be a changeling."

Louise wriggled with delight.

"Oh, tell about her, Miss Hartill. What was she like?"

"Tiny and black, with a very white skin. They were a fair family. Nurse said they all disliked her, though she never did them any harm. She used to be out in the woods all day-and she ate strange food."

"What?"

"Fungi, and nettle-tops, and young bracken, and blackberries, my nurse said."

"Blackberries?"

"She was Irish; the Irish peasants won't touch blackberries, you know. We're just as bad, Louise. Heaps of fungi are delicious-wait till you've been in Germany. They know what's good: but, then, they won't touch rabbits, so there you are! I expect my nurse's aunt thought us an odd lot, us humans."

"Was she really a fairy?" Louise was breathless.

"How do I know? A witch perhaps. I should think a young witch, by all accounts."

"What happened to her?"

"She was 'swept' on her wedding-day."

"Crossing water?"

"No. She was to marry an old farmer. She went into the woods at dawn to wash in dew, and gather bindweed for her wreath ——" She paused dramatically, her eyes dancing with fun; but Louise was wholly in earnest.

"Go on! Oh, go on!"

"She was never seen again."

"Oh, how lovely!" Louise shivered ecstatically. "I wish I'd been her. What did her foster people do?"

"What could they? I think they were glad to be rid of her." (Clare suppressed a certain tall young gipsy, who had figured suspiciously in the original narrative.) "Fairy blood is ill to live with, Louise. I don't envy Mrs. Blake, or Mrs. Thomas Rhymer."

"No. But it's so difficult to live in two worlds at once."

"Shouldering the wise man's burden already?"

"You get absent-minded, and forget-ink-stains, you know, and messages."

"I know," said Clare.

"You see, I have such a gorgeous world inside my head, Miss Hartill: I go there when I'm rather down, here. It's a sort of Garden of the Hesperides, and you are there, and Mother, and all my special friends."

"Who, for instance?" Clare was curious; it was the first she had heard of Louise with friends of her own.

"Well-Elizabeth Bennett, and the Little Women, and Garm, and Amadis of Gaul ——"

"Oh-not real people?" Clare was amused at herself for being relieved.

"Oh, but Miss Hartill-they are real." Louise was indignant. "Ever so much more than-oh, most people! Look at Mrs. Bennett and Mamma! Nobody will think of Mamma in a hundred years-but who'd ever forget Mrs. Bennett?"

"Mrs Bennett in the Garden of the Hesperides, Louise?" Clare began to chuckle. "I can't swallow that."

Louise pealed with laughter.

"You should have seen her the other day, with the dragon after her. She'd been trying to sneak some apples, because Bingley was coming to tea."

"Who came to the rescue?"

"Oh, I did." Louise was revelling in her sympathetic listener. "I have to keep order, you know. She was awfully blown, though. Siegfried helped me."

"I wish I could get to fairyland as easily as you do."

Louise considered.

"I don't. My country is only in my head. Fairyland must be somewhere, mustn't it? Do you know what I think, Miss Hartill?"

"In patches, Louise."

Louise blushed.

"No, but seriously-don't laugh. You know you explained the fourth dimension to us the other day?"

"That I'm sure I never did." Clare was lying back in her chair, her arms behind her head, smiling inscrutably.

"Oh, but Miss Hartill — —"

"Never, Louise!"

"Oh, but honestly—I'm not contradicting you, of course-but you did. Last Thursday fortnight, in second lesson."

"I wish you were as accurate over all your dates, Louise! Your History paper was not all that it should be."

"It's holidays, Miss Hartill! But don't you remember?"

"I explained to you that the fourth dimension was inexplicable —a very different thing."

"*The Plattner Story* explains it-clearly." Louise's tone was distinctly reproachful.

"Oh no, it doesn't, Louise. Mr. Wells only deludes you into thinking it does."

"Well, anyhow, I think-don't you think that it's rather likely that fairyland is the fourth dimension? It would all fit in so beautifully with all the old stories of enchantment and disappearances. Then there was another book I read about it. *The Inheritors* — —"

"Have done, Louise! You make me dizzy. Don't try to live exclusively on truffles. If you could continue to confine your attention to books you have some slight chance of understanding, for the next few years, it would be an excellent thing. Neither Meredith nor the fourth dimension is meat for babes, you know."

"I like what I don't understand. It's the finding out is the fun." Louise looked mutinous.

"And having found out?"

"Then I start on something else."

Clare considered her.

"Louise, I don't know if it's a compliment to either of us-but I believe we're very much alike."

Louise gave a child's delighted chuckle, but she showed no surprise.

"That's nice, Miss Hartill." She hesitated. "Miss Hartill, did you know my Mother?"

"Mrs. Denny?" Clare hesitated.

Louise gave an impatient gesture.

"Not Mamma. My very own Mother."

"No, my dear." Clare's voice was soft.

Louise sighed.

"No one does. There are no pictures. Father was angry when I asked about her once: and Miss Murgatroyd-she was our governess-she said I had no tact. I miss her, you know, though I don't remember her. I had a nurse: she told me a little. Mother had grey eyes too, you know," said Louise, gazing into Clare's. "I expect she was rather like you."

She watched Clare a little breathlessly. There was more of tenderness in her face than many who thought they knew Clare Hartill would have credited, but no hint of awakening memory, of the recognition the child sought. She went on —

"People never come back when they're dead, do they?" She had no idea of the longing in her voice.

"No, you poor baby!" Clare rose hastily and began to walk up and down the room, as her fashion was when she was stirred.

"Never?"

"'*Stieg je ein Freund Dir aus dem Grabe wieder?*'" murmured Clare.

"What, Miss Hartill?"

"Never, Louise."

Louise's thistledown fancies were scattered by her tone. Impossible to discredit any statement of Miss Hartill's. Yet she protested timidly.

"There was the Witch of Endor, Miss Hartill. Samuel, you know."

"Is that Meredith?" said Clare absently. Then she caught Louise's expression. "What's the matter?"

"But it's the Bible!" cried Louise horrified.

Clare sat down again and began to laugh pleasantly.

"What am I to do with you, Louise? Are you five or fifty? You want to discuss Meredith with me —(not that I shall let you, my child-don't think I approve of all this reading —I did it myself at your age, you see) and five minutes later you look at me round-eyed because I've forgotten my Joshua or my Judges! Kings? I beg your pardon; Kings be it! Never mind, Louise. Tell me about the Witch of Endor."

"Only that she called up Samuel, I meant, from the dead."

Louise was evidently abstracted; she was picking her words.

"Don't you believe it, Miss Hartill, quite?"

"It's the Old Testament, after all," temporised Clare. She began to see Louise's difficulty. She had no beliefs herself but she thought she would find out how fourteen handled the problem.

"Then the New is different? There was Dorcas, you know, and the widow's son. That is all true, Miss Hartill?"

Clare fenced.

"Many people think so."

"I want to know the truth," said Louise tensely. "I want to know what you think." She spoke as if the two things were synonymous.

Clare shook her head.

"I won't help you, Louise. You must find out for yourself. Leave it alone, if you're wise."

"How can I? I've been reading — —"

"Ah?"

"The *Origin of Species* —and *We Two*."

Clare's gravity fled. She lay back shaking with laughter.

"Louise, you're delightful! Anything else?"

Louise pulled up her footstool to Clare's knee.

"Miss Hartill, I've been reading a play. It's horrible. I can't bear it, though it was thrilling to read — —"

Clare interrupted.

"Where do you get all these books, Louise?"

"They are all Mother's, you know. Nobody else wants them. And then there's the Free Library."

Clare shuddered. She would sooner have drunk from the tin cup of a public fountain than have handled the greasy volumes of a public library.

"How can you?" she said disgustedly. "Dirt and dog-ears!"

Louise opened her eyes. She was too young to be squeamish.

"'A book's a book for a' that,'" she laughed. "How else am I to get hold of any-that I like?"

Clare jerked her head to the lined walls.

"Help yourself," she said.

Louise was radiant.

"May I? Oh, you are good! I will take such care. I'll cover them in brown paper."

She jumped up and, running across the room, flung herself on her knees before the wide shelves. Timidly, at first, but with growing forgetfulness of Clare, she pulled out here a volume and there a volume, handling them tenderly, yet barely opening each, so eager was she for fresh discoveries. She reminded Clare of *Alice* with the scented rushes. Clare was amused by her absorption, and a little touched. The child's attitude to books hinted at the solitariness of her life: she relaxed to them, greeting them as intimates and companions; there was a new appearance on her; she was obviously at home, welcomed by her friends; a very different person to the shy-eyed, prim little prodigy her school-fellows knew.

Clare, glancing at her now and then, sympathised benevolently, and left her to herself; she understood that side of the child; her remark to Louise about the resemblance between them had not been made at random; she was constantly detecting traits and tastes in her similar to her own. She was interested; she had thought herself unique. Their histories were not dissimilar; she, too, different as her environment had been, could look back on a lonely, self-absorbed childhood; she, too, had had forced and premature successes. They had not been empty ones, she reflected complacently; she had used those schoolgirl triumphs as stepping-stones. She doubted if Louise could do the same: there was something unpractical about Louise —a hint of the visionary in her air. She had at present none of Clare's passion for power and the incense of success. Clare, quite aware of her failing, aware that it was a failing and perversely proud of it, yet hoped that she should not see it sprouting in the character of Louise. She hated to see her own defects reproduced (ineffably vulgarised) in others; it jarred her pride. The discovery of the resemblance between herself and Louise amused and charmed her, as long as it was confined to the qualities that Clare admired; but if the girl began to reflect her faults, Clare knew that she should be irritated.

She considered these things as she sat and sewed. She was an exquisite needlewoman. The frieze of tapestry that ran round the low-ceilinged room was her own work. Alwynne had designed it —a history of the loves of Deirdre and Naismi some months before, when she and Clare had discovered Yeats together; and Clare had adapted the rough, clever sketches, working with her usual amazing speed. The foot-deep strips of needlework and painted silk, with their golden skies and dark foregrounds, along which the dim, rainbow figures moved, were just what Clare had wanted to complete her panelled room; for she was beauty-loving and house-proud, though her love of originality, or more correctly her tendency to be superior and aloof, often enticed her into bizarrerie. But the Deirdre frieze was as harmonious as it was unusual; and Clare, as she daily feasted her eyes on the rich, mellow colours, was only annoyed that the idea of it had been Alwynne's. That fact, though she would not own it, was able, though imperceptibly, to taint Clare's pleasure. She was quite unnecessarily scrupulous in mentioning Alwynne's share in the work to any one who admired it; but it piqued her to do so, none the less. If any one had told her that it piqued her she would have been extremely amused at the absurdity of the idea.

She was at the time working out a medallion of her own design, and growing interested, she soon forgot all about Louise, sitting Turkish fashion at the big book-case. The light had long since faded and the enormous fire, gilding walls and furniture, rendered the candles' steady light almost superfluous. Candlelight was another predilection of Clare's —there was neither electricity nor gas in her tiny, perfect flat. The tick of the clock in the hall and the flutter of turning pages alone broke the silence. Outside, the snow fell steadily.

Half-a-mile away Alwynne Durand, drumming on the window-pane, while her aunt dozed in her chair, thought incessantly of Clare, and was filled with restless longing to be with her. She tried to count the snowflakes till her brain reeled. She felt cold and dreary, but she would not rouse Elsbeth by making up the fire. She wished she had something new to read. She thought it the longest Christmas Day she had ever spent.

The neat maid, bringing in the tea-tray, roused Clare. She pushed aside her work and began to pour out; but Louise in her corner, made no sign.

Clare laughed.

"Louise, wake up! Don't you want any tea?"

Louise, as if the conversation had not ceased for an instant, scrambled to her feet and came to the table, a load of books in her arms, saying as she did so —

"I'll be awfully careful. May I take these, perhaps?"

Clare nodded.

"Presently. I'll look them over first. Muffins?"

She gave Louise a delightful meal and taught her to take tea with a slice of lemon. She was particular, Louise noticed; some of the muffins were not toasted to her liking, and were instantly banished; she criticised the cakes and the flavouring of the dainty sandwiches; then she laughed wickedly at Louise for her round eyes.

"What's the matter, child?"

"Nothing," said Louise, embarrassed.

"I believe you're shocked because I talked so much about food?"

Louise blushed scarlet.

"I like eating, Louise."

"Yes-yes, of course," she concurred hastily.

Clare was entertained. She knew quite well that Louise, like all children, considered a display of interest in food, if not indelicate, at least extremely human. She knew, too, that in Louise's eyes she was too entirely compounded of ideals and noble qualities to be more than officially human. She enjoyed upsetting her ideas.

"If you come to actual values, I'd rather do without Shakespeare than Mrs. Beeton," she remarked blandly.

"Oh, Miss Hartill!" Louise was protesting-suspecting a trap-ready to ripple into laughter. "You do say queer things."

"I?"

"Yes. As if you meant that!"

"But I do! Eating's an art, Louise, like painting or writing. I had a pheasant last Sunday — —" She gave the entire menu, and enlarged on the etceteras with enthusiasm.

Louise looked bewildered.

"I never thought you thought about that sort of thing," she remarked. "I thought you just didn't notice —I thought you would always be thinking of poetry and pictures — —" She subsided, blushing.

Clare laughed at her pleasantly.

"I thought, I thought, I think, I thought! What a lot of thoughts. I'm sorry, Louise! Is all my star-dust gone?"

Louise shook her head vigorously, but she was still embarrassed. She changed the subject with agility.

"I've read that!"

"What?"

"The star-dust book-but I've picked out two others of his. May I? All these?"

Clare ran her finger along the titles.

"Yes-yes-Fiona Mcleod-yes —*Peer Gynt* —yes, if you like, you won't understand it, or Yeats-but all right. No, not Nietzsche! Not on any account, Louise."

Louise protested.

"Oh, why not, Miss Hartill? I'm nearly fourteen."

"Are you really?" said Clare, with respect.

"He looks so jolly-Old Testament — —"

"He does, Louise! That's his little way. But he's not for the Upper Fifth."

"He's in the Free Library," said Louise, with a twinkle. Clare turned.

"You can have all the books you want, if you come to me. But no more Free Library, Louise. You understand? I don't wish it."

Louise tingled like a bather under a cold spray. She liked and disliked the autocratic tone. Clare went on.

"I detest trash-and there's a good deal, even in a Carnegie collection. There's no need for you to dull your imagination on melodrama like-what was it?"

"What, Miss Hartill?"

"The play you began to tell me about-you thought it horrible, you said."

Louise opened her eyes.

"Miss Hartill, it wasn't melodrama-it was good stuff. That's why it worried me. It's by a Norwegian or a Dane or some one. *Pastor Sang* it's called."

"That? I don't follow. I should have thought the theology would have bored you, but there's nothing horrible in it."

"It worried me. Oh, Miss Hartill, what does it all mean? Darwin says, we just grew-doesn't he? and that the Bible's all wrong. But you say that doesn't matter-it's just Old Testament? And this play says-do you remember? the wife is ill-and the husband, who cures people by praying-he can't cure her——"

"Well?" said Clare impatiently.

"And he says, if the apostles did miracles, we ought to be able to-he kills his wife, trying. He can't, you see. But the point is, if he couldn't, with all his faith-could the apostles? And if the apostles couldn't, could Christ Himself? The miracles are just only a tale, perhaps?"

"Perhaps," said Clare. "You're not clear, Louise, but I know what you mean."

"It frightened me, that play," said the child in a low voice. "If there were no miracles-and everything one reads makes one sure there weren't —why, then, the Bible's not true! Jesus was just a man! He didn't rise? Perhaps there isn't an afterwards? Perhaps there isn't God?"

"Perhaps," said Clare.

The child's eyes were wide and frightened. She put her hand timidly on Clare's knee.

"Miss Hartill-you believe in God?"

Clare looked at her, weighing her.

Louise spoke again; her voice had grown curiously apprehensive.

"Miss Hartill-you do believe in God?"

Clare shrugged her shoulders.

Louise stared at her appalled.

"If *you* don't believe in God——" she began slowly, and then stopped.

They sat a long while in silence.

Clare felt uncomfortable. She had not intended to express any opinion, to let her own attitude to religion appear. But Louise, with her sudden question, had forced one from her. After all, if Louise had begun to doubt and to inquire, no silence on Clare's part would stop her.... Every girl went through the phase-with Louise it had begun early, that was all.... Yet in her heart she knew that Louise, with her already overworked mind, should have been kept from the mental distress of religious doubt.... She knew that for some years she could have been so kept; that, as the mouth can eat what the body will not absorb, so, though her intelligence might have assimilated all the books she chose to read, her soul need not necessarily have been disturbed by them. Her acquired knowledge that the world is round need not have jostled her rule of thumb conviction that it is flat. Her interest in 'ologies and 'osophies could have lived comfortably enough, with her child's belief in four angels round her head, for another two or three years-strengthening, maturing years.

Clare knew her power. At a soothing word from her, Louise would have shelved her speculations, or at least have continued them impersonally. Clare could have guaranteed God to her. But Clare had shrugged her shoulders, and Louise had grown white-and she had felt like a murderess. Do children really take their religion so seriously?... After all, what real difference could it make to Louise?... She, Clare, had been glad to be rid of her clogging and irrational beliefs.... Louise, too, when she recovered from the shock, would enjoy the sense of freedom and self-respect.... If Louise talked like a girl of eighteen she could not be expected to receive the careful handling you gave a child of twelve.... Anyhow, it was done now....

Suddenly and persuasively she began to talk to Louise. She touched gently on the history, the growth and inevitable decay of all religions-the contrasting immutability of the underlying code of ethics, upon which they, one and all, were founded. She told her vivid little stories of the religious struggles of the centuries, had her breathless over the death of Socrates, nailed up for her anew the ninety-five theses to the Wittenberg church door. Exerting all her powers, all her knowledge, all her descriptive and dramatic skill, to charm away one child's distress, Clare was, for an hour, a woman transformed, sound and honey-sweet. Against all that happened later, she could at least put the one hour, when, remorsefully, she had given Louise of the best that was in her.

Incidentally, she delivered to her audience of one the most brilliant lecture of her career. Later she wrote down what she remembered of it, and it became the foundation for her monograph on religions that was to become a minor classic. Its success was immediate-that was typical of Clare-but she never wrote another line. That also was typical of Clare. It bored her to repeat a triumph.

She soon had Louise happy again: it was not in Louise to stick to the high-road of her own thoughts, with Miss Hartill opening gates to fairyland at every sentence. Clare kept her for the rest of the evening, and took her home at last, weighed down by her parcel of books, sleepy from the effects of excitement and happiness. She poured out her incoherent thanks as they waited on the doorstep of her home. There had never been such a Christmas-she had never had such a glorious time-she couldn't thank Miss Hartill properly if she talked till next Christmas came.

Clare, nodding and laughing, handed her over to the maid, and went home, not ill-pleased with her Christmas either. She thought of the child as she walked down the snowy, star-lighted streets, and wondered whimsically what she was doing at the moment. Would she say her prayers on her way to bed still, or had Clare's little, calculated shrug stopped that sort of thing for many a long day? She rather thought so. She shook off her uneasy sense of compunction and laughed aloud. The cold night air was like wine to her. After all, for an insignificant spinster, she had a fair share of power-real power-not the mere authority of kings and policemen. Her mind, not her office, ruled a hundred other minds, and in one heart, at least, a shrug of her shoulders had toppled God off His throne; and the vacant seat was hers, to fill or flout as she chose.

CHAPTER XIII

With the opening of the spring term began the final and most arduous preparations for the Easter examinations.

The school had been endowed, some years before, under the will of a former pupil, with a scholarship, a valuable one, ensuring not only the freedom of the school, but substantial help in the subsequent college career, that the winning of it entailed.

The rules were strict. The papers were set and corrected by persons chosen by the trustees of the bequest. The scholarship was open to the school, but no girl over seventeen might enter: and though an unsuccessful candidate might compete a second time, she must gain a percentage of marks in the first attempt. Total failure debarred her from making a second. This last rule limited in effect, the entries to members of the Sixths and Fifths, for the scholarship was too valuable for a chance of it to be risked through insufficient training. The standard, too, was high, and the rules so strictly enforced that withheld the grant if it were not attained, that Miss Marsham was accustomed to make special arrangements for those competing. They were called the "Scholarship Class," and had certain privileges and a great amount of extra work. To most of them the particular privilege that compensated for six months' drudgery was the fact that they were almost entirely under Miss Hartill's supervision. She considered their training her special task and spared neither time nor pains. She loved the business. She understood the art of rousing their excitement, pitting ambition against ambition. She worked them like slaves, weeding out remorselessly the useless members. Theoretically all had the right to enter; but none remained against Miss Hartill's wishes.

In spite of the work, the members of the Scholarship Class had an envied position in the school. Clare saw to that. Without attackable bias, she differentiated subtly between them and the majority. Each of the group was given to understand, without words, impalpably, yet very definitely, that if Miss Hartill, the inexorable, could have a preference, one had but to look in the glass to find it; and that to outstrip the rest of the class, to be listed an easy first, would be the most exquisite justification that preference could have. And as the type of girl who succumbed the most surely to Clare's witchcraft was also usually of the type to whom intellectual work was in itself attractive, it was not surprising if her favourite class were a hot-bed of emulation and enthusiasm-enthusiasm that was justified of its origin, for not even Henrietta Vigers denied that Clare contributed her full share to the earning of the scholarship, Miss Marsham, towards the end of the spring, was wont to declare, with her usual kindly concern, that she was thankful that the examination was not an annual affair.... Their good Miss Hartill was too anxious, too conscientious.... Miss Marsham must really forbid her to make herself ill. And, indeed, when the class was a large one, Clare was as reckless of her own strength as of that of her pupils, and suffered more from its expenditure. Where they were responsible, each for herself, Clare toiled early and late for them all. She fed them, moreover, from her own resources of energy, was entirely willing to devitalise herself on their behalf. The strain once over, she appeared slack, gaunt, debilitated. She had, however, her own methods of recuperation. Her ends gained, she could take back what she had given-take back more than ever she had given. Moreover, the supply of child-life never slackened. Old scholars might go-but ever the new ones came. Was it not Clare who gave the school its latter-day reputation? By the end of the summer term Clare would be once more in excellent condition.

When the promotion of Louise to the Upper School had first been mooted, Miss Hartill had not forgotten that the scholarship examination was once more drawing near. She saw no reason why Louise should not compete. That Louise, the whilom dullard of the Third, the youngest girl in the Upper School, should snatch the prize from the expectants of the Sixths and Fifths, would be an effective retort on Clare's critics, would redound very pleasantly to Clare's credit.

If she let the opportunity pass, Louise must wait two years: at thirteen it would be a triumph for Louise and Clare; at fifteen there would be nothing notable in her success. And the baby herself would be delighted. Clare was already sufficiently taken with Louise to enjoy the anticipation of her delight.

She was quite aware that it would entail special efforts on her own part, as well as on the child's, and that she had a large class already on her hands, and in need of coaching. But there was always Alwynne. Alwynne was so reliable; she could safely leave Louise's routine work in Alwynne's hands. It remained to consult Louise and incidentally the parent Dennys.

Louise was awestruck, overwhelmed by the honour of being allowed to compete, absurdly and touchingly delighted. No doubt as to Louise's sentiments. No doubt as to the sincerity of her efforts. No doubt, until the spring term began, of the certainty of her success.

The spring term opened with Clare in Miss Marsham's carved seat at morning prayers. The school had grown accustomed to its head-mistress's occasional absence. Miss Marsham, who had for some time felt the strain of school routine too much for her advanced years, was only able to sustain the fiction of her unimpaired powers by taking holidays, as a morphineuse takes her drug, in ever-increasing doses. She was confident in the discretion alike of Clare Hartill and Henrietta Vigers, and, indeed, but for their efficiency, the school would have suffered more quickly than it actually did. Nevertheless, the absence of supreme authority had, though but slightly, the usual disintegrating effect. There was always, naturally, an increase of friction between the two women, especially when the absence of the directress occurred at the beginning of a term. There would be the usual agitations-problems of housing and classification. There would arrive parents to be interviewed and impressed, new girls to be gracefully and graciously welcomed. Clare (to whom Henrietta, for all her hostility, invariably turned in emergencies), showing delicately yet unmistakably that she considered herself unwarrantably hampered in her own work, would submit to being on show with an air of bored acquiescence, tempered with modest surprise at the necessity for her presence. It was sufficiently irritating to Henrietta, under strict, if indirect, orders to leave the decorative side of the vice-regency to her rival. She was quite aware of Clare's greater effectiveness. She did not believe that it weighed with Miss Marsham against her own solid qualities. She affected to despise it. Yet despising, she envied.

She was unjust to Clare, however, in believing the latter's reluctance entirely assumed. Clare enjoyed ruffling the susceptibilities of Henrietta, but she was none the less genuinely annoyed at being even partially withdrawn from her classes and was relieved when, at the end of a fortnight, Miss Marsham returned to her post. Clare had been forced to neglect her special work. Classes had been curtailed and interrupted, the many extra lessons postponed or turned over to Alwynne, whom more than any other mistress she had trained and could trust.

It was Alwynne who, reporting to her at the end of the first fortnight, had made her more than ever eager to be rid of her deputyship.

There were new girls in the Fifth in whom Alwynne was interested. One, at least, she prophesied, would be found to have stuff in her. It was a pity she was not in the Scholarship Class.... She was too good for the Lower Fifth.... Alwynne supposed it would be quite impossible to let her enter?

"At this time of day? Impossible! Do you realise that we've only another three months?"

"I don't suppose she'd want to, anyhow," said Alwynne. "She's a quaint person! Talk about independence! She informed me to-day that she shouldn't stay longer than half-term, unless she liked us."

"Oho! Young America!" Clare was alert. "I didn't know you referred to Cynthia Griffiths. I interviewed the parents last week. Immensely rich! She was demure enough, but I gathered even then that she ruled the roost. Her mother was quite tearful-implored me to keep her happy for three months anyhow, while they both indulged in a rest cure abroad. She seemed doubtful of our capacities. But she was not explicit."

"Cynthia is. I've heard the whole story while I tried to find out how much she knew. She's a new type. Her French and her German are perfect-and her clothes. Her bedroom is a pig-sty and she gets up when she chooses. I gather that she has reduced Miss Vigers to a nervous wreck already. Thank goodness I'm a visiting mistress! I wonder what the girls will make of her!"

"Or she of them."

"That won't be the question," surmised Alwynne shrewdly. "Clare, she has five schools behind her, American and foreign-and she's fifteen! We are an incident. I know. There were two Americans at my school."

"It remains to be seen." Clare's eyes narrowed. "Well, what else?"

Alwynne fidgeted.

"I'm glad you're taking over everything again. I prefer my small kids."

"Why?"

"Easier to understand-and manage."

Clare looked amused.

"Been getting into difficulties? Who's the problem? Agatha?"

"That wind-bag! She only needs pricking to collapse," said Alwynne contemptuously. Then, with a frown: "I wish poor little Mademoiselle Charette would realise it. Have you ever seen a Lower Fifth French lesson? But, of course, you haven't. It's a farce."

Clare frowned.

"If she can't keep order ——"

"She can teach anyhow," said Alwynne quickly. "I was at the other end of the room once, working. I listened a little. It's only Agatha. Mademoiselle can tackle the others. She's effective in a delicate way; but senseless, noisy rotting-it breaks her up. She loses her temper. Of course, it's funny to watch. But I hate that sort of thing. I did when I was a schoolgirl even, didn't you?"

"I don't remember." But in the back of Clare's mind was a class-room and herself, contemptuously impertinent to a certain ineffective Miss Loveday.

Alwynne continued, frowning—

"Anyhow, I wish you'd do something."

Clare yawned.

"One mustn't interfere with other departments-unasked."

"Well, I ask you." Alwynne was in earnest.

"Why?"

"I want you to."

"Why?"

Alwynne blushed.

"Why this championship? I didn't know you and Mademoiselle Charette were such intimates?"

"It's just because we aren't. I like her, but ——"

"But what?"

"Well-we had a row. You see-You won't tell, Clare?"

Clare smiled.

"She doesn't like you," blurted out Alwynne indignantly. "And I just want to show her how altogether wrong ——"

"What a crime! How did you find it out?" Clare was amused.

"She was telling me about Agatha. And I said-why on earth didn't she complain to you? And she said-nothing on earth would induce her to. I said —I was sure you would be only too glad for her to ask you. And she said ——" Alwynne paused dramatically: "She said-she hadn't the faintest doubt you would, and that I was a charming child, but that she happened to understand you. Then we had a row of course."

Clare pealed with laughter.

"She's quite right, Alwynne. You are a charming child. So that is Mademoiselle Charette, is it? And I never guessed." She mused, a curious little smile on her lips.

"She's a dear, really," said Alwynne apologetically. "Only she's what Mrs. Marpler calls 'aughty.' I can't think why her knife's into you."

"Suppose ——" Clare's eyes lit up, she showed the tip of her tongue-sure sign of mischief afloat. "Suppose I pull it out? What do you bet me, Alwynne?"

Alwynne laughed.

"I wish you would. I don't like it when people don't appreciate you. Anyhow, I wish you'd settle Agatha. You know, it's not doing the scholarship French any good. The class slacks. Mademoiselle is worried, I know."

Clare was serious at once.

"That must stop. The standard's too high for trifling. And one or two of them are weak as it is. Especially Louise. Isn't she? Don't you coach her for the grammar? How is her extra work getting on, by the way? Like a house on fire, I suppose?"

"Not altogether." Alwynne looked uneasy.

"What?" Clare looked incredulous.

"She's the problem," said Alwynne.

She had a piece of paper on the table before her and was drawing fantastic profiles as she spoke, sure sign of perturbation with Alwynne, as Clare knew.

"Well?" demanded Clare, after an interval.

Alwynne paused, pencil hovering over an empty eyesocket. She seemed nervous, opened her lips once or twice and closed them again.

"What's wrong?" Clare prompted her.

"Nothing's wrong exactly." Alwynne flushed uncomfortably. "After all, you've seen her in class. Her work is as good as usual?"

"I think so. Her last essay was a little exotic, by the bye, not quite as natural-but you corrected them. I was so busy."

"You don't think she's getting too keen, working too hard?" Alwynne's tone was tentative.

"Do you think so?" Clare was thoroughly interested. She was tickled at Alwynne's anxious tones. She always enjoyed her occasional bursts of responsibility. But she was nevertheless intrigued by Alwynne's hints. She had certainly not given her class its usual attention lately. To Louise she had scarcely spoken unofficially since term began; no opportunity had occurred, and she had been too busy to make one. Louise had returned a bundle of books to her on the opening day of the term, and had been bidden to fetch herself as many more as she chose. But Clare had been out when Louise had called. Clare, to tell the truth, had not once given a thought to Louise since Christmas Day. She had taken a trip to London with Alwynne soon after. The two had enjoyed themselves. The holidays had flown. But she had been glad to find her class radiantly awaiting her. She had found it much as usual. Alwynne's perturbation was the more intriguing.

"Do you think so?" she repeated, with a lift of her eyebrows that reduced Alwynne's status to that of a Kindergarten pupil teacher. She enjoyed seeing her grow pink.

"Of course, it's no affair of mine," said Alwynne aggrievedly. She went on with her drawing.

Clare swung herself on to the low table and sat, skirts a-sway, gazing down at Alwynne's head, bent over its grotesques. There was a curl at the nape of the neck that fascinated her. It lay fine and shining like a baby's. She picked up a pencil and ran it through the tendril. Alwynne jumped.

"Clare, leave me alone. You only think I'm impertinent."

"Does she want a finger in the pie, then?" said Clare softly. "Poor old Alwynne!" The pencil continued its investigations.

Alwynne tried not to laugh. She could never resist Clare's soft voice, as Clare very well knew.

"I don't! I only thought ——"

"That Louise-your precious Louise ——"

"She's trying so awfully hard ——"

"Yes?"

"She's overdoing it. The work's not so good. She's too keen, I think ——"

"Yes?"

"I think ——"

"Yes, Alwynne?"

"You won't be annoyed?"

"That depends."

"Then I can't tell you."

"I think you can," said Clare levelly.

Alwynne was silent. Clare took the paper from her and examined it.

"You've a fantastic imagination, Alwynne. When did you dream those faces? Well-and what do you think? Be quick."

"I think she's growing too fond of you," said Alwynne desperately.

She faced Clare, red and apprehensive. She expected an outburst. But Clare never did what Alwynne expected her to do.

"Is that all? Pooh!" said Clare lightly and began to laugh. She swung backwards, her fingertips crooked round the edge of the table, her neat shoes peeping and disappearing beneath her skirts as she rocked herself. She regarded Alwynne with sly amusement.

"So I've a bad influence, Alwynne? Is that the idea?"

Alwynne protested redly. Clare continued unheeding.

"Well, it's a novel one, anyhow. Could you indicate exactly how my blighting effect is produced? Don't mind me, you know." Then, with a chuckle: "Oh, you delicious child!"

Alwynne was silent.

"Tell me all about it, Alwynne dear!" cooed Clare.

Alwynne shrugged her shoulders with a curiously helpless gesture.

"I can't," she said. "I thought I could-but I can't. You don't help me. I was worried over Louise. I thought—I think she alters. I think she gets a strained look. I know she thinks about you all the time. I thought-but, of course, if you see nothing, it's my fancy. There's nothing definite, I know. If you don't know what I mean — —"

"I don't!" said Clare shortly. "Do you know yourself?"

"No!" said Alwynne. She searched Clare's face wistfully. "I just thought perhaps-she was too fond of you —I can't put it differently. I'm a fool! I wish I hadn't said anything."

"So do I," said Clare gravely.

"I didn't mean to interfere: it wasn't impertinence, Clare," said Alwynne, her cheeks flaming.

Clare hesitated. She was annoyed at Alwynne's unnecessary display of insight, yet tickled by her penetration, not displeased by the jealousy which, as it seemed to her, must be at the root of the protest. Alwynne had evidently not forgotten her chilly Christmas afternoon.... Louise, as obviously, had talked.... There must have been some small degree of friction for Alwynne to complain of Louise.... Curiously, it never occurred to Clare that Alwynne's remarks hid no motive, that Alwynne was genuinely anxious and meant exactly what she had said, or tried to say. Possibly in Alwynne's simplicity lay her real attraction for Clare. It made her as much of a sphinx to Clare as Clare was to her.

As she stood before her, apprehensive of her displeasure, obviously afraid that she had exceeded those bounds to their intercourse that she, more than Clare, had laid down, yet withal, a curiously dogged look upon her face, Clare was puzzled as to her own wisest attitude. She was inclined to batter her into a retraction; it would have relieved her own feelings. Clare could not endure criticism. But she was not yet so sure of Alwynne as to allow herself the relief of invective. She thought that she might easily reserve her annoyance for Louise. It was Louise, after all, who had exposed her to criticism....And if Alwynne chose to be jealous, it was at least a flattering display....She supposed she must placate Alwynne....After all, fifty Louises and her own dignity could not weigh against the possession of Alwynne....She spoke slowly, choosing her words,

"As if I could think you impertinent! But, my dear —I'm older than you. Can't you trust me to understand my girls? After all, I devote my life to them, Alwynne." Clare's quiet dignity was in itself a reproof.

"I know." Alwynne lifted distressed eyes. "I didn't mean —I didn't imply-of course, you know best. I only thought — —"

"That I took more notice of Louise than was wise?"

"No, no!" protested Alwynne unhappily.

Clare continued —

"If you think I'm to blame for encouraging a lonely child-she has no mother, Alwynne-lending her a few books-asking her to tea with me-because I felt rather sorry for her — —"

"I didn't mean that — —" Alwynne twisted her fingers helplessly.

"Then what did you mean?" Clare asked her. She had slipped on to the floor, and was facing Alwynne, very tall and grave and quiet. "Won't you tell me just exactly what you did mean?" she allowed a glimmer of displeasure to appear in her eyes.

And Alwynne, tongue-tied and cornered, had nothing whatever to say. She had been filled with vague uneasiness and had come to Clare to have it dispelled. The uneasiness was still there, formless yet insistent-but the only effect of her clumsy phrases was to hurt Clare's feelings. After all, was she not worrying herself unduly? Was she to know better than Clare? She had felt for some moments that she had made a fool of herself. There remained to capitulate. Her anxiety over Louise melted before the pain in Clare's eyes-the reproof of her manner.

"Would you like me to speak to Louise, before you?" went on Clare patiently. "Perhaps she could explain what it is that worries you — —"

"No, no! for goodness' sake, Clare!" cried Alwynne, appalled. Then surrendering, "Clare —I didn't mean anything. I do see —I've been fussing-impertinent-whatever you like. I didn't mean any harm. Oh, let's stop talking about it, please."

"I'd rather you convinced yourself first," said Clare frigidly. "I don't want the subject re-opened once a week." Then relenting, "Poor old Alwynne! The trials of a deputy! Has she worried herself to death? But I'm back now. I think I can manage my class, Alwynne-as long as you stand by to give me a word of advice now and then."

Alwynne squirmed. Clare laughed tenderly.

"My dear-give Louise a little less attention. It won't hurt either of you. Are you going to let me feel neglected?" Then, with a change of tone. "Now we've had enough of this nonsense." She curled herself in her big chair. "Alwynne, there's a box of Fuller's in the cupboard, and an English Review. Don't you want to hear the new Masefield before you go home?"

And Alwynne's eyes grew big, and she forgot all about Louise, as Clare's "loveliest voice" read out the rhyme of *The River*.

Yet Clare had a last word as she sent her home to Elsbeth.

"Sorry?" said Clare whimsically, as Alwynne bade her good-bye.

"I always was a fool," said Alwynne, and hugged her defiantly.

But Clare, for once, made no protest. She patted her ruffled hair as she listened to the noises of the departure.

"Too fond of me?" she said softly. "Too fond of me? Alwynne-what about you?"

But if Alwynne heard, she made no answer.

CHAPTER XIV

Miss Marsham was accustomed to recognise that it was the brief career of Cynthia Griffiths that first induced her to consider the question of her own retirement.

It is certain that the school was never again quite as it had been before her advent. The Cynthia Griffiths term remained a school date from which to reckon as the nation reckons from the Jubilee. In an American school Cynthia Griffiths must have been at least a disturbing element–in the staid English establishment, with its curious mixture of modern pedagogy and Early Victorian training, she was seismic.

With their usual adaptability, the new girls, as they accustomed themselves subduedly to the strange atmosphere, had found nothing to cavil at in the school arrangements. They had not thought it incongruous to come from Swedish exercises to prolonged and personal daily prayers, kneeling for ten minutes at a time while their head mistress wrestled with Deity. It might have bored girls of sixteen and eighteen to learn their daily Bible verse, and recite it alternately with the Kindergarten and Lower School, but it never occurred to them to protest, any more than they were likely to object to the little note-book which each girl carried, with its printed list of twenty-five possible crimes, and the dangling pencil wherewith, at tea-time, to mark herself innocent or guilty. The hundred and one rules that Edith Marsham had found useful in the youth of her seminary, forty years before, and that time had rendered obsolete, irritating, or merely unintelligible, were nevertheless endured with entire good nature by her successions of pupils. Alwynne and her contemporaries might fume in private and Clare shrug her shoulders in languid tolerance, but nobody thought it worth while to question directly the entire sufficiency of a bygone system to the needs of the new century's hockey-playing generations.

But a little leaven leaveneth the whole lump.

What, if you please, is an old lady to do? An old lady, declining on her pleasant seventies, owning sixty, not a day more, traditionally awe-inspiring and unapproachable, whose security lies in the legends that have grown up of the terrors of her eye and tongue, when Young America clamours at her intimidating door? Young America, calm-eyed, courteous, coaxing, squatting confidentially at the feet of Authority, demanding counsel and comfort. Useless for harried Authority to suggest consultation with equally harried assistants. Young America, with a charming smile and the prettiest of gestures, would rather talk it over quietly with Authority's self. Authority, who is the very twin of her dear old Grannie at home, will be sure to understand. Such fusses about nothing all day and every day! Can it be that Authority expects her to keep her old bureau tidy, when she's had a maid all her life? Young America will be married as soon as she quits Europe (follows a confidential sketch of the more promising of Young America's best boys), and have her own maid right on. Can Authority, as a matter of cold common-sense, see any use in bothering over cupboards for just three months or so? If so-right! Young America will worry along somehow, but it seemed kind of foolish, didn't it? Or could Young America hire a girl-like she did in Paris? Anyway it was rough luck on the lady in the glasses to get an apoplexy every day, as Authority might take it was the case at present. Another point-could Authority, surveying matters impartially, see any harm in running down town when she was out of candy? It only meant missing ten minutes French, and if there was one thing Young America (lapsing suddenly, with bedazing fluency, into that language) was sure of, it was French. These English-French classes meant well-but, her God! how they were slow! There had been-Young America confessed it with candid regret-some difficulties with the cute little mark-books. Young America had mislaid three in a fortnight. She just put them down, and they lay around awhile, and then they weren't there. Some of the ladies had been real annoyed. And once on the subject of mark-books, did Authority really mean that she was to chalk it up each time she was late for breakfast, or said "Darn it," or talked in class? Would, in her place, Authority be able to keep tally? Couldn't Young America just mark off the whole concern and be done with it? Young America apologised for worrying Authority with these quaint matters-but, on her honour, every lady in the school seemed to have gone plum crazy about them.... They just sat around and yapped at her. Young America was genuinely scared. She had thought a heart-to-heart chat with Authority ought to put things right. She would be real grateful to Authority for fixing things....

And so, with the odd curtsey she had learned among "the Dutchies," as she called her German pensionat, and a hearty kiss on either cheek, Young America, affable as ever, beamed upon Authority and withdrew.

Authority felt as if it had been out in a high wind. Instinctively it clutched at its imposing head-dress. All was in place. Authority lay back in its chair and gasped fishily.

But Miss Vigers, frenzied into confession of inability to deal with the situation-got scant sympathy.

"What am I to do? I hate troubling you—I am sure, though, it's a relief to us all to have you back. Of course, if you had been at home she would never have been admitted.... You would have realised the unsuitability-but it was not my decision.... Miss Hartill.... But what am I to do? I flatter myself I can control our English girls-but these Americans! Open defiance, Miss Marsham! Her room! She refuses to attend to it. She comes and goes when she chooses. She treats me, positively, as an equal. Her influence is unspeakable! It must be stopped! Ten minutes late for breakfast-oh, every day! Once, I could excuse. And on the top of it all to offer me chocolates! I must ask you to punish her severely.... Keep her in? Miss Marsham, I did.... I sent her to her room. Miss Marsham, will you believe me? When I went up to her later, she was fast asleep! On the bed! In the daytime!! Without taking off the counterpane!!! Miss Marsham, I leave the matter to you!"

She paused for the comments her tale deserved. But to outraged Authority, it had called up a picture-an impudent picture of Young America, curled kitten-fashion on its austere white pallet-pink cheek on rounded arm, guileless eyes opening sleepily under a sour and scandalised gaze.

Henrietta started. She could not believe her ears.

Benevolently-unmistakably-Authority had chuckled.

But the scandal was short-lived. Before the term was over: before Henrietta had braced herself to her usual resource, a threat of resignation, or Miss Marsham, hesitating between the devil of her protesting subordinates and the deep sea of Young America's unshakable conviction that in her directress she had an enthusiastic partisan, could allow her maid to suggest to her that she needed a change, the end had arrived.

Cynthia, as Alwynne had surmised, found ten weeks of an English private school more than enough for her; and an imperious telegram had summoned her docile parents.

She departed as she had come, in a joyous flurry. The school mourned, and the Common-room, in its relief, sped the parting guest with a cordiality that was almost effusive.

A remark of Henrietta's, as the mistress sat over their coffee on the afternoon of Cynthia's departure, voiced the attitude of the majority to its late pupil.

"I'm thankful," Miss Vigers was unusually talkative, "deeply thankful that she's gone. An impossible young woman. Oh, no-you couldn't call her a girl. Would any girl-any English girl-conceivably behave as she has? They have begun to imitate her, of course. That was to be expected. She demoralised the school. It will take me a month to get things straight. I have three children in bed to-day. Headaches? Fiddlesticks! Over-eating! I suppose you heard that there was a midnight feast last night?"

The Common-room opened its eyes.

"I'm not astonished. A farewell gathering, I suppose! I'm sure it's not the first," said Clare, her eyes alight with amusement. "But go on. How did you find it out?"

"Miss Marsham informed me of it," said Henrietta, with desperate calmness. "It appears that Cynthia asked her permission. Miss Marsham-er-contributed a cake. Seed!"

Clare gurgled.

"This is priceless. Did she tell you? I wonder she had the face."

Henrietta grew pink.

"No. Cynthia herself. She-er-offered me a slice. She had the impertinence-the entirely American impertinence-to come to my room-after midnight-to borrow a tooth-glass. To eat ices in. It appeared that they were short of receptacles."

"Ices?" came the chorus.

"Her mother provided them, I believe. In a pail," said Henrietta stiffly.

"Did you lend the tooth-glass?" asked Clare.

Henrietta coughed.

"It was difficult to refuse. She had bare feet. I did not wish her to catch cold."

Clare turned away abruptly. Her shoulders shook.

"I do not wish to be unjust. I do not think she was intentionally insubordinate." Henrietta fingered one of the tall pink roses that had appeared on her desk that morning. "I believe she meant well."

"She was a dear!" said the little gym mistress.

"She was an impossible young woman," retorted Henrietta with spirit. "At the same time — —"

"At the same time?" Clare spoke with unusual friendliness.

"She certainly had a way with her," said Henrietta.

CHAPTER XV

Cynthia Griffiths had set a fashion.

Her kewpie hair-ribbons and abbreviated blouses were an unofficial uniform long after she had ceased, probably, to know that such articles of dress existed. Her slang phrases incorporated themselves in the school vocabulary. Her deeds of derring-do were imitated from afar. To have been on intimate terms with her would have been an impressive distinction, had not every member of the school been able to lay claim to it. For Cynthia's jolly temperament laughed at schoolgirl etiquette, could never be brought to realise the existence of caste and clique. She darted into their lives and out again, like a dragon-fly through a cloud of gnats. It was not strange that her beauty, her prodigality, in conjunction with the all-excusing fact of her nationality, should have attracted the weather-cock enthusiasm of her companions: should have made her, short as her career had been, the rage.

Yet the one person on whom that career was to have a lasting influence was, to all appearance, the least affected by it.

Cynthia and Louise Denny were class-mates, for Clare, amused and interested by the new type, had, after all, arranged for Cynthia to join the Scholarship Class, though there could be no idea of her entering. She agreed with Alwynne that there was not much likelihood of Cynthia's sojourn being a long one. In the meantime, as she had explained to Miss Marsham, it was better to have the fire-brand under her own eye. Miss Marsham agreed with alacrity, and contrasted Clare's calmly capable manner with the protests of Henrietta. She realised joyfully that Cynthia would not be permitted to appeal from any decision of Miss Hartill. She recalled, not for the first time, that in all Clare's years there had never come a crisis for which she had been found unprepared. Details of a campaign might finally reach the ears of Authority-there would be always birds of the air to carry the matter-but from Miss Hartill herself, no word; if pressed, there would be a brief summary, a laughing comment, never an appeal for help. Miss Marsham had built up her school by sheer force of personality. She was old now, grown slack and easy, but instinctively she recognised a ruling spirit, a kindred mind. One day she must choose her successor.... She was rich. Her school need not fall to the highest bidder.... There were Henrietta and Clare. Henrietta had scraped and saved, she knew.... Henrietta was fond of trying on Authority's shoes.... Of Clare's wishes she was less sure.... But Clare was a capable girl—a capable girl.... Clare had never let any one worry her....

She read Clare correctly. Clare had no intention of allowing Cynthia Griffiths to lessen her prestige. But she had her own method of solving the American problem. She treated her new pupil with the easy good humour, the mocking friendliness of an equal. She realised the impossibility of counteracting the effects of a haphazard education, but recognising equally the inherent kindliness and lawlessness of the character, played on both qualities in her management of the girl. Her classes were not demoralised, but stimulated, by the new-comer's presence: yet Clare had said nothing to Cynthia of rules and regulations. But Miss Hartill's manner had certainly implied that while to her, too, they were a folly and a weariness, after all it was easy to conform. It saved trouble and pleased people. All conveyed without prejudice to the morals of her other pupils in a shrug, and a twinkle, and a half-finished phrase.

Cynthia was charmed. Here was common-sense. For the first time she felt herself at home. She appalled the classes by her loud encomiums, her delighted discovery of qualities that it was blasphemy to connect with Miss Hartill. For Cynthia, with the pitiful shrewdness that her cosmopolitan years had instilled, admired Clare for reasons that bewildered the worshippers. To them Clare moved through the school, apart, Olympian, a goddess, condescending delightfully. To Cynthia, accustomed to intrigue, she was obviously and admirably Macchiavellian. It amazed her that the English girls could not perceive Miss Hartill's cleverness, that they should adore her for qualities as foreign to her character as they were essentially insipid, and be indignant at understanding and discriminating praise.

But Cynthia was above all philosophical. She shrugged her shoulders over the crazy crew, and reserved her comments for-Louise. For in Louise, incredible as Alwynne Durand, for instance, would have thought it, she did find a listener-an antagonist, easily pricked into amusing indignation, into white-hot denials-nevertheless, a listener. Indeed, it was the attitude of Cynthia to Clare Hartill rather than her personal attraction that was responsible for Louise's departure from her original and sincere attitude of indifference to the advances of the popular American.

Louise was less in the foreground than she had been in the previous term. She had come back to school, less talkative, less brilliant, but working with a dogged persistence that had on Alwynne, at least, a depressing effect. But Alwynne, also, was seeing less of the girl. Cynthia Griffiths obstructed her view-Cynthia, taking one of her vociferous likings to a sufficiently unresponsive Louise. For the *rapprochement* was scarcely a normal, schoolgirl intimacy. Cynthia Griffiths had been intrigued by Louise's personality. She had been quick to grasp the importance of the child's position-to guess her there by reason of her brains and temperament. Yet to Cynthia, judging life, as she did, chiefly by exterior appearances, Louise, insignificant, timid, shadowy, was an incessant denial of her nevertheless recognisable influence in school politics. In the language of Cynthia, she was a dark horse. Cynthia was charmed-school life was dull-the mildest of mysteries was better than none. She would devote herself to deciphering a new type. This little English kid had undoubted influence with girl and mistress alike. Cynthia had intercepted glances between her and Miss Hartill, and Miss Durand too, that spoke of mutual understanding. Perhaps it was money-half the school in her pay? Or secret influences of the most sinister? Hypnotism, maybe? Cynthia Griffiths, fed on dime novels and magazine literature, was not ten minutes concocting the hopefullest of mare's nests. She approached Louise between excitement and suspicion.

Cynthia was not scrupulous. She forced her way through the reserves and defences of the younger girl like a bumble-bee clawing and screwing and buzzing into the heart of a half-shut flower.

She found much to puzzle her, more to amuse, but nothing to justify her gorgeous suspicions. She confessed them one day to Louise, in a burst of confidence, and Louise was hugely delighted. Cynthia always delighted her. She liked her jolly ways, and her sense of fun, and was quite convinced that she had no sense of humour at all. The conviction saved her some suffering. She was jealous, inevitably jealous, of the brilliant new-comer, painfully alive to, exaggerating and writhing at Clare's preoccupation with her; yet the warped shrewdness proper to her state of mind, she could calculate with painful accuracy how long it would take Clare to tire of her new toy, what qualities would soonest induce satiety. She guessed, hoped, prayed, that Miss Hartill would discover, as she had done, Cynthia's lack of conscious humour, the obtuseness that underlay her boisterous ease. She was not fine enough to hold Miss Hartill long: she would grow too fond of Miss Hartill: would, in the terrible craving to render up her whole soul, expose herself in all her crudity. Louise did, for a while, soothe the jealousy, the tearing, clawing beast in her breast, with that comfortable conviction. That her reasoning was subconscious, that she was unaware of the process of analysation and deduction that led to her conclusions, is immaterial; she felt-and as she felt, she acted; her reasons for her actions were sounder than she dreamed.

She made mistakes often enough: her profound occupation with Clare Hartill had induced a spiritual myopia; the rest of the world was out of focus; and it was her initial misunderstanding of Cynthia Griffiths that led to their curious, unaffectionate alliance. In all Louise's ponderings, she had never doubted but that Cynthia would, like the rest of the world, fall down and worship at the shrine of Clare Hartill. Cynthia Griffiths, amused spectator of an alien life, did nothing of the kind. And Louise-amazed, fiercely incredulous, all-suspicious, yet finally convinced of the inconceivable fact-it had a curious effect. She should have been indignant, contemptuous of the obtuse creature-as, indeed, in a sense, she was-but chiefly she was conscious of a lifted weight-of an enormous and hysterical gratitude.

Cynthia was a fool—a purblind philistine. But what relief was in her folly, what immense security! Jealousy could not die out in Louise, but it entered on a new phase-became passive, enduring resignedly inevitable pain. But its vigilance, its fierce pugnacity was dead; for Cynthia-dear fool-did not care. Pearls had been cast before Americans. Louise was ready enough to be gracious to such exquisite insensibility. She became friendly. She had guarded her secret jealousy from the world. She was "keen" on Miss Hartill, certainly, but so was half the school, at least. She was merely in the fashion. Insignificant and circumspect, giving no confidences, no one but Clare herself, and Alwynne Durand, guessed at the intensity of her affection. But with Cynthia Griffiths she was reckless. Ostrich-like, she trusted to the protection of her formal disclaimer, while with each new discussion, each half-confidence, she exposed herself and her feelings more completely.

And Cynthia, dropping her theories, began to be interested in the strange, vehement imp, with its alternating fits of frankness and reticence, wit and childishness, its big brain and its inexplicable yet obvious unhappiness. She affected Louise, was accustomed to pet and parade her, long before she had solved the problem of her character; indeed, it was not until she had confided to the child her plans for an early departure, that Louise relaxed her self-protective vigilance. She had begun, in her walks with Cynthia, to realise the relief and healing of self-expression. If Cynthia were going away to Paris, America, never to be seen again, what harm in talking-in saying for once what she felt? There was wry pleasure in it, and, oh, what harm?

Louise found an odd satisfaction in leading Cynthia-on her side, if you please, alert for evidence, the amateur detective still-to sit in judgment on Clare Hartill; would sit, horrified, thrilled, drinking in blasphemy. She would have allowed no other human being to impeach the smallest detail of Clare Hartill's conduct, but from Cynthia, though she raged hotly, she did allow, and in some queer fashion, enjoy it. She had, perhaps, a vague assurance that Cynthia, being a foreigner, could not be taken seriously.

So the pair discussed Clare Hartill from all possible angles till Louise occasionally forgot to keep up her elaborate pretence of indifference, to insist on its being understood that the discussion was rhadamanthine in its impersonality.

"Yes, I'm off soon," Cynthia had confided. They were sitting together in her cubicle. "All this is slow-slow. Ne' mind! Wait till this child gets going!" She stretched herself lazily, and flung back on her little white bed, arms behind her. Louise studied her magnificent torso.

"Why did you come?" she demanded.

Cynthia laughed.

"Italy-France-Deutschland—I'd done everywhere but England. Now comes a tour round the world-and so home. I'm Californian, you know. I'll have great times then. You don't live, over here. You're afraid of your own shadows. Now an American girl——"

"How do you mean?"

"Aren't you? Always afraid of breaking rules? Haven't I asked you-haven't I begged you to come out with me one day? Oh, Louise, it would be great! I saw a taxi-man yesterday, outside church, with the duckiest eyes! Lunch somewhere, and 'phone through for the new show at Daly's. An American show! Dandy! Only taken you four years to transfer here! Let's go, Louise? We'd be back to supper."

Louise twinkled.

"Rot! We'd be expelled."

Cynthia opened her china-blue eyes.

"For a little thing like that? Why? We wouldn't miss a class. Besides, we'd say you asked me home to tea."

Louise looked distressed. Their ideas of veracity had clashed before.

Cynthia, watching mischievously, giggled.

"Poor kid! Doesn't it want to tell lies, then?"

"You see-English people don't! Of course, I know it's different abroad," said Louise delicately.

"Haven't you ever, Louise?"

Louise flushed crimson.

"You have?" Cynthia was amused. "What was it, Louise? Oh, what was it? Tell! Oh, you needn't mind me-my average is-well, quite average. What was it?"

Louise's lips closed.

"I call you the limit, you know! 'English people don't!' With a red-hot tarradiddle on your little white conscience all the time. You're a good pupil, Louise."

Louise, blushing, turned suspiciously.

"What are you at now!" she demanded.

"I was thinking of Clarissa." Cynthia smiled with intention.

"Clarissa who?"

"Clare, kid! Clare! Sweet Clare! Sugar-sweet Clare! Our dear Dame Double!"

"I wish you wouldn't talk like that," said Louise, in her lowest voice. "You know I hate it."

"All right, honey!" Cynthia rolled lazily on to her side and pulled a box of chocolates from the shelf beside her.

The room was quiet for a while.

"Cynthia?"

"Um?"

"What did you mean just now?"

"Have a candy?"

"No, thanks!"

Cynthia munched on.

"About Miss Hartill?" Louise's tone was half defiant, half guilty. She felt disloyal in re-opening the subject. Yet Cynthia's hints rankled.

"I don't know. Nothing, I guess."

"Oh, but you did mean something," said Louise uneasily.

"Maybe."

"Tell me."

"Want to know?"

"Yes."

"Badly?"

"It's not true, of course! But I'd like to know."

Cynthia's eyes danced. She could be grave enough otherwise, but her eyes and her dimples could never be kept in order.

"Tell about the tarradiddle first, and I will."

But to Louise a lie was a lie and no joking matter. She fidgeted.

"If you must know——"

"I must."

"Well-you know how Miss Hartill hates birthdays?"

"Why?"

"At least, school ones. You know, there's such a fuss at Miss Marsham's —a holiday, presents, and all that. So Miss Hartill won't let hers be known."

"'Splendid Isolation' stunt."

"If you're going to be a hatefully unjust pig, I won't tell you."

"I apologise. Have a candy?"

"Well, you know, Agatha found out that Miss Hartill was giving a party last week, and, of course, every one thought it was for hers. But it turned out it was Daffy's birthday: Miss Hartill gave it for her. It was Agatha's fault. She was so dead certain about it."

"But what did it matter?"

"Well, you see, I'd got some roses——"

"Pale pink and yellow? Beauties?"

"Yes."

"Oho! So that's where they came from. I did Dame Double an injustice. I thought it was a best boy." Cynthia gurgled.

"You saw them?"

"I went to tea with her-it must have been that day-the eighth?"

Louise nodded.

"A party! Agatha is a coon. There was only Daffy there! I wonder she didn't ask you."

Louise said nothing. Her face was expressionless.

"Mean old thing!" Cynthia grew indignant as the situation dawned on her.

"She can't ask every one. There was no reason whatever to ask me." But Louise's voice had a suspicious quiver in it, which Cynthia, with unusual tact, ignored.

"Well-about the roses? They were beauties, kid!"

"Oh, I brought 'em round, going to school. I thought she'd started, but she hadn't. She opened the door. So there I was, stuck." Louise began to laugh. "I'd meant to leave them, just without any name."

"I see." Cynthia twinkled.

"She was rather-rather breakfasty, you know-and I got flustered and forgot to wish her 'many happy.' Wasn't it lucky? I was thankful afterwards. I only said they were out of the greenhouse and I thought she'd like them. She did, too." Louise smiled to herself.

"Well?"

"That's all."

"But where did the lie come in?"

"Oh! Oh-well —I'd bought them, you see. As if Mamma would let me pick flowers. Besides, we haven't even got a greenhouse. But I had five shillings at Christmas, and sixpence in the pudding-and sixpence a week pocket-money—and I never have anything to buy. I could well afford it," said Louise, with dignity.

"That's not a lie," said Cynthia, disappointed. "It's barely an-an evasion."

"I didn't mean to-evade. I was only afraid she'd be cross, and yet I couldn't resist getting them. Do you know the feeling, when you ache to give people things? But it was a lie, of course."

"Oh, well! You needn't mind. She tells plenty herself-acts them, at least ——"

Louise caught her up.

"There! That's it! That's one of the things! You're always hinting things! Why do you? I won't have it! Of course, I know you're only in fun, but if anybody hears you ——"

"I'm not! Oh, but it's no use talking! You think she's a god almighty. What's the use of my telling you that she's a conceited ——"

"She's not!"

"Oh, she's a right to be. She'd be a peach if I had the dressing of her ——"

"She doesn't like American fashions. We don't want her to. We like her as she is."

"And she knows it-you bet your bottom dollar! There's not much she doesn't know. Why, she simply lives for effect! She's the most gorgeous hypocrite ——"

"You're a beastly one yourself-you pretend you like her ——"

"But I do! I admire her heaps! But I understand her. You don't. She likes to be top dog. She'll do anything for that. She likes to know every woman and child in the school is a bit of putty, to knead into shape. I know! I've met her sort before-only generally it was men they were after. And yet it bores her too——" parenthesised Cynthia shrewdly. "That's why she likes me. I don't care two pins for her tricks. That stings her up a bit. She'll be mighty bored when I go."

Louise listened, angry, yet fascinated. It gave her a curious pleasure to hear Miss Hartill belied. She would hug herself for her own superior discernment. A phrase from a half-digested story often recurred to her: "One doesn't defend one's god! One's god is a defence in himself." But Cynthia was going too far-abandoning innuendo for direct assault. She struck back.

"It's easy to say things. Just saying so doesn't make it so. And if it did, I shouldn't believe it."

"Oh! I can prove it." Cynthia laughed. "Have you noticed the Charette comedy?"

"Mademoiselle? Oh, she hates Miss Hartill. But she's French, of course."

"Does she just? H'm——!"

"Well, there was a French girl-she left last term-she told Marion that Mademoiselle had said things to her about Miss Hartill. Agatha told me. Agatha loathes Mademoiselle. Of course, Mademoiselle is rather down on her."

"I don't wonder. You know how Agatha hazes her in class."

"I can't stand Agatha." Louise shook herself. "Last French Grammar it was awful-silly, you know, not funny. One simply couldn't work. Mademoiselle kept her in. I suppose Agatha didn't like that. She's been a lamb since, anyway. About time too!"

"Shucks! It wasn't being kept in. It was Clarissa. Oh, my dear, it was fun! There was poor little Mademoiselle, storming away in her absurd English, and Agatha cheeking her for all she was worth."

"How did you hear?"

"Why, I was in the studio! Agatha didn't know we were there, of course. The glass doors were open. You know, Daffy gives me extra drawing. And just when Agatha was in full swing, and Mademoiselle speechless with rage, Miss Hartill turned up-wanted Daffy."

"Oh, go on!" Louise cried breathlessly.

"It really was funny, you know. Miss Hartill was talking to Daffy and the row going on next door-you couldn't help hearing-and suddenly Daffy said-Daffy had been fidgeting for some time —'Listen!' and Clarissa said, 'Oho-o!' You know her way, with about ten o's at the end; and Daffy said, 'There! Now do you believe me?' kind of crowing. And Miss Hartill, she just smiled, like a cat with cream, and said, 'All right, Alwynne! All right, my dear!' and went into the next room. Say, it was exciting! She didn't raise her voice, but she just let herself go, and in about two minutes Agatha came out like a ripe cheese-literally crawling. I wish she hadn't shut the door. I couldn't hear any more. I could see, of course, and you bet I watched out of the tail of my eye. Daffy never noticed me."

"What happened then?"

"Oh! They stood and talked, and Mademoiselle was scarlet and seemed to be pitching into Miss Hartill, as far as I could see, and Miss Hartill was letting her talk herself out, and sometimes she smiled and said something; that always started Mademoiselle off again. And at last Mademoiselle went and sat in one of the window-seats, and I couldn't see her face, but I imagined she was howling. French people always do. Clarissa went and patted her shoulder."

"She is a dear!" Loyally Louise bit back her instant jealousy.

"Oh, she was enjoying herself," said Cynthia coolly. "You should have seen her face. Sort of smiling at her own thoughts. Have you ever seen a spider smile?"

Louise disdained an answer.

"Nor have I! Have a candy? But I bet I know what it looks like."

"Well, what happened?" demanded Louise impatiently.

"Oh, it was annoying! Daffy came and sat down in my place, to correct. I couldn't see any more. Only when Miss Hartill came out (she didn't notice me, I was putting away the group), she said to Daffy, 'She's coming to tea on Friday.' And Daffy said, 'Clare, you're a wonder!' And Miss Hartill said, 'I didn't do it for her, Alwynne!' And Daffy got pink. Clarissa did look pleased with herself."

"Well, so she ought! Wouldn't you be-if you could make people happy?"

Cynthia threw up her hands. "Happy! Oh, Momma! Are you happy?"

Louise winced.

"Is Daffy? Mademoiselle? Any of you fools? Oh, it's no use talking! You won't believe me when I tell you that she's a cat. Yes, a pussy-cat, Louise! A silky, purring pussy-cat, pawing you, pat-pat-so softly, like kisses. But if you wriggle-my! Look out for claws! Have a candy?"

Louise gathered herself together. She came close to the bed, and leaning over the older girl, spoke —

"I don't understand what you're driving at-but you're wrong. It's you that's a fool. You misjudge her, utterly. You don't understand her-you're not fit to."

"Are you?" Cynthia laughed at her openly.

"Of course not. No one-Daffy does, of course. But us?—girls? Just because she's been heavenly to you, you take advantage, to watch her, to judge, to twist all she says and does. Why do you hate her so?"

"I don't." Cynthia pulled herself upright. "My dear, you're wrong there. I like her immensely. She's a real treat. But I don't worship her like you do."

"I don't! I—I just love her." Louise glowed.

Cynthia laughed jollily.

"Oh, well! You'll get over that. Wait till you get a best boy."

"If you think I'd look at any silly man, after knowing her——"

"My dear girl! Has it never occurred to you that you'll marry some day?"

Louise shook her head.

"I've thought it all out. I never could love anybody as much as I do Miss Hartill. I know I couldn't."

"But it's not the same! Falling in love with a man——"

"Love's love," said Louise with finality. "Where's the difference?"

Cynthia sat up.

"Where's the difference? Where's the——?" She giggled. But something in the quality of her laughter disturbed. Louise frowned.

"I didn't say anything funny. You'll love your husband, I suppose, that you're always talking about having-and I'll stick to Miss Hartill. It's perfectly simple."

But Cynthia was still laughing. Louise grew irritable under her amused glances, and would have turned away, but Cynthia flung her arm about her.

"Stop! Don't you really know?"

"What?"

"The difference."

Cynthia's eyes shone oddly. Louise moved uneasily, disconcerted by their expression.

Cynthia continued.

"Hasn't any one told you? Why, with the books you've read——Haven't you read the Bible ever?"

"Of course!" Louise was indignant. "I've been right through-four times."

"And you've never noticed? Good Lord! That's all I read it for."

"I haven't an idea what you're driving at," said Louise. Cynthia was making her thoroughly uncomfortable.

Cynthia was flushed, laughing, pure devilry in her eyes. Her lips were pouted, her little teeth gleamed. She looked a child licking its lips over forbidden dainties. She had pulled Louise into her lap and her voice had dropped to a whisper.

"Shall I tell you? Would you like to know? You ought to-you're fourteen-it's absurd-not knowing about things-shall I tell you?"

Louise fidgeted. Cynthia's manner had aroused her curiosity, but none the less she was repelled. Why, she could not have said. She hesitated, aroused, yet half frightened.

"I'll tell you," said Cynthia lusciously.

With a sudden effort Louise freed herself from the encircling arm. She edged away from the elder girl, stammering a little.

"I don't think I want to know anything. It's awfully sweet of you. I'd rather—I always ask Daffy things. Do you mind?"

Cynthia, good-tempered as ever, laughed aloud.

"Lord, no! But what a little saint! Aren't you ever curious, Louise? All right! I won't tease. Have a candy?"

And Louise, eating chocolates, was not long in forgetting the conversation and all the curious discomfort it had aroused. If a leaf had fallen on the white garment of her innocence—a leaf from the tree of the knowledge of good and evil-she had brushed it aside, all unconscious, before it could leave a stain.

CHAPTER XVI

The spring term was nearly over, holidays and a trip to Italy deliciously near; yet Clare Hartill sat at breakfast and frowned over a neatly-written letter.

Clare Hartill did not encourage the re-entry of old friends into her life. She did not forget them. She would look back upon the far-off flaming intimacy with regret, would quote its pleasures to the friend of the hour with disconcerting enthusiasm; but she was never eager for the reappearance of any whose ways had once diverged from her own. Pleasant memories, if you will; but, in the flesh, old friends were tiresome. They claimed instant intimacy; were free-tongued, fond, familiar; could not realise that though they might choose to stand still, she, Clare, had grown out of their knowledge, beyond their fellowship. She, indeed, would find them terribly unaltered; older, glamourless, yet amazingly, humiliatingly the same. She would look at them furtively as she entertained them, and shudder at the lapse from taste that surely must have explained her former affection. She would be gracious, kind, yet inimitably distant, and would send them away at last, subdued, vaguely disquieted, loyal still, yet very sure that they would never trouble her again. Which was exactly what Clare Hartill intended. Yet she had her fits of remorse withal, her secret bitter railing at fate and her own nature, for that she could neither keep a friend nor live without one. Recovering, she would be complacent at having contrived, without loss of prestige, to rid herself of bores.

There was one fly in her ointment. Who knows not that fly, earnest and well-intentioned, which, when it is dug out with a hairpin, cleanses itself exhaustively and forthwith returns to the vaseline jar? Such a fly, optimistic and persistent, was the correspondent who invariably signed herself, "Ever, dear Clare, your affectionate little friend, Olivia Pring. P.S. Do you remember...?" There would follow a reminiscence, at least twenty years old, that Clare never did remember.

Olivia Pring was a school-mate. There had been a term together in the Lower Third. For a few weeks she had been Clare's best friend and she never let Clare forget it. Clare, with removes and double removes, had disappeared speedily from Olivia's world, but she never quite shook off Olivia. Olivia, amiable, admiring, impervious to snubs, refused to be shaken off. She went her placid way, became a governess, and an expert in the more complicated forms of crochet. She wrote to Clare about twice a year-dull, affectionate letters. Clare, that involute character, amazed herself by invariably answering them. At long intervals Olivia would be passing through London, and would announce herself, if quite convenient, as intending to visit her dear Clare that afternoon. She would describe the lengthy tussle between herself and her employer, before she had wrested the requisite permission to stay the night-and did Clare remember the last visit but three, and the amusing evening they had had? And the letter was invariably delayed in the posting, and its arrival would precede that of Olivia by a bare half-hour. Olivia, growing even fatter and more placid, would apologise breathlessly between broad smiles at the sight of Clare and recollections of the dear old days. And Clare, as one hypnotised, would go to her linen cupboard and give out sheets for the spare room. There would follow an evening of interminable small-talk for Clare, of sheer delight for Olivia Pring, who, consciously and conscientiously commonplace, enjoyed dear Clare's daring views as a youthful curate might enjoy, strictly as an onlooker, what he imagines to be the less respectable aspects of an evening in Paris.

And Clare would retire to bed at ten-fifteen and sleep as she had not slept for weeks. Olivia would be regretfully obliged to catch the eight-eleven, and would depart amid embraces. And Clare would order up a second breakfast and wonder why she stood it. Yet the pile of unused doileys in her linen cupboard increased yearly. A doiley was Olivia's invariable tribute, and arrived, intricate and unlovely, within a week of her visit.

Clare fingered her letter in quaint helplessness. She had a sleepless night behind her, and a big morning's work before, and her usual end-of-term headache. Olivia was arriving-she glanced at the hopelessly legible sheets-at three-fifty. No chance of mistake there. Clare decided that it was quite impossible for her to survive a seven hours' *tête-à-tête* with her affectionate friend Olivia Pring. If only Alwynne could help her out. But Alwynne, she knew, was taking the skimmings of the Sixths and Fifths to a suitable Shakespeare performance. She had taken the pick of the classes herself the evening before. No chance of Alwynne, then. And Cynthia! Alack for Cynthia! who could have been trusted to amuse Olivia Pring as much as Olivia Pring would have amused her-Cynthia must be aboard ship by now. Clare, in regretful parenthesis, hoped Cynthia would send a few compatriots to Utterbridge....Americans gave a fillip to one's duties....Anyhow Alwynne and Cynthia were out of the question.

There was Louise! She brightened. Louise, queer little thing, was always amusing....Louise would serve her turn....Louise would be so charmed to come....Clare laughed a little consciously. Perhaps she had neglected Louise a trifle of late, perhaps it was not altogether fair of her. A happy thought buffered the prick of her yawning conscience. It was Alwynne's fault....Alwynne, with her ridiculous, well-meaning objections....She, Clare, had given in to them, for peace and quiet sake....And now, most probably, Louise was not too content with life....One knew what schoolgirls were....Never mind! Clare would be very nice to Louise this evening....Louise should enjoy herself, and, incidentally, preserve Clare from expiring of boredom at poor Olivia's large, flat feet.

The invitation was given during the eleven o'clock break. Clare would occasionally join the school in Big Hall, and share its milk and biscuits. Often enough to make it any day's delightful possibility, not often enough for it to be other than an event. She would sit on the platform steps, watching the gay promenaders below, informal, approachable, tossing the ball to the daring few, hedged about, in turn, by the tentative many. Sometimes she would stroll about the hall with a girl on either side, or one only. She had a curious little trick of catching the girl she spoke with by the elbow, and pushing her gently along as she talked, bending over (she was very tall) and enveloping. Everybody knew the "Gendarme Stunt" as Cynthia Griffiths irreverently termed it, and no one would have dreamed of approaching or interrupting such a tête-à-tête.

Nevertheless, Miss Hartill had not exchanged three sentences with Louise Denny on the morning of Olivia Pring's arrival, before every girl in Big Hall knew of it, and twice the number of eyes were following them, with an elaborately accidental gaze, in their progress.

Possibly Clare was a little touched by Louise's delight at the invitation. At any rate she managed, in spite of her headache, to be a very charming companion. She confessed to the headache, and asked Louise for advice. And Louise, deeply concerned, could think of nothing but a recipe she had found in Clare's own Culpeper, in which rhubarb and powdered dormice figured largely. She suggested it in a doubtful little voice. The school would have given a good deal to know what made Miss Hartill laugh so.

Miss Hartill told Louise all about her visitor, whom, she declared, she depended on Louise to entertain, and added a couple of comical tales of their mutual schooldays. Unfortunately Clare's *novelli* owed their charm more to her inventive touches and graphic manner than to the actual underlying fact. Louise was left with the impression of an Olivia Pring who had been Friar Tuck to Clare's Robin Hood. She appreciated the honour of being asked to meet her to a degree that would have tickled Clare, had she guessed it.

"Miss Olivia Pring!" Louise meditated all day over Miss Olivia Pring. Evidently Miss Hartill's best friend....She hoped Miss Olivia Pring would like her....How dreadful it would be if she didn't ...for what might she not say of her to Miss Hartill? Louise must be careful, oh, so careful, of her manners and her speech....It was rather hard luck that she would not have Miss Hartill to herself....It would be dreadfully uncomfortable-talking before a stranger....Except for the delightfulness of being asked by Miss Hartill, she could have wished that Miss Hartill had not asked her. Rather an ordeal for a thirteen-year-old—supper with Miss Hartill and Miss Olivia Pring.

Now shyness, like any other painful sensation, is inexplicable to such as have not experienced it, is at once forgotten by such as outgrow it, but to those at its mercy, to sheer suffering, paralysing, stultifying, a spiritual Torture of the Pear.

Clare Hartill should have understood; she had her own furtive childhood for reference; but Clare Hartill had a headache, and she was very tired of Olivia Pring. Olivia was so placid, so shapeless, so ridiculous, in her pink flannel blouse, and the reckless glasses, that were ever on the point of toppling over the precipice of her abbreviated nose into the abyss of her half-open mouth. It certainly did not occur to Clare that Louise could feel the slightest discomfort on account of Olivia Pring.

But Louise was blind to the flannel blouse, and the foolish face, and the unmanageable glasses. She was wearing glasses of her own, rose-coloured affairs, through which Miss Pring appeared, not only as a "grown-up" and a stranger, but as the intimate of Deity in Undress. Miss Pring did nothing to dispel the illusion-she had conscientiously flattened the high spirits out of too many little girls to be interested in a new specimen. She addressed herself chiefly to Clare-recalling incessantly, and enlarging upon, trifling incidents of their mutual past, which every fresh sentence of the badgered hostess contrived to recall to her elastic memory. Louise, always sensitive, her shyness growing with every word, could but take each unexplained allusion as a personal snub, and feeling herself entirely superfluous, began to imagine that Miss Hartill was already regretting the invitation. Panic-struck she tried to remedy matters by effacing herself as completely as possible. It was wonderful what a small and insignificant person Louise could sometimes look, and did look that evening in one of Clare's big arm-chairs. Her prim little whisper and deprecatory smile might have struck Clare as pathetic if Clare had not been so very tired of the affectionate reminiscences of Olivia Pring. As it was, she was annoyed. She had asked Louise of the bright eyes and quick stammer and extravagant imagery, to supper with her-the panther-cub, not the leveret. She had talked of Louise too-had looked forward to putting the child through its paces, if only for the benefit of Olivia Pring. She had even surmised that Louise would take Olivia's measure, and at a nod from Clare would be delicately, deliciously impertinent. Indeed, she had thought her capable of it. But it was only a schoolgirl after all—a silly tongue-tied schoolgirl-that she had for an instant compared with Alwynne: Alwynne, monstrously absent, a match for ten Olivias.

She yawned, shrugged her shoulders, and suggested, in fine ironic fit, a game of "Old Maid." Olivia was extremely pleased. She so much preferred Old Maid-or Beggar-my-Neighbour, perhaps?—to Bridge. She did not approve of Bridge. In her position it did not do. Clare would remember that she had always said....

Clare fetched the cards.

Louise! Louise! You have done yourself no good to-night. Shy? Nonsense! What is there to be shy about? A few words from Miss Hartill—a prompting or two—a leading question-could have broken the ice of your shyness for you, eh? And Miss Hartill knows it, as well as you, if not better. That shall not avail you. Who are you, to set Miss Hartill's conscience itching? Miss Hartill has a headache. Pull up your chair, and deal your cards, and stop Miss Hartill yawning, if you can. Believe me, it's your only chance of escape.

Louise was a clumsy dealer. Her careful setting out of cards irritated Clare to snatching point. Olive triumphed in every game. On principle, Clare disliked losing, even at Beggar-my-Neighbour. And they played Beggar-my-Neighbour till ten o'clock.

Louise grew more cheerful as the evening progressed, ventured a few sentences now and then. Clare was dangerously suave with both her guests; but Louise, taking all in good faith, hoped after all, that she had not appeared as stupid as she felt. It had been dreadful at first, she reflected, as she put on coat and hat. But it had gone better afterwards.... She didn't believe Miss Hartill was cross with her.... That had been a silly idea of her own.... Miss Hartill was just as usual.

She made her farewells. Clare came out into the hall and ushered her forth.

"Good-bye!" Louise smiled up at her. "It was so kind of you to have me. I have so much enjoyed myself." Then, the formula off her tongue: "Miss Hartill, I do hope your head's better?"

"Thank you!" said Clare inscrutably. "Good-night!" Then, as the maid went down the stairs: "Louise!"

"Yes, Miss Hartill?"

Clare was smiling brilliantly.

"Don't come again, Louise, until you can be more amusing. At any rate, natural. Goodnight!"

She shut the door.

CHAPTER XVII

Louise spent her Easter holidays among her lesson books. Miss Hartill and Miss Durand were in Italy, all responsibilities put aside for four blessed weeks, but for Louise there could be no relaxation. The examinations were to take place a few days before the summer term began, and their imminence overshadowed her. Useless for Miss Durand to extract a promise to rest, to be lazy, to forget all about lessons. Louise promised readily and broke her promise half-an-hour after she had waved the train out of the station. Impossible to keep away from one's History and Latin and Mathematics with examinations three weeks ahead. Miss Durand might preach; her overtaxed brain cry pax; her cramped body ache for exercise; but Louise knew herself forced to ignore all protests. She would rest when the examinations were over. Till then-revision, repetition-repetition, revision-with as little time as might be grudged to eating and sleeping and duty walks with Mrs. Denny.

There was no time to lose. The nights swallowed up the days all too swiftly.

Yet, waking one morning with a start to realise that the day of days had dawned at last, she found it incredible. The morning was exactly like other mornings, with the sun streaming blindingly in upon her, because she had forgotten, as usual, to drawn her blind at night, her head already aching a little, hot and heavy from uneasy sleep. All night long her brain had been alert, restless, beyond control. All night long it had tugged and fretted, like a leashed dog, at the surface slumber that tethered it. She felt confused, burdened with a half-consciousness of vivid, forgotten dreams.

She dressed abstractedly, lesson books propped against her looking-glass, and wedged between soap-dish and pitcher. For the hundredth time she conned the technicalities of her work, and making no slips, grew more cheerful for it had been the letter, not the spirit, that had troubled her-little matters of rules and exceptions, of dates and derivations, that would surely trip her up. But she was feeling sure of herself at last, and thrilling as she was with nervous excitement, could yet be glad that the great day had dawned, and ready to laugh at all her previous despondencies. Things were turning out better than she had expected. There was bracing comfort in beginning with her own subject-Miss Hartill's own subject. She could have no fears for herself in the Literature examination. French in the afternoon, that was less pleasant. But she would manage-must, literally. "Miss Hartill expects ——" She laughed. She supposed the sailors felt just the same about Nelson as she did about Miss Hartill. She wondered if Lady Hamilton had minded his only having one eye and one arm? Suppose Miss Hartill had only one eye and one arm? Oh! If anything happened to Miss Hartill...! She shivered at the idea and instantly witnessed, with all imaginable detail, the wreck of the train as it entered Utterbridge station, and she herself rescuing Miss Hartill, armless and blind, from the blazing carriage. She had her on the sofa, five years later, in the prettiest of invalid gowns, contentedly reliant on her former pupil. And Louise, blissfully happy, was her hands and feet and eyes, her nurse, her servant, her —(hastily Louise deprived her alike of income and friends) her bread-winner and companion. Here her French Grammar, slithering over the soap to the floor, woke her from that delicious reverie.

She picked it up, and applied herself for a while to its dazing infinitives. But teeth-brushing is a rhythmic process: her thoughts wandered again perforce. She had got to be first.... Miss Hartill would be so pleased.... It would be heavenly to please Miss Hartill again as she used to do.... Nothing had been the same since Cynthia came.... She flushed to the eyes at the recollection of her last unlucky visit ——"You needn't come again unless you can be more amusing. You might at least be natural...." Yet Miss Hartill had been so kind at the last ... had waved to her from the train....

The postman's knock startled her, disturbed her meditations anew. Letters! Was it possible? Would Miss Hartill have remembered? Have sent her, perhaps, a postcard? Stranger things had been. She had for weeks envisaged the possibility. She finished her dressing and tore downstairs.

The maid was hovering over the breakfast-table.

"Are there any letters, Baxter? Are there any letters?" But she had already caught sight of a foreign postcard on her plate, a postcard with an unfamiliar stamp. She scurried round the table, her heart thumping.

But the big, adventurous handwriting was hatefully familiar. The postcard was from Miss Durand.

She waited a moment, her lips parted vacantly, as was her fashion when controlling emotion; waited till the maid had gone.

Then she crumpled and tore the thin cardboard in her hand and flung it at last on the floor, in a passion of disappointment.

"She might have written!" cried Louise. "Oh, she might have written! It wouldn't have hurt her —a postcard."

Presently a thought struck her. She groped under the table for the torn scraps of paper and spread them in her lap, piecing them eagerly, laboriously. Miss Hartill might have written on Miss Durand's postcard.

She had the oblong fitted together at last and read the scrawl with impatient eagerness. Miss Durand was just sending her a line to wish her all imaginable luck. She and Miss Hartill were having a glorious time. They were sitting at that moment where she had made a cross on the picture postcard. She wished Louise could be with them to see the wonderful view over the valley and with good wishes from them both, was her Alwynne Durand....

Louise's eyes softened —"from them both." That was something! Miss Hartill had sent her a message. She sighed as she wrapped the scraps carefully in her handkerchief. Life was queer.... Here was Miss Durand, so kind, so friendly always-yet her kindness brought no pleasure....And Miss Hartill, who could open heaven with a word-was not half so kind as Miss Durand. Louise marvelled that Miss Hartill could be so miserly. She was sure that if she, Louise, could make people utterly happy by kind looks and kind words, stray messages and occasional postcards, that she would be only too glad to be allowed to do it. To possess the power of giving happiness.... And with no more trouble to yourself than the writing of a postcard! Queer that Miss Hartill did not realise what her mere existence meant to people....She couldn't realise it, of course ... that was it....She thought so little about herself....It was her own beautiful selflessness that made her seem, occasionally, hard-unkind even....She didn't realise what she meant to people....If she had, she would have written....Of course she would have written ...just a word ... on Daffy's postcard....

Louise sighed again. One didn't ask much....But it seemed the more humble one grew-the less one asked-the more unlikely people were to throw one even that little....At any rate there was the examination to tackle....If she did well —! She lost herself again in speculations as to the form Miss Hartill's approval might take.

The family trooped in to breakfast as the brisk maid dumped a steaming dishful of liver and bacon upon the table.

Louise occupied her place and began to spread her bread-and-butter, avoiding her father's eye. But, as she foresaw, she was not permitted to escape.

Mr. Denny pounced upon the butter-dish.

"Not with bacon," he remarked, with reproachful satisfaction, and removed it.

Louise said nothing. She was careful not to look at her parent, for she knew that her expression was not permissible. His harmless tyrannies irritated her as invariably as her tricks of personality grated upon him. She thought him smug and petty, and despised him for his submissive attitude to her step-mother. His noisy interferences with her personal habits she thought intolerable, though she had learned to endure them stolidly. But most of all, she hated to see his fat, pudgy hands touching her food. She was accustomed to cut bread for the family. No one guessed why she had arrogated to herself that duty.

And he, good man, would look at his daughter occasionally, and wonder why she was so unlike his satisfactory sons and their capable mother: would be vaguely annoyed by her silences, and by a certain expression that reminded him uncomfortably of his first "fine-lady" wife; would have an emotion of disquieted responsibility; would hesitate: would end by presenting his daughter with a five-shilling-piece, or be delivered from a dawning sense of responsibility by crumbs on the carpet, the muddy boots of a son and heir, or, as in the present instance, an unjustifiable predilection for butter.

"Bread with your meat," he said firmly and handed her a full plate.

Then he watched her with interest. His conception of the duties of fatherhood was realised in seeing that his children slightly over-ate themselves at every meal. He did as he would be done by.

Louise picked up knife and fork unwillingly. She was dry-mouthed with excitement and the beginnings of a headache, and the liberal portion of hot, rich food sickened her. But anything was better than a fuss. She sliced idly at the slab of liver.

Opportunity beckoned Mr. Denny.

"Don't play with your food," said the father sharply.

She ate a few mouthfuls, conscious of his supervision. Satisfied, he turned at last to his own breakfast.

There was a peaceful interval.

The children talked among themselves. Mrs. Denny, hidden behind her tea-cosy, was exclusively concerned with the table manners of the youngest boy. The moment was propitious.

Softly Louise rose and slipped to the sideboard. Her plate once hidden behind the biscuit-tin....

Mr. Denny looked up. He was ever miraculously alert at breakfast.

"More bacon, Louise?"

"No, thank you, Father," said Louise fervently.

"Have you finished your plate?"

"Yes, Father."

Her brothers gave tongue joyously.

"Oh-h! You whopper!"

"Oh, Father, she hasn't!"

"Mother, did you hear? Louise says she's finished her bacon. She hasn't."

"Not near!"

"Not half!"

"Not a quarter!"

"Well-of all the whopping lies!"

Mr. Denny sprang up, his eyes glistening. He, too, enjoyed a scene. The plate was retrieved from its hiding-place and its guilty burden laid bare.

"Emma, do you see this? Emma! Leave that child alone and attend to me! Flagrant! Flagrant disobedience! Louise, I told you to eat it. Turning up your nose at good food! There's many a child would be thankful-Emma! Am I to be disobeyed by my own children? And a lie into the bargain! If that is the way you are taught at your fine school, I'll take you away. Disgraceful! Eat it up now. Emma! Are you or are you not going to back me up? Is all that food to be wasted?"

Mrs. Denny's calm eyes surveyed the excited table.

"Don't fuss, Edwin. Louise, eat up your bacon."

"I can't," said Louise sullenly.

"Then you shouldn't have taken so much."

"I didn't. It was Father——"

"Eat it up at once," said Mrs. Denny peremptorily, as the baby cast his spoon upon the carpet. The tone of her voice ended the discussion.

Mr. Denny watched his daughter triumphantly, as she toiled over her task, called her attention to a piece of bacon she had left on the edge of her plate, and when she had finished told her she was a good girl and that it would do her good. After which he gave her a shilling.

"I don't want it," muttered Louise.

"You don't want it?" repeated Mr. Denny incredulously.

Louise looked at him. There was a world of uncomprehending contempt in the eyes of father and child alike, though the father's were amused, where the child's were bitter.

Mr. Denny laughed jollily.

"I say, kids! Hear that? Your sister here hasn't any use for a shilling. Bet you haven't either! Eh? I don't think!"

Ensued clamour, with jostling and laughter and clutching of coins, from which the head of the house retired to his chair by the fire, chuckling and content. He enjoyed distributing largesse, especially where there was no great need for it, though he was liberal enough to famous charities. He never gave to beggars, on principle.

Louise slipped out of the room under cover of the noise, and was dressed and departing when her step-mother called her back.

"Louise! You stay to lunch to-day, don't you?"

"At school? Oh no, Mamma. Holidays, you know! They only open a class-room for the exam."

"The fifty-pound job, eh?" Her father eyed her over the top of his paper approvingly. For once his daughter was showing a proper spirit. "Go in and win, my girl! I've given you the best education money could buy. If you don't get it, you jolly well ought to. Fifty quid, eh? I wasn't given the chance of earning fifty quid when I was thirteen. Shop-boy, I was. Started as shop-boy like me father before me."

His wife cut in sharply.

"Isn't there an afternoon examination? I understood ——"

"Yes, Mamma. But no dinners. It's all shut."

Mrs. Denny frowned.

"It's annoying. I wanted you out of the way. Nurse is taking the children for an outing. I've enough to do without providing lunches-you must take some sandwiches-spring cleaning-maids all busy——"

"I'd rather take sandwiches!" Louise's face brightened.

"I thought the cleaning was over-not a comfortable room in the house for the last fortnight." Mr. Denny was testy.

His wife answered them thickly, her mouth full of pins as she adjusted her dusting apron.

"Very well! Ask cook to-no, she's upstairs. Cut them yourself. There's plenty of liver. Perfectly absurd! Do you want the house a foot deep in dust? You leave the household arrangements to me! The top-floor hasn't been done for years-not thoroughly."

"The top floor? Not the attics?" said Louise.

"Yes! I'm re-arranging the rooms. John's getting too big for the nursery. He needs a room to himself. I'm putting him in cook's old room."

Louise paused, the slice of bread half cut.

"Where's cook going?" said her father.

She awaited the answer, a fear catching at her breath.

"Oh, in the lumber-room," said Mrs. Denny easily. "It only wants papering. A nice, big room! A sloping roof, of course. But with her wages, if she can't put up with a sloping roof—! But it'll take some clearing! You wouldn't believe what an amount of rubbish has collected."

"It's not rubbish," said Louise. Her voice was low with passion. "It's not rubbish! You shan't touch it."

Mrs. Denny spun round amazedly: Her step-daughter, the loaf clutched to her breast with an unconscious gesture, the big knife gleaming, was a tragi-comic figure.

"What on earth ——?" she began.

Louise leaned forward, hot-eyed.

"Mamma! You won't! You can't! You mustn't! Father, don't let her! That's Mother's room! If you put cook in Mother's room——" She choked. A priestess defending her altars could have used her accents.

Mr. Denny put down his paper.

"What's the matter with the girl?" he demanded.

Mrs. Denny shrugged her shoulders.

"I've no idea! I don't know what she means. Put down that knife; Louise-you'll cut yourself. And mind your own business, please."

"You don't understand!" Louise fought for calmness, for words that should enlighten and persuade. "I didn't mean to interfere. But the big attic! Mamma! Father! That's my room. I always go there-do my lessons there—I love it! You don't know how I love it. You see——" She paused helplessly.

"But you've got the nursery to sit in," said Mrs. Denny, equally helpless. "I'm sorry, Louise, if you've taken a fancy to the room-but I want it for cook."

Louise made her way to the hearth and stood between the pair.

"Mamma-please! Please! Please! There's the other attic for cook-not this one!"

"Now be quiet, Louise!" Mrs. Denny was getting impatient.

Suddenly Louise lost grip of herself.

"It's not right! It's not right! You've got all the house! Every room is yours and you grudge me that one! Nobody's ever wanted it but me! It's mine! You've got your lovely rooms-drawing-room, and dining-room, and morning-room, and bedroom, and summerhouse, and the boys have got the nursery and the maids have got the kitchen, and yet you won't let me have the attic! It's not fair! It's mean! Why can't cook have the other attic? Not this one! Not this one!"

"But why? Why?" Mrs. Denny was more bewildered than angry. She looked down at her step-daughter as a St. Bernard looks at an aggressive kitten. Desperately Louise tore off her veils.

"Because of Mother. Can't you understand? All her things are there. She's there! So I've always played up there. Oh, won't you understand?"

Mrs. Denny flushed.

"You talk a lot of nonsense, Louise. Finish your sandwiches. You'll be late."

"Then you will leave it, as it is?"

"Certainly not. I told you—I need it for cook."

Louise turned to her father with a frenzied gesture.

"Father! Don't let her! Don't let her touch it! Oh, how can you let her touch it?"

Mr. Denny put down his paper, staring from one to the other.

"Emma? What's she driving at?"

"To control the household, apparently. She's a very impertinent child," said Mrs. Denny impatiently.

"Father! I'm not! I don't! Father! I only want her to leave my attic alone! Father——"

"Don't worry your father now," began Mrs. Denny.

"He's my father! I can speak to him if I choose," cried Louise shrilly.

"Now then, now then!" reasoned Mr. Denny heavily. "Can't have you rude to your mother, you know."

Louise gave herself up to her passion.

"She's not my mother! I call her Mamma! She's not my mother! Mother wouldn't be so cruel! To take away all I've got like that. Her books are there! Her things! It's always been our room-hers and mine! And to take it away! To put cook-it's horrible! It's wicked! It's stealing! I hate her! I hate you-all of you! I'll never forget-never-never-never!"

She stopped abruptly on a high note, stared blindly at the outraged countenances that opposed her, and fled from the room.

They listened to the clatter of umbrellas in the hall stand, to the furious hands fumbling for mackintosh and satchel, to the bang of the hall door.

Mr. Denny whistled.

"Hot stuff! What? I never knew she had it in her." There was a curious element of approval in his tone. He respected volubility.

His wife frowned; then, she, too, began to laugh. She was as incapable as he of imagining the state of nerves that could lead, in Louise, to such an outburst. To speak one's mind, noisily and emphatically, was a daily occurrence for her. Silence was stupidity, and meekness irritating. This "row" was unusual because Louise had taken part in it, but she certainly thought no worse of her step-daughter on that account. The child should be sent to bed early as a punishment, she decided, but good-humouredly enough. She was too thick-skinned to be pricked by Louise's repudiation. She dismissed it as "temper." Its underlying criticism of her character escaped her utterly.

By the time the attic was cleared and the paperhanger at work, she had forgotten the matter.

CHAPTER XVIII

It is not impossible to sympathise with Ahab.

It must have been difficult for him, with his varied possessions, to realise the value to Naboth of his vineyard. He had offered compensation. Naboth would undoubtedly have gained by the exchange. Ahab, owning half Palestine, must have been genuinely puzzled by this blind attachment to one miserable half-acre. One wonders what would have happened if they had met to talk over the matter. Ahab, convinced of the generosity of his offer, courteously argumentative, carefully repressing his not unnatural impatience, would have contrasted favourably with the peasant, black, fierce, dumb, incapable of explaining himself, conscious only of his own bitter helplessness in the face of oppression and loss.

The Naboth mood is a dangerous one. Fierce emotions, unable to disperse themselves in speech, can turn in again upon the mind that bred them, to work strange havoc. The affair of the attic, outwardly so trivial, shook the child's nature to its foundation. Though one's house be built of cards, it is none the less bedazing to have it knocked about one's ears. To Louise, the loss of her holy place, but yet more the manner of its loss, was catastrophic. Her nerves, frayed and strained by weeks of overwork and excitement, snapped under the shock. Her sense of proportion failed her. Miss Hartill, the examination, all that made up her life, faded before this monstrous desecration of an ideal. She suffered as Naboth, forgetting also his greater goods of life and kith and kin, suffered before her.

Before she reached the school the violence of her emotion had faded, and she was in the first stage of the inevitable physical reaction. She felt weak and shaken. She was going, she knew, to her examination. She wondered idly why she did not feel nervous. She tried to impress the importance of the occasion upon herself, but her thoughts eluded her-sequence had become impossible. She gave up the attempt, and her mind, released, returned to the scene of the morning in incessant, miserable rehearsal.

Mechanically she made her way into the school by the unfamiliar mistresses' entrance, greeted the little knot of competitors assembled in the hall. But if she were introspective and distraught, so were they: her silence was unnoticed.

The nervous minutes passed jerkily. Louise thought that the clock must be enjoying himself. He was playing overseer; he wheezed and grunted as her father did at breakfast; had just such a bland, fat face. Her father would be a fat, horrible old man in another ten years. She was glad. Every one would hate him, then, as she hated him, show it as she dared not do.

Miss Vigers interrupted her meditations; Miss Vigers, utterly unreal in holiday smiles and the first hobble-skirt in which her decent limbs had permitted themselves to be outlined. She marshalled the procession.

The Lower Fifth class-room, newly scrubbed and reeking of naphthaline, with naked shelves and treble range of isolated desks, was unfamiliar, curiously disconcerting. Louise, ever perilously susceptible to outward conditions, was dismayed by the lack of atmosphere. She wriggled uneasily in her desk. It was uncomfortable, far too big for her: Agatha's initials, of an inkiness that had defied the charwoman, stared at her from the lid. She was at the back of the room. Between Marion's neat head and the coiffure of the little Jewess, the bored face of the examiner peered and shifted. He was speaking—

"You will find the questions on your desks. Write your names in the top right-hand corner of each page. Full name. Kindly number the sheets. You are allowed two and a half hours."

A pause. Some rustling of papers and the snap and rattle of pencil-boxes. Then the voice of the examiner again—

"You may begin."

Instantly a furious pen-scratching broke the hush. Louise glanced in the direction of the sound, and smiled broadly. Agatha had begun. Miss Hartill would have seen the joke, but the examiner was already absorbed in the book he had taken from his pocket. Louise gazed idly about her. So this was what the ordeal was like! There were her clean, blank papers on the desk before her, and the printed list of questions. She supposed she had better begin.... But there was plenty of time. She had a curious sense of detachment. Her body surrounded her, rigid, quiescent, dreading exertion. Her mind, on the contrary, was bewilderingly active, consciously alive with thoughts, as she had once, under a microscope, seen a drop of water alive with animalculi: thoughts, however, that had no connection with real life as it at the moment presented itself: thoughts that admitted the fact of the examination with a dreamy impersonality that precluded any idea of participation. Her mind felt comfortable in its warm bed of motionless flesh, would not disturb its repose for all the ultimate gods might offer: but was interested nevertheless in its surroundings, gazing out into them with the detached curiosity of an attic-dweller, peering out and down at a dwarfed and distant street. Yet each trivial object on which her eyes alighted gave birth to a train of thought that led separately, yet quite inevitably, to the memories that would shatter her quietude, as conscious and subconscious self struggled for possession of her mind.

She stared at the intent backs of her neighbours. One by one they hunched forward, as each in turn settled to work. Louise considered them critically. What ugly things backs were! It was funny, but girls with dark skirts always pinned them to their blouses with white safety-pins, and *vice versa*. It made them look skewered....Yet Miss Durand had said that backs were the most expressive part of the whole body....That was the day they had seen the Watts pictures. But then the draperies of the great white figure in "Love and Death" were not fastened up in the middle with safety-pins....That had been a wonderful picture....She knew how the boy felt, how he fought....How long had he been able to hold the door? she wondered. Characteristically, she never questioned the ultimate defeat. It was terrible to be so weak....But the Death was beautiful....pitying....One wouldn't hate it while one resisted it, as one hated Mamma.... Mamma, forcing her way into an attic....Louise writhed as she thought of it.

The girl in front of her coughed, a hasty, grudging cough, recovered herself, and bent again to her work. Louise was amused. What a hurry she was in! What a hurry every one was in! How hot Marion's cheeks were! And Agatha....Agatha was up to her wrists in ink....Like the women in the French Revolution....Though that was blood, of course....They were steeped in gore.... It would be fascinating to write a story about the knitting women ... click-click-clicking-like a lot of pens scraping....What were they all scribbling like that for? Of course, it was the examination....There was a paper on her own desk too....How funny!

"Distinguish between Shelley the poet, and Shelley the politician. Illustrate your meaning by quotations."

Shelley? The name was familiar....She sells sea-shells....

"Give a short account of the life of Shakespeare."

He had a wife, hadn't he? A narrow, grudging woman, who couldn't understand him....A woman like Mamma....Mamma, who was turning out the attic and laughing at Louise....Not that that mattered-but to clear the attic-to take away Mother's things....What would Mother do-little, darling Mother...? It was holidays....Mother would know....Mother would be there, waiting for Louise. A hideous picture rose up in Louise's mind. With photographic clearness she saw the attic and the faint shadow of her mother wavering from visibility to nothingness as the sunlight caught and lost her impalpable outlines: there was a sound of footsteps-Louise heard it: the faint thing held out sweet arms and Louise strained towards them; but the door opened, and Mrs. Denny and the maids came in. Mamma pointed, while the maids laughed and took their brooms and chased the forlorn appearance, and it fled before them about the room, cowering, afraid, calling in its whisper to Louise. But the maids closed in, and swept that shrinking nothingness into the dark corner behind the old trunk: but when they had moved the trunk, there was nothing to be seen but a delicate cobweb or two. So they swept it into the dustpan and settled down to the scrubbing of the floor.

The picture faded. Louise crouched over her desk, her head in her hands. About her the pens scratched rhythmically.

For a space she existed merely. She could not have told how long it was before thoughts began once more to drift across the blankness of her mind like the first imperceptible flakes that herald a fall of snow.

She moved stiffly in her seat. The thoughts came thicker-thoughts of her mother still, of the dream presence that she would not feel again.... Never again? There was the Last Judgment, of course.... She would see her then.... And who knew when the Judgment would come.... In a thousand years? In the next five seconds? She counted slowly, holding her breath: "One-two-three-four-five ——" and stared out expectantly into space through the lashes of her dropped lids.

All about her sat forms, bowed like her own, scarcely moving. Of course, of course-she nodded to herself-satisfied with her own acuteness. Obviously, the Last Judgment.... They were all waiting for God.... He hadn't arrived yet, it seemed.... Well, one might look about a little first.... How queer Heaven smelt! The heart of Louise leapt within her.... Now was the opportunity to find Mother.... Mother would be somewhere among the dead.... But they all had ugly backs.... But Mother.... Of course Mother would be standing on that high platform place like a throne.... It was her place.... She always stood there.... Or did she? Was there not some one else? very like her ... with eyes ... and a smile ... whom Louise knew so well? Wasn't it Mother? With patient deliberation she strove to disentangle the two personalities, that combined and divided and blurred again into one. There was Mother-and the Other-one was shape and one was shadow-but which was real? There was Mother-and the Other-who was Mother? No, who was-who was-The Other was not Mother-but if not, who? —who? —who? —

A chorus of angels took up the chant: Who? who? who? They had flat, faint voices, that gritted and whispered, like pens passing over paper.

Who? who? who?

The answer came thundering back out of infinite space in the awaited voice of God....

"You have ten minutes more."

Louise gave a faint gasp. Reality enveloped her once more, licking up her illusion as instantly and fiercely as an unnoticed candle will shrivel up a woman's muslins. She stood naked amid the ashes of her dreams.

She glanced wildly about her. The girls at her elbows were furiously at work. The little examiner had put away his book and was staring at her. Her eyes fell. Before her lay foolscap, fair and blank, save for her name in the corner, and a close-printed paper that she did not recognise, clamouring for information anent Shelley, and Carlyle, and the Mermaid Tavern. Because, of course, she was at the Literature examination, and there were ten minutes more.

And she had written nothing.

An instant she sat appalled. Then she snatched up her pen and wrote....

Her pen fled across the paper at Tam o' Shanter speed, leaving its trail of shapeless, delirious sentences. She never paused to consider-she wrote. She knew only that she had ten-twelve-fifteen questions to answer, and ten minutes in which to do it. Ten minutes for a two and a half hours' paper! No matter-if one stopped to think.... Hurry! hurry! Shelley was born in 1792 —he was the son of Sir Timothy Shelley, of Field Place, near Horsham ——

When the examiner collected the papers, she had written exactly two pages.

CHAPTER XIX

The examination had taken place early in May, but the summer term was nearly over before news of the results arrived. When it came, it made but a small sensation. The school had tired of waiting. Not only was its own more intimate examination drawing near, but its many heads were filled, to the exclusion of all else, with the excitements and rivalries of the summer theatricals.

The school play was an institution. Of late years-ever since she had joined the staff indeed-it had grown into an annual personal triumph for Miss Hartill.

Clare was blessed-cursed-with that sixth sense, the *sens du théâtre*. Her own nature was, in essence, theatrical; her frigid and fastidious reserve warring incessantly with her irrepressible love of the scene for its own sake. She was aware of the trait and humiliated by its presence in her character. Usually she would curb her inclination with a severity that was in itself histrionic: at times she indulged it with voluptuous recklessness.

As a girl, the stage had appealed to her strongly; but her excessive squeamishness, with her acute sense of personal, bodily dignity, closed it to her as a career. Also her love of power. Though she knew little of stage life she had sufficient intuition to gauge correctly what she might become. Successful necessarily-dominant never. And she required a dais. But the compelling woman, she knew, is successful through her combination of intellectual strength with sexual charm. She must not scruple to use all the weapons at her service. Clare had told herself that there were some weapons to which she would never condescend. If sting had lain in the fact that, though she would, they were not hers to use, she did not acknowledge it, even to herself. Resolutely she put from her the idea of fostering a useless talent; and the desire to exploit it, save surreptitiously in social intercourse, dulled as she grew older.

Nevertheless, the yearly plays were to Clare a source of excitement and gratification. She alone was responsible for the production. In five successful years they had become an event, a festival-not only to the school, but to the entire neighbourhood. Two, and then three public performances were given each summer, and the proceeds benefited the school charities. *As You Like It*, *Twelfth Night*, *Verona*, and *The Merchant of Venice*, followed upon the *Midsummer Night's Dream*, and exhausted the list of entirely suitable plays; but after some hesitation, Clare had devised for her next venture scenes from *King John*. Several forms were studying the period, the Sixths and Fifths were reading the play, politically also it was apropos. (Clare had ever sound reasons to gild her decisions.) Privately she had been slightly embarrassed by the fact that the classes she supervised had that year proved themselves unusually poor in dramatic ability. She could depend, indeed, on a score of keen and capable children, but in Louise Denny alone had she glimpsed an actress who could do her credit. The child's physique precluded her from rôles that, otherwise, she could easily have filled, but as Prince Arthur, she could be made the central, unforgettable figure of an otherwise trite performance. "*King John*," quoth Clare; "decidedly, the very play." And *King John* was chosen.

Since the beginning of the term, with Clare as generalissimo and Alwynne most ingenious of adjutants, staff and school had worked enthusiastically. Costumes were finished, staging painted and planned, and the various scenes were, at length, receiving their final polish. Alwynne was responsible for the interpretation of the minor parts, while Clare, in her spare time, devoted herself to the principals, attacking alternately the exaggerations of Agatha's "Constance," Marion's stolid "Hubert," a certain near-sighted amiability in the spectacled "King John."

Clare was a born stage-manager, patient, resourceful, compelling. The children trusted her; she had the habit of success. Her air of authority cushioned them, denied the possibility of failure. Clare, wholly in earnest, Clare at usual hours, intimate and relaxed, Clare appealing, exhorting, inspiring, was irresistible. She got what she wanted from them and was not ill content. She knew to the last ounce their capabilities.

With Louise alone she had difficulties. The child was almost too easily trained. Responsive, quickly fired or chilled, she was, in fact, too delicately and completely attuned to Clare herself.

Clare could be crude: she had her gusty moods: the little æolian harp quivered to snapping point before them. Originally this extreme sensitiveness had fascinated Clare; she felt like a musician exploring the possibilities of an unknown instrument; but she tired of it in time. As Louise became saturated with the stronger personality, she had, in her passionate desire to satisfy Clare, grown into her mere replica; reproducing her phraseology, voicing her opinions, reflecting her moods, stifling, in the exquisite delight of abnegation, all in her that had originally attracted the older woman. That the effect had been, first to amuse, then to irritate, finally to bore Clare's fickle humour, was natural enough. Clare, had she cared, could have guided the child, despite the great disparity of age, into a pleasant path of affection and friendship, but that she did not choose. She was disappointed, and showed it: and there, for her, the matter ended. That she was in any way responsible, she would not admit.

She did not, indeed, fully realise the extent of the change in Louise until the rehearsals began. For all her growing indifference, in spite of the marked deterioration that automatically it had caused in the girl's work, she had still a high and just opinion of her capabilities. She was positive that as Prince Arthur, Louise would give a fine and original performance, and anticipated with amused interest her initial rendering of the character.

At the first rehearsal Louise did not disappoint her. She was neither stiff nor self-conscious, and her acting, which proved to be entirely instinctive, carried conviction. Though Clare worked from the head, she could appreciate the more primitive method, but even then, the character as portrayed by Louise amazed her. The deliberate pathos, the cloying charm, did not seem to exist for Louise. She played as in an ecstasy of terror. The text, Clare knew, could permit the reading, and the conception interested her; but the temptation to criticise, alter and improve, was natural. Here and there, as rehearsals progressed, she pulled and patched and patted-quite genuinely in the interest of the play as a whole. But the result was discouraging. The Louise of former days would have defended her own version, delighting Clare with shy impudences and flashes of insight, naïve parries and counter-attacks, till between them they had attained notable results. But the sparkle had been drilled out of Louise. She was humble, anxiously acquiescent, agreeing with every alteration, accepting every suggestion, however foreign to her own instinctive convictions, while the vividness faded slowly from her reading, leaving it lifeless and forced.

"It's patchwork," said Clare disgustedly to Alwynne, at the end of the third week, "pure patchwork. She does everything I tell her-and the result is dire. What it will be like on the night, heaven knows! And there's nobody else. Yet she *can* act. That first performance was quite excellent."

"And she tries."

"She slaves! She would be less irritating if she didn't. You know, Alwynne, I let myself go yesterday. I told her how impossible she was. And all she did was to look at me like a mournful monkey!"

"Inarticulate. Exactly."

Clare lifted her eyebrows. Alwynne looked at her quaintly.

"You know perfectly well what's wrong. Why on earth don't you leave her alone?"

"Uncoached?"

"That as well, of course. You said yourself she was excellent at first. Why don't you leave her to herself? It's safe. She's not like the others. She's a nectarine, not a potato. Give her a free hand till the dress-rehearsal. It won't be your reading—I prefer yours, too; at least I think I do ———"

"I'm glad you say 'think.' But think again. There's no question of which you ought to prefer. But I, my good child, must consider my public! It wants to enjoy itself! It wants to weep salt tears! Louise's reading would cheat it of its emotions!"

"At least it will be a reading, not a repetition. I don't mean that, though, when I say-leave her alone. Clare-you won't realise what you mean to people!"

"I don't follow——" but Clare laughed a little.

"You do. You know you've made Louise crazy about you." Clare shrugged impatiently.

"I dislike these enthusiasms."

"But you cause them. I think it is rather mean to shirk the consequences."

"Really, Alwynne!" But Clare was still smiling.

"You do. You begin by being heavenly to people-and then you tantalise them."

"Does it hurt, Alwynne? Are you going to run away?"

Alwynne smiled.

"Oh, you won't get rid of me so easily. I'm a limpet. Do you know, I couldn't imagine existence without you now. I've never been so gloriously happy in my life. You wouldn't ever get really tired of me, would you?"

"I wonder."

"I know."

"I've warned you that I'm changeable. Instance your Louise."

"Oh, Clare, do be nicer to Louise."

"Oh, Alwynne, do mind your own business. I'm as nice as is good for her. But I believe you're right about this acting. I'll wash my hands of her till the dress-rehearsal, if you like. You can tell her I said so."

But Alwynne, whispering to Louise that perhaps the old way was better after all, that Miss Hartill had said she didn't mind, achieved little.

"Oh, Miss Durand-don't let her think I'm hopeless. I shall get it right in time. I'd rather stick to the way she showed me. Miss Durand-do you think she's angry? Honestly, I will get it right. Miss Durand —I suppose there's no news?"

The child's face was very drawn; her eyes seemed larger than ever; she looked like a little old woman! Alwynne was concerned; she felt vaguely responsible. She, too, wished that the news, good or bad, would come, and put an end at least to the tension.

And one morning, all unexpectedly, the news did come.

The performances were but two days away. The decorous Big Hall was in confusion. The school sat, picnic-fashion, for its prayers; and the head mistress, entering between half-hung cloths, mounted a battlemented rostrum to address it. She carried a sheaf of papers. Louise, sitting with her class at the further end of the hall, outwardly decorous enough, was in reality paying little attention. Her vague, unhappy thoughts were concerned with the coming rehearsal; she could not remember what Miss Hartill's last directions had been; she was sure she should stumble. Sometimes the mere words seemed to evade her. Yet the play was on her shoulders-Miss Durand had said so. She supposed Prince Arthur was really fond of Hubert? Not pretending, because he was afraid? But of course it was easy to love a person and yet be terrified of them. She stole a look at Clare, prominent in the grave group of mistresses. They were all very intent. It dawned on her that the head mistress had been speaking for several minutes.

Suddenly there was an outburst of clapping. The spectacled girl at the end of the row grew pink and stared at her hands.

"What is it?" breathed Louise. "Oh, what is it? What is it?"

A neighbour caught the murmur and looked down at her curiously.

"Are you asleep? It's the lists. Your exam. You'll be second, I expect."

But Marion was second.

The clapping crackled up anew.

So the news was come!

It was cruel to let it spring upon you thus.... You would have asked so little ... ten minutes ... a bare ... in which to brace yourself.... Surprise was horrible ... it caught you with your soul half-naked ... it shocked like sudden noise....

There came a fresh outburst.

It was wicked to make such sounds ... like all the policeman's-rattles in the world....

The reading proceeded; it calmed her; it barely stirred the beautiful silence. But presently the neat voice altered. Old Edith Marsham was a kindly soul. She had not quite forgotten her own schooldays. She realised, perfunctorily, as the successful do, the blankness of defeat. Louise heard her name pronounced, a trifle hurriedly. Louise Denny-failed.

She made no sign. She sat erect, listening to the conclusion of that matter, clapped in due course, stood, kneeled, rose again, as applause, hymns and prayers buzzed about her, filed with her class from the hall and added her shy word to the clamour of congratulation in the long corridors. Inwardly, she was stunned by the evil that was upon her.

The irregular morning classes (the imminent entertainment had disorganised the entire system of work) gave her time to rouse, to review her position.

She turned helplessly within herself, wondering how she should begin to think-and where. She wondered idly if this was how soldiers felt, when a shell had blown them to pieces? She wondered how they collected themselves afterwards? Where did they begin? Did an arm pick up the legs and head, or how?

The picture thus conjured up struck her as excessively funny. She began to giggle. The mistress's astonished voice roused her to the necessity for self-control. She picked up her pen. The thoughts flowed more clearly-yes, like ink in a pen.

So it had come.

All along she had known that she must have failed: known it from the day of the examination itself. The burden of that knowledge had been upon her for weeks like a secret guilt. Daily she had gone to prayers in cold fear, thinking: "Now-now-now-they will read it out." Daily she had studied Clare's face, to each change of expression, each abstraction or transient sternness, her heart beating out its one thought: "She had heard! she knows!" And yet behind her academic certainty of failure had lain a little illogical hope. There was just a chance-an examiner more kind than just ... a spilled ink-bottle ... an opportune fire. The child in her could still pray for miracles, for help from fairyland, and half believe it on the way.

And now the daily terrors, the daily reliefs, were alike over. Louise, who had learned, as she thought, to do without hope these many weeks, realised pitifully her self-deception. This hopelessness, this dead weight of certainty, was a new burden —a Sisyphus rock which would never roll for her. She was at the end.

Her mind, for all its forced and hot-house development, had, in matters of raw fact, the narrow outlook of the schoolgirl, superimposed upon the passions, the more intense for their utter innocence, of the child. Her sense of proportion, that latest developed and most infallible sign of maturity, was embryonic. The examination, so intrinsically unimportant, appeared to her a Waterloo. She could not see beyond it.

Clare, inexplicably altering, daily sterner and more indifferent, save for stray gleams of whimsical kindness, that stung and maddened the child by their sweetness and rarity, would, Louise considered, be effectually alienated. But Louise could not conceive life possible without Clare. The future was a night of black misery, without a hint of dawn.

CHAPTER XX

The morning wore to an end. Clare had come in at the mid-morning break to announce that the dress rehearsal would take place on the afternoon of the following day. All costumes were to be ready. The day-girls were to lunch at the school. She was brief and businesslike, inaccessible to questions. She did not look at Louise.

Alwynne, later in the morning, supplementing her instructions, paused a moment at the child's desk. But Louise gave no sign. Alwynne hesitated. She herself was averse from verbal sympathy. Also she was pressed for time, and Clare, she knew, wanted her. The one o'clock bell shattered her indecision. She gave her directions and hurried away.

Louise packed her books together and went home.

She endured the cheerful noisy lunch; carried out some small commissions for her stepmother; shepherded the troop of small boys into the paddock behind the garden and saw them established at their games. She stayed a moment with the round two-year-old, sprawling by the pile of coats, but he, too, had his amusements. Every pocket tempted his enquiring fingers. He ignored her.

She went back to the house. Habit brought her for the fiftieth time to the attic, and she had opened the door before she remembered. She looked about her. An iron bedstead, covered by a crude quilt, stood where the trunk of books had lain. A square of unswept carpet lay before it. There was a deal night-table and a candlestick of blue tin, with matches and a guttered candle. Across a chair lay a paper-back, face downwards, and a pair of soiled red corsets. The ivy had been cut away from the window, and the sunlight cast no fantastic frieze, but a squared, black shadow on the floor. The air was close, and a little rank. Louise shrank from it.

"Mother?" she said; and then: "You've gone away, haven't you? It's no use calling?"

She waited. The uneven water-jug rattled in its basin.

She spoke again —

"Mother, I know it's all spoiled here, but couldn't you come? Just for a little while, Mother? I'm most miserable. Please, Mother?"

There was no answer.

"What shall I do?" cried Louise wildly. "What shall I do? Oh, what shall I do?"

She turned from that empty place, stumbled to her room, and flung herself across her bed. She was shaken by her misery, as a dog shakes a rat. She cried, her head on her arms, till she was sick and blinded. Loneliness and longing seared her as with irons.

The clock ticked, and the sunshine poured into the room. The shouts of the children, the crack of the ball on bat sounded faintly. The house slept. Two hours passed.

Somewhere a clock chimed and boomed. Four o'clock.

Slowly and stiffly Louise roused herself and got off her bed. She was cramped and shivering. She stood in the middle of the room and held out her hands to the brassy sunlight, but it did not warm her. She felt dazed and giddy; her head burned as if there were live coals in it. Her thoughts flowed sluggishly; she found it impossible to hurry them; they split apart into fragments that were words and meaningless phrases, or stuck like cogged wheels. Her mind moved across immense spaces to adjust these difficulties, but she policed them in vain. There was one sentence, in particular, that she could not deal with. It would not move along and make room for other thoughts. It danced before her; its grin spanned the horizon; it inhabited her mind; it was reversible like a Liberty satin; it ticked like a clock: "What next? What next? What next? Next what? Next what? Next what?"

What next?...Dully she reckoned it up. The tea-bell—homework-bedtime. Night-and the false dreams. Morning-and the anger of Miss Hartill. Day and week and month-and the anger of Miss Hartill. The years stretched out before her in infinite repetition of the afternoon's agony, till her raw nerves shrank appalled. Kneeling down, she told God that it was impossible for her to endure this desolation. She implored Him, if He should in truth exist, not to reckon her doubt against her, but to be merciful and let her die. It was not the first time that she had prayed thus, but never before with such fierce insistence. If He existed He could impossibly refuse....

Speaking her thoughts, even to so indefinite a Listener, steadied her. A ghost of hope had drifted through her mind. A ghost indeed; a messenger that whispered not of waking but of sleep, not of arduous renewing but of an end. Death was life upon his lips and life, death; yet he was none the less a hope.

The familiar text upon the wall above her bed caught her eye. The message seemed no more miraculous than the pansies and mistletoe that wreathed about its gilt and crimson capitals. "God is our Refuge and Strength, a very present Help in Trouble." "Ask and it shall be given unto you" confirmed her from the other wall.

She sat between those tremendous statements and considered them.

God had never yet answered any prayer of hers.... Not, she supposed, that He could not, but because He did not choose.... He was rather like Miss Hartill.... But Miss Hartill would never understand.... At least one could explain things to God-if God were.... And she asked so little of Him-just to let her die and be at peace.... She thought He might-if He had even time for sparrows.... She wondered how He would manage it! If He would only be quick-because red-hot wires ran through her head when she tried to think, and she was afraid-afraid-afraid-of to-morrow and Miss Hartill....

The tea-bell pealed across the garden.

She tidied her hair, and fetching the sponge and towel stood before the glass, trying to trim her marred face into some semblance of composure. The boys would be clamouring-and one never knew.... There might be tainted food —a loose baluster —a tag of carpet.... He had his ways.... She must not baulk Him....

She went downstairs.

The children were tired and cross and quarrelsome-the heat had soured even cheerful Mrs. Denny. It was not a pleasant meal. But it could not oppress Louise. Outwardly docile and attentive, her mind had withdrawn into itself and sat aloof, inviolate, surveying its surroundings much as it would have watched the actors in a moving picture. She was impervious to bickerings and querulous comment. What did it matter? She would never have tea with them again.... She was going away from it all.... If only God did not forget....

All through the breathless evening she awaited His pleasure.

Long after the house was quiet, and Mrs. Denny tucking up her children, had come and gone, Louise lay wakeful-still waiting.

It was an airless night. Every other moment the little unaccountable noises of a sleeping building broke the warm silence. Shadows scurried across the counterpane and over her face like ghostly mice, as the trees outside her window bent and nodded to a radiant moon.

She was weary to the point of exhaustion. Momently her body seemed to shrink away from her into the depths of the bed-warm, fathomless depths-leaving her essential self to float free and uncontained. She would resign herself luxuriously to the sensation of disintegration, but with maddening regularity her next breath clicked body and soul together anew. Yet, as she drowsed, the space between breath and breath lengthened slowly, till they lay divided by incredible æons in which her thoughts wandered and lost themselves, grew hoar and died and were born again; while the dead-weight of her body sank ever deeper into sleep, was recalled to consciousness with ever increasing effort.

She speculated languidly upon her sensations. They recalled a day at the dentist's, years before. A tube had been placed over her mouth and she had struggled, remembering a hideous story of a woman —a French marquise-that she had read in a magazine. The name began with a "B" or a "V." "Brin—" something. The Funnel —*The Leather Funnel* —that was the name of the story.... But there came no choking water-only sweet, buzzing air.... And then her body had dropped away from her, as it was doing now.... She recalled the sensation of rest and freedom; she had passed, like a bird planing down warm breezes, into exquisite oblivion....

She had returned, centuries later, to a dull aching pain, harsh noises, and lights that were like blows....But if she had not returned? She would have been dead....They would have buried her.... Such things had happened....So that was death-that cradling, beautiful sleep. And God was sending it to her now; flooding her, drowning her in its warm comfort....God was very good.... She was sorry-sorry that she had often not believed in Him....But Miss Hartill didn't....But she would never see Miss Hartill any more....Perhaps, years after, when she was tired of sleeping, she would go back and see her again....There was All Souls' Night, when you woke up....But she would not frighten Miss Hartill....She laughed a little, to think that she could ever frighten Miss Hartill....She would just kiss her, a little ghost's kiss that would feel like a puff of air ... and then she would go back and sleep and sleep and sleep ... with only the yew-berries pattering on to her gravestone to tell her when another year had drifted past....It was funny that people could be afraid to die....She wondered if ghosts snored, and if you heard them, if your grave were very close? It was her last thought as she slid into slumber.

Instantly the breakfast gong came crashing across her peace. She fought against waking. Her eyelids lifted the weight upon them as violets press upwards against a clod of rotten leaves. She lay dazedly, her mind cobwebbed with dreams, her thoughts trickling back into the channels of the previous night. Slowly she took in her situation. There was the window, and a shining day without: she could hear the starlings quarrelling on the lawn, and the squeak of an angry robin....There was her room, and the tidy pile of clothes by the bed ... the bed, and she herself lying in it....So she was not dead! There was to-day to be faced, and Miss Hartill's anger, and all the other hundreds and thousands of days....

And she must get up at once.

Her sick mind shrank from that, as from a culminating terror. She was desperately tired; her body ached as if it had been beaten. Dressing was a monstrous and impossible feat....It could not be....Yet her step-mother would come-she was between God and Mrs. Denny-and God had left her in the lurch.

She lay shielding her eyes from the strong light.

The pressure on her eyeballs was causing the usual kaleidoscopic ring of light to form within her closed lids. The phenomenon had always been a childish amusement to her; she was adept at the shifting pressure that could vary colour and pattern. She watched idly. Red changed to green, purple followed yellow, and the ring narrowed to a pin-point of light on its background of watered silk; then it broke up as usual into starry fragments. But they danced no dazzling fire-dance for her ere they merged again into the yellow ring; to her distracted fancy they were letters-fiery letters, that formed and broke and formed again. G —O —D —then an H and a P and an L. She puzzled over them. "God hopes?" "God helps?" But He hadn't...."God helps?" A Voice in her ears exactly like her own took it up —"Those that help themselves." It spoke so loudly that she shrank. The universe echoed to Its boom: yet she knew so well that the Voice was only in her own head.

No wonder her head ached, when it was all full of Lights and Voices....And Miss Hartill would be angry if she took Them to school....If only she need not go to school....Why-why had God cheated her? "He helped those ——" Was that what They meant?

She looked about her, brightening yet uncertain; then her long plait of hair caught her eye. Lazily she lifted it, disentangled a strand no thicker than coarse string, and doubling it about her throat, began to tighten it, using her fingers as a lever, till the blood sang in her ears. She had sat upright in bed for the greater ease. Suddenly she caught sight of her face in the wardrobe mirror. It was growing pink and puffy; the eyes goggled a little. The sensation of choking grew unendurable. Instinctively her fingers freed themselves and the noose fell apart. She swung forward, panting, and watched her features grow normal again.

"It's no good. Oh, I am a coward," cried Louise, wearily.

Her mother's old-fashioned travelling clock, chiming the quarter, answered her, and for a moment forced her thoughts back from those borderlands where sanity ends. Habit asserted itself; she was filled with everyday anxieties. She was late, certainly for breakfast, probably for school. She jumped out of bed, washed and dressed in panic speed, collected her belongings and hurried from the house.

Her father, hearing the gate clack, glanced up from his newspaper.

"Has that child had any breakfast?" he demanded, uneasily.

There was no answer. He was late himself, and his wife had poured his coffee and left the room. He could hear her heavy footfall in their bedroom overhead.

He returned to his reading.

CHAPTER XXI

Louise ran up the steep hill, her satchel padding at her back, the soft wind disordering her hair and whipping a colour into her white cheeks. She gained the deserted cloakroom, flung off her hat, and fled upstairs. But she was later than she guessed. Racing, against all rules, through the upper hall and down the long corridor, the drone of voices as she passed the glass-panelled doors warned her that no hurrying could avail her. She was definitely late. Her speed slackened.

The passage ended at right-angles to a small landing, into which her class-room opened. She paused, sheltering in the curve of the hall, listening. The class was still. The single voice of a mistress rang muffled through the walls. She could not distinguish the accents.

It was Miss Durand's class; but when everything was so upset ... one never knew ... it might be Miss Hartill herself.... That would be just Louise's luck.... She hated you to be late.... But there was no point in hesitating....

Yet she hesitated, shifting her weight uneasily from foot to foot, till a far-off step in the corridor without, ended her uncertainty. Some one was coming.... That again might be Miss Hartill.... Louise must be in her place.... Yet surely it was Miss Hartill's voice in the form-room?

She crept to the door and peered through the glass.

Miss Durand was standing at the blackboard.

Louise entered, brazen with relief, and began her apologies. But Alwynne was no Rhadamanthus, and her official reprobation was marred by a twinkle. She would have been late herself that morning, but for Elsbeth-poor dear Elsbeth, who conceded, without remotely comprehending, the joys of that extra twenty minutes. And when had Louise been late before? Little, good, frightened Louise! She entered the name in the defaulters' book, but her manner sent the child to her desk quieted.

Alwynne, at sentry-go between blackboard and rostrum, dictating, supervising, expounding, yet found time to watch her. Louise was always a little on her motherly young mind. The child's shrinking manner worried her-and her pain-haunted eyes. Pain was Alwynne's devil. She was selfish, as youth must be, but at least, unconsciously. Hint trouble, and all of her was eager to serve and save. She was the instinctive Samaritan. But her perception was blurred by her profound belief in Clare. Louise, she knew, was in good hands, in wise hands; where she had known ten children, Clare had trained a hundred; if Clare's ways were not hers-so much the worse for hers.

Yet this disciplining of Louise was a long business; she wished it need not make the child so wretched. Surely Clare forgot how young she was.... There would be new trouble over the affair of the papers.... If Clare would but be commonplace for once, laugh, and say it didn't matter, and perhaps ask Louise to tea.... The child would be radiant for another six months-and work better too.... But, of course, it was absurd for her to dictate to Clare.... Louise had had such a pretty colour when she came in; it was all gone now.... She looked dreadfully thin.... Alwynne wondered if it would do any good to speak to Clare again.... Dear Clare-she was so proud of her girls, so eager to see them successful.... Louise was a bitter disappointment to her.... Yet, if she could have been gentler-but, of course, Clare knew best.... Alwynne only hoped the rehearsal would be a success. If Louise did well, it might adjust the tension....

She watched the child, sitting apparently attentive, noted the moving lips, the little red volume half hidden in her lap. Shakespeare had no business in a physiology lesson, but Alwynne let her alone.

The hour was over all too quickly for Louise. Earlier in the year, when she had been at her most brilliant, and Miss Hartill's classes the absorbing joy of her day, she had yet welcomed the hours with Miss Durand. They alone had not seemed, in comparison, a waste of priceless time. They were jolly hours, quick-stepping, cheerful, laughter-flecked; void of excitements, yet never savourless; above all restful. Unconsciously she had counted on them for their recuperative value. Even now, exhausted, overwrought, beyond all influence, the kindly atmosphere could at least soothe her. Wistfully her eyes followed Alwynne, as the young mistress left the room.

Clamour arose; slamming of desk-lids, thud of satchels and rattle of pencil-cases mingling with the babble of tongues. The next lesson was French Grammar. The little Frenchwoman was invariably late. She dreaded the lesson as much as her audience enjoyed it. They welcomed it as a pleasant interlude-the hour for conversation. Agatha did not even trouble to keep an eye on the door, as she turned to Louise, immobile beside her.

"I say, were you late?"

"Didn't you see?"

"Why were you late? Weren't you called? Didn't you wake up?"

"No."

"Why?"

"Oh, the housemaid died in the night. Smallpox." Louise stooped over her book, her shoulders hunched against questions.

"No, but tell me. Did you get in a row?"

"You heard what Daffy said. I want to learn, Agatha."

"Oh, not that. Did you get in a row about the rehearsal?"

"What rehearsal?"

"The rehearsal yesterday."

Louise sat up, her eyes widening.

"There was no rehearsal yesterday?" she said anxiously.

"Wasn't there just!"

"But I never heard; nobody told me."

"Why, Daffy came in herself, yesterday morning. Every one was there. I suppose you were moonstruck as usual. Do you mean to say you didn't hear? I don't envy you."

"Was she angry?" said Louise, in her smallest voice.

Agatha began to enjoy herself.

"Angry? She was raving!"

"What did she say?"

"Well, she didn't say much," admitted Agatha. "Just asked where you were, and if not, why not-you know her way. Then we got started and went all through it, and had a gorgeous afternoon. She read your part. I say, she can act, can't she? But she was pretty mad, of course."

"Was she —" said Louise. But it was not a question.

"Oh, and you're to go to her at break, this morning. Don't go and forget, and then say I didn't tell you." And she turned to greet the entering mistress with a flood of Anglo-French.

Louise had three parts of an hour in which to assimilate the message. How unlucky she was! She remembered the previous morning as one remembers a nightmare....Miss Durand had certainly drifted through its dreadfulness-but of what she had said or done, Louise remembered nothing. But it was certain that she had managed to annoy Miss Hartill more than ever. To miss a special rehearsal! Now she was to go to her, and Miss Hartill would be so angry already, that when the question of the papers arose, the last chance of her leniency was gone....For, of course, she would speak of the examination....What would she say? Her imagination stubbed; it could not pierce the terror of what Miss Hartill would say.

The break was half over before she had wrenched herself out of her desk, along the length of the school, and up the staircase to Clare's little sanctum.

She knocked timidly. Clare's answering bell, that invariably startled her, rang sharply. She hesitated-the bell rang again, a prolonged, shrill peal. She pulled herself together, opened the door, and went in.

The floor was littered with gay costumes. Miss Durand, in a big apron, laughter-flushed, with her pretty hair tumbling down her back, was sorting them into neat heaps.

Clare, at ease in a big arm-chair, directing operations, while her quick fingers cut and pasted at a tinsel crown, was laughing also.

"How happy they look," thought Louise.

Clare glanced up.

"Well, Louise," she said, not unkindly.

Louise stammered a little.

"Miss Hartill—I'm very sorry—I'm most awfully sorry. They said-the girls said-there was rehearsal yesterday, and you wanted me. I honestly didn't know. I've only just heard there was one."

Clare kept her waiting while she clipped at the indentations of the crown. The scissors clicked and flashed. It seemed an interminable process.

Finally she spoke to Alwynne, her eyes on her work.

"Miss Durand! You gave my message to the Fifths?"

Yes, Alwynne had told the girls.

"Wasn't Louise in the room at the time?"

Alwynne's unwilling eyes took in every detail of the forlorn figure between them. She lied swiftly, amazing herself—

"As a matter of fact—I believe Louise was not in the room at the time. It was my fault: I should have seen that she was told. I'm so sorry."

Louise gave a little gasp of relief-more audible than she realised.

Clare roused at it. She disliked a check. She disliked also the obvious sympathy between the child and the girl.

"No, it was my fault. I should have gone myself. It's always wiser. It saves trouble in the long run. Never mind, Louise. You couldn't help it. Are you sure of your words?"

Louise, infinitely relieved, was quite sure of her words.

"Very well. Shut the door after you-oh, Louise!"

Louise turned in the doorway.

"Yes, Miss Hartill."

"I may as well explain to you now. I am re-arranging the classes."

Louise questioned her mutely.

"You will be in the Upper Fourth next term."

Louise stood petrified. She had never thought of this.

"You are moving me down? I am third still."

"We think-Miss Marsham agrees with me-that the work in the Fifth is too much for you. It is not your fault."

"Miss Hartill, I have tried—I am trying."

Clare smiled quite pleasantly.

"I am quite sure of it. I tell you that I'm not blaming you. I blame myself. If I expected more of you than you could manage-no one but myself is to blame. I am sure you will do well in the Fourth."

Louise broke out passionately—

"It is because of the examination."

Clare held out her crown at arm's length, and eyed it between criticism and approval as she answered Louise.

"I think," said Clare smoothly, "we had better not discuss the examination."

Louise stood in the doorway, her mouth quivering.

Alwynne could stand the scene no longer. She jerked herself upright, and, going to the child, slipped her arm about her and pushed her gently from the room.

Clare was still admiring her crown, as Alwynne shut the door again. Alwynne must try it on. It would suit Alwynne.

Alwynne peeped at herself in the little mirror, but her thoughts were with Louise on the other side of the door.

"Clare," said Alwynne uneasily, "you hurt that child."

Clare looked at her oddly.

"Do her good," she said. "Do you think no one has ever hurt me?"

Alwynne was silent. At times her goddess puzzled her.

CHAPTER XXII

To the schoolgirls the dress rehearsal was, if possible, more of an ordeal than the performances themselves. The head mistress attended in state with the entire staff and such of the girls as were not themselves acting. Stray relatives, unable to be present at the play proper, dotted the more distant benches, or were bestowed in the overhanging galleries, while the servants, from portly matron to jobbing gardener, clustered at the back of the hall.

The platform at the upper end had been built out to form a stage, and when, late in the afternoon, the final signal had been given and the improvised curtains drew audibly apart, Clare had fair reason to plume herself on her stage-management.

The long blinds of the windows had been let down and shut out the sceptical sunshine; and the candle footlights, flickering unprofessionally, mellowed the paintwork and patterned the home-made scenery with re-echoing lights, pools of unaccountable shadow, and shaftlike, wavering, prismatic gleams, flinging over the crude stage-setting a veil of fantastic charm.

The play opened, however, dully enough. The scenes chosen had had inevitably to be compressed, run together, mangled, and Clare had not found it easy work. Faulconbridge, bowdlerised out of all existence, could not tickle his hearers, and King John, not yet broken in to crown and mantle, gave him feeble support. But with the entrance of Constance, Arthur and the French court, actors and audience alike bestirred themselves.

Agatha, her dark eyes flashing, her lank figure softened and rounded by the generous sweep of her geranium-coloured robes, looked an authentic stage queen. Her exuberant movements and theatrical intonation had been skilfully utilised by Clare, who, playing on her eager vanity, had alternately checked and goaded her into a plausible rendering of the part. She was the reverse of nervous; her voice rolled her opening speech without a tremor; her impatient, impetuous delivery (she hardly let her fellow-actors finish their lines) fitted the character and was effective enough.

Yet to Clare, note-book in hand, prepared to pounce, cat-like, on deficiencies, neither she nor her foil dominated the stage, nor the row of schoolgirl princes. Her critical appreciation was for the little figure, wavering uncertainly between the shrieking queens, with scared anxious eyes, that swept the listening circle in faint appeal, quivering like a sensitive plant at each verbal assault, shrinking beneath the hail of blandishments and reproaches. The one speech of the scene, the reproof of Constance, was spoken with un-childlike, weary dignity —

> "Good my mother, peace!
> I would that I were low laid in my grave;
> I am not worth this coil that's made for me."

Yet it was not Arthur that spoke, nor Louise-no frightened boy or overwrought, precocious girl. It was the voice of childhood itself, sexless, aloof; childhood the eternal pilgrim, wandering passive and perplexed, an elf among the giants: childhood, jostled by the uncaring crowd, swayed by gross energies and seared by alien passions.

"She's got it," muttered Clare to Alwynne, reporting progress in the interval; "oh, how she's got it!" She laughed shortly. "So that's her reading. Impudent monkey! But she's got her atmosphere. Uncanny, isn't it? It reminds me-do you remember that performance of hers last autumn with *Childe Roland*? I told you about it. Well, this brings it back, rather. Clever imp. I wonder how much of my coaching in this act she'll condescend to leave in?"

"You gave her a free hand, you know," deprecated Alwynne.

"I did. But it's impudence——"

"Inspiration——"

"Impudence all the same. When the rehearsal is over I must have a little conversation with Miss Denny." She showed her white teeth in a smile.

Alwynne caught her up uneasily —

"Clare-you're not going to scold? It wouldn't be fair. You know you're as pleased as Punch, really."

Clare shot a look at her, but Alwynne's face was innocent and anxious. She shrugged her shoulders.

"Am I? I suppose I am. I don't know. On my word, Alwynne, I don't know! But run along, my deputy. There's an agitated orb rolling in your direction from the join of the curtains."

Alwynne fled.

The opening scene of the second division of the play-as Clare had planned it-showed Arthur a prisoner to John and the old queen. The child's face was changed, his manner strained; his startled eyes darted restlessly from Hubert to the king and back again to Hubert; the pair seemed to fascinate him. Yet he shrank from their touch and from Elinor's embrace, only to check the instinctive movement with pitiful, propitiatory haste, and to submit, his small fists clenched, to their caresses. His eyes never left their faces; you saw the tide of fear rising in his soul. Not till the interview with Hubert, however, was the morbid drift of the conception fully apparent. He hung upon the man, smiling with white lips; he fawned; he babbled; he cajoled; marshalled his poor defences of tears and smiles, frail defiance and wooing surrender, with an awful, childish cunning. He watched the man as a frightened bird watches a cat; turned as he turned, confronting him with every muscle tense. His high whisper premised a voice too weak with terror to shriek. Yet at the entrance of the attendants there came a cry that made Clare shiver where she sat. It was fear incarnate.

Clare fidgeted. It was too bad of Louise....And what had Alwynne been thinking of? A free hand, indeed! Too much of a free hand altogether! The fact that she was listening to a piece of acting, that, in a theatre, would have overwhelmed her with admiration, added to her annoyance. A school performance was not the place for brilliant improprieties. Certainly impropriety-this laborious exposure of a naked emotion was, in such a milieu, essentially improper-Louise must be crazy! And in what unholy school had she learned it all-this baby of thirteen? And what on earth would staff and school say?

She stole a look at her colleagues. Some were interested, she could see, but obviously puzzled. A couple were whispering together. A third had chosen the moment to yawn.

Her contradictory mind instantly despised them for fools that could not appreciate what manner of work they were privileged to watch. She saw her path clear-her attitude outlined for her. She would glorify a glorious effort (it was pleasant that for once justice might walk with expediency) and her sure, instant tribute would, she knew, suffice to quiet the carpers. But, for all that, the performances themselves should be, she promised herself, on less dangerous lines than the dress-rehearsal. She would have a word with Louise: the imp needed a cold douche.... But what an actress it would make later on! Clare sighed enviously.

The scene was nearly over. With the glad cry—"Ah! now you look like Hubert," the enchantment of terror broke. A few more sentences and Arthur was left alone on the stage.

As the door clanged (Alwynne was juggling with hardware in the wings) the child's strained attitude relaxed and the audience unconsciously relaxed with it. He swayed a moment, then collapsed brokenly into a chair. The long pause was an exquisite relief.

But before long the small face puckered into frowns; a back-wash of subsiding fear swept across it. The hands twitched and drummed. You felt that a plan was maturing.

At last, after furtive glances at the door, he rose with an air of decision, and crossed quickly to the alcove of the window. For an instant the curtains hid him, and the audience stared expectantly at an empty stage. When he turned to them again, holding the great draperies apart with little, resolute fists, his face was alight with hope, and, for the first time, wholly youthful. In the soft voice ringing out the last courageous sentences, detailing the plan of the escape, there was a little quiver of excitement, of childish delight in an adventure. He ended; stood a moment smiling; then the heavy folds hid him again as they swept into position.

There was a tense pause.

Suddenly as from a great distance, came a faint wailing cry. Thereon, silence.

225

The curtains wheezed and rattled into place.

Alwynne, hurrying on to the stage to shift scenery for the following act, nearly tripped, as she dismantled the alcove, over a huddle of clothes crouched between backing and wall. She stooped and shook it. A small arm flung up in instant guard.

"Louise? Get up! The act's over. Run out of the way. Stop-help me with this, as you're here."

Obediently the child scrambled to her feet. She gripped an armful of curtain, and trailed across the stage in Alwynne's wake. Till the curtains rose on the final act, she trotted after her meekly, helping where she could.

With King John embarked on his opening speech, Alwynne drew breath again. She ran her eye over the actors, palpitant at their several entrances, saw the prompter still established with book and lantern, and decided that all could go on without her for a moment. She put her hand on Louise's shoulder and drew her into the passage.

"What is it, Louise?"

"Nothing."

"What were you doing just now? Were you scared? Was it stage fright?"

"Oh no." Louise smiled faintly.

"Then what were you doing?"

Louise considered.

"I was dead. I had jumped, you know. I was finding out how it would feel."

"Louise! You gruesome child!"

"I liked it-it was so quiet. I'd forgotten about shifting the scenery. I'm sorry. Does it-did it hurt him, do you think, the falling?"

Alwynne put both her hands on the thin shoulders and shook her gently.

"Louise! Wake up! You're not Prince Arthur now! Gracious me, child-it's only a play. You mustn't take it so seriously."

Louise made no answer; she did not seem to understand.

Alwynne was struck by a new idea. She took the child's face in her hand and turned it to the gaslight.

"Did I see you at lunch, Louise? I don't believe I did. Do you know you're a very naughty child to take advantage of the confusion?"

"Miss Durand, I had to learn. I was forgetting it all. I slipped the last two lines as it was-you know, the 'My uncle's spirit is in these stones' bit. I wasn't hungry."

"And you were very late, too. What did you have for breakfast?"

An agitated face peered round the corner.

"Miss Durand, which side do I come on from? Hubert's nearly off."

"The left." Alwynne hurried to the rescue, dragging Louise after her. She hustled the anxious courier to his entrance, twitched his mantle into position, and saw him safely on the stage. Then she turned to Louise.

"Louise, will you please go to the kitchen and ask Mrs. Random for two cups of tea and some buns-at once. There is some tea made, I know. I'm tired and thirsty-two cups, please. Bring it to me here, and don't run into any one with your hands full. Be quick —I'm dying for some."

Louise darted away on her errand. Poor Daffy did look hot and flustered.... Daffy was such a dear ... every one worried her ... it was a shame.... Wouldn't Daffy have been a pleasant mother? Better than shouting Constance.... What was it she had asked for? A plum, a cherry and a fig? No, that wasn't it. Oh, of course, tea-tea and buns.

Alwynne looked after her, smiling and frowning; she was not in the least thirsty. What a baby it was.... But nothing to eat all day! Mrs. Denny ought to be ashamed of herself.... She, Alwynne, would keep a vigilant eye on her to-morrow, poor little soul.... Had she really lost herself so entirely in the part-or was there a touch of pose? No, that was more Agatha's line.... Agatha was enjoying herself.... She listened amusedly, watching through a crack in the screen, till a far-away chink caught her ear. She went out again into the passage, and met Louise with a laden tray.

Alwynne drank with expressive pantomime and motioned to the other cup.

"Drink it up," she commanded.

"It's a second cup-for you ——" began Louise.

"Be a good child and do as you're told! I must fly in a minute."

The child looked doubtful; but the steaming liquid was tempting and the new-baked, shining cakes. She obeyed. Alwynne watched the faint colour flush her cheeks with a satisfaction that surprised herself.

"Finish it all up—d'you hear? I must go." She hesitated: "Louise-you were very good to-day. I am sure Miss Hartill must have been awfully pleased."

She went back to the stage. She had had the pleasure of bringing a look of relief to Louise's face. Alwynne could never remember that the kindest lie is a lie none the less.

In the part of Arthur the child, unconsciously, had seen embodied her own psychological situation. She had enacted the spirit, if not the letter, of her own state of mind, and in the mock death had experienced something of the sensations, the sense of release, of a real one. Left to herself, she might gradually have dreamed and imagined and acted herself out of her troubles, have drifted back to real life again, cured and sane. But Alwynne, with her suggestion of good cheer, had destroyed the skin of make-believe that was forming healingly upon the child's sore heart. Louise awoke, with a pang of hope, to her real situation.

"I am sure Miss Hartill must have been awfully pleased." ... So pleased that, who knew, she might yet forgive the crime of the examination? If it might be.... "What might be must be," cried the child within her.

There came a crash of clapping; the rehearsal was over at last, and in a few moments flocks of girls, chattering and excited, came trouping past Louise on their way to tea.

She did not follow them. She was suddenly aware of boy's clothes. She must change them.... She could not find Miss Hartill till she was tidy, and she had determined to speak with her.

Miss Durand had said.... She would do as Arthur did to Hubert-she would besiege Miss Hartill, force her to be kind, till she could say, "Oh, now you look Miss Hartill! all this while you were disguised." She shivered at the idea of undergoing once more the emotional experience of the scene-but the vision of Miss Hartill transfigured drew her as a magnet pulls a needle.

She went towards the stairs.

The big music-room at the top of the house had been temporarily converted into a dressing-room, and she thought she would go quickly and change, while it was still quiet and spacious. But as she pushed open the swinging doors that divided staircase from passage, she saw Clare coming down the long corridor. There was no one else in sight. Again wild, unreasoning hopes flooded her. She would seize the opportunity ... she would speak to Miss Hartill there and then.... She would ask her why she was always angry.... Perhaps she would be kind? "I am sure Miss Hartill must have been awfully pleased...." She must have speech with her at once-at once....

She waited, holding open the door, her heart beating violently, her face steeled to composure.

Clare, passing with a nod, found her way barred by a white-faced scrap of humanity, whose courage, obviously and pitifully, was desperation. But Clare could be very blind when she did not choose to see.

"Miss Hartill, may I speak to you?"

"I can't wait, Louise. I'm busy."

"Miss Hartill, was it all right? Were you pleased? I tried furiously. Was it as you wanted it?"

"Oh, you played your own version." Clare caught her up sharply.

"But Miss Durand said-you said I was to."

"I expect it was all right," said Clare lightly. "I'm afraid I was too busy to attend much, even to your efforts, Louise." She smiled crookedly. "And now run along and change."

She pushed against the door, but Louise, beyond all control, caught back the handles.

"Miss Hartill-you shall listen. Are you always going to be angry? What have I done? Will you never be good to me again as you used to be?"

Clare's face grew stern.

"Louise, you are being very silly. Let me pass."

"Because I can't bear it. It's killing me. Couldn't you stop being angry?"

Clare, ignoring her, wrenched open the door. Louise, flung sideways, slipped on the polished floor. She crouched where she fell, and caught at Clare's skirts. She was completely demoralised.

"Miss Hartill! Oh, please-please-if you would only understand. You hurt me so. You hurt me so."

Clare stood looking down at her.

"Once and for all, Louise, I dislike scenes. Let me go, please."

For a moment their eyes strove. And suddenly Louise, relaxing all effort, let her go. Without another look, Clare retraced her steps and entered the Common-room. Louise, still crouching against the wall, watched her till she disappeared. The doors swung and clicked into rigidity.

There was a sudden uproar of voices and laughter and scraping chairs. A distant door had opened.

Louise started to her feet, and sped swiftly up the stairs, flight on flight, of the tall old house, till she reached the top floor and the music-room. It was empty. She flung-to the door, and fumbled with the stiff key. It turned at last, and she leaned back against the lock, shaking and breathless, but with a sense of relief.

She was safe.... Not for long-they would be coming up soon-but long enough for her purpose.

But first she must recover breath. It was foolish to tremble so. It only hindered one ... when there was so little time to lose.

Hurriedly she sorted out her little pile of everyday clothes-some irrelevant instinct insisting on the paramount necessity of changing into them. Mrs. Denny would be annoyed if she spoiled the new costume. She re-dressed hastily and, clasping her belt, crossed to the window.

It was tall and divided into three casements. The centre door was open. A low seat ran round the bay. She climbed upon it and stood upright, peering out.

How high up she was! There was a blue haze on the horizon, above the line of faint hills, that melted in turn into a weald, chequered like the chessboard counties in *Alice*. So there was a world beyond the school! Nearer still, the suburb spread map-like. She craned forward. Directly under her lay the front garden, and a row of white steps that grinned like teeth. It was on them that she would fall-not on the grass....

She imagined the sensation of the impact, and shuddered. But at least they would kill one outright.... One would not die groaning in rhymed couplets, like Arthur....

Clasping the shafts, she hoisted herself upwards, till she stood upon the inner sill. Instantly the fear of falling caught her by the throat. She swayed backwards, gasping and dizzy, steadying herself against the stout curtains.

"I can't do it," whispered Louise hoarsely. "I can't do it."

Slowly the vertigo passed. She fought with her rampant fear, wrenching away her thoughts from the terror of the death she had chosen, to the terror of the life she was leaving. She stood a space, balanced between time and eternity, weighing them.

With an effort she straightened herself, and put a foot on the outer ledge. Again, inevitably, she sickened. Huddled in the safety of the window-seat, stray phrases thrummed in her head: "My bones turn to water" —"There is no strength in me." He knew-that Psalmist man....

She slipped back on to the floor, and walked unsteadily to the littered table. Her hands were so weak that she could hardly lift them to pour out a glass of water.

She leaned against the table and drank thirstily. What a fool she was.... What a weak fool.... An instant's courage-one little second-and peace for ever after.... Wasn't it worth while? Wasn't it? Wasn't it? She turned again to her deliverance.

As she pulled herself on to the seat, she heard a noise of footsteps in the passage without, and the handle of the door was rattled impatiently. In an instant she was on the sill. This was pursuit-Miss Hartill, and all the terrors! There must be no more hesitation. Once more she crouched for the leap, only, with a supreme effort, to swing herself back to safety again.

Her hands were so slippery with sweat that they could barely grip the window-shafts. There was a banging at the door and a sound of voices calling. She swayed in a double agony, as fear strove against fear.

She heard the voice of a prefect—

"Who is it in there? Open the door at once."

They would break open the door....They would find her....They would stop her....Coward that she was-fool and coward....One instant's courage-one little movement!

She stiffened herself anew. Poised on the extreme edge of the outer sill, she pushed her two hands through the belt of her dress, lest they should save her in her own despite. She stood an instant, her eyes closed.

Then she sprang....

CHAPTER XXIII

Clare was enjoying tea and triumph. She had worked hard for both, and was virtuously fatigued. The rocking-chair was comfortable, and the little gym mistress had brought her her favourite cakes. The Common-room, tinkling its tea-cups, buzzed criticism and approval. The rehearsal had been a success.

The talk centred, while opinion divided, on the Constance and the Prince Arthur. The general standpoint seemed to be that Agatha had reached the heights. Her royal robes had been effective; she reminded nearly every one of a favourite actress. Louise was less popular. A curious performance-very clever, of course-only one had not thought of Arthur quite like that! Now the Constance ——

Clare, watching and listening, purred like a sleepy cat. She wondered why Alwynne was absent ... she was missing a lot.... Louise was annoying-she had been excessively irritated with her ten minutes before-and there was the debacle of the scholarship papers-but to class her with Agatha! What fools these women were!

The discussion had become argument, and was growing faintly acrimonious, when a deep voice cut across it.

Miss Hamilton, a visiting music mistress, always had a hearing when she chose to speak. She was a big woman, with a fine massive head and shrewd eyes. She dressed tweedily and carried her hands in her pockets, slouching a little. It was her harmless vanity to have none. Teaching music was her business; her recreations, hockey, and the more law-abiding forms of suffrage agitation. She was a level-headed and convincing speaker, with a triumphant sense of humour that could, and had, carried her successfully through many a fantastic situation. Rumours of her adventures had spread among the staff, if not through the school, and beglamoured her; she could have had a following if she had chosen. But her healthy twelve stone crashed through pedestals, and she established comradeship, as she helped you, laughter-shaken, to pick up the pieces.

A postponed lesson had given her time to attend the rehearsal, and she had afterwards joined the flock of mistresses at tea. Clare, who thought more of her opinion than she chose to own, had eyed her once or twice already, and at the sound of her voice she stopped her lazy rocking.

"But they are not in the same category! Any schoolgirl could have played Constance as What's-her-name played it, given the training she has had." Miss Hamilton nodded pleasantly to the rocking-chair. She appreciated Clare's capacities. "But Arthur ——"

"Well, I thought Agatha was splendid," repeated a junior mistress stubbornly.

"She was. An excellent piece of work! 'But the hands were the hands of Esau.'"

"They always are," said the little gym mistress fervently.

Clare gave her a quick, brilliant smile. She blushed scarlet.

The music mistress laughed; she enjoyed her weekly glimpse of school interdependencies.

"Why did you single out *King John*, Miss Hartill?" she inquired politely.

Clare was demure, but her eyes twinkled.

"The decision lay with Miss Marsham," she murmured.

"Of course. But having a Cinderella on the premises-eh?"

"If you know of a glass slipper ——"

"You fit it on! Exactly! Where did you discover her?"

"Starving-literally starving, in the Lower Third." Clare thawed to the congenial listener. "It was an amazing performance, wasn't it? Of course, there was nothing of the actual Arthur in it ——"

Miss Hamilton nodded.

"That struck me. It was a child in trouble-not a boy. Not a girl either-but, of course, only a girl would be precocious enough to conceive and carry out the idea. If she did, that is!"

"Oh, it was original," Clare disclaimed prettily. "It had little to do with me. I had to let her go her own way."

Miss Hamilton liked her generosity.

"You're wise. It's all very well to trim the household lamps, but a burning bush is best left alone. I don't altogether envy you. Genius must be a disturbing factor in a school."

"You think she has genius?"

"It was more than precocity to-day—or talent. The Constance had talent."

"And was third in the scholarship papers. Louise failed completely. Isn't it inexplicable? What is one to do? Of course, it was disgraceful: she should have been first. I expected it. I coached her myself. I know her possibilities. Frankly, I am deeply disappointed."

Miss Hamilton pulled her chair nearer. She was interested; Clare was not usually so communicative. But their further conversation was interrupted by the opening of the door, and old Miss Marsham appeared on a visit of congratulation, accepting tea and dispensing compliments with equal stateliness.

"An excellent performance! We must felicitate each other-and Miss Hartill. But we are accustomed to great things from Miss Hartill. There can be no uneasiness to-morrow. The child in the green coat, in that scene-ah, you remember? I thought her a trifle indistinct. Perhaps a hint——? Altogether it was excellent. Especially the Constance-most dramatic. If I may criticise-acting is not my department-but the Prince Arthur? Now, were you satisfied? Louise is a dear child, but hardly suitable, eh?"

Clare stiffened.

"I thought her acting remarkable."

"Did you? Now I can't help feeling that Shakespeare never intended it like that. He makes him such a dear little boy. It's so pathetic, you know, where he begs the man not to put out his eyes. So childlike and touching. Like little Lord Fauntleroy. I know I cried when I saw it, years ago. Now this child was not at all appealing."

Clare shrugged her shoulders.

"It is not a pretty scene, Miss Marsham, though the managers conspire to make us think so. A child at the mercy of brutes, knowing its own danger, terrorised into the extreme of cunning, parading its poor little graces with the skill of a mondaine-it's not pretty! And Louise spared us nothing."

Miss Marsham fidgeted.

"If that is your view of the scene, Miss Hartill, I wonder that you consider it fit for a school performance."

Clare hedged.

"My private view doesn't matter, after all. Traditionally it is inadmissible, of course. But if you would like the treatment altered a little, I will speak to Louise. It is only the dress rehearsal, of course."

Miss Marsham looked relieved.

"Perhaps it would be better. A little more childlike, you know. But don't let her think me annoyed, Miss Hartill; I am sure she has worked so hard. Just a hint, you know. I should not like her feelings to be hurt. Poor child, the results were a sad disappointment to her, I'm afraid. You spoke to her about the change of class?"

"Yes."

"I hope she was not distressed?"

Clare remembered the look on Louise's face. She hesitated.

"She will get over it," she said.

The kind old woman looked worried.

"You must not let her feel that she has failed over this, Miss Hartill-on the top of the other trouble. You will be judicious?"

A door slammed in the distance; there was a blurr of voices, a sound of hurrying footsteps.

Clare rose impatiently; she was tired of the subject.

"It will be all right, Miss Marsham. I understand Louise. What in the world is that disgraceful noise?"

But the door was flung open before she could reach it. Alwynne stood in the aperture, panting a little. In her arms lay Louise, her head falling limply, like a dead bird's. Behind them, peering faces showed for a moment, white against the dusk of the passage. Then Alwynne, staggering beneath the dead weight, stumbled forward, and the door swung to with a crash.

The roomful of women stared in horrified silence.

"She's dead," said Alwynne. "I found her on the steps. She fell from a window. One of the children saw it. She's dead."

She swayed forward to the empty rocking-chair, and sat down, the child's body clasped to her breast. She looked like a young mother.

Clare, watching half stupified, saw a thin trickle of blood run out across her bare arm.

It woke her.

"Send for a doctor!" screamed Clare. "Send for a doctor! Will nobody send for a doctor?"

CHAPTER XXIV

The sudden death of Louise Denny had shocked, each in her degree, every member of the staff. The general view was that such a deplorable accident could and should have been impossible. Every one remembered having long ago thought that the old-fashioned windows were unsafe, and having wondered why precautions had never been taken. Every one, the first horror over, canvassed the result of the unavoidable inquest, and speculated whether any one would be censured for carelessness. The younger mistresses were so sure that it was nobody's business to be on duty in the dressing-room at that particular hour that they spent the rest of the hushed, horror-stricken day in telling each other so, proclaiming, a trifle too insistently, their relief that they at least had nothing, however remote, to do with the affair: while inwardly they ransacked their memories to recall if perchance some half-heard order, some forgotten promise of standing substitute or relieving guard could, at the last moment, implicate them.

But the task of quieting and occupying the frightened children, and of clearing away, as far as might be, all traces of the dress rehearsal, was at least distraction. On the heads of the school, real and nominal, the strain was immeasurably greater. It was first truly felt, indeed, many hours later. Old Miss Marsham, in whom the shock had awakened something of her old-time decision of character, had conducted the interview with the decorously grieving parents with sufficient dignity; had overseen the temporary resting-place of the dead child; had communicated with doctors, lawyers and officials. But the spurt of energy had subsided with the necessity for it. She had retired late at night to her own apartments and the ministrations of her efficient maid, a broken old commander, facing tremulously the calamity that had befallen her life-work: foreseeing and exaggerating its effect on the future of the school, planning feverishly her defence from the gossip that must ensue. An accident ...of course, an accident ...a terrible yet unforeseeable accident....That was the point....At all costs it must be shown that it was an accident pure and simple, with never a whisper of negligence against authority or underling.... But she was an old woman....She needed, she supposed bitterly, a shock of this kind to humble her into realising that her day was over....She had been driving with slack reins this many a long year....She had known it and had hoped that no one shared her knowledge. And none had known....So there came this pitiful occurrence to advertise her weakness to the world.... The poor child! Ah, the poor little child! There had been a lack of supervision, no doubt ... some such gross carelessness as she, in her heyday, would never have tolerated....And she was grown too old, too feeble to hold enquiry-to dispense strict justice....She must depend on the lieutenants who had failed her, to hush the matter up-to make the administration of the school appear blameless....They could do that, she did not doubt, and so she must be content....But in the day of her strength she would not have been content....But she was old....It was time for her to abdicate....She must put her affairs in order, name her successor-Clare Hartill or the secretary, she supposed....They knew her ways....There was that bright girl who had faced her to-day with the little child in her arms ...what was her name? Daughter or niece of some old pupil of her own....She could more easily have seen her in her seat than either of her vice-regents....So young and strong and eager....She had been like that once....Now she was a weak old woman, and because of her weakness a little child lay dead in her house....Yes, Martha might put her to bed....Why not? She was very tired.

Henrietta Vigers had also her anxieties. She had so long claimed the position of virtual head that there was no doubt in her own mind that other people would consider her as responsible as if she had been the actual one. She worried incessantly. Should she have had bars put up to those old-fashioned windows? She, who was responsible for all the household arrangements? Ought she not to have foreseen the danger and guarded against it? And there was the matter of the dressing-room mistress....For the school machinery she had made herself even more pointedly responsible....She should have arranged for some one to oversee the children....But the dressing-room had been a temporary one and she had overlooked the necessity....Yet if some one had been in the room the accident could impossibly have happened....She felt that she would be lucky to escape public censure, that loss of prestige in the eyes at least of the head mistress was inevitable.

But the more or less selfish perturbation, as distinct from the emotion of sheer humanity, that was aroused by the death of the little schoolgirl in the two older women, was as nothing to the sensation of sick dismay that it awoke in Clare Hartill. She, too, through the night that followed on the accident, lay awake till sunrise, considering her position. She was stunned by the unexpectedness of the catastrophe; a little grieved for the loss of Louise, but, above all, intensely and quite selfishly frightened. She felt guilty. She remembered, remorselessly enlightened, the afternoon, the expression in Louise's eyes, and not for one instant did she share the general belief in the accidental nature of her death. Her conscience would not allow her the comfort of such self-deception. Later she might lull it to sleep again, but for the moment it was awake, and her master. This same keen-witted conscience of hers, this quintessence of her secret admirations and considered opinions, her epicurean appreciation of what was guileless and beautiful and worthy, co-existing, as it did, with the intellectualised sensuality of her imperious and carnal personality, was no small trial to Clare. Though it could not sway her decisions nor influence her actions by one hair's-breadth, it was at least cynically active, as now, to prick and fret at her peace. It was, indeed, at the root of the whimsical irritability that, for all her charm, made her an impossible housemate.

Essentially, her attitude to life was simple. It was an orange, to be squeezed for her pleasure. It must serve her; but she owed it, therefore, no duty. She found that she achieved a maximum of pleasurable sensations by following the dictates of that mind which is the mouthpiece of body, while indulging, as Lucullus ate turnips, in austere flirtations with that other mind, which is the mouthpiece of spirit. So she served Mammon, or rather, she allowed Mammon to serve her, but she was, on occasions, critically interested in God. And this was her undoing. Could she have been content to be frankly selfish, she might have been happy enough, but her very interest in the kingdom of Heaven had created her conscience, and had laid her open to its attacks. She ignored it, and it made her wretched: she compromised with it, and became a hypocrite.

She resented the death of Louise because it challenged her whole scheme of life. She was furiously angry with the dead child for what she felt to be an indictment of her legitimate amusements. Louise, so meek and ineffectual, had yet been able to steal a march on her, had stabbed in the back and run away, beyond reach of Clare's retaliation.... Louise had fooled her.... She, Clare, proud of her insight, her complete knowledge of character, her alert intuition, had yet had no inkling of what was passing in that childish mind.... If she had guessed, however vaguely, she could have taken measures, have scourged the mere suggestion of such monstrous rebellion out of that subject soul.... But Louise, secure in her insignificance, had tricked her, planned her sure escape.... But how unhappy she must have been!...

In a sudden revulsion of feeling Clare grew faint with pity, as she tried to realise the child's state of mind during the past months. Her thoughts went back to the Christmas Day they had spent together. She had been happy enough then.... Half sincerely she tried to puzzle out the change in Louise, the gradual deterioration that had led to the tragedy. Had she been to blame? Louise had grown tiresome, and she had snubbed her.... There was the thing in a nutshell.... If she was to be so tender of the feelings of all the silly girls who sentimentalised over her, where would it end, at all?

Poor little Louise.... She had been really fond of her at the beginning.... She had thought for a time that she might even supplant Alwynne.... But Louise had disappointed her.... She had let her work go to the dogs.... All her originality and charm fizzled out.... She had ceased to be interesting.... And she, Clare, had naturally been bored and had shown it.... Why couldn't the child take it quietly? If Louise had only known-and had conducted herself with tact-Clare had been preparing to be nicer to her again.... She had been deeply interested in her performance of the morning, had recognised its uncanny sincerity-had thought, with a distinct quickening of interest, that Louise was recovering herself at last, and that it might be as well to take her in hand again.... Oh, she had been full of benevolent impulses! But then Louise had been tiresome again...had stopped her and made a scene....She hated scenes...at least (with a laugh) scenes that were not of her own devising....

She supposed she should have recognised that the child was overwrought-terribly overwrought by the emotions aroused by such an interpretation as she had insisted upon giving....She ought never to have been allowed to play it like that....That was Alwynne's doing....Alwynne had persuaded Clare to leave Louise to her own devices....Alwynne was so headstrong....She hoped that Alwynne would never need to realise how much she was to blame....

Here she became aware that her conscience was convulsed with cynical laughter. She flushed in the darkness, her opportune sense of injury increasing.

Alwynne might well be distressed....If any awkward questions should be asked, Alwynne might find herself uncomfortably placed....People would wonder that she had not noticed how unbalanced Louise was growing....Every one knew how intimate, how ridiculously intimate, she and Louise had become....Alwynne had fussed over her like an old hen...had even on occasion questioned her, Clare's, method with her....She must have known what was in Louise's mind.... Yet Clare had no doubt that people would be only too ready to accuse her, rather than Alwynne, of criminal obtuseness....Henrietta Vigers, for instance....Henrietta would be less prejudiced than many others, though....She was no friend to Alwynne....It might do no harm to talk over the matter with Henrietta Vigers....A word or two would be enough....

Of course it would be considered an accident....But if by any chance, vague suspicions were rife, a judicious talk with Henrietta would have served, at least, to prevent Clare from being made their object....She had her enemies, she knew....Alwynne, with her easy popularity, had none save Henrietta....A few waspish remarks from Henrietta would not hurt Alwynne....Clare would protect Alwynne from serious annoyance, of course....If the mistresses-the school-oh, if the whole world turned against Alwynne, Clare would make it up to her....What did Alwynne want, after all, with any one but Clare? The less the world gave Alwynne, the more she would be content with Clare, the more entirely she would be Clare's own property....It was a good idea....She would certainly speak to Miss Vigers....

She was outlining that conversation till she fell asleep.

CHAPTER XXV

On the following afternoon Clare and Henrietta were sitting together in the mistresses' room. The afternoon classes were over and the day pupils and mistresses had gone home. The boarders were at supper and the staff with them.

But Henrietta had taken no notice of the supper-hour. She had more work in hand than she could well compass-letters to write and answer, of explanation, and enquiry, and condolence. She could have found time for her supper, nevertheless, but when she was overworked she liked her world to be aware of it. Clare, contrary to her custom, had stayed late. She was waiting for Alwynne. She had offered, perfunctorily enough, her assistance, but Henrietta had refused all help from her. Yet Henrietta had turned over the bulk of her formal correspondence to Alwynne, who sat, hard at work, in the adjacent office. She disliked Alwynne, but accepted the very necessary help from her more easily than from Clare Hartill. Yet she was softened by Clare's offer, which she had refused, and not at all grateful for Alwynne's help, though she accepted it.

She wrote busily for more than an hour, and Clare, silent, scarcely moving, sat watching her. Henrietta had, for once, no feeling of impatience at her idle supervision. She did not experience her usual sensation of intimidated antagonism. It was as if the stress of the last twenty-four hours had temporarily atoned the two incongruous characters. Neither by look or gesture had Clare flouted any suggestion or arrangement of Henrietta's —indeed, her presence had been quite distinctly a support. Henrietta had appealed more than once, and even confidently, to her. Henrietta had thought, with a touch of compunction, how strangely trouble brought out the best in people. Miss Hartill had been very proud of Louise Denny; evidently felt her death. The shock was causing her to unbend. Not, as one would have expected, to Alwynne Durand-she hoped, by the way, that Miss Durand was addressing those envelopes legibly: she did so dislike an explosive handwriting-no, Miss Hartill was turning, very properly, to herself in the emergency.... She was pleased.... There should be free-masonry between the heads of the school.... And Clare Hartill, for all her lazy indifference, was influential and enormously capable.... Henrietta wondered if it would be safe to consult her.... She might, without acknowledging a definite uneasiness, find out cautiously whether it had occurred to Miss Hartill that she, Henrietta, might be considered to have been negligent.

She glanced across at her inscrutable colleague. Clare was staring thoughtfully at her. Her lips were puffed a little, as if in doubt.

Their eyes met for a moment in a glance that was almost one of understanding.

Henrietta hesitated, for the first time not at all disconcerted by Clare's direct gaze. But the sparkle of gay malice that attracted half her world, and disconcerted the other half, was gone from Clare's eyes. Their expression, for the time being, was calm, possibly friendly; at any rate, irreproachably matter-of-fact.

Henrietta flung down her pen with a sigh of fatigue, and bent and unbent her cramped fingers. But it was not fatigue that made her stop work. She wanted to talk to Clare Hartill, and had a queer conviction that Clare Hartill wanted to talk to her.

"Finished?" Clare spoke from the shadow of her deep chair. Her back was to the light, but Henrietta faced the west window. The evening sun laid bare her face for Clare's inspection. Not a flicker of expression could escape her, if she chose to look.

"More or less. I want half-an-hour's rest."

"I don't wonder. You've had everything to see to." Clare's voice was delicately sympathetic. Henrietta unbent.

"A secretary's work isn't showy, Miss Hartill, but it's necessary: and any happening that's out of the common doubles it. The correspondence over this unhappy affair alone — —"

"I know. Of course, at Miss Marsham's age — —"

"It all falls on me! People don't realise that. The extra work is enormous. Miss Marsham depends on me so entirely, of course."

"Yes, yes," murmured Clare appreciatively.

Henrietta played with her papers.

"I feel the responsibility very strongly," she said abruptly; but her tone was confidential.

Clare nodded.

"Yet, of course-as far as nominal responsibility goes—I am not the head of the school. I cannot be held responsible-any oversight——"

Clare nodded.

"Oh, Miss Vigers-you merely carry out instructions, like the rest of us"—she hesitated imperceptibly—"officially," she added slowly.

Henrietta looked relieved.

"I am so glad you see what I mean."

"Oh, I do, entirely," Clare assured her grimly.

"I'm not heartless," said Henrietta suddenly, flushing. Her tone justified herself against unuttered criticism. "And the poor child's death was as much a shock to me as to any one. But I was not fond of her-as you were, for instance——"

Clare's pose never altered.

"I was very proud of her," she said gently. "I thought her an exceptional child. But, as Miss Durand said to me only a few days ago—I didn't really know her: not, at least, as she did. Alwynne, I know, thinks we have lost a genius. But you're right-it was a shock to me—a terrible shock."

"It was that to everybody, naturally. But in a way it's curious," said Henrietta meditatively, "how much we all feel it-how oppressively, at least: for I don't think any one was very fond of Louise."

"Oh, Miss Durand was deeply attached to her," Clare protested, her beautiful voice low with emotion.

"Yes, of course! Oh, I've noticed that." Clare's unusual accessibility made Henrietta anxious to agree. Also, though she had noticed nothing unusual, she did not wish to appear lacking in penetration. She recalled Alwynne's haggard face; recollected how much she had had to do with the child; and decided that Clare was probably right.

"But except for her," she went on, "and your interest in her——"

"I've never had such a pupil," said Clare calmly. "Industrious-original-oh, I shall miss her, I know. But you're right-she was not popular——"

"Yet everybody feels her death-among ourselves, I mean-to an extraordinary degree. After all-an accident is only an accident, however dreadful! But there's a sort of oppression on us—a kind of fear. Do you know what I mean? I think we all feel it. It draws us together in a curious way."

"'The Tie of Common Funk,'" rapped out Clare, forgetting her rôle.

Henrietta stiffened.

"I don't think it is an occasion for slang," she said. "The child's not buried yet."

Clare bit back a flippancy.

"I thought you would realise," continued Henrietta severely, "that the situation is trying for us all——"

"Of course I do." Clare hastened to soothe her. "But seriously, Miss Vigers, I do not think you need be anxious. The inquest-oh, a painful ordeal, if you like. But you, at least, can have no reason to reproach yourself."

Henrietta relaxed again.

"No! As I say, I'm not the head of the school. I'm not responsible for regulations-only for carrying them out. And accidents will happen."

"I only hope," said Clare, as if to herself, "that it will be considered an accident——"

Henrietta stared.

"But Miss Hartill! Of course it was an accident!"

Clare looked at her wistfully.

"Yes! It was, wasn't it? Yes, of course! It must have been an accident." Her tone dismissed the matter.

But Henrietta was on the alert. Her own anxieties had been skilfully allayed. Her mind was recovering poise. She nosed a mystery and her reviving sense of importance insisted on sharing the knowledge of it.

"Miss Hartill-you are not suggesting ——?" Her tone invited confidence.

Clare gave a little natural laugh.

"Oh, my dear woman —I'm all nerves just at present. Of course I'm not suggesting anything. One gets absurd ideas into one's head. I'm only too relieved to hear you laugh at me. Your common sense is always a real support to me, you know. I've grown to depend on it all these years. I'm afraid I've got into the way of taking it too much for granted."

She gave a charming little deprecatory shrug.

Henrietta flushed: she felt herself warming unaccountably to Clare Hartill. She wondered why she had never before taken the trouble to draw her out.... She was evidently a woman of heart as well as brain. She felt vaguely that she must constantly have been unjust to her. But these sensations only whetted her eager curiosity. She pulled in her chair to the hearth.

"But what ideas, Miss Hartill? If you will tell me —I should be the last person to laugh. I have far too much respect for —I wish you would tell me what is worrying you. Does anything make you think it was not an accident?"

Clare was the picture of reluctance.

"Impressions-vague ideas-is it fair to formulate them? Even if Louise were unbalanced-but, of course, I did not see much of her out of class. I confess I thought her manner strained at times. But I teach. I have nothing to do with the supervision of the younger children."

"That is Miss Durand's business," remarked Henrietta crisply.

"Oh, but if she had noticed anything——" began Clare. Then, lamely, "Obviously she didn't——"

"It was her business to. She should have reported to me. Why, she coached Louise, didn't she?"

"Of course, if Louise had really overworked-badly ——" reflected Clare, with the distressed air of one on whom unwelcome ideas are dawning. "One hears of cases-in Germany-but it's impossible!"

Henrietta looked genuinely shocked, but none the less she was excited.

"She failed in that exam. ——" she adduced.

"Yes! Miss Durand coached her for that, you know. Poor Miss Durand! How she slaved over her! She was dreadfully disappointed," said Clare indulgently.

"Of course, she let her overdo herself!" cried Henrietta triumphantly. "But you coached her too-didn't you notice either?"

"I coach the whole class. You know how busy I am. I'm afraid I left Louise a good deal to Alwynne," said Clare regretfully.

"But she's supposed to be grown up-an asset to the school, according to Miss Marsham," said Henrietta tartly. "But, I must say, if she couldn't see that the child was doing too much, she's not fit to teach ——"

"Oh, my dear!" cried Clare, distressed. "You mustn't say such things. You've no idea how conscientious Alwynne is. She may have worked Louise too hard-but with the best intentions. She would be heartbroken if you suggested it."

"Oh, you are always very lenient to Miss Durand," began Henrietta, with a touch of jealousy.

"Ah! She's so young! So full of the zeal of youth. Besides, I'm very fond of her." Clare's smile took Henrietta into her confidence-confessed to an amiable weakness.

Henrietta brooded.

"Oh, Miss Hartill, you talk of my common sense. I wish —I wish you could see Miss Durand from my point of view for a moment." She eyed Clare, attentive and plastic in her shadows, and took courage. "This-appalling-probability ——"

"Possibility— —" Clare deprecated.

"Oh, but it seems terribly probable to me-only carries on my idea of Miss Durand. She is so ignorant-so inexperienced-so undisciplined-she cannot possibly have a good influence on young children— —"

"She is my friend!" Clare reminded her, with gentle dignity.

"And if your suspicions are correct-if Louise's death were not accidental-if it had anything to do with her state of mind-if it were the effect of overwork—I consider—I must consider Miss Durand in some measure responsible. I feel that Miss Marsham should be told."

Clare shook her head. Her solemn, candid eyes abashed Henrietta.

"Miss Vigers-we are speaking in confidence. I should never forgive myself if anything I've said to you were repeated."

"Of course, of course!" Henrietta appeased her hastily. "But I've had my own suspicions-oh, for a long time, I assure you. I've not been blind. And I might feel it my duty-on my account, you understand-after all Miss Marsham depends on me implicitly-to speak to her-for the sake of the school— —"

Clare considered.

"That, of course—I can't prevent. But Miss Vigers-forgive me-but-don't let your sense of responsibility make you unfair. And for heaven's sake, don't let my vague uneasiness-it's really nothing more-affect your judgment. We may both be utterly mistaken. I am sure the result of the inquest will prove us mistaken after all-it will be found to have been an accident."

Henrietta closed her lips obstinately.

Clare rose in her place.

"It was an accident!" she cried passionately. "In my heart I am sure. I wish I'd never said anything to you. I'd no right to be suspicious. Think of what Miss Durand's feelings would be if she realised— —" She flung out her hands appealingly. "Oh, we're two overwrought women, aren't we? Sitting in the dusk and scaring ourselves with bogies. It was an accident, Miss Vigers—a tragic accident! Make yourself think so! Make me think so too!" Her beautiful eyes implored comfort.

Henrietta, quite touched, patted her awkwardly on the arm. She enjoyed her transient superiority.

"Of course, of course, we'll try to think so. Now you must go home. You are quite overwrought. It will be a trying day for us all to-morrow. I shall go to bed early too. Won't you go home now?"

Clare nodded, mute, grateful. She went to her peg, and took down her hat and jacket.

"Have you finished with Miss Durand? She was going home with me."

"Oh! Miss Durand!" Henrietta's tone grew crisper. "Yes, of course. I'll see if she has done. I'll send her to you. And you mustn't let yourself worry, Miss Hartill. Leave it all to me. These things are more my province. Good-night!" said Henrietta cordially.

She left the room.

Clare, pinning on her hat, stared critically at herself in the inadequate mirror.

"I think," she said confidentially, "we did that rather well."

She smiled. The cynical lips smiled back at her.

"You beast!" cried Clare, with sudden passion. "You beast! You beast!"

She was still staring at herself when Alwynne came for her.

CHAPTER XXVI

Clare Hartill's precautions proved to be unnecessary as the alarms of her colleagues. The inquest was a formal and quickly concluded affair, and the only corollary to the verdict of accidental death was an expression of sympathy with all concerned.

Whereon, there being no further cause for the detaining of Louise Denny above ground, she was elegantly and expeditiously buried.

The whole school attended the funeral. The flowers required a second carriage, and for the first time in his life, Mr. Denny was genuinely proud of his daughter. He did not believe that his own death could have extracted more lavish tributes from the purses of his acquaintances.

Clare Hartill, writing a card for her wreath of incredible orchids, did not regret her extravagance. After all–one must keep up one's position.... There would certainly not be such another wreath in the churchyard.... How Louise would have exclaimed over it! Poor child.... It was all one could do for her now. Clare hesitated, pen arrested —"With deepest sympathy." It was not necessary to write anything more.... Her name was printed already.... But Louise would have liked a message.... After all, she had been very proud of Louise....

She reversed the card, and wrote, almost illegibly, in a corner, "Louise-with love. C. H." She paused, lips pursed. Sentimental, perhaps? Possibly.... But let it go....

Hastily she impaled her card on its attendant pin, and thrust it, print upward, among the flowers. The message was for Louise; no one else need see it.

Alwynne, too, sent flowers. But as usual she had spent all but a fraction of her salary. Seven and sixpence does not make a show, even if the garland be home-made. The shabby wreath was forgotten among the crowd of hot-house blooms. It lay in a corner till the day after the funeral. Then the housemaid threw it away.

So Louise had no message from Alwynne.

By the end of a fortnight Louise was barely a memory in the school. A month had obliterated her entirely.

Yet her short career and sudden death had its influence on school and individual alike. Miss Marsham had had her lesson; she began to make her preliminary preparations for giving up her head mistress-ship, and selling her interest in the school; though it was the following spring before she began to negotiate definitely with Clare, on whom her choice had finally fallen. She would not be hurried; she would not appear anxious to settle her affairs; but she had determined, between regret and relief, that the next summer should be the last of her reign.

Henrietta, though her anxieties were abated by the turn affairs had taken, was still doubtful whether Miss Marsham were as blindly reliant upon her as usual. But, though feeling her position still somewhat insecure, her spirits had risen, and her natural love of interference had risen with them. She could not forget her conversation with Miss Hartill: an amazing conversation —a conversation teeming with suggestions and possibilities.... Of course, Miss Hartill had had no idea, poor distracted woman, of how skilfully Henrietta had drawn her out.... Henrietta felt pleased with herself. Without once referring to Miss Hartill, she could follow out her own plans as far as Miss Durand was concerned.... Later, Miss Hartill might remember that apparently innocent conversation and realise that Henrietta had stolen a march on her.... Yet, though she might be loyally angry, for her friend's sake, she could not do anything to cross Henrietta's arrangements ... could not wish to do anything, because essentially, if reluctantly, she had approved them, had recognised that it was time to curtail Miss Durand's activities....

Henrietta felt virtuous. Miss Durand had brought it on herself.... She wished her no harm.... But it was right that Marsham should realise how far she was from an ideal school-mistress.... She had been engaged as scholastic maid-of-all-work.... Yet in a few terms she had become second only to Miss Hartill herself.... It was not fit.... Let her go back to her beginnings.... She, Henrietta, had only to open Miss Marsham's eyes.... But to that end there must be evidence....

For the rest of the term, patient and peering as a rag-picker, she went about collecting her evidence.

Clare did not give another thought to her conversation with the gimlet-eyed secretary. It had served its purpose-had been a barrier between herself and the possibility of attack-had given her a feeling of security. She perceived, nevertheless, that her transient affability had made Henrietta violently her adherent. Clare was resigned to knowing that the change of face would be temporary-she could not allow a parading of herself as an intimate, and thither, she shrewdly suspected, would Henrietta's amenities lead. But she found it amusing to be gracious, as long as no more was expected of her. She did not like Henrietta one whit the better; felt herself, indeed, degraded by the expedient to which she had resorted, and fiercely despised her tool. Henrietta should be given rope, might attack Alwynne unhindered, nevertheless she should hang herself at the last.... Clare would ensure that.... Once-Henrietta had called her a cat.... Oh, she had heard of it! Well-for the present, she would purr to Henrietta, blank-eyed, claws sheathed.... Let her serve her turn.

But Clare, beneath her schemes and jealousies, was, nevertheless, deeply and sincerely unhappy. The removal of the entirely selfish and cold-blooded panic that had been upon her since Louise's death, left her free to entertain deeper and sincerer feelings. She thought of Louise incessantly, with a growing feeling of regret and responsibility. She hated responsibility, though she loved authority-she had always shut her eyes to the effects of her caprices. But the more she thought of Louise, the more insistent grew her qualms. That the child was dead of its own will, she never doubted; but she fought desperately against the suggestion that her own conduct could have affected its state of mind, was ready to accept the most preposterous premise, whose ensuing chain of reasoning could acquit her. But nobody having accused her, no ingenuity of herself or another, could, for the time being, acquit her. She was merely a prey to her own intangible uneasinesses. Yet it needed but a key to set the whole machinery of her conscience in motion against her. The key was to be found.

The term was drawing to an end, and Alwynne, rounding off her special classes and generally making up arrears, was proportionately busy. She still spent her week-ends with Clare, but she brought her work along with her. She had her corner of the table, and Clare her desk, and the two would work till the small hours.

But by the last Sunday evening, Clare's piles of reports and examination papers had disappeared, and she was free to lie at ease on her sofa, and to laugh at Alwynne, still immersed in exercise books, and tantalise her with airy plans for the long, delicious holidays. It had been, in spite of the season, a day of rain and cold winds. The skies had cleared at the sunset, with its red promise of fine weather once more, but the remnant of a fire still smouldered on the hearth. Alwynne was flushed with the interest of her work, but ever and again Clare shivered, and pulled the quilted sofa-wrap more closely about her. She wished that Alwynne would be quick.... Surely Alwynne could finish off her work some other time.... It wouldn't hurt her to get up early for once, for that matter.... She was bored.... She was dull.... She wanted amusement.... She wanted Alwynne, and attention, and affection, and a little butterfly kiss or two.... Alwynne ought to be awake to the fact that she was wanted....

She watched her, between fretfulness and affection, æsthetically appreciative of the big young body in the lavender frock, and the crown of shining hair, pleased with her property, intensely impatient of its interest in anything but herself.

"Alwynne — —?" There was a hint of neglect in her voice.

Alwynne beamed, but her eyes were abstracted.

"Only another half-hour, Clare. I must just finish these. You don't mind, do you?"

"I? Mind?" Clare laughed elaborately. She picked up a book, and there was silence once more. Leaves fluttered and a pen scraped. The light began to fade.

Suddenly Alwynne gave a smothered exclamation. Clare looked up and pulled herself upright, angry enough.

"Alwynne! Your carelessness-you've dropped your wet pen on my carpet. It's too bad."

Alwynne groped hastily beneath the table. But even the prolonged stooping had not brought back the colour to her cheek, as she replaced her pen on the stand.

"I'm sorry. I was startled. It hasn't marked it. Clare-just listen to this."

"What have you got hold of?" demanded Clare irritably. She disliked spots and spillings and mess, as Alwynne might know.

"It's Louise's composition book. I always wondered where it had got to, when I cleared out her desk. It must have lain about and got collected in with the rest, yesterday."

"Well?" said Clare, with a show of indifference.

"Here's that essay on King John and his times. Do you remember? You gave it to them to do just before the play. It's not corrected. Not finished." She hesitated. "Clare! It's rather queer."

"Is it any good?" said Clare meditatively.

"What for?"

"The School Magazine. We're short of copy. The child wrote well. But I suppose it wouldn't do to use it-though I don't see why not."

Suddenly Alwynne began to read aloud.

> *"Another way by which King John got money from the Jews was by threatening them with torture. He was all-powerful. He could draw their teeth, tooth by tooth, twist their thumbs, or leave them to rot in dark, silent prisons. They could not do anything against him. If he could not force them to yield up their treasure he would have them burned, or cause them to be pressed to death. This is a horrible torture. I read about a woman who was killed in this way in the 'Hundred Best Books'; and there was a man in Good King Charles's days whom they killed like this. It is the worst death of any. They tie you down, so that you cannot move at all, and there is a slab of stone that hangs a little above you. This sinks very slowly, so that all the first day you just lie and stare at it and wonder if it really moves. People come and give you food and laugh at you. You are scarcely afraid, because it moves so little and you think nobody could be really so cruel and hurt you so horribly, and that you will be saved somehow. But all the time the stone is sinking-sinking-and the day goes by and the night comes and they leave you alone. And perhaps you go to sleep at last. You are horribly tired, because of the weeks of fear that are behind you. Perhaps you dream. You dream you are free and people love you, and you have done nothing wrong and you are frightfully happy, and the one you love most kisses your forehead. But then the kiss grows so cold that you shrink away, only you cannot, and it presses you harder and harder, and you wake up and it is the stone. It is the sinking stone that is pressing you, pressing you, pressing you to death-and you cannot move. And you shriek and shriek for help within your gagged mouth, and no one comes, and always the stone is pressing you, pressing you, pressing you — —"*

Clare caught the exercise-book from Alwynne's hand and thrust it into the heart of the half-dead fire. It lay unlighted, charring and smouldering. The unformed handwriting stood out very clearly. Clare caught at a matchbox, and tore it open; the matches showered out over her hand on to the rug and grate. She struck one after another, breaking them before they could light. Silently Alwynne took the box from her shaking fingers, lit a match and held it to the twisting papers. A thin little flame flickered up, overran them eagerly, wavered a second, and died with a faint whistling sigh.

"Do you hear that? Did you see that?" Clare knelt upright on the hearth. She held up her forefinger. "Listen! Like a voice! Like a child's voice! A child sighing! Light the candles-light all the candles! I want light everywhere. No room for any shadow."

But as Alwynne moved obediently, she caught at her hand.

"Alwynne! Stay with me! Don't go into another room. Alwynne, I'm frightened of my thoughts."

Alwynne put her hand shyly on her shoulders, talking at random.

"Clare, dear, do get up. Come on to the sofa. You mustn't kneel there. You'll strain yourself. I always get tired kneeling in church. It makes one's heart ache."

Clare would not move.

"Don't you think my heart aches?" she said. "Don't you think it aches all day? You're young-you're cold-you can sit there reading, reading-with a ghost at your shoulder——"

An undecipherable expression flashed across Alwynne's face. It came but to go-and Clare, absorbed in her own passion, saw nothing.

"It's Louise!" she cried, between sincerity and histrionics. "Calling to some one. Calling from her grave. They call it an accident, like fools. Oh, can't you hear? She died because she was forced. She's complaining-plaining-plaining——I tell you it's nothing to do with me. It wasn't my fault!"

She flung her arms about Alwynne's waist and clutched her convulsively. She was sincere enough at last.

"Alwynne! Alwynne! Say it was not my fault."

Alwynne sank to her knees beside her and held her close. They clung to each other like scared children. But Clare's abandonment awoke all Alwynne's protective instincts. She crushed down whatever emotions had hollowed her eyes and whitened her cheeks in the last long weeks, and addressed herself to quieting Clare. Clare, stepped off her pedestal, unpoised, clinging helplessly, was a new experience. In the face of it she felt herself childish, inadequate. But Clare was in trouble and needed her. The very marvel of it steadied. All her love for Clare rose within her, overflowed her, like a warm tide.

By sheer strength she pulled Clare into a chair and dropped on to the floor beside her, face upturned, talking fast and eagerly.

"You're not to talk like that. Of course it's not your fault. If anything could be your fault. Clare, darling, don't look like that. You must lean back and rest. You're just tired, you know. We've talked of it so often. You know it was an accident. Why can't you believe it, if every one else does?"

"Do you?" said Clare intently.

Alwynne's eyes met hers defiantly.

"I do. Of course I do. It's wicked to torment yourself. But if I didn't—if the poor baby was overtired and overworked-is it your fault? You only saw her in class at the last. You couldn't help it if the exams, and the play were suddenly too much-if something snapped——"

"You see, you do think so," said Clare bitterly. "I've always known you did. Well-think what you like-what do I care?" She put up her clenched hands and rubbed and kneaded at her dry aching eyes.

Alwynne watched her, desperately. Here was her lady wanting comfort, and she had found none. She wracked her brains as the sluggish minutes passed.

Clare's hands dropped at last. She met Alwynne's anxious gaze and laughed harshly.

"Well? The verdict? That I was a brute to Louise, I suppose?"

Alwynne looked at her wistfully.

"Clare, I do love you so."

Clare stiffened.

"Then I warn you-stop! I'm not good for you. I hurt people who love me. You always pestered me about hurting Louise. You needn't protest. You always did. And now you lay her death at my door. I see it in your face. Can't I read you like a book? Can't I? Can't I?" Her face was distorted by the conflict within her.

Alwynne's simplicity was convinced. Here, she felt, was tragedy. Awe and pity tore at her sense of reality. Love loosened her tongue. Her words rushed forth in a torrent of incoherent argument. She was so eager that her fallacies had power to convince herself, much more Clare.

"Clare, I won't have it. You don't know what you say. What is this mad idea you've got? What would poor Louise think if she heard? Why, she adored you. And you were kind-always kind-only when you thought it better for her, you were strict. It's folly to torment yourself. If you do-what about me?"

"You?" Clare's eyes glinted suddenly.

"Me! If you are to blame, how much more I? Oh, don't you see?" Alwynne's face grew rapt. Here was inspiration; her path grew suddenly clear. "Clare, don't you see? If she did —" she paused imperceptibly —"I ought to have seen what was coming. I knew her so much better than you."

Clare repressed a denial.

"Oh, darling-you mustn't worry. It's my responsibility. Try and think-at the play, for instance. Did you think her manner strained? No, of course you didn't. But I did. I thought at the time it had all been too much for her. I did notice —I did! I thought-that child will get brain-fever if we're not careful — —I meant to speak to Elsbeth. I meant to speak to you. Oh, I'd noticed before. Only I was busy, and lazy, and put it off. She was unhappy at failing —I knew. I wanted to tell you that I know how much it meant to her-and I didn't. I was afraid — —" She broke off abruptly; her eloquence ended as suddenly as it had begun.

But she had succeeded in her desire. Clare was recovering poise; would soon have herself all the more rigidly in control for her recent collapse. She stiffened as she spoke.

"Afraid of whom?"

"I mean I was afraid all along of what might happen," Alwynne concluded lamely. "You see, it was my fault?" There was an odd half-query in her voice.

"If you noticed so much and never tried to warn me, you are certainly to blame." Clare's voice was full of reluctant conviction. "I can't remember that you tried very hard."

"Oh, Clare!" began Alwynne. Their eyes met. Clare's face was hard and impassive-all trace of emotion gone. Her eyes challenged. Alwynne's lids dropped as she finished her sentence. "That is-no, I didn't try very hard."

"And why not?"

Inconceivably an answer suggested itself to Alwynne, an unutterable iconoclasm. Her mind edged away from it horrified and in an instant it was not. But it had been.

"I don't know," she stammered.

"You realised the responsibility you incurred?" Clare went on.

"I didn't. No, never!" Alwynne supplicated her.

"You do now?"

"Oh, yes," she said despairingly. She rejoiced that Clare could believe and be comforted, but it hurt her that she believed so easily. It alarmed her, too, made her, knowing her own motives, yet doubt herself. She felt trapped.

"I'm sorry you told me," said Clare abruptly.

They sat a moment in silence. A ray from the dying sun illuminated their faces. In Alwynne an innocent air of triumph fought with distress, and a growing uneasiness. Clare was expressionless.

Clare put up her hand to shelter herself, and her face was scarcely visible as she went on. She spoke softly.

"My dear, I can't say I'm not relieved. I feel exonerated-completely. Yet I wish you hadn't told me. I'd have rather thought it my fault than known it — —"

"Mine," said Alwynne huskily.

Clare bent towards her, tender, gracious, yet subtly aloof; confessor, not friend.

"Oh, Alwynne! Why will you always be so sure of yourself? Why not have come to me for advice as you used to? What are we elder folk for? I love your impetuosity-your self-reliance — and I believe, I shall always believe, that you wanted to spare me trouble and worry. I know you. But you're not all enough, Alwynne, to decide everything for yourself. You won't believe it, I suppose-oh, I was just the same. But doesn't all this dreadful business show you? A few words-and Louise might have been with us now. Of course you acted for the best, but — — There, my dear, there, there — —" for her beautiful, pitiful voice had played too exquisitely on Alwynne's nerves, and the girl was sobbing helplessly.

And Clare was very kind to Alwynne, and let her cry in peace. And when she was tired of watching her, she braced her with deft praises of courage and self-control. Self-control appealed very strongly to Clare, Alwynne knew. While she dried her eyes, Clare whispered to her that the past was past and that one couldn't repair one's mistakes by dwelling on them. Let devotion to the living blot out a debt to the dead. She must try and forget. Clare would help her. Clare would try to forget too. They would never speak of it again. Never by word or look would Clare refer to it. It should be blotted out and forgotten.

And after a discreet interval, when there was no chance of big, irrepressible tears dropping into the gravy, or salting the butter, Clare thought she would like her supper.

She made quite a hearty meal, and Alwynne crumbled bread and drank thirstily, and watched her with humble, adoring eyes.

Clare, in soft undertones, was delicately amusing, full of dainty quips that coaxed Alwynne gently back to smiles and naturalness. She spared no pains, and sent Alwynne home at last, with, metaphorically speaking, her blessing.

But Alwynne stooped as she walked, as though she carried a burden.

CHAPTER XXVII

The summer holidays came and went, eight cloudless weeks of them. Clare loved the sun; was well content to be out, day after day, cushioned and replete, on the sunniest strip of sand in the sunniest corner of a parched and gasping England. She found it wonderfully soothing to listen with shut eyes to the purr of the sea and the distant cries of gulls and children, with Alwynne to fan her and shade her, and clamber up and down two hundred feet of red cliff for her when the corkscrew was forgotten, or the salt, or Clare's bathing-dress, or a half-read magazine. Clare grew brown and plump as the drowsy days went by. Alwynne grew brown, too, but she certainly did not grow plumper. But then the heat never suited Alwynne. She had often said so, as she reminded Elsbeth. For, when Alwynne came back to her for the three weeks at home that she had persuaded Clare were due to Elsbeth, Elsbeth was difficult to satisfy. Elsbeth was inclined to be indignant. What sort of a holiday had it been, if Alwynne could come back so thin, and tired, and colourless under her tan? What had Miss Hartill been about to allow it?

But Alwynne's account of their pleasant lazy days was certainly appeasing....It must have been the heat....Not even the most suspicious of aunts could conscientiously suspect Clare of having anything to do with it....Wait till September came, with its cooling skies....Alwynne would be better then.

In the meantime Elsbeth tried what care and cookery and coddling could do, and Alwynne submitted more patiently than usual.

Alwynne, indeed, was unusually gentle with Elsbeth in the three weeks they spent together before the autumn term began. She was always good to Elsbeth, considerate of her bodily comforts, lovingly demonstrative. But Clare had taught Alwynne very carefully that she was growing up at last, becoming financially and morally independent, free to lead her own life, that if she stayed with Elsbeth it was by favour, not by duty. And Alwynne, immensely flattered by the picture of herself as a woman of the world, had lived up to it with her usual drastic enthusiasm. Elsbeth, not unused to disillusionment and hopes deferred, could sigh and smile and acquiesce, knowing it for the phase that it was and forgiving Alwynne in advance. But Clare, who owed her neither gratitude nor duty, she never forgave. She was a very human woman, for all her saintliness.

She got her reward that summer, when Alwynne came back, quieted, grave, very tender with Elsbeth, clinging to her sometimes as if she were nearer nine than nineteen. But Elsbeth was fated never to have her happiness untainted. She was haunted by the conviction that Alwynne's subduement was not natural. Her pleasure in being with her aunt was so obvious that Elsbeth was worried, and knowing how infallibly Alwynne turned to her in any trouble, she expected revelations. But none came-only the manner was there that always accompanied them. Yet something was wrong....A quarrel with Clare Hartill.

But Alwynne, delicately questioned, chattered happily enough of their holiday, and there were frequent letters — —She was over-anxious, too, to protest that she was perfectly well, and, in proof, exhausted herself in unnecessary housework. But she continued restless and abstracted, jumped absurdly at any sudden noise, and followed Elsbeth about like a homeless dog.

And she had contracted an odd habit of coming late at night into Elsbeth's room, trailing blankets and a pillow under her arm, to beg to sleep on Elsbeth's sofa-just this once! She would laugh at herself and pull Elsbeth's face down to her for a kiss, but she never gave any good reason for her whim. But she came so often that Elsbeth had a bed made up for her at last, and she slept there all the holidays, or lay awake. Elsbeth suspected that she lay awake two nights out of three.

With the autumn term Alwynne seemed to rouse herself, and flung herself into her work with her usual energy. Elsbeth saw less of her. The school claimed all her days, and Clare the bulk of her evenings. She had moved back into her own room again, and Elsbeth, her door ajar, would lie and watch the crack of light across the passage, and grieve over her darling's sleeplessness, and the shocking waste of electric light.

She wondered if the girl were working too hard.... Could that be at the root of the matter? She grew so anxious that she could even consult Clare on one of the latter's rare and formal calls.

"I am so glad to see you. Alwynne is changing; she'll be down in a minute. I made her lie down. Miss Hartill, I'm very distressed about the child. Do you think she looks well?"

Clare, less staccato than usual, certainly didn't think so.

"So thin-she's growing so dreadfully thin! Her neck! You should see her neck-salt-cellars, literally! And she had such a beautiful neck! But you've never seen her in evening dress."

Yes, Clare had seen her.

"And so white and listless! I don't know what to make of her. I don't know what to do."

Clare, with unusual gentleness, would not advise Elsbeth to worry herself. Possibly Alwynne was doing a little too much. Clare would make enquiries. But she was sure that Elsbeth was over-anxious.

But Elsbeth was not to be comforted. She nodded to the open door.

"Look at her now-dragging across the hall."

But Alwynne, in her gay frock, cheeks, at sight of Clare, suddenly aflame, did not look as if there were much amiss. She was thinner, of course....

Elsbeth, however, had made Clare uneasy. She attacked Alwynne on the following day.

"Your aunt says you're dying, Alwynne. What's the matter?"

"Dear old Elsbeth!" Alwynne laughed lightly.

"*Is* anything wrong?" Clare did not appear to look at her; nevertheless she did not miss the slight change in Alwynne's face, as she answered with careful cheeriness —

"What should be wrong in this best of all possible ——"

Clare caught her up.

"I'm not a fool, Alwynne. What's the matter?"

"I wish you wouldn't discuss me with Elsbeth," said Alwynne uneasily. "I don't like it. I won't have you bothered."

"I'm not," said Clare coolly. "At the same time ——"

Alwynne braced herself. She knew the tone.

"—I don't like any one about me with a secret grief and a pale, courageous smile. I can't stand a martyr."

"I'm not!" Alwynne was wincing. Then, suddenly: "What has Elsbeth been saying? Honestly, I didn't know she'd noticed anything."

"What is the matter?" said Clare again, gently enough. "Tell me, silly child!"

Alwynne shrugged her shoulders.

"Nothing! Just life!"

Clare waited.

"I'm sorry if I've been horrid —" she paused —"to Elsbeth."

Clare opened her eyes.

"What about me?"

"I'm never horrid to you," said Alwynne with compunction. "That's what's so beastly of me."

"Well, upon my word!" cried Clare blankly.

"Oh, you know what I mean." Alwynne jumbled her words. "I always want to be nice to you. It's perfectly easy. And then I go home to Elsbeth, the darling, and am grumpy and snappy, and show her all the hateful side of me. Heaven knows why! Only yesterday she said, 'You wouldn't speak to Clare Hartill like that,' in her dear, hurt voice. I felt such a brute."

A little smile hovered at the corners of Clare's mouth.

"I was always so sorry," said Clare smoothly, "that you couldn't spend Christmas Day with me last year."

Alwynne wrinkled her forehead.

"What's that got to do ——?"

Clare caught her up.

"With your secret griefs? Nothing whatever! You're quite right. But what are they, Alwynne? Who's been worrying you? Have you got too much to do?"

"It's not that," said Alwynne unwillingly.

"Then what?"

"Oh, things!"

"What things?"

"Miss Vigers, for one," Alwynne began. Then she burst out: "Clare, I don't know what I've done to her. She never leaves me alone."

Clare stiffened.

"Miss Vigers? What has she to say to you? You're responsible to me-after Miss Marsham."

"She doesn't seem to think so. It's nag, nag, nag-fuss, fuss, fuss. Are the girls working properly? Am I not neglecting this? Or overdoing that? Do I remember that Dolly Brown had measles three terms ago? Why is Winifred Hawkins allowed to sit with the light in her eyes? Do I make a habit of keeping So-and-so in? and if so, why so? And Miss Marsham doesn't approve of this, and Miss Marsham evidently doesn't know of that-and my manner is excessively independent-and will I kindly remember...? Oh, Clare, it's simply awful. I get no peace. And you know how driven I am, with Miss Hutchins away. You'd think I'd done something awful from the way she treats me. Everlastingly spying and hinting——"

"Hinting what?" Clare's voice was icy.

"That's what I can't make out. That's the maddening part of it. Do you think I'm such a failure? Do you think I'm not to be trusted? I get on with the children-they work well! Truly, Clare, I don't know why she dislikes me so. You'd think she was trying to worry me into leaving."

"You should have told me before," said Clare curtly, and changed the subject so abruptly that Alwynne feared she was angry, and wished that she had held her tongue.

She was right. Clare was angry. Clare had conveniently forgotten her little conversation with Henrietta on that panic-stricken summer day: was naturally surprised and indignant to find it bearing the fruit she had intended it to bear. This was what came of confiding in people! And Henrietta, she had no doubt, would be prepared to give chapter and verse for her surveillance, if Clare should, directly or indirectly, call it in question.... Henrietta would appear to have Clare in a cleft stick: and Alwynne was to suffer in consequence. Clare (a great deal fonder of Alwynne than she, or Alwynne, or any one save Elsbeth, guessed) laughed to herself, once, softly, and her eyes snapped. Wait a while, Henrietta ... wait a wee while!

Thoughtfully she approached the question of the counter-attack. That was inevitable, a sop to her own conscience. Besides, it would be amusing.... It was necessary, however, to decide upon the weapon.

It was a small matter-the refusal of a boarder for lack of space-that provided it. Quietly, she went to work.

For the first time, for her own departments had allowed her energy its outlet, she set herself to disentangle the lines on which the school was run. She found many knots. Half day, half boarding school, grown from a timid beginning into one of the most flourishing of its kind, it was, indeed, like the five hundred-year-old town in which it stood, a marvellous compound of ancient custom and modern usage. The "Seminary for Young Ladies" of the 'seventies was three parts obliterated by the 'nineties High School regimen, on which, in its turn, was superimposed the cricket and hockey of the twentieth century's effemination of the public-school system; the whole swollen, patchwork concern held together by the personality of its creator, and its own reputation.

Clare nodded. It was obvious to her, that with the retirement of Miss Marsham, accomplished already in all save name, the school would fall to pieces. A pity ... it had a fine past ... was a valuable property still.... With a vigorous woman at its head, judiciously iconoclastic, no stickler for tradition, it would revive its youth.... She herself, for instance.... She toyed with the idea.

Miss Marsham was looking out for a successor.... She herself had been sounded.... Should she? She shook her head. Life was very pleasant as it was.... She knew that she hated responsibility as much as she liked power.... She sat on the school's shoulders, at present.... As head mistress the school would sit on hers.... No, thank you! She had better uses for her spare time.... There were books ... idleness ... Alwynne.... Imagine never having time to play with Alwynne!

Nevertheless it would be fascinating to plan out the reorganisation of the school ... and carry it out, for that matter. She could do it, she knew. She would get all pat and then have some talks-some suggestive talks-with Miss Marsham.... She, Clare, had some little influence.... And there was life in the old warhorse yet.... Anything that she could be persuaded to believe would benefit her school would have her instant sanction.... She would be nominally responsible, of course, and would give Clare, nevertheless, a free hand.... And Clare, sweeping clean, would sweep away whatever withstood her.... Henrietta would have little energy left for Alwynne when Clare had finished her spring-cleaning....

For the next few weeks, Clare spent nearly all her spare time at the school. She would stay to supper, and even, on occasion, superintend "lights out." She would ask artless questions, and the matron and the young mistresses found her "so sympathetic when you really got her to yourself. So sensible, you know-always sees what you mean."

Finally, Clare shut herself up for a Saturday and a Sunday with a neat little note-book, and drew up plans and made some calculations. Then she went to see Miss Marsham. She went to see Miss Marsham several times.

The plan was certainly an excellent one.... Miss Marsham could not follow the details very well ... but that, of course, would be dear Clare's affair.... A great saving ... an immense improvement.... There would be changes, of course.... This idea of separate houses, for instance.... It would mean taking extra premises-but Clare was quite right, they were overcrowded-had had to turn away girls.... She quite agreed with Clare ... she had always preferred boarders herself; one had a freer hand.... With a mistress responsible for each house, though, what would there be left for Miss Vigers to do?... Yes-she might take over a house, of course.... But Miss Marsham paused uneasily. She anticipated trouble with Henrietta.

She was justified. Henrietta refused utterly to discuss the suggested alterations. Miss Marsham must excuse her; she had her position.... One house? after controlling the entire school's economy? She did not suggest that Miss Marsham could be serious-that was impossible.... Miss Marsham was serious? Then there was no more to be said....

She said a good deal, however, and at considerable length; ended, breathless, waspish, leaving her resignation in her principal's hands. Neither she nor Miss Marsham dreamed that it would be accepted.

But Clare Hartill, consulted by Miss Marsham, was puzzlingly relieved. Very delicately she congratulated her chief on being extricated from a difficult position; praised Miss Vigers's tact-or her sense of fitness. Unusual good sense.... People so seldom realised their limitations, unprompted ... poor Miss Vigers was certainly no longer young ... hardly the woman for a modern house-mistress-ship.... Old fashioned ... in these days of degrees and college-training so much more was expected ... and after that affair in the summer no doubt she had lost confidence in herself.... Clare was sure that Miss Vigers had appreciated Miss Marsham's forbearance, but of course, she must know, in her own heart, that if she had taken proper precautions-it was her business to arrange for a mistress to be on duty, wasn't it? —the accident could not have happened. Poor little Louise! Oh, and of course, poor Miss Vigers too!... Well, it was for the best, she supposed ... and Miss Vigers seemed to feel that it was time for her to go.... Perhaps it was.... But they would all be sorry to lose her.... Clare really thought that she would like to get up a presentation from the school.... Now what did Miss Marsham consider appropriate?

So Henrietta found herself taken at her word. She left, passionately resentful, at the half-term; hoping, at least, to embarrass her employer thereby. (But Clare Hartill knew of such a nice suitable woman-Newnham.)

Henrietta Vigers was forty-seven when she left. She had spent youth and prime at the school, and had nothing more to sell. She had neither certificates nor recommendations behind her. She was hampered by her aggressive gentility. Out of a £50 salary she had scraped together £500. Invested daringly it yielded her £25 a year. She had no friends outside the school. She left none within it.

Miss Marsham presented her with a gold watch, decorously inscribed; the school with a handsomely bound edition of Shakespeare.

Heaven knows what became of her.

CHAPTER XXVIII

Said Clare to Elsbeth at their next meeting—
"I found out what the trouble was. Henrietta Vigers has been slave-driving her. I should have guessed before, but you know that sort of thing can go on in a school unnoticed."

"Oh, yes," said Elsbeth.

Clare shot a suspicious glance at her, but Elsbeth's face was impassive.

"But she'll be all right now. Miss Vigers is leaving us at half-term."

"So I hear."

Their eyes met. Clare flushed faintly.

"I couldn't have Alwynne bullied."

"I know exactly how you feel," said Elsbeth quietly. Then, with a direct glance, "Has Miss Vigers got another post?"

"I haven't enquired."

"You're a bad enemy," Elsbeth's tone was quaintly reflective, almost admiring.

"But a good friend, I hope?" Clare laughed.

"I hope so," said Elsbeth doubtfully, and Clare laughed again. It amused her to cross swords with Elsbeth. At times she felt, that had it not been for Alwynne-that bone of contention she could have liked her.

"You can't be one without the other," she instructed her. "I don't pretend to be a saint. And you'll see how much better Alwynne will be next term."

But the spring term came, and Alwynne was no better. She flagged like a transplanted tree. She went about her business as usual, but even Clare, not too willing to acknowledge what interfered with her scheme of things, realised that her efficiency was laborious, that her high spirits were forced, her comicalities not spontaneous, that she was in fact, not herself, but merely an elaborate imitation.

But where Elsbeth grew anxious Clare grew irritated. She spied a mystery. Some obscure, yet powerful instinct prevented her from probing it, but she was none the less piqued at being left in the dark. It annoyed her too, that Alwynne should be obviously and daily losing her health and good looks. Clare required above all vitality in her associates. It had been, in her eyes, one of Alwynne's most attractive characteristics. This changing Alwynne, whitened, quieted, submissive, the sparkle gone from her eyes and the snap from her tongue, was less to her taste. Alwynne, very conscious of her shortcomings and of Clare's irritation at them, grew daily more nervously propitiatory-ever a fatal attitude to Clare. It roused the petty tyrant in her. There were jarrings, misunderstandings, exhausting scenes and more exhausting reconciliations. Yet the two were always together. Clare, viciously adroit as she grew in those days in piercing the armour of Alwynne's peace, exacted nevertheless her incessant service. And never had Alwynne so strained every nerve to please her.

Elsbeth, guessing at the situation, could give thanks when influenza, sweeping over the school, claimed Alwynne as its earliest victim. Her turn had come. She nursed Alwynne through the attack, prolonged her convalescence, excluded all enquirers, censored messages and letters. When Alwynne grew better, and talked, restless yet unwilling, of fixing the date of her return, Elsbeth, lips firmly set, went out one afternoon to pay a call upon Miss Marsham, and returning, sat down to write a letter. She busied herself for the rest of that day and all the next over Alwynne's wardrobe, mending and pressing and freshening.

Alwynne protested.

"Elsbeth dear, do leave my things alone. I'll mend them some time-honestly. They're all right. I wish you wouldn't fuss."

But Elsbeth fussed placidly on.

In the evening came letters for them both. Alwynne read hers hurriedly.

"Elsbeth, it's from Clare! She wants to know why I'm not coming back. What does she mean? Of course I'm coming back. Mademoiselle Charette is already, and she was ill after I was!"

Elsbeth sniffed.

"She was only in bed two days-Miss Marsham said so. You're not going back this term, Alwynne. I've seen Miss Marsham myself. I told her what the doctor said. I've arranged things. She agrees with me-you're not fit to. It's only a month to end of term. They can manage. You've simply got to have a change. So I wrote to Dene-to the Lumsdens, and Alicia's answer has just come. They're delighted to have you. I knew they would be, of course. They have asked us so often. Such a lovely place. Now, my dear, be a sensible child and don't argue, because I've made up my mind. It'll do you good to get away."

For in Alwynne's face astonishment had been succeeded by indignation. Elsbeth prepared herself resignedly to face a storm of protest, if not a blank refusal. To be arranged for as if she were a child-unconsulted-Clare-the school-the coaching-leaving Elsbeth alone-Dene-utter strangers-perfectly well-simply ridiculous. Elsbeth saw it all coming.

"My dear Elsbeth! What a preposterous — —" began Alwynne. Then the weakness of convalescence swamped her. She sank back in her chair.

"Perhaps it will," said Alwynne wearily. "All right, Elsbeth! I'll go if you want me to. Anyway, I don't much care."

CHAPTER XXIX

A week later Alwynne was sitting in a diminutive go-cart drawn by a large pony, and driven by a large lady with a wide smile and bulgy knees, with which, as the little cart jolted over the stony road, she unconsciously nudged Alwynne, imparting an air of sly familiarity to her pleasant, formal talk. This, Alwynne supposed, was Alicia. She liked her, liked her fat kind face, her comfortable rotundity, and her sweet voice. She liked her cool disregard of her own comical appearance, wedged in among portmanteaux and Alwynne and a basket of market produce, with an old sun-hat tied bonnet-fashion to shade her eyes, and her scarf ends fluttering madly, as she thwacked and tugged at the iron-mouthed pony.

She was more than middle-aged, a woman of flopping draperies and haphazard hookings, and scatter-brained grey locks, that had been a fringe in the days of fringes. She moved, as Alwynne noticed later, like a hurried cow, and tripped continually over her long skirts. Yet, in spite of her ramshackle exterior, she was not ridiculous. The good-men and stray children they encountered greeted her with obvious respect. Alwynne, comparing the keen eyes and their cheerful crowsfeet, with the chin, firm enough in its cushion of fat, guessed her the ruling spirit of the Dene household, and wondered why she had not married a vicar.

But Alicia, though Alwynne listened politely to her flow of talk, and answered prettily when she must, did not long occupy her attention.

She was in her own country again. She loved the country-woods, fields, hedges and lanes-as she loved no city or sea-town of them all. London, Paris, Rome-Swiss mountains or Italian lakes-she would have given them all for Kent and Hampshire and the Sussex Weald. But Clare would never hear of a country holiday. Alwynne took deep breaths of the clean, kindly air, and wondered to herself that she had taken the proposal of her holiday so dully. She had not realised that she was going into the country-she had not realised anything, except that she was tired, and that Elsbeth would not leave her alone. She had shrunk painfully from the idea of meeting strangers, from the exertion of accommodating herself to them. But this good air made one feel alive again....

She stared over the pony's ears at the gay spring landscape.

"Those are the Dene fields," said Alicia, following her glance. "There are two Denes, you know-Dene Village and Dene Fields. There's a couple of miles between them. We are in the hollow, where the road dips, at the foot of Witch Hill."

"Witch Hill?"

Alicia flourished her whip at the sky-line. The fields were spread over the hillside in sections of chocolate and magenta and silver-green, with here and again a parti-coloured patch, where oats and dandelions, pimpernel and sky-blue flax choked and strangled on an ash-heap. From the slopes Witch Hill lifted a brow of blank white chalk, crowned and draped in woodland, lying against pillows of cloud, for all the world like a hag abed, knees hunched, and patchwork quilt drawn up to ragged eyebrows. Round her neck the road wound like a silver riband; looped, dipped, disappeared, for two unfenced miles-to flash into view but a parrot's flight away, and swerve, with a steep little rush, round a house with French windows thatched in yellow jessamine.

Alwynne's eyes lit up.

"What a good name! Who was she before she was turned into that?" She stopped, flushing. Alicia would think her stupid.

Alicia laughed pleasantly.

"Do you like fairy tales? You've come to the right place-the country-side's full of them. There's a fairy fort-Roman I suppose, really, and a haunted barn out beyond Dene Compton, besides Witch Hill and the Witch Wood just behind our house. There's a story, of course. I don't know it-you must ask Roger. He's always picking up stories."

"Roger?"

"My nephew, Roger Lumsden. Hasn't Elsbeth ——?"

"Oh yes, of course."

"He's away just now. Look, now you can see the house properly."

"Behind the hill?" Alwynne had caught sight of a group of buildings crowning a secondary slope.

"No, no-that's the school, Dene Compton."

"A school?" Alwynne screwed up her eyes to look at it. "What a big place! Girls or boys?"

"Both."

"Oh! A board school!" Alwynne's interest flagged.

"Scarcely!" Alicia laughed. "Haven't you heard of Dene Compton? And you a school-mistress!"

Alwynne was politely blank.

"The thin end of the co-educational wedge. It's unique-or was, till a few years ago. There are several now, dotted about England. You ladies' seminaries should be trembling in your shoes."

"Boys and girls! What a mad idea! Yes, I believe Clare —I believe I did hear something about it. It's all cranks and simple lifers and socialists though, isn't it?"

"You'd better come up one day and see. I'll take you."

"Why, do you know them?"

"I teach there."

"You? Oh —I beg your pardon," cried Alwynne strickenly.

Alicia laughed.

"I'm accustomed to it. Jean will be delighted with an ally. She pretends to disapprove. But Roger and I are generally too much for her."

"Is he a master, then?"

"Good gracious, no! But he has a lot of friends at the school. He ought to be interested-it's his land, you know. His people lived there for generations-the Lumsdens of Dene Compton. The head master has the old house, but the school itself is new-all those buildings you see. No, not those —" Alwynne's eyes were caught by a glitter of glass roofs —"those are Roger's houses. He's a gardener, you know. He lives for his bulbs and his manures."

The tiny cart rocked as the pony bucketed down the dip of the road and whirled it through the gates and up the short drive. Alwynne clutched the inadequate rail.

"He will do it," said Alicia resignedly. "He wants his tea. There's Jean. Mind the door."

She pulled up the rocketing pony as the ridiculous little door burst open and Alwynne and her baggage were precipitated on to the gravel.

A little woman ran out from the porch.

"Are you hurt? It always does that. I'm always asking Alicia to tell Bryce to take it to be seen to. Alicia —I shall speak to Roger if you don't. My dear, I hope you haven't hurt yourself. That pretty frock-but it will all brush off. And how is Elsbeth, and why didn't you bring her with you? Come in at once and have some tea. Alicia has driven round to the stables. It's Bryce's afternoon off."

Jean was a prim little red-haired woman, some years younger than Alicia, with brisk ways, and a clacking tongue. She had Alwynne in a chair, had given her tea, deplored her white looks, suggested three infallible remedies, recounted their effect on her own constitution and Alicia's and her nephew's, and, digressing easily, was beginning a detailed history of Roger's health since, at the age of five or thereabouts, he had come under her care, before Alwynne had had time to realise more than that the room was very cheerful, Jean very talkative, and she herself very, very tired. She could not help being relieved when Alicia returned. Jean, with her neat dress and knowledgeable ways and little air of apologising for her slap-dash elder, should, by all the rules, have been the more reliable of the cousins. Yet Alwynne turned instinctively to Alicia; and Alicia, spread upon a chair, fanning herself cyclonically with her enormous hat, did not fail her.

"Jean! The child's as white as a sheet. You can ask about Elsbeth to-morrow, and Roger will keep. Take her up to her room, leave her to unpack and lie down in peace and quiet, and come back and give me my tea. Supper's at seven, Alwynne. Take my advice and have a good rest. There are plenty of books-oh, yes, I know all about your likes and dislikes. Elsbeth's a talker too-on paper! Jean-if you're not down in five minutes, I'll come and fetch you."

Alwynne, half an hour later, curled comfortably upon a sofa, in front of a blazing fire, with a lazy hour before her and a Copperfield upon her knee, thought that Alicia was a perfect dear. And Jean? Jean, pulling out the sofa, poking the fire, pattering about her like a too intelligent terrier-Jean was a dear too.... They were a couple of comical dears.

And "The Dears" was Alwynne's name for them from that day on.

CHAPTER XXX

Alwynne settled down with an ease that surprised herself. Much as she loved the country, a country life would have bored her to death, Clare had often assured her, as a permanent state; but for a few weeks it was certainly delightful. She enjoyed pottering about the garden with Jean, and jogging into the village on her own account behind the obstinate pony, who, approving her taste in apples, allowed her to believe that she more or less regulated his direction and pace. She enjoyed the complicated smells of the village store, half post office, half emporium, and the taste of its gargantuan bulls'-eyes. She sent, in the first enthusiasm of discovery, a tinful heaped about with early primroses to Clare; but Clare was not impressed.

Clare disapproved strongly of Alwynne's holiday, needed her too much to allow it necessary. Her first letters were a curious mixture-half fretfulness over Alwynne's absence, half assurance of how perfectly well she, Clare, got on without her. Alwynne would have been exquisitely amazed could she have known how eagerly Clare awaited her bi-weekly budget. Alwynne was afraid her letters were dull enough. She apologised constantly—

> Of course, Clare, this will seem very small beer to you-but little things are important down here. It's all so quiet, you see. I've been perfectly happy this morning because I found a patch of white violets in a clearing, and Jean and Alicia were just as excited when I told them at lunch: and we went off with a tea-basket afterwards, and dug violet roots for an hour, or more, and then spread our mackintoshes over a felled trunk and made tea. The ground was sopping, but it was fun. You'd love my cousins. They're as old as Elsbeth but full of beans, and they've travelled and are interesting-only they will talk incessantly about this nephew they've got. It's "Roger" this and "Roger" that-he seems to rule them with a rod of iron-can't do wrong! He comes back next week. I rather wonder what he'll be like. The Dears make him out a paragon; but I'm expecting a prig, myself! There are photographs of him all over the place. He's quite good-looking.

But before Alwynne could tire of the lanes and village, of gardening with Jean, and hints of how Roger stubbed up roots and handled bulbs, Alicia had provided her with a new interest. She remembered her promise one morning and took her up to Dene Compton.

Alicia gave Italian lessons twice a week, and from her Alwynne had gleaned many quaint details of the school and its workings. What she heard interested her, though she was prepared to be merely, if indulgently, amused. She looked forward to the visit if only to get copy for a letter to Clare. Clare, too, liked to be amused.

The gong was clanging for the mid-morning break when Alicia, Alwynne in her wake, led the way into the main building, and waving her airily towards a mound of biscuits, bade her help herself and look about her for a while, because she, Alicia, had got to speak to-She dived into the crowd.

Alwynne, thus deserted, stood shyly enough in a roofed corner of the great brick quadrangle, munching a fair imitation of a dog-biscuit, and watching the boys and girls who swarmed past her as undisturbed by her presence as if she were invisible. At the boys she smiled indulgently as she would have smiled at a string of lively terriers, but of the girls she was sharply critical. They wore curious, and as she thought hideous, serge tunics: she jibbed at their utilitarian plaits: but she conceded a good carriage to most of them and was impressed by a certain pleasant fearlessness of manner. A couple of men, Alicia, and a bright, emphatic woman in a nurse's uniform, wandered through the crowd, which made way courteously enough, but seemed otherwise in no degree embarrassed by their propinquity. Alwynne had a sudden memory of Clare's triumphal processions; compared them uneasily with the fashion of these quiet people.

She watched a small girl dash panting to the loggia at the opposite side of the quadrangle, where a slight man in disreputable tennis-shoes, leaned against a shaft and observed the pleasant tumult. There was a moment's earnest consultation, and the small girl darted away again and disappeared down a corridor. The man resumed his former pose-head on one side, smiling a little.

Alwynne ventured out of her corner and caught at Alicia as she passed.

"Cousin Alice! I like all this. I'm glad you brought me. Who's that?" She nodded towards the man in tennis-shoes.

"The Head."

"The head-master?"

"Why not?"

"But-but-when Miss Marsham comes in-you can hear a pin drop——Is he nice?"

Alicia laughed.

"I'll introduce you."

She did.

"Well," said Alicia with a twinkle as they walked home together later, "what did you think of him?"

Alwynne flushed, but she laughed too.

"Cousin Alice-it was too bad of you. He just said 'How do you do?' and smiled politely. Then he said nothing at all for five minutes, and then he clutched at one of the girls and handed me over to her with another smile-an immensely relieved one-and drifted away. I've never been so snubbed in my life."

"You're not the first one. So you didn't like him?"

"Oh—I liked him," conceded Alwynne grudgingly.

They walked on in silence for a while.

"What's that?" Alwynne pointed to a large grey building half way down the avenue.

"The girls' house, Hill Dene. They sleep there; and have the needlework classes, and house-wifery, I believe."

"Do they have everything else with the boys?"

"Practically."

"Does it answer?"

"Why not? Girls with brothers and boys with sisters have an advantage over the solitary specimens, everybody knows. This is only extending the principle."

Alwynne giggled suddenly.

"You know that girl he dumped me on to-she was showing me round, and we ran into some boys in the gym. I couldn't make out why, but she jolly well sent them flying."

"Out of hours, I expect."

"But the coolness of it, Cousin Alice! She was a bit of a thing-the boys were half as high again!"

"But not prefects."

"Oh, I see." Alwynne meditated. "Oh, Cousin Alicia, that girl asked me to go with them next Saturday for a tramp. Over Witch Hill. She and another girl and some boys. Imagine! they're going by themselves-without a master or a mistress or anything!"

"Why not?"

"We don't. We crocodile. Two and two, and two and two, and two and two. And I trot along at the side and see that they don't take arms. But of course, you can't control the day-girls. One of them asked two of the boarders out for the day one Sunday, at least her mother did, and we met them after church on the promenade, arm in arm-all three! I tell you, there was a row. They were locked up in their bedrooms for three days, and nobody might speak to them for the rest of the term. Miss Marsham said it was defiance and that they might remember they were ladies."

"I don't think they want 'ladies' here," said Alicia. "They're quite content if they produce gentlewomen. Your school must be peculiar."

"Oh, no," said Alwynne, opening her eyes. "There are dozens of schools like Utterbridge. I was at two myself when I was young. It's this place that's peculiar. It's like nothing I've heard of. I want to explore. He said I could. Yes, I forgot-he did say that-that I was to come up whenever I liked."

And for the next week Alwynne spent a good half of her days at Dene Compton. She clung to Alicia's skirts at the first, afraid of appearing to intrude. But she soon found that she might go where she would without arousing curiosity or even notice, though boys and girls alike were friendly enough when she spoke to them. Accustomed to her mistress-ship, she was half-piqued, half-amused to find herself so entirely unimportant.

But the great school fascinated her. It was scarce a third larger than her own in point of numbers, but the perfection of its proportions made it impressive. The arrangements for the children's physical well-being reflected the methods employed for their spiritual development. There was an insistence on sunlight and fresh air and space-above all, space. There was no calculation of the legal minimum of cubic feet: body and mind alike were given room in which to turn, to stretch themselves, to grow.

Gradually she realised that she had been living for years in a rabbit warren.

With her discoveries she filled many sheets of notepaper. But Clare's letters were nicely calculated to divert enthusiasm. Their tone was changing; they allowed Alwynne to guess herself missed. There was in them a hint of appeal: a suggestion of lonely evenings — —Never a word of Alwynne's doings. Yet, by implication, description of her new friends and their outlook was dismissed as unnecessary. Clare, Alwynne was to realise, would smile pleasantly as she read, and think it all rather silly.

Elsbeth —*so pleased that they are so kind to you at Alicia's school* —was more genuinely uninterested. Dene Compton had been the home of a certain John Lumsden for Elsbeth. She did not care for descriptions of its metamorphosis. She wanted to hear about Dene, and her cousins, and how Alwynne was eating and sleeping, and if Roger Lumsden had come back yet. She asked twice if Roger Lumsden had come back yet. But Alwynne had an annoying habit of leaving her questions unanswered through eight closely written sheets. It was not only Clare who was very tired of co-education and Dene Compton.

But Elsbeth got her news at last, and was satisfied with it as Macchiavellis usually are, whose plots are being developed by unconscious and self-willed instruments. Alwynne, who in her spare time had discovered what spring in the country could mean, tucked in the news at the end of an epistle that was purely botanical — —

> *... and cuckoo-pint and primroses and violets! Have you ever seen larches in bud? Oh, Elsbeth, why can't we live in the country? Every collection of buildings bigger than Dene Village ought to be razed by Act of Parliament. I expect the earth hates cities as I hated warts on my hands when I was little. Well, I must stop. Oh-the Lumsden man turned up a day or two ago. The Dears were in ecstasies, and he let himself be fussed over in the calmest way, as if he had a perfect right to it. I think he's conceited. I don't think you'd like him. He's back for good, apparently, but he won't worry me much. I'm only in at meals. The Dears are always busy and let me do as I like, and I either go up to Compton, or prowl, or take a rug and book into the garden. It's quite hot, although it's barely April- so you needn't worry. The garden is jolly, big and half wild: only "Roger" is beginning to trim it-the vandal! He's by way of being a gardener, you know. Great on bulbs and roses, I believe.*
>
> *By the way is he a relation? Even The Dears are only very distant cousins, aren't they? Because he will call me "Alwynne" as if he were. I call it cheek. I was very stiff, but he's got a hide like a rhinoceros. When I said "Mr. Lumsden," he just grinned. So now I say "Roger" very markedly whenever he says "Alwynne." I can't see what Jean and Alicia see in him; but of course I have to be polite. They are dears, if you like-are giving me a lovely time.*
>
> *I hope you're not very dull, Elsbeth dear. You must try and get out this lovely weather. Why not have Clare to tea one day? You'd both enjoy it. I heard from her yesterday-such a jolly letter!*

Heaps of love from Jean and Alicia-and you know what a lot from me.

Alwynne.

P.S. —I found these violets to-day on a bank behind the church. They'll be squashed when you get 'em, but they'll smell still.

P.S. —The Lumsden man saw me writing, and said, would I send you his love, and do you remember him? I told him I'd scarcely heard you mention his name, so it wasn't probable-but he just smiled his superior smile. He reminds me of Mr. Darcy in P. and P. I can't say I like him.

CHAPTER XXXI

Roger Lumsden had been home a week. Alwynne, save at meals, had seen little of him, and that little she did not intend to like. There was a memory of a passage of arms at their first meeting which rankled.

Roger had been inquiring when the Compton holidays began. Alicia hesitated —

"Let me see-the play's Tuesday week— —"

"Wednesday week," put in Alwynne.

"Tuesday— —"

"No, Wednesday," Alwynne persisted. "Because, you know, Mr. Bryant is so afraid that Gertrude Clarke won't be out of the 'San.' He says he can never coach up another Alkestis in the time. Besides, there isn't any one. He's been tearing his hair."

Alicia laughed.

"She knows more about it than I do, Roger! She's been half living there, haven't you, Alwynne?"

Roger turned to her with a smile and the first touch of personal interest that he had shown. "Jolly place, isn't it? You teach, don't you? I wonder how it strikes you!"

But he was a stranger and Alwynne was nervous. She answered flippantly, as she always did when she was not at her ease —

"Oh, I can't get over their dresses! Appalling garments! Imagine that poor girl trying to rehearse Alkestis in a pea-green potato sack! It must be delicious. And their hair! Doesn't anybody ever teach them to do their hair?"

He eyed her thoughtfully, from her carefully dressed head to her shining shoe-buckles, and shrugged his shoulders.

"Is that all you see?" said Roger dispassionately, and withdrew interest.

Alwynne grew hot with annoyance. Idiot! All she saw....As if she had meant anything of the kind....One said things like that....One just said them....Especially when one was nervous.... Taking a remark like that seriously....Oh well, if he liked to think her a fool-let him! Silly prig!

She endeavoured to put him out of her mind. But his mere existence disturbed her. She was not accustomed to tobacco, for instance ... and it was disconcerting to find him in her favourite corner of the library or occupying the writing-table that no one had seemed to use but herself. He appeared to have forgotten that he had snubbed her and was unquenchably friendly. She found herself being pleasanter than she intended, but she made it a point of honour never to agree with him. That, at least, she owed herself.

She watched him furtively, alert for justification of her ill-humour. She told herself that it would be easier to be nice to him if everybody else did not fuss over him so....It was ridiculous to see how Jean, especially, brightened at the sight of him....He was good to her, certainly: she was argumentative, without being shrewd, but he never lost patience, as Alwynne, in secret was inclined to do. Even Alicia, so stoutly the head of her household, submitted every difficulty, from an unexpected legacy to a dearth of eggs. And he would sit down solidly and think the matter out. And his advice, from a flutter in rubber to pepper in the chicken pail, would be followed literally, and generally, Alwynne admitted, with success.

But she jibbed furiously when the sisters began to consult him about her personal affairs.

"Roger, don't you think that Alwynne— —?"

But here Roger was invariably offhand and non-committal. Curiously, however, this attitude, correct as it was, did not appease Alwynne. But she was forced, at least, to admit that he could, on occasion, be tactful.

The last week of the term had begun. Alicia, at breakfast behind the coffee urn, was making her plans.

"It's a busy week. The Swains want us to go to lunch, Jean, only we haven't a day before Sunday, have we? At least-there's Tuesday; it's only the dress-rehearsal. I can get out of that. Alwynne can represent me." She nodded benevolently.

There was a slight pause. Roger, glancing up, stared openly. Alwynne had turned as white as paper. Her words came stickily.

"Cousin Alice, I can't. I mean —I'd rather —I don't want to go much, if you don't mind." Alicia blessed herself.

"But, my dear! Why not? I thought you'd be looking forward — —Oh, I suppose you've watched it so often, already."

"No —I haven't seen it; I'm afraid rehearsals bore me — —" Alwynne broke off with an attempt at a light laugh.

"But you've been up to Compton so much," Alicia's tone was reproachful. "I should have thought you would have been sufficiently interested — —"

"Oh, I am! Only-you see I've got letters to write-to Elsbeth — —"

"Well, you've got all the week to write in! Are you so afraid of being bored? Compton wouldn't be flattered. We rather pride ourselves on our acting, you know! My dear, we're expected to go-must give the performers some sort of an audience to get them into training for the night. You ought to understand, of all people! Don't you ever give plays at your school?"

Alwynne was silent, but prompted by an instinct she could not have explained, she turned to Roger, stolid behind his eggs and bacon. She said nothing, but she looked at him desperately. He gave an imperceptible nod. He had been watching her intently.

"But, dear Alwynne — —" Jean was chirruping her version of Alicia's remarks when Roger's calm voice interrupted —

"I say, Alicia! I thought you and Jean were coming with me! I can't go on the night itself. Of course you must come. Go to your lunch on Sunday —I'll look after Alwynne. But I'm not going up to Compton without you. Spoil all the fun."

"Of course, if Roger wants us — —" began Jean quickly.

"Oh, I didn't want to miss it," retreated Alicia hastily. "I only thought the Swains — —But of course Sunday would do."

"I met old Swain yesterday," said Roger, "travelled up to town with him. He was very full of his daughter's engagement."

"Engagement!" Alicia and Jean swooped to the news, like gulls to a falling crust. It kept them busy till breakfast was over.

And Roger returned to his eggs and bacon with never a glance at Alwynne.

Alwynne, half an hour later in her own room, fighting certain memories, arguing herself fiercely out of her weakness, had yet time to puzzle her head over Roger Lumsden. How quick he had been-and how kind.... Or had he noticed nothing? Had that adroit change of subject been accidental? That was much more likely.

She dismissed him from her mind. She wished she could dismiss all the thoughts that filled her mind as easily.

Alwynne was grateful enough to Roger, however, when Tuesday came and he set out for Compton, an aunt on either arm: but on Sunday she had to pay for her non-attendance. Hurrying down, a little late, to lunch, she was half-way through her usual apologies before she realised that neither Jean nor Alicia were in their places. Of course-they were going to the Swain's.... Their nephew, however, waiting gravely behind his chair, admitted her excuses with a little air of acknowledging them to be necessary that ruffled her at once, though she had promised herself to be pleasant. After all, she was staying, as she had told herself several times already, with Jean and Alicia. Once more she applied herself, quite unsuccessfully, to snubbing his air of host. Roger listened to her in some amusement; her ungracious ways disturbed him no more than the rufflings and peckings of an angry bird, and her charming manner to his aunts and occasional whim of friendliness to himself, had prevented him from pigeon-holing her definitely as a pretty young shrew. He was inclined to like her, for Jean and Alicia had confessed themselves absurdly taken with the girl, and he was accustomed to be influenced by their judgment; but the touch of hostility that usually showed itself in her manner to him puzzled as much as it amused him.

He enjoyed baiting her, yet he thought, carelessly, that it was a pity she should have inaugurated guerilla warfare. She looked as if she could have been pleasant company for his spare time if she had chosen. However, he would have little enough spare time, for the next few weeks, anyhow ... he had promised Jean to set to work seriously at the renovation of her garden.... He should be thankful for a visitor requiring neither escort nor attention.

Yet, naturally, her independence piqued him. He eyed her swiftly, as she sat at his right hand. She was a curious girl, he thought, to be so pretty and well-dressed, and yet so self-sufficing. Girls, apparently of her type, (he thought of his American cousins) usually needed a good deal of admiration to keep them contented.

She did not look altogether contented, though ... there were lines and puckers at the corners of her large eyes, that were surely out of place ... nineteen, wasn't she? She had had a breakdown, of course ... rather absurd, for such a child....Jean had hinted a guess at some trouble.... A love affair, he supposed. That would account for her thorniness, her occasional air of absence and depression, that contrasted with her usual cheerfulness....Yet that curious whim the other day-what had it meant? More than a whim, he imagined-her very lips had grown white.... He was quite sure that he had helped her out of a hole.... She might at least show a certain decent gratitude.... He wondered what she was thinking about, sitting there so silently ... she was generally talkative enough ... pretty quarrelsome, too. He supposed she was having a fit of the blues.... He had better talk to her, perhaps....

Alwynne, eating her wing of chicken, was merely and sheerly shy. She was garrulous enough with women, but she did not in the least know how to talk to men. Therefore and naturally she was full of theories. She had vague ideas that they had to be amused as babies have to be amused, but confronted with the prospect of a prolonged *tête-à-tête*, without Alicia or Jean to retire upon, she had nothing whatever to say. Yet she had been taught by Elsbeth to consider a lack of table-talk as a lack of manners, and was irritated with herself for her silence, and still more irritated with Roger for his.

She met his belated attempts at a conversation none too graciously-was bored by the boat-race, and would have nothing to say to the weather; though she thawed to his catalogue of copses and plantations in the neighbourhood, where certain wild flowers she had not yet discovered might be found.

But it was impossible for Alwynne to be silent long, and by the time they had adjourned to the drawing-room, the pair were talking easily enough. Roger did not find himself bored. He had, from the beginning, recognised that she was no fool, that her remarks owed their comicality to her phrasing of them, and that essentially they were shrewd, her acrobatic intellect swinging easily across the gaps in her education. The gaps were certainly there. He would marvel at her amazing ignorance, only to be tripped up by her unexpected display of authoritative knowledge. Gradually he began to analyse and discriminate, to see that she was naturally observant. Her remarks on life as she knew it, were as illuminating as original. She had humour and a nice sense of caricature. But when she, as it were, hoisted herself on the shoulders of the women about her, and from that level peered curiously at an outer, alien world, her insight failed her, her views grew distorted and merely grotesque. He thought he guessed the reason. She was no longer gazing, critical and clear-eyed, at known surroundings, but, still supported by the opinions of the women of her circle, was seeing what she had expected to see, what she had been told by them that she would see.

For all her air of modern girl, her independence, her store of book experience, she was comically convental in her curiosities and intolerances, in her prim company manners and uncontrollable lapses into unconventionality. She had an air of not being at her ease; yet he guessed that it was merely the unaccustomed environment that disturbed her poise. He could see her handling surely enough a crowd of schoolgirls. He was equally certain that she ruled through sheer, easy popularity. She had dignity in spite of her whimsies, but he could not imagine her intimidating even a schoolgirl.

But most of all her attitude to himself amused him. She had a certain veiled antagonism of manner, that was allied to the antagonism of the small child to any innovation. She talked to him readily enough (and he, for that matter, to her) yet she was always on the defensive, inquisitive yet wary. He felt that if she had been ten years younger, she would have circled about him and poked.

A stray phrase explained her to him.

They had discussed the latest raid. At Alwynne's age and period all conversational roads led to the suffrage question, and he had found her re-hash of Mona Hamilton's arguments sufficiently entertaining. He guessed a plagiarism of the matter, but the manner was obviously her own. She was full of second-hand indignation over the conduct of a certain Cabinet Minister.

"He won't even see them!" she explained grievously. "Not even a deputation from the constitutional section! Just because some women are fools-and burn things——" The pause was eloquent. "It's so utterly unreasonable," declaimed Alwynne. "But of course men are unreasonable," said Alwynne, pensively reflective.

"Are they?"

"All I know are, anyhow."

He considered her ingenuous countenance—

"If it's not a delicate question-how many do you know?" said Roger softly.

She looked at him, mildly surprised.

"Hundreds! In books, that is."

"Oh-books! I meant real life."

"Surely a page of Shakespeare is more real than dozens of real people's lives."

"Side issue! I'm not to be deflected. How many men do you know, in real life, well enough to discuss the suffrage with?"

"I'm always kept at school the day the vicar comes to tea," she said suggestively.

"Who else?"

She saw his drift, but defended herself, smiling.

"The assistants are most intelligent at the circulating library."

"Who else?"

"There were music masters at school. I didn't mean *you* were unreasonable," she deprecated.

He began to laugh, openly, mischievously, delighting in her discomfiture.

"Anyhow, I know a lot about women," said Alwynne heatedly.

He eyed her respectfully.

"I'm sure you do. But we were talking of men. And on the whole-you make me a polite exception-as a result of your wide knowledge, your complicated experience of Us-as a class-you consider that we are unreasonable?"

But he spoke into space. Alwynne had retired, pinkly, to a sofa and a novel. But he thought, as he settled to his own reading, that he heard a strangled chuckle. Alwynne, caught napping, always tickled Alwynne.

Over the top of his book, he considered her bent head approvingly. He liked her sense of fun. It was not every girl who could appreciate the smut on her own nose ...quite a pretty nose too ...indeed the whole profile was unexceptionable....He noticed how well the patch of sky and the slopes of Witch Hill framed it ...and her hair ... it regularly mopped up the sunlight! He felt that he wanted to take the great heavy rope and twist it like a wet cloth till the gold dropped out on to the floor in shining pools.

He supposed she would be called a beautiful woman....He had always looked upon a beautiful woman as an improbable possibility, like a millionaire or an archbishop-whom you might meet any day, but somehow never did....Yet he was in the same house with one-and she his semi-demi cousin....Yes-she was certainly beautiful....

Here Alwynne, who had not been entirely absorbed, looked up and caught his eye. Neither quite knew how to meet the other's unexpected scrutiny. Roger, less agile than Alwynne, stared solemnly until she looked away.

263

Alwynne gave a little inaudible sigh. She was boring him, of course.... It was pretty obvious.... Yet he had been quite nice all through lunch.... It was a pity.... She wondered if he wanted to read, or if she ought to go on talking? She racked her brains for something to say to him. It was not so easy to talk if he would not do his share.... She supposed she had talked too much about the suffrage.... Men never liked to be contradicted.... She glanced at him swiftly, and met his look once more, and once more he stared, till her dropping lids released him. Then he lit his pipe.

She shrugged her shoulders.

She thought it very rude of him to leave off talking.... Silence was oppressive unless you knew people well.... It snubbed you.... Especially when you had been, as Alwynne feared she had, holding forth a trifle.... She supposed he had put her down as a talkative bore.... Elsbeth always said that strangers thought her enthusiasms were pose ... as if it mattered what strangers thought! She hated strangers.... She was always fantastic with new acquaintances.... It was the form her shyness took. If Roger chose to think she was posing.... It didn't affect her anyway.... She was only too glad to be able to read in peace.... Hang Roger!

She settled herself to her reading.

For five long minutes they both read steadily. But Alwynne's book was not interesting; she began to flutter the pages, her thoughts once more astray.

It was rather a shame of The Dears to desert her ... to leave her to entertain a strange man who didn't like her.... It made her look a fool.... She hated boring people.... If she bored their precious nephew as much as the book on her lap bored her!... She wondered why, with all the library to choose from, she had pitched on it. Of course, it was Roger's suggestion.... Well, she didn't think much of his taste.... Or perhaps he imagined it was the sort of stuff to appeal to her? She flung up her chin indignantly, to find his serious and critical eyes once more concerned with her. She met them with a raising of eyebrows —a hint of cool defiance. It was Roger's turn to retire into his book.

He was an odd sort of a man.... She wondered what Clare would think of him? As if Clare would bother her head.... But then he wasn't Clare's cousin. But Clare would be out in the woods after the wild hyacinths.... Somebody had said it was blue with them in the little wood behind the house.... She must send Clare a boxful to-morrow ... or to-day? She supposed there was an evening post.... It was a pity to waste such a heavenly afternoon....

She stole yet another glance at Roger; he was evidently engrossed at last. It would not be rude? After all, what did it matter? He wasn't too polite himself! She drove her book viciously down the yielding side of the Chesterfield, swished to the open French window, and so out. The gravel crunched moistly beneath her thin shoes; she could feel every pebble. She glanced back into the drawing-room. All quiet. But by the time she had changed, the man might have come out.... She would change afterwards.... The smooth lawn sloped invitingly-beyond lay the rose walk and the wood, little Witch Wood that she had never yet explored, just because it was always at hand.

She picked up her silken skirts and took to her heels.

It was exactly half an hour later that Roger's book also grew dull to the point of imbecility. He shut it with a bang, stirred the sun-drowned fire, and knocked out his pipe against the shining dogs. Then he too walked out on to the terrace.

He wondered where the girl had got to. Then he frowned. Little half-moons dinted the wet yellow path and the stretch of grass beyond it. It was very careless, cutting up the turf like that.... If there was one thing he hated.... Of course she was town-bred ... could not be expected to realise the sacredness of a lawn.... But he must certainly tell her.... He might as well find her and tell her at once.... Then he laughed. Alwynne's high heels had betrayed her. The tracks led straight to the wood. So that was the lure.... He remembered saying that the hyacinths would probably be out....

He wondered if she knew her way.... It wasn't a large wood.... Perhaps he had better go and see ... and warn her off the lawn coming back? He hesitated. His eyes fell on Jean's forgotten bodge, lying by the border. If the hyacinths were out, she would need a basket.... She had not taken one....Trust her to forget such a detail....She would be glad of it though....He tipped out the weeds into a neat pile and jumping the narrow bed, ran down in his turn, towards the wood.

Alicia and Jean, home to tea, were annoyed to find the fire out.

The gardener, rolling the lawn next day, thought as ill of hobnailed boots as of high French heels.

CHAPTER XXXII

Alwynne left the garden behind her and crossed the stretch of grass, half lawn, half paddock, that lay between kitchen-garden and wood. It was fenced with riotous hedges, demure for the moment in dove-grey honeysuckle and star of Bethlehem, with no hint in their puritan apparel of the brionies and eglantines that were to follow. About the hedge borders the grass grew tall and rank, and, as she watched, the wind would stir it into a sea of emerald and the parsley-blossoms sway above it like snatches of drifting foam. Beyond the hedge shadow, "Nicholas Nye," the one-eyed donkey, reposed Celestially among the buttercups, which, making common cause with the afternoon sun, had turned his grazing ground into a Field of the Cloth of Gold.

For a moment she was minded to content herself with all the buttercups on earth to gather, and to go no further that day; but staring down the dazzling slope, her eyes rested once more upon the pleasant darkness of the goal for which she had been bound. Among the nearer tree trunks were stripes and chequerings of blue-the blue that is lovelier than the sea, the one blue in the world to the flower-lover. At once, indifferently, she left the buttercups to Nicholas Nye and hurried on and into the wood.

There were hyacinths everywhere, hyacinths by the million. It was as if the winds had torn her robes from the faint, spring sky, and had flung them to earth, and she now bent above them naked and shivering.

Alwynne wandered from patch to patch in an ecstasy of delight. As usual, her pleasure shaped itself into exclamations, phrases, whole sentences of the letters she would write to Clare Hartill of her experiences. If only she could have Clare with her, she thought, to see and hear and touch and smell-to share the loveliness she was enjoying. Her thoughts flew to Italy, to their crowded month of beautiful sights together. She laughed-she would discard all those memories for love of this present vision....If only Clare could see it....She could never describe it properly...adjectives welled up in her mind and dispersed again, like bubbles in a glass of water. The stalks and the hoarse ring of the hyacinth bells fascinated her. Clare was forgotten. She began to pick for the sake of picking.

The hot silence of early afternoon lay upon tree and bird and air. Alwynne, moving from blue clump to blue clump, grew ashamed of the rustle of her dress and the scrunch of twigs and soaked leaves beneath her feet, and trod softly; even her own calm breathing sounded too loudly for the perfect peace of the place and the hour.

She picked steadily, greedily-she had never before had as many flowers as she wanted, and there was inexpressible pleasure in filling her arms till she could hold no more; yet, some twenty minutes later, as she straightened herself at last, a little giddily, and looked about her over the pile of azure bells, there was no sign of bareness, for all she had gathered; she still stood to her knees in a lake of blue and green and gold.

She stretched herself lazily as she considered the flowers about her and wondered at their luxuriance. They were thicker and longer-stemmed than the mass of those she carried: the leaves were juicy and shining like dark swords: the last dozen of her armful had flecked her hands and dress with milky syrup. The ground, too, was black and boggy, and sucked at her feet as she moved. Suddenly she realised that the trees grew thick and close together-that the patches of sunlight were far apart-and that she had wandered farther into the wood than she had intended. She thought that she had picked enough, more than enough for Elsbeth as well as Clare; that it was time to be getting home. She had no idea of the hour....It would not do to risk being late....

She moved forward uncertainly.

She had had a blessed afternoon: she had surrendered herself to the sounds and sights and smells of the spring, to the warmth of the sun and the touch of the wind, till every sense was drunken with pleasure. But her ecstasy had been impersonal and thoughtless: she had enjoyed too completely to have had knowledge of her enjoyment. With the return to realisation of place and time, her mood was changing. She was no longer of the wood, but in it merely; wandering in the dark heart of it, no dryad returned and welcome, but a stranger, one Alwynne Durand, in thin shoes and an unsuitable dress, with the wood's flowers, not her own, in her hands. Stolen flowers-their weight was suddenly a burden to her. She felt guilty, and had an odd, sudden wish to put them down tenderly at the foot of a tree, hide them with grasses and run for her life. She laughed at the idea as she looked for the path-what were flowers for, but picking? Yet she could not get rid of the feeling that she had been doing wrong, and that even now she was being watched, and would, in due time, be caught and punished, her stolen treasures still in her hands.

But wild flowers are free to all-and the wood was Roger Lumsden's wood! He had told her that he rented it.

She moved backwards and forwards, turning hurriedly hither and thither, trampling the hyacinths and stumbling on the uneven ground, unreasonably flurried that she could not find any path. She could not even track her own footsteps.

It was very strange, she thought, when she had penetrated so easily the depths of the wood, that the return should be so difficult. She had thought it a mere copse. She put her free hand to her eyes, scanning the wall of greenery in all directions. She fancied that at one point the trees grew less densely, and set out, scrambling over rough ground towards the faint light.

But in spite of her hurry she advanced slowly. The thin switches of the undergrowth whipped her as she pushed them aside, and the huge briars twisted themselves about her like live things. Twice the slippery moss brought her to her knees, and the faint light grew no stronger as she pressed forward. She began to feel frightened, though she knew the sensation to be absurd. It was impossible to be lost in a little wood, half a mile across....It was merely a question of walking straight on till one emerged on open fields....

She told herself so, and tried to be amused at her adventure, and hummed a confident little tune as she plodded on, very careful not to look behind her. Her shoes, thudding and squelching in the wet mess of mould and green stuff, made more noise than one would have thought possible for one pair of feet, and woke the oddest echoes.

Of course, it was impossible that any one could be following her....But the wood was so horribly silent that her own breathing and clumsy footfalls (there could be nothing else) counterfeited the noises of pursuit....She could have sworn there was a presence at her elbow, in her rear, moving as she moved, stumbling as she stumbled. Twice she faced round abruptly, standing still-but she saw nothing but the wall of vegetation, motionless, silent, yet insistently alive. She felt that every tree, every leaf, every blade of grass, was watching her with green, unwinking eyes. There was nothing more in the wood than there had been a pleasant hour ago-less indeed, for she realised suddenly that the sun had gone in and that it was cold; yet she owned to herself at last that she was nervous, vaguely uneasy. Instantly, by that mere act of recognition, fright was born in her-unreasonable and unreasoning fright, that, in the length of a thought, pervaded her entire personality, crisping her hair, catching at her throat, paralysing her mind. The wood-panic had her in its grip-the age-old terror that still lies in wait where trees are gathered together, though the god that begot it be dead these nineteen hundred years.

She began to run.

It was impossible to pass quickly through the tangled undergrowth; but sheer fright gave her skill to avoid real obstacles, strength to crash over and through the mere wreckage of the wood. She turned and doubled like a hare, yet desperately, with the hare's terror of the sudden turn that might confront her with the presence at her heels. She could endure its pursuit, but she knew that its revelation would be more than she could bear. She was so far merely and indefinitely frightened, but to face the unknown would be to confront fear itself. And she was more frightened of fear than of any evil she knew. She could, she thought, meet pain or sickness, or any mere misery, with sufficient calmness, but the fear of fear was an obsession. She tore through the wood, shaken and gasping with terror of the greater terror she every moment expected to be forced to undergo; for almost the only clear thought remaining to her, in that onrush of panic, was the realisation that there was, at her elbow, in her heart, physical or metaphysical, she knew not which, some as yet veiled fact waiting to be revealed, in view of which her present agitation was trivial and meaningless.

She ran on, blind and blundering; yet her feet were so clogged by the weight of earth and wet, her thoughts by the sweat of the fear that was on them, that neither seemed to move for all her willing. And all the while, another part of her consciousness sat aloof, critical and detached, laughing at her for an excitable fool, analysing, in Clare's crispest accents, the illusions which were bewildering her, and wondering coolly that any girl of her age could so let her imagination run away with her.

She pulled herself together with an immense effort of will.

That was the truth.... It was her own imagination that was literally and physically running away with her, whipping her tired body into unnecessary exertion, flogging her into mad flight from this pleasant, harmless place, with its hideous and horrible suggestion of evil at hand.... But the evil was in her own mind.... There was nothing pursuing her, no vague ghost at her elbow.... The horror was in herself, to be faced, and fought, and trampled.... Running would not help her ... she would only carry her terror with her.... For an instant she had a lightning glimpse of the reasons of the Sadducean attitude to personality, and its desperate denials of future existence. She was suddenly appalled at the hideous possibility of existing eternally with her own undying thoughts for company. She wondered if there were really such a thing as soul suicide, and thought that, if so, many must have chosen to commit it.

Here her shifting, crowding thoughts blotted out the glimmer of understanding, as flies clustering on a window-pane can blot out light; yet the word *suicide* remained in her mind, disturbing, vaguely suggestive. It was connected with something terrible-she could not remember what-that in its turn was one with the vague horror at her elbow, that walked with the echo of her footsteps and panted with the echoes of her breaths, and yet was not real at all, but only in her mind.

She did not believe she should ever find her way out of the wood.... The hyacinths in her arms were so heavy—a queerly familiar weight: and the sun had gone in, which had, somehow, something to do with the trouble.... She felt the black depression of the winter months that she had left Utterbridge to escape settling down on her once more. She turned hopelessly to elude it, but it surrounded her like a fog, as indeed she half believed it to be. She supposed they had sudden fogs in the country, when the sun went in.... And the sun had gone in because she had picked all the hyacinths.... She remembered the story clearly enough now.... The sun had played at quoits with a child, and had thrown amiss, and killed it, and the purple blood had trickled down from the child's forehead.... So the sun had turned it into purple hyacinths.... But she, Alwynne, had been gathering all the hyacinths, and they were a heavy bunch, heavy as a dead child's body ... and in another minute they would be disenchanted, and she would be carrying a dead child's body in her arms....

She stood still, gazing down at the flowers, white and glassy-eyed with terror, wondering that she was still alive and not yet mad. For she knew that the fear she had feared was upon her at last. She dared not blink lest in that second the change should take place, and she should find Louise, long buried, in her arms. Because, of course, it was Louise who had been following her all the while.... Louise-who had committed suicide.... She was following Alwynne, because it was Alwynne's fault.... Clare had said so.... Well-at least she could tell Louise that she had meant no harm....

She waited, swayed back against a tree trunk, the flowers a dead weight over her arm. She held them gently, lest a rough movement should wake the horror they hid. With what was left of sanity she prayed.

The trees encircled her, watching. From far away there came once more a sound of footsteps.

CHAPTER XXXIII

Roger set out at a quick pace for the wood, the basket rattling lightly on his arm; but the track of Alwynne's shoes was lost in the deep grass of the paddock, and he hesitated, wondering where he should look for her. Followed a cupboard-love scene with Nicholas Nye, who accompanied him to the boundary of his kingdom, snuffling windily in the empty bodge. He brayed disgustedly when Roger left him, his ancient lips curling backward over yellow stumps, in a smile that was an insult. He had the air of knowing exactly where Roger was going, and of being leeringly amused.

For ten minutes Roger wandered about, starting aside from the pathway half a dozen times, deceived by a swaying branch, or the deceptive pink and white of distant birch bark. He tramped on into the thickness of the wood, till at last, through a thinning of trees, a hundred yards to his left, he caught a glimpse of gold, that could only, he told himself, be Alwynne's hair. He frowned. It was just like the girl to go floundering into the only boggy bit of the wood, when two thirds were drained and dry, and thick with flowers....It was sheer spirit of contradiction! She would catch cold of course; and he would, not to mince matters, be stunk out with eucalyptus for the next ten days...and The Dears would fuss...he knew them! His fastidiousness was always revolted by a parade of handkerchiefs and bleared eyes. He was accustomed to insist that disease was as disgraceful as dirt: and that there was not a pin to choose between Dartmoor and the London Hospital as harbourage for criminals. But he could always dismount from his hobby-horse for any case of suffering that came his way. He could give his time, his money, or his tenderness, with a matter-of-course promptitude that relieved all but a tender-skinned few of any belief that they had reason to be grateful to him.

Roger, his eye on the distant halo, crashed through the undergrowth at a great rate, emerging into a little natural clearing, to find Alwynne facing him, a bare half-dozen yards away.

The full sight of her pulled him up short.

She was standing—lying upright, rather, for she seemed incapable of self-support—flattened against a big grey oak. One arm, flung backwards, clutched and scrabbled at the bark; the other, crooked shelteringly, supported a mass of bluebells. Her face was grey, her mouth half open, her eyes wide and pale. Very obviously she did not see him.

"Alwynne!" he exclaimed.

She cowered. He exclaimed again, astonished and not a little alarmed ——

"Alwynne! Are you ill? What on earth has happened?"

She flung up her head, staring.

"Roger?" she said incredulously.

Then her face began to work. He never forgot the expression of relief that flowed across it. It was like the breaking up of a frozen pool.

"Why, it's you!" cried Alwynne. "It's you! It's only you!" The flowers dropped lingeringly from her slack hands, and she swayed where she stood. He crossed hastily to her and she clung helplessly to his arm. She looked dazed and stupid.

"Of course it is," he said. "Who did you think it was?"

Alwynne looked at him.

"Louise," she said, "I thought it was Louise. She's come before, but never in the daytime. A ghost can't walk in the daytime. But this place is so dark, she might think it was night here, don't you think?"

He gave her arm a gentle shake.

"Let's get out of this, Alwynne," he began persuasively. "I think you're rather done for. There's been a hot sun to-day, and you've been stooping till you're dizzy. Come on. What a lot of flowers you've picked! Come, let's get out of this place."

"Yes," she said; "let's get out of this place."

"What about your bunch?" he questioned, glancing down at the hyacinths' heaped disorder. "Don't you want it?"

He felt her shiver.

"No," she said, "no." She hesitated. "Could we hide it? Cover it up? It ought to be buried. I can't leave it-just lying there— —" There was a catch in her voice.

He concealed his astonishment and looked about him.

"Of course not," he said cheerfully. "Here-what about this?"

A huge tussock of bleached grass, its sodden leaves as long as a woman's hair, caught his eye. He parted the heavy mass and showed her the little cave of dry soil below.

"What about this? They'll be all right here," he suggested gravely.

Alwynne nodded.

"Yes-put it in quickly," she said.

Without a word, as if it were the most natural thing in the world, he did as she asked. Then, rising and slipping her arm through his own, he pushed on quite silently, holding back the strong pollard shoots, clearing aside the brambles, till they reached the uneven footpath once more, that led them in less than five minutes to the further edge of the wood. As they emerged into the open fields, he felt the weight on his arm lessening. He glanced at his companion, and saw that there was once more a tinge of colour in her cheek.

She drew a deep breath and looked at him.

"I thought I should never get out again," she said dispassionately, as one stating a bald fact.

"Get where?"

"Out of that wood. You were just in time. I thought I was caught. I should have been, if you hadn't come."

Then she grew conscious of his expression, and answered it —

"I suppose you think I'm mad."

"I do rather."

"I don't wonder. It doesn't much matter— —" Her voice flagged and strained.

They walked on in silence.

She began again abruptly.

"Of course you thought I was mad. I knew you would. I do myself, sometimes. Any one would. Even Clare. That's why I never told any one. But it never happened when I was awake before."

"I wonder if you would tell me exactly what happened?"

"I was frightened," she began irresolutely.

"For a moment I wondered if a tramp— —"

She laughed shakily.

"I'm a match for the average tramp, I think. I'm head of the games."

He was amused.

"You'd tell him what you thought of him, I'm sure."

But already her smile had grown absent; she was relapsing into her abstraction.

They had crossed the field as they talked, and struck into the little gravelled path that led to the monster glass-houses on the other side of the hedge. A wide gate barred their progress. Roger manipulated the rusty chain in silence for a moment, then, as the gate yawned open, turned to her pleasantly— —

"Won't you have a look round, as we've come so far? You're in my territory now, and I've a houseful of daffodils just bursting."

His calm matter-of-fact manner had its effect. Alwynne absorbed in her sick thoughts, found herself listening to his account of his houses and his experiments, as one listens subconsciously to the slur of a distant water-course. She did not take in the meaning of his words, but his even voice soothed her fretted nerves.

Roger was perfectly aware of her inattention. He was not brilliant, but he was equipped with experience and common-sense and kindness of heart; and above all he was observant. The Alwynne of his acquaintance, pretty, amusing, clever, had attracted him sufficiently, had even, as he admitted to himself as he went in search of her, been able to entice him from his Sunday comfort to wander quarrelling in wet fields. But the Alwynne he had come upon half-an-hour later was a revelation; at a glance every preconceived notion of her character was swept away.

His first idea was that she had been frightened by roughs, but her manner and expression speedily contradicted it. She was, he perceived, struggling, and not for the first time, with some overwhelming trouble of the mind. He had been appalled by the fear in her eyes. He remembered Jean's account. Elsbeth had been worried about her for a long time: ill-health and depression: she believed there had been some sort of a shock—a child had died suddenly at the school....

Alwynne's gay and piquant presence had made him forget, till that moment, such rudiments of her history as he had heard. But seeing her distress, he was angry that he had been obtuse, and amazed at her skill in concealing whatever trouble it might be that was oppressing her. All the kindliness of his nature awoke at sight of her haunted, hunted air; he bestirred himself to allay her agitation; he resolved then and there to help her if he could.

He had recognised at once that she was in no state for argument or explanation, and had devoted himself to calming her, falling in with her humour, and showing no surprise at the extravagance of her remarks. He had her quieted, almost herself, by the time they had reached his nursery and descended brick steps into a bath of sweet-smelling warmth.

Alwynne exclaimed.

The glass-house was very peaceful. Above a huge Lent lily the spring's first butterfly hovered and was still awhile, then quivered again and fluttered away, till his pale wings grew invisible against the aisles of yellow bloom. The short, impatient barks of Roger's terrier outside the door came to them, dulled and faint. The sun poured down upon the already heated air.

Alwynne walked down the long narrow middle way, hesitating, enjoying, and moving on again, much, Roger thought, as the butterfly had done. She said little, but her delight was evident. Roger was pleased; he liked his flowers to be appreciated. But he, too, said little; he was considering his course of action.

At the end of the conservatory was a square of brick flooring on which stood a table with a tobacco jar, and a litter of magazines; beside it an ancient basket-chair. Roger pulled it forward.

"This is my sanctum," he said. "Won't you sit down? I do a lot of work here in the winter."

Alwynne sank into the creaking wicker-work with a sigh of relief.

"I shall never get up again," she said. "It's too comfortable. I'm tired."

"Of course." He smiled at her. "Don't you worry. You needn't budge till you want to. I'll get some tea."

"You mustn't bother. It'll be cold. It's miles to the house," said Alwynne wearily.

He made no answer, but began to clear away the rubbish on the table. He moved deftly, light-footed, without clumsy or unnecessary noise; in spite of his size, his movements were always silent and assured.

She closed her eyes indifferently. She had said that she was tired; the word was as good as another where none were adequate to express her utter exhaustion. She felt that, in a sense, she was in luck to be so tired that she could not think.... She knew that later she must brace herself to an examination of the nightmare experience of the afternoon, to renew her struggle against the devils of her imagination; but for the moment her weakness was her safe-guard, and she could lie relaxed and thoughtless, mesmerised by the flooding sunshine and the pulsing scents and the quick movements of the man beside her. She wondered what he was doing, but she was too tired to open her eyes, or to interpret to herself the faint sounds she heard. She thought dreamily that he was as kind as Elsbeth. She was grateful to him for not talking to her. He was a wonderfully understanding person.... He might have known her for years.... He made her feel safe ... that was a great gift.... If she, Alwynne, had been like that, kind and reassuring, to poor little Louise-if only she had understood-Louise would have come to her, then, instead of brooding herself to death.... Poor Louise.... Poor unhappy Louise.... And after all she had not been able to kill herself.... She was still alive, lying in wait for her, though she knew that Alwynne could not help her.... She would never go away, though they had left her outside in the cold-in the cold of the wood-and were safe in this warm summerland ... she would be waiting when they came out again.... She shuddered as she thought of retracing her steps. She would ask Roger to take her home another way.... She would not have to explain.... He had not wanted explanation.... She was passionately grateful to him because he had not overwhelmed her with questions at their meeting. She could never explain, of course, because people would think her mad.... They might even send her to an asylum, if she told them.... She longed for the relief of confession, yet who would believe that she was merely a sane woman rendered desperate by evil dreams? Not Clare, certainly-not Elsbeth, though they loved her.... She would just have to go on fighting her terrors as best she could, till she or they were crushed....

She sighed hopelessly and opened her eyes.

"Had a doze? Good! Tea's ready! I expect you want it," said Roger cheerfully.

She was surprised into normality, and began to smile as she looked about her.

The rickety table had been covered by a gay, chequered cloth. There was crockery, and a little green tea-pot, and a pile of short-bread at her elbow. A spirit-lamp and kettle were shelved incongruously between trays of daffodils.

Roger sat upon an upturned flower-pot, and beamed at her.

"Oh, how jolly!" cried Alwynne, the Alwynne once more of his former acquaintance. "Where did it come from?"

He showed her a cupboard against the wall, half hidden by a canopy of smilax.

"I always keep stores here," he confessed boyishly. "I used to when I was a kid. This is the old glass-house, you know, on Great House land. I've built all the others. I used to be Robinson Crusoe then, and now it's useful, when I'm busy, not to have to go up to the house always. Won't you pour out?"

Alwynne flashed a look at him.

"I don't believe it's that. You enjoy the-the marooning still. I should. I think it's perfectly delightful here."

"Well, Harris-my head-gardener—doesn't approve. Thinks it's *infra dig*. He told me once that he knew ladies enjoyed making parlours of their conservatories, and letting in draughts and killing the plants; but he was a nursery-man himself. However, I've broken him in to it. Oh, I say, there's no milk!"

"I don't take it. Clare—a friend of mine-never does, so I've got accustomed to it." She drank thirstily. "Oh, it's good! I didn't know I wanted my tea so."

"I did," he said significantly.

She coloured painfully: she would not look at him.

"I was very tired," she said lamely.

"Were you?" he asked her. "You weren't gone half an hour. Do you know it's only half-past three?"

He was very gentle; but she felt herself accused. She played uneasily with her rope of beads as she chose her words. Roger, for all his intentness, could not help noticing how white and slender her hands showed, stained though they were with hyacinth-milk, as they fingered the blue, glancing chain. They were thin though; and following the outline of her wrist and arm and bare neck, he thought her cheek, for all its smooth youthfulness, was thin also, too thin-altogether too austere, for her age and way of life. She had always been flushed in his presence, delightfully flushed with laughter, or anger, or embarrassment, and he had noticed nothing beyond her pretty colour. But now, he saw uneasily that there were hollows round her eyes, as if she slept little, and that there were hollows as well as dimples in her cheeks. He was astonished to find himself not a little perturbed at his discovery, so perturbed that he did not, for a moment, realise that she was speaking to him.

"I am very sorry," she was saying. "I'm afraid you thought—I'm afraid I was rather silly-in the wood. I was disturbed when you found me." Her words came jerkily. "I had not expected-that is—I did not expect——" She broke off. Her eyes implored him to leave her alone.

He would not understand their appeal.

"Yes, you expected——" he prompted her.

She controlled her voice with difficulty.

"Heavens knows!" She laughed, with a pitiful little air of throwing him off the scent. "One gets frightened for no reason sometimes."

"Does one?"

"In the country—I'm town-bred." She smiled at him.

He made up his mind, though he felt brutal.

"You were expecting-Louise?"

There was a silence. Slowly she lifted shaking hands, warding him off.

"No, no!" she said. "For pity's sake. You are calling her back." Then, struck with a new idea, she grew, if possible, whiter still. "Unless," she said, whispering, "you saw her-you too? Then there is no hope. I thought it was in my mind-only in my mind-but if you saw her too——" Her voice failed.

He thrust in hastily, ready enough to comfort her, but knowing well that the time had not come. Yet he felt like a surgeon at his first operation.

"No, you are mistaken. There was no one. I don't even know who Louise is. Only you mentioned her-once or twice, you see."

"Did I?" she said. Then, with an effort at a commonplace tone: "I was stupidly upset. You must excuse——"

He broke in.

"Who is Louise?" he asked her bluntly.

"A ghost," said Alwynne, white to the lips.

Again they were blankly silent.

Then she spoke, with extraordinary passion—

"If you laugh-it will be wicked if you laugh at me."

"I'm not thinking of laughing," he said, with the petulance of extreme anxiety.

She met his look and shrugged her shoulders.

"Then you think I'm crazy," she began defiantly. "I can't help it, what you think." She changed the subject transparently. "Roger, it's nice here. What are the names of all these flowers? Are those big ones daffodils, or jonquils, or narcissi? I never know the difference. I never remember——" Her voice trailed into silence.

"But look here," he began, and stopped again abruptly, deep in thought.

The flame of the spirit-lamp on the shelf between them flickered and failed, and sputtered up again noisily. Mechanically he rose to extinguish it, and, still absently, cleared the little table of its china and eatables.

Then he sat down once more, and leant forward, his arms on the table, his expression determined, yet very friendly.

"Alwynne," he said, in his most matter-of-fact voice, "hadn't you better tell me all about it?"

"You?"

"Why not?" he said comfortably. "You'll feel ever so much better if you get if off your chest."

For an instant she hesitated: then she shook her head wearily.

"I would like to tell some one. But I can't. I sound mad, even to myself. I couldn't tell any one. I couldn't tell Elsbeth even."

"Of course not," he agreed. "You can't worry your own people."

"No, you can't, can you?" she said, grateful for his comprehension.

"Of course not. But you see—I'm different. Whatever your trouble is, it won't worry me-because I don't care for you like Elsbeth and your friends. So you can just ease off on me—d'you see? If I do think you mad, it just doesn't matter, does it? What does it matter telling some one a secret when you'll never see them again? Don't you see?" he argued reassuringly.

She nodded dumbly. The cheerful, impersonal kindness of his voice and air made her want to cry. She realised how she had been aching for sympathy.

"Don't you see?" he repeated.

"You wouldn't make fun?" she asked him. "You wouldn't tell any one? You wouldn't talk me over?"

"No, Alwynne," he said gravely.

For a moment her eyes searched his face wistfully; then with sudden decision, she began to speak.

CHAPTER XXXIV

Alwynne's words, after the months of silence, came rushing out, breaking down all barriers, sweeping on in unnatural fluency. Yet she was simple and direct, entirely sincere; accepting him at his own valuation, impersonally, as confessor and comforter, without a side glance at the impression she might make, or its effect on their after relations.

She told him the story of Louise; and he felt sick as he listened. Unintentionally, for she was obviously absorbed in her school and uncritical in her attitude to it, she gave him a vivid enough impression of the system in force, of the deliberate encouragement of much that he considered unhealthy, if not unnatural. He detected an hysterical tendency in the emulations and enthusiasms to which she referred. The gardener in him revolted at the thought of such congestion of minds and bodies. He felt as indignant as if he had discovered a tray of unthinned seedlings. Alwynne conveyed to him, more clearly than she knew, an idea of the forcing-house atmosphere that she, and those still younger than she, had been breathing. The friend she so constantly mentioned, repelled him; he thought of her with distaste, as of an unscrupulous and unskilful hireling; he was amazed at the affection of Alwynne's references to her. Only in connection with the dead child was there a hint of uncertainty in her attitude. There perhaps, she admitted, had "Clare" been, not unkind-never and impossibly unkind-but perhaps, with the best of motives, mistaken. She had not understood Louise. Roger agreed silently and grimly enough. She had not understood Louise, whom she had killed, nor this loyal and affectionate child, whom she was driving into melancholia, nor any one it appeared, nor anything, but the needs of her own barrenly emotional nature.... He was horrified at the idea of such a woman, such a type of woman, in undisputed authority, moulding the mothers of the next generation.... He had never considered the matter seriously, but he supposed she was but one of many.... There must be something poisonous in a system that could render possible the placing of such women in such positions....

"Then what happened, after that poor child's death?" he asked. "She left, of course?"

"Who?"

"Your friend —'Clare' —Miss ——?"

"Hartill. Oh, no! Why should she?"

"I should have thought-suicide-bad for the school's reputation?"

"Then you think it was-that-too? It was supposed to be an accident."

"How do you mean, 'supposed'?"

"There was an inquest, you see. I had to go. I was so frightened all the time, of what I might slip into saying. But they all agreed that it was an accident. She was fond of curling up in the window-seats with her books. Oh, she was a queer little thing! When you came on her suddenly, she used to look up like a startled baby colt. She always looked as if she wanted some one to run to. Well, there was no guard, you see, only an inch of ledge-she had not been well-she must have felt faint-and fallen. They all said it was that. I was so thankful-for Clare's sake. She could not reproach herself-after such a verdict. It was 'Accidental Death.' Only —I —of course —I knew. Some of them guessed-Clare-and I believe Elsbeth, though we never discussed it-and I knew. But nobody said anything-nobody has, ever since, except once Clare told me-what she feared. I never managed to persuade her that it was an accident, but at least she doesn't know for certain, and at least she knows she couldn't help it. And now we never speak of it. But *I* know——"

"What do you know?" he said. "You found out something?"

"She did-she did kill herself," said Alwynne. "Oh, Roger, she did. I've known it all along —I should have guessed anyway, I think, because I knew how unhappy she was. I knew how awfully she cared about Clare. Clare was very good to her sometimes. Clare was fond of her, you know. Clare takes violent fancies like that, to clever people. And Louise was brilliant, of course. Clare was charmed with her. Only Louise-this is how I've thought it out; oh, I've had time to think it out-she just got drunk on it, the happiness, I mean, of being cared for. She hadn't much of

275

a home. She was rather an ugly duckling to her people, I think. Then Clare made a fuss of her, and you see, she was so little, she couldn't see that-it didn't mean much to Clare. And I don't think grown-up people understand how girls are-they have to worship some one, at that age. Clare doesn't quite understand, I think. She is too sensible herself to realise how girls can be silly. She is awfully good to them, but, of course, she never dreams how miserable they get when she gets bored with them. She can't help it."

Roger's face was expressive-but Alwynne was staring at the uneasy butterfly.

"It doesn't matter, as a rule. Only Louise had no one else-and it just broke her heart. If she had been grown-up it would have been like being in love."

Roger made an inarticulate remark.

"Don't you see?" said Alwynne innocently.

"I see." He was carefully expressionless.

"And then she was run down and did her work badly. And Clare hates illness-besides-she thought Louise was slacking. I tried to make her see——Oh," she cried passionately, "why didn't I try harder? It's haunting me, Roger, that I didn't try hard enough. I ought to have known how she felt—I was near her age. Clare couldn't be expected to-but Louise talked to me sometimes—I ought to have seen. I did see. All that summer she went about so white and miserable-and Clare was angry with her-and I hadn't the pluck to tackle either of them. I was afraid of being a busybody—I was afraid of upsetting Clare. You see—I'm awfully fond of Clare. She makes you forget everything but herself. And, of course, she never realised what was wrong with Louise. I didn't altogether, either-you do believe that?" She broke off, questioning pitifully, as if he were her judge.

He nodded.

"Right till the day of the play, I never really saw how crazily miserable she was growing. She was crazy-don't you think?"

"You want to think so?" He considered her curiously.

"It mitigates it."

"That she killed herself?"

"It's deadly sin? Or don't you believe——?"

"No," he said. "There's such a thing as the right of exit-but go on."

"What do you mean?"

"I'll tell you what I think presently. I want all your thoughts now—— There were signs——?"

"Of insanity? No. But she was-exaggerated-too intelligent-too babyish-too brilliant-too everything. She felt things too much. She failed in an exam. —sheer overwork-just before."

"I see. Was she ambitious?"

"Only to please Clare. Clare didn't like her failing."

"Did she tell the child so?" His tone was stern.

"Oh, no!"

"You're sure?"

"Clare would have told me if they had had a row. She tells me everything."

He smiled a little.

"How old is your friend?"

She looked surprised.

"Oh-thirty-three-thirty-four-thirty-five. I don't really know. She never talks about ages and looks and that sort of thing. She rather despises all that. She laughs at me for-for liking clothes...." Her little blush made her look natural again. "But why?"

"I wondered. Then there was nothing to upset the child?"

"Only the failing. And then the play. I told you. She was awfully strange afterwards. That's where I blame myself. I ought to have seen that she was overwrought. But she drank the tea, and cheered up so when I told her Clare was pleased with her acting——"

"Was she?" He was frowning interestedly.

"I'm sure she must have been-it was brilliant, you know."

"She said so?"

"Oh, not actually-but I could tell. And it cheered the child up. I was quite easy about her-and then ten minutes later — —" She shuddered.

"Then it might have been an accident," he suggested soothingly.

"It wasn't," she said, with despairing conviction.

"My dear girl! Either you're indulging in morbid imaginings-or you've something to go on?"

She shook her head with a frightened look at him.

"No!" she said hurriedly. "No!"

"Then why," he said quietly, meeting her eyes, "were you frightened at the inquest?"

She averted her eyes.

"I wasn't — I mean — I was nervous, of course."

"You were frightened of what you might slip into saying. You told me so ten minutes ago."

"Oh, if you're trying to trap me?" she flashed out wrathfully.

He rejoiced at the tone. It was the impetuous Alwynne of his daily intercourse again. The mere relief of discussion was, as he had guessed, having a tonic effect on her nerves.

He smiled at her pleasantly.

"Don't tell me anything more, if you'd rather not."

She subsided at this.

"I didn't mean to be angry," she faltered. "Only I've guarded myself so from telling. You see, I lied at the inquest. It was perjury, I suppose." There was a little touch of importance in her tone. "But I'll tell you."

She hesitated, her older self once more supervening.

"Afterwards-when the doctor had come, and they took Louise away-after that ghastly afternoon was over — —" She whitened. "It was ghastly, you know-so many people-crowding and gaping — I dream of all those crowded faces — —"

"Well?" he urged her forward.

"I went up to the room where she had changed, to see that the children had gone — —"

"She fell from that room?"

"She must have. After she had changed. She'd locked the door-to change. I broke it open. I thought she had fainted — a baby told me something about Louise falling-lisping so, I couldn't make out what she meant-and I'd run up to see. It turned out afterwards that little Joan had been in a lower room, and had seen her body as it fell past the window."

"How beastly!" he said, with an involuntary shudder.

"And when I got the door open-an empty room. Something made me look out of the window. She was down below-right under me-on the steps."

She was silent.

"But afterwards?" he urged her. "You went up again?"

"I had to. I was afraid already-recollecting little things. I looked about, in case she'd left a message. And on the window-ledge — there were great scratches. Then I knew."

She was forgetting him, staring into space, peopled as it was with her memories.

"I don't understand," he said.

She did not answer.

"Alwynne!" he said urgently.

She looked at him absently.

"Scratches? What are you driving at?"

"Oh," she said dully, "there was a nail in her shoe. She had tried to hammer it in at the morning school. It had made scratches all over the rostrum. I was rather cross about it."

"But I don't see," he began, and stopped, realising suddenly her meaning.

"You mean-she must have stood on the ledge-to make those marks?"

"Yes," said Alwynne. Then, fiercely, "Well?"

"Yes, that's conclusive," he admitted. He looked at her pityingly. "You poor child! And you never told?"

"I got a paint-box," she said defiantly, "and painted them brown-like the paintwork. It would have broken up Clare to know-and all the questions and comments. What would you have done?"

He ignored the challenge, answered only the misery in the tone.

"It can't have been easy for you-that week," he said gently.

"Easy?" She began to laugh harshly. "And yet I don't know," she reflected. "I don't think I felt anything much at the time. It was like being in a play. Almost interesting. Entirely unreal. At the inquest —I lied as easily as saying grace. I wasn't a bit worried. What did worry me was a bit of sticking-plaster on the coroner's chin. One end was uncurled, and I was longing for him to stick it down again. It seemed more important than anything else that he should stick it down. It would have been a real relief to me. I'm not trying to be funny."

"I know," he said.

"And when it was over —I was quite cheerful. And at the funeral —I know they thought I was callous. But I didn't feel sad. Only cold-icy cold-in my hands and my feet and my heart. And I felt desperately irritated with them all for crying. People look appalling when they cry." She paused. "So they banked up Louise with wreaths and we left her." She paused again.

"Well?" he prompted.

"I went home at the end of that week. Elsbeth sent me to bed early. I was log-tired all of a sudden. Oh, I was tired! I had hardly slept at all since she died. I'd stayed at Clare's, you know. She's a bad sleeper, too, and it always infects me-and we used to sit up till daylight, forgetting the time, talking. We've always heaps to talk about. Clare's a night-bird. She's always most brilliant about midnight." She smiled reminiscently. "We picnic, you know, in our dressing-gowns. She has a great white bearskin on the hearth. Her fires are piled up, and never go out all night. And I brew coffee-and we talk. It's jolly. I wish you knew Clare. She's an absorbing person."

"You're giving me quite a good idea of her," he said. Then carelessly: "But she must have realised that after such a shock-and the strain— —"

"Oh, it was much worse for Clare," she broke in quickly. "Think-her special pupil! She had had such hopes of Louise. And Clare's so terribly sensitive-she was getting it on her mind. Do you know, she almost began to think it was her fault, not to have seen what was going on? Once, she was absolutely frantic with depression, poor darling, until I made her understand that, if it was any one's, it must be mine. Of course, when I told her everything, how I'd guessed Louise was pretty miserable, and tried to tell her again and then funked it-well, then she saw. As she said, if I'd only spoken out.... She was very kind-but, of course, I soon felt that she thought I was responsible-indirectly-for the whole thing— —" Her voice quavered.

Roger, watching her simple face, wanted to do something vigorous. At that moment it would have given him great satisfaction to have interviewed Miss Hartill. Failing that, he wanted to take Alwynne by the shoulders and shake the nonsense out of her. He repressed himself, however. He was in his way, as simple as Alwynne, but where she was merely direct, he was shrewd. He knew that she must show him all the weeds that were choking her before he could set about uprooting them and planting good seed in their stead.

She went on.

"But even then, though I had been neglectful-oh, Roger, what made Louise do it? Just then? She looked happier! It couldn't have been anything I'd said! I know I cheered her up. It's inconceivable! She was smiling, contented-and she went straight upstairs and killed herself!"

He shook his head.

"Inconceivable, as you say. You're sure-of your facts!"

"How?"

"I mean-you were the last person to see her?"

"Oh, yes, Roger! every one was at tea."

"Miss Hartill?"

"Clare would have said ——"

"Of course," he said, "she tells you everything."

She nodded, in all good faith —

"Besides, Clare was in the mistresses' room."

"Impossible for her to have spoken with Louise?"

"Quite. Clare would have told me ——"

"Yet there remains the fact that Louise was, as you say, happier after seeing you. Within fifteen minutes, she is dead. Either she went mad-which I don't believe, do you?"

"I want to ——"

"But you don't—knowing the child. Neither do I, from what you tell me. She seems to have been horribly sane. Sane enough, anyhow, to throw off a burden. So if, as we agree, she didn't suddenly go mad-something occurred to change her mood of comparative happiness to actual despair. I think, if you ask me, that she did see Miss Hartill after she left you."

"But Clare would have told me," repeated Alwynne stubbornly.

"I'm not so sure."

"But she said nothing at the inquest, either."

"Did you?" he retorted. "If she had had a row with the child it would have sounded pretty bad."

"But Clare's incapable of deceit."

"She might say the same of you."

"But-if your guess were true, it would be Clare's fault-all Clare's fault-not mine at all!" she deducted slowly.

"It's not your fault, anyway," he assured her.

"But it would have been too utterly cruel of Clare not to have told me. She knew what I felt at the time-why not have told me?"

"She might have been afraid-you might have shrunk ——"

"From Clare?" She smiled securely. Then, with a change of tone: "No, Roger. All this is guessing, far-fetched guessing."

"Anyhow, Alwynne," he said sharply, "there was gross cruelty in her treatment of that child. You can't excuse it. Directly or indirectly, she is responsible for her death."

She flushed.

"You have not the shadow of right to say that."

"I do say it."

She put out her hand to him with a touch of appeal.

"Please-won't you leave Clare out of it? You are utterly wrong. You see, you don't know her. If you did you would understand. I am so grateful to you for being kind. I don't want to be angry. But I must, if you talk like that. Please-if you can, make me sure it wasn't my fault. But if it involves Clare —I'd rather go on being-not not quite happy. Yet I hoped, perhaps, you would help me."

"Of course I'm helping you," he said, quick to catch and adopt her tone. He had no wish to intimidate her. He liked her pathetic little dignities and loyalties. He was, so far, content; he had, he knew, in spite of her protestations, sown a seed of distrust in her mind. Time would ripen it. He felt no compunction in enlightening her blind devotion. He had quick antipathies, and he had conceived an idea of Clare Hartill that would have appalled Alwynne, and which justified to himself any measure that he might see fit to take. In his own mind he referred to her as "that poisonous female." There were no half-measures with Roger.

CHAPTER XXXV

Alwynne leant back in her chair and regarded Roger with some intentness.

"Well?" he said politely.

"I was thinking——" she said lamely.

"Obviously."

"That it was rather queer-that I should tell you all this, when I couldn't even tell Elsbeth."

"Don't you think it's often easier to talk to strangers? One's personality can make its own impression-it has no preconception to fight against."

"Yes. But I hate strangers, till they've stopped being strange. And, you know"—she hesitated—"I haven't really liked you. Have you noticed it?"

"In streaks," he admitted. "But why?"

"You patronise so!" she flared. "You make me feel a fool. This afternoon——Of course, it's quite true that I don't know much about men. I suppose you knew I was-inexperienced; but you needn't have rubbed it in. And you've always talked down to me."

"I don't think I did," he considered the matter unsmiling. "I think it's rather the other way-the tilt of your nose disturbs my complacence. You listen to me at meals like Disapproval incarnate. You make me nervous."

"Do I?" she asked delightedly.

"Yes." He laughed. "I hide it under a superior air, of course."

"Yes, of course," she sympathised. "That's what I do always."

"It is useful," he agreed.

"People may think you disagreeable, but at least you're dignified. *You have chosen your fault well, I really cannot laugh at it.* Do you remember? I told Elsbeth that you were like Mr. Darcy."

"And that you don't like me?"

"Well—I didn't. That's why it's so queer-that I can talk to you so easily. I am grateful. It has helped, just talking."

"I knew it would."

"I feel better." She stirred in her seat. "Is it late? Ought we to be going home?"

He chose his words, his eyes on her, though he spoke casually enough.

"No hurry. We can always take a cut through the wood, you know."

She flinched at that, as he expected; spoke uneasily, furtive-eyed.

"I think I'd rather go at once-round by the road. Isn't there a road?" She rose and looked about her, taking farewell of the daffodils.

"Yes, there's a road. Wouldn't you like a bunch?" He took a pair of scissors from the wall, and began to select his blooms. Alwynne followed him delightedly. She thought she would have a surprise for Clare, after all. And Elsbeth! Elsbeth was an after-thought. But she hoped there would be enough for Elsbeth.

"Why won't you go back through the wood?" he said quietly, as, hands full, he at last replaced the scissors on their particular nail, and twitched a strand from the horse-tail of bass that hung beside them. "Tell me." Then, calmly, "Here-put your finger here, will you?"

Mechanically she obeyed and he tied the knot that secured the great yellow sheaf and gave it to her.

"Now tell me. What frightened you in the wood? What was wrong?" He spoke quietly, but his tone compelled her.

"If you dreamed a dream——" she began unwillingly, "night after night-month after month-something ghastly——"

"Yes—" he encouraged her.

"Ah, well-at least you've the comfort of knowing it's a dream. But suppose, one day-you dreamt it while you were awake——?"

"Dreamt what?" He guessed her meaning, but he was deliberately forcing her to reduce her terrors into words-the more they crystallised, the easier she would find it to face and destroy them.

"Do you believe in hell?" she flung at him.

"I should jolly well think so."

"For children?" Her tone implored comfort.

"I'm afraid so."

"But how can it be fair? They're so little. They don't know right from wrong."

"I knew a kid," he said meditatively, an eye on her tormented face, "only eight-used to act, if you please. Hung about London stage-doors, and bearded managers in their dens for a living. Quick little chap! Father drunk or ill; incapable, anyhow. The child supported them both. I've seen that child kept hanging about three or four hours on end. And what he knew! It made you sick and sorry. He must be twelve by now-getting on, I believe, poor kid! And a cheerful monkey! He's certainly had his hell, though."

She had hardly listened, she was absorbed in her thoughts; but she caught at his last words — —

"In this life? Oh, yes! That's cruel enough. But not afterwards? Not eternal damnation! I don't mind it for myself so much-but for a baby that can't understand why — —It isn't possible, is it?"

He began to laugh jollily.

"Alwynne-you utter fool! Don't you believe in God?"

"I suppose so," she admitted.

"Of course, if you didn't — —"

"Yes," she thrust in. "Then it would be all right. I could be sure she was asleep-dead-like last year's leaves — —"

"But why should God complicate matters?"

"Well-heaven follows-and hell-don't they? *Their worm dieth not* —and all the rest."

"Oh, I follow."

"Miss Marsham-the head mistress, you know-of course she's very old-but she believes-terribly. It's an awfully religious school. It scares some of the children. I used to laugh, but now, since Louise died, it scares me, though I am grown up. I've no convictions-and she is certain-and then I get these nightmares. I hear her calling-for water."

The flat matter-of-fact tone alarmed him more than emotion would have done.

"Water?"

"*For I am tormented in this flame.* I hear her every night-wailing." Her eyes strained after something that he could not see.

He found no words.

She returned with an effort.

"Of course, when it's over —I know it's imagination. My sense tells me so-in the daytime. Only I can't be sure. If only I could be sure! If some one would tell me to be sure. It's the reasoning it out for myself-all day-and going back to the dreams all night."

"How long has this been going on?" he asked curtly.

"Ever since-when I came home from Clare's —that night. I'd slept like a log. Then I woke up suddenly. I thought I heard Louise calling. I'd forgotten she was dead. Every night it happens-as soon as I go to sleep, she comes. Always trying to speak to me. I hear her screaming with pain-wanting help. Never any words. Do you think I'm mad? I know it's only a dream-but every night, you know — —"

"You're not going to dream any more," he said, with a determination that belied his inward sense of dismay. "But go on-let's have the rest of it."

"There isn't much. Just dreams. It's been a miserable year. I couldn't be cheerful always, you know-and I used to dread going to bed so. It made me stupid all day. And Clare-Clare didn't quite understand. Oh —I did want to tell her so. But you can't worry people. I'm afraid Elsbeth got worried-she hates it if you don't eat and have a colour. She packed me off here at last."

She drew a long breath.

"This blessed place! You don't know how I love it. I feel a different girl. All this space and air and freedom. What is it that the country does to one's mind? I've slept. No dreaming. Sleep that's like a hot bath. Can you imagine what that is after these months? Oh, Roger! I thought I'd stopped dreaming for good —I was forgetting — —"

"Go on forgetting," he said. "You can. I'll help you. You had a shock. It made you ill. You're getting well again. That's all."

"I'm not," she said. "I'm going mad. To-day, in that wood....Louise came running after me-and I was awake...."

Suddenly she gave a little ripple of high-pitched laughter.

"Oh, Mr. Lumsden! Isn't this a ridiculous conversation? And your face-you're so absurd when you frown....You make me laugh....You make me laugh...."

She broke off. Roger, with a swift movement, had turned and was standing over her.

"Now shut up!" he said sharply. "Shut up! D'you hear? Shut up this instant, and sit down." He put his hand on her shoulder and jerked her back into the chair.

The shock of his roughness checked her hysterics, as he had intended it should. She sat limply, her head in her hand, trying not to cry. He watched her.

"Pull yourself together, Alwynne," he said more gently.

Her lips quivered, but she nodded valiantly.

"I will. Just wait a minute. I don't want to make a fool of myself." Then, with a quavering laugh, "Oh, Roger, this is pleasant for you!"

He laughed.

"You needn't mind me," he said calmly. "Any more than I mind you. Except when you threaten hysterics. I bar hysterics. I wouldn't mind if they did any good. But we've got lots to do. No time at all for them. We've got to work this thing out. Ready?"

Alwynne waited, her attention caught.

"Now listen," he said. "First of all, get it into your head that I know all about it, and that I'm going to see you through. Next-whenever you get scared-though you won't again, I hope-that you are just to come and talk it over. You won't even have to tell me —I shall see by your face, you know. Do you understand? You're not alone any more. I'm here. Always ready to lay your ghosts for you. Will you remember?"

He spoke clearly and patiently-very cheerful and reassuring.

"You've got to go home well, Alwynne. Because, you know, though you're as sane as I am, you've been ill. This last year has been one long illness. You had a shock —a ghastly shock-and, of course, it skinned your nerves raw. My dear, I wonder it didn't send you really mad, instead of merely making you afraid of going mad. If you hadn't put up such a fight — —Honestly, Alwynne! I think you've been jolly plucky."

The sincere admiration in his voice was wonderfully pleasant to hear.

Alwynne opened her eyes widely.

"I don't know what you mean," she began shyly.

"I'm not imaginative," he said, "but if I'd been hag-ridden as you have — —" He broke off abruptly. "But, at least, you've fought yourself free," he continued cheerfully. "Yes, in spite of to-day." And his complete assurance of voice and manner had its effect on Alwynne, though she did not realise it.

"You're better already. You say yourself you're a different girl since you got away from-since you came here. And when you're quite well, it'll be your own work, not mine. I'm just tugging you up the bank, so to speak. But you've done the real fighting with the elements. I think you can be jolly proud of yourself."

Alwynne looked at him, half smiling, half bewildered.

"What do you mean? You talk as if it were all over. Shall I never be frightened again? Think of to-day?"

"Of course it's all over," he assured her truculently. "To-day? To-day was the last revolt of your imagination. You've let it run riot too long. Of course it hasn't been easy to call it to heel."

"You think it's all silly imaginings, then?"

"Alwynne," he said. "You've got to listen to this, just this. You say I'm not to talk about your friend, that I don't know her-that I'm unjust. But listen, at least, to this. I won't be unfair. I'll grant you that she was fond of the little girl, and meant no harm, no more than you did. But you say yourself that she was miserable till you relieved her mind by taking all the blame on yourself. Can't you conceive that in so doing you did assume a burden, a very real one? Don't you think that her fears, her terrors, may have haunted you as well as your own? I believe in the powers of thought. I believe that fear-remorse-regret-may materialise into a very ghost at your elbow. Do you remember Macbeth and Banquo? Do you believe that a something really physical sat that night in the king's seat? Do you think it was the man from his grave? I think it was Macbeth's thoughts incarnate. He thought too much, that man. But let's leave all that. Let's argue it out from a common-sense point of view. You said you believed in God?"

"Yes," she said.

"And the devil?"

"I suppose so."

"Well—I'm not so sure that I do," he remarked meditatively. "But if I do—I must say I cannot see the point of a God who wouldn't be more than a match for him: and a God who'd leave a baby in his clutches to expiate in fire and brimstone and all the rest of the beastliness——Well, is it common sense?" he appealed to her.

"If you put it like that——" she admitted.

"My dear, would you let Louise frizzle if it were in your hands? Why, you've driven yourself half crazy with fear for her, as it is. Can't you give God credit for a little common humanity? I'm not much of a Bible reader, but I seem to remember something about a sparrow falling to the ground——Now follow it up," he went on urgently. "If Louise's life was so little worth living that she threw it away-doesn't it prove she had her hell down here? If you insist on a hell. And when she was dead, poor baby, can't you trust God to have taken charge of her? And if He has-as He must have-do you think that child-that happy child, Alwynne, for if God exists at all, He must exist as the very source and essence of peace and love-that that child would or could wrench itself apart from God, from its happiness, in order to return to torment you? Is it possible? Is it probable? In any way feasible?"

Alwynne caught her breath.

"How you believe in God! I wish I could!"

Roger flushed suddenly like an embarrassed boy.

"You know, it's queer," he confided, subsiding naïvely, "till I began to talk to you, I didn't know I did. I never bother about church and things. You know——"

But Alwynne was not attending.

"Of course —I see what you mean," she murmured. "It applies to Louise too. Why, Roger, she was really fond of me-not as she was of Clare-of course-but quite fond of me. She never would have hurt me. Hurt? Poor mite! She never hurt any one in all her life."

"I wonder you didn't think of that before," remarked Roger severely. "I hope you see what an idiot you've been?"

"Yes," said Alwynne meekly. She did not flash out at him as he had hoped she would: but her manner had grown calm, and her eyes were peaceful.

"Poor little Louise!" said Alwynne slowly. "So we needn't think about her any more? She's to be dead, and buried, and forgotten. It sounds harsh, doesn't it? But she is dead-and I've only been keeping her alive in my mind all this year. Is that what you mean?"

"Yes," he said. "And if it were not as I think it is, sheer imagination-if your grieving and fear really kept a fraction of her personality with you, to torment you both-let her go now, Alwynne. Say good-bye to her kindly, and let her go home."

She looked at him gravely for a moment. Then she turned from him to the empty house of flowers.

"Good-bye, Louise!" said Alwynne, simply as a child.

About them was the evening silence. The sun, sinking over the edge of the world, was a blinding glory.

Out of the flowers rose the butterfly, found an open pane and fluttered out on the evening air, straight into the heart of the sunlight.

They watched it with dazzled eyes.

CHAPTER XXXVI

Alwynne had gone to bed early. She confessed to being tired, as she bade her cousins goodnight, and, indeed, she had dark rings about her eyes; but her colour was brilliant as she waited at the foot of the stairs for her candle. Roger had followed her into the hall and was lighting it. The thin flame flickered between them, kindling odd lights in their eyes.

"Good-night," said Alwynne, and went up a shallow step or two.

"Good-night," said Roger, without moving.

She turned suddenly and bent down to him over the poppy-head of the balustrade.

"Good-night," said Alwynne once more, and put out her hand.

"You're to sleep well, you know," he said authoritatively.

She nodded. Then, with a rush —

"Roger, I do thank you. I do thank you very much."

"That's all right," said Roger awkwardly.

Alwynne went upstairs.

He watched her disappear in the shadows of the landing, and took a meditative turn up and down the long hall before he returned to the drawing-room.

He felt oddly responsible for the girl; wished that he had some one to consult about her.... His aunts? Dears, of course, but ... Alicia, possibly.... Certainly not Jean.... Nothing against them ... dearest women alive ... but hardly capable of understanding Alwynne, were they? Without at all realising it he had already arrived at the conviction that no one understood Alwynne but himself.

He caught her name as he re-entered the room.

"Ever so much better! A different creature! Don't you think so, Roger?"

"Think what?"

"That Alwynne's a new girl? It's the air. Nothing like Dene air. But, of course, you didn't see her when she first came. A poor white thing! She'd worked herself to a shadow. How Elsbeth allowed it — —"

Jean caught her up.

"Overwork! Fiddlesticks! It wasn't that. I'm convinced in my own mind that there's something behind it. A girl doesn't go to pieces like that from a little extra work. Look at your Compton women at the end of a term. Bursting with energy still, I will say that for them. No — I'm inclined to agree with Parker. I told you what she said to me? 'She must have been crossed in love, poor young lady, the way she fiddle-faddles with her food!'"

Alicia laughed.

"When you and Parker get together there's not a reputation safe in the three Denes. If there had been anything of the kind, Elsbeth would have given me a hint."

"I should have thought Elsbeth would be the last person — —" Jean broke off significantly.

Roger glanced at her, eyebrows lifted.

"What's she driving at, Aunt Alice?"

"Lord knows!" said Alicia shortly.

Jean grew huffed.

"It's all very well, Alicia, to take that tone. You know what I mean perfectly well. Considering how reticent Elsbeth was over her own affairs to us-she wouldn't be likely to confide anything about Alwynne. But Elsbeth always imagined no one had any eyes."

Alicia moved uneasily in her chair.

"Jean, will you never let that foolish gossip be? It wasn't your business thirty years ago-at least let it alone now."

Jean flushed.

"It's all very well to be superior, Alicia, but you know you agreed with me at the time."

Roger chuckled.

"What are you two driving at? Let's have it."

Alicia answered him.

285

"My dear boy, you know what Jean is. Elsbeth stayed with us a good deal when we were all girls together-and because she and your dear father were very good friends — —"

"Inseparable!" snapped Jean. She was annoyed that the telling of the story was taken from her.

"Oh, they had tastes in common. But we all liked him. I'm quite certain Elsbeth was perfectly heart-whole. Only Jean has the servant-girl habit of pairing off all her friends and acquaintances. I don't say, of course, that if John had never met your dear mother-but she came home from her French school-she'd been away two years, you know-and turned everybody's head. Ravishing she was. I remember her coming-out dance. She wore the first short dress we'd seen-every one wore trains in those days-white gauze and forget-me-nots. She looked like a fairy. All the gentlemen wanted to dance with her, she was so light-footed. Your father fell head over ears! They were engaged in a fortnight. And nobody, in her quiet way, was more pleased than Elsbeth, I'm sure. Why, she was one of the bridesmaids!"

"She never came to stay with them afterwards," said Jean obstinately, "always had an excuse."

"Considering she had to nurse her father, with her mother an invalid already — —" Alicia was indignant. "Ten years of sick-nursing that poor girl had!"

"Anyhow, she never came to Dene again till after John died. Then she came, once. When she heard we were all going out to Italy. Stayed a week."

"I remember," said Roger unexpectedly.

"You! You were only five," cried Jean. The clock struck as she spoke. She jumped up. "Alicia! It's ten o'clock! Where's Parker? Why hasn't Parker brought the biscuits? You really might speak to her! She's always late!"

She flurried out of the room.

Roger drew in his chair.

"Aunt Alice, I say-how much of that is just-Aunt Jean?"

Alicia sighed.

"My dear boy! How should I know? It's all such a long while ago. Jean's no respecter of privacy. I never noticed anything-hate prying-always did."

"She never married?"

"She was over thirty before her mother died. She aged quickly-faded somehow. At that visit Jean spoke of—I shall never forget the change in her. She was only twenty-six, two years older than your mother, but Rosemary was a girl beside her, in spite of you and her widow's weeds. And then Alwynne was left on her hands and she absorbed herself in her. She's one of those self-effacing women-But there-she's quite contented, I think. She adores Alwynne. Her letters are cheerful enough. I always kept up with her. I'd like to see her again."

"Why didn't you ask her with Alwynne?"

"I did. She wouldn't come. Spring-cleaning, and one of her whimsies. Wanted the child to have a change from her. That's Elsbeth all over. She was always painfully humble. I imagine she'd sell her immortal soul for Alwynne."

"Well-and so would you for me," said Roger, with a twinkle.

"Don't you flatter yourself," retorted Alicia with spirit. Then she laughed and kissed him, and lumbered off to scold Jean up to bed.

Roger sat late, staring into the fire, and reviewing the day's happenings.

There was Alwynne to be considered.... Alwynne in the wood.... Alwynne in the daffodil house.... Alwynne hanging over the bannisters, a candle in her hand.... And Elsbeth.... Elsbeth had become something more than a name.... Elsbeth had known his mother-had been "pals" with his father.... He chuckled at the recollection of Jean's speculations.... Poor old Jean! She hadn't altered much.... He remembered her first horror at Compton and its boys and girls.... But Elsbeth was evidently a good sort ... appreciated Alwynne.... He would like to have a talk with Elsbeth.... He would like to have her version of that disastrous summer; have her views on Alwynne and this school of hers ... and that woman ... what was her name?... Hartill! Clare Hartill! Yes, he must certainly get to know Alwynne's Elsbeth.... In the meantime....

He hesitated, fidgeting at his desk; spoiled a sheet or two; shrugged his shoulders; began again; and finally, with a laugh at his own uncertainty, settled down to the writing of a long letter to his second cousin Elsbeth.

Elsbeth, opening a boot-boxful of daffodils on the following evening, had no leisure for any other letter till Alwynne's was read.

> *I hope they'll arrive fresh. Roger packed them for me himself. He's frightfully clever with flowers, you know; you should just see his greenhouses! But he goes in chiefly for roses; he's going to teach me pruning and all that, he says, later on. The Dears were out all day, but he looked after me. He's really awfully nice when you get to know him. One of those sensible people. I'm sure you would like him,* etcetera, etcetera, etcetera.

Elsbeth smiled over her daffodils. She had to put them in water, and arrange them, and rearrange them, and admire them for a full half-hour before she had time for the rest of her post, for her two circulars and the letter in the unfamiliar handwriting.

But when, at last, it was opened, she had no more eyes for daffodils; and though she spent her evening letter-writing, Alwynne got no thanks for them next day.

"Not even a note!" declaimed Alwynne indignantly. "She might at least have sent me a note! It isn't as if she had any one else to write to!"

Roger was most sympathetic.

CHAPTER XXXVII

Alwynne's visit had been prolonged in turn by Alicia, Jean and Roger; and Elsbeth had acquiesced-her sedate letters never betrayed how eagerly-in each delay.

Alicia was flatteringly in need of her help for the Easter church decorations, and how could Alwynne refuse? Jean was in the thick of preparations for the bazaar: Alwynne's quick wits and clever fingers were not to be dispensed with. Alwynne wondered what Clare would say to her interest in a bazaar and a mothers' meeting, and was a little nervous that it would be considered anything but a reasonable excuse for yet another delay. Clare's letters were getting impatient-Clare was wanting her back. Clare was finding her holidays dull. Yet Alwynne, longing to return to her, was persuaded to linger-for a bazaar—a village bazaar! That a bazaar of all things should tempt Alwynne from Clare! She felt the absurdity of it as fully as ever Clare could do. Yet she stayed. After all, The Dears had been very good to her.... She should be glad to make some small return by being useful when she could....

And Alwynne was pleasantly conscious that she was uncommonly useful. A fair is a many-sided gaiety. There are tableaux-Alwynne's suggestions were invaluable. Side-shows—Alwynne, in a witch's hat, told the entire village its fortunes with precision and point. Alwynne's well-drilled school-babies were pretty enough in their country dances and nursery rhymes; and the stall draperies were a credit to Alwynne's taste. Alwynne's posters lined the walls; and her lightning portraits-fourpence each, married couples sixpence-were the success of the evening. The village notabilities were congratulatory: The Dears beamed: it was all very pleasant.

Her pleasure in her own popularity was innocent enough. Nevertheless she glanced uneasily in the direction of Roger Lumsden more than once during the evening. He was very big and busy in his corner helping his aunts, but she felt herself under observation. She had an odd idea that he was amused at her. She thought he might have enquired if she needed help during the long evening, when the little Parish Hall was grown crowded. Once, indeed, she signed to him across the room to come and talk to her, but he laughed and shook his head, and turned again to an old mother, absorbed in a pile of flannel petticoats. Alwynne was not pleased.

But when the sale had come to its triumphant end, and the stall-holders stood about in little groups, counting coppers and comparing gains-it was Roger who discovered Alwynne, laughing a trifle mechanically at the jokes of the ancient rector, and came to her rescue.

She found herself in the cool outer air, hat and scarf miraculously in place.

"Jean and Alicia are driving, they won't be long after us. I thought you'd rather walk. That room was a furnace," said Roger, with solicitude.

She drew a deep breath.

"It was worth it to get this. Isn't it cool and quiet? I like this black and white road. Doesn't the night smell delicious?"

"It's the cottage gardens," he said.

"Wallflowers and briar and old man. Better than all your acres of glass, after all," she insinuated mischievously. Then, with a change of tone, "Oh, dear, I am tired."

"You'd better hang on to my arm," said Roger promptly. "That's better. Of course you're tired. If you insist on running the entire show——"

"Then you did think that?" Alwynne gave instant battle. "I knew you did. I saw you laugh. I can walk by myself, thank you."

But her dignity edged her into a cart-rut, for Roger did not deviate from the middle of the lane.

He laughed.

"You're a consistent young woman—I'm as sure of a rise——You'd better take my arm. Alwynne! You're not to say 'Damn.'" A puddle shone blackly, and Alwynne, nose in air, had stepped squarely into it.

She ignored his comments.

"I wasn't interfering. I had to help where I could. They asked me to. Besides—I liked it."

"Of course you did."

She looked up quickly.

"Did I really do anything wrong? Did I push myself forward?"

"You made the whole thing go," he said seriously. "A triumph, Alwynne. The rector's your friend for life."

"Then why do you grudge it?" She was hurt.

"Do I?"

"You laugh at me."

"Because I was pleased."

"With me?"

"With my thoughts. You've enjoyed yourself, haven't you?"

She nodded.

"I never dreamed it would be such fun." She laughed shyly. "I like people to like me."

"Now, come," he said. "Wasn't it quite as amusing as a prize-giving?"

She looked up at him, puzzled. He was switching with his stick at the parsley-blooms, white against the shadows of the hedge.

"I suppose your goal is a head mistress-ship?" he suggested off-handedly.

"Why?" began Alwynne, wondering. Then, taking the bait: "Not for myself—I couldn't. I haven't been to college, you know. But if Clare got one—I could be her secretary, and run things for her, like Miss Vigers did for Miss Marsham. We've often planned it."

"Ah, that's a prospect indeed," he remarked. "I suppose it would be more attractive, for instance, than to be Lady Bountiful to a village?"

"Oh, yes," said Alwynne, with conviction. "More scope, you know. And, besides, Clare hates the country."

"Ah!" said Roger.

They walked awhile in silence.

But before they reached home, Roger had grown talkative again. He had heard from his aunts that she was planning to go back to Utterbridge on the following Saturday—a bare three days ahead. Roger thought that a pity. The bazaar was barely over-had Alwynne any idea of the clearing up there would be to do? Accounts-calls-congratulations. Surely Alwynne would not desert his aunts till peace reigned once more. And the first of his roses would be out in another week; Alwynne ought to see them; they were a sight. Surely Alwynne could spare another week.

Alwynne had a lot to say about Elsbeth. And Clare. Especially Clare. Alwynne did not think it would be kind to either of them to stay away any longer. It would look at last as if she didn't want to go home. Elsbeth would be hurt. And Clare. Especially Clare.

But the lane had been dark and the hedges had been high, high enough to shut out all the world save Roger and his plausibilities. By the time they reached the garden gate Alwynne's hand was on Roger's arm-Alwynne was tired-and Alwynne had promised to stay yet another week at Dene. On the following day, labouring over her letters of explanation, she wondered what had possessed her. Wondered, between a chuckle of mischief and a genuine shiver, what on earth Clare would say.

But if Roger had gained his point, he gained little beside it. The week passed pleasantly, but some obscure instinct tied Alwynne to his aunts' apron-strings. He saw less of her in those last days than in all the weeks of her visit. He had assured her that The Dears would need help, and she took him at his word. She absorbed herself in their concerns, and in seven long days found time but twice to visit Roger's roses.

Yet who so pleasant as Alwynne when she was with him? Roger should have appreciated her whim of civility. It is on record that she agreed with him one dinner-time, on five consecutive subjects. On record, too, that in that last week there arose between them no quarrel worthy of the name. Yet Roger was not in the easiest of moods, as his gardeners knew, and his coachman, and his aunts. The gardeners grumbled. The coachman went so far as to think of talking of giving notice. Alicia said it was the spring. Jean thought he needed a tonic-or a change. Roger, cautiously consulted, surprised her by agreeing. He said it was a good idea. He might very well take a few days off, say in a fortnight, or three weeks....

Only Alwynne, very busy over the finishing touches of Clare's birthday present, paid no attention to the state of Roger's temper. She was entirely content. The anticipation of her reunion with Clare accentuated the delights of her protracted absence. Indeed, it was not until the last morning of her visit that she noticed any change in him. That last morning, she thought resentfully, as later she considered matters in the train, he had certainly managed to spoil. Roger, her even-minded, tranquil Roger-Roger, prime sympathiser and confederate-Roger, the entirely dependable-had failed her. She did not know what had come over him.

For Roger had been in a bad temper, a rotten bad temper, and heaven knew why....Alwynne didn't....She had been in such a jolly frame of mind herself....She had got her packing done early, and had dashed down to breakfast, beautifully punctual-and then it all began....She re-lived it indignantly, as the telegraph poles shot by.

The bacon had sizzled pleasantly in the chafing-dish. She was standing at the window, crumbling bread to the birds.

"Hulloa! You're early!" remarked Roger, entering.

"Done all my packing already! Isn't that virtue?" Alwynne was intent on her pensioners. "Oh, Roger-look! There's a cuckoo. I'm sure it's a cuckoo. Jean says they come right on to the lawn sometimes. I've always wanted to see one. Look! The big dark blue one."

"Starling," said Roger shortly, and sat himself down. "First day I've known you punctual," he continued sourly.

"I'm going home," cried Alwynne. "I'm going home! Do you know I've been away seven weeks? It's queer that I haven't been homesick, isn't it?"

"Is it?" said Roger blankly.

"So, of course, I'm awfully excited," she continued, coming to the table. "Oh, Roger! In six hours I shall see Clare!"

"Congratulations!" He gulped down some coffee.

Alwynne looked at him, mildly surprised at his taciturnity.

"I've had a lovely time," she remarked wistfully. "You've all been so good to me."

Roger brightened.

"The Dears are such dears," continued Alwynne with enthusiasm. "I've never had such a glorious time. It only wanted Clare to make it quite perfect. And Elsbeth, of course."

"Of course," said Roger.

"So often I've thought," she went on: "'Now if only Clare and Elsbeth could be coming down the road to meet us——'" she paused effectively. "I do so like my friends to know each other, don't you?"

Roger was cutting bread-stale bread, to judge by his efforts. His face was growing red.

"Because then I can talk about them to them," concluded Alwynne lucidly.

"Jolly for them!" he commented indistinctly.

Alwynne looked up.

"What, Roger?"

"I said, 'Jolly for them!'"

"Oh!" Alwynne glanced at him in some uncertainty. Then, with a frown—

"Have you finished-already?"

"Yes, thank you."

"I haven't," remarked Alwynne, with sufficient point. Roger rose.

"You'll excuse me, won't you? I've a busy morning ahead of me."

He got up. But in spite of his protestations of haste he still stood at the table, fidgeting over his pile of circulars and seed catalogues, while he coughed the preliminary cough of a man who has something to say, and no idea of how to say it.

290

Alwynne, meanwhile, had discovered the two letters that her napkin had hidden, and had neither ears nor eyes for him and his hesitations.

Roger watched her gloomily as she opened the envelopes. The first enclosure was read and tossed aside quickly enough, but the other was evidently absorbing. He shrugged his shoulders at last, and, crossing the room, took his warmed boots from the hearth. The supporting tongs fell with a crash.

Alwynne jumped.

"Oh, Roger, you are noisy!"

"Sorry," said Roger, but without conviction.

She looked across at him with a hint of perturbation in her manner. She distrusted laconics.

"I say-is anything the matter?"

"Nothing whatever!" he assured her. "Why?" He bent over his boots.

"I don't know. You're rather glum to-day, aren't you?"

"Not at all," said Roger, with a dignity that was marred by the sudden bursting of his over-tugged bootlace. His ensuing exclamation was vigorous and not inaudible. Alwynne giggled. It is not easy to tie a knot in four-sided leather laces. She watched his struggles without excessive sympathy. Presently a neat twist of twine flicked through space and fell beside him.

"'Just a little bit of string,'" murmured Alwynne flippantly. But getting no thanks, she returned to her letter. Roger fumbled in silence.

"The Dears are late," remarked Alwynne at last, as she folded her sheets.

"No-it's we who are early. I got down early on purpose. I thought you might be, too. I wanted — —" he broke off abruptly.

"Yes, I always wake up at daybreak when I'm excited," she said joyously. "Oh, Roger! How I'm looking forward to getting home! Clare says she may meet me-if she feels like it," she beamed.

"Oh!" said Roger.

Alwynne tapped her foot angrily.

"What's the matter with you?" she demanded. "Why on earth do you sit there and grunt at me like that? Why won't you talk? You're an absolute wet blanket-on my last morning. I wish The Dears would come down."

"I think I hear them moving," he said, and stared at the ceiling.

"I hope you do." Alwynne flounced from the table and picked up a paper.

He stood looking at her-between vexation and amusement, and another sensation less easily defined.

"Well, I must be off," he said at last.

He got no answer.

"Good-bye, Alwynne. Pleasant journey."

Alwynne turned in a flash.

"Good-bye? Aren't you coming to see me off?" she demanded blankly.

He hesitated, looking back at her from the open window, one foot already on the terrace.

"I'm awfully busy. It's market-day, you know-and the new stuff's coming in. The Dears will see you off."

"Oh, all right." Alwynne was suddenly subdued. She held out a limp hand.

He disregarded it.

"Do you want me to come?" He spoke more cheerfully.

"One always likes one's friends to see one off," she remarked sedately.

"And meet one?" He glanced at the letter in her hand.

"And meet one. Certainly." Her chin went up. "I hadn't to ask Clare. But you needn't come. Good-bye!"

"Oh, I'm coming-now," he assured her, smiling.

Alwynne's eyebrows went up.

"But it's market-day, you know — —"

"Yes."

"You're awfully busy."

"Yes."

"The new stuff's coming in."

"Yes."

"Are you coming, Roger?"

"Yes, Alwynne."

"Then, Roger dear-if you are coming, and it's no bother, and you can spare them, would you bring me a tiny bunch of your roses? Not for me-for Clare. She does love them so. Do, Roger!"

"I'm hanged if I do," cried Roger, and went his wrathful way.

But he did. A big bunch. More than enough for Clare.

CHAPTER XXXVIII

Alwynne was out of the train a dangerous quarter minute before it came to a standstill, and making for the bunch of violets that bloomed perennially in Elsbeth's bonnet. There followed a sufficiency of kissing. It was like a holiday home-coming, thought Alwynne, of not so very long ago. But not so long ago she would have been exclusively occupied with Elsbeth, and her luggage, and her forgotten compartment; would not have turned impatiently from her aunt to scan the length of the platform. Not a sign of Clare? And Clare had promised to meet her....

She prolonged as long as she might her business with porters and ticket collectors and outsidemen, but Clare did not appear; and she left the station at last, at her aunt's side, sedately enough, with the edge off the pleasure of her home-coming.

A telegram on the hall stand, however, contented her. Clare was sorry; Clare was delayed; would be away another four days; was writing. Alwynne shook off her black dog, and the meeting with Clare still delightfully ahead of her, was able to devote herself altogether to Elsbeth. Elsbeth spent a gay four days with an Alwynne grown rosy and cheerful, affectionate and satisfyingly garrulous again; found it very pleasant to have Alwynne to herself, her own property, even for four days. Elsbeth might know that she was second fiddle still, but though it cost her something to realise that she could never be first fiddle again, she could be content to give place to Roger Lumsden. She shook her head over her inconsistency. She could school herself, rather than lose the girl's confidence, to accept Clare Hartill as the main theme of Alwynne's conversation, till she was weary of the name, but she could not hear enough of Roger. All that Alwynne let fall of incident, description, or approval-Roger, Elsbeth discovered, had, in common with Clare, no faults whatever-she stored up to compare, when Alwynne had gone to bed, with letters, half-a-dozen by this time, that she kept locked up, with certain other, older letters, in the absurd little secret drawer of her desk. And she would patter across into Alwynne's room at last, to tuck in a sheet or twitch back a coverlet or merely to pretend to herself that Alwynne was a baby still, and so, with a smile and a sigh, to her own room, to make her plain toilet and to say her selfless prayers to God and her counterpane. Happy days and nights-four happy days and nights for Elsbeth.

Then Clare came back.

It was natural that Alwynne should meet her and go home with her, portmanteau in hand, to spend a night or two.... Elsbeth agreed that it was natural.... Three nights or even four.... But when a week passed, with no sign from Alwynne but a meagre, apologetic postcard, Elsbeth thought that she had good cause for anger. Not, of course, with Alwynne ... never, be it understood, with Alwynne ... but most certainly with Clare Hartill. Alwynne was so fatally good-natured.... Clare, she supposed, had kept the child by a great show of needing her help.... Of course, school was beginning, had begun already.... Clare would find Alwynne useful enough.... No doubt it was pleasant to have some one at her beck and call again in these busy first days of term.... Possibly-probably-oh, she conceded the "probably" —Clare had missed Alwynne badly.... Had not Elsbeth, too, missed Alwynne?

But she answered Alwynne's postcard affectionately as usual. If Alwynne were happier with Clare, Elsbeth would given no hint of loneliness. A hint, she knew, would suffice. Alwynne had a sense of duty. But she wanted free-will offering from Alwynne, not tribute.

In spite of herself, however, something of bitterness crept into her next note to Roger Lumsden, who had inveigled her, she hardly knew how, into regular correspondence. Her remark that *Alwynne has been away ten days now*, was set down baldly, with no veiling sub-sentences of explanation or excuse.

Had she but known it, however, she was not altogether just to Alwynne. The first hours of reunion did certainly drive her aunt out of Alwynne's mind, but after a couple of days she was ready to remind herself and Clare that Elsbeth, too, had some claim on her time. It is possible, however, that had she been happier, she would have been less readily scrupulous. Clare had certainly been glad to see her, had, for an hour or two, been entirely delightful. But with the

293

resumption of their mutual life Clare was not long in falling back into her old bad ways, and in revenge for her two months' boredom, in sheer teasing high spirits at Alwynne's return, as well as in unreasoning, petulant jealousy, led Alwynne a pretty enough dance. For Clare was jealous, jealous of these eight weeks of Alwynne's youth that did not belong to her, and between her jealousy and her own contempt for her jealousy, was in one of the moods that she and Alwynne alike dreaded.

The mornings at the school came as a relief to them both, but no sooner were they together again than Clare's pricking devil must out. Scenes were incessant-wanton, childish scenes. Yet Alwynne, sore and bewildered as she was by Clare's waxing unreasonableness, was yet not proof against the sudden surrenders that always contrived to put her in the wrong. She would repeat to herself that it must be she who was unreasonable, that she should be flattered rather than distressed, for instance, that Clare would not let her go home.... She would rather be with Clare than Elsbeth, wouldn't she? Of course! well, then!... Nevertheless she could not help wondering if any letters had come for her; if Elsbeth, expecting her daily, would bother to send them on.... Roger had promised to write.... She thought that really she ought to go home.

But Clare would not hear of her leaving. Elsbeth wanted Alwynne? So did she. Didn't Elsbeth always have Alwynne? Surely Alwynne was old enough to be away from Elsbeth for a fortnight, without leave granted! Really, with all due respect to her, Alwynne's aunt was a regular Old Man of the Sea.

"Clare!" Alwynne's tone had a hint of remonstrance.

"Oh, I said 'with all respect.' But if she were not your aunt I should really be tempted to get rid of her-have you here altogether. You would like that, Alwynne, eh?"

Alwynne refused to nod, but she laughed.

"'Get rid'? Clare, don't be absurd."

Clare looked at her, smiling, eyes narrowed in the old way.

"Do you think I couldn't get rid of her if I wanted to? I always do what I set out to do. Look at Henrietta Vigers."

Alwynne sat bolt upright.

"Miss Vigers? But she resigned! She had been meaning to leave! She told us so! Do you mean that she didn't want to leave? Do you mean that she had to?"

"Have you ever seen a liner launched? You press an electric button, you know-just a touch-it's awfully simple ——" She paused, eyes dancing.

But Alwynne had no answering twinkle.

"I wouldn't have believed it," she said slowly. Then, distractedly, "But why, Clare, why? What possessed you?"

"She got in my way," said Clare indolently.

Alwynne turned on her, eyes blazing.

"You mean to say-you deliberately did that poor old thing out of her job? If you did ——But I don't believe it. If you did ——Clare, excuse me-but I think it was beastly."

"*Demon! With the highest respect to you* ——" quoted Clare, tongue in cheek.

But Alwynne was not to be pacified.

"Clare-you didn't, did you?"

"My dear, she was in the way. She worried you and you worried me. I don't like being worried."

Alwynne shivered.

"Don't, Clare! I hate you to talk like that-even in fun. It's—it's so cold-blooded."

"In fun!" Clare laughed lightly. Alwynne's youthful severity amused her. But she had gone, she perceived, a trifle too far. "Well, then, in earnest-joking apart ——"

Alwynne's face relaxed. Of course, she had known all along that Clare was in fun....

"Joking apart-it was time for Miss Vigers to go. I admit saying what I thought to Miss Marsham. I am quite ready to take responsibility. She was too old-too fussy-too intolerant—I can't stand intolerance. She had to go."

Alwynne looked wicked.

"Clare, you remind me of a man I met, down at Compton. You ought to get on together. He's great on tolerance too. So tolerant that five hundred years ago he'd have burned every one who wasn't as tolerant as he. As it is, he shrugs them out of existence, *à la* Podsnap. Just as you did Miss Vigers just now."

"Who was he?"

"Don't know-only met him once. But he tickled me awfully. He hadn't the faintest idea how funny he was."

"Did he shrug you out of existence?"

"My dear Clare-could any one snub me? You might as well snub a rubber ball."

"Yes, you're pretty thick-skinned." Clare paid her back reflectively.

Alwynne winced.

"Am I? I'm sorry. I didn't mean to be. How, just now?"

Clare yawned.

"Well, for one thing, you needn't flavour your conversation exclusively with Denes. They bore me worse than if they had an 'a' in them."

"I'm sorry." Alwynne paused. Then she plucked up courage. "Clare, I stayed there two months. The Dene people are my friends, my great friends. I don't think you need sneer at them."

Clare yawned again.

"I wonder you ever came back, if they're so absorbing. What is the particular attraction there, by the way? The old women or the young men?"

Alwynne's lips quivered.

"Clare, what has happened? What is the matter with you nowadays? Why are you grown so different? Why are you always saying unkind things?"

Clare shrugged her shoulders.

"Really, Alwynne, I am not accustomed to be cross-examined. Such a bore, giving reasons. Besides, I haven't got any. Oh, don't look such a martyr."

"I think I'll go home," said Alwynne in a low voice. "I don't think you want me."

"But Elsbeth does, doesn't she?"

Clare settled herself more comfortably in the comfortable Chesterfield as she watched Alwynne out of the room. She lay like a sleepy cat, listening to the muffled sounds of Alwynne's packing; let her get ready to her hat and her gloves and the lacing of her boots, before she called her back, and played with her, and forgave her at the last. Yet she found Alwynne less pliable than usual: convicted of sin, she was yet resolved on departure, if not to-day—no, of course she would not go to-day, after behaving so ill to her Clare-then, the day following. That would be Friday—a completed fortnight-and Saturday was Clare's birthday-had Clare forgotten? Alwynne hadn't, anyhow. Oh, she must come for Saturday, and what would Elsbeth say to that? There must be one evening, at least, given to Elsbeth in between. After all, it was jolly dull for Elsbeth all by herself.

Clare, good-tempered for the first time that afternoon, supposed it was, rather.

But on that particular day, Alwynne's qualms of conscience were unnecessary. Elsbeth was not at all dull. Elsbeth, on the contrary, was tremendously excited. And Elsbeth had forgotten all about Alwynne, was not missing her in the least. Elsbeth had received a letter from Dene that morning, and was expecting Roger Lumsden to supper.

CHAPTER XXXIX

Elsbeth spent her day in that meticulous and unnecessary arrangement and re-arrangement of her house and person, with which woman, since time was, has delighted to honour man, and which he, the unaccountable, has as inevitably failed to notice. The clean cretonnes had arrived in time and were tied and smoothed into place; the vases new-filled; and the fire, though spring-cleaning had been, sprawled opulently in a brickless grate. The matches, with the fifty cigarettes Elsbeth had bought that forenoon, hesitating and all too reliant upon the bored tobacconist, lay, aliens unmistakable, near Roger's probable seat, and the knowledge of the supper laid out in the next room fortified Elsbeth as, years ago, a new frock might have done. Alwynne, in every age and stage, dotted the piano and occasional tables, and a photograph that even Alwynne had never seen was placed on the mantelshelf, that Roger, greeting Elsbeth, might see it and forget to be shy.

But it was Elsbeth that was shy, when Roger, very punctual, arrived amid the chimes of the evening service. Yet Elsbeth had been ready since five. They greeted each other in dumb show and sat a moment, smiling and taking stock, while the clamour swelled, insisted, ebbed and died away.

Roger, still silent, began to fumble at a case he carried, while Elsbeth found herself apologetically and for the thousandth time wondering to her guest why she had taken root so near a church, while within herself a hard voice cried exultantly, "He's his father, his father over again! Nothing of Rosemary there!" and she tasted a little strange flash of triumph over the dead woman she had been too gentle to hate.

But suddenly her lap was filled with roses, bunch upon tight masculine bunch, and the formal sentences broke up into incoherence as Roger stooped and kissed his second cousin Elsbeth.

They soon made friends. Roger, who had never quite forgotten her, found the pleasant-faced spinster as attractive as the pretty lady of his childhood. He examined her as he ate his supper. A spare figure, soft grey hair, and square, capable hands; a kind mouth, not a strong one, set in lines firmer than were natural to it; gentle eyes, no longer beautiful, and a cheerful, tired smile; a sweet face, thought Roger, not a happy one. Yet she had Alwynne! She fluttered a little over the meal, and was anxious about his coffee, and full of little enquiries and attentions that were never irritating. There was a faint scent of verbena as she moved about him, and her silk gown did not crackle like younger women's dresses. She listened well, but he guessed her no talker, and later in the evening, gauged her affection for Alwynne by her breathless fluency. He thought her charming and a little pathetic, and wondered why nobody had ever insisted on marrying her.

Elsbeth's shyness soon dwindled; she slipped quickly into the informal "aunt and nephew" attitude that he evidently expected, and found his friendliness and obvious pleasure in her as delightful as it was astonishing. She supposed, with a wistful little shrug, that she was near the rose! Nevertheless she enjoyed herself.

They talked in narrowing circles: of his father a little; more of his mother; of Dene, and Elsbeth's former visits. He described Compton and The Dears, and his gardens and his roses. Then, with a chuckle, an unauthorised attempt of Alwynne at pruning that had ended in disaster; and so plunged into confidences.

"I expect you've guessed that I intend-that I want to marry Alwynne, —with her permission," he added hastily, smiling down at her.

Elsbeth envied him his inches. For Alwynne's sake she did not intend to be dominated; but she found his mere masculinity a little overpowering, and did not guess that her frail dignity had made its own impression.

She smiled back at him.

"I'm glad you put that in. You should respect grey hairs."

"But I do."

"No. You imply that I'm a very blind and foolish guardian! My dear boy," her pretty voice shook a little, "I've hoped and prayed for this. You, John's boy, and-and dear Rosemary's, of course-and Alwynne, who's dearer to me than a daughter! Why, that's why I sent her down to Dene!" She blushed the rare blush of later middle age. "Oh, my dear-it was shameless! I was matchmaking! I was! And I've always considered it so indelicate. But I wished so strongly that you two might come together. When Alwynne wrote of you so often, I hoped: and then your letters made me sure. You had got on so well without me these twenty-five years-and then to feel the ties of kinship so very strongly all of a sudden-it was transparent, Roger."

He laughed.

"I hadn't forgotten really-though it's the vaguest memory. You gave me a rabbit in a green cabbage that opened. And one Sunday we shared Prayer Books. You had a blue dress —a pale blue that one never sees nowadays, and very pink cheeks."

"Ah! the *crêpe de Chine*," said Elsbeth absently.

"I always remembered-though I'd forgotten I did. Alwynne brought it back. She's like you in some ways, you know. She made me awfully curious to see you again. From the way she talked I knew you'd be decent to me." He smiled. "Elsbeth —I'm tremendously in love."

"Have you told her so?"

"Alwynne's rather difficult to get hold of. She doesn't understand anything but black and white."

"Clare Hartill —I suppose you've heard of Clare Hartill?"

"Have I not!"

"Clare Hartill says she has an uncanny ear for nuances."

"Also that she's thick-skinned! The woman's a fool."

"Oh, she's quite right, Roger, though I expect she was in a temper when she said it. But it only means that Alwynne has been trained to listen to women. She can't follow men yet. She has been advised that they are grown-up children and that her rôle is to be superior but tactful."

He chuckled.

"Yes. When Alwynne's tactful-she's tactful! You can't mistake it, can you? Have you ever seen her sidling out of a room when she thought she wasn't wanted? Still, she can hold her own, on occasion. She simply walked through my hints. But-how does she talk of me, Elsbeth, if she does at all, that is?"

"She likes you, in the 'good old Roger' fashion."

"But you do think I have a chance?"

"That's why I wanted to see you. Frankly, at present I don't think you have."

He looked at her coolly, not at all depressed.

"Why not?"

"Clare Hartill."

"Ah!" He sat down at the table again, his chin in his fist. "You think her the obstacle?"

"I taught her once. Alwynne has been absorbed in her for two years. Alwynne talks ——" they both smiled. "I could compare. I ought to know her pretty well."

"Yes. But how can she affect Alwynne and me? Of course I know what a lot Alwynne thinks of her. She's rather delightful on the subject. Thinks her perfection, and so on. Alwynne is naïve; conveys more than she knows or intends, sometimes. And she never looks at her god's feet, does she? 'Clare' and 'Clare' and 'Clare.' Personally, I imagine her a bit of a brute."

"I try to be fair. She is fond of Alwynne."

"Why not? But what's that got to do with Alwynne's caring for me, if I am lucky enough to make her? And I'm —conceitedly sure-that it's only a question of waking Alwynne up."

"You don't know Clare. If once she knows, she'll never let the child go."

"But if Alwynne were engaged to me?"

"She'll never allow it. She'll play on Alwynne's affection for her."

"But why? I shouldn't interfere with their friendship."

"My dear Roger-marriage ends friendship automatically. Clare would be shrewd enough to see that. And even-otherwise-she would never share. You don't guess how jealous women are."

Roger leant back in his chair with a gesture of bewilderment.

"My dearest cousin! The age of sorcery is over. You talk as if Alwynne were under a spell."

"Practically she is. Of course Clare would put it on the highest grounds-unsuitability— a waste of talents. She pretends to despise domesticity. Alwynne would be hypnotised into repeating her arguments as her own opinion."

"Hypnotism?"

"Oh, not literally. But she really does influence some women, and young girls especially, in the most uncanny way. I've watched it so often."

"She's not married?"

"She hardly ever speaks to a man. I've seen her at gaieties, when she was younger. She was always rather stranded. Men left her alone. Something in her seems to repel them. I think she fully realised it. And she's a proud woman. There's tragedy in it."

"Does she repel you?"

"Not in that way. I dislike her. I think her dangerous. I'm intensely sorry for her. And I do understand something of the attraction she exercises, better than you can, though it has never affected me. You see-eccentricity-abnormality-does not affect women as it does men. And she's brilliantly clever."

"So is Alwynne-you wouldn't call her abnormal?"

"Alwynne? Never! She's as sound and sweet as an apple. But-and it means a good deal at her age-she's in abnormal hands. Clare Hartill is abnormal, spiritually perverse-and she's fastened on the child. They adore each other. It's terribly bad for Alwynne. As it is, it will take her months to shake off Clare's influence, even with you to help her. That is, if you succeed in detaching her. I'm useless, of course. Loving-just loving-is no good. You can only influence if you are strong enough to wound. I merely irritate. I'm weak. But you could do as you like, I believe. Take her away from that selfish woman, Roger! It's blighting her."

"You think," he said, "that she would be content with me-with marriage as a career? Of course, Miss Hartill's right about her talents."

"Alwynne? I don't think—I know. All her gifts are so much surface show; she's a very simple child underneath. Content? Can't you see her, Roger-with children? Her own babies?"

Roger beamed.

"It's rather a jolly prospect. Well, I must take my chance."

"Of course, you must wait; it's too soon yet. Even later, if Clare really wants her-wants her enough to suppress her own perverse impulses—I'm afraid you've little chance. But it's possible that she will not want her as much as that."

"I don't follow."

"I mean that Clare, with that impish nature of hers, may hurt Alwynne."

"I should think she has already, often enough."

"Yes-but Alwynne has never realised it, never realised that it was deliberate. She is always so sure that it was her fault somehow. If once she found out that Clare was hurting her for-for the fun of it, you know-for the pleasure of watching her suffer-as I'm sure she does-it might end everything. Alwynne hates cruelty. That poor child's death shook her. A little more, and she will be disillusioned."

"But loyal still?"

"Probably. But the glamour would be gone. She would be extremely unhappy. There your chance would come. Though I don't think Clare will give it you-for I believe Alwynne does mean more to her than most things. But she's an unaccountable person: there is the chance."

"I see," Roger rose and straightened himself. "Practically I'm not to depend on my own-attractions-at all." He laughed a little. "I am to watch the whims of this-this unpleasant school-marm, and be grateful to her for forcing Alwynne to prefer my deep sea to her devil. The situation is hardly dignified."

Elsbeth laughed too.

"Love is always undignified, Roger. What does it matter if you want her?" But she watched him anxiously as he walked to the window, and stood staring out.

There was a silence. At last he turned —

"Elsbeth, dear, it's a beautiful scheme, and a woman could carry it through, I daresay-but it's no good to me. It's too-too tortuous, too feminine. I don't mean anything rude. It's merely that I'm not-subtle enough, or patient. At least, I haven't got that cat-and-mouse kind of patience. I can wait, you know. That's different. I can wait all right. But I can't intrigue."

Elsbeth flushed.

"There is no intrigue. It's a question of understanding Alwynne and of using the opportunity when it comes."

"To trick and surprise and over-persuade her into caring for me! It's no good, Elsbeth. It isn't possession I want-it's Alwynne. Can't you see? We should neither of us be happy. She would always distrust me and remember that I'd taken an advantage. I should end by hating her, I believe. Can't you see?"

Elsbeth was shaken by her own thoughts.

"I see," she said finally. "And I see that you don't love her-or you'd take her on any terms."

"Would you?"

"Yes."

"Well, I wouldn't. And I do love her. But I want Alwynne on my terms. Do I sound an awful prig? Cousin Elsbeth, hear my way! I'm going to have it out with Alwynne."

"At once?"

"At once. As soon as I see her-no beating about the bush."

"Roger-she may be utterly out of the mood."

"Hang moods! I beg your pardon, Elsbeth. But I'm going to tell her-certain things. If she doesn't like it I'm going back to Dene. She'll know where to find me when she changes her mind. Elsbeth, don't look so hopeless."

"You don't understand Alwynne."

"I don't want to understand her—I want to marry her. I must stick to my own way. Can't you conceive that all this consideration, all this deference to moods and dissection of motives, this horribly feminine atmosphere that she seems to have lived in, of subtleties, and reservations, and simulations-may be bad for her? It seems to me that she's always being thought about. You, with your anxious affection-that unholy woman with her lancet and probe-you neither of you leave her alone for a second. She's always being touched. Well, I'm going to leave her alone. It gives her a chance."

"I've never spoiled her." Elsbeth was off at a tangent.

"I'm sure of it. I can remember Father holding you up to Mother once. He said you were the most judicious woman with children that he knew."

"Did he?" said Elsbeth.

"Mother was awfully annoyed." Roger chuckled. "I'd been bawling for my fourth doughnut-and got it."

"I've never spoiled Alwynne," repeated Elsbeth tonelessly.

"No one could," remarked Roger with conviction.

Elsbeth looked up and laughed at him.

"So you are human!" she said. "I was beginning to doubt it."

"When I get on the subject of Alwynne's adorableness ———" he laughed back at her, "we're obviously cousins, aren't we? But, really, I've been trying to be detached, and critical, and analytical, and all the things you feel are important. I wanted to see what you meant, Cousin Elsbeth; and I do see that we both want the same thing. But as to the means—I believe I must go my own way."

She eyed him doubtfully. But he looked very big and solid in the little room, comfortingly sure of himself.

"You think me a frantic old clucking hen, don't you? And are just a little sorry for the duckling."

"I think you're a perfect dear," said Roger.

"You'll come to-morrow? Alwynne will be back, I hope."

"What time is she likely to turn up?"

"About four, if she comes. She would lunch with Clare, I expect."

He nodded whimsically.

"Very well. To-morrow, at four precisely, there will be a row royal. To-morrow I am calling on Miss Hartill to fetch Alwynne home. Good-bye, Cousin Elsbeth."

He turned again in the doorway.

"Elsbeth, there's a house at Dene I've got my eye on. There's a turret room. My best roses will clamber right into it. That's to be yours. And Elsbeth! Nobody but you shall run the nursery."

He had shut the door before she could answer, and she heard him laugh as he ran, two at a time, down the shallow steps.

She went to the window and watched till his strong figure had disappeared in the dusk.

"He is very like his father," said Elsbeth wistfully, glancing across at the faded likeness.

The dusk deepened and the stars began to twinkle.

"He will never be the man his father was," cried Elsbeth, suddenly and defiantly.

Her hands shook as she cleared away the remnants of the meal. She swept up the hearth, picked the coals carefully apart, and tidied the tidy room. Roger's roses still lay in a heap in the basket chair. She gathered them up and carried them into the tiny bathroom, that they might drink their fill all night. Their scent was strong and sweet. Then she lit her candle and prepared for bed.

The sheets were very cold. She tried not to think of Roger's father lying in the grave she had never seen. The old, cruel longing was upon her for the sound of his voice and the sight of his face and the sweetness of his smile. She broke into painful weeping.

The hours wore past.

Of course he would marry Alwynne.... Alwynne would be happy ... there was comfort in that.... Roger would be kind to her.... A good boy ... a dear boy....

"And he might have been my son," cried out Elsbeth to the uncaring night.

CHAPTER XL

Roger never fought his battle-royal with Clare, for at the turn of Friar's Lane he met Alwynne herself, dragging wearily along the cobblestones, weighed down by paper parcels and the heavy folds of the waterproof hanging on her arm. Her hair was roughened by the wind that tugged and strained at her loosened hat; her face was drawn and shadowy; she had an air of exhaustion, of indefinable demoralisation that Roger recognised angrily. He had seen it in the first weeks of her visit to Dene. Her thoughts were evidently far away, and she would have passed him without a look if he had not stopped her. She started violently as he spoke-it was like rousing a nightmare-ridden sleeper-then her face grew radiant.

"Roger!" she cried, and beamed at him like a delighted child.

He possessed himself of her parcels and they walked on, Alwynne's questions and exclamations tumbling over each other. Roger at Utterbridge! Why had he come? How long was he staying? How were The Dears and how did Dene spare him? When had he arrived?

Roger dropped his bomb.

"Yesterday. I went to supper with Elsbeth. We had a long talk."

His tone conveyed much. The brightness died out of Alwynne's face. She looked surprised and excessively annoyed.

"She knew you were coming?"

"She did."

"Why on earth didn't she let me know? Why, she doesn't know you! She hasn't seen you since you were a kid! It's extraordinary of Elsbeth."

"I wouldn't let her."

"Wouldn't let her?" Alwynne looked at him blankly. "Roger —I think you're cracked."

"Terse and to the point! Don't you worry. Elsbeth and I understand each other. Besides, we've been corresponding."

"You and Elsbeth?"

"Yes. That's partly why I came. I wanted to get to know her. You see, your description and her letters didn't tally. So I came. We got on jolly well. I burst in on her again at breakfast this morning. She didn't fuss-took it like a lamb. I fancy you underrate our cousin-in more ways than one. She knows it too; she's no fool! I found that out when we talked about you."

"Elsbeth discussed me? —with you?" Alwynne's tone foreboded a bad half-hour to Elsbeth.

"Why not? You're not sacred, are you?" Roger chuckled.

Alwynne felt inclined to box his ears. Here was a new Roger. Roger-her own property-to take such an attitude-to ally himself with Elsbeth-to leave her in the dark! Roger! It was unthinkable....And she had been so awfully glad to see him ...absurdly glad to see him ...he had made her forget even Clare....Clare....She began to occupy her mind once more with the scene of the previous day, recalling what she had said; contrasting it with what she had intended to say; stabbed afresh by Clare's manner; writhing at her own helplessness; when Roger's slow voice brought her thoughts back to the present.

"You've been away from Elsbeth a fortnight," he said accusingly, as they entered the Town Gardens.

She flared anew at his tone.

"Certainly. I've been staying with friends. Have you any objection?"

"A friend," he corrected.

She flushed.

"Clare Hartill is my best friend——"

"Your worst, you mean."

She turned on him.

"How dare you say that? How dare you speak of my friends like that? How dare you speak to me at all?"

He continued, quite unmoved—

"Don't be silly, Alwynne. Your best friend is your Aunt Elsbeth-you ought to know that. You don't treat her well, I think. You've been away a fortnight with that-friend of yours; you stayed on without consulting her——"

"I telephoned," cried Alwynne, in spite of herself.

"Since then you've sent her one post card. She isn't even sure that you're coming back to-day; she's just had to sit tight and wait until it's your-no, I'll give you your due-until it's your friend's pleasure to send you back to her, fagged out, miserable-just like my dog after a thrashing. And Elsbeth's to comfort you, and cosset you, and put you to rights-and then you'll go back to that woman again, to have the strength and the spirit drained out of you afresh-and you walk along talking of your best friend. I call it hard luck on Elsbeth."

Alwynne's careful dignity was forgotten in her anger. She turned on him like a furious schoolgirl.

"Will you stop, please? How dare you speak of Clare? If Elsbeth chooses to complain —— What affair is it of yours anyhow? I'll never speak to you again-never-or Elsbeth either." Her voice broke-she was on the verge of tears.

Roger took her by the arm, and drew her to a seat.

"You'd better sit down," he said. "We've heaps to talk over yet, more than you've a notion of. And if we're to have a row, let's get it over in the open-far less dangerous. Never get to cover in a thunderstorm. I know what you want." He had watched her fumbling unavailingly in the bag and pocket and had chuckled. He knew his Alwynne. He produced a clean silk handkerchief and dangled it before her. She clutched at it with undignified haste.

"'Thank you,' first," he said, holding it firmly. A moment victory hung in the balance. Then —

"Oh! Oh, thank you," said Alwynne, with fine unconcern, and secured it. Their eyes met. It was impossible not to smile.

"At the same time," remarked Alwynne, a little later, "you've no right to talk to me like that, Roger, whatever you choose to think. You're not my cousin."

"I'm Elsbeth's. It strikes me she needs defending."

Alwynne laughed.

"You know I'm awfully fond of Elsbeth. You know I am. I am a beast sometimes to her, you're quite right-but she doesn't really need defending. Honestly."

"Not from you, I know. But frankly, without wanting to be rude to your friend—I think she makes you careless of Elsbeth's feelings. Elsbeth was awfully hurt this week, and she's the sort of dear one hates to see hurt."

Alwynne looked at him wistfully.

"Roger," she said hesitatingly, "suppose some one were unkind to me-hurt me-hurt me badly, very often, almost on purpose-would you defend me? Would you care at all?"

"I shouldn't let 'em," he grunted.

"If you couldn't help it?"

"I shouldn't let 'em," he repeated doggedly.

"But should you care?"

"Of course I should. What rot you talk. Of course I should. But I shouldn't let them."

"Oh, Roger," she cried, suddenly and pitifully, "they do hurt me sometimes-they do, they do."

Roger looked around him with unusual caution. The Gardens were empty. There was not even a loafer in sight. He put his arm round her, and drew her clumsily to him. She yielded like a tired child, and lay quietly, staring with brimming eyes at the gaudy tulip-bed on the further side of the walk.

"I believe you're about fed up with that school of yours," he said, after a time, as if he had not followed the allusion to Clare.

She nodded.

"I'm not lazy, Roger; you know it's not that. It's just the atmosphere, and the awful crowding. Such a lot of women at close quarters, all enthusiasm and fussing and importance. They're all hard-working, and all unselfish and keen-more than a crowd of men would be, I believe. But that's just it-they're dears when you get them alone, but somehow, all together, they stifle you. And they all have high voices, that squeak when they're keenest. D'you know, that was what first made me like you, Roger-your voice? It's slow, and deep, and restful-such a reasonable voice. You mustn't think me disloyal to the school. The girls are all frightfully interesting, and the women are dears, and there's always Clare-only we do get on each other's nerves."

"A boys' school is just the same."

"Is it? I've only seen Compton. I don't know how co-education affects the boys, but I'm sure it's good for the girls, and the mistresses too. Of course, they're not really different to my lot, but they seemed so. They had room to move. They weren't always rubbing up against each other like apples in a basket. It all seemed so natural and jolly. Fresh air everywhere. And since I've been back, I've felt I couldn't breathe. I believe it's altered me, just seeing it all; and I can't make Clare understand. She thinks I liked Dene because I wanted to flirt."

"That type would."

"Yes, I know you think that," she answered uneasily, "but she isn't —that horrid type. That's why it hurts so that she can't understand. As if I ever thought of such a thing until she talked of it! Only I like talking to men, you know, Roger; because they've often got quite interesting minds, and it's easier to find out what they really think than with women. But they bore Clare."

"Do they?" Roger had his own opinion on the question. But he found that it was difficult to refrain from kissing Alwynne when she looked at him with innocent eyes and made preposterous statements; so he stared at the tulips.

"You see, she thinks-we both think, that if you've got a —a really real woman friend, it's just as good as falling in love and getting married and all that-and far less commonplace. Besides the trouble-smoking, you know-and children. Clare hates children."

"Do you?" Roger looked at her gravely.

"Me? I love them. That's the worst of it. When I grew old, I'd meant to adopt some-only Clare wouldn't let me, I'm sure. Of course, as long as Clare wanted me, I shouldn't mind. To live with Clare all my life-oh, you know how I'd love it. I just —I love her dearly, Roger, you know I do-in spite of things I've told you. Only-oh, Roger, suppose she got tired of me. And, since I've been back, sometimes I believe she is."

"Poor old girl!"

"It's a shame to grizzle to you; it can't be interesting; and, of course, I don't mean for one moment to attack Clare; only everything I do seems wrong. When she sneers, I get nervous; and the more nervous I get, the more I do things wrong-you know, silly things, like spilling tea and knocking into furniture. And she gets furious and then we have a scene. It's simply miserable. We had one yesterday, and again this morning. It's my fault, of course —I get on her nerves."

"You never get on my nerves," said Roger suggestively.

"Not when I chop up your best pink roses?" She looked at him sideways, dimpling a little.

"As long as you don't chop up your own pink fingers-you've got pretty fingers, Alwynne —"

"Roger, you're a comforting person. I wish —I wish Clare would treat me as you do, sometimes. You pull me up too, but you never make me nervous. I'm sure I shouldn't disappoint her so often, if she did."

"Alwynne," he returned with a twinkle, "stop talking. I've made a discovery."

"Well?"

"You're ten times fonder of me than you are of that good lady. Now, own up."

"Roger!" Alwynne was outraged. She made efforts to sit upright, but Roger's arm did not move. It was a strong arm and it held her, if anything, a trifle more firmly. "You're talking rot. Please let me sit up."

"You're all right. It's quite true, my child, and you know it. Ah, yes-they're a lovely colour, aren't they?"

303

For Alwynne was gazing at the tulips with elaborate indifference. Secretly she was a little excited. Here was a new Roger....He was quite mad, of course, but rather a dear....She wondered what he would say next....

"To examine our evidence. You were very glad to see me-now weren't you?"

"I'm always pleased," remarked Alwynne sedately to the tulips, "to see old friends."

"Yes-but we're not old friends exactly, if you refer to length of acquaintanceship. If to age —I was thirty last March. I'm not doddering yet."

"I wasn't speaking of ages. Thirty is perfectly young. Clare's thirty-five. You do fish, Roger."

"Yes. I'm going to have a haul some day soon, I hope. But to resume. Firstly, you were jolly glad to see me. Secondly, you took your lecture very fairly meekly-for you! and you've already had one talking-to to-day during which, I gather, you were anything but meek."

"I never told you ——"

"But there was a glint in your eye ——You've no idea how invariably your face gives you away, Alwynne. Thirdly, you've hinted quite half-a-dozen times that Miss Hartill would be all the better for a few of my virtues. Tenth, and finally, you've made my coat collar thoroughly damp-you needn't try to move-and I don't exactly see you spoiling your Clare's Sunday blouse that way, often, eh?"

Alwynne was obliged to agree with the tulips.

"I thought so. Therefore I say, after considering all the evidence-in your heart of hearts you are ten times fonder of me than of Miss Clare Hartill."

The trap was attractively baited. Impossible for an Alwynne to resist analysis of her own emotions. She walked into it.

"I don't know —I wonder if you're right? Perhaps I am *fonder* of you. I love Clare-that's quite a different thing. One couldn't be fond of Clare. That would be commonplace. She's the sort of wonderful person you just worship. She's like a cathedral —a sort of mystery. Now you're like a country cottage, Roger. Of course, one couldn't be fond of a cathedral."

"A cottage," remarked Roger to the tulips in his turn, "can be made a very comfortable place. Especially if it's a good-sized one-Holt Meadows, for instance. My tenants leave in June, did you know? There's a south wall and a croquet ground."

"Tennis?"

Roger was afraid the tulips would find it too small for tennis.

"But a court could be made in Nicholas Nye's paddock," Alwynne reminded them.

Roger thought it would be rather fun to live there, tennis or no tennis-didn't the tulips think so?

The tulips did, rather.

"One could buy Witch Wood for a song, I believe; you know it runs along the paddock. Think of it, all Witch Wood for a wild garden."

"And no trespassers! No trampled hyacinths any more! Or ginger-beer bottles! Oh, Roger!" A delighted, delightful Alwynne was forgetting all about the tulips; but they nodded very pleasantly for all that.

"A footpath through to The Dears' garden, and my glass-houses. And chickens in a corner of the paddock. You'd have to undertake those."

"All white ones!"

"Better have Buff Orpingtons. Lay better. Remember Jean's troubles: 'Really, the Amount of Eggs ——'"

"Dear Jean. And besides, I shall want some for clutches. I adore them when they're all fluff and squeak; and ducklings too, Roger. We won't have incubators, will we?"

"Rather not. Lord, it will be sport. You're to wear print dresses at breakfast, Alwynne-lilac, with spots."

"You're very particular ——"

"Like that one you wore at the Fair ——you know."

"Oh, that one! Do you mean to say——All right. But I shall wear tea-gowns every afternoon-with lace and frillies. Elsbeth says they're theatrical."

"All right! We'll eat muffins——"

"And read acres of books——"

"May I smoke?"

"It'll get into the curtains——"

"I'll get you a new lot once a week——"

"And we won't ever be at home to callers——"

"Just us two."

Alwynne sighed contentedly.

"Oh, Roger, it would be rather nice. You can invent beautifully."

He laughed.

"Then we'll consider that settled."

He bent his head and kissed her.

A very light kiss—a very airy and fugitive attempt at a kiss—a kiss that suited the moment better than his mood; but Roger could be Fabian in his methods. Alwynne rather thought that it was a curl brushing her forehead: the tulips rather thought it wasn't. Roger could have settled the matter, but they did not like to appeal to him. They were all a little disturbed-more than a little uncertain how to act. The tulips' attitude was frankly alarming to Alwynne, who (if the kiss had really happened) was prepared to be dignified and indignant. The tulips, however, appeared to think a kiss a pleasant enough indiscretion. "To some one, at any rate, we are worth the kissing," quoth the tulips defiantly, with irreverent eyes on a vision of Clare's horrified face. Then, veering smartly, they reminded Alwynne, that from a patient, protective Roger it was the most brotherly and natural of sequels to their make-believe. Alwynne was not so sure; Roger was developing characteristics of which the kiss (had it taken place) was not the least exciting and alarming symptom. He was no longer the Roger of Dene days, not a month dead; or rather, the Dene Roger was proving himself but a facet of a many-sided personality-big, too-that was more than a match for a many-sided Alwynne, with moods that met and enveloped hers, as a woman's hands will catch and cover a baby's aimless fist. More than his strength, his gentleness disturbed her. So long a prisoner to Clare, ever bruising herself against the narrow walls of that labyrinthine mind-she would have been indifferent to any harshness from him; but his kindliness, his simplicity, unnerved her. He had been right-she had her pride. Clare did not often guess when her self-control was undermined. But with Roger-what was the use of pretending to Roger? It had been comforting to have a good cry. His kiss had been comforting too. She remembered the first of Clare's rare kisses-the thin fingers that gripped her shoulders; the long, fierce pressure, mouth to mouth; the rough gesture that released her, flung her aside.

But Roger-if, indeed, she had not dreamed-had been comforting. Here the tulips broke in whimsically with the brazen suggestion that it would be delightful to put one's arms round Roger's neck and return that supposititious kiss. A remark, of course, of which no flower but a flaunting scarlet tulip could be capable. Alwynne was horrified at the tulips. Horrified by the tulips, worried by her own uncertainties, puzzled by the imperturbable face smiling down at her. Certainly not a conscience-stricken face. Probably the entire incident was a wild imagining of the tulips. She had watched those nodding spring devils long enough. Time to go home: at any rate it was time to go home.

It puzzled her anew that Roger's arm was no longer about her, that he should make no effort to detain her, or to reopen the conversation; that he should walk at her side in his usual fashion, originating nothing. Once or twice, glancing up at him, she surprised a smile of inscrutable satisfaction, but he did not speak; he merely met her eyes steadily, still smiling, till she dropped her own once more. A month ago she would have challenged that smile, cavilled and cross-examined. To-day she was quaintly intimidated by it. Indeed a new Roger! She never dreamed of a new Alwynne.

Yet for all her perplexity and very real physical fatigue, Alwynne walked with a light step and a light heart. As usually she was absurdly touched by his unconscious protective movements-the touch on her arm at crossings-the juggle of places on the fresh pathway-the little courtesies which the woman-bred girl had practised, without receiving, appealed to her enormously. She felt like a tall school-child, "gentleman" perforce at all her dancing lessons, who, at her first ball, comes delightedly into her own.

She gave Roger little friendly glances as they walked home, but no words; though she could have talked had he invited. But Roger was resolutely silent, and for some obscure reason this embarrassed her more than his previous loquacity. Gradually she grew conscious of her crumpled dress and loosened hair; that a button was missing on her glove! trifles not often wont to trouble her. She wondered if Roger had noticed the button's absence; she hoped fervently that he had not. She glanced obscurely at shop-windows, whose blurred reflections could not help her to the conviction that her hat was straight. Also it dawned upon her that Roger was weighed down by preposterous parcels; that the parcels were her own. She was sure the string was cutting his fingers. She was penitent, knowing that she would not be allowed to relieve him, and hugely annoyed with herself. She had been scolded often enough for her parcel habit, and had laughed at Elsbeth; and here was Elsbeth proved entirely right. Weighing down Roger like this! What would he think of her? He had not spoken for ten minutes.... Of course-he was annoyed.... They had better get home as quickly as might be....

CHAPTER XLI

Elsbeth, sitting at the window, had seen them come down the street, and was at the door to welcome them. Alwynne was kissed, rather gravely, but Elsbeth and Roger greeted each other like the oldest of trusted friends. Alwynne's eyebrows lifted, but Elsbeth ignored her. She scolded Roger for being late, showed him his roses, revived and fragrant in their blue bowls; and when Alwynne turned to go and dress, declared that he looked starved, that supper was long overdue, and must be eaten at once. Roger seconded her, and to supper they went.

Alwynne raged silently. What was the matter with Elsbeth? She had barely greeted her.... And now to be so inconsiderate.... To insist on sitting down to supper then and there, without giving her time to make herself decent! Couldn't she see how tired Alwynne was, how badly in need of soap and water and a brush and comb, let alone a prettier frock? It wasn't fair! Elsbeth might know she would want to look nice-with Roger there.... She did not choose to look a frump, however Elsbeth dressed herself....

It dawned on her, however, as Elsbeth, resigning the joint to Roger, began to mix a salad under his eye, after some particular recipe of his imparting, that Elsbeth, on this occasion, was looking anything but a frump. She wore her best dress of soft, dark purple stuff, and the scarf of fine old lace, that, as Alwynne very well knew, saw the light on high and holy days only; and a bunch of Roger's roses were tucked in her belt. Her hair was piled high in a fashion new to Alwynne: a tiny black velvet bow set off its silvery grey; it was waved, too, and clustered becomingly at the temples. Alwynne, gasping, realised that Elsbeth must have paid a visit to the local coiffeur. She realised also, for the first time, how pretty, in delicate, pink-may fashion, her aunt must once have been.

At any other time Alwynne would have been delighted at the improvement, for she was proud of Elsbeth, in daughterly fashion, and had wrestled untiringly with her indifference to dress. She knew she should have hailed the change, but, to her own annoyance, she found it irritating. It displeased her that she herself should be dishevelled and day-worn, while Elsbeth faced her, cool and dainty and dignified. Roger was obviously impressed.... Roger, to whom Elsbeth had been so carefully, deprecatingly explained.... It made Alwynne look such a fool.... How was she to know that Elsbeth would have this whim? She had never guessed that Elsbeth could make herself look so charming.... And she to be in her street clothes ... with her hair like a mouse's nest! It was too bad! However, it didn't seem to matter.... Roger, it was clear enough, had no eyes for her....

Her resentment grew. She attempted to join in the conversation, but though Roger listened gravely, and answered politely-she never caught the twinkle in his eye-he invariably flung back the ball to Elsbeth as quickly as might be. She mentioned Dene; made intimate allusions to their walks and adventures; and he turned to explain them, to include Elsbeth, with a pointedness that made Alwynne pink with vexation. She began to long to get him to herself ... to quarrel or make peace, as he pleased ... but anyhow to get him to herself.... Couldn't one have a moment's conversation without dragging Elsbeth into it? So absurd of Roger....

Slowly she realised that neither Roger nor Elsbeth were finding her indispensable, and her surprise was only rivalled by her indignation. Elsbeth particularly-it was simply beastly of Elsbeth-was being, in her impalpable way, unapproachable.... She was angry about something.... Alwynne knew the signs.... She, Alwynne, supposed that she ought to have written.... But she did write a postcard.... One couldn't be everlastingly writing letters.... Any one but Elsbeth would have waived the matter, with a visitor present, but Elsbeth was so vindictive.... Here Alwynne's rebellious conscience allied itself with her sense of humour, to protest against the picture of a vindictive Elsbeth. They bubbled with tender laughter at the idea. Alwynne must needs laugh with them, a trifle remorsefully, and admit that the idea was fantastic; that Elsbeth, in all the years she had known her, had been the most meek and forgiving of guardians; and that she, Alwynne, had been undeniably negligent. Nevertheless, why must Elsbeth show Roger the kitchen? What was he saying to her out there? And why were they both laughing like that?

307

"Cackle, cackle, cackle," muttered Alwynne viciously; "awfully funny, isn't it?"
She continued her reflections.

Fussing over clearing the supper still! One of Elsbeth's absurd ideas, just because it was the maid's evening out.... Let her do it when she came back! Such a fuss and excitement always! What would Roger think of them? What a long time they were! She might take the opportunity of going to change her frock.... She hesitated. What was that? What was Roger saying? She caught the murmur of his deep voice and her aunt's staccato in answer, but the words were blurred.

After all-why should she bother to change? Elsbeth would be sure to make unnecessary remarks.... And Roger wouldn't care-he was too occupied with Elsbeth.... Nobody cared-nobody wanted her.... She would go back to Clare to-morrow.... But if Clare were in to-day's humour still?

What a wretched week it had been.... Even if Clare had not been so moody, Alwynne would have felt ill at ease ... she had known perfectly well that she owed the first weeks of her return to her aunt ... but at a hint from Clare she had stifled her conscience and stayed.... And now Elsbeth, she could tell, was deeply hurt.... Once away from Clare, Alwynne could reflect and be sorry.... She wouldn't have believed that she could be so careless of Elsbeth's feelings.... She was suddenly and generously furious with herself. How selfish, how abominably selfish she had been.... No wonder Roger had been shocked! Of course neither he nor Elsbeth could ever understand how difficult it was to withstand Clare.... It had been possible once.... Her thought strayed to that early Christmas when she had resisted all Clare's arguments.... But now she had no choice.... However determined one might be beforehand-and she had intended to return that first day-one's will was beaten aside, blown about like a straw in a strong wind.... If only Roger would understand that.... She hated him to think her so selfish.... Elsbeth needn't have told him, she thought resentfully ... it was not like Elsbeth to give her away.... She supposed she had hurt Elsbeth's feelings pretty badly.... Why, oh why, hadn't she been firmer with Clare? She had only to say, quite quietly, that she must do what she felt to be right.... Clare couldn't have eaten her....

She began to rehearse the conversation; it soothed her to compose the telling phrases she might have uttered. They sounded all right ... but, of course, face to face with Clare she could never have said them.... Clare, in indifference, displeasure or appeal, would have conquered without battle given ... in her heart she knew that.

She moved uneasily about the room, deep in thought. For the first time her attitude to Clare struck her as contemptible.... What had Roger said? "Like a dog after a thrashing." Intolerable! She flung up her head, her pride writhing under the phrase. So that was how it struck outsiders! Outsiders? She didn't care a dead leaf for outsiders.... Let them think what they chose! But Roger? And Elsbeth? Did they really think her weak and enslaved? It stung her that Roger should think so meanly of her. She told herself that the loss of his opinion in no way affected her-and instantly began to revolve within herself phrases, explanations, actions, wherewith to regain it. And there was Elsbeth.... He had thought her unkind to Elsbeth.... He was right there! She saw, remorsefully, with her usual thoroughness, that she had been, for many a long year, as the plagues of Egypt to her Elsbeth.

She flung herself on the prim little sofa, and stared at the closed door uncertainly. She was too proud to do what she wanted to do-invade the kitchen, and regardless of Roger's eyes and presence, confess to Elsbeth, and receive absolution. A word, she knew, would be enough.... If Elsbeth felt as miserable as she did — a word would be more than enough....

Elsbeth and Roger, returning to the sitting-room, ended her indecision. Their manner had changed-Roger was quieter-less talkative-but Elsbeth was so radiant that Alwynne decided that contrition could wait. More than ever she realised that two were company....

Her anger grew again as she watched and listened.

Elsbeth had produced cards, and suggested three-handed bridge. Alwynne excused herself, and Roger, who had been her partner on occasion at Dene, was obviously relieved. His Alwynne was the One Woman-but she could not play bridge!

He settled down to double-dummy with Elsbeth. The conversation became a rapt and technical duet, punctuated with interminable pauses.

Alwynne fumed.

So this was Elsbeth's idea of a really pleasant evening! Cards! Beastly, idiotic cards! Roger, her Roger, had come up all the way from Dene to play cards with Elsbeth! Had he just? All right then! He should have all the cards he wanted-and more! As for Elsbeth-catch Alwynne telling her she was sorry now!

The striking of the clock gave her her opportunity. She rose, yawning elaborately.

"I'm going to bed," she remarked to the card-table.

"Are you, dear?" said Elsbeth.

"Oh! Oh, good-night," said Roger casually rising, and sitting down again. "Your shout, Elsbeth."

Elsbeth went "no trumps."

Alwynne lingered.

"Of course the kitchen fire's out?" she said, with sour suggestiveness.

"Do you want a bath? Yes, of course. Do you know, my dear, you're looking rather grubby?" Elsbeth paid her sweetly. "I expect the water will still be hot, if you're quick. Don't forget to turn the light off, will you, when you've finished?"

Alwynne made no answer, but she still lingered. Elsbeth, finishing her hand, spoke over her shoulder—

"Alwynne, dear, either go out, or come in and sit down. There's such a draught."

There was a swish of skirts, and all the innumerable ornaments rattled on their shelves. Alwynne had permitted herself the luxury of banging the door.

Roger laughed like a schoolboy.

"'All is not well!'" he quoted.

Elsbeth laughed too, yet half against her will.

"My poor Alwynne! She hates me to be annoyed with her. It infuriates her. She'll be awfully penitent to-morrow. It's really rather comical, you know. She'll take criticism from any one else-but I must approve implicitly! And you being here didn't improve matters. She was longing to be nice, and I didn't help her. She was quite aware that she was showing you her worst side, and quite unable to get out of the mood. I knew, bless her heart!"

She looked at him with a quick little gesture of appeal.

"Roger-you do understand? That-tantrum-meant nothing. She's such an impulsive child."

He smiled.

"I know. Don't you worry. Besides, it was my fault. I was teasing her all the evening. It was not what she expected. Oh, I'm growing subtle enough to please even you, Elsbeth. You know, she's had rather a full day. Evidently a scorching afternoon with that delightful friend of hers, to start with——"

"Ah?" said Elsbeth, her eyes brightening.

"Oh, yes; she was distinctly chastened. I improved the occasion, and you've about finished her off, the poor old girl! I was expecting that little exhibition."

"I believe—I believe you enjoy upsetting her," began Elsbeth, rather indignantly.

"Of course I do. It's as good as a play!"

Elsbeth sighed.

"Well—I suppose it's all right. You'll have to manage her for the future, not I."

"Oh, she'll do all the managing," said Roger ruefully. "I foresee that this is my last stand. She's just a trifle in awe of me, at present, you know, though she doesn't know it. But it won't last. And then-heaven help me! But, you know, Cousin Elsbeth-to be henpecked by Alwynne-don't you think it will be quite pleasant?"

"It is. She's bullied me since she was three. Oh, Roger, I shall miss her." She blinked rapidly.

Roger stared away from her in awkward sympathy.

"You shan't, not very much," he said. "We'll fix things. You'll have to come and settle with us."

Elsbeth fidgeted.

"You know, you took my breath away in the kitchen just now," she said. "Are you quite sure it's all right? Does Alwynne *know* she's engaged to you?"

He perpended.

"Well, frankly—I don't think she did quite take it in."

"Roger!"

"But I'm buying the engagement ring to-morrow," he added hastily. "That'll clear things up."

Elsbeth looked at him helplessly.

"Roger, either you're a genius or a lunatic. I'm not sure which-but, I think, a lunatic."

"Oh, well! We shall know to-morrow," he observed consolingly. "I shall turn up about eleven. Keep Alwynne for me, won't you?"

Elsbeth struck her hands together.

"It's Clare Hartill's birthday! I'd almost forgotten her! Alwynne will be engrossed. Oh, Roger! You've been telling me fairy tales. We've forgotten Clare Hartill!"

Roger picked up the scattered cards. With immense caution he poised a couple, tent fashion, and builded about them, till a house was complete. He added storey after storey, frowning and absorbed. At the sixth, the structure collapsed. He looked up and met Elsbeth's eyes.

"People in card-houses shouldn't raise Cain. It's an expensive habit," he remarked sententiously. "Elsbeth, don't worry! But keep Alwynne till I come to-morrow, won't you?"

"I'll try."

"Of course, if she's still in a temper——Hulloa!"

The door had been softly opened. Alwynne, in her gay dressing-gown stood on the threshold. Her hair was knotted on the top of her head, and small damp curls strayed about her forehead. The folds of her wrapper, humped across her arm, with elaborate care, hinted at the towels and sponges concealed beneath. She looked, in spite of her bigness, like an extremely small child masquerading as a grown-up person.

Her eyes sought her aunt's appealingly. Roger, she ignored.

"Elsbeth," she said meekly, "please won't you come and tuck me up?"

She disappeared again.

Elsbeth laughed as she rose.

"I knew she wouldn't be content. Isn't she a dear, Roger, for all her little ways?"

"She's all right," said Roger, with immense conviction.

CHAPTER XLII

Alwynne was spending a contented morning. She had made her peace with Elsbeth over-night, and at the ensuing breakfast had been something of a feasted prodigal. Elsbeth had made no objection to her plans for the afternoon, but had suggested that, as Roger was coming to lunch, Alwynne might take him for a walk in the morning. He was sure to arrive by twelve. Alwynne, her head full of Clare's birthday and Clare's birthday present, acquiesced graciously. Indeed, she was herself anxious to talk to him again, to show him how completely she and Elsbeth were in accord, to prove to him, once and for all, though with kindly firmness, how uncalled for his comments had been. She believed that they had not parted the best of friends last night.... A pity-Roger could be such a dear when he chose.... Yesterday afternoon, for instance.... She found herself blushing hotly, as she recalled the details of yesterday afternoon.

Her thoughts were divided evenly between Roger and Clare as she sat at her work-table, running the last ribbon through the foamy laces and embroideries. She was proud of her work, and thrilled with pleasurable anticipations of Clare's comments. Clare would be pleased, wouldn't she?

Elsbeth, helping her to fold the dainty garment, and wondering wistfully if Alwynne would ever be found spending a tenth of the time and trouble on her own trousseau that she lavished on presents for people who did not appreciate them, was quite sure that Clare would be more than pleased. She could not cloud Alwynne's happy face; but she hoped to goodness that Roger would come soon.... She was sick of the word Clare.

Alwynne despatched her parcel by messenger-boy. She would not trust it to the post-yet it must arrive before she did. Clare hated to be confronted with you and your gift together. She hoped that Clare would not be in a mood when gifts were anathema. You never knew with Clare.

She paid the boy with a bright shilling and a slice of inviolate company cake, and was guiltily endeavouring so to squeeze and compress its girth, that Elsbeth would not notice the enlarged gap at tea-time, when Roger arrived.

She slid the tin hastily back into the cupboard.

"I won't shake hands," she said. "But it's stickiness, not ill-feeling."

Roger frowned aside the remark. He was looking excited, extremely pleased with himself, yet a trifle worried. He had the air of a man who had been priding himself on doing the right thing, and is suddenly stricken with doubt as to whether, after all, he had not made a mess of the business. He confronted her.

"I expect I've got it wrong," he remarked, with gloomy triumph. "I hate coloured stones myself."

"What are you talking about?" demanded Alwynne.

"Which is it, anyhow?"

"Which is what?"

"Which is your favourite stone?"

Alwynne gazed at him blankly.

"What on earth — —?" she began.

Roger frowned anew.

"Don't argue with me. Which is your favourite stone?"

"I don't know-emeralds, I think."

He gave a sigh of relief, not entirely make-believe.

"Of course! I knew I was right. Elsbeth swore to pearls."

"Oh, I've always coveted her string. She's going to give it to me when I'm forty. I'd like to know what you're talking about, Roger, if you don't mind?"

"Why forty?"

"Years of discretion! You are tidy and never lose anything once you're forty. But why? Were you having a bet?"

"Not exactly." Roger searched his pockets. "Here, catch hold!"

311

He had produced a small package, gay with sealing-wax and coloured string. He handed it to her awkwardly, with immense detachment.

She opened it curiously.

In a little white kid case lay an emerald, round and shining like a safety signal. It was set in silver, quaintly carven.

Alwynne exclaimed.

"Oh, Roger! How gorgeous! How perfectly ripping! Where did you pick it up? Was it awfully expensive?"

Roger had been beaming in a gratified fashion, but at her question his jaw dropped.

"Well," he began. "Well—I———"

His expression struck her.

"Do you mind my asking? It's only because it is so exactly what I've always longed to give Clare. I'm saving. I'm going to, some day. Clare loves emeralds."

"Perhaps," said Roger, with elaborate irony, "you'd like to give her this? Don't mind me."

She glanced up at him, startled, puzzled.

"This?"

"It happens to be your engagement ring," he remarked offendedly.

Alwynne began to laugh, but a trifle uncertainly. To laugh without accompaniment or encouragement is uneasy work, and Roger's face was entirely expressionless. She felt that her laughter was sounding affected, and ceased abruptly, her foot tapping the floor, a glint of annoyance in her eye.

"What are you talking about?" she attacked him.

"Your engagement ring, wasn't it?" he said.

"Are you by any chance serious?"

"Perfectly." Roger's schoolboy awkwardness, due to his encounter with an unexpectedly facetious jeweller, was wearing off.

"*My* engagement ring?"

"We'll change it, of course," he said, with maddening politeness, "if you really prefer pearls."

"Presupposing an engagement?" Alwynne was on her high horse.

"To me. That was the idea, I think. Elsbeth is delighted."

Alwynne dismounted hastily again, though she kept a hand on the bridle.

"Roger-this is beyond a joke. What have you been saying to Elsbeth?"

"Why, my dear," he said gently, "very much what I told you yesterday afternoon."

Alwynne grew scarlet.

"Roger-we were in fun yesterday. We were joking. I forget what it was all about. There was nothing to tell Elsbeth."

"Yes, you do forget," he said.

"Yes. I have. I want to," she answered unsteadily. "You know you weren't serious. Why, you were laughing at me-you know you were."

"Do you never laugh when you're serious?"

"Never!" said Alwynne earnestly.

"Well, then, we're like the Cheshire cat and dog. But I laugh when I'm most amazingly serious sometimes, Alwynne. I was yesterday, and I think you knew it."

"I didn't," said Alwynne stubbornly. "We only just talked nonsense. All about Holt Meadows-you know it was nonsense."

"I didn't," said Roger, with equal stubbornness.

"You did," said Alwynne.

"I didn't," said Roger.

"Oh, of course, if you're going to lose your temper——" cried Alwynne.

Roger shrugged his shoulders. It was deadlock.

Alwynne looked at him. He was grave enough now.

"I didn't mean to be rude," she said unhappily.

"Didn't you?" He was all polite surprise.

"I expect I was——" she ventured.

"It all depends on what one's used to," he returned philosophically.

"Yes, I know I was. But you are so horrid to-day."

"Sorry," said Roger stiffly.

She turned to him impulsively.

"Roger—I've missed you awfully since I came back. It was quite absurd, when I'd got Clare all to myself. But I did. It was so nice seeing you. I was simply miserable yesterday, and then you turned up and were perfectly sweet. It cheered me up. And then you turned horrid. All the evening you were horrid. And now you're horrid, quarrelling and arguing. Why can't you be nice to me always?"

She was very close to him. Her hand was on the arm of his chair. Her skirts swished against his knee.

"Alwynne, you're too illogical for a school-marm. Haven't you been bullying me since I came on account of yesterday?"

"Roger," she said unsteadily, "don't tease me. I do so want to be friends with you."

He put his arms about her as she stood beside him, and looked up at her, with laughing, tender eyes.

"And I do so want to marry you. Why not, Miss Le Creevy? *Let's be a comfortable couple.*"

She struggled away from him.

"No, Roger! No. No. I don't want to get married. Why aren't you content to be friends, as we were at Dene? Friendship's a lot. If I can see you very often, and write to you twice a week, and tell you everything—I should be awfully content. Wouldn't you?"

He looked at her with amusement.

"Your idea of friendship is pretty comprehensive. What's wrong with getting married, Alwynne?"

"Oh—I don't know."

"What's wrong with getting married, Alwynne?"

"How can I get married," cried Alwynne, in sudden exasperation, "when I'm not in love with you? You're silly sometimes, Roger."

"I suppose you're quite sure about it," he ventured cautiously.

"Oh, yes."

He looked utterly unconvinced.

"Why, I've hardly ever even dreamed about you," she remonstrated. "And I know all your faults."

"Oh, you do, do you? Out with the list."

"It would take too long." Alwynne dimpled.

"Love must be blind-is that the idea? Couldn't that be got over? One uses blinkers, you know, in double harness. I never dream, Alwynne, normally. Must I eat lobster salad every night?"

"There-you see!" Alwynne waved her hand complacently. "You're just as bad. You couldn't talk like that if——"

"If what?"

"Nothing!"

"If what?"

Alwynne looked at him.

"If what, Alwynne?" Roger's tone was a little stern.

She had taken a rose from the bowl at her elbow, and was slowly pulling off the petals. Her eyes were on her work.

He waited.

Her hands cupped the little pile of rose-leaves. She buried her face in them-watching him an instant, through her fingers.

"They are very sweet, Roger-are they from home-from Dene, I mean? Smell!"

She held out her hands to him.

He caught them in his own. The red petals fluttered noiselessly to the ground.

"If what, Alwynne?" he insisted.

"Oh, Roger! Do you really care-so much?"

"Yes, dear," he said soberly, "so much."

Alwynne looked up at him anxiously. She was very conscious of the big warm hands that held hers so firmly. She wished that he would not look so intent and grave; he made her feel frightened and unhappy. No-not frightened, exactly. There was something strong and serene about him, that upheld her, even when she opposed him; but certainly, unhappy. She realised suddenly how immensely she liked him-how entirely his nature satisfied hers.

"Oh, Roger!" she said wistfully. "I do like you. It isn't that I wouldn't like to marry you."

His face lit up.

"Would-liking awfully-do, Roger? Would it be fair? Must one be in love like a book?"

His face relaxed.

"I shall be content," he said. Then, impetuously, "Alwynne, I'll make you so happy. You shall do-nearly everything-you want to. Alwynne, if you only knew——"

She stopped him hurriedly, pulling away her hands.

"Don't, Roger! Don't! I didn't mean that. I only meant I'd like to. But I can't, of course. Of course, I can't. There's Clare."

"Clare!" His tone abolished Clare.

Alwynne flushed.

"Why do you sneer at Clare? You always sneer. I won't have it."

Her tone, in spite of her sudden anger, was unconsciously and comically proprietary. He repressed a smile as he answered her.

"All right, dear. But I wasn't sneering-not at Clare."

"At me, then?"

"Not sneering-chuckling. My dear, what has Clare-oh, yes, she's your dearest friend-but what has any friend, any woman, got to say to us two? We're going to get married."

"We're not. It's no good, Roger." Alwynne spoke slowly and emphatically, as one explaining things to a foreigner. "Why won't you understand? Clare wants me. We've been friends for years."

"Two years!" he interjected contemptuously.

"Well! You needn't talk! I've known you two months," she flashed out. "Do you think I'm going to desert Clare for you, even if-even if——" She stopped suddenly.

He beamed.

"You do. Don't you, darling?" he said.

"I don't. I don't. I don't want to. I mustn't. I don't know why I'm even talking to you like this. It's ridiculous. Of course, there can never be any one but Clare."

"Yes, it is ridiculous," he said impatiently.

She faced him angrily.

"Yes, very ridiculous, isn't it? Not to leave a person in the lurch —a person whom you love dearly, and who loves you. You can laugh. It's easy to laugh at women being friends. Men always do. They think it funny, to pretend women are always catty, and spiteful, and disloyal to each other."

"I've never said so or thought so," said Roger.

"You have! You do! Look at the way you've talked about Clare. That looks as if you thought me loyal and a good friend, doesn't it? What would Clare think of me-when I've let her be sure she can have me always-when I've promised her——"

"At nineteen! Miss Hartill's generous to allow you to sacrifice yourself——"

"It's no sacrifice! Can't you understand that I care for her-awfully. Why —I owe her everything. I was a silly, ignorant schoolgirl, and she took me, and taught me-pictures, books, everything. She made me understand. Of course, I love my dear old Elsbeth-but Clare woke me up, Roger. You don't know how good she's been to me. I owe her-all my mind— —"

"And your peace?" he asked significantly.

She softened.

"You know I'm grateful. I don't forget. But she's such a dreadfully lonely person. You've got The Dears, at least. She's queer. She can't help it. She doesn't make friends, though every one adores her. She's only got me. She wants me. How could I go when she wants me-when she's so good to me?"

"Is she?" he said. "Yesterday— —"

"I was a fool yesterday," said Alwynne quickly. "Of course, I get on her nerves sometimes. But it's always my fault-honestly. You don't know what she's like, Roger, or you wouldn't say such things. I hate you to misunderstand her. How could I care for her so, if she were what you and Elsbeth think?"

He looked at her innocent, anxious face, and sighed.

"All right, my dear. Stick to your Clare. As long as you're happy, I suppose it's all right. Well, I'd better be off. Where's Elsbeth?"

"Be off? Where?" Alwynne looked startled.

"To pack my traps. I'm going home."

"Oh, Roger, you're not angry with me?"

"I am, rather," he said. "But you needn't mind me. You don't, do you?"

She looked at him piteously.

"Good-bye," he said. He shook hands perfunctorily and turned away.

"You're angry-oh, you are!" cried Alwynne, following him.

He laughed.

"You can't pay Clare without robbing Roger. Don't worry, Alwynne."

"Are you really going?" she said wistfully.

"Yes. Any message?"

"You'll write to me, won't you?"

"Good Lord, no!" said Roger, with immense decision.

Alwynne jumped. It was not the answer she had expected.

"But-but you must write to me," she stammered. "How shall I know about you, if you don't write to me?"

He was silent.

A new idea struck Alwynne.

"D'you mean-you don't want to hear from me either?" she asked incredulously.

"I think it would be better," he said.

"Oh, Roger-why? Aren't you going to be friends?"

Alwynne was looking alarmed.

"I wonder," he began, with elaborate patience, "if you could contrive, without straining yourself, to look at things from my point of view-for a moment-only a moment?"

"That's mean. You make me feel a beast."

"That won't hurt you— —"

"Roger!"

"Alwynne?"

"You're being very rude."

"You kick at the privileges of friendship already? I knew you would. Let's drop it, Alwynne. You've got your good lady: you're quite satisfied. I've not got you: I'm not. So the best thing I can do is to go back to Dene and forget about you."

"If you can," said Alwynne's widening, indignant eyes.

"After all," he said meditatively, "you're a dear, but you aren't the only woman in the world, are you?"

"Oh, no," said Alwynne.

315

"I might go back to America," he said, "for a time. I've heaps of friends out there."

"Oh?" said Alwynne.

"Yes, I shall get over it," he concluded comfortably. "You mustn't worry, my child. Well, good-bye again-wish me good luck, Alwynne."

"Good luck," said Alwynne.

He took up his hat-looked at her-smiled a little, and walked to the door.

But before he could open it, he felt a touch on his arm.

"Roger," said a soft and wheedling voice, "wouldn't you *like* to write to me? Now and then, Roger?"

He dissented with admirable gravity.

"All right! Don't then!" cried Alwynne wrathfully. She turned her back on him and sat down.

The luncheon-bell tinkled across the ensuing pause, like a peal of puckish laughter.

CHAPTER XLIII

Elsbeth's voice, raised tactfully at the further end of the passage, warned them of her approach.

Said Alwynne over her shoulder —

"Anyhow, you must stay to lunch now, Elsbeth would be furious if you went. She'll say I've driven you away or something. Unless you want to get me into another row?"

She spoke ungraciously enough, for she disliked having to ask a favour of him at such a juncture; but she disliked even more the notion of a *tête-à-tête* lunch with Elsbeth. Elsbeth, by right of aunthood, would ask questions, demand confession.... Elsbeth, she knew instinctively, would be on Roger's side.... She told herself that she did not mind being bullied by Roger, because, after all, it was Roger's affair; but she would not be otherwise interfered with.... Elsbeth had a way of putting you in the wrong.... She would rather not talk with Elsbeth until she had seen Clare.... Clare would fortify her.... If only Roger would keep Elsbeth occupied till she got away to Clare....

"You must stay, you know," she repeated uneasily.

"You made me forget about lunch," he said cheerfully. "Of course I must! You know, you're a terror, Alwynne. I never know which makes me hungrier, a football match or an argument with you. I'm ravenous."

Alwynne was speechless.

"Is no one coming in to lunch?" asked Elsbeth, entering. She looked quickly from one to the other. Alwynne was at the glass, tidying her hair, and Roger seemed cheerful. Elsbeth smiled a significant smile: her eyebrows were question-marks.

Roger shook his head, but not before Elsbeth had caught sight of the scattered rose and disarranged vases. She was instantly engaged in restoring order, and missed the movement.

Suddenly she exclaimed, and pounced on a small object lying on the floor, half hidden in petals.

"Oh! Oh, how lovely! What an exquisite ring! Why, Roger-why, Alwynne-look! I might have trodden on it. How careless of you both."

But she beamed on them with immense satisfaction, as she held out the emerald ring.

"It's not mine," said Alwynne icily.

"Nothing to do with me," Roger assured her.

Elsbeth looked bewildered.

"One of you must have dropped it," she began.

"No!" said Alwynne.

"Oh, no!" said Roger.

But there was a glimmer of fun in his eye, that enlightened Elsbeth, or she thought, at least, that it did.

"In my young days," she remarked severely, "young people didn't leave a valuable engagement ring lying about on the floor."

"A disengaged engagement ring," he corrected her sadly. "At least, it's disengaged at present."

"I think, Elsbeth," said Alwynne firmly, "that the lunch must be getting cold." And preceded them in all dignity to the dining-room.

Alwynne found the meal a trying one. Roger was talkative, and Elsbeth, though obviously puzzled, was too much occupied with him, to be critical of her niece. Alwynne was divided between gratitude to Roger for relieving the situation, and pique that he could be equal to so doing. A man in his position should be far too crushed by disappointment for social amenities. She would have been genuinely distressed, yet undeniably gratified, if his appetite had failed him; but she noticed that he was able to eat a hearty meal. He could laugh, too, with Elsbeth, and make ridiculous jokes, and draw Alwynne, silent and unwilling, into the conversation. He seemed to have no objection to catching her eye, though she found it difficult to meet his. He was a queer man.... She supposed he wasn't very much in love with her, really, that was the truth of it.... She found the idea depressing. She wondered if he were really going back to Dene at once, and was relieved to hear her aunt challenging his decision. Elsbeth was expostulating. She had plans for the next day ... there was a concert that evening.... Roger appeared to waver. Alwynne, contemptuous that he could be so easily turned, annoyed that Elsbeth should sway him where she herself had failed, was yet conscious of a feeling of relief. At least she should see him again, if only to quarrel with him.... She was due to supper with Clare as well as tea, though she had not told Elsbeth so....It would be quite simple-she would run round to Clare at once, and spend a long afternoon, and get back for another peep at Roger in the evening.... Clare wouldn't mind....

She hesitated. Clare would be rather surprised if she didn't stay.... She had never been known to curtail a visit to Clare before....But she would explain things to her....Clare would be as sorry for Roger as she herself ...for, of course, she must tell Clare all about it....She hoped Clare would not say she had been flirting....But she must make her at least understand what a dear Roger was....She should like Clare to appreciate Roger ...she was afraid she would never be able to make Roger appreciate Clare....It was a great pity!...If it had not been for Roger's unlucky prejudice, she might have introduced them to each other, and it would have all been so jolly.... She would have loved to show Clare to Roger, if Clare had been in a good mood, and had worn her new peacock-coloured frock and had looked and been as adorable as she sometimes could be. They might have gone to-day—and now Roger had spoiled everything.... But at least he was not going till to-morrow.... She would slip away at once while he and Elsbeth were talking-she would be back all the sooner....

She left the pair at their coffee, and hurried to her room to put on her new coat and skirt and her prettiest hat. It was Clare's birthday ...and Clare liked her to be fine.... She wondered, with a little skip of excitement, if Clare had got her parcel yet?

She was no sooner gone than Roger turned to Elsbeth, his laughing manner dropped from him like a mask.

"It's all off, Elsbeth," he said. "You were right. It's that woman. She's infatuated."

The pleasure died out of Elsbeth's face.

"I was afraid so," she said. "I saw something had happened. But you were so comical, I couldn't be sure."

"I didn't want an explanation just then ——"

"Of course not," she interpolated hastily.

"But I think I'll go straight back to Dene. Have you a time-table?"

"Have you quarrelled badly?"

"Not exactly! Alwynne's rather annoyed with me, though."

"Annoyed? With you?"

"Well, you see," he explained, with a touch of amusement, "I think she rather wants to retain me as a tame cat ——"

"Oh, but Alwynne's not like that," Elsbeth protested.

"Don't you think every woman is, if she gets the chance? She has to kow-tow to the Hartill woman, and it would be a relief to have some one to do the same to her-as well as an amusement. But she's had to understand that I won't be her friend's whipping-boy. I decline the post."

"Oh,—well, if you put it that way-but it's hardly fair to Alwynne. Of course, you're angry and disappointed ——"

"I'm not!" he protested heatedly.

"Oh, but you are. Don't pretend you're not human. I don't blame you; I'm angry too. But you must be fair. Alwynne's motives are obvious enough. There's no cat-and-mouse business about it. She simply can't bear the idea of losing you."

"Yet she won't marry me."

"She would, if it weren't for Clare. Didn't you get that impression? Roger, if you really care, wait here a little longer. Stay with us. Let her have a chance of contrasting you with Clare Hartill."

"No, I won't," he said obstinately.

"You care more for your own dignity than for Alwynne, I think," said Elsbeth, in her lowest voice.

"Cousin Elsbeth, I care more for Alwynne than for anything else in the world. You know that. Also, though you'll call me a conceited ass, I believe I know your ewe-lamb ten thousand times better than you do. And I've simply got to sit tight for a bit. The less she sees of me at present, the more she'll think of me-in two senses. If I can make her miss me, it'll be a profitable exile. Oh, you dear, worried woman," he cried, laughing at her intent face, "do you think I want to go away from Alwynne? Nevertheless-where's the time-table?"

She rose and fetched it, and gave it him, without a word.

He ran his finger down the page.

"There's a four o'clock," he announced.

"If only I could do something," mused Elsbeth.

He smiled at her gratefully.

"You're a pretty staunch friend," he said. "What more can one ask?"

"Oh, but I ought to think of something," she said impatiently. "I sit here and let you go—I see two people's lives being spoiled-for the want of a——"

"What?"

"That's it! What? What can I do? Nothing, nothing, nothing. Oh, Roger, it's hard. It's very hard to see people you love unhappy, and not to be able to help them. It's the hardest thing I know. It would be such happiness to be allowed to bear things for them. But to watch....It's harder for us than for men, you know-we're such born meddlers. We think it's our mission to put things to rights."

"When we've made a mess of 'em. I'm not sure that it isn't!"

"I've got to do something," she went on, without heeding him. "There you'll be at Dene, miserable-you will be miserable, Roger?" she interrupted herself, with a faint twinkle.

"Don't you worry," he reassured her. "It was bad enough when she left. She's managed to make every nook and corner of the place remind one of her. I don't know how she does it. Oh, it will be rotten, all right."

"Then there will be Alwynne here," she continued, "pretending she doesn't care. Working herself into a fever each time Clare is unkind to her-and pretending she doesn't care. Watching the posts for a letter from you—I know her-and pretending she doesn't care. Thoroughly miserable, and quite satisfied that I see nothing, as long as she laughs and jokes at meals. Oh, life's a comedy," cried Elsbeth. "You young folk have your troubles, and think we are too old and blind to see them; and we old folk have our troubles, and know you are too young and blind to see them. Yes, Roger—I'm having a grumble, and it's doing me good. One suffers vicariously as one gets older, but one suffers just the same. You children forget that."

"Do we?" he said gently. "I won't again-we won't, later on, Elsbeth-Alwynne and I."

"I want you two to be happy," she cried piteously. "I want it so. Oh, Roger, what can I do?"

"Nothing," he said.

She was silenced. But he was touched and a little amused to see how entirely she was unconvinced. He admired her persistence, and wondered if she had fought as vehemently for her own happiness, as she now fought for Alwynne's. Failure was instinct in her, in her faded colouring and eager, unassured manner. He thought it probable that the memory of failure was spurring her now.

He roused her gently.

"Elsbeth! It's past three o'clock. Will you come and see me off? I must go back to the White Horse for my bag first. Shall I call for you? I shan't be more than twenty minutes."

She nodded assent and promised to be ready.

Left to herself, she went to her room and dressed with mechanical care. Her mind tossed the while like an oarless boat in the sea of her restless thoughts.

What could she do? Wait-wait and hope, and watch things go wrong....Roger was in love now, and prepared to be patient; but Roger was only a man....He would get over it in time;

and Alwynne, finally released from Clare's influence-that, too, surely, was only a question of time-would find out what she had lost.... She understood Alwynne well enough to know that if she cared, however unconsciously, for Roger, she would never be content to attach herself to any later comer.... Alwynne was terribly tenacious. So she, too, would waste and spoil her life; and for the sake of an infatuation, a piece of girlish quixotry.... It was criminal of Clare Hartill to allow it.... She supposed that the situation amused Clare; at least, if Alwynne's version had allowed her to guess it.... She wondered exactly how much Alwynne would tell Clare....

Suddenly and wonderfully she was illumined by an idea.

Roger, returning punctually with his bag, found Elsbeth awaiting him on the step, in calling costume, pulling and patting at a new pair of gloves with extraordinary energy. Her cheeks were bright; she had the air of frightened bravery of a cornered sheep.

"Come away quickly, Roger," she whispered, with a glance at the windows. "I don't want Alwynne to catch me. I can't come with you to the station, Roger. I'm going to see Clare Hartill."

CHAPTER XLIV

Alwynne, for all her eagerness, took more than her usual breathless ten minutes in reaching Clare Hartill's flat. Underneath her pleasure at seeing Clare again ran a little current of uneasiness. There was so much to be told, not only in deference to the intimacy of their relationship, but in order to procure the proof that had never before seemed necessary, that Roger's, and incidentally Elsbeth's, view of that relationship was wrong....Clare, of course, was reserved, undemonstrative, not, Alwynne was prepared to admit, so kindly or considerate a companion as-well, as Roger....But why it should therefore follow that Roger loved her better, and was more worthy-preposterous word-of her own love, Alwynne could not see....Clare Hartill cared for her, had told her so, had-had not as yet proved it, because there had been no need of proof.... Alwynne could love for two....But to-day she felt only an aching desire that Clare should realise the importance of what she had just done; should reward her sacrifice with little softenings and intimacies, some such signs as she had shown her in the earlier days of their friendship, of affection and sympathy....She did not ask much, she told herself; if Clare were only a little kind, she should not miss Roger. Even as she so decided, her cheek flushing at the idea of Clare's kindness, at the possibility of a return to their earlier relationship, she saw suddenly, with flashlight distinctness, how much, even then, she should miss Roger, how great her sacrifice would still be....She saw, as in a vision, the man and woman drowning in waste seas, and she herself at rescue work with room for one and one only in the boat beside her....She felt herself torn by the agony of choice, knowing the while, that a year ago it had not been so; that a year ago she would have outstretched arms for Clare alone; that even now, Elsbeth, The Dears, all alike might drown in that dream sea, so long as Clare were saved....She acknowledged, she exulted in the narrowness of her affection....Clare before the world! But Clare before Roger? Clare safe and Roger drowning? She chuckled as it occurred to her that Roger would certainly be able to swim....Yes, he would swim comfortably alongside and spare her the fantastic trouble of a choice....Blessed old Roger!

As she passed the little kiosk at the corner of Friar's Lane, where a red-haired girl sat behind branches of white and mauve lilac, and high-piled mounds of violets, she hesitated and turned back. It was a breaking of unwritten rules, and Clare would give her no thanks, but to-day at least she would not scold....She would say nothing, but how big her dear eyes would grow at sight of that armful of scented colour! She bought lavishly, and forgot to stay for change, for she was picturing her own arrival as she hurried on: the open door; the pell-mell of flowers and sunlight; Clare's smile; Clare's kiss. In spite of moods Clare could not do without her! She tore up the stairs and pealed the bell, with never another thought of Roger.

Clare was at her writing-table and had but a bare nod for Alwynne, as she stood in the doorway, flushed, smiling, expectant. The girl was accustomed to finding her preoccupied; there was a time, indeed, when there had been subtle flattery in the cavalier welcome, when the lack of ceremony had seemed but a proof of intimacy, and she would bide her time happily enough, exploring book-shelves, darning stockings, tiptoeing from parlour to pantry to refill vases and valet neglected plants, or, curled in the big arm-chair, would sketch upon imaginary canvases Clare's profile, dark against the sun-filled window, or stare half-hypnotised, at the twinkling diamond on her finger. But to-day, for the first time, Clare's reception of her jarred.

She sat down quietly, the flowers in a heap at her feet, her excitement subsiding and leaving her jaded and sorehearted. She felt herself disregarded, reduced to the level of an importunate schoolgirl....She wondered how much longer Clare intended to write, and told herself, with a little, petulant shrug, that for two pins she would surprise Clare, wrench away her pen, take her by the shoulders and anger her into attention. Roger was right....One could be too meek....She rose with a little quiver of excitement, her irrepressible phantasy limning with lightning speed an imaginary Clare —a Clare beleaguered, with barriers down, a Clare with wide maternal arms, enclosing, comforting, sufficing....

The real Clare shifted in her seat and Alwynne sank back again. No, that was not the way to take Clare.... One must be patient, only patient, like Roger.... Clare would give all one needed, that was sure, but in her own time, her own way.... One must be patient....

She loosed her coat.... How close the room was.... She would have liked to fling open the window, but Clare always protested.... She heard Elsbeth's voice: "Fresh air? Her idea of fresh air is an electric fan." ...Queer, how those two jarred! But Elsbeth was not just....

Her head throbbed. Listlessly she picked up a spray of lilac and crushed it against her face. It was deliciously cool.... She supposed that the lilacs were out by now at Dene....

Tic, tac! Tic, tac! The tick of the clock would not keep time with the scratch of Clare's pen.... How stupid! Stupid, stu-pid, stu-pid, stu — —

"Clare!" she cried desperately, "won't you even talk to me?"

Clare wrote on for a moment as if she had not heard her, finished her letter, blotted it, stamped and addressed the cover and wiped her pen deliberately; then she rose, smiling a little. She had been perfectly conscious of Alwynne's unrest.

"What is it?" she said. Alwynne flushed and gathered up her flowers.

"It's your birthday," she apologised. "Look, Clare, aren't they darlings? I know you hate the school fusses, but your own birthday is important. Must you go on writing? It ought to be a holiday. May I get vases? Clare, I've such heaps to tell you, heaps and heaps, only I can't if you stand and look at me from such a long way off. Won't you sit down and smell your lilacs and let me talk to you comfortably?"

With enormous daring she put her arm round Clare and drew her on to the sofa. Clare made no resistance, but she sat stiffly, unsupported, still smiling, her eyes glittering oddly. But the acquiescence was enough for Alwynne and she slid to the ground and sat there sorting her flowers, her face level with Clare's knee, radiant and fearless again.

"I wonder what you will say? It's about Roger."

Clare raised her eyebrows.

"Oh, Clare, don't you know? I wrote such a lot about him from Dene."

"I am to remember every detail of your epistles?"

Alwynne looked up quaintly —

"I suppose there is a good deal to wade through. There always seems so much to say to you. Do you really mind?"

"You remind me that I've letters to finish."

Alwynne looked at the clock in sudden alarm.

"Am I awfully early? You did expect me to tea?"

"And you're never on the late side, are you?" Clare was still smiling, but her tone stung.

Alwynne got up quickly.

"I'm very sorry. Don't bother about me. I'll arrange these things while you finish. I didn't know you were really busy."

Clare put out her hand to the table behind her.

"I'm not busy. It seems one mayn't tease you since you've stayed at Dene."

Alwynne's eyes flashed.

"That's not fair. It's only that-that sometimes now you tease with needles-you used to tease with straws."

"So I had better not tease at all?"

"You know I don't mean that."

Clare lifted an opened parcel from the table. Alwynne recognised it and beamed. So Clare was pleased!

"If I tease with needles," she smoothed the paper and began to straighten the little heap of knotted string, "it's because you annoy me so often. Why did you send me this, Alwynne?"

She shrugged her shoulders.

"It was your birthday."

"I hate birthdays."

"I know." She spoke flatly, a lump in her throat. She might have known and saved herself her trouble and her pleasure....She thought of the weeks of careful work and her delight in it; of the little sacrifices; the early rising; the walks with Roger curtailed and foregone....Everybody had admired it, even Elsbeth had been sure that Clare would be charmed....But Clare was angry.... Perhaps it was only that Clare did not understand....She roused herself.

"Clare, it's different. Don't you remember?"

Clare gave no sign. She had disentangled the string and was retying it with elaborate care. Alwynne spoke with eyes fixed upon the dexterous fingers —

"You challenged me, don't you remember, Clare? When Marion showed us the things she was making for her sister's trousseau? And you said, would I ever have the patience, let alone my clumsy fingers? And I said I could, and you said you would wear all I made. And you did laugh at me so. So I thought I'd surprise you, and Elsbeth taught me the pillow-lace, and I was frightfully careful. It's taken months and months, and you love lace, and oh, Clare! I thought you would be a little bit pleased."

Her lip quivered; she was very childlike in her eagerness and disappointment.

"Did you think I should wear it?"

Alwynne dimpled.

"It's your size, Clare. Wouldn't you just try it?"

Clare looked at her inscrutably.

"You've taken great pains," she said. "I've been pleased to see it. But you've shown it to me and I've told you that you've learned to work well, so it has fulfilled its purpose, hasn't it? And now you'd better take it back with you. I'm sure you will be able to use it."

She held out the neatly fastened package.

Alwynne's face hardened. She put her hands behind her back.

"I shall do nothing of the kind," she said.

Clare did not seem ruffled.

"Of course you will. And you'll look very pretty in it." She smiled amiably.

But Alwynne's face did not relax.

"I won't take it back. I gave it to you. I made it to give you pleasure. If you don't want it, burn it, give it to your maid, throw away. Do you think I care what becomes of it? But I won't take it back. That is an insult. You say that to hurt me."

"You'll take it back because I wish you to."

"I won't. You shouldn't wish me to."

"You know I dislike presents."

"I never labelled it a present in my mind. You talk as if we were strangers."

"Perhaps, then," murmured Clare, still smiling, "I dislike the hint that you consider my wardrobe inadequate."

Alwynne caught her breath. For the last ten minutes she had been growing angry, not in her usual summer-tempest fashion, but with a slow, cold anger that was pain. She felt Clare's attitude an indelicacy-the discussion a degradation. She sickened at its pettiness. She seemed to be defending, not herself, but some shrinking, weaponless creature, from attack and outrage.... The fight had been sudden, desperate; but at Clare's last sentence she knew herself vanquished, knew that the first love of her life had been most mortally wounded.

She turned blindly. She had no tears, no regret: her sensations were purely physical. She was numbed, breathless, choking, conscious only of an overpowering desire for fresh air, for escape into the open. But first she must say good-bye, head erect, betraying nothing ... say good-bye to the dark figure that was no longer Clare....A sentence from a child's book danced through her mind in endless repetition, *They rubbed her eyes with the ointment, and she saw it was only a stock.* Of course! And now she must go away quickly....She should choke if she could not get into the air....

She heard her own voice, flat and tiny —

"Have you finished with me? May I go now?"

Clare's laugh was quite unforced.

"You're not to go yet!"

"Yes. Yes—I think so. May I go now, please?"

She had retreated to the door and clung to the handle looking back with blank eyes.

"But, you foolish child, you've had no tea. Why are you running away? Are you going to spoil my afternoon?"

She lied blunderingly, mad to escape.

"But I told you I couldn't stay long. Because-because of Elsbeth. She's to meet me. I only ran up for a minute. Really, I have to go." She made a tremendous effort: "I—I can come back later."

Clare shrugged her shoulders.

"Oh, very well. Will you come to supper?"

Alwynne forced a smile.

"Yes." She crossed the threshold, Clare watching from the doorway.

"I shall wait for you, we'll have a lazy evening. Supper at eight."

There was no answer. Alwynne was stumbling down into the darkness of the stairs and did not seem to hear. Clare turned back into her flat, hesitated uneasily, and came out again. She leaned far over the balustrade, peering down.

"Alwynne!" she cried. "Alwynne! Wait a moment, Alwynne!"

But Alwynne was gone, gone beyond recall.

CHAPTER XLV

Alwynne fled down Friar's Lane in amazement, conscious only of the need of escape. She had heard the outer door of the flat close behind her, yet she felt herself pursued. Clare's voice rang in her ears. Momently she awaited the touch of Clare's hand upon her shoulder. She felt herself exhausted; knew that, once overtaken, she would be powerless to resist; that she would be led back; would submit to reconciliation and caresses. And yet she was sure that she would never willingly see Clare again. She was free, and her terror of recapture taught her what liberty meant to her. There was the whole world before her, and Elsbeth-and Roger.... She must find Roger.... She was capable of no clear thought, but very sure that with him was safety.

She hurried along in the shadow of the overhanging lilac-hedge, ears a-prick, eyes glancing to right and left. Oblivious of probabilities she saw Clare in every passer-by. At the turn of the blind lane she ran into a woman, walking towards her. She bit back a cry.

But it was only Elsbeth-Elsbeth in her Sunday gown, very determined, gripping her card-case as if it were a dagger. She spoke between relief and distress.

"Alwynne! Why did you disappear? Where have you been?"

"With Clare."

"It was more than rude. You could surely have foregone one afternoon. No one to see Roger off! After all his kindness to you at Dene!"

"See Roger off?"

Elsbeth was pleased to see her concern.

"I should have gone myself, of course, but he would not allow it. The heat-as I have to pay a call. So he saw me on my way and then went off by himself, poor Roger!"

"Where is he going? Why is he going?"

"Back to Dene. The four-five. I am afraid, Alwynne, he has been hurt and upset. Alwynne!"

But Alwynne, tugging at her watch-chain, was already running down the road with undignified speed. The four-five! Another ten minutes ... no, nine and a half.... Cutting through the gardens she might do it yet.... She prayed for her watch to be fast-the train late. She ran steadily, doggedly, oblivious of the passers-by, oblivious of heat and dust and choking breathlessness, of everything but the idea that Roger was deserting her.

As she bent round the sweep of the station yard past the shelter with its nodding cabmen, and ran down the little wall-flower-bordered asphalt path, she heard the engine's valedictory puff. The platform was noisy and crowded, alive with shouting porters, crates of poultry and burdened women, but at the upper end was Roger, his foot on the step of the carriage, obviously bribing a guard.

She pushed past the outraged ticket collector, and darted up the platform.

Roger had disappeared when she reached the door of his compartment, and the whistle had sounded, but the door was still a-swing. The train began to move as she scrambled in. The door banged upon their privacy.

"Roger!" cried Alwynne. "Roger!"

She was shaking with breathlessness and relief.

"You were right. I was wrong. It's you I want. I will do everything you want, always. I've been simply miserable. Oh, Roger-be good to me."

And for the rest of his life Roger was good to her.

CHAPTER XLVI

Clare had paused a moment, half expecting Alwynne to return; but it was draughty on the landing and she did not wait long. Silly of Alwynne to dash off like that.... She had wanted to discuss Miss Marsham's letter with her before writing her answer.... Not that she was really undecided, of course.... The offer was an excellent one no doubt, and it was fitting that it should have been made.... But to accept the head mistress-ship was another matter.... Life was pleasant enough as it was.... She had plenty of money and Alwynne was hobby enough.... She wondered what Alwynne would say to it ... urge her to accept, probably.... Alwynne was so terribly energetic.... Well, she would let Alwynne talk ... (she picked up her pen) and when she had expended herself, Clare would produce her already written refusal.... Alwynne would pout and be annoyed.... Alwynne hated being made to look a fool.... Clare laughed as she bent over her letter.

She had achieved preliminary compliments and was hesitating as to how she should continue, when a violent rat-tat, hushing immediately to a tremulous tat-a-tat-tat, as if the success of the attack upon Clare's door had proved a little startling to the knocker, announced a visitor, and to their mutual astonishment, Elsbeth Loveday fluttered into the room. Though Elsbeth's naïve amazement at herself and her own courage was more apparent, it was scarcely greater than Clare's politely veiled surprise at the invasion, for since Alwynne's attempts to reconcile the oil and water of their reluctant personalities had ceased with her absence, there had been practically no intercourse between them. With a crooked smile for her first fleeting conviction of the imminence of a church bazaar or Sunday-school treat on gargantuan lines, Clare applied herself to the preparation of Elsbeth's tea, in no great hurry for the disclosure of the visit's object, but already slightly amused at her visitor's unease, and foreseeing a whimsical half-hour in watching her pant and stumble, unassisted, to her point.

Elsbeth was dimly aware of her hostess's attitude, and not a little nettled by it. She waved away cake and toast with a vague idea of breaking no bread in the enemy's house, but she was not the woman to resist tea, though Hecate's self brewed it. Fortified, she returned the empty cup; readjusted her veil, and opened fire.

"My dear Miss Hartill," she began, a shade too cordially, "I've come round — I do hope you're not too busy; I know how occupied you always are."

Clare was not at all busy; entirely at Miss Loveday's service.

"Ah, well, I confess I came round in the hope of finding you alone-in the hope of a quiet chat — —"

Clare was expecting no visitors. But would not Miss Loveday take another cup of tea?

"Oh no, thank you. Though I enjoyed my cup immensely-delicious flavour. China, isn't it? Alwynne always quotes your tea. Poor Alwynne-she can't convert me. I've always drunk the other, you know. Not but that China tea is to be preferred for those who like it, of course. An acquired taste, perhaps-at least — —" She finished with an indistinct murmur uncomfortably aware that she had not been particularly lucid in her compliments to Clare's tea.

Might Clare order a cup of Indian tea to be made for Miss Loveday? It would be no trouble; her maid drank it, she believed.

"Oh, please don't. I shouldn't dream — —You know, I didn't originally intend to come to tea. But you are so very kind. I am sure you are wondering what brings me."

Clare disclaimed civilly.

"Well, to tell you the truth — I am afraid you will think me extremely roundabout, Miss Hartill — —"

Clare's mouth twitched.

"But it is not an easy subject to begin. I'm somewhat worried about Alwynne — —"

"Again?" Clare had stiffened, but Elsbeth was too nervous to be observant.

"Oh, not her health. She is splendidly well again-Dene did wonders." Clare found Elsbeth's quick little unexplained smile irritating. "No, this is-well, it certainly has something to do with Dene, too!"

"Indeed," said Clare.

Elsbeth continued, delicately tactless: she was always at her worst with her former pupil.

"I daresay you are surprised that I consult you, for we need not pretend, need we, that we have ever quite agreed over Alwynne? You, I know, consider me old-fashioned ——" She paused a moment for a disclaimer, but Clare was merely attentive. With a little less suavity she resumed: "And of course I've always thought that you ——But that, after all, has nothing to do with the matter."

"Nothing whatever," said Clare.

"Exactly. But knowing that you are fond of Alwynne, and realising your great, your very great, influence with her, I felt-indeed we both felt-that if you once realised ——"

"We?"

"Roger. Mr. Lumsden."

"Oh, the gardener at Dene."

"My cousin, Miss Hartill."

"Oh. Oh, really. But what has he to do with Alwynne?"

"My dear, he wants to marry her. Didn't she tell you?" Elsbeth had the satisfaction of seeing Clare look startled. "Now I was sure Alwynne had confided the matter to you. Hasn't she just been here? That is really why I came. I was so afraid that you, with the best of motives, of course, might incline her to refuse him. And you know, Miss Hartill, she mustn't. The very man for Alwynne? He suits her in every way. Devoted to her, of course, but not in the least weak with her, and you know I always say that Alwynne needs a firm hand. And between ourselves, though I am the last person to consider such a thing, he is an extremely good match. I can't tell you, Miss Hartill, the joy it was to me, the engagement. I had been anxious —I quite foresaw that Alwynne would be difficult, though I am convinced she is attached to him-underneath, you know. So I made up my mind to come to you. I said to myself: 'I am sure —I am quite sure-Miss Hartill would not misunderstand the situation. I am quite sure Miss Hartill would not intend to stand in the child's light. She is far too fond of Alwynne to allow her personal feelings ——' After all, feminine friendship is all very well, very delightful, of course, and I am only too sensible of your goodness to Alwynne-and taking her to Italy too-but when it is a question of Marriage-oh, Miss Hartill, surely you see what I mean?"

Clare frowned.

"I think so. The gard——This Mr. Lumpkin ——"

"Lumsden."

"Of course. I was confusing him ——Mr. Lumsden has proposed to Alwynne. She has refused him, and you now wish for my help in coercing her into an apparently distasteful engagement?"

"Oh no, Miss Hartill! No question of coercion. I think there is no possible doubt that she is fond of him, and if it were not for you ——But Alwynne is so quixotic."

Clare lifted her eyebrows, politely blank.

"Oh, Miss Hartill-why beat about the bush? You know your influence with Alwynne. It is very difficult for me to talk to you. Please believe that I intend nothing personal-but Alwynne is so swayed by you, so entirely under your thumb; you know what a loyal, affectionate child she is, and as far as I can gather from what Roger let fall-for she is in one of her moods and will not confide in me-she considers herself bound to you by-by the terms of your friendship. All she would say to Roger was, 'Clare comes first. Clare must come first' —which, of course, is perfectly ridiculous."

Clare reddened.

"You mean that I, or you, for that matter, who have known Alwynne for years, must step aside, must dutifully foster this liking for a comparative stranger."

Elsbeth smiled.

"Well, naturally. He's a man."

"I am sorry I can't agree. Alwynne is a free agent. If she prefers my friendship to Mr. Lumsden's adorations ——"

"But I've told you already, it's a question of Marriage, Miss Hartill. Surely you see the difference? How can you weigh the most intimate, the most ideal friendship against the chance of getting married?" Elsbeth was wholly in earnest.

Clare mounted her high horse.

"I can —I do. There are better things in life than marriage."

"For the average woman? Do you sincerely say so? The brilliant woman-the rich woman —I don't count them, and there are other exceptions, of course; but when her youth is over, what is the average single woman? A derelict, drifting aimlessly on the high seas of life. Oh —I'm not very clear; it's easy to make fun of me; but I know what I mean and so do you. We're not children. We both know that an unmated woman-she's a failure-she's unfulfilled."

Clare was elaborately bored.

"Really, Miss Loveday, the subject does not interest me."

"It must, for Alwynne's sake. Don't you realise your enormous responsibility? Don't you realise that when you keep Alwynne entangled in your apron strings, blind to other interests, when you cram her with poetry and emotional literature, when you allow her to attach herself passionately to you, you are feeding, and at the same time deflecting from its natural channel, the strongest impulse of her life-of any girl's life? Alwynne needs a good concrete husband to love, not a fantastic ideal that she calls friendship and clothes in your face and figure. You are doing her a deep injury, Miss Hartill-unconsciously, I know, or I should not be here-but doing it, none the less. If you will consider her happiness ——"

Clare broke in angrily —

"I do consider her happiness. Alwynne tells you that I am essential to her happiness."

"She may believe so. But she's not happy. She has not been happy for a long time. But she believes herself to be so, I grant you that. But consider the future. Shall she never break away? Shall she oscillate indefinitely between you and me, spend her whole youth in sustaining two old maids? Oh, Miss Hartill, she must have her chance. We must give her what we've missed ourselves."

Clare appeared to be occupied in stifling a yawn. Her eyes were danger signals, but Elsbeth was not Alwynne to remark them.

"In one thing, at least, I do thoroughly agree with you. I don't think there is the faintest likelihood of Alwynne's wishing to marry at all at present, but I do feel, with you, that it is unfair to expect her to oscillate, as you rhetorically put it, between two old maids. I agree, too, that I have responsibilities in connection with her. In fact, I think she would be happier if she were with me altogether, and I intend to ask her to come and live here. I shall ask her to-night. Don't you think she will be pleased?"

Clare's aim was good. Elsbeth clutched at the arms of her chair.

"You wouldn't do such a thing."

Clare laughed shrilly.

"I shall do exactly what your Mr. Lumsden wants to do. I'm not poor. I can give her a home as well as he, if you are so anxious to get her off your hands. She seems to be going begging."

Elsbeth rose.

"I'm wasting time. I'll say good-bye, Miss Hartill. I shouldn't have come. But it was for Alwynne's sake. I hoped to touch you, to persuade you to forego, for her future's sake, for the sake of her ultimate happiness, the hold you have on her. I sympathised with you. I knew it would be a sacrifice. I knew, because I made the same sacrifice two years ago, when you first began to attract her. I thought you would develop her. I am not a clever woman, Miss Hartill, and you are; so I made no stand against you; but it was hard for me. Alwynne did not make it easier. She was not always kind. But hearing you to-day, I understand. You made Alwynne suffer more than I guessed. I don't blame her if sometimes it recoiled on me. You were always cruel. I remember you. The others were always snails for you to throw salt upon. I might have known you'd never change. Do you think I don't know your effect on the children at the school? Oh, you are a good teacher! You force them successfully; but all the while you eat up their souls. Sneer if you like! Have you forgotten Louise? I tell you, it's vampirism. And now you are to take Alwynne. And when she is squeezed dry and flung aside, who will be the next victim be? And the next, and the next? You grow greedier as you grow older, I suppose. One day you'll be old. What will you do when your glamour's gone? I tell you, Clare Hartill, you'll die of hunger in the end."

The small relentless voice ceased. There was a silence. Clare, who had remained quiescent for sheer amaze at the attack from so negligible a quarter, pulled herself together. Rather white, she began to clap her hands gently, as a critic surprised into applause.

"My dear woman, you're magnificent! Really you are. I never thought you had it in you. The Law and the Prophets incarnate. How Alwynne will laugh when I tell her. I wish she'd been here. You ought to be on the stage, you know, or in the pulpit. Have you quite finished? Quite? Do unburden yourself completely, you won't be given another opportunity. You understand that, of course? If Alwynne wishes to see you, she must make arrangements to do so elsewhere. That is the one condition I shall make. This is the way out."

Elsbeth rose. She was furious with herself that her lips must tremble and her hands shake, as she gathered up scarf and reticule; but she followed her hostess with sufficient dignity.

Clare flung open the door with a gesture a shade too ample.

Elsbeth laughed tremulously as she passed her and crossed the hall.

"Oh, you are not altered," she said, and bent to fumble at the latch. "But it doesn't impress me. You've not won yet. You count too much on Alwynne. And you have still to reckon with Mr. Lumsden."

"And his three acres and a cow!" Clare watched her contemptuously. It did not seem worth while to keep her dignity with Elsbeth. She felt that it would be a relief to lose her temper completely, to override this opponent by sheer, crude invective. She let herself go.

"What a fool you are! Do you flatter yourself that you understand Alwynne? Go back to your Cœlebs and tell him from Alwynne —I tell you I speak for Alwynne-that he's wasting his time. Let him take his goods to another market: Alwynne won't buy. I've other plans for her-she has other plans for yourself. She doesn't want a husband. She doesn't want a home. She doesn't want children. She wants me-and all I stand for. She wants to use her talents-and she shall-through me. She wants success-she shall have it-through me. She wants friendship-can't I give it? Affection? Haven't I given it? What more can she want? A home? I'm well off. A brat to play with? Let her adopt one, and I'll house it. I'll give her anything she wants. What more can your man offer? But I won't let her go. I tell you, we suffice each other. Thank God, there are some women who can do without marriage-marriage-marriage!"

Elsbeth, as if she heard nothing, tugged at the catch. The door swung open, and she stepped quietly into the sunny passage. Then she turned to Clare, a grey, angry shadow in the dusk of the hall.

"Poor Clare!" she said. "Are the grapes very sour?"

She pulled-to the door behind her.

* * * * *

Later in the evening, as she sat, flushed, tremulous, utterly joyful over Roger's telegram, she considered the manner of her exit and was shocked at herself.

"I don't know what possessed me," said Elsbeth apologetically. "And if I had only known. It was unladylike-it was unwomanly-it was unchristian." She shook her head at her mild self in the glass. "But she made me so angry! If I'd only known that this was coming!" She fingered the pink envelope. "She'll think I knew. She'll always think I knew. And then to say what I did? It was unpardonable.

"But I was right, all the same," cried Elsbeth incorrigibly; "and I don't care. I'm glad I said it —I'm glad —I'm glad!"

CHAPTER XLVII

The sun slid over the edge of the sweating earth. Its red-hot plunge into the sea behind the hills was almost audible. The black cloud, fuming up from its setting-place, was as the steam of the collision. In great clots and coils it rolled upwards, spreading as it thinned, till it was a pall of vapour that sheeted all the lemon-coloured sky. Suddenly a cold wind sprang up, raced down the silent heavens, and, by way of Eastern Europe and the North Sea and the straight Roman road that drives down England, tore along the Utterbridge byways, and into the open window of Clare Hartill's parlour. A touch of its cold lips on her hair, and brow, and breast, and it was out again, driving the dust before it.

Clare shivered. She was very tired of waiting....It was inexplicable that Alwynne should be late; but Clare with a half laugh, promised Alwynne to forego her scolding if she would but come....The dusk and the wind and the silence were getting on her nerves....The tick of the hall clock, for instance, was aggressive, insistent, maddening in its precise monotony....Oh, unbearable! With a gesture that was hysterical in its abandonment, Clare rose suddenly and flung into the hall, plucked open the clock door, and removed the pendulum. The released wire waggled foolishly into silence, like an idiot, tongue a-loll.

As the quiet hunted Clare into her sitting-room again, a little silver wire flickered down the sky like a scared snake, and for an instant she saw herself reflected in a convex mirror, a Clare bleached and shining and askew, like a St. Michael in a stained-glass window. Dusk and the thunder followed. The storm was beginning.

Clare moved about restlessly. She disliked storms. Her eyes ached, and she was cramped with waiting, and Alwynne had not come. She would, of course....That woman had detained her, purposely, no doubt, and now there was the storm to delay her....But Alwynne would come....Clare smiled securely.

Again the lightning whipped across the heavens, and thunder roared in its wake.

Clare went to the window and watched the sky. The pane of glass was grateful to her hot forehead. She was too tired, too bruised and shaken by her own recent anger to arrange her thoughts, to pose for the moment, even to herself-of all audiences the most critical. The interview with Elsbeth Loveday rehearsed itself incessantly, pricking, probing, bludgeoning, in crescendo of intonation, innuendo, open attack, to the final triumphant insult. Triumphant, because true. The insult could cut through her defences and strike at her very self, because it was true. Her pride agonised. She had thought herself shrouded, invulnerable. And yet Elsbeth, whom of all women she had reckoned negligible, had guessed, had pitied....Yet even her enemy was forgotten, as she sat and shuddered at the wound dealt; plucked and shrank, and plucked again at the arrow-tip rankling in it still.

The hours had passed in an evil mazement. But Alwynne was to come....She thought of Alwynne with shifting passions of relief and longing and sheer crude lust for revenge. Alwynne would come....Alwynne would soothe and comfort, intuitive, never waiting for the cry for help.

And Alwynne should pay....Oho! Alwynne should pay Elsbeth's debts ...should wince, and shrink, and whiten. *Scientific vivisection of one nerve.* Wait a little, Alwynne! —Ah, Alwynne-the dearest-the beloved-the light and laughter of one's life....What fool is whispering that Clare can hurt her?...Alwynne shall see when she comes, who loves her....There shall be a welcome, the royalest welcome she has ever had....For what in all the world has Clare but Alwynne, and having Alwynne, has not Clare the world?

Ah, well....Perhaps, she had not been always good to Alwynne....To-day, for instance, she might have been kinder....But Alwynne always understood....That was the comfort of Alwynne, that she always understood....Why didn't she come? Wasn't there an echo of a step far down the street?

When Alwynne came, they would make plans....It would not be easy to wean the girl from her aunt, at least while they lived in the same town, the same country....But one could travel, could take Alwynne quite away....Italy....Greece....Egypt....they would go round the world together, shake off the school and all it stood for....In a new world, begin a new life....Why not? She had money enough to burn....It would not be hard to persuade Alwynne, adventurous, infatuate.... Once gone, Elsbeth might whistle for her niece....They would talk it over to-morrow ... to-night ... as soon as Alwynne came....

Was that thunder or a knocking? Rat-tat! Rat-tat! She had not been mistaken after all.... Alwynne! Alwynne!

And Clare, with an appearance on her that even Alwynne had never seen, ran like a child to open the door.

On the threshold stood a messenger boy, proffering a telegram. She took it.

"Any answer, Miss!" for she had offered to close the door.

"Oh, of course!" She frowned, and pulled open the flimsy sheet.

The boy waited. He peered past her, interested in the odd pictures on the walls, and the glimpse of a table luxuriously set. The minutes sped. He had soon seen all he could, and began to fidget.

"Any answer, Miss?" he hinted.

"Oh!" said Clare vaguely. "Answer? No. No answer. No answer at all."

The boy knuckled his forehead and clattered away down the staircase.

Mechanically Clare shut the door, locked and bolted it and secured it with the chain. Then she returned to the sitting-room and crossed to her former station by the open window.

The storm was ending in a downpour of furious tropical rain. It beat in unheeded upon her thin dress and bare neck and the open telegram in her hands, as, with lips parted and a faint, puzzled pucker between her brows, she conned over the message —

I cannot come to-night. —I have gone to Dene. I am going to marry Roger.

She read it and re-read, twisting it this way and that, for it was barely visible in the wet dusk. It seemed an eternity before its full meaning dawned upon her. And yet she had known all there was to know when she confronted the messenger boy (Oh, Destiny is up to date) and took her sentence from his grimy hand.

I am going to marry Roger.

"Very well, Alwynne!" Clare flung up her head, up and back. Her face was drowned in the shadows of the crimson curtain, but her neck caught the last of the light, shone like old marble. The whole soul of her showed for an instant in its defiant outline, in the involuntary pulsation that quivered across its rigidity, in the uncontrollable flutter beneath the chin.

The thin, capable fingers twisted and clenched over the sodden paper.

She moved at last, spoke into space. Passion, anger, and the cool contempt of the school-mistress for a mutinous class, mingled grotesquely in her voice.

"Very well, Alwynne! Just as you please, of course. There is no more to be said." She tossed away the little ball of paper as she spoke.

She wandered aimlessly about the room; turned to her book-shelves after a while, and stood a long time, pulling out volume after volume, opening each at random, reading a page, closing the book again, letting it slide from her hand, never troubling to replace it. She was tired at last and turned to her writing-table.

It was piled high with exercise-books, and she corrected a couple before she swept them also aside.

The rain had not faltered in its swishing downfall. It beat against the panes, and on to the sill, and dripped down into a pool beneath the open window.

"She will have to come back on Monday," said Clare suddenly. "She can't go off like that. There's the school ——" She broke off abruptly, as a gust of wind soughed by.

I cannot come. I have gone to Dene. I am going to marry Roger. She could hear Alwynne's voice in it, answering.

"But why?" cried Clare piteously. "Why? What is it? What have I done?"

"S'hush!" sighed the rain. "S'hush!"

"I loved her," cried Clare. "I loved her. What have I done?"

331

"S'hush!" sobbed the rain. "S'hush! S'hush!"

She turned to the darkening windows, and started, and shuddered away again, stricken dumb and shaking. A pool of something red and wet was spreading over the polished boards, and a thin trickle was stealing forward to her feet.

Blood?

Fool.... The red of the curtains reflected, tingeing a pool of rain-water.... Blood, nevertheless.... She had forgotten Louise.

What had Alwynne heard? A garbled version of that last interview? Fool again-unless the dead can speak.... But Alwynne knew.... Something had been revealed to her, suddenly, during their idle talk.... But when? But how? She had come as a lover ... she had left as a stranger ... what in any god's name, had she guessed? Clare's subconscious memory reproduced for her instantly, with photographic accuracy, details of the scene that she had not even known she had observed. Alwynne had changed, in an instant, between a word and a reply.... What was it that Clare had said-what trifling, teasing nothing, flung out in pure wantonness? But Alwynne's face, her dear face, had become, for an instant-Clare strained to the memory-as the face of Louise.... Louise had looked at her like that, that other day.... What had they seen then, both of them? Was she Gorgon to bring that look into their faces? Louise-yes-she could understand Louise.... She did not care to think about Louise.... But Alwynne-what had she ever done to Alwynne? At least Alwynne might tell her what she had done.... She would not submit to it.... She would not be put aside.... She would at least have justice....

I am going to marry Roger.

Useless! All useless! The struggle was over before she had known she was fighting.... She knew that in Alwynne's life there was no longer any part for her. And Clare had travelled far that evening, to phrase it thus. Sharing was a strange word for her to use. But she recognised dully that even sharing was out of her power. What had she to do with a husband, and housewifery, and the bearing of children? Alwynne married was Alwynne dead.

Alwynne in love.... Alwynne married.... Alwynne putting any living thing before Clare! She broke into bitter laughter at the idea. What had happened? What had Clare done or left undone? She realised grimly that of this at least she might be sure-it had been her own doing.... No influence could have wrought against her own.... Alwynne, at least, was where she was, because Clare had sent her, not because another had beckoned.... And that was the comfort she had stored up for herself, to last her in the lean years to come....

What was the use of regretting?

Alwynne was gone.... Then forget her.... There were other fish in the sea.... There was a promising class this term.... That child in the Fourth.... She wondered if Alwynne had noticed her.... She must ask Alwynne.... Alwynne had gone away, had gone to Dene, was going to marry Roger....

Well, there was always work.... Where was that letter to Miss Marsham?

She moved stiffly in her seat, lit a candle, and drew towards her the half-written sheet that lay open on the blotter. She re-read it.

You will, I am sure, understand how much I appreciate your offer of the partnership, but after much consideration I have decided —— —

She hesitated, crossed out the *but* and wrote an *and* above it, and continued —

—to accept it. I will come to tea to-morrow, as you kindly suggest.

She finished the letter, signed it, stamped and addressed, and sat idle at last, staring down at it.

The neat handwriting danced, and flickered, and grew dim.

With an awkward gesture she put her hands to her eyes, and brought them away again, wet. She smiled at that, a twisted, mocking smile. She supposed she was crying.... She did not remember ever having done such a thing....

So her future was decided....It was to be work and loneliness-loneliness and work ...because, it seemed, she had no friends left....Yet Alwynne had promised many things....What had she done to Alwynne? What had she done?

She turned within herself and reviewed her life as she remembered it, thought by thought, word by word, action by action. Faces rose about her, whispering reminders, forgotten faces of the many who had loved her: from her old nurse, dead long ago, to Louise, and Alwynne, and foolish Olivia Pring.

The candle at her elbow flared and dribbled, and died at last with a splutter and a gasp. She paid no heed.

When the dawn came, she was still sitting there, thinking-thinking.

March 1914—September 1915.

Carmilla

by Sheridan Le Fanu

Prologue

Upon a paper attached to the Narrative which follows, Doctor Hesselius has written a rather elaborate note, which he accompanies with a reference to his Essay on the strange subject which the MS. illuminates.

This mysterious subject he treats, in that Essay, with his usual learning and acumen, and with remarkable directness and condensation. It will form but one volume of the series of that extraordinary man's collected papers.

As I publish the case, in this volume, simply to interest the "laity," I shall forestall the intelligent lady, who relates it, in nothing; and after due consideration, I have determined, therefore, to abstain from presenting any precis of the learned Doctor's reasoning, or extract from his statement on a subject which he describes as "involving, not improbably, some of the profoundest arcana of our dual existence, and its intermediates."

I was anxious on discovering this paper, to reopen the correspondence commenced by Doctor Hesselius, so many years before, with a person so clever and careful as his informant seems to have been. Much to my regret, however, I found that she had died in the interval.

She, probably, could have added little to the Narrative which she communicates in the following pages, with, so far as I can pronounce, such conscientious particularity.

Chapter 1
An Early Fright

In Styria, we, though by no means magnificent people, inhabit a castle, or schloss. A small income, in that part of the world, goes a great way. Eight or nine hundred a year does wonders. Scantily enough ours would have answered among wealthy people at home. My father is English, and I bear an English name, although I never saw England. But here, in this lonely and primitive place, where everything is so marvelously cheap, I really don't see how ever so much more money would at all materially add to our comforts, or even luxuries.

My father was in the Austrian service, and retired upon a pension and his patrimony, and purchased this feudal residence, and the small estate on which it stands, a bargain.

Nothing can be more picturesque or solitary. It stands on a slight eminence in a forest. The road, very old and narrow, passes in front of its drawbridge, never raised in my time, and its moat, stocked with perch, and sailed over by many swans, and floating on its surface white fleets of water lilies.

Over all this the schloss shows its many-windowed front; its towers, and its Gothic chapel.

The forest opens in an irregular and very picturesque glade before its gate, and at the right a steep Gothic bridge carries the road over a stream that winds in deep shadow through the wood. I have said that this is a very lonely place. Judge whether I say truth. Looking from the hall door towards the road, the forest in which our castle stands extends fifteen miles to the right, and twelve to the left. The nearest inhabited village is about seven of your English miles to the left. The nearest inhabited schloss of any historic associations, is that of old General Spielsdorf, nearly twenty miles away to the right.

I have said "the nearest *inhabited* village," because there is, only three miles westward, that is to say in the direction of General Spielsdorf's schloss, a ruined village, with its quaint little church, now roofless, in the aisle of which are the moldering tombs of the proud family of Karnstein, now extinct, who once owned the equally desolate chateau which, in the thick of the forest, overlooks the silent ruins of the town.

Respecting the cause of the desertion of this striking and melancholy spot, there is a legend which I shall relate to you another time.

I must tell you now, how very small is the party who constitute the inhabitants of our castle. I don't include servants, or those dependents who occupy rooms in the buildings attached to the schloss. Listen, and wonder! My father, who is the kindest man on earth, but growing old; and I, at the date of my story, only nineteen. Eight years have passed since then.

I and my father constituted the family at the schloss. My mother, a Styrian lady, died in my infancy, but I had a good-natured governess, who had been with me from, I might almost say, my infancy. I could not remember the time when her fat, benignant face was not a familiar picture in my memory.

This was Madame Perrodon, a native of Berne, whose care and good nature now in part supplied to me the loss of my mother, whom I do not even remember, so early I lost her. She made a third at our little dinner party. There was a fourth, Mademoiselle De Lafontaine, a lady such as you term, I believe, a "finishing governess." She spoke French and German, Madame Perrodon French and broken English, to which my father and I added English, which, partly to prevent its becoming a lost language among us, and partly from patriotic motives, we spoke every day. The consequence was a Babel, at which strangers used to laugh, and which I shall make no attempt to reproduce in this narrative. And there were two or three young lady friends besides, pretty nearly of my own age, who were occasional visitors, for longer or shorter terms; and these visits I sometimes returned.

These were our regular social resources; but of course there were chance visits from "neighbors" of only five or six leagues distance. My life was, notwithstanding, rather a solitary one, I can assure you.

My gouvernantes had just so much control over me as you might conjecture such sage persons would have in the case of a rather spoiled girl, whose only parent allowed her pretty nearly her own way in everything.

The first occurrence in my existence, which produced a terrible impression upon my mind, which, in fact, never has been effaced, was one of the very earliest incidents of my life which I can recollect. Some people will think it so trifling that it should not be recorded here. You will see, however, by-and-by, why I mention it. The nursery, as it was called, though I had it all to myself, was a large room in the upper story of the castle, with a steep oak roof. I can't have been more than six years old, when one night I awoke, and looking round the room from my bed, failed to see the nursery maid. Neither was my nurse there; and I thought myself alone. I was not frightened, for I was one of those happy children who are studiously kept in ignorance of ghost stories, of fairy tales, and of all such lore as makes us cover up our heads when the door cracks suddenly, or the flicker of an expiring candle makes the shadow of a bedpost dance upon the wall, nearer to our faces. I was vexed and insulted at finding myself, as I conceived, neglected, and I began to whimper, preparatory to a hearty bout of roaring; when to my surprise, I saw a solemn, but very pretty face looking at me from the side of the bed. It was that of a young lady who was kneeling, with her hands under the coverlet. I looked at her with a kind of pleased wonder, and ceased whimpering. She caressed me with her hands, and lay down beside me on the bed, and drew me towards her, smiling; I felt immediately delightfully soothed, and fell asleep again. I was wakened by a sensation as if two needles ran into my breast very deep at the same moment, and I cried loudly. The lady started back, with her eyes fixed on me, and then slipped down upon the floor, and, as I thought, hid herself under the bed.

I was now for the first time frightened, and I yelled with all my might and main. Nurse, nursery maid, housekeeper, all came running in, and hearing my story, they made light of it, soothing me all they could meanwhile. But, child as I was, I could perceive that their faces were pale with an unwonted look of anxiety, and I saw them look under the bed, and about the room, and peep under tables and pluck open cupboards; and the housekeeper whispered to the nurse: "Lay your hand along that hollow in the bed; someone *did* lie there, so sure as you did not; the place is still warm."

I remember the nursery maid petting me, and all three examining my chest, where I told them I felt the puncture, and pronouncing that there was no sign visible that any such thing had happened to me.

The housekeeper and the two other servants who were in charge of the nursery, remained sitting up all night; and from that time a servant always sat up in the nursery until I was about fourteen.

I was very nervous for a long time after this. A doctor was called in, he was pallid and elderly. How well I remember his long saturnine face, slightly pitted with smallpox, and his chestnut wig. For a good while, every second day, he came and gave me medicine, which of course I hated.

The morning after I saw this apparition I was in a state of terror, and could not bear to be left alone, daylight though it was, for a moment.

I remember my father coming up and standing at the bedside, and talking cheerfully, and asking the nurse a number of questions, and laughing very heartily at one of the answers; and patting me on the shoulder, and kissing me, and telling me not to be frightened, that it was nothing but a dream and could not hurt me.

But I was not comforted, for I knew the visit of the strange woman was *not* a dream; and I was *awfully* frightened.

I was a little consoled by the nursery maid's assuring me that it was she who had come and looked at me, and lain down beside me in the bed, and that I must have been half-dreaming not to have known her face. But this, though supported by the nurse, did not quite satisfy me.

I remembered, in the course of that day, a venerable old man, in a black cassock, coming into the room with the nurse and housekeeper, and talking a little to them, and very kindly to me; his face was very sweet and gentle, and he told me they were going to pray, and joined my hands together, and desired me to say, softly, while they were praying, "Lord hear all good prayers for us, for Jesus' sake." I think these were the very words, for I often repeated them to myself, and my nurse used for years to make me say them in my prayers.

I remembered so well the thoughtful sweet face of that white-haired old man, in his black cassock, as he stood in that rude, lofty, brown room, with the clumsy furniture of a fashion three hundred years old about him, and the scanty light entering its shadowy atmosphere through the small lattice. He kneeled, and the three women with him, and he prayed aloud with an earnest quavering voice for, what appeared to me, a long time. I forget all my life preceding that event, and for some time after it is all obscure also, but the scenes I have just described stand out vivid as the isolated pictures of the phantasmagoria surrounded by darkness.

Chapter 2
A Guest

I am now going to tell you something so strange that it will require all your faith in my veracity to believe my story. It is not only true, nevertheless, but truth of which I have been an eyewitness.

It was a sweet summer evening, and my father asked me, as he sometimes did, to take a little ramble with him along that beautiful forest vista which I have mentioned as lying in front of the schloss.

"General Spielsdorf cannot come to us so soon as I had hoped," said my father, as we pursued our walk.

He was to have paid us a visit of some weeks, and we had expected his arrival next day. He was to have brought with him a young lady, his niece and ward, Mademoiselle Rheinfeldt, whom I had never seen, but whom I had heard described as a very charming girl, and in whose society I had promised myself many happy days. I was more disappointed than a young lady living in a town, or a bustling neighborhood can possibly imagine. This visit, and the new acquaintance it promised, had furnished my day dream for many weeks

"And how soon does he come?" I asked.

"Not till autumn. Not for two months, I dare say," he answered. "And I am very glad now, dear, that you never knew Mademoiselle Rheinfeldt."

"And why?" I asked, both mortified and curious.

"Because the poor young lady is dead," he replied. "I quite forgot I had not told you, but you were not in the room when I received the General's letter this evening."

I was very much shocked. General Spielsdorf had mentioned in his first letter, six or seven weeks before, that she was not so well as he would wish her, but there was nothing to suggest the remotest suspicion of danger.

"Here is the General's letter," he said, handing it to me. "I am afraid he is in great affliction; the letter appears to me to have been written very nearly in distraction."

We sat down on a rude bench, under a group of magnificent lime trees. The sun was setting with all its melancholy splendor behind the sylvan horizon, and the stream that flows beside our home, and passes under the steep old bridge I have mentioned, wound through many a group of noble trees, almost at our feet, reflecting in its current the fading crimson of the sky. General Spielsdorf's letter was so extraordinary, so vehement, and in some places so self-contradictory, that I read it twice over — the second time aloud to my father — and was still unable to account for it, except by supposing that grief had unsettled his mind.

It said "I have lost my darling daughter, for as such I loved her. During the last days of dear Bertha's illness I was not able to write to you.

"Before then I had no idea of her danger. I have lost her, and now learn *all*, too late. She died in the peace of innocence, and in the glorious hope of a blessed futurity. The fiend who betrayed our infatuated hospitality has done it all. I thought I was receiving into my house innocence, gaiety, a charming companion for my lost Bertha. Heavens! what a fool have I been!

"I thank God my child died without a suspicion of the cause of her sufferings. She is gone without so much as conjecturing the nature of her illness, and the accursed passion of the agent of all this misery. I devote my remaining days to tracking and extinguishing a monster. I am told I may hope to accomplish my righteous and merciful purpose. At present there is scarcely a gleam of light to guide me. I curse my conceited incredulity, my despicable affectation of superiority, my blindness, my obstinacy — all — too late. I cannot write or talk collectedly now. I am distracted. So soon as I shall have a little recovered, I mean to devote myself for a time to enquiry, which may possibly lead me as far as Vienna. Some time in the autumn, two months hence, or earlier if I live, I will see you — that is, if you permit me; I will then tell you all that I scarce dare put upon paper now. Farewell. Pray for me, dear friend."

In these terms ended this strange letter. Though I had never seen Bertha Rheinfeldt my eyes filled with tears at the sudden intelligence; I was startled, as well as profoundly disappointed.

The sun had now set, and it was twilight by the time I had returned the General's letter to my father.

It was a soft clear evening, and we loitered, speculating upon the possible meanings of the violent and incoherent sentences which I had just been reading. We had nearly a mile to walk before reaching the road that passes the schloss in front, and by that time the moon was shining brilliantly. At the drawbridge we met Madame Perrodon and Mademoiselle De Lafontaine, who had come out, without their bonnets, to enjoy the exquisite moonlight.

We heard their voices gabbling in animated dialogue as we approached. We joined them at the drawbridge, and turned about to admire with them the beautiful scene.

The glade through which we had just walked lay before us. At our left the narrow road wound away under clumps of lordly trees, and was lost to sight amid the thickening forest. At the right the same road crosses the steep and picturesque bridge, near which stands a ruined tower which once guarded that pass; and beyond the bridge an abrupt eminence rises, covered with trees, and showing in the shadows some grey ivy-clustered rocks.

Over the sward and low grounds a thin film of mist was stealing like smoke, marking the distances with a transparent veil; and here and there we could see the river faintly flashing in the moonlight.

No softer, sweeter scene could be imagined. The news I had just heard made it melancholy; but nothing could disturb its character of profound serenity, and the enchanted glory and vagueness of the prospect.

My father, who enjoyed the picturesque, and I, stood looking in silence over the expanse beneath us. The two good governesses, standing a little way behind us, discoursed upon the scene, and were eloquent upon the moon.

Madame Perrodon was fat, middle-aged, and romantic, and talked and sighed poetically. Mademoiselle De Lafontaine — in right of her father who was a German, assumed to be psychological, metaphysical, and something of a mystic — now declared that when the moon shone with a light so intense it was well known that it indicated a special spiritual activity. The effect of the full moon in such a state of brilliancy was manifold. It acted on dreams, it acted on lunacy, it acted on nervous people, it had marvelous physical influences connected with life. Mademoiselle related that her cousin, who was mate of a merchant ship, having taken a nap on deck on such a night, lying on his back, with his face full in the light on the moon, had wakened, after a dream of an old woman clawing him by the cheek, with his features horribly drawn to one side; and his countenance had never quite recovered its equilibrium.

"The moon, this night," she said, "is full of idyllic and magnetic influence — and see, when you look behind you at the front of the schloss how all its windows flash and twinkle with that silvery splendor, as if unseen hands had lighted up the rooms to receive fairy guests."

There are indolent styles of the spirits in which, indisposed to talk ourselves, the talk of others is pleasant to our listless ears; and I gazed on, pleased with the tinkle of the ladies' conversation.

"I have got into one of my moping moods tonight," said my father, after a silence, and quoting Shakespeare, whom, by way of keeping up our English, he used to read aloud, he said:

"'In truth I know not why I am so sad. It wearies me: you say it wearies you; But how I got it — came by it.'

"I forget the rest. But I feel as if some great misfortune were hanging over us. I suppose the poor General's afflicted letter has had something to do with it."

At this moment the unwonted sound of carriage wheels and many hoofs upon the road, arrested our attention.

They seemed to be approaching from the high ground overlooking the bridge, and very soon the equipage emerged from that point. Two horsemen first crossed the bridge, then came a carriage drawn by four horses, and two men rode behind.

It seemed to be the traveling carriage of a person of rank; and we were all immediately absorbed in watching that very unusual spectacle. It became, in a few moments, greatly more interesting, for just as the carriage had passed the summit of the steep bridge, one of the leaders, taking fright, communicated his panic to the rest, and after a plunge or two, the whole team broke into a wild gallop together, and dashing between the horsemen who rode in front, came thundering along the road towards us with the speed of a hurricane.

The excitement of the scene was made more painful by the clear, long-drawn screams of a female voice from the carriage window.

We all advanced in curiosity and horror; me rather in silence, the rest with various ejaculations of terror.

Our suspense did not last long. Just before you reach the castle drawbridge, on the route they were coming, there stands by the roadside a magnificent lime tree, on the other stands an ancient stone cross, at sight of which the horses, now going at a pace that was perfectly frightful, swerved so as to bring the wheel over the projecting roots of the tree.

I knew what was coming. I covered my eyes, unable to see it out, and turned my head away; at the same moment I heard a cry from my lady friends, who had gone on a little.

Curiosity opened my eyes, and I saw a scene of utter confusion. Two of the horses were on the ground, the carriage lay upon its side with two wheels in the air; the men were busy removing the traces, and a lady, with a commanding air and figure had got out, and stood with clasped hands, raising the handkerchief that was in them every now and then to her eyes.

Through the carriage door was now lifted a young lady, who appeared to be lifeless. My dear old father was already beside the elder lady, with his hat in his hand, evidently tendering his aid and the resources of his schloss. The lady did not appear to hear him, or to have eyes for anything but the slender girl who was being placed against the slope of the bank.

I approached; the young lady was apparently stunned, but she was certainly not dead. My father, who piqued himself on being something of a physician, had just had his fingers on her wrist and assured the lady, who declared herself her mother, that her pulse, though faint and irregular, was undoubtedly still distinguishable. The lady clasped her hands and looked upward, as if in a momentary transport of gratitude; but immediately she broke out again in that theatrical way which is, I believe, natural to some people.

She was what is called a fine looking woman for her time of life, and must have been handsome; she was tall, but not thin, and dressed in black velvet, and looked rather pale, but with a proud and commanding countenance, though now agitated strangely.

"Who was ever being so born to calamity?" I heard her say, with clasped hands, as I came up. "Here am I, on a journey of life and death, in prosecuting which to lose an hour is possibly to lose all. My child will not have recovered sufficiently to resume her route for who can say how long. I must leave her: I cannot, dare not, delay. How far on, sir, can you tell, is the nearest village? I must leave her there; and shall not see my darling, or even hear of her till my return, three months hence."

I plucked my father by the coat, and whispered earnestly in his ear: "Oh! papa, pray ask her to let her stay with us — it would be so delightful. Do, pray."

"If Madame will entrust her child to the care of my daughter, and of her good gouvernante, Madame Perrodon, and permit her to remain as our guest, under my charge, until her return, it will confer a distinction and an obligation upon us, and we shall treat her with all the care and devotion which so sacred a trust deserves."

"I cannot do that, sir, it would be to task your kindness and chivalry too cruelly," said the lady, distractedly.

"It would, on the contrary, be to confer on us a very great kindness at the moment when we most need it. My daughter has just been disappointed by a cruel misfortune, in a visit from which she had long anticipated a great deal of happiness. If you confide this young lady to our care it will be her best consolation. The nearest village on your route is distant, and affords no such inn as you could think of placing your daughter at; you cannot allow her to continue her journey for any considerable distance without danger. If, as you say, you cannot suspend your journey, you must part with her tonight, and nowhere could you do so with more honest assurances of care and tenderness than here."

There was something in this lady's air and appearance so distinguished and even imposing, and in her manner so engaging, as to impress one, quite apart from the dignity of her equipage, with a conviction that she was a person of consequence.

By this time the carriage was replaced in its upright position, and the horses, quite tractable, in the traces again.

The lady threw on her daughter a glance which I fancied was not quite so affectionate as one might have anticipated from the beginning of the scene; then she beckoned slightly to my father, and withdrew two or three steps with him out of hearing; and talked to him with a fixed and stern countenance, not at all like that with which she had hitherto spoken.

I was filled with wonder that my father did not seem to perceive the change, and also unspeakably curious to learn what it could be that she was speaking, almost in his ear, with so much earnestness and rapidity.

Two or three minutes at most I think she remained thus employed, then she turned, and a few steps brought her to where her daughter lay, supported by Madame Perrodon. She kneeled beside her for a moment and whispered, as Madame supposed, a little benediction in her ear; then hastily kissing her she stepped into her carriage, the door was closed, the footmen in stately liveries jumped up behind, the outriders spurred on, the postilions cracked their whips, the horses plunged and broke suddenly into a furious canter that threatened soon again to become a gallop, and the carriage whirled away, followed at the same rapid pace by the two horsemen in the rear.

Chapter 3
We Compare Notes

We followed the *cortege* with our eyes until it was swiftly lost to sight in the misty wood; and the very sound of the hoofs and the wheels died away in the silent night air.

Nothing remained to assure us that the adventure had not been an illusion of a moment but the young lady, who just at that moment opened her eyes. I could not see, for her face was turned from me, but she raised her head, evidently looking about her, and I heard a very sweet voice ask complainingly, "Where is mamma?"

Our good Madame Perrodon answered tenderly, and added some comfortable assurances.

I then heard her ask:

"Where am I? What is this place?" and after that she said, "I don't see the carriage; and Matska, where is she?"

Madame answered all her questions in so far as she understood them; and gradually the young lady remembered how the misadventure came about, and was glad to hear that no one in, or in attendance on, the carriage was hurt; and on learning that her mamma had left her here, till her return in about three months, she wept.

I was going to add my consolations to those of Madame Perrodon when Mademoiselle De Lafontaine placed her hand upon my arm, saying:

"Don't approach, one at a time is as much as she can at present converse with; a very little excitement would possibly overpower her now."

As soon as she is comfortably in bed, I thought, I will run up to her room and see her.

My father in the meantime had sent a servant on horseback for the physician, who lived about two leagues away; and a bedroom was being prepared for the young lady's reception.

The stranger now rose, and leaning on Madame's arm, walked slowly over the drawbridge and into the castle gate.

In the hall, servants waited to receive her, and she was conducted forthwith to her room. The room we usually sat in as our drawing room is long, having four windows, that looked over the moat and drawbridge, upon the forest scene I have just described.

It is furnished in old carved oak, with large carved cabinets, and the chairs are cushioned with crimson Utrecht velvet. The walls are covered with tapestry, and surrounded with great gold frames, the figures being as large as life, in ancient and very curious costume, and the subjects represented are hunting, hawking, and generally festive. It is not too stately to be extremely comfortable; and here we had our tea, for with his usual patriotic leanings he insisted that the national beverage should make its appearance regularly with our coffee and chocolate.

We sat here this night, and with candles lighted, were talking over the adventure of the evening.

Madame Perrodon and Mademoiselle De Lafontaine were both of our party. The young stranger had hardly lain down in her bed when she sank into a deep sleep; and those ladies had left her in the care of a servant.

"How do you like our guest?" I asked, as soon as Madame entered. "Tell me all about her?"

"I like her extremely," answered Madame, "she is, I almost think, the prettiest creature I ever saw; about your age, and so gentle and nice."

"She is absolutely beautiful," threw in Mademoiselle, who had peeped for a moment into the stranger's room.

"And such a sweet voice!" added Madame Perrodon.

"Did you remark a woman in the carriage, after it was set up again, who did not get out," inquired Mademoiselle, "but only looked from the window?"

"No, we had not seen her."

Then she described a hideous black woman, with a sort of colored turban on her head, and who was gazing all the time from the carriage window, nodding and grinning derisively towards the ladies, with gleaming eyes and large white eyeballs, and her teeth set as if in fury.

"Did you remark what an ill-looking pack of men the servants were?" asked Madame.

"Yes," said my father, who had just come in, "ugly, hang-dog looking fellows as ever I beheld in my life. I hope they mayn't rob the poor lady in the forest. They are clever rogues, however; they got everything to rights in a minute."

"I dare say they are worn out with too long traveling — said Madame.

"Besides looking wicked, their faces were so strangely lean, and dark, and sullen. I am very curious, I own; but I dare say the young lady will tell you all about it tomorrow, if she is sufficiently recovered."

"I don't think she will," said my father, with a mysterious smile, and a little nod of his head, as if he knew more about it than he cared to tell us.

This made us all the more inquisitive as to what had passed between him and the lady in the black velvet, in the brief but earnest interview that had immediately preceded her departure.

We were scarcely alone, when I entreated him to tell me. He did not need much pressing.

"There is no particular reason why I should not tell you. She expressed a reluctance to trouble us with the care of her daughter, saying she was in delicate health, and nervous, but not subject to any kind of seizure — she volunteered that — nor to any illusion; being, in fact, perfectly sane."

"How very odd to say all that!" I interpolated. "It was so unnecessary."

"At all events it *was* said," he laughed, "and as you wish to know all that passed, which was indeed very little, I tell you. She then said, 'I am making a long journey of *vital* importance — she emphasized the word — rapid and secret; I shall return for my child in three months; in the meantime, she will be silent as to who we are, whence we come, and whither we are traveling.' That is all she said. She spoke very pure French. When she said the word 'secret,' she paused for a few seconds, looking sternly, her eyes fixed on mine. I fancy she makes a great point of that. You saw how quickly she was gone. I hope I have not done a very foolish thing, in taking charge of the young lady."

For my part, I was delighted. I was longing to see and talk to her; and only waiting till the doctor should give me leave. You, who live in towns, can have no idea how great an event the introduction of a new friend is, in such a solitude as surrounded us.

The doctor did not arrive till nearly one o'clock; but I could no more have gone to my bed and slept, than I could have overtaken, on foot, the carriage in which the princess in black velvet had driven away.

When the physician came down to the drawing room, it was to report very favorably upon his patient. She was now sitting up, her pulse quite regular, apparently perfectly well. She had sustained no injury, and the little shock to her nerves had passed away quite harmlessly. There could be no harm certainly in my seeing her, if we both wished it; and, with this permission I sent, forthwith, to know whether she would allow me to visit her for a few minutes in her room.

The servant returned immediately to say that she desired nothing more.

You may be sure I was not long in availing myself of this permission.

Our visitor lay in one of the handsomest rooms in the schloss. It was, perhaps, a little stately. There was a somber piece of tapestry opposite the foot of the bed, representing Cleopatra with the asps to her bosom; and other solemn classic scenes were displayed, a little faded, upon the other walls. But there was gold carving, and rich and varied color enough in the other decorations of the room, to more than redeem the gloom of the old tapestry.

There were candles at the bedside. She was sitting up; her slender pretty figure enveloped in the soft silk dressing gown, embroidered with flowers, and lined with thick quilted silk, which her mother had thrown over her feet as she lay upon the ground.

What was it that, as I reached the bedside and had just begun my little greeting, struck me dumb in a moment, and made me recoil a step or two from before her? I will tell you.

I saw the very face which had visited me in my childhood at night, which remained so fixed in my memory, and on which I had for so many years so often ruminated with horror, when no one suspected of what I was thinking.

It was pretty, even beautiful; and when I first beheld it, wore the same melancholy expression. But this almost instantly lighted into a strange fixed smile of recognition.

There was a silence of fully a minute, and then at length she spoke; I could not.

"How wonderful!" she exclaimed. "Twelve years ago, I saw your face in a dream, and it has haunted me ever since."

"Wonderful indeed!" I repeated, overcoming with an effort the horror that had for a time suspended my utterances. "Twelve years ago, in vision or reality, I certainly saw you. I could not forget your face. It has remained before my eyes ever since."

Her smile had softened. Whatever I had fancied strange in it, was gone, and it and her dimpling cheeks were now delightfully pretty and intelligent.

I felt reassured, and continued more in the vein which hospitality indicated, to bid her welcome, and to tell her how much pleasure her accidental arrival had given us all, and especially what a happiness it was to me.

I took her hand as I spoke. I was a little shy, as lonely people are, but the situation made me eloquent, and even bold. She pressed my hand, she laid hers upon it, and her eyes glowed, as, looking hastily into mine, she smiled again, and blushed.

She answered my welcome very prettily. I sat down beside her, still wondering; and she said:

"I must tell you my vision about you; it is so very strange that you and I should have had, each of the other so vivid a dream, that each should have seen, I you and you me, looking as we do now, when of course we both were mere children. I was a child, about six years old, and I awoke from a confused and troubled dream, and found myself in a room, unlike my nursery, wainscoted clumsily in some dark wood, and with cupboards and bedsteads, and chairs, and benches placed about it. The beds were, I thought, all empty, and the room itself without anyone but myself in it; and I, after looking about me for some time, and admiring especially an iron candlestick with two branches, which I should certainly know again, crept under one of the beds to reach the window; but as I got from under the bed, I heard someone crying; and looking up, while I was still upon my knees, I saw you — most assuredly you — as I see you now; a beautiful young lady, with golden hair and large blue eyes, and lips — your lips — you as you are here.

"Your looks won me; I climbed on the bed and put my arms about you, and I think we both fell asleep. I was aroused by a scream; you were sitting up screaming. I was frightened, and slipped down upon the ground, and, it seemed to me, lost consciousness for a moment; and when I came to myself, I was again in my nursery at home. Your face I have never forgotten since. I could not be misled by mere resemblance. *You are* the lady whom I saw then."

It was now my turn to relate my corresponding vision, which I did, to the undisguised wonder of my new acquaintance.

"I don't know which should be most afraid of the other," she said, again smiling —"If you were less pretty I think I should be very much afraid of you, but being as you are, and you and I both so young, I feel only that I have made your acquaintance twelve years ago, and have already a right to your intimacy; at all events it does seem as if we were destined, from our earliest childhood, to be friends. I wonder whether you feel as strangely drawn towards me as I do to you; I have never had a friend — shall I find one now?" She sighed, and her fine dark eyes gazed passionately on me.

Now the truth is, I felt rather unaccountably towards the beautiful stranger. I did feel, as she said, "drawn towards her," but there was also something of repulsion. In this ambiguous feeling, however, the sense of attraction immensely prevailed. She interested and won me; she was so beautiful and so indescribably engaging.

I perceived now something of languor and exhaustion stealing over her, and hastened to bid her good night.

"The doctor thinks," I added, "that you ought to have a maid to sit up with you tonight; one of ours is waiting, and you will find her a very useful and quiet creature."

"How kind of you, but I could not sleep, I never could with an attendant in the room. I shan't require any assistance — and, shall I confess my weakness, I am haunted with a terror of robbers. Our house was robbed once, and two servants murdered, so I always lock my door. It has become a habit — and you look so kind I know you will forgive me. I see there is a key in the lock."

She held me close in her pretty arms for a moment and whispered in my ear, "Good night, darling, it is very hard to part with you, but good night; tomorrow, but not early, I shall see you again."

She sank back on the pillow with a sigh, and her fine eyes followed me with a fond and melancholy gaze, and she murmured again "Good night, dear friend."

Young people like, and even love, on impulse. I was flattered by the evident, though as yet undeserved, fondness she showed me. I liked the confidence with which she at once received me. She was determined that we should be very near friends.

Next day came and we met again. I was delighted with my companion; that is to say, in many respects.

Her looks lost nothing in daylight — she was certainly the most beautiful creature I had ever seen, and the unpleasant remembrance of the face presented in my early dream, had lost the effect of the first unexpected recognition.

She confessed that she had experienced a similar shock on seeing me, and precisely the same faint antipathy that had mingled with my admiration of her. We now laughed together over our momentary horrors.

Chapter 4
Her Habits — A Saunter

I told you that I was charmed with her in most particulars.

There were some that did not please me so well.

She was above the middle height of women. I shall begin by describing her.

She was slender, and wonderfully graceful. Except that her movements were languid — very languid — indeed, there was nothing in her appearance to indicate an invalid. Her complexion was rich and brilliant; her features were small and beautifully formed; her eyes large, dark, and lustrous; her hair was quite wonderful, I never saw hair so magnificently thick and long when it was down about her shoulders; I have often placed my hands under it, and laughed with wonder at its weight. It was exquisitely fine and soft, and in color a rich very dark brown, with something of gold. I loved to let it down, tumbling with its own weight, as, in her room, she lay back in her chair talking in her sweet low voice, I used to fold and braid it, and spread it out and play with it. Heavens! If I had but known all!

I said there were particulars which did not please me. I have told you that her confidence won me the first night I saw her; but I found that she exercised with respect to herself, her mother, her history, everything in fact connected with her life, plans, and people, an ever wakeful reserve. I dare say I was unreasonable, perhaps I was wrong; I dare say I ought to have respected the solemn injunction laid upon my father by the stately lady in black velvet. But curiosity is a restless and unscrupulous passion, and no one girl can endure, with patience, that hers should be baffled by another. What harm could it do anyone to tell me what I so ardently desired to know? Had she no trust in my good sense or honor? Why would she not believe me when I assured her, so solemnly, that I would not divulge one syllable of what she told me to any mortal breathing.

There was a coldness, it seemed to me, beyond her years, in her smiling melancholy persistent refusal to afford me the least ray of light.

I cannot say we quarreled upon this point, for she would not quarrel upon any. It was, of course, very unfair of me to press her, very ill-bred, but I really could not help it; and I might just as well have let it alone.

What she did tell me amounted, in my unconscionable estimation — to nothing.

It was all summed up in three very vague disclosures:

First — Her name was Carmilla.

Second — Her family was very ancient and noble.

Third — Her home lay in the direction of the west.

She would not tell me the name of her family, nor their armorial bearings, nor the name of their estate, nor even that of the country they lived in.

You are not to suppose that I worried her incessantly on these subjects. I watched opportunity, and rather insinuated than urged my inquiries. Once or twice, indeed, I did attack her more directly. But no matter what my tactics, utter failure was invariably the result. Reproaches and caresses were all lost upon her. But I must add this, that her evasion was conducted with so pretty a melancholy and deprecation, with so many, and even passionate declarations of her liking for me, and trust in my honor, and with so many promises that I should at last know all, that I could not find it in my heart long to be offended with her.

She used to place her pretty arms about my neck, draw me to her, and laying her cheek to mine, murmur with her lips near my ear, "Dearest, your little heart is wounded; think me not cruel because I obey the irresistible law of my strength and weakness; if your dear heart is wounded, my wild heart bleeds with yours. In the rapture of my enormous humiliation I live in your warm life, and you shall die — die, sweetly die — into mine. I cannot help it; as I draw near to you, you, in your turn, will draw near to others, and learn the rapture of that cruelty, which yet is love; so, for a while, seek to know no more of me and mine, but trust me with all your loving spirit."

And when she had spoken such a rhapsody, she would press me more closely in her trembling embrace, and her lips in soft kisses gently glow upon my cheek.

Her agitations and her language were unintelligible to me.

From these foolish embraces, which were not of very frequent occurrence, I must allow, I used to wish to extricate myself; but my energies seemed to fail me. Her murmured words sounded like a lullaby in my ear, and soothed my resistance into a trance, from which I only seemed to recover myself when she withdrew her arms.

In these mysterious moods I did not like her. I experienced a strange tumultuous excitement that was pleasurable, ever and anon, mingled with a vague sense of fear and disgust. I had no distinct thoughts about her while such scenes lasted, but I was conscious of a love growing into adoration, and also of abhorrence. This I know is paradox, but I can make no other attempt to explain the feeling.

I now write, after an interval of more than ten years, with a trembling hand, with a confused and horrible recollection of certain occurrences and situations, in the ordeal through which I was unconsciously passing; though with a vivid and very sharp remembrance of the main current of my story.

But, I suspect, in all lives there are certain emotional scenes, those in which our passions have been most wildly and terribly roused, that are of all others the most vaguely and dimly remembered.

Sometimes after an hour of apathy, my strange and beautiful companion would take my hand and hold it with a fond pressure, renewed again and again; blushing softly, gazing in my face with languid and burning eyes, and breathing so fast that her dress rose and fell with the tumultuous respiration. It was like the ardor of a lover; it embarrassed me; it was hateful and yet over-powering; and with gloating eyes she drew me to her, and her hot lips traveled along my cheek in kisses; and she would whisper, almost in sobs, "You are mine, you *shall* be mine, you and I are one for ever." Then she has thrown herself back in her chair, with her small hands over her eyes, leaving me trembling.

"Are we related," I used to ask; "what can you mean by all this? I remind you perhaps of someone whom you love; but you must not, I hate it; I don't know you — I don't know myself when you look so and talk so."

She used to sigh at my vehemence, then turn away and drop my hand.

Respecting these very extraordinary manifestations I strove in vain to form any satisfactory theory — I could not refer them to affectation or trick. It was unmistakably the momentary breaking out of suppressed instinct and emotion. Was she, notwithstanding her mother's volunteered denial, subject to brief visitations of insanity; or was there here a disguise and a romance? I had read in old storybooks of such things. What if a boyish lover had found his way into the house, and sought to prosecute his suit in masquerade, with the assistance of a clever old adventuress. But there were many things against this hypothesis, highly interesting as it was to my vanity.

I could boast of no little attentions such as masculine gallantry delights to offer. Between these passionate moments there were long intervals of commonplace, of gaiety, of brooding melancholy, during which, except that I detected her eyes so full of melancholy fire, following me, at times I might have been as nothing to her. Except in these brief periods of mysterious excitement her ways were girlish; and there was always a languor about her, quite incompatible with a masculine system in a state of health.

In some respects her habits were odd. Perhaps not so singular in the opinion of a town lady like you, as they appeared to us rustic people. She used to come down very late, generally not till one o'clock, she would then take a cup of chocolate, but eat nothing; we then went out for a walk, which was a mere saunter, and she seemed, almost immediately, exhausted, and either returned to the schloss or sat on one of the benches that were placed, here and there, among the trees. This was a bodily languor in which her mind did not sympathize. She was always an animated talker, and very intelligent.

She sometimes alluded for a moment to her own home, or mentioned an adventure or situation, or an early recollection, which indicated a people of strange manners, and described customs of which we knew nothing. I gathered from these chance hints that her native country was much more remote than I had at first fancied.

As we sat thus one afternoon under the trees a funeral passed us by. It was that of a pretty young girl, whom I had often seen, the daughter of one of the rangers of the forest. The poor man was walking behind the coffin of his darling; she was his only child, and he looked quite heartbroken.

Peasants walking two-and-two came behind, they were singing a funeral hymn.

I rose to mark my respect as they passed, and joined in the hymn they were very sweetly singing.

My companion shook me a little roughly, and I turned surprised.

She said brusquely, "Don't you perceive how discordant that is?"

"I think it very sweet, on the contrary," I answered, vexed at the interruption, and very uncomfortable, lest the people who composed the little procession should observe and resent what was passing.

I resumed, therefore, instantly, and was again interrupted. "You pierce my ears," said Carmilla, almost angrily, and stopping her ears with her tiny fingers. "Besides, how can you tell that your religion and mine are the same; your forms wound me, and I hate funerals. What a fuss! Why you must die — *everyone* must die; and all are happier when they do. Come home."

"My father has gone on with the clergyman to the churchyard. I thought you knew she was to be buried today."

"She? I don't trouble my head about peasants. I don't know who she is," answered Carmilla, with a flash from her fine eyes.

"She is the poor girl who fancied she saw a ghost a fortnight ago, and has been dying ever since, till yesterday, when she expired."

"Tell me nothing about ghosts. I shan't sleep tonight if you do."

"I hope there is no plague or fever coming; all this looks very like it," I continued. "The swineherd's young wife died only a week ago, and she thought something seized her by the throat as she lay in her bed, and nearly strangled her. Papa says such horrible fancies do accompany some forms of fever. She was quite well the day before. She sank afterwards, and died before a week."

"Well, *her* funeral is over, I hope, and *her* hymn sung; and our ears shan't be tortured with that discord and jargon. It has made me nervous. Sit down here, beside me; sit close; hold my hand; press it hard-hard-harder."

We had moved a little back, and had come to another seat.

She sat down. Her face underwent a change that alarmed and even terrified me for a moment. It darkened, and became horribly livid; her teeth and hands were clenched, and she frowned and compressed her lips, while she stared down upon the ground at her feet, and trembled all over with a continued shudder as irrepressible as ague. All her energies seemed strained to suppress a fit, with which she was then breathlessly tugging; and at length a low convulsive cry of suffering broke from her, and gradually the hysteria subsided. "There! That comes of strangling people with hymns!" she said at last. "Hold me, hold me still. It is passing away."

And so gradually it did; and perhaps to dissipate the somber impression which the spectacle had left upon me, she became unusually animated and chatty; and so we got home.

This was the first time I had seen her exhibit any definable symptoms of that delicacy of health which her mother had spoken of. It was the first time, also, I had seen her exhibit anything like temper.

Both passed away like a summer cloud; and never but once afterwards did I witness on her part a momentary sign of anger. I will tell you how it happened.

She and I were looking out of one of the long drawing room windows, when there entered the courtyard, over the drawbridge, a figure of a wanderer whom I knew very well. He used to visit the schloss generally twice a year.

It was the figure of a hunchback, with the sharp lean features that generally accompany deformity. He wore a pointed black beard, and he was smiling from ear to ear, showing his white fangs. He was dressed in buff, black, and scarlet, and crossed with more straps and belts than I could count, from which hung all manner of things. Behind, he carried a magic lantern, and two boxes, which I well knew, in one of which was a salamander, and in the other a mandrake. These monsters used to make my father laugh. They were compounded of parts of monkeys, parrots squirrels, fish, and hedgehogs, dried and stitched together with great neatness and startling effect. He had a fiddle, a box of conjuring apparatus, a pair of foils and masks attached to his belt, several other mysterious cases dangling about him, and a black staff with copper ferrules in his hand. His companion was a rough spare dog, that followed at his heels, but stopped short, suspiciously at the drawbridge, and in a little while began to howl dismally.

In the meantime, the mountebank, standing in the midst of the courtyard, raised his grotesque hat, and made us a very ceremonious bow, paying his compliments very volubly in execrable French, and German not much better.

Then, disengaging his fiddle, he began to scrape a lively air to which he sang with a merry discord, dancing with ludicrous airs and activity, that made me laugh, in spite of the dog's howling.

Then he advanced to the window with many smiles and salutations, and his hat in his left hand, his fiddle under his arm, and with a fluency that never took breath, he gabbled a long advertisement of all his accomplishments, and the resources of the various arts which he placed at our service, and the curiosities and entertainments which it was in his power, at our bidding, to display.

"Will your ladyships be pleased to buy an amulet against the oupire, which is going like the wolf, I hear, through these woods," he said dropping his hat on the pavement. "They are dying of it right and left and here is a charm that never fails; only pinned to the pillow, and you may laugh in his face."

These charms consisted of oblong slips of vellum, with cabalistic ciphers and diagrams upon them.

Carmilla instantly purchased one, and so did I.

He was looking up, and we were smiling down upon him, amused; at least, I can answer for myself. His piercing black eye, as he looked up in our faces, seemed to detect something that fixed for a moment his curiosity. In an instant he unrolled a leather case, full of all manner of odd little steel instruments.

"See here, my lady," he said, displaying it, and addressing me, "I profess, among other things less useful, the art of dentistry. Plague take the dog!" he interpolated. "Silence, beast! He howls so that your ladyships can scarcely hear a word. Your noble friend, the young lady at your right, has the sharpest tooth — long, thin, pointed, like an awl, like a needle; ha, ha! With my sharp and long sight, as I look up, I have seen it distinctly; now if it happens to hurt the young lady, and I think it must, here am I, here are my file, my punch, my nippers; I will make it round and blunt, if her ladyship pleases; no longer the tooth of a fish, but of a beautiful young lady as she is. Hey? Is the young lady displeased? Have I been too bold? Have I offended her?"

The young lady, indeed, looked very angry as she drew back from the window.

"How dares that mountebank insult us so? Where is your father? I shall demand redress from him. My father would have had the wretch tied up to the pump, and flogged with a cart whip, and burnt to the bones with the castle brand!"

She retired from the window a step or two, and sat down, and had hardly lost sight of the offender, when her wrath subsided as suddenly as it had risen, and she gradually recovered her usual tone, and seemed to forget the little hunchback and his follies.

My father was out of spirits that evening. On coming in he told us that there had been another case very similar to the two fatal ones which had lately occurred. The sister of a young peasant on his estate, only a mile away, was very ill, had been, as she described it, attacked very nearly in the same way, and was now slowly but steadily sinking.

"All this," said my father, "is strictly referable to natural causes. These poor people infect one another with their superstitions, and so repeat in imagination the images of terror that have infested their neighbors."

"But that very circumstance frightens one horribly," said Carmilla.

"How so?" inquired my father.

"I am so afraid of fancying I see such things; I think it would be as bad as reality."

"We are in God's hands: nothing can happen without his permission, and all will end well for those who love him. He is our faithful creator; He has made us all, and will take care of us."

"Creator! *Nature!*" said the young lady in answer to my gentle father. "And this disease that invades the country is natural. Nature. All things proceed from Nature — don't they? All things in the heaven, in the earth, and under the earth, act and live as Nature ordains? I think so."

"The doctor said he would come here today," said my father, after a silence. "I want to know what he thinks about it, and what he thinks we had better do."

"Doctors never did me any good," said Carmilla.

"Then you have been ill?" I asked.

"More ill than ever you were," she answered.

"Long ago?"

"Yes, a long time. I suffered from this very illness; but I forget all but my pain and weakness, and they were not so bad as are suffered in other diseases."

"You were very young then?"

"I dare say, let us talk no more of it. You would not wound a friend?"

She looked languidly in my eyes, and passed her arm round my waist lovingly, and led me out of the room. My father was busy over some papers near the window.

"Why does your papa like to frighten us?" said the pretty girl with a sigh and a little shudder.

"He doesn't, dear Carmilla, it is the very furthest thing from his mind."

"Are you afraid, dearest?"

"I should be very much if I fancied there was any real danger of my being attacked as those poor people were."

"You are afraid to die?"

"Yes, every one is."

"But to die as lovers may — to die together, so that they may live together.

"Girls are caterpillars while they live in the world, to be finally butterflies when the summer comes; but in the meantime there are grubs and larvae, don't you see — each with their peculiar propensities, necessities and structure. So says Monsieur Buffon, in his big book, in the next room."

Later in the day the doctor came, and was closeted with papa for some time.

He was a skilful man, of sixty and upwards, he wore powder, and shaved his pale face as smooth as a pumpkin. He and papa emerged from the room together, and I heard papa laugh, and say as they came out:

"Well, I do wonder at a wise man like you. What do you say to hippogriffs and dragons?"

The doctor was smiling, and made answer, shaking his head —

"Nevertheless life and death are mysterious states, and we know little of the resources of either."

And so the walked on, and I heard no more. I did not then know what the doctor had been broaching, but I think I guess it now.

Chapter 5
A Wonderful Likeness

This evening there arrived from Gratz the grave, dark-faced son of the picture cleaner, with a horse and cart laden with two large packing cases, having many pictures in each. It was a journey of ten leagues, and whenever a messenger arrived at the schloss from our little capital of Gratz, we used to crowd about him in the hall, to hear the news.

This arrival created in our secluded quarters quite a sensation. The cases remained in the hall, and the messenger was taken charge of by the servants till he had eaten his supper. Then with assistants, and armed with hammer, ripping chisel, and turnscrew, he met us in the hall, where we had assembled to witness the unpacking of the cases.

Carmilla sat looking listlessly on, while one after the other the old pictures, nearly all portraits, which had undergone the process of renovation, were brought to light. My mother was of an old Hungarian family, and most of these pictures, which were about to be restored to their places, had come to us through her.

My father had a list in his hand, from which he read, as the artist rummaged out the corresponding numbers. I don't know that the pictures were very good, but they were, undoubtedly, very old, and some of them very curious also. They had, for the most part, the merit of being now seen by me, I may say, for the first time; for the smoke and dust of time had all but obliterated them.

"There is a picture that I have not seen yet," said my father. "In one corner, at the top of it, is the name, as well as I could read, 'Marcia Karnstein,' and the date '1698'; and I am curious to see how it has turned out."

I remembered it; it was a small picture, about a foot and a half high, and nearly square, without a frame; but it was so blackened by age that I could not make it out.

The artist now produced it, with evident pride. It was quite beautiful; it was startling; it seemed to live. It was the effigy of Carmilla!

"Carmilla, dear, here is an absolute miracle. Here you are, living, smiling, ready to speak, in this picture. Isn't it beautiful, Papa? And see, even the little mole on her throat."

My father laughed, and said "Certainly it is a wonderful likeness," but he looked away, and to my surprise seemed but little struck by it, and went on talking to the picture cleaner, who was also something of an artist, and discoursed with intelligence about the portraits or other works, which his art had just brought into light and color, while I was more and more lost in wonder the more I looked at the picture.

"Will you let me hang this picture in my room, papa?" I asked.

"Certainly, dear," said he, smiling, "I'm very glad you think it so like. It must be prettier even than I thought it, if it is."

The young lady did not acknowledge this pretty speech, did not seem to hear it. She was leaning back in her seat, her fine eyes under their long lashes gazing on me in contemplation, and she smiled in a kind of rapture.

"And now you can read quite plainly the name that is written in the corner. It is not Marcia; it looks as if it was done in gold. The name is Mircalla, Countess Karnstein, and this is a little coronet over and underneath A.D. 1698. I am descended from the Karnsteins; that is, mamma was."

"Ah!" said the lady, languidly, "so am I, I think, a very long descent, very ancient. Are there any Karnsteins living now?"

"None who bear the name, I believe. The family were ruined, I believe, in some civil wars, long ago, but the ruins of the castle are only about three miles away."

"How interesting!" she said, languidly. "But see what beautiful moonlight!" She glanced through the hall door, which stood a little open. "Suppose you take a little ramble round the court, and look down at the road and river."

"It is so like the night you came to us," I said.

She sighed; smiling.

She rose, and each with her arm about the other's waist, we walked out upon the pavement.

In silence, slowly we walked down to the drawbridge, where the beautiful landscape opened before us.

"And so you were thinking of the night I came here?" she almost whispered.

"Are you glad I came?"

"Delighted, dear Carmilla," I answered.

"And you asked for the picture you think like me, to hang in your room," she murmured with a sigh, as she drew her arm closer about my waist, and let her pretty head sink upon my shoulder. "How romantic you are, Carmilla," I said. "Whenever you tell me your story, it will be made up chiefly of some one great romance."

She kissed me silently.

"I am sure, Carmilla, you have been in love; that there is, at this moment, an affair of the heart going on."

"I have been in love with no one, and never shall," she whispered, "unless it should be with you."

How beautiful she looked in the moonlight!

Shy and strange was the look with which she quickly hid her face in my neck and hair, with tumultuous sighs, that seemed almost to sob, and pressed in mine a hand that trembled.

Her soft cheek was glowing against mine. "Darling, darling," she murmured, "I live in you; and you would die for me, I love you so."

I started from her.

She was gazing on me with eyes from which all fire, all meaning had flown, and a face colorless and apathetic.

"Is there a chill in the air, dear?" she said drowsily. "I almost shiver; have I been dreaming? Let us come in. Come; come; come in."

"You look ill, Carmilla; a little faint. You certainly must take some wine," I said.

"Yes. I will. I'm better now. I shall be quite well in a few minutes. Yes, do give me a little wine," answered Carmilla, as we approached the door.

"Let us look again for a moment; it is the last time, perhaps, I shall see the moonlight with you."

"How do you feel now, dear Carmilla? Are you really better?" I asked.

I was beginning to take alarm, lest she should have been stricken with the strange epidemic that they said had invaded the country about us.

"Papa would be grieved beyond measure." I added, "if he thought you were ever so little ill, without immediately letting us know. We have a very skilful doctor near this, the physician who was with papa today."

"I'm sure he is. I know how kind you all are; but, dear child, I am quite well again. There is nothing ever wrong with me, but a little weakness.

"People say I am languid; I am incapable of exertion; I can scarcely walk as far as a child of three years old: and every now and then the little strength I have falters, and I become as you have just seen me. But after all I am very easily set up again; in a moment I am perfectly myself. See how I have recovered."

So, indeed, she had; and she and I talked a great deal, and very animated she was; and the remainder of that evening passed without any recurrence of what I called her infatuations. I mean her crazy talk and looks, which embarrassed, and even frightened me.

But there occurred that night an event which gave my thoughts quite a new turn, and seemed to startle even Carmilla's languid nature into momentary energy.

Chapter 6
A Very Strange Agony

When we got into the drawing room, and had sat down to our coffee and chocolate, although Carmilla did not take any, she seemed quite herself again, and Madame, and Mademoiselle De Lafontaine, joined us, and made a little card party, in the course of which papa came in for what he called his "dish of tea."

When the game was over he sat down beside Carmilla on the sofa, and asked her, a little anxiously, whether she had heard from her mother since her arrival.

She answered "No."

He then asked whether she knew where a letter would reach her at present.

"I cannot tell," she answered ambiguously, "but I have been thinking of leaving you; you have been already too hospitable and too kind to me. I have given you an infinity of trouble, and I should wish to take a carriage tomorrow, and post in pursuit of her; I know where I shall ultimately find her, although I dare not yet tell you."

"But you must not dream of any such thing," exclaimed my father, to my great relief. "We can't afford to lose you so, and I won't consent to your leaving us, except under the care of your mother, who was so good as to consent to your remaining with us till she should herself return. I should be quite happy if I knew that you heard from her: but this evening the accounts of the progress of the mysterious disease that has invaded our neighborhood, grow even more alarming; and my beautiful guest, I do feel the responsibility, unaided by advice from your mother, very much. But I shall do my best; and one thing is certain, that you must not think of leaving us without her distinct direction to that effect. We should suffer too much in parting from you to consent to it easily."

"Thank you, sir, a thousand times for your hospitality," she answered, smiling bashfully. "You have all been too kind to me; I have seldom been so happy in all my life before, as in your beautiful chateau, under your care, and in the society of your dear daughter."

So he gallantly, in his old-fashioned way, kissed her hand, smiling and pleased at her little speech.

I accompanied Carmilla as usual to her room, and sat and chatted with her while she was preparing for bed.

"Do you think," I said at length, "that you will ever confide fully in me?"

She turned round smiling, but made no answer, only continued to smile on me.

"You won't answer that?" I said. "You can't answer pleasantly; I ought not to have asked you."

"You were quite right to ask me that, or anything. You do not know how dear you are to me, or you could not think any confidence too great to look for. But I am under vows, no nun half so awfully, and I dare not tell my story yet, even to you. The time is very near when you shall know everything. You will think me cruel, very selfish, but love is always selfish; the more ardent the more selfish. How jealous I am you cannot know. You must come with me, loving me, to death; or else hate me and still come with me, and *hating* me through death and after. There is no such word as indifference in my apathetic nature."

"Now, Carmilla, you are going to talk your wild nonsense again," I said hastily.

"Not I, silly little fool as I am, and full of whims and fancies; for your sake I'll talk like a sage. Were you ever at a ball?"

"No; how you do run on. What is it like? How charming it must be."

"I almost forget, it is years ago."

I laughed.

"You are not so old. Your first ball can hardly be forgotten yet."

"I remember everything it — with an effort. I see it all, as divers see what is going on above them, through a medium, dense, rippling, but transparent. There occurred that night what has confused the picture, and made its colours faint. I was all but assassinated in my bed, wounded here," she touched her breast, "and never was the same since."

"Were you near dying?"

"Yes, very — a cruel love — strange love, that would have taken my life. Love will have its sacrifices. No sacrifice without blood. Let us go to sleep now; I feel so lazy. How can I get up just now and lock my door?"

She was lying with her tiny hands buried in her rich wavy hair, under her cheek, her little head upon the pillow, and her glittering eyes followed me wherever I moved, with a kind of shy smile that I could not decipher.

I bid her good night, and crept from the room with an uncomfortable sensation.

I often wondered whether our pretty guest ever said her prayers. I certainly had never seen her upon her knees. In the morning she never came down until long after our family prayers were over, and at night she never left the drawing room to attend our brief evening prayers in the hall.

If it had not been that it had casually come out in one of our careless talks that she had been baptised, I should have doubted her being a Christian. Religion was a subject on which I had never heard her speak a word. If I had known the world better, this particular neglect or antipathy would not have so much surprised me.

The precautions of nervous people are infectious, and persons of a like temperament are pretty sure, after a time, to imitate them. I had adopted Carmilla's habit of locking her bedroom door, having taken into my head all her whimsical alarms about midnight invaders and prowling assassins. I had also adopted her precaution of making a brief search through her room, to satisfy herself that no lurking assassin or robber was "ensconced."

These wise measures taken, I got into my bed and fell asleep. A light was burning in my room. This was an old habit, of very early date, and which nothing could have tempted me to dispense with.

Thus fortified I might take my rest in peace. But dreams come through stone walls, light up dark rooms, or darken light ones, and their persons make their exits and their entrances as they please, and laugh at locksmiths.

I had a dream that night that was the beginning of a very strange agony.

I cannot call it a nightmare, for I was quite conscious of being asleep.

But I was equally conscious of being in my room, and lying in bed, precisely as I actually was. I saw, or fancied I saw, the room and its furniture just as I had seen it last, except that it was very dark, and I saw something moving round the foot of the bed, which at first I could not accurately distinguish. But I soon saw that it was a sooty-black animal that resembled a monstrous cat. It appeared to me about four or five feet long for it measured fully the length of the hearthrug as it passed over it; and it continued to-ing and fro-ing with the lithe, sinister restlessness of a beast in a cage. I could not cry out, although as you may suppose, I was terrified. Its pace was growing faster, and the room rapidly darker and darker, and at length so dark that I could no longer see anything of it but its eyes. I felt it spring lightly on the bed. The two broad eyes approached my face, and suddenly I felt a stinging pain as if two large needles darted, an inch or two apart, deep into my breast. I waked with a scream. The room was lighted by the candle that burnt there all through the night, and I saw a female figure standing at the foot of the bed, a little at the right side. It was in a dark loose dress, and its hair was down and covered its shoulders. A block of stone could not have been more still. There was not the slightest stir of respiration. As I stared at it, the figure appeared to have changed its place, and was now nearer the door; then, close to it, the door opened, and it passed out.

I was now relieved, and able to breathe and move. My first thought was that Carmilla had been playing me a trick, and that I had forgotten to secure my door. I hastened to it, and found it locked as usual on the inside. I was afraid to open it — I was horrified. I sprang into my bed and covered my head up in the bedclothes, and lay there more dead than alive till morning.

Chapter 7
Descending

It would be vain my attempting to tell you the horror with which, even now, I recall the occurrence of that night. It was no such transitory terror as a dream leaves behind it. It seemed to deepen by time, and communicated itself to the room and the very furniture that had encompass the apparition.

I could not bear next day to be alone for a moment. I should have told papa, but for two opposite reasons. At one time I thought he would laugh at my story, and I could not bear its being treated as a jest; and at another I thought he might fancy that I had been attacked by the mysterious complaint which had invaded our neighborhood. I had myself no misgiving of the kind, and as he had been rather an invalid for some time, I was afraid of alarming him.

I was comfortable enough with my good-natured companions, Madame Perrodon, and the vivacious Mademoiselle Lafontaine. They both perceived that I was out of spirits and nervous, and at length I told them what lay so heavy at my heart.

Mademoiselle laughed, but I fancied that Madame Perrodon looked anxious.

"By-the-by," said Mademoiselle, laughing, "the long lime tree walk, behind Carmilla's bedroom window, is haunted!"

"Nonsense!" exclaimed Madame, who probably thought the theme rather inopportune, "and who tells that story, my dear?"

"Martin says that he came up twice, when the old yard gate was being repaired, before sunrise, and twice saw the same female figure walking down the lime tree avenue."

"So he well might, as long as there are cows to milk in the river fields," said Madame.

"I daresay; but Martin chooses to be frightened, and never did I see fool more frightened."

"You must not say a word about it to Carmilla, because she can see down that walk from her room window," I interposed, "and she is, if possible, a greater coward than I."

Carmilla came down rather later than usual that day.

"I was so frightened last night," she said, so soon as were together, "and I am sure I should have seen something dreadful if it had not been for that charm I bought from the poor little hunchback whom I called such hard names. I had a dream of something black coming round my bed, and I awoke in a perfect horror, and I really thought, for some seconds, I saw a dark figure near the chimney-piece, but I felt under my pillow for my charm, and the moment my fingers touched it, the figure disappeared, and I felt quite certain, only that I had it by me, that something frightful would have made its appearance, and, perhaps, throttled me, as it did those poor people we heard of."

"Well, listen to me," I began, and recounted my adventure, at the recital of which she appeared horrified.

"And had you the charm near you?" she asked, earnestly.

"No, I had dropped it into a china vase in the drawing room, but I shall certainly take it with me tonight, as you have so much faith in it."

At this distance of time I cannot tell you, or even understand, how I overcame my horror so effectually as to lie alone in my room that night. I remember distinctly that I pinned the charm to my pillow. I fell asleep almost immediately, and slept even more soundly than usual all night.

Next night I passed as well. My sleep was delightfully deep and dreamless.

But I wakened with a sense of lassitude and melancholy, which, however, did not exceed a degree that was almost luxurious.

"Well, I told you so," said Carmilla, when I described my quiet sleep, "I had such delightful sleep myself last night; I pinned the charm to the breast of my nightdress. It was too far away the night before. I am quite sure it was all fancy, except the dreams. I used to think that evil spirits made dreams, but our doctor told me it is no such thing. Only a fever passing by, or some other malady, as they often do, he said, knocks at the door, and not being able to get in, passes on, with that alarm."

"And what do you think the charm is?" said I.

"It has been fumigated or immersed in some drug, and is an antidote against the malaria," she answered.

"Then it acts only on the body?"

"Certainly; you don't suppose that evil spirits are frightened by bits of ribbon, or the perfumes of a druggist's shop? No, these complaints, wandering in the air, begin by trying the nerves, and so infect the brain, but before they can seize upon you, the antidote repels them. That I am sure is what the charm has done for us. It is nothing magical, it is simply natural."

I should have been happier if I could have quite agreed with Carmilla, but I did my best, and the impression was a little losing its force.

For some nights I slept profoundly; but still every morning I felt the same lassitude, and a languor weighed upon me all day. I felt myself a changed girl. A strange melancholy was stealing over me, a melancholy that I would not have interrupted. Dim thoughts of death began to open, and an idea that I was slowly sinking took gentle, and, somehow, not unwelcome, possession of me. If it was sad, the tone of mind which this induced was also sweet.

Whatever it might be, my soul acquiesced in it.

I would not admit that I was ill, I would not consent to tell my papa, or to have the doctor sent for.

Carmilla became more devoted to me than ever, and her strange paroxysms of languid adoration more frequent. She used to gloat on me with increasing ardor the more my strength and spirits waned. This always shocked me like a momentary glare of insanity.

Without knowing it, I was now in a pretty advanced stage of the strangest illness under which mortal ever suffered. There was an unaccountable fascination in its earlier symptoms that more than reconciled me to the incapacitating effect of that stage of the malady. This fascination increased for a time, until it reached a certain point, when gradually a sense of the horrible mingled itself with it, deepening, as you shall hear, until it discolored and perverted the whole state of my life.

The first change I experienced was rather agreeable. It was very near the turning point from which began the descent of Avernus.

Certain vague and strange sensations visited me in my sleep. The prevailing one was of that pleasant, peculiar cold thrill which we feel in bathing, when we move against the current of a river. This was soon accompanied by dreams that seemed interminable, and were so vague that I could never recollect their scenery and persons, or any one connected portion of their action. But they left an awful impression, and a sense of exhaustion, as if I had passed through a long period of great mental exertion and danger.

After all these dreams there remained on waking a remembrance of having been in a place very nearly dark, and of having spoken to people whom I could not see; and especially of one clear voice, of a female's, very deep, that spoke as if at a distance, slowly, and producing always the same sensation of indescribable solemnity and fear. Sometime there came a sensation as if a hand was drawn softly along my cheek and neck. Sometimes it was as if warm lips kissed me, and longer and longer and more lovingly as they reached my throat, but there the caress fixed itself. My heart beat faster, my breathing rose and fell rapidly and full drawn; a sobbing, that rose into a sense of strangulation, supervened, and turned into a dreadful convulsion, in which my senses left me and I became unconscious.

It was now three weeks since the commencement of this unaccountable state.

My sufferings had, during the last week, told upon my appearance. I had grown pale, my eyes were dilated and darkened underneath, and the languor which I had long felt began to display itself in my countenance.

My father asked me often whether I was ill; but, with an obstinacy which now seems to me unaccountable, I persisted in assuring him that I was quite well.

In a sense this was true. I had no pain, I could complain of no bodily derangement. My complaint seemed to be one of the imagination, or the nerves, and, horrible as my sufferings were, I kept them, with a morbid reserve, very nearly to myself.

It could not be that terrible complaint which the peasants called the oupire, for I had now been suffering for three weeks, and they were seldom ill for much more than three days, when death put an end to their miseries.

Carmilla complained of dreams and feverish sensations, but by no means of so alarming a kind as mine. I say that mine were extremely alarming. Had I been capable of comprehending my condition, I would have invoked aid and advice on my knees. The narcotic of an unsuspected influence was acting upon me, and my perceptions were benumbed.

I am going to tell you now of a dream that led immediately to an odd discovery.

One night, instead of the voice I was accustomed to hear in the dark, I heard one, sweet and tender, and at the same time terrible, which said, "Your mother warns you to beware of the assassin." At the same time a light unexpectedly sprang up, and I saw Carmilla, standing, near the foot of my bed, in her white nightdress, bathed, from her chin to her feet, in one great stain of blood.

I wakened with a shriek, possessed with the one idea that Carmilla was being murdered. I remember springing from my bed, and my next recollection is that of standing on the lobby, crying for help.

Madame and Mademoiselle came scurrying out of their rooms in alarm; a lamp burned always on the lobby, and seeing me, they soon learned the cause of my terror.

I insisted on our knocking at Carmilla's door. Our knocking was unanswered.

It soon became a pounding and an uproar. We shrieked her name, but all was vain.

We all grew frightened, for the door was locked. We hurried back, in panic, to my room. There we rang the bell long and furiously. If my father's room had been at that side of the house, we would have called him up at once to our aid. But, alas! he was quite out of hearing, and to reach him involved an excursion for which we none of us had courage.

Servants, however, soon came running up the stairs; I had got on my dressing gown and slippers meanwhile, and my companions were already similarly furnished. Recognizing the voices of the servants on the lobby, we sallied out together; and having renewed, as fruitlessly, our summons at Carmilla's door, I ordered the men to force the lock. They did so, and we stood, holding our lights aloft, in the doorway, and so stared into the room.

We called her by name; but there was still no reply. We looked round the room. Everything was undisturbed. It was exactly in the state in which I had left it on bidding her good night. But Carmilla was gone.

Chapter 8
Search

At sight of the room, perfectly undisturbed except for our violent entrance, we began to cool a little, and soon recovered our senses sufficiently to dismiss the men. It had struck Mademoiselle that possibly Carmilla had been wakened by the uproar at her door, and in her first panic had jumped from her bed, and hid herself in a press, or behind a curtain, from which she could not, of course, emerge until the majordomo and his myrmidons had withdrawn. We now recommenced our search, and began to call her name again.

It was all to no purpose. Our perplexity and agitation increased. We examined the windows, but they were secured. I implored of Carmilla, if she had concealed herself, to play this cruel trick no longer — to come out and to end our anxieties. It was all useless. I was by this time convinced that she was not in the room, nor in the dressing room, the door of which was still locked on this side. She could not have passed it. I was utterly puzzled. Had Carmilla discovered one of those secret passages which the old housekeeper said were known to exist in the schloss, although the tradition of their exact situation had been lost? A little time would, no doubt, explain all — utterly perplexed as, for the present, we were.

It was past four o'clock, and I preferred passing the remaining hours of darkness in Madame's room. Daylight brought no solution of the difficulty.

The whole household, with my father at its head, was in a state of agitation next morning. Every part of the chateau was searched. The grounds were explored. No trace of the missing lady could be discovered. The stream was about to be dragged; my father was in distraction; what a tale to have to tell the poor girl's mother on her return. I, too, was almost beside myself, though my grief was quite of a different kind.

The morning was passed in alarm and excitement. It was now one o'clock, and still no tidings. I ran up to Carmilla's room, and found her standing at her dressing table. I was astounded. I could not believe my eyes. She beckoned me to her with her pretty finger, in silence. Her face expressed extreme fear.

I ran to her in an ecstasy of joy; I kissed and embraced her again and again. I ran to the bell and rang it vehemently, to bring others to the spot who might at once relieve my father's anxiety.

"Dear Carmilla, what has become of you all this time? We have been in agonies of anxiety about you," I exclaimed. "Where have you been? How did you come back?"

"Last night has been a night of wonders," she said.

"For mercy's sake, explain all you can."

"It was past two last night," she said, "when I went to sleep as usual in my bed, with my doors locked, that of the dressing room, and that opening upon the gallery. My sleep was uninterrupted, and, so far as I know, dreamless; but I woke just now on the sofa in the dressing room there, and I found the door between the rooms open, and the other door forced. How could all this have happened without my being wakened? It must have been accompanied with a great deal of noise, and I am particularly easily wakened; and how could I have been carried out of my bed without my sleep having been interrupted, I whom the slightest stir startles?"

By this time, Madame, Mademoiselle, my father, and a number of the servants were in the room. Carmilla was, of course, overwhelmed with inquiries, congratulations, and welcomes. She had but one story to tell, and seemed the least able of all the party to suggest any way of accounting for what had happened.

My father took a turn up and down the room, thinking. I saw Carmilla's eye follow him for a moment with a sly, dark glance.

When my father had sent the servants away, Mademoiselle having gone in search of a little bottle of valerian and salvolatile, and there being no one now in the room with Carmilla, except my father, Madame, and myself, he came to her thoughtfully, took her hand very kindly, led her to the sofa, and sat down beside her.

"Will you forgive me, my dear, if I risk a conjecture, and ask a question?"

"Who can have a better right?" she said. "Ask what you please, and I will tell you everything. But my story is simply one of bewilderment and darkness. I know absolutely nothing. Put any question you please, but you know, of course, the limitations mamma has placed me under."

"Perfectly, my dear child. I need not approach the topics on which she desires our silence. Now, the marvel of last night consists in your having been removed from your bed and your room, without being wakened, and this removal having occurred apparently while the windows were still secured, and the two doors locked upon the inside. I will tell you my theory and ask you a question."

Carmilla was leaning on her hand dejectedly; Madame and I were listening breathlessly.

"Now, my question is this. Have you ever been suspected of walking in your sleep?"

"Never, since I was very young indeed."

"But you did walk in your sleep when you were young?"

"Yes; I know I did. I have been told so often by my old nurse."

My father smiled and nodded.

"Well, what has happened is this. You got up in your sleep, unlocked the door, not leaving the key, as usual, in the lock, but taking it out and locking it on the outside; you again took the key out, and carried it away with you to someone of the five-and-twenty rooms on this floor, or perhaps upstairs or downstairs. There are so many rooms and closets, so much heavy furniture, and such accumulations of lumber, that it would require a week to search this old house thoroughly. Do you see, now, what I mean?"

"I do, but not all," she answered.

"And how, papa, do you account for her finding herself on the sofa in the dressing room, which we had searched so carefully?"

"She came there after you had searched it, still in her sleep, and at last awoke spontaneously, and was as much surprised to find herself where she was as any one else. I wish all mysteries were as easily and innocently explained as yours, Carmilla," he said, laughing. "And so we may congratulate ourselves on the certainty that the most natural explanation of the occurrence is one that involves no drugging, no tampering with locks, no burglars, or poisoners, or witches — nothing that need alarm Carmilla, or anyone else, for our safety."

Carmilla was looking charmingly. Nothing could be more beautiful than her tints. Her beauty was, I think, enhanced by that graceful languor that was peculiar to her. I think my father was silently contrasting her looks with mine, for he said:

"I wish my poor Laura was looking more like herself"; and he sighed.

So our alarms were happily ended, and Carmilla restored to her friends.

Chapter 9
The Doctor

As Carmilla would not hear of an attendant sleeping in her room, my father arranged that a servant should sleep outside her door, so that she would not attempt to make another such excursion without being arrested at her own door.

That night passed quietly; and next morning early, the doctor, whom my father had sent for without telling me a word about it, arrived to see me.

Madame accompanied me to the library; and there the grave little doctor, with white hair and spectacles, whom I mentioned before, was waiting to receive me.

I told him my story, and as I proceeded he grew graver and graver.

We were standing, he and I, in the recess of one of the windows, facing one another. When my statement was over, he leaned with his shoulders against the wall, and with his eyes fixed on me earnestly, with an interest in which was a dash of horror.

After a minute's reflection, he asked Madame if he could see my father.

He was sent for accordingly, and as he entered, smiling, he said:

"I dare say, doctor, you are going to tell me that I am an old fool for having brought you here; I hope I am."

But his smile faded into shadow as the doctor, with a very grave face, beckoned him to him.

He and the doctor talked for some time in the same recess where I had just conferred with the physician. It seemed an earnest and argumentative conversation. The room is very large, and I and Madame stood together, burning with curiosity, at the farther end. Not a word could we hear, however, for they spoke in a very low tone, and the deep recess of the window quite concealed the doctor from view, and very nearly my father, whose foot, arm, and shoulder only could we see; and the voices were, I suppose, all the less audible for the sort of closet which the thick wall and window formed.

After a time my father's face looked into the room; it was pale, thoughtful, and, I fancied, agitated.

"Laura, dear, come here for a moment. Madame, we shan't trouble you, the doctor says, at present."

Accordingly I approached, for the first time a little alarmed; for, although I felt very weak, I did not feel ill; and strength, one always fancies, is a thing that may be picked up when we please.

My father held out his hand to me, as I drew near, but he was looking at the doctor, and he said:

"It certainly is very odd; I don't understand it quite. Laura, come here, dear; now attend to Doctor Spielsberg, and recollect yourself."

"You mentioned a sensation like that of two needles piercing the skin, somewhere about your neck, on the night when you experienced your first horrible dream. Is there still any soreness?"

"None at all," I answered.

"Can you indicate with your finger about the point at which you think this occurred?"

"Very little below my throat — here," I answered.

I wore a morning dress, which covered the place I pointed to.

"Now you can satisfy yourself," said the doctor. "You won't mind your papa's lowering your dress a very little. It is necessary, to detect a symptom of the complaint under which you have been suffering."

I acquiesced. It was only an inch or two below the edge of my collar.

"God bless me! — so it is," exclaimed my father, growing pale.

"You see it now with your own eyes," said the doctor, with a gloomy triumph.

"What is it?" I exclaimed, beginning to be frightened.

"Nothing, my dear young lady, but a small blue spot, about the size of the tip of your little finger; and now," he continued, turning to papa, "the question is what is best to be done?"

"Is there any danger?" I urged, in great trepidation.

"I trust not, my dear," answered the doctor. "I don't see why you should not recover. I don't see why you should not begin immediately to get better. That is the point at which the sense of strangulation begins?"

"Yes," I answered.

"And — recollect as well as you can — the same point was a kind of center of that thrill which you described just now, like the current of a cold stream running against you?"

"It may have been; I think it was."

"Ay, you see?" he added, turning to my father. "Shall I say a word to Madame?"

"Certainly," said my father.

He called Madame to him, and said:

"I find my young friend here far from well. It won't be of any great consequence, I hope; but it will be necessary that some steps be taken, which I will explain by-and-by; but in the meantime, Madame, you will be so good as not to let Miss Laura be alone for one moment. That is the only direction I need give for the present. It is indispensable."

"We may rely upon your kindness, Madame, I know," added my father.

Madame satisfied him eagerly.

"And you, dear Laura, I know you will observe the doctor's direction."

"I shall have to ask your opinion upon another patient, whose symptoms slightly resemble those of my daughter, that have just been detailed to you — very much milder in degree, but I believe quite of the same sort. She is a young lady — our guest; but as you say you will be passing this way again this evening, you can't do better than take your supper here, and you can then see her. She does not come down till the afternoon."

"I thank you," said the doctor. "I shall be with you, then, at about seven this evening."

And then they repeated their directions to me and to Madame, and with this parting charge my father left us, and walked out with the doctor; and I saw them pacing together up and down between the road and the moat, on the grassy platform in front of the castle, evidently absorbed in earnest conversation.

The doctor did not return. I saw him mount his horse there, take his leave, and ride away eastward through the forest.

Nearly at the same time I saw the man arrive from Dranfield with the letters, and dismount and hand the bag to my father.

In the meantime, Madame and I were both busy, lost in conjecture as to the reasons of the singular and earnest direction which the doctor and my father had concurred in imposing. Madame, as she afterwards told me, was afraid the doctor apprehended a sudden seizure, and that, without prompt assistance, I might either lose my life in a fit, or at least be seriously hurt.

The interpretation did not strike me; and I fancied, perhaps luckily for my nerves, that the arrangement was prescribed simply to secure a companion, who would prevent my taking too much exercise, or eating unripe fruit, or doing any of the fifty foolish things to which young people are supposed to be prone.

About half an hour after my father came in — he had a letter in his hand — and said:

"This letter had been delayed; it is from General Spielsdorf. He might have been here yesterday, he may not come till tomorrow or he may be here today."

He put the open letter into my hand; but he did not look pleased, as he used when a guest, especially one so much loved as the General, was coming.

On the contrary, he looked as if he wished him at the bottom of the Red Sea. There was plainly something on his mind which he did not choose to divulge.

"Papa, darling, will you tell me this?" said I, suddenly laying my hand on his arm, and looking, I am sure, imploringly in his face.

"Perhaps," he answered, smoothing my hair caressingly over my eyes.

"Does the doctor think me very ill?"

"No, dear; he thinks, if right steps are taken, you will be quite well again, at least, on the high road to a complete recovery, in a day or two," he answered, a little dryly. "I wish our good friend, the General, had chosen any other time; that is, I wish you had been perfectly well to receive him."

"But do tell me, papa" I insisted, "what does he think is the matter with me?"

"Nothing; you must not plague me with questions," he answered, with more irritation than I ever remember him to have displayed before; and seeing that I looked wounded, I suppose, he kissed me, and added, "You shall know all about it in a day or two; that is, all that I know. In the meantime you are not to trouble your head about it."

He turned and left the room, but came back before I had done wondering and puzzling over the oddity of all this; it was merely to say that he was going to Karnstein, and had ordered the carriage to be ready at twelve, and that I and Madame should accompany him; he was going to see priest who lived near those picturesque grounds, upon business, and as Carmilla had never seen them, she could follow, when she came down, with Mademoiselle, who would bring materials for what you call a picnic, which might be laid for us in the ruined castle.

At twelve o'clock, accordingly, I was ready, and not long after, my father, Madame and I set out upon our projected drive.

Passing the drawbridge we turn to the right, and follow the road over the steep Gothic bridge, westward, to reach the deserted village and ruined castle of Karnstein.

No sylvan drive can be fancied prettier. The ground breaks into gentle hills and hollows, all clothed with beautiful wood, totally destitute of the comparative formality which artificial planting and early culture and pruning impart.

The irregularities of the ground often lead the road out of its course, and cause it to wind beautifully round the sides of broken hollows and the steeper sides of the hills, among varieties of ground almost inexhaustible.

Turning one of these points, we suddenly encountered our old friend, the General, riding towards us, attended by a mounted servant. His portmanteaus were following in a hired wagon, such as we term a cart.

The General dismounted as we pulled up, and, after the usual greetings, was easily persuaded to accept the vacant seat in the carriage and send his horse on with his servant to the schloss.

Chapter 10
Bereaved

It was about ten months since we had last seen him: but that time had sufficed to make an alteration of years in his appearance. He had grown thinner; something of gloom and anxiety had taken the place of that cordial serenity which used to characterize his features. His dark blue eyes, always penetrating, now gleamed with a sterner light from under his shaggy grey eyebrows. It was not such a change as grief alone usually induces, and angrier passions seemed to have had their share in bringing it about.

We had not long resumed our drive, when the General began to talk, with his usual soldierly directness, of the bereavement, as he termed it, which he had sustained in the death of his beloved niece and ward; and he then broke out in a tone of intense bitterness and fury, inveighing against the "hellish arts" to which she had fallen a victim, and expressing, with more exasperation than piety, his wonder that Heaven should tolerate so monstrous an indulgence of the lusts and malignity of hell.

My father, who saw at once that something very extraordinary had befallen, asked him, if not too painful to him, to detail the circumstances which he thought justified the strong terms in which he expressed himself.

"I should tell you all with pleasure," said the General, "but you would not believe me."

"Why should I not?" he asked.

"Because," he answered testily, "you believe in nothing but what consists with your own prejudices and illusions. I remember when I was like you, but I have learned better."

"Try me," said my father; "I am not such a dogmatist as you suppose. Besides which, I very well know that you generally require proof for what you believe, and am, therefore, very strongly predisposed to respect your conclusions."

"You are right in supposing that I have not been led lightly into a belief in the marvelous — for what I have experienced is marvelous — and I have been forced by extraordinary evidence to credit that which ran counter, diametrically, to all my theories. I have been made the dupe of a preternatural conspiracy."

Notwithstanding his professions of confidence in the General's penetration, I saw my father, at this point, glance at the General, with, as I thought, a marked suspicion of his sanity.

The General did not see it, luckily. He was looking gloomily and curiously into the glades and vistas of the woods that were opening before us.

"You are going to the Ruins of Karnstein?" he said. "Yes, it is a lucky coincidence; do you know I was going to ask you to bring me there to inspect them. I have a special object in exploring. There is a ruined chapel, ain't there, with a great many tombs of that extinct family?"

"So there are — highly interesting," said my father. "I hope you are thinking of claiming the title and estates?"

My father said this gaily, but the General did not recollect the laugh, or even the smile, which courtesy exacts for a friend's joke; on the contrary, he looked grave and even fierce, ruminating on a matter that stirred his anger and horror.

"Something very different," he said, gruffly. "I mean to unearth some of those fine people. I hope, by God's blessing, to accomplish a pious sacrilege here, which will relieve our earth of certain monsters, and enable honest people to sleep in their beds without being assailed by murderers. I have strange things to tell you, my dear friend, such as I myself would have scouted as incredible a few months since."

My father looked at him again, but this time not with a glance of suspicion — with an eye, rather, of keen intelligence and alarm.

"The house of Karnstein," he said, "has been long extinct: a hundred years at least. My dear wife was maternally descended from the Karnsteins. But the name and title have long ceased to exist. The castle is a ruin; the very village is deserted; it is fifty years since the smoke of a chimney was seen there; not a roof left."

"Quite true. I have heard a great deal about that since I last saw you; a great deal that will astonish you. But I had better relate everything in the order in which it occurred," said the General. "You saw my dear ward — my child, I may call her. No creature could have been more beautiful, and only three months ago none more blooming."

"Yes, poor thing! when I saw her last she certainly was quite lovely," said my father. "I was grieved and shocked more than I can tell you, my dear friend; I knew what a blow it was to you."

He took the General's hand, and they exchanged a kind pressure. Tears gathered in the old soldier's eyes. He did not seek to conceal them. He said:

"We have been very old friends; I knew you would feel for me, childless as I am. She had become an object of very near interest to me, and repaid my care by an affection that cheered my home and made my life happy. That is all gone. The years that remain to me on earth may not be very long; but by God's mercy I hope to accomplish a service to mankind before I die, and to subserve the vengeance of Heaven upon the fiends who have murdered my poor child in the spring of her hopes and beauty!"

"You said, just now, that you intended relating everything as it occurred," said my father. "Pray do; I assure you that it is not mere curiosity that prompts me."

By this time we had reached the point at which the Drunstall road, by which the General had come, diverges from the road which we were traveling to Karnstein.

"How far is it to the ruins?" inquired the General, looking anxiously forward.

"About half a league," answered my father. "Pray let us hear the story you were so good as to promise."

Chapter 11
The Story

"With all my heart," said the General, with an effort; and after a short pause in which to arrange his subject, he commenced one of the strangest narratives I ever heard.

"My dear child was looking forward with great pleasure to the visit you had been so good as to arrange for her to your charming daughter." Here he made me a gallant but melancholy bow. "In the meantime we had an invitation to my old friend the Count Carlsfeld, whose schloss is about six leagues to the other side of Karnstein. It was to attend the series of fetes which, you remember, were given by him in honor of his illustrious visitor, the Grand Duke Charles."

"Yes; and very splendid, I believe, they were," said my father.

"Princely! But then his hospitalities are quite regal. He has Aladdin's lamp. The night from which my sorrow dates was devoted to a magnificent masquerade. The grounds were thrown open, the trees hung with colored lamps. There was such a display of fireworks as Paris itself had never witnessed. And such music — music, you know, is my weakness — such ravishing music! The finest instrumental band, perhaps, in the world, and the finest singers who could be collected from all the great operas in Europe. As you wandered through these fantastically illuminated grounds, the moon-lighted chateau throwing a rosy light from its long rows of windows, you would suddenly hear these ravishing voices stealing from the silence of some grove, or rising from boats upon the lake. I felt myself, as I looked and listened, carried back into the romance and poetry of my early youth.

"When the fireworks were ended, and the ball beginning, we returned to the noble suite of rooms that were thrown open to the dancers. A masked ball, you know, is a beautiful sight; but so brilliant a spectacle of the kind I never saw before.

"It was a very aristocratic assembly. I was myself almost the only 'nobody' present.

"My dear child was looking quite beautiful. She wore no mask. Her excitement and delight added an unspeakable charm to her features, always lovely. I remarked a young lady, dressed magnificently, but wearing a mask, who appeared to me to be observing my ward with extraordinary interest. I had seen her, earlier in the evening, in the great hall, and again, for a few minutes, walking near us, on the terrace under the castle windows, similarly employed. A lady, also masked, richly and gravely dressed, and with a stately air, like a person of rank, accompanied her as a chaperon.

"Had the young lady not worn a mask, I could, of course, have been much more certain upon the question whether she was really watching my poor darling.

"I am now well assured that she was.

"We were now in one of the salons. My poor dear child had been dancing, and was resting a little in one of the chairs near the door; I was standing near. The two ladies I have mentioned had approached and the younger took the chair next my ward; while her companion stood beside me, and for a little time addressed herself, in a low tone, to her charge.

"Availing herself of the privilege of her mask, she turned to me, and in the tone of an old friend, and calling me by my name, opened a conversation with me, which piqued my curiosity a good deal. She referred to many scenes where she had met me — at Court, and at distinguished houses. She alluded to little incidents which I had long ceased to think of, but which, I found, had only lain in abeyance in my memory, for they instantly started into life at her touch.

"I became more and more curious to ascertain who she was, every moment. She parried my attempts to discover very adroitly and pleasantly. The knowledge she showed of many passages in my life seemed to me all but unaccountable; and she appeared to take a not unnatural pleasure in foiling my curiosity, and in seeing me flounder in my eager perplexity, from one conjecture to another.

"In the meantime the young lady, whom her mother called by the odd name of Millarca, when she once or twice addressed her, had, with the same ease and grace, got into conversation with my ward.

"She introduced herself by saying that her mother was a very old acquaintance of mine. She spoke of the agreeable audacity which a mask rendered practicable; she talked like a friend; she admired her dress, and insinuated very prettily her admiration of her beauty. She amused her with laughing criticisms upon the people who crowded the ballroom, and laughed at my poor child's fun. She was very witty and lively when she pleased, and after a time they had grown very good friends, and the young stranger lowered her mask, displaying a remarkably beautiful face. I had never seen it before, neither had my dear child. But though it was new to us, the features were so engaging, as well as lovely, that it was impossible not to feel the attraction powerfully. My poor girl did so. I never saw anyone more taken with another at first sight, unless, indeed, it was the stranger herself, who seemed quite to have lost her heart to her.

"In the meantime, availing myself of the license of a masquerade, I put not a few questions to the elder lady.

"'You have puzzled me utterly,' I said, laughing. 'Is that not enough? Won't you, now, consent to stand on equal terms, and do me the kindness to remove your mask?'

"'Can any request be more unreasonable?' she replied. 'Ask a lady to yield an advantage! Beside, how do you know you should recognize me? Years make changes.'

"'As you see,' I said, with a bow, and, I suppose, a rather melancholy little laugh.

"'As philosophers tell us,' she said; 'and how do you know that a sight of my face would help you?'

"'I should take chance for that,' I answered. 'It is vain trying to make yourself out an old woman; your figure betrays you.'

"'Years, nevertheless, have passed since I saw you, rather since you saw me, for that is what I am considering. Millarca, there, is my daughter; I cannot then be young, even in the opinion of people whom time has taught to be indulgent, and I may not like to be compared with what you remember me. You have no mask to remove. You can offer me nothing in exchange.'

"'My petition is to your pity, to remove it.'

"'And mine to yours, to let it stay where it is,' she replied.

"'Well, then, at least you will tell me whether you are French or German; you speak both languages so perfectly.'

"'I don't think I shall tell you that, General; you intend a surprise, and are meditating the particular point of attack.'

"'At all events, you won't deny this,' I said, 'that being honored by your permission to converse, I ought to know how to address you. Shall I say Madame la Comtesse?'

"She laughed, and she would, no doubt, have met me with another evasion — if, indeed, I can treat any occurrence in an interview every circumstance of which was prearranged, as I now believe, with the profoundest cunning, as liable to be modified by accident.

"'As to that,' she began; but she was interrupted, almost as she opened her lips, by a gentleman, dressed in black, who looked particularly elegant and distinguished, with this drawback, that his face was the most deadly pale I ever saw, except in death. He was in no masquerade — in the plain evening dress of a gentleman; and he said, without a smile, but with a courtly and unusually low bow: —

"'Will Madame la Comtesse permit me to say a very few words which may interest her?'

"The lady turned quickly to him, and touched her lip in token of silence; she then said to me, 'Keep my place for me, General; I shall return when I have said a few words.'

"And with this injunction, playfully given, she walked a little aside with the gentleman in black, and talked for some minutes, apparently very earnestly. They then walked away slowly together in the crowd, and I lost them for some minutes.

"I spent the interval in cudgeling my brains for a conjecture as to the identity of the lady who seemed to remember me so kindly, and I was thinking of turning about and joining in the conversation between my pretty ward and the Countess's daughter, and trying whether, by the time she returned, I might not have a surprise in store for her, by having her name, title, chateau, and estates at my fingers' ends. But at this moment she returned, accompanied by the pale man in black, who said:

"'I shall return and inform Madame la Comtesse when her carriage is at the door.'

"He withdrew with a bow."

Chapter 12
A Petition

"'Then we are to lose Madame la Comtesse, but I hope only for a few hours,' I said, with a low bow.

"'It may be that only, or it may be a few weeks. It was very unlucky his speaking to me just now as he did. Do you now know me?'

"I assured her I did not.

"'You shall know me,' she said, 'but not at present. We are older and better friends than, perhaps, you suspect. I cannot yet declare myself. I shall in three weeks pass your beautiful schloss, about which I have been making enquiries. I shall then look in upon you for an hour or two, and renew a friendship which I never think of without a thousand pleasant recollections. This moment a piece of news has reached me like a thunderbolt. I must set out now, and travel by a devious route, nearly a hundred miles, with all the dispatch I can possibly make. My perplexities multiply. I am only deterred by the compulsory reserve I practice as to my name from making a very singular request of you. My poor child has not quite recovered her strength. Her horse fell with her, at a hunt which she had ridden out to witness, her nerves have not yet recovered the shock, and our physician says that she must on no account exert herself for some time to come. We came here, in consequence, by very easy stages — hardly six leagues a day. I must now travel day and night, on a mission of life and death — a mission the critical and momentous nature of which I shall be able to explain to you when we meet, as I hope we shall, in a few weeks, without the necessity of any concealment.'

"She went on to make her petition, and it was in the tone of a person from whom such a request amounted to conferring, rather than seeking a favor.

"This was only in manner, and, as it seemed, quite unconsciously. Than the terms in which it was expressed, nothing could be more deprecatory. It was simply that I would consent to take charge of her daughter during her absence.

"This was, all things considered, a strange, not to say, an audacious request. She in some sort disarmed me, by stating and admitting everything that could be urged against it, and throwing herself entirely upon my chivalry. At the same moment, by a fatality that seems to have pre-determined all that happened, my poor child came to my side, and, in an undertone, besought me to invite her new friend, Millarca, to pay us a visit. She had just been sounding her, and thought, if her mamma would allow her, she would like it extremely.

"At another time I should have told her to wait a little, until, at least, we knew who they were. But I had not a moment to think in. The two ladies assailed me together, and I must confess the refined and beautiful face of the young lady, about which there was something extremely engaging, as well as the elegance and fire of high birth, determined me; and, quite overpowered, I submitted, and undertook, too easily, the care of the young lady, whom her mother called Millarca.

"The Countess beckoned to her daughter, who listened with grave attention while she told her, in general terms, how suddenly and peremptorily she had been summoned, and also of the arrangement she had made for her under my care, adding that I was one of her earliest and most valued friends.

"I made, of course, such speeches as the case seemed to call for, and found myself, on reflection, in a position which I did not half like.

"The gentleman in black returned, and very ceremoniously conducted the lady from the room.

"The demeanor of this gentleman was such as to impress me with the conviction that the Countess was a lady of very much more importance than her modest title alone might have led me to assume.

"Her last charge to me was that no attempt was to be made to learn more about her than I might have already guessed, until her return. Our distinguished host, whose guest she was, knew her reasons.

"'But here,' she said, 'neither I nor my daughter could safely remain for more than a day. I removed my mask imprudently for a moment, about an hour ago, and, too late, I fancied you saw me. So I resolved to seek an opportunity of talking a little to you. Had I found that you had seen me, I would have thrown myself on your high sense of honor to keep my secret some weeks. As it is, I am satisfied that you did not see me; but if you now suspect, or, on reflection, should suspect, who I am, I commit myself, in like manner, entirely to your honor. My daughter will observe the same secrecy, and I well know that you will, from time to time, remind her, lest she should thoughtlessly disclose it.'

"She whispered a few words to her daughter, kissed her hurriedly twice, and went away, accompanied by the pale gentleman in black, and disappeared in the crowd.

"'In the next room,' said Millarca, 'there is a window that looks upon the hall door. I should like to see the last of mamma, and to kiss my hand to her.'

"We assented, of course, and accompanied her to the window. We looked out, and saw a handsome old-fashioned carriage, with a troop of couriers and footmen. We saw the slim figure of the pale gentleman in black, as he held a thick velvet cloak, and placed it about her shoulders and threw the hood over her head. She nodded to him, and just touched his hand with hers. He bowed low repeatedly as the door closed, and the carriage began to move.

"'She is gone,' said Millarca, with a sigh.

"'She is gone,' I repeated to myself, for the first time — in the hurried moments that had elapsed since my consent — reflecting upon the folly of my act.

"'She did not look up,' said the young lady, plaintively.

"'The Countess had taken off her mask, perhaps, and did not care to show her face,' I said; 'and she could not know that you were in the window.'

"She sighed, and looked in my face. She was so beautiful that I relented. I was sorry I had for a moment repented of my hospitality, and I determined to make her amends for the unavowed churlishness of my reception.

"The young lady, replacing her mask, joined my ward in persuading me to return to the grounds, where the concert was soon to be renewed. We did so, and walked up and down the terrace that lies under the castle windows.

"Millarca became very intimate with us, and amused us with lively descriptions and stories of most of the great people whom we saw upon the terrace. I liked her more and more every minute. Her gossip without being ill-natured, was extremely diverting to me, who had been so long out of the great world. I thought what life she would give to our sometimes lonely evenings at home.

"This ball was not over until the morning sun had almost reached the horizon. It pleased the Grand Duke to dance till then, so loyal people could not go away, or think of bed.

"We had just got through a crowded saloon, when my ward asked me what had become of Millarca. I thought she had been by her side, and she fancied she was by mine. The fact was, we had lost her.

"All my efforts to find her were vain. I feared that she had mistaken, in the confusion of a momentary separation from us, other people for her new friends, and had, possibly, pursued and lost them in the extensive grounds which were thrown open to us.

"Now, in its full force, I recognized a new folly in my having undertaken the charge of a young lady without so much as knowing her name; and fettered as I was by promises, of the reasons for imposing which I knew nothing, I could not even point my inquiries by saying that the missing young lady was the daughter of the Countess who had taken her departure a few hours before.

"Morning broke. It was clear daylight before I gave up my search. It was not till near two o'clock next day that we heard anything of my missing charge.

"At about that time a servant knocked at my niece's door, to say that he had been earnestly requested by a young lady, who appeared to be in great distress, to make out where she could find the General Baron Spielsdorf and the young lady his daughter, in whose charge she had been left by her mother.

"There could be no doubt, notwithstanding the slight inaccuracy, that our young friend had turned up; and so she had. Would to heaven we had lost her!

"She told my poor child a story to account for her having failed to recover us for so long. Very late, she said, she had got to the housekeeper's bedroom in despair of finding us, and had then fallen into a deep sleep which, long as it was, had hardly sufficed to recruit her strength after the fatigues of the ball.

"That day Millarca came home with us. I was only too happy, after all, to have secured so charming a companion for my dear girl."

Chapter 13
The Woodman

"There soon, however, appeared some drawbacks. In the first place, Millarca complained of extreme languor — the weakness that remained after her late illness — and she never emerged from her room till the afternoon was pretty far advanced. In the next place, it was accidentally discovered, although she always locked her door on the inside, and never disturbed the key from its place till she admitted the maid to assist at her toilet, that she was undoubtedly sometimes absent from her room in the very early morning, and at various times later in the day, before she wished it to be understood that she was stirring. She was repeatedly seen from the windows of the schloss, in the first faint grey of the morning, walking through the trees, in an easterly direction, and looking like a person in a trance. This convinced me that she walked in her sleep. But this hypothesis did not solve the puzzle. How did she pass out from her room, leaving the door locked on the inside? How did she escape from the house without unbarring door or window?

"In the midst of my perplexities, an anxiety of a far more urgent kind presented itself.

"My dear child began to lose her looks and health, and that in a manner so mysterious, and even horrible, that I became thoroughly frightened.

"She was at first visited by appalling dreams; then, as she fancied, by a specter, sometimes resembling Millarca, sometimes in the shape of a beast, indistinctly seen, walking round the foot of her bed, from side to side.

"Lastly came sensations. One, not unpleasant, but very peculiar, she said, resembled the flow of an icy stream against her breast. At a later time, she felt something like a pair of large needles pierce her, a little below the throat, with a very sharp pain. A few nights after, followed a gradual and convulsive sense of strangulation; then came unconsciousness."

I could hear distinctly every word the kind old General was saying, because by this time we were driving upon the short grass that spreads on either side of the road as you approach the roofless village which had not shown the smoke of a chimney for more than half a century.

You may guess how strangely I felt as I heard my own symptoms so exactly described in those which had been experienced by the poor girl who, but for the catastrophe which followed, would have been at that moment a visitor at my father's chateau. You may suppose, also, how I felt as I heard him detail habits and mysterious peculiarities which were, in fact, those of our beautiful guest, Carmilla!

A vista opened in the forest; we were on a sudden under the chimneys and gables of the ruined village, and the towers and battlements of the dismantled castle, round which gigantic trees are grouped, overhung us from a slight eminence.

In a frightened dream I got down from the carriage, and in silence, for we had each abundant matter for thinking; we soon mounted the ascent, and were among the spacious chambers, winding stairs, and dark corridors of the castle.

"And this was once the palatial residence of the Karnsteins!" said the old General at length, as from a great window he looked out across the village, and saw the wide, undulating expanse of forest. "It was a bad family, and here its bloodstained annals were written," he continued. "It is hard that they should, after death, continue to plague the human race with their atrocious lusts. That is the chapel of the Karnsteins, down there."

He pointed down to the grey walls of the Gothic building partly visible through the foliage, a little way down the steep. "And I hear the axe of a woodman," he added, "busy among the trees that surround it; he possibly may give us the information of which I am in search, and point out the grave of Mircalla, Countess of Karnstein. These rustics preserve the local traditions of great families, whose stories die out among the rich and titled so soon as the families themselves become extinct."

"We have a portrait, at home, of Mircalla, the Countess Karnstein; should you like to see it?" asked my father.

"Time enough, dear friend," replied the General. "I believe that I have seen the original; and one motive which has led me to you earlier than I at first intended, was to explore the chapel which we are now approaching."

"What! see the Countess Mircalla," exclaimed my father; "why, she has been dead more than a century!"

"Not so dead as you fancy, I am told," answered the General.

"I confess, General, you puzzle me utterly," replied my father, looking at him, I fancied, for a moment with a return of the suspicion I detected before. But although there was anger and detestation, at times, in the old General's manner, there was nothing flighty.

"There remains to me," he said, as we passed under the heavy arch of the Gothic church — for its dimensions would have justified its being so styled —"but one object which can interest me during the few years that remain to me on earth, and that is to wreak on her the vengeance which, I thank God, may still be accomplished by a mortal arm."

"What vengeance can you mean?" asked my father, in increasing amazement.

"I mean, to decapitate the monster," he answered, with a fierce flush, and a stamp that echoed mournfully through the hollow ruin, and his clenched hand was at the same moment raised, as if it grasped the handle of an axe, while he shook it ferociously in the air.

"What?" exclaimed my father, more than ever bewildered.

"To strike her head off."

"Cut her head off!"

"Aye, with a hatchet, with a spade, or with anything that can cleave through her murderous throat. You shall hear," he answered, trembling with rage. And hurrying forward he said:

"That beam will answer for a seat; your dear child is fatigued; let her be seated, and I will, in a few sentences, close my dreadful story."

The squared block of wood, which lay on the grass-grown pavement of the chapel, formed a bench on which I was very glad to seat myself, and in the meantime the General called to the woodman, who had been removing some boughs which leaned upon the old walls; and, axe in hand, the hardy old fellow stood before us.

He could not tell us anything of these monuments; but there was an old man, he said, a ranger of this forest, at present sojourning in the house of the priest, about two miles away, who could point out every monument of the old Karnstein family; and, for a trifle, he undertook to bring him back with him, if we would lend him one of our horses, in little more than half an hour.

"Have you been long employed about this forest?" asked my father of the old man.

"I have been a woodman here," he answered in his patois, "under the forester, all my days; so has my rather before me, and so on, as many generations as I can count up. I could show You the very house in the village here, in which my ancestors lived."

"How came the village to be deserted?" asked the General.

"It was troubled by revenants, sir; several were tracked to their graves, there detected by the usual tests, and extinguished in the usual way, by decapitation, by the stake, and by burning; but not until many of the villagers were killed.

"But after all these proceedings according to law," he continued —"so many graves opened, and so many vampires deprived of their horrible animation — the village was not relieved. But a Moravian nobleman, who happened to be traveling this way, heard how matters were, and being skilled — as many people are in his country — in such affairs, he offered to deliver the village from its tormentor. He did so thus: There being a bright moon that night, he ascended, shortly after sunset, the towers of the chapel here, from whence he could distinctly see the churchyard beneath him; you can see it from that window. From this point he watched until he saw the vampire come out of his grave, and place near it the linen clothes in which he had been folded, and then glide away towards the village to plague its inhabitants.

"The stranger, having seen all this, came down from the steeple, took the linen wrappings of the vampire, and carried them up to the top of the tower, which he again mounted. When the vampire returned from his prowlings and missed his clothes, he cried furiously to the Moravian, whom he saw at the summit of the tower, and who, in reply, beckoned him to ascend and take them. Whereupon the vampire, accepting his invitation, began to climb the steeple, and so soon as he had reached the battlements, the Moravian, with a stroke of his sword, clove his skull in twain, hurling him down to the churchyard, whither, descending by the winding stairs, the stranger followed and cut his head off, and next day delivered it and the body to the villagers, who duly impaled and burnt them.

"This Moravian nobleman had authority from the then head of the family to remove the tomb of Mircalla, Countess Karnstein, which he did effectually, so that in a little while its site was quite forgotten."

"Can you point out where it stood?" asked the General, eagerly.

The forester shook his head, and smiled.

"Not a soul living could tell you that now," he said; "besides, they say her body was removed; but no one is sure of that either."

Having thus spoken, as time pressed, he dropped his axe and departed, leaving us to hear the remainder of the General's strange story.

Chapter 14
The Meeting

"My beloved child," he resumed, "was now growing rapidly worse. The physician who attended her had failed to produce the slightest impression on her disease, for such I then supposed it to be. He saw my alarm, and suggested a consultation. I called in an abler physician, from Gratz.

"Several days elapsed before he arrived. He was a good and pious, as well as a leaned man. Having seen my poor ward together, they withdrew to my library to confer and discuss. I, from the adjoining room, where I awaited their summons, heard these two gentlemen's voices raised in something sharper than a strictly philosophical discussion. I knocked at the door and entered. I found the old physician from Gratz maintaining his theory. His rival was combating it with undisguised ridicule, accompanied with bursts of laughter. This unseemly manifestation subsided and the altercation ended on my entrance.

"'Sir,' said my first physician, 'my learned brother seems to think that you want a conjuror, and not a doctor.'

"'Pardon me,' said the old physician from Gratz, looking displeased, 'I shall state my own view of the case in my own way another time. I grieve, Monsieur le General, that by my skill and science I can be of no use. Before I go I shall do myself the honor to suggest something to you.'

"He seemed thoughtful, and sat down at a table and began to write.

"Profoundly disappointed, I made my bow, and as I turned to go, the other doctor pointed over his shoulder to his companion who was writing, and then, with a shrug, significantly touched his forehead.

"This consultation, then, left me precisely where I was. I walked out into the grounds, all but distracted. The doctor from Gratz, in ten or fifteen minutes, overtook me. He apologized for having followed me, but said that he could not conscientiously take his leave without a few words more. He told me that he could not be mistaken; no natural disease exhibited the same symptoms; and that death was already very near. There remained, however, a day, or possibly two, of life. If the fatal seizure were at once arrested, with great care and skill her strength might possibly return. But all hung now upon the confines of the irrevocable. One more assault might extinguish the last spark of vitality which is, every moment, ready to die.

"'And what is the nature of the seizure you speak of?' I entreated.

"'I have stated all fully in this note, which I place in your hands upon the distinct condition that you send for the nearest clergyman, and open my letter in his presence, and on no account read it till he is with you; you would despise it else, and it is a matter of life and death. Should the priest fail you, then, indeed, you may read it.'

"He asked me, before taking his leave finally, whether I would wish to see a man curiously learned upon the very subject, which, after I had read his letter, would probably interest me above all others, and he urged me earnestly to invite him to visit him there; and so took his leave.

"The ecclesiastic was absent, and I read the letter by myself. At another time, or in another case, it might have excited my ridicule. But into what quackeries will not people rush for a last chance, where all accustomed means have failed, and the life of a beloved object is at stake?

"Nothing, you will say, could be more absurd than the learned man's letter.

"It was monstrous enough to have consigned him to a madhouse. He said that the patient was suffering from the visits of a vampire! The punctures which she described as having occurred near the throat, were, he insisted, the insertion of those two long, thin, and sharp teeth which, it is well known, are peculiar to vampires; and there could be no doubt, he added, as to the well-defined presence of the small livid mark which all concurred in describing as that induced by the demon's lips, and every symptom described by the sufferer was in exact conformity with those recorded in every case of a similar visitation.

"Being myself wholly skeptical as to the existence of any such portent as the vampire, the supernatural theory of the good doctor furnished, in my opinion, but another instance of learning and intelligence oddly associated with someone hallucination. I was so miserable, however, that, rather than try nothing, I acted upon the instructions of the letter.

"I concealed myself in the dark dressing room, that opened upon the poor patient's room, in which a candle was burning, and watched there till she was fast asleep. I stood at the door, peeping through the small crevice, my sword laid on the table beside me, as my directions prescribed, until, a little after one, I saw a large black object, very ill-defined, crawl, as it seemed to me, over the foot of the bed, and swiftly spread itself up to the poor girl's throat, where it swelled, in a moment, into a great, palpitating mass.

"For a few moments I had stood petrified. I now sprang forward, with my sword in my hand. The black creature suddenly contracted towards the foot of the bed, glided over it, and, standing on the floor about a yard below the foot of the bed, with a glare of skulking ferocity and horror fixed on me, I saw Millarca. Speculating I know not what, I struck at her instantly with my sword; but I saw her standing near the door, unscathed. Horrified, I pursued, and struck again. She was gone; and my sword flew to shivers against the door.

"I can't describe to you all that passed on that horrible night. The whole house was up and stirring. The specter Millarca was gone. But her victim was sinking fast, and before the morning dawned, she died."

The old General was agitated. We did not speak to him. My father walked to some little distance, and began reading the inscriptions on the tombstones; and thus occupied, he strolled into the door of a side chapel to prosecute his researches. The General leaned against the wall, dried his eyes, and sighed heavily. I was relieved on hearing the voices of Carmilla and Madame, who were at that moment approaching. The voices died away.

In this solitude, having just listened to so strange a story, connected, as it was, with the great and titled dead, whose monuments were moldering among the dust and ivy round us, and every incident of which bore so awfully upon my own mysterious case — in this haunted spot, darkened by the towering foliage that rose on every side, dense and high above its noiseless walls — a horror began to steal over me, and my heart sank as I thought that my friends were, after all, not about to enter and disturb this triste and ominous scene.

The old General's eyes were fixed on the ground, as he leaned with his hand upon the basement of a shattered monument.

Under a narrow, arched doorway, surmounted by one of those demoniacal grotesques in which the cynical and ghastly fancy of old Gothic carving delights, I saw very gladly the beautiful face and figure of Carmilla enter the shadowy chapel.

I was just about to rise and speak, and nodded smiling, in answer to her peculiarly engaging smile; when with a cry, the old man by my side caught up the woodman's hatchet, and started forward. On seeing him a brutalized change came over her features. It was an instantaneous and horrible transformation, as she made a crouching step backwards. Before I could utter a scream, he struck at her with all his force, but she dived under his blow, and unscathed, caught him in her tiny grasp by the wrist. He struggled for a moment to release his arm, but his hand opened, the axe fell to the ground, and the girl was gone.

He staggered against the wall. His grey hair stood upon his head, and a moisture shone over his face, as if he were at the point of death.

The frightful scene had passed in a moment. The first thing I recollect after, is Madame standing before me, and impatiently repeating again and again, the question, "Where is Mademoiselle Carmilla?"

I answered at length, "I don't know — I can't tell — she went there," and I pointed to the door through which Madame had just entered; "only a minute or two since."

"But I have been standing there, in the passage, ever since Mademoiselle Carmilla entered; and she did not return."

She then began to call "Carmilla," through every door and passage and from the windows, but no answer came.

"She called herself Carmilla?" asked the General, still agitated.

"Carmilla, yes," I answered.

"Aye," he said; "that is Millarca. That is the same person who long ago was called Mircalla, Countess Karnstein. Depart from this accursed ground, my poor child, as quickly as you can. Drive to the clergyman's house, and stay there till we come. Begone! May you never behold Carmilla more; you will not find her here."

Chapter 15
Ordeal and Execution

As he spoke one of the strangest looking men I ever beheld entered the chapel at the door through which Carmilla had made her entrance and her exit. He was tall, narrow-chested, stooping, with high shoulders, and dressed in black. His face was brown and dried in with deep furrows; he wore an oddly-shaped hat with a broad leaf. His hair, long and grizzled, hung on his shoulders. He wore a pair of gold spectacles, and walked slowly, with an odd shambling gait, with his face sometimes turned up to the sky, and sometimes bowed down towards the ground, seemed to wear a perpetual smile; his long thin arms were swinging, and his lank hands, in old black gloves ever so much too wide for them, waving and gesticulating in utter abstraction.

"The very man!" exclaimed the General, advancing with manifest delight. "My dear Baron, how happy I am to see you, I had no hope of meeting you so soon." He signed to my father, who had by this time returned, and leading the fantastic old gentleman, whom he called the Baron to meet him. He introduced him formally, and they at once entered into earnest conversation. The stranger took a roll of paper from his pocket, and spread it on the worn surface of a tomb that stood by. He had a pencil case in his fingers, with which he traced imaginary lines from point to point on the paper, which from their often glancing from it, together, at certain points of the building, I concluded to be a plan of the chapel. He accompanied, what I may term, his lecture, with occasional readings from a dirty little book, whose yellow leaves were closely written over.

They sauntered together down the side aisle, opposite to the spot where I was standing, conversing as they went; then they began measuring distances by paces, and finally they all stood together, facing a piece of the sidewall, which they began to examine with great minuteness; pulling off the ivy that clung over it, and rapping the plaster with the ends of their sticks, scraping here, and knocking there. At length they ascertained the existence of a broad marble tablet, with letters carved in relief upon it.

With the assistance of the woodman, who soon returned, a monumental inscription, and carved escutcheon, were disclosed. They proved to be those of the long lost monument of Mircalla, Countess Karnstein.

The old General, though not I fear given to the praying mood, raised his hands and eyes to heaven, in mute thanksgiving for some moments.

"Tomorrow," I heard him say; "the commissioner will be here, and the Inquisition will be held according to law."

Then turning to the old man with the gold spectacles, whom I have described, he shook him warmly by both hands and said:

"Baron, how can I thank you? How can we all thank you? You will have delivered this region from a plague that has scourged its inhabitants for more than a century. The horrible enemy, thank God, is at last tracked."

My father led the stranger aside, and the General followed. I know that he had led them out of hearing, that he might relate my case, and I saw them glance often quickly at me, as the discussion proceeded.

My father came to me, kissed me again and again, and leading me from the chapel, said:

"It is time to return, but before we go home, we must add to our party the good priest, who lives but a little way from this; and persuade him to accompany us to the schloss."

In this quest we were successful: and I was glad, being unspeakably fatigued when we reached home. But my satisfaction was changed to dismay, on discovering that there were no tidings of Carmilla. Of the scene that had occurred in the ruined chapel, no explanation was offered to me, and it was clear that it was a secret which my father for the present determined to keep from me.

The sinister absence of Carmilla made the remembrance of the scene more horrible to me. The arrangements for the night were singular. Two servants, and Madame were to sit up in my room that night; and the ecclesiastic with my father kept watch in the adjoining dressing room.

The priest had performed certain solemn rites that night, the purport of which I did not understand any more than I comprehended the reason of this extraordinary precaution taken for my safety during sleep.

I saw all clearly a few days later.

The disappearance of Carmilla was followed by the discontinuance of my nightly sufferings.

You have heard, no doubt, of the appalling superstition that prevails in Upper and Lower Styria, in Moravia, Silesia, in Turkish Serbia, in Poland, even in Russia; the superstition, so we must call it, of the Vampire.

If human testimony, taken with every care and solemnity, judicially, before commissions innumerable, each consisting of many members, all chosen for integrity and intelligence, and constituting reports more voluminous perhaps than exist upon any one other class of cases, is worth anything, it is difficult to deny, or even to doubt the existence of such a phenomenon as the Vampire.

For my part I have heard no theory by which to explain what I myself have witnessed and experienced, other than that supplied by the ancient and well-attested belief of the country.

The next day the formal proceedings took place in the Chapel of Karnstein.

The grave of the Countess Mircalla was opened; and the General and my father recognized each his perfidious and beautiful guest, in the face now disclosed to view. The features, though a hundred and fifty years had passed since her funeral, were tinted with the warmth of life. Her eyes were open; no cadaverous smell exhaled from the coffin. The two medical men, one officially present, the other on the part of the promoter of the inquiry, attested the marvelous fact that there was a faint but appreciable respiration, and a corresponding action of the heart. The limbs were perfectly flexible, the flesh elastic; and the leaden coffin floated with blood, in which to a depth of seven inches, the body lay immersed.

Here then, were all the admitted signs and proofs of vampirism. The body, therefore, in accordance with the ancient practice, was raised, and a sharp stake driven through the heart of the vampire, who uttered a piercing shriek at the moment, in all respects such as might escape from a living person in the last agony. Then the head was struck off, and a torrent of blood flowed from the severed neck. The body and head was next placed on a pile of wood, and reduced to ashes, which were thrown upon the river and borne away, and that territory has never since been plagued by the visits of a vampire.

My father has a copy of the report of the Imperial Commission, with the signatures of all who were present at these proceedings, attached in verification of the statement. It is from this official paper that I have summarized my account of this last shocking scene.

Conclusion

I write all this you suppose with composure. But far from it; I cannot think of it without agitation. Nothing but your earnest desire so repeatedly expressed, could have induced me to sit down to a task that has unstrung my nerves for months to come, and reinduced a shadow of the unspeakable horror which years after my deliverance continued to make my days and nights dreadful, and solitude insupportably terrific.

Let me add a word or two about that quaint Baron Vordenburg, to whose curious lore we were indebted for the discovery of the Countess Mircalla's grave.

He had taken up his abode in Gratz, where, living upon a mere pittance, which was all that remained to him of the once princely estates of his family, in Upper Styria, he devoted himself to the minute and laborious investigation of the marvelously authenticated tradition of Vampirism. He had at his fingers' ends all the great and little works upon the subject.

"Magia Posthuma," "Phlegon de Mirabilibus," "Augustinus de cura pro Mortuis," "Philosophicae et Christianae Cogitationes de Vampiris," by John Christofer Herenberg; and a thousand others, among which I remember only a few of those which he lent to my father. He had a voluminous digest of all the judicial cases, from which he had extracted a system of principles that appear to govern — some always, and others occasionally only — the condition of the vampire. I may mention, in passing, that the deadly pallor attributed to that sort of revenants, is a mere melodramatic fiction. They present, in the grave, and when they show themselves in human society, the appearance of healthy life. When disclosed to light in their coffins, they exhibit all the symptoms that are enumerated as those which proved the vampire-life of the long-dead Countess Karnstein.

How they escape from their graves and return to them for certain hours every day, without displacing the clay or leaving any trace of disturbance in the state of the coffin or the cerements, has always been admitted to be utterly inexplicable. The amphibious existence of the vampire is sustained by daily renewed slumber in the grave. Its horrible lust for living blood supplies the vigor of its waking existence. The vampire is prone to be fascinated with an engrossing vehemence, resembling the passion of love, by particular persons. In pursuit of these it will exercise inexhaustible patience and stratagem, for access to a particular object may be obstructed in a hundred ways. It will never desist until it has satiated its passion, and drained the very life of its coveted victim. But it will, in these cases, husband and protract its murderous enjoyment with the refinement of an epicure, and heighten it by the gradual approaches of an artful courtship. In these cases it seems to yearn for something like sympathy and consent. In ordinary ones it goes direct to its object, overpowers with violence, and strangles and exhausts often at a single feast.

The vampire is, apparently, subject, in certain situations, to special conditions. In the particular instance of which I have given you a relation, Mircalla seemed to be limited to a name which, if not her real one, should at least reproduce, without the omission or addition of a single letter, those, as we say, anagrammatically, which compose it.

Carmilla did this; so did Millarca.

My father related to the Baron Vordenburg, who remained with us for two or three weeks after the expulsion of Carmilla, the story about the Moravian nobleman and the vampire at Karnstein churchyard, and then he asked the Baron how he had discovered the exact position of the long-concealed tomb of the Countess Mircalla? The Baron's grotesque features puckered up into a mysterious smile; he looked down, still smiling on his worn spectacle case and fumbled with it. Then looking up, he said:

"I have many journals, and other papers, written by that remarkable man; the most curious among them is one treating of the visit of which you speak, to Karnstein. The tradition, of course, discolors and distorts a little. He might have been termed a Moravian nobleman, for he had changed his abode to that territory, and was, beside, a noble. But he was, in truth, a native of Upper Styria. It is enough to say that in very early youth he had been a passionate and favored lover of the beautiful Mircalla, Countess Karnstein. Her early death plunged him into inconsolable grief. It is the nature of vampires to increase and multiply, but according to an ascertained and ghostly law.

"Assume, at starting, a territory perfectly free from that pest. How does it begin, and how does it multiply itself? I will tell you. A person, more or less wicked, puts an end to himself. A suicide, under certain circumstances, becomes a vampire. That specter visits living people in their slumbers; they die, and almost invariably, in the grave, develop into vampires. This happened in the case of the beautiful Mircalla, who was haunted by one of those demons. My ancestor, Vordenburg, whose title I still bear, soon discovered this, and in the course of the studies to which he devoted himself, learned a great deal more.

"Among other things, he concluded that suspicion of vampirism would probably fall, sooner or later, upon the dead Countess, who in life had been his idol. He conceived a horror, be she what she might, of her remains being profaned by the outrage of a posthumous execution. He has left a curious paper to prove that the vampire, on its expulsion from its amphibious existence, is projected into a far more horrible life; and he resolved to save his once beloved Mircalla from this.

"He adopted the stratagem of a journey here, a pretended removal of her remains, and a real obliteration of her monument. When age had stolen upon him, and from the vale of years, he looked back on the scenes he was leaving, he considered, in a different spirit, what he had done, and a horror took possession of him. He made the tracings and notes which have guided me to the very spot, and drew up a confession of the deception that he had practiced. If he had intended any further action in this matter, death prevented him; and the hand of a remote descendant has, too late for many, directed the pursuit to the lair of the beast."

We talked a little more, and among other things he said was this:

"One sign of the vampire is the power of the hand. The slender hand of Mircalla closed like a vice of steel on the General's wrist when he raised the hatchet to strike. But its power is not confined to its grasp; it leaves a numbness in the limb it seizes, which is slowly, if ever, recovered from."

The following Spring my father took me a tour through Italy. We remained away for more than a year. It was long before the terror of recent events subsided; and to this hour the image of Carmilla returns to memory with ambiguous alternations — sometimes the playful, languid, beautiful girl; sometimes the writhing fiend I saw in the ruined church; and often from a reverie I have started, fancying I heard the light step of Carmilla at the drawing room door.

Mrs. Dalloway

by Virginia Woolf

Mrs. Dalloway said she would buy the flowers herself.

For Lucy had her work cut out for her. The doors would be taken off their hinges; Rumpelmayer's men were coming. And then, thought Clarissa Dalloway, what a morning-fresh as if issued to children on a beach.

What a lark! What a plunge! For so it had always seemed to her, when, with a little squeak of the hinges, which she could hear now, she had burst open the French windows and plunged at Bourton into the open air. How fresh, how calm, stiller than this of course, the air was in the early morning; like the flap of a wave; the kiss of a wave; chill and sharp and yet (for a girl of eighteen as she then was) solemn, feeling as she did, standing there at the open window, that something awful was about to happen; looking at the flowers, at the trees with the smoke winding off them and the rooks rising, falling; standing and looking until Peter Walsh said, "Musing among the vegetables?" —was that it? —"I prefer men to cauliflowers" —was that it? He must have said it at breakfast one morning when she had gone out on to the terrace-Peter Walsh. He would be back from India one of these days, June or July, she forgot which, for his letters were awfully dull; it was his sayings one remembered; his eyes, his pocket-knife, his smile, his grumpiness and, when millions of things had utterly vanished-how strange it was! —a few sayings like this about cabbages.

She stiffened a little on the kerb, waiting for Durtnall's van to pass. A charming woman, Scrope Purvis thought her (knowing her as one does know people who live next door to one in Westminster); a touch of the bird about her, of the jay, blue-green, light, vivacious, though she was over fifty, and grown very white since her illness. There she perched, never seeing him, waiting to cross, very upright.

For having lived in Westminster-how many years now? over twenty, —one feels even in the midst of the traffic, or waking at night, Clarissa was positive, a particular hush, or solemnity; an indescribable pause; a suspense (but that might be her heart, affected, they said, by influenza) before Big Ben strikes. There! Out it boomed. First a warning, musical; then the hour, irrevocable. The leaden circles dissolved in the air. Such fools we are, she thought, crossing Victoria Street. For Heaven only knows why one loves it so, how one sees it so, making it up, building it round one, tumbling it, creating it every moment afresh; but the veriest frumps, the most dejected of miseries sitting on doorsteps (drink their downfall) do the same; can't be dealt with, she felt positive, by Acts of Parliament for that very reason: they love life. In people's eyes, in the swing, tramp, and trudge; in the bellow and the uproar; the carriages, motor cars, omnibuses, vans, sandwich men shuffling and swinging; brass bands; barrel organs; in the triumph and the jingle and the strange high singing of some aeroplane overhead was what she loved; life; London; this moment of June.

For it was the middle of June. The War was over, except for some one like Mrs. Foxcroft at the Embassy last night eating her heart out because that nice boy was killed and now the old Manor House must go to a cousin; or Lady Bexborough who opened a bazaar, they said, with the telegram in her hand, John, her favourite, killed; but it was over; thank Heaven-over. It was June. The King and Queen were at the Palace. And everywhere, though it was still so early, there was a beating, a stirring of galloping ponies, tapping of cricket bats; Lords, Ascot, Ranelagh and all the rest of it; wrapped in the soft mesh of the grey-blue morning air, which, as the day wore on, would unwind them, and set down on their lawns and pitches the bouncing ponies, whose forefeet just struck the ground and up they sprung, the whirling young men, and laughing girls in their transparent muslins who, even now, after dancing all night, were taking their absurd woolly dogs for a run; and even now, at this hour, discreet old dowagers were shooting out in their motor cars on errands of mystery; and the shopkeepers were fidgeting in their windows with their paste and diamonds, their lovely old sea-green brooches in eighteenth-century settings to tempt Americans (but one must economise, not buy things rashly for Elizabeth), and she, too, loving it as she did with an absurd and faithful passion, being part of it, since her people were courtiers once in the time of the Georges, she, too, was going that very night to kindle and illuminate; to give her party. But how strange, on entering the Park, the silence; the mist; the hum; the slow-swimming happy ducks; the pouched birds waddling; and who should be coming along with his back against the Government buildings, most appropriately, carrying a despatch box stamped with the Royal Arms, who but Hugh Whitbread; her old friend Hugh-the admirable Hugh!

"Good-morning to you, Clarissa!" said Hugh, rather extravagantly, for they had known each other as children. "Where are you off to?"

"I love walking in London," said Mrs. Dalloway. "Really it's better than walking in the country."

They had just come up-unfortunately-to see doctors. Other people came to see pictures; go to the opera; take their daughters out; the Whitbreads came "to see doctors." Times without number Clarissa had visited Evelyn Whitbread in a nursing home. Was Evelyn ill again? Evelyn was a good deal out of sorts, said Hugh, intimating by a kind of pout or swell of his very well-covered, manly, extremely handsome, perfectly upholstered body (he was almost too well dressed always, but presumably had to be, with his little job at Court) that his wife had some internal ailment, nothing serious, which, as an old friend, Clarissa Dalloway would quite understand without requiring him to specify. Ah yes, she did of course; what a nuisance; and felt very sisterly and oddly conscious at the same time of her hat. Not the right hat for the early morning, was that it? For Hugh always made her feel, as he bustled on, raising his hat rather extravagantly and assuring her that she might be a girl of eighteen, and of course he was coming to her party tonight, Evelyn absolutely insisted, only a little late he might be after the party at the Palace to which he had to take one of Jim's boys, —she always felt a little skimpy beside Hugh; schoolgirlish; but attached to him, partly from having known him always, but she did think him a good sort in his own way, though Richard was nearly driven mad by him, and as for Peter Walsh, he had never to this day forgiven her for liking him.

She could remember scene after scene at Bourton-Peter furious; Hugh not, of course, his match in any way, but still not a positive imbecile as Peter made out; not a mere barber's block. When his old mother wanted him to give up shooting or to take her to Bath he did it, without a word; he was really unselfish, and as for saying, as Peter did, that he had no heart, no brain, nothing but the manners and breeding of an English gentleman, that was only her dear Peter at his worst; and he could be intolerable; he could be impossible; but adorable to walk with on a morning like this.

(June had drawn out every leaf on the trees. The mothers of Pimlico gave suck to their young. Messages were passing from the Fleet to the Admiralty. Arlington Street and Piccadilly seemed to chafe the very air in the Park and lift its leaves hotly, brilliantly, on waves of that divine vitality which Clarissa loved. To dance, to ride, she had adored all that.)

For they might be parted for hundreds of years, she and Peter; she never wrote a letter and his were dry sticks; but suddenly it would come over her, If he were with me now what would he say? —some days, some sights bringing him back to her calmly, without the old bitterness; which perhaps was the reward of having cared for people; they came back in the middle of St. James's Park on a fine morning-indeed they did. But Peter-however beautiful the day might be, and the trees and the grass, and the little girl in pink-Peter never saw a thing of all that. He would put on his spectacles, if she told him to; he would look. It was the state of the world that interested him; Wagner, Pope's poetry, people's characters eternally, and the defects of her own soul. How he scolded her! How they argued! She would marry a Prime Minister and stand at the top of a staircase; the perfect hostess he called her (she had cried over it in her bedroom), she had the makings of the perfect hostess, he said.

So she would still find herself arguing in St. James's Park, still making out that she had been right-and she had too-not to marry him. For in marriage a little licence, a little independence there must be between people living together day in day out in the same house; which Richard gave her, and she him. (Where was he this morning for instance? Some committee, she never asked what.) But with Peter everything had to be shared; everything gone into. And it was intolerable, and when it came to that scene in the little garden by the fountain, she had to break with him or they would have been destroyed, both of them ruined, she was convinced; though she had borne about with her for years like an arrow sticking in her heart the grief, the anguish; and then the horror of the moment when some one told her at a concert that he had married a woman met on the boat going to India! Never should she forget all that! Cold, heartless, a prude, he called her. Never could she understand how he cared. But those Indian women did presumably-silly, pretty, flimsy nincompoops. And she wasted her pity. For he was quite happy, he assured her-perfectly happy, though he had never done a thing that they talked of; his whole life had been a failure. It made her angry still.

She had reached the Park gates. She stood for a moment, looking at the omnibuses in Piccadilly.

She would not say of any one in the world now that they were this or were that. She felt very young; at the same time unspeakably aged. She sliced like a knife through everything; at the same time was outside, looking on. She had a perpetual sense, as she watched the taxi cabs, of being out, out, far out to sea and alone; she always had the feeling that it was very, very dangerous to live even one day. Not that she thought herself clever, or much out of the ordinary. How she had got through life on the few twigs of knowledge Fräulein Daniels gave them she could not think. She knew nothing; no language, no history; she scarcely read a book now, except memoirs in bed; and yet to her it was absolutely absorbing; all this; the cabs passing; and she would not say of Peter, she would not say of herself, I am this, I am that.

Her only gift was knowing people almost by instinct, she thought, walking on. If you put her in a room with some one, up went her back like a cat's; or she purred. Devonshire House, Bath House, the house with the china cockatoo, she had seen them all lit up once; and remembered Sylvia, Fred, Sally Seton-such hosts of people; and dancing all night; and the waggons plodding past to market; and driving home across the Park. She remembered once throwing a shilling into the Serpentine. But every one remembered; what she loved was this, here, now, in front of her; the fat lady in the cab. Did it matter then, she asked herself, walking towards Bond Street, did it matter that she must inevitably cease completely; all this must go on without her; did she resent it; or did it not become consoling to believe that death ended absolutely? but that somehow in the streets of London, on the ebb and flow of things, here, there, she survived, Peter survived, lived in each other, she being part, she was positive, of the trees at home; of the house there, ugly, rambling all to bits and pieces as it was; part of people she had never met; being laid out like a mist between the people she knew best, who lifted her on their branches as she had seen the trees lift the mist, but it spread ever so far, her life, herself. But what was she dreaming as she looked into Hatchards' shop window? What was she trying to recover? What image of white dawn in the country, as she read in the book spread open:

> Fear no more the heat o' the sun
> Nor the furious winter's rages.

This late age of the world's experience had bred in them all, all men and women, a well of tears. Tears and sorrows; courage and endurance; a perfectly upright and stoical bearing. Think, for example, of the woman she admired most, Lady Bexborough, opening the bazaar.

There were Jorrocks' *Jaunts and Jollities;* there were *Soapy Sponge* and Mrs. Asquith's *Memoirs* and *Big Game Shooting in Nigeria*, all spread open. Ever so many books there were; but none that seemed exactly right to take to Evelyn Whitbread in her nursing home. Nothing that would serve to amuse her and make that indescribably dried-up little woman look, as Clarissa came in, just for a moment cordial; before they settled down for the usual interminable talk of women's ailments. How much she wanted it-that people should look pleased as she came in, Clarissa thought and turned and walked back towards Bond Street, annoyed, because it was silly to have other reasons for doing things. Much rather would she have been one of those people like Richard who did things for themselves, whereas, she thought, waiting to cross, half the time she did things not simply, not for themselves; but to make people think this or that; perfect idiocy she knew (and now the policeman held up his hand) for no one was ever for a second taken in. Oh if she could have had her life over again! she thought, stepping on to the pavement, could have looked even differently!

She would have been, in the first place, dark like Lady Bexborough, with a skin of crumpled leather and beautiful eyes. She would have been, like Lady Bexborough, slow and stately; rather large; interested in politics like a man; with a country house; very dignified, very sincere. Instead of which she had a narrow pea-stick figure; a ridiculous little face, beaked like a bird's. That she held herself well was true; and had nice hands and feet; and dressed well, considering that she spent little. But often now this body she wore (she stopped to look at a Dutch picture), this body, with all its capacities, seemed nothing-nothing at all. She had the oddest sense of being herself invisible; unseen; unknown; there being no more marrying, no more having of children now, but only this astonishing and rather solemn progress with the rest of them, up Bond Street, this being Mrs. Dalloway; not even Clarissa any more; this being Mrs. Richard Dalloway.

Bond Street fascinated her; Bond Street early in the morning in the season; its flags flying; its shops; no splash; no glitter; one roll of tweed in the shop where her father had bought his suits for fifty years; a few pearls; salmon on an iceblock.

"That is all," she said, looking at the fishmonger's. "That is all," she repeated, pausing for a moment at the window of a glove shop where, before the War, you could buy almost perfect gloves. And her old Uncle William used to say a lady is known by her shoes and her gloves. He had turned on his bed one morning in the middle of the War. He had said, "I have had enough." Gloves and shoes; she had a passion for gloves; but her own daughter, her Elizabeth, cared not a straw for either of them.

Not a straw, she thought, going on up Bond Street to a shop where they kept flowers for her when she gave a party. Elizabeth really cared for her dog most of all. The whole house this morning smelt of tar. Still, better poor Grizzle than Miss Kilman; better distemper and tar and all the rest of it than sitting mewed in a stuffy bedroom with a prayer book! Better anything, she was inclined to say. But it might be only a phase, as Richard said, such as all girls go through. It might be falling in love. But why with Miss Kilman? who had been badly treated of course; one must make allowances for that, and Richard said she was very able, had a really historical mind. Anyhow they were inseparable, and Elizabeth, her own daughter, went to Communion; and how she dressed, how she treated people who came to lunch she did not care a bit, it being her experience that the religious ecstasy made people callous (so did causes); dulled their feelings, for Miss Kilman would do anything for the Russians, starved herself for the Austrians, but in private inflicted positive torture, so insensitive was she, dressed in a green mackintosh coat. Year in year out she wore that coat; she perspired; she was never in the room five minutes without making you feel her superiority, your inferiority; how poor she was; how rich you were; how she lived in a slum without a cushion or a bed or a rug or whatever it might be, all her soul rusted with that grievance sticking in it, her dismissal from school during the War-poor embittered unfortunate creature! For it was not her one hated but the idea of her, which undoubtedly had gathered in to itself a great deal that was not Miss Kilman; had become one of those spectres with which one battles in the night; one of those spectres who stand astride us and suck up half our life-blood, dominators and tyrants; for no doubt with another throw of the dice, had the black been uppermost and not the white, she would have loved Miss Kilman! But not in this world. No.

It rasped her, though, to have stirring about in her this brutal monster! to hear twigs cracking and feel hooves planted down in the depths of that leaf-encumbered forest, the soul; never to be content quite, or quite secure, for at any moment the brute would be stirring, this hatred, which, especially since her illness, had power to make her feel scraped, hurt in her spine; gave her physical pain, and made all pleasure in beauty, in friendship, in being well, in being loved and making her home delightful rock, quiver, and bend as if indeed there were a monster grubbing at the roots, as if the whole panoply of content were nothing but self love! this hatred!

Nonsense, nonsense! she cried to herself, pushing through the swing doors of Mulberry's the florists.

She advanced, light, tall, very upright, to be greeted at once by button-faced Miss Pym, whose hands were always bright red, as if they had been stood in cold water with the flowers.

There were flowers: delphiniums, sweet peas, bunches of lilac; and carnations, masses of carnations. There were roses; there were irises. Ah yes-so she breathed in the earthy garden sweet smell as she stood talking to Miss Pym who owed her help, and thought her kind, for kind she had been years ago; very kind, but she looked older, this year, turning her head from side to side among the irises and roses and nodding tufts of lilac with her eyes half closed, snuffing in, after the street uproar, the delicious scent, the exquisite coolness. And then, opening her eyes, how fresh like frilled linen clean from a laundry laid in wicker trays the roses looked; and dark and prim the red carnations, holding their heads up; and all the sweet peas spreading in their bowls, tinged violet, snow white, pale-as if it were the evening and girls in muslin frocks came out to pick sweet peas and roses after the superb summer's day, with its almost blue-black sky, its delphiniums, its carnations, its arum lilies was over; and it was the moment between six and seven when every flower-roses, carnations, irises, lilac-glows; white, violet, red, deep orange; every flower seems to burn by itself, softly, purely in the misty beds; and how she loved the grey-white moths spinning in and out, over the cherry pie, over the evening primroses!

And as she began to go with Miss Pym from jar to jar, choosing, nonsense, nonsense, she said to herself, more and more gently, as if this beauty, this scent, this colour, and Miss Pym liking her, trusting her, were a wave which she let flow over her and surmount that hatred, that monster, surmount it all; and it lifted her up and up when-oh! a pistol shot in the street outside!

"Dear, those motor cars," said Miss Pym, going to the window to look, and coming back and smiling apologetically with her hands full of sweet peas, as if those motor cars, those tyres of motor cars, were all *her* fault.

The violent explosion which made Mrs. Dalloway jump and Miss Pym go to the window and apologise came from a motor car which had drawn to the side of the pavement precisely opposite Mulberry's shop window. Passers-by who, of course, stopped and stared, had just time to see a face of the very greatest importance against the dove-grey upholstery, before a male hand drew the blind and there was nothing to be seen except a square of dove grey.

Yet rumours were at once in circulation from the middle of Bond Street to Oxford Street on one side, to Atkinson's scent shop on the other, passing invisibly, inaudibly, like a cloud, swift, veil-like upon hills, falling indeed with something of a cloud's sudden sobriety and stillness upon faces which a second before had been utterly disorderly. But now mystery had brushed them with her wing; they had heard the voice of authority; the spirit of religion was abroad with her eyes bandaged tight and her lips gaping wide. But nobody knew whose face had been seen. Was it the Prince of Wales's, the Queen's, the Prime Minister's? Whose face was it? Nobody knew.

Edgar J. Watkiss, with his roll of lead piping round his arm, said audibly, humorously of course: "The Proime Minister's kyar."

Septimus Warren Smith, who found himself unable to pass, heard him.

Septimus Warren Smith, aged about thirty, pale-faced, beak-nosed, wearing brown shoes and a shabby overcoat, with hazel eyes which had that look of apprehension in them which makes complete strangers apprehensive too. The world has raised its whip; where will it descend?

387

Everything had come to a standstill. The throb of the motor engines sounded like a pulse irregularly drumming through an entire body. The sun became extraordinarily hot because the motor car had stopped outside Mulberry's shop window; old ladies on the tops of omnibuses spread their black parasols; here a green, here a red parasol opened with a little pop. Mrs. Dalloway, coming to the window with her arms full of sweet peas, looked out with her little pink face pursed in enquiry. Every one looked at the motor car. Septimus looked. Boys on bicycles sprang off. Traffic accumulated. And there the motor car stood, with drawn blinds, and upon them a curious pattern like a tree, Septimus thought, and this gradual drawing together of everything to one centre before his eyes, as if some horror had come almost to the surface and was about to burst into flames, terrified him. The world wavered and quivered and threatened to burst into flames. It is I who am blocking the way, he thought. Was he not being looked at and pointed at; was he not weighted there, rooted to the pavement, for a purpose? But for what purpose?

"Let us go on, Septimus," said his wife, a little woman, with large eyes in a sallow pointed face; an Italian girl.

But Lucrezia herself could not help looking at the motor car and the tree pattern on the blinds. Was it the Queen in there-the Queen going shopping?

The chauffeur, who had been opening something, turning something, shutting something, got on to the box.

"Come on," said Lucrezia.

But her husband, for they had been married four, five years now, jumped, started, and said, "All right!" angrily, as if she had interrupted him.

People must notice; people must see. People, she thought, looking at the crowd staring at the motor car; the English people, with their children and their horses and their clothes, which she admired in a way; but they were "people" now, because Septimus had said, "I will kill myself"; an awful thing to say. Suppose they had heard him? She looked at the crowd. Help, help! she wanted to cry out to butchers' boys and women. Help! Only last autumn she and Septimus had stood on the Embankment wrapped in the same cloak and, Septimus reading a paper instead of talking, she had snatched it from him and laughed in the old man's face who saw them! But failure one conceals. She must take him away into some park.

"Now we will cross," she said.

She had a right to his arm, though it was without feeling. He would give her, who was so simple, so impulsive, only twenty-four, without friends in England, who had left Italy for his sake, a piece of bone.

The motor car with its blinds drawn and an air of inscrutable reserve proceeded towards Piccadilly, still gazed at, still ruffling the faces on both sides of the street with the same dark breath of veneration whether for Queen, Prince, or Prime Minister nobody knew. The face itself had been seen only once by three people for a few seconds. Even the sex was now in dispute. But there could be no doubt that greatness was seated within; greatness was passing, hidden, down Bond Street, removed only by a hand's-breadth from ordinary people who might now, for the first and last time, be within speaking distance of the majesty of England, of the enduring symbol of the state which will be known to curious antiquaries, sifting the ruins of time, when London is a grass-grown path and all those hurrying along the pavement this Wednesday morning are but bones with a few wedding rings mixed up in their dust and the gold stoppings of innumerable decayed teeth. The face in the motor car will then be known.

It is probably the Queen, thought Mrs. Dalloway, coming out of Mulberry's with her flowers; the Queen. And for a second she wore a look of extreme dignity standing by the flower shop in the sunlight while the car passed at a foot's pace, with its blinds drawn. The Queen going to some hospital; the Queen opening some bazaar, thought Clarissa.

The crush was terrific for the time of day. Lords, Ascot, Hurlingham, what was it? she wondered, for the street was blocked. The British middle classes sitting sideways on the tops of omnibuses with parcels and umbrellas, yes, even furs on a day like this, were, she thought, more ridiculous, more unlike anything there has ever been than one could conceive; and the Queen herself held up; the Queen herself unable to pass. Clarissa was suspended on one side of Brook Street; Sir John Buckhurst, the old Judge on the other, with the car between them (Sir John had laid down the law for years and liked a well-dressed woman) when the chauffeur, leaning ever so slightly, said or showed something to the policeman, who saluted and raised his arm and jerked his head and moved the omnibus to the side and the car passed through. Slowly and very silently it took its way.

Clarissa guessed; Clarissa knew of course; she had seen something white, magical, circular, in the footman's hand, a disc inscribed with a name,—the Queen's, the Prince of Wales's, the Prime Minister's?—which, by force of its own lustre, burnt its way through (Clarissa saw the car diminishing, disappearing), to blaze among candelabras, glittering stars, breasts stiff with oak leaves, Hugh Whitbread and all his colleagues, the gentlemen of England, that night in Buckingham Palace. And Clarissa, too, gave a party. She stiffened a little; so she would stand at the top of her stairs.

The car had gone, but it had left a slight ripple which flowed through glove shops and hat shops and tailors' shops on both sides of Bond Street. For thirty seconds all heads were inclined the same way-to the window. Choosing a pair of gloves-should they be to the elbow or above it, lemon or pale grey?—ladies stopped; when the sentence was finished something had happened. Something so trifling in single instances that no mathematical instrument, though capable of transmitting shocks in China, could register the vibration; yet in its fulness rather formidable and in its common appeal emotional; for in all the hat shops and tailors' shops strangers looked at each other and thought of the dead; of the flag; of Empire. In a public house in a back street a Colonial insulted the House of Windsor which led to words, broken beer glasses, and a general shindy, which echoed strangely across the way in the ears of girls buying white underlinen threaded with pure white ribbon for their weddings. For the surface agitation of the passing car as it sunk grazed something very profound.

Gliding across Piccadilly, the car turned down St. James's Street. Tall men, men of robust physique, well-dressed men with their tail-coats and their white slips and their hair raked back who, for reasons difficult to discriminate, were standing in the bow window of Brooks's with their hands behind the tails of their coats, looking out, perceived instinctively that greatness was passing, and the pale light of the immortal presence fell upon them as it had fallen upon Clarissa Dalloway. At once they stood even straighter, and removed their hands, and seemed ready to attend their Sovereign, if need be, to the cannon's mouth, as their ancestors had done before them. The white busts and the little tables in the background covered with copies of the *Tatler* and syphons of soda water seemed to approve; seemed to indicate the flowing corn and the manor houses of England; and to return the frail hum of the motor wheels as the walls of a whispering gallery return a single voice expanded and made sonorous by the might of a whole cathedral. Shawled Moll Pratt with her flowers on the pavement wished the dear boy well (it was the Prince of Wales for certain) and would have tossed the price of a pot of beer—a bunch of roses-into St. James's Street out of sheer light-heartedness and contempt of poverty had she not seen the constable's eye upon her, discouraging an old Irishwoman's loyalty. The sentries at St. James's saluted; Queen Alexandra's policeman approved.

A small crowd meanwhile had gathered at the gates of Buckingham Palace. Listlessly, yet confidently, poor people all of them, they waited; looked at the Palace itself with the flag flying; at Victoria, billowing on her mound, admired her shelves of running water, her geraniums; singled out from the motor cars in the Mall first this one, then that; bestowed emotion, vainly, upon commoners out for a drive; recalled their tribute to keep it unspent while this car passed and that; and all the time let rumour accumulate in their veins and thrill the nerves in their thighs at the thought of Royalty looking at them; the Queen bowing; the Prince saluting; at the thought of the heavenly life divinely bestowed upon Kings; of the equerries and deep curtsies; of the Queen's old doll's house; of Princess Mary married to an Englishman, and the Prince-ah! the Prince! who took wonderfully, they said, after old King Edward, but was ever so much slimmer. The Prince lived at St. James's; but he might come along in the morning to visit his mother.

So Sarah Bletchley said with her baby in her arms, tipping her foot up and down as though she were by her own fender in Pimlico, but keeping her eyes on the Mall, while Emily Coates ranged over the Palace windows and thought of the housemaids, the innumerable housemaids, the bedrooms, the innumerable bedrooms. Joined by an elderly gentleman with an Aberdeen terrier, by men without occupation, the crowd increased. Little Mr. Bowley, who had rooms in the Albany and was sealed with wax over the deeper sources of life but could be unsealed suddenly, inappropriately, sentimentally, by this sort of thing-poor women waiting to see the Queen go past-poor women, nice little children, orphans, widows, the War-tut-tut-actually had tears in his eyes. A breeze flaunting ever so warmly down the Mall through the thin trees, past the bronze heroes, lifted some flag flying in the British breast of Mr. Bowley and he raised his hat as the car turned into the Mall and held it high as the car approached; and let the poor mothers of Pimlico press close to him, and stood very upright. The car came on.

Suddenly Mrs. Coates looked up into the sky. The sound of an aeroplane bored ominously into the ears of the crowd. There it was coming over the trees, letting out white smoke from behind, which curled and twisted, actually writing something! making letters in the sky! Every one looked up.

Dropping dead down the aeroplane soared straight up, curved in a loop, raced, sank, rose, and whatever it did, wherever it went, out fluttered behind it a thick ruffled bar of white smoke which curled and wreathed upon the sky in letters. But what letters? A C was it? an E, then an L? Only for a moment did they lie still; then they moved and melted and were rubbed out up in the sky, and the aeroplane shot further away and again, in a fresh space of sky, began writing a K, an E, a Y perhaps?

"Glaxo," said Mrs. Coates in a strained, awe-stricken voice, gazing straight up, and her baby, lying stiff and white in her arms, gazed straight up.

"Kreemo," murmured Mrs. Bletchley, like a sleep-walker. With his hat held out perfectly still in his hand, Mr. Bowley gazed straight up. All down the Mall people were standing and looking up into the sky. As they looked the whole world became perfectly silent, and a flight of gulls crossed the sky, first one gull leading, then another, and in this extraordinary silence and peace, in this pallor, in this purity, bells struck eleven times, the sound fading up there among the gulls.

The aeroplane turned and raced and swooped exactly where it liked, swiftly, freely, like a skater —

"That's an E," said Mrs. Bletchley-or a dancer —

"It's toffee," murmured Mr. Bowley —(and the car went in at the gates and nobody looked at it), and shutting off the smoke, away and away it rushed, and the smoke faded and assembled itself round the broad white shapes of the clouds.

It had gone; it was behind the clouds. There was no sound. The clouds to which the letters E, G, or L had attached themselves moved freely, as if destined to cross from West to East on a mission of the greatest importance which would never be revealed, and yet certainly so it was —a mission of the greatest importance. Then suddenly, as a train comes out of a tunnel, the aeroplane rushed out of the clouds again, the sound boring into the ears of all people in the Mall, in the Green Park, in Piccadilly, in Regent Street, in Regent's Park, and the bar of smoke curved behind and it dropped down, and it soared up and wrote one letter after another-but what word was it writing?

Lucrezia Warren Smith, sitting by her husband's side on a seat in Regent's Park in the Broad Walk, looked up.

"Look, look, Septimus!" she cried. For Dr. Holmes had told her to make her husband (who had nothing whatever seriously the matter with him but was a little out of sorts) take an interest in things outside himself.

So, thought Septimus, looking up, they are signalling to me. Not indeed in actual words; that is, he could not read the language yet; but it was plain enough, this beauty, this exquisite beauty, and tears filled his eyes as he looked at the smoke words languishing and melting in the sky and bestowing upon him in their inexhaustible charity and laughing goodness one shape after another of unimaginable beauty and signalling their intention to provide him, for nothing, for ever, for looking merely, with beauty, more beauty! Tears ran down his cheeks.

It was toffee; they were advertising toffee, a nursemaid told Rezia. Together they began to spell t...o...f...

"K...R..." said the nursemaid, and Septimus heard her say "Kay Arr" close to his ear, deeply, softly, like a mellow organ, but with a roughness in her voice like a grasshopper's, which rasped his spine deliciously and sent running up into his brain waves of sound which, concussing, broke. A marvellous discovery indeed-that the human voice in certain atmospheric conditions (for one must be scientific, above all scientific) can quicken trees into life! Happily Rezia put her hand with a tremendous weight on his knee so that he was weighted down, transfixed, or the excitement of the elm trees rising and falling, rising and falling with all their leaves alight and the colour thinning and thickening from blue to the green of a hollow wave, like plumes on horses' heads, feathers on ladies', so proudly they rose and fell, so superbly, would have sent him mad. But he would not go mad. He would shut his eyes; he would see no more.

But they beckoned; leaves were alive; trees were alive. And the leaves being connected by millions of fibres with his own body, there on the seat, fanned it up and down; when the branch stretched he, too, made that statement. The sparrows fluttering, rising, and falling in jagged fountains were part of the pattern; the white and blue, barred with black branches. Sounds made harmonies with premeditation; the spaces between them were as significant as the sounds. A child cried. Rightly far away a horn sounded. All taken together meant the birth of a new religion—

"Septimus!" said Rezia. He started violently. People must notice.

"I am going to walk to the fountain and back," she said.

For she could stand it no longer. Dr. Holmes might say there was nothing the matter. Far rather would she that he were dead! She could not sit beside him when he stared so and did not see her and made everything terrible; sky and tree, children playing, dragging carts, blowing whistles, falling down; all were terrible. And he would not kill himself; and she could tell no one. "Septimus has been working too hard"—that was all she could say to her own mother. To love makes one solitary, she thought. She could tell nobody, not even Septimus now, and looking back, she saw him sitting in his shabby overcoat alone, on the seat, hunched up, staring. And it was cowardly for a man to say he would kill himself, but Septimus had fought; he was brave; he was not Septimus now. She put on her lace collar. She put on her new hat and he never noticed; and he was happy without her. Nothing could make her happy without him! Nothing! He was selfish. So men are. For he was not ill. Dr. Holmes said there was nothing the matter with him. She spread her hand before her. Look! Her wedding ring slipped-she had grown so thin. It was she who suffered-but she had nobody to tell.

Far was Italy and the white houses and the room where her sisters sat making hats, and the streets crowded every evening with people walking, laughing out loud, not half alive like people here, huddled up in Bath chairs, looking at a few ugly flowers stuck in pots!

"For you should see the Milan gardens," she said aloud. But to whom?

There was nobody. Her words faded. So a rocket fades. Its sparks, having grazed their way into the night, surrender to it, dark descends, pours over the outlines of houses and towers; bleak hillsides soften and fall in. But though they are gone, the night is full of them; robbed of colour, blank of windows, they exist more ponderously, give out what the frank daylight fails to transmit-the trouble and suspense of things conglomerated there in the darkness; huddled together in the darkness; reft of the relief which dawn brings when, washing the walls white and grey, spotting each window-pane, lifting the mist from the fields, showing the red-brown cows peacefully grazing, all is once more decked out to the eye; exists again. I am alone; I

391

am alone! she cried, by the fountain in Regent's Park (staring at the Indian and his cross), as perhaps at midnight, when all boundaries are lost, the country reverts to its ancient shape, as the Romans saw it, lying cloudy, when they landed, and the hills had no names and rivers wound they knew not where-such was her darkness; when suddenly, as if a shelf were shot forth and she stood on it, she said how she was his wife, married years ago in Milan, his wife, and would never, never tell that he was mad! Turning, the shelf fell; down, down she dropped. For he was gone, she thought-gone, as he threatened, to kill himself-to throw himself under a cart! But no; there he was; still sitting alone on the seat, in his shabby overcoat, his legs crossed, staring, talking aloud.

Men must not cut down trees. There is a God. (He noted such revelations on the backs of envelopes.) Change the world. No one kills from hatred. Make it known (he wrote it down). He waited. He listened. A sparrow perched on the railing opposite chirped Septimus, Septimus, four or five times over and went on, drawing its notes out, to sing freshly and piercingly in Greek words how there is no crime and, joined by another sparrow, they sang in voices prolonged and piercing in Greek words, from trees in the meadow of life beyond a river where the dead walk, how there is no death.

There was his hand; there the dead. White things were assembling behind the railings opposite. But he dared not look. Evans was behind the railings!

"What are you saying?" said Rezia suddenly, sitting down by him.

Interrupted again! She was always interrupting.

Away from people-they must get away from people, he said (jumping up), right away over there, where there were chairs beneath a tree and the long slope of the park dipped like a length of green stuff with a ceiling cloth of blue and pink smoke high above, and there was a rampart of far irregular houses hazed in smoke, the traffic hummed in a circle, and on the right, dun-coloured animals stretched long necks over the Zoo palings, barking, howling. There they sat down under a tree.

"Look," she implored him, pointing at a little troop of boys carrying cricket stumps, and one shuffled, spun round on his heel and shuffled, as if he were acting a clown at the music hall.

"Look," she implored him, for Dr. Holmes had told her to make him notice real things, go to a music hall, play cricket-that was the very game, Dr. Holmes said, a nice out-of-door game, the very game for her husband.

"Look," she repeated.

Look the unseen bade him, the voice which now communicated with him who was the greatest of mankind, Septimus, lately taken from life to death, the Lord who had come to renew society, who lay like a coverlet, a snow blanket smitten only by the sun, for ever unwasted, suffering for ever, the scapegoat, the eternal sufferer, but he did not want it, he moaned, putting from him with a wave of his hand that eternal suffering, that eternal loneliness.

"Look," she repeated, for he must not talk aloud to himself out of doors.

"Oh look," she implored him. But what was there to look at? A few sheep. That was all.

The way to Regent's Park Tube station-could they tell her the way to Regent's Park Tube station-Maisie Johnson wanted to know. She was only up from Edinburgh two days ago.

"Not this way-over there!" Rezia exclaimed, waving her aside, lest she should see Septimus.

Both seemed queer, Maisie Johnson thought. Everything seemed very queer. In London for the first time, come to take up a post at her uncle's in Leadenhall Street, and now walking through Regent's Park in the morning, this couple on the chairs gave her quite a turn; the young woman seeming foreign, the man looking queer; so that should she be very old she would still remember and make it jangle again among her memories how she had walked through Regent's Park on a fine summer's morning fifty years ago. For she was only nineteen and had got her way at last, to come to London; and now how queer it was, this couple she had asked the way of, and the girl started and jerked her hand, and the man-he seemed awfully odd; quarrelling, perhaps; parting for ever, perhaps; something was up, she knew; and now all these people (for she returned to the Broad Walk), the stone basins, the prim flowers, the old men and women, invalids most of them in Bath chairs-all seemed, after Edinburgh, so queer. And Maisie Johnson, as she joined that gently trudging, vaguely gazing, breeze-kissed company-squirrels perching and preening, sparrow fountains fluttering for crumbs, dogs busy with the railings, busy with each other, while the soft warm air washed over them and lent to the fixed unsurprised gaze with which they received life something whimsical and mollified-Maisie Johnson positively felt she must cry Oh! (for that young man on the seat had given her quite a turn. Something was up, she knew.)

Horror! horror! she wanted to cry. (She had left her people; they had warned her what would happen.)

Why hadn't she stayed at home? she cried, twisting the knob of the iron railing.

That girl, thought Mrs. Dempster (who saved crusts for the squirrels and often ate her lunch in Regent's Park), don't know a thing yet; and really it seemed to her better to be a little stout, a little slack, a little moderate in one's expectations. Percy drank. Well, better to have a son, thought Mrs. Dempster. She had had a hard time of it, and couldn't help smiling at a girl like that. You'll get married, for you're pretty enough, thought Mrs. Dempster. Get married, she thought, and then you'll know. Oh, the cooks, and so on. Every man has his ways. But whether I'd have chosen quite like that if I could have known, thought Mrs. Dempster, and could not help wishing to whisper a word to Maisie Johnson; to feel on the creased pouch of her worn old face the kiss of pity. For it's been a hard life, thought Mrs. Dempster. What hadn't she given to it? Roses; figure; her feet too. (She drew the knobbed lumps beneath her skirt.)

Roses, she thought sardonically. All trash, m'dear. For really, what with eating, drinking, and mating, the bad days and good, life had been no mere matter of roses, and what was more, let me tell you, Carrie Dempster had no wish to change her lot with any woman's in Kentish Town! But, she implored, pity. Pity, for the loss of roses. Pity she asked of Maisie Johnson, standing by the hyacinth beds.

Ah, but that aeroplane! Hadn't Mrs. Dempster always longed to see foreign parts? She had a nephew, a missionary. It soared and shot. She always went on the sea at Margate, not out o' sight of land, but she had no patience with women who were afraid of water. It swept and fell. Her stomach was in her mouth. Up again. There's a fine young feller aboard of it, Mrs. Dempster wagered, and away and away it went, fast and fading, away and away the aeroplane shot; soaring over Greenwich and all the masts; over the little island of grey churches, St. Paul's and the rest till, on either side of London, fields spread out and dark brown woods where adventurous thrushes hopping boldly, glancing quickly, snatched the snail and tapped him on a stone, once, twice, thrice.

Away and away the aeroplane shot, till it was nothing but a bright spark; an aspiration; a concentration; a symbol (so it seemed to Mr. Bentley, vigorously rolling his strip of turf at Greenwich) of man's soul; of his determination, thought Mr. Bentley, sweeping round the cedar tree, to get outside his body, beyond his house, by means of thought, Einstein, speculation, mathematics, the Mendelian theory-away the aeroplane shot.

Then, while a seedy-looking nondescript man carrying a leather bag stood on the steps of St. Paul's Cathedral, and hesitated, for within was what balm, how great a welcome, how many tombs with banners waving over them, tokens of victories not over armies, but over, he thought, that plaguy spirit of truth seeking which leaves me at present without a situation, and more than that, the cathedral offers company, he thought, invites you to membership of a society; great men belong to it; martyrs have died for it; why not enter in, he thought, put this leather bag stuffed with pamphlets before an altar, a cross, the symbol of something which has soared beyond seeking and questing and knocking of words together and has become all spirit, disembodied, ghostly-why not enter in? he thought and while he hesitated out flew the aeroplane over Ludgate Circus.

It was strange; it was still. Not a sound was to be heard above the traffic. Unguided it seemed; sped of its own free will. And now, curving up and up, straight up, like something mounting in ecstasy, in pure delight, out from behind poured white smoke looping, writing a T, an O, an F.

393

"What are they looking at?" said Clarissa Dalloway to the maid who opened her door.

The hall of the house was cool as a vault. Mrs. Dalloway raised her hand to her eyes, and, as the maid shut the door to, and she heard the swish of Lucy's skirts, she felt like a nun who has left the world and feels fold round her the familiar veils and the response to old devotions. The cook whistled in the kitchen. She heard the click of the typewriter. It was her life, and, bending her head over the hall table, she bowed beneath the influence, felt blessed and purified, saying to herself, as she took the pad with the telephone message on it, how moments like this are buds on the tree of life, flowers of darkness they are, she thought (as if some lovely rose had blossomed for her eyes only); not for a moment did she believe in God; but all the more, she thought, taking up the pad, must one repay in daily life to servants, yes, to dogs and canaries, above all to Richard her husband, who was the foundation of it-of the gay sounds, of the green lights, of the cook even whistling, for Mrs. Walker was Irish and whistled all day long-one must pay back from this secret deposit of exquisite moments, she thought, lifting the pad, while Lucy stood by her, trying to explain how

"Mr. Dalloway, ma'am"—

Clarissa read on the telephone pad, "Lady Bruton wishes to know if Mr. Dalloway will lunch with her to-day."

"Mr. Dalloway, ma'am, told me to tell you he would be lunching out."

"Dear!" said Clarissa, and Lucy shared as she meant her to her disappointment (but not the pang); felt the concord between them; took the hint; thought how the gentry love; gilded her own future with calm; and, taking Mrs. Dalloway's parasol, handled it like a sacred weapon which a Goddess, having acquitted herself honourably in the field of battle, sheds, and placed it in the umbrella stand.

"Fear no more," said Clarissa. Fear no more the heat o' the sun; for the shock of Lady Bruton asking Richard to lunch without her made the moment in which she had stood shiver, as a plant on the river-bed feels the shock of a passing oar and shivers: so she rocked: so she shivered.

Millicent Bruton, whose lunch parties were said to be extraordinarily amusing, had not asked her. No vulgar jealousy could separate her from Richard. But she feared time itself, and read on Lady Bruton's face, as if it had been a dial cut in impassive stone, the dwindling of life; how year by year her share was sliced; how little the margin that remained was capable any longer of stretching, of absorbing, as in the youthful years, the colours, salts, tones of existence, so that she filled the room she entered, and felt often as she stood hesitating one moment on the threshold of her drawing-room, an exquisite suspense, such as might stay a diver before plunging while the sea darkens and brightens beneath him, and the waves which threaten to break, but only gently split their surface, roll and conceal and encrust as they just turn over the weeds with pearl.

She put the pad on the hall table. She began to go slowly upstairs, with her hand on the bannisters, as if she had left a party, where now this friend now that had flashed back her face, her voice; had shut the door and gone out and stood alone, a single figure against the appalling night, or rather, to be accurate, against the stare of this matter-of-fact June morning; soft with the glow of rose petals for some, she knew, and felt it, as she paused by the open staircase window which let in blinds flapping, dogs barking, let in, she thought, feeling herself suddenly shrivelled, aged, breastless, the grinding, blowing, flowering of the day, out of doors, out of the window, out of her body and brain which now failed, since Lady Bruton, whose lunch parties were said to be extraordinarily amusing, had not asked her.

Like a nun withdrawing, or a child exploring a tower, she went upstairs, paused at the window, came to the bathroom. There was the green linoleum and a tap dripping. There was an emptiness about the heart of life; an attic room. Women must put off their rich apparel. At midday they must disrobe. She pierced the pincushion and laid her feathered yellow hat on the bed. The sheets were clean, tight stretched in a broad white band from side to side. Narrower and narrower would her bed be. The candle was half burnt down and she had read deep in Baron Marbot's *Memoirs*. She had read late at night of the retreat from Moscow. For the House sat so long that Richard insisted, after her illness, that she must sleep undisturbed. And really she preferred to read of the retreat from Moscow. He knew it. So the room was an attic; the bed narrow; and lying there reading, for she slept badly, she could not dispel a virginity preserved through childbirth which clung to her like a sheet. Lovely in girlhood, suddenly there came a moment-for example on the river beneath the woods at Clieveden-when, through some contraction of this cold spirit, she had failed him. And then at Constantinople, and again and again. She could see what she lacked. It was not beauty; it was not mind. It was something central which permeated; something warm which broke up surfaces and rippled the cold contact of man and woman, or of women together. For *that* she could dimly perceive. She resented it, had a scruple picked up Heaven knows where, or, as she felt, sent by Nature (who is invariably wise); yet she could not resist sometimes yielding to the charm of a woman, not a girl, of a woman confessing, as to her they often did, some scrape, some folly. And whether it was pity, or their beauty, or that she was older, or some accident-like a faint scent, or a violin next door (so strange is the power of sounds at certain moments), she did undoubtedly then feel what men felt. Only for a moment; but it was enough. It was a sudden revelation, a tinge like a blush which one tried to check and then, as it spread, one yielded to its expansion, and rushed to the farthest verge and there quivered and felt the world come closer, swollen with some astonishing significance, some pressure of rapture, which split its thin skin and gushed and poured with an extraordinary alleviation over the cracks and sores! Then, for that moment, she had seen an illumination; a match burning in a crocus; an inner meaning almost expressed. But the close withdrew; the hard softened. It was over-the moment. Against such moments (with women too) there contrasted (as she laid her hat down) the bed and Baron Marbot and the candle half-burnt. Lying awake, the floor creaked; the lit house was suddenly darkened, and if she raised her head she could just hear the click of the handle released as gently as possible by Richard, who slipped upstairs in his socks and then, as often as not, dropped his hot-water bottle and swore! How she laughed!

But this question of love (she thought, putting her coat away), this falling in love with women. Take Sally Seton; her relation in the old days with Sally Seton. Had not that, after all, been love?

She sat on the floor-that was her first impression of Sally-she sat on the floor with her arms round her knees, smoking a cigarette. Where could it have been? The Mannings? The Kinloch-Jones's? At some party (where, she could not be certain), for she had a distinct recollection of saying to the man she was with, "Who is *that?*" And he had told her, and said that Sally's parents did not get on (how that shocked her-that one's parents should quarrel!). But all that evening she could not take her eyes off Sally. It was an extraordinary beauty of the kind she most admired, dark, large-eyed, with that quality which, since she hadn't got it herself, she always envied —a sort of abandonment, as if she could say anything, do anything; a quality much commoner in foreigners than in Englishwomen. Sally always said she had French blood in her veins, an ancestor had been with Marie Antoinette, had his head cut off, left a ruby ring. Perhaps that summer she came to stay at Bourton, walking in quite unexpectedly without a penny in her pocket, one night after dinner, and upsetting poor Aunt Helena to such an extent that she never forgave her. There had been some quarrel at home. She literally hadn't a penny that night when she came to them-had pawned a brooch to come down. She had rushed off in a passion. They sat up till all hours of the night talking. Sally it was who made her feel, for the first time, how sheltered the life at Bourton was. She knew nothing about sex-nothing about social problems. She had once seen an old man who had dropped dead in a field-she had seen cows just after their calves were born. But Aunt Helena never liked discussion of anything (when Sally gave her William Morris, it had to be wrapped in brown paper). There they sat, hour after hour, talking in her bedroom at the top of the house, talking about life, how they were to reform the world. They meant to found a society to abolish private property, and actually had a letter written, though not sent out. The ideas were Sally's, of course-but very soon she was just as excited-read Plato in bed before breakfast; read Morris; read Shelley by the hour.

Sally's power was amazing, her gift, her personality. There was her way with flowers, for instance. At Bourton they always had stiff little vases all the way down the table. Sally went out, picked hollyhocks, dahlias-all sorts of flowers that had never been seen together-cut their heads off, and made them swim on the top of water in bowls. The effect was extraordinary-coming in to dinner in the sunset. (Of course Aunt Helena thought it wicked to treat flowers like that.) Then she forgot her sponge, and ran along the passage naked. That grim old housemaid, Ellen Atkins, went about grumbling —"Suppose any of the gentlemen had seen?" Indeed she did shock people. She was untidy, Papa said.

The strange thing, on looking back, was the purity, the integrity, of her feeling for Sally. It was not like one's feeling for a man. It was completely disinterested, and besides, it had a quality which could only exist between women, between women just grown up. It was protective, on her side; sprang from a sense of being in league together, a presentiment of something that was bound to part them (they spoke of marriage always as a catastrophe), which led to this chivalry, this protective feeling which was much more on her side than Sally's. For in those days she was completely reckless; did the most idiotic things out of bravado; bicycled round the parapet on the terrace; smoked cigars. Absurd, she was-very absurd. But the charm was overpowering, to her at least, so that she could remember standing in her bedroom at the top of the house holding the hot-water can in her hands and saying aloud, "She is beneath this roof... . She is beneath this roof!"

No, the words meant absolutely nothing to her now. She could not even get an echo of her old emotion. But she could remember going cold with excitement, and doing her hair in a kind of ecstasy (now the old feeling began to come back to her, as she took out her hairpins, laid them on the dressing-table, began to do her hair), with the rooks flaunting up and down in the pink evening light, and dressing, and going downstairs, and feeling as she crossed the hall "if it were now to die 'twere now to be most happy." That was her feeling-Othello's feeling, and she felt it, she was convinced, as strongly as Shakespeare meant Othello to feel it, all because she was coming down to dinner in a white frock to meet Sally Seton!

She was wearing pink gauze-was that possible? She *seemed,* anyhow, all light, glowing, like some bird or air ball that has flown in, attached itself for a moment to a bramble. But nothing is so strange when one is in love (and what was this except being in love?) as the complete indifference of other people. Aunt Helena just wandered off after dinner; Papa read the paper. Peter Walsh might have been there, and old Miss Cummings; Joseph Breitkopf certainly was, for he came every summer, poor old man, for weeks and weeks, and pretended to read German with her, but really played the piano and sang Brahms without any voice.

All this was only a background for Sally. She stood by the fireplace talking, in that beautiful voice which made everything she said sound like a caress, to Papa, who had begun to be attracted rather against his will (he never got over lending her one of his books and finding it soaked on the terrace), when suddenly she said, "What a shame to sit indoors!" and they all went out on to the terrace and walked up and down. Peter Walsh and Joseph Breitkopf went on about Wagner. She and Sally fell a little behind. Then came the most exquisite moment of her whole life passing a stone urn with flowers in it. Sally stopped; picked a flower; kissed her on the lips. The whole world might have turned upside down! The others disappeared; there she was alone with Sally. And she felt that she had been given a present, wrapped up, and told just to keep it, not to look at it—a diamond, something infinitely precious, wrapped up, which, as they walked (up and down, up and down), she uncovered, or the radiance burnt through, the revelation, the religious feeling! —when old Joseph and Peter faced them:

"Star-gazing?" said Peter.

It was like running one's face against a granite wall in the darkness! It was shocking; it was horrible!

Not for herself. She felt only how Sally was being mauled already, maltreated; she felt his hostility; his jealousy; his determination to break into their companionship. All this she saw as one sees a landscape in a flash of lightning-and Sally (never had she admired her so much!)

gallantly taking her way unvanquished. She laughed. She made old Joseph tell her the names of the stars, which he liked doing very seriously. She stood there: she listened. She heard the names of the stars.

"Oh this horror!" she said to herself, as if she had known all along that something would interrupt, would embitter her moment of happiness.

Yet, after all, how much she owed to him later. Always when she thought of him she thought of their quarrels for some reason-because she wanted his good opinion so much, perhaps. She owed him words: "sentimental," "civilised"; they started up every day of her life as if he guarded her. A book was sentimental; an attitude to life sentimental. "Sentimental," perhaps she was to be thinking of the past. What would he think, she wondered, when he came back?

That she had grown older? Would he say that, or would she see him thinking when he came back, that she had grown older? It was true. Since her illness she had turned almost white.

Laying her brooch on the table, she had a sudden spasm, as if, while she mused, the icy claws had had the chance to fix in her. She was not old yet. She had just broken into her fifty-second year. Months and months of it were still untouched. June, July, August! Each still remained almost whole, and, as if to catch the falling drop, Clarissa (crossing to the dressing-table) plunged into the very heart of the moment, transfixed it, there-the moment of this June morning on which was the pressure of all the other mornings, seeing the glass, the dressing-table, and all the bottles afresh, collecting the whole of her at one point (as she looked into the glass), seeing the delicate pink face of the woman who was that very night to give a party; of Clarissa Dalloway; of herself.

How many million times she had seen her face, and always with the same imperceptible contraction! She pursed her lips when she looked in the glass. It was to give her face point. That was her self-pointed; dartlike; definite. That was her self when some effort, some call on her to be her self, drew the parts together, she alone knew how different, how incompatible and composed so for the world only into one centre, one diamond, one woman who sat in her drawing-room and made a meeting-point, a radiancy no doubt in some dull lives, a refuge for the lonely to come to, perhaps; she had helped young people, who were grateful to her; had tried to be the same always, never showing a sign of all the other sides of her-faults, jealousies, vanities, suspicions, like this of Lady Bruton not asking her to lunch; which, she thought (combing her hair finally), is utterly base! Now, where was her dress?

Her evening dresses hung in the cupboard. Clarissa, plunging her hand into the softness, gently detached the green dress and carried it to the window. She had torn it. Some one had trod on the skirt. She had felt it give at the Embassy party at the top among the folds. By artificial light the green shone, but lost its colour now in the sun. She would mend it. Her maids had too much to do. She would wear it tonight. She would take her silks, her scissors, her-what was it? —her thimble, of course, down into the drawing-room, for she must also write, and see that things generally were more or less in order.

Strange, she thought, pausing on the landing, and assembling that diamond shape, that single person, strange how a mistress knows the very moment, the very temper of her house! Faint sounds rose in spirals up the well of the stairs; the swish of a mop; tapping; knocking; a loudness when the front door opened; a voice repeating a message in the basement; the chink of silver on a tray; clean silver for the party. All was for the party.

(And Lucy, coming into the drawing-room with her tray held out, put the giant candlesticks on the mantelpiece, the silver casket in the middle, turned the crystal dolphin towards the clock. They would come; they would stand; they would talk in the mincing tones which she could imitate, ladies and gentlemen. Of all, her mistress was loveliest-mistress of silver, of linen, of china, for the sun, the silver, doors off their hinges, Rumpelmayer's men, gave her a sense, as she laid the paper-knife on the inlaid table, of something achieved. Behold! Behold! she said, speaking to her old friends in the baker's shop, where she had first seen service at Caterham, prying into the glass. She was Lady Angela, attending Princess Mary, when in came Mrs. Dalloway.)

"Oh Lucy," she said, "the silver does look nice!"

"And how," she said, turning the crystal dolphin to stand straight, "how did you enjoy the play last night?" "Oh, they had to go before the end!" she said. "They had to be back at ten!" she said. "So they don't know what happened," she said. "That does seem hard luck," she said (for her servants stayed later, if they asked her). "That does seem rather a shame," she said, taking the old bald-looking cushion in the middle of the sofa and putting it in Lucy's arms, and giving her a little push, and crying:

"Take it away! Give it to Mrs. Walker with my compliments! Take it away!" she cried.

And Lucy stopped at the drawing-room door, holding the cushion, and said, very shyly, turning a little pink, Couldn't she help to mend that dress?

But, said Mrs. Dalloway, she had enough on her hands already, quite enough of her own to do without that.

"But, thank you, Lucy, oh, thank you," said Mrs. Dalloway, and thank you, thank you, she went on saying (sitting down on the sofa with her dress over her knees, her scissors, her silks), thank you, thank you, she went on saying in gratitude to her servants generally for helping her to be like this, to be what she wanted, gentle, generous-hearted. Her servants liked her. And then this dress of hers-where was the tear? and now her needle to be threaded. This was a favourite dress, one of Sally Parker's, the last almost she ever made, alas, for Sally had now retired, living at Ealing, and if ever I have a moment, thought Clarissa (but never would she have a moment any more), I shall go and see her at Ealing. For she was a character, thought Clarissa, a real artist. She thought of little out-of-the-way things; yet her dresses were never queer. You could wear them at Hatfield; at Buckingham Palace. She had worn them at Hatfield; at Buckingham Palace.

Quiet descended on her, calm, content, as her needle, drawing the silk smoothly to its gentle pause, collected the green folds together and attached them, very lightly, to the belt. So on a summer's day waves collect, overbalance, and fall; collect and fall; and the whole world seems to be saying "that is all" more and more ponderously, until even the heart in the body which lies in the sun on the beach says too, That is all. Fear no more, says the heart. Fear no more, says the heart, committing its burden to some sea, which sighs collectively for all sorrows, and renews, begins, collects, lets fall. And the body alone listens to the passing bee; the wave breaking; the dog barking, far away barking and barking.

"Heavens, the front-door bell!" exclaimed Clarissa, staying her needle. Roused, she listened.

"Mrs. Dalloway will see me," said the elderly man in the hall. "Oh yes, she will see *me*," he repeated, putting Lucy aside very benevolently, and running upstairs ever so quickly. "Yes, yes, yes," he muttered as he ran upstairs. "She will see me. After five years in India, Clarissa will see me."

"Who can-what can," asked Mrs. Dalloway (thinking it was outrageous to be interrupted at eleven o'clock on the morning of the day she was giving a party), hearing a step on the stairs. She heard a hand upon the door. She made to hide her dress, like a virgin protecting chastity, respecting privacy. Now the brass knob slipped. Now the door opened, and in came-for a single second she could not remember what he was called! so surprised she was to see him, so glad, so shy, so utterly taken aback to have Peter Walsh come to her unexpectedly in the morning! (She had not read his letter.)

"And how are you?" said Peter Walsh, positively trembling; taking both her hands; kissing both her hands. She's grown older, he thought, sitting down. I shan't tell her anything about it, he thought, for she's grown older. She's looking at me, he thought, a sudden embarrassment coming over him, though he had kissed her hands. Putting his hand into his pocket, he took out a large pocket-knife and half opened the blade.

Exactly the same, thought Clarissa; the same queer look; the same check suit; a little out of the straight his face is, a little thinner, dryer, perhaps, but he looks awfully well, and just the same.

"How heavenly it is to see you again!" she exclaimed. He had his knife out. That's so like him, she thought.

He had only reached town last night, he said; would have to go down into the country at once; and how was everything, how was everybody-Richard? Elizabeth?

"And what's all this?" he said, tilting his pen-knife towards her green dress.

He's very well dressed, thought Clarissa; yet he always criticises *me*.

Here she is mending her dress; mending her dress as usual, he thought; here she's been sitting all the time I've been in India; mending her dress; playing about; going to parties; running to the House and back and all that, he thought, growing more and more irritated, more and more agitated, for there's nothing in the world so bad for some women as marriage, he thought; and politics; and having a Conservative husband, like the admirable Richard. So it is, so it is, he thought, shutting his knife with a snap.

"Richard's very well. Richard's at a Committee," said Clarissa.

And she opened her scissors, and said, did he mind her just finishing what she was doing to her dress, for they had a party that night?

"Which I shan't ask you to," she said. "My dear Peter!" she said.

But it was delicious to hear her say that-my dear Peter! Indeed, it was all so delicious-the silver, the chairs; all so delicious!

Why wouldn't she ask him to her party? he asked.

Now of course, thought Clarissa, he's enchanting! perfectly enchanting! Now I remember how impossible it was ever to make up my mind-and why did I make up my mind-not to marry him? she wondered, that awful summer?

"But it's so extraordinary that you should have come this morning!" she cried, putting her hands, one on top of another, down on her dress.

"Do you remember," she said, "how the blinds used to flap at Bourton?"

"They did," he said; and he remembered breakfasting alone, very awkwardly, with her father; who had died; and he had not written to Clarissa. But he had never got on well with old Parry, that querulous, weak-kneed old man, Clarissa's father, Justin Parry.

"I often wish I'd got on better with your father," he said.

"But he never liked any one who-our friends," said Clarissa; and could have bitten her tongue for thus reminding Peter that he had wanted to marry her.

Of course I did, thought Peter; it almost broke my heart too, he thought; and was overcome with his own grief, which rose like a moon looked at from a terrace, ghastly beautiful with light from the sunken day. I was more unhappy than I've ever been since, he thought. And as if in truth he were sitting there on the terrace he edged a little towards Clarissa; put his hand out; raised it; let it fall. There above them it hung, that moon. She too seemed to be sitting with him on the terrace, in the moonlight.

"Herbert has it now," she said. "I never go there now," she said.

Then, just as happens on a terrace in the moonlight, when one person begins to feel ashamed that he is already bored, and yet as the other sits silent, very quiet, sadly looking at the moon, does not like to speak, moves his foot, clears his throat, notices some iron scroll on a table leg, stirs a leaf, but says nothing-so Peter Walsh did now. For why go back like this to the past? he thought. Why make him think of it again? Why make him suffer, when she had tortured him so infernally? Why?

"Do you remember the lake?" she said, in an abrupt voice, under the pressure of an emotion which caught her heart, made the muscles of her throat stiff, and contracted her lips in a spasm as she said "lake." For she was a child, throwing bread to the ducks, between her parents, and at the same time a grown woman coming to her parents who stood by the lake, holding her life in her arms which, as she neared them, grew larger and larger in her arms, until it became a whole life, a complete life, which she put down by them and said, "This is what I have made of it! This!" And what had she made of it? What, indeed? sitting there sewing this morning with Peter.

She looked at Peter Walsh; her look, passing through all that time and that emotion, reached him doubtfully; settled on him tearfully; and rose and fluttered away, as a bird touches a branch and rises and flutters away. Quite simply she wiped her eyes.

"Yes," said Peter. "Yes, yes, yes," he said, as if she drew up to the surface something which positively hurt him as it rose. Stop! Stop! he wanted to cry. For he was not old; his life was not over; not by any means. He was only just past fifty. Shall I tell her, he thought, or not? He would like to make a clean breast of it all. But she is too cold, he thought; sewing, with her scissors; Daisy would look ordinary beside Clarissa. And she would think me a failure, which I am in their sense, he thought; in the Dalloways' sense. Oh yes, he had no doubt about that; he was a failure, compared with all this-the inlaid table, the mounted paper-knife, the dolphin and the candlesticks, the chair-covers and the old valuable English tinted prints-he was a failure! I detest the smugness of the whole affair, he thought; Richard's doing, not Clarissa's; save that she married him. (Here Lucy came into the room, carrying silver, more silver, but charming, slender, graceful she looked, he thought, as she stooped to put it down.) And this has been going on all the time! he thought; week after week; Clarissa's life; while I—he thought; and at once everything seemed to radiate from him; journeys; rides; quarrels; adventures; bridge parties; love affairs; work; work, work! and he took out his knife quite openly-his old horn-handled knife which Clarissa could swear he had had these thirty years-and clenched his fist upon it.

What an extraordinary habit that was, Clarissa thought; always playing with a knife. Always making one feel, too, frivolous; empty-minded; a mere silly chatterbox, as he used. But I too, she thought, and, taking up her needle, summoned, like a Queen whose guards have fallen asleep and left her unprotected (she had been quite taken aback by this visit-it had upset her) so that any one can stroll in and have a look at her where she lies with the brambles curving over her, summoned to her help the things she did; the things she liked; her husband; Elizabeth; her self, in short, which Peter hardly knew now, all to come about her and beat off the enemy.

"Well, and what's happened to you?" she said. So before a battle begins, the horses paw the ground; toss their heads; the light shines on their flanks; their necks curve. So Peter Walsh and Clarissa, sitting side by side on the blue sofa, challenged each other. His powers chafed and tossed in him. He assembled from different quarters all sorts of things; praise; his career at Oxford; his marriage, which she knew nothing whatever about; how he had loved; and altogether done his job.

"Millions of things!" he exclaimed, and, urged by the assembly of powers which were now charging this way and that and giving him the feeling at once frightening and extremely exhilarating of being rushed through the air on the shoulders of people he could no longer see, he raised his hands to his forehead.

Clarissa sat very upright; drew in her breath.

"I am in love," he said, not to her however, but to some one raised up in the dark so that you could not touch her but must lay your garland down on the grass in the dark.

"In love," he repeated, now speaking rather dryly to Clarissa Dalloway; "in love with a girl in India." He had deposited his garland. Clarissa could make what she would of it.

"In love!" she said. That he at his age should be sucked under in his little bow-tie by that monster! And there's no flesh on his neck; his hands are red; and he's six months older than I am! her eye flashed back to her; but in her heart she felt, all the same, he is in love. He has that, she felt; he is in love.

But the indomitable egotism which for ever rides down the hosts opposed to it, the river which says on, on, on; even though, it admits, there may be no goal for us whatever, still on, on; this indomitable egotism charged her cheeks with colour; made her look very young; very pink; very bright-eyed as she sat with her dress upon her knee, and her needle held to the end of green silk, trembling a little. He was in love! Not with her. With some younger woman, of course.

"And who is she?" she asked.

Now this statue must be brought from its height and set down between them.

"A married woman, unfortunately," he said; "the wife of a Major in the Indian Army."

And with a curious ironical sweetness he smiled as he placed her in this ridiculous way before Clarissa.

(All the same, he is in love, thought Clarissa.)

"She has," he continued, very reasonably, "two small children; a boy and a girl; and I have come over to see my lawyers about the divorce."

There they are! he thought. Do what you like with them, Clarissa! There they are! And second by second it seemed to him that the wife of the Major in the Indian Army (his Daisy) and her two small children became more and more lovely as Clarissa looked at them; as if he had set light to a grey pellet on a plate and there had risen up a lovely tree in the brisk sea-salted air of their intimacy (for in some ways no one understood him, felt with him, as Clarissa did) —their exquisite intimacy.

She flattered him; she fooled him, thought Clarissa; shaping the woman, the wife of the Major in the Indian Army, with three strokes of a knife. What a waste! What a folly! All his life long Peter had been fooled like that; first getting sent down from Oxford; next marrying the girl on the boat going out to India; now the wife of a Major in the Indian Army-thank Heaven she had refused to marry him! Still, he was in love; her old friend, her dear Peter, he was in love.

"But what are you going to do?" she asked him. Oh the lawyers and solicitors, Messrs. Hooper and Grateley of Lincoln's Inn, they were going to do it, he said. And he actually pared his nails with his pocket-knife.

For Heaven's sake, leave your knife alone! she cried to herself in irrepressible irritation; it was his silly unconventionality, his weakness; his lack of the ghost of a notion what any one else was feeling that annoyed her, had always annoyed her; and now at his age, how silly!

I know all that, Peter thought; I know what I'm up against, he thought, running his finger along the blade of his knife, Clarissa and Dalloway and all the rest of them; but I'll show Clarissa- and then to his utter surprise, suddenly thrown by those uncontrollable forces thrown through the air, he burst into tears; wept; wept without the least shame, sitting on the sofa, the tears running down his cheeks.

And Clarissa had leant forward, taken his hand, drawn him to her, kissed him, —actually had felt his face on hers before she could down the brandishing of silver flashing-plumes like pampas grass in a tropic gale in her breast, which, subsiding, left her holding his hand, patting his knee and, feeling as she sat back extraordinarily at her ease with him and light-hearted, all in a clap it came over her, If I had married him, this gaiety would have been mine all day!

It was all over for her. The sheet was stretched and the bed narrow. She had gone up into the tower alone and left them blackberrying in the sun. The door had shut, and there among the dust of fallen plaster and the litter of birds' nests how distant the view had looked, and the sounds came thin and chill (once on Leith Hill, she remembered), and Richard, Richard! she cried, as a sleeper in the night starts and stretches a hand in the dark for help. Lunching with Lady Bruton, it came back to her. He has left me; I am alone for ever, she thought, folding her hands upon her knee.

Peter Walsh had got up and crossed to the window and stood with his back to her, flicking a bandanna handkerchief from side to side. Masterly and dry and desolate he looked, his thin shoulder-blades lifting his coat slightly; blowing his nose violently. Take me with you, Clarissa thought impulsively, as if he were starting directly upon some great voyage; and then, next moment, it was as if the five acts of a play that had been very exciting and moving were now over and she had lived a lifetime in them and had run away, had lived with Peter, and it was now over.

Now it was time to move, and, as a woman gathers her things together, her cloak, her gloves, her opera-glasses, and gets up to go out of the theatre into the street, she rose from the sofa and went to Peter.

And it was awfully strange, he thought, how she still had the power, as she came tinkling, rustling, still had the power as she came across the room, to make the moon, which he detested, rise at Bourton on the terrace in the summer sky.

"Tell me," he said, seizing her by the shoulders. "Are you happy, Clarissa? Does Richard —"

The door opened.

"Here is my Elizabeth," said Clarissa, emotionally, histrionically, perhaps.

"How d'y do?" said Elizabeth coming forward.

The sound of Big Ben striking the half-hour struck out between them with extraordinary vigour, as if a young man, strong, indifferent, inconsiderate, were swinging dumb-bells this way and that.

"Hullo, Elizabeth!" cried Peter, stuffing his handkerchief into his pocket, going quickly to her, saying "Good-bye, Clarissa" without looking at her, leaving the room quickly, and running downstairs and opening the hall door.

"Peter! Peter!" cried Clarissa, following him out on to the landing. "My party tonight! Remember my party tonight!" she cried, having to raise her voice against the roar of the open air, and, overwhelmed by the traffic and the sound of all the clocks striking, her voice crying "Remember my party tonight!" sounded frail and thin and very far away as Peter Walsh shut the door.

Remember my party, remember my party, said Peter Walsh as he stepped down the street, speaking to himself rhythmically, in time with the flow of the sound, the direct downright sound of Big Ben striking the half-hour. (The leaden circles dissolved in the air.) Oh these parties, he thought; Clarissa's parties. Why does she give these parties, he thought. Not that he blamed her or this effigy of a man in a tail-coat with a carnation in his buttonhole coming towards him. Only one person in the world could be as he was, in love. And there he was, this fortunate man, himself, reflected in the plate-glass window of a motor-car manufacturer in Victoria Street. All India lay behind him; plains, mountains; epidemics of cholera; a district twice as big as Ireland; decisions he had come to alone-he, Peter Walsh; who was now really for the first time in his life, in love. Clarissa had grown hard, he thought; and a trifle sentimental into the bargain, he suspected, looking at the great motor-cars capable of doing-how many miles on how many gallons? For he had a turn for mechanics; had invented a plough in his district, had ordered wheel-barrows from England, but the coolies wouldn't use them, all of which Clarissa knew nothing whatever about.

The way she said "Here is my Elizabeth!" —that annoyed him. Why not "Here's Elizabeth" simply? It was insincere. And Elizabeth didn't like it either. (Still the last tremors of the great booming voice shook the air round him; the half-hour; still early; only half-past eleven still.) For he understood young people; he liked them. There was always something cold in Clarissa, he thought. She had always, even as a girl, a sort of timidity, which in middle age becomes conventionality, and then it's all up, it's all up, he thought, looking rather drearily into the glassy depths, and wondering whether by calling at that hour he had annoyed her; overcome with shame suddenly at having been a fool; wept; been emotional; told her everything, as usual, as usual.

As a cloud crosses the sun, silence falls on London; and falls on the mind. Effort ceases. Time flaps on the mast. There we stop; there we stand. Rigid, the skeleton of habit alone upholds the human frame. Where there is nothing, Peter Walsh said to himself; feeling hollowed out, utterly empty within. Clarissa refused me, he thought. He stood there thinking, Clarissa refused me.

Ah, said St. Margaret's, like a hostess who comes into her drawing-room on the very stroke of the hour and finds her guests there already. I am not late. No, it is precisely half-past eleven, she says. Yet, though she is perfectly right, her voice, being the voice of the hostess, is reluctant to inflict its individuality. Some grief for the past holds it back; some concern for the present. It is half-past eleven, she says, and the sound of St. Margaret's glides into the recesses of the heart and buries itself in ring after ring of sound, like something alive which wants to confide itself, to disperse itself, to be, with a tremor of delight, at rest-like Clarissa herself, thought Peter Walsh, coming down the stairs on the stroke of the hour in white. It is Clarissa herself, he thought, with a deep emotion, and an extraordinarily clear, yet puzzling, recollection of her, as if this bell had come into the room years ago, where they sat at some moment of great intimacy, and had gone from one to the other and had left, like a bee with honey, laden with the moment. But what room? What moment? And why had he been so profoundly happy when the clock was striking? Then, as the sound of St. Margaret's languished, he thought, She has been ill, and the sound expressed languor and suffering. It was her heart, he remembered; and the sudden loudness of the final stroke tolled for death that surprised in the midst of life, Clarissa falling where she stood, in her drawing-room. No! No! he cried. She is not dead! I am not old, he cried, and marched up Whitehall, as if there rolled down to him, vigorous, unending, his future.

He was not old, or set, or dried in the least. As for caring what they said of him-the Dalloways, the Whitbreads, and their set, he cared not a straw-not a straw (though it was true he would have, some time or other, to see whether Richard couldn't help him to some job). Striding, staring, he glared at the statue of the Duke of Cambridge. He had been sent down from Oxford-true. He had been a Socialist, in some sense a failure-true. Still the future of civilisation lies, he thought, in the hands of young men like that; of young men such as he was, thirty years ago; with their love of abstract principles; getting books sent out to them all the way from London to a peak in the Himalayas; reading science; reading philosophy. The future lies in the hands of young men like that, he thought.

A patter like the patter of leaves in a wood came from behind, and with it a rustling, regular thudding sound, which as it overtook him drummed his thoughts, strict in step, up Whitehall, without his doing. Boys in uniform, carrying guns, marched with their eyes ahead of them, marched, their arms stiff, and on their faces an expression like the letters of a legend written round the base of a statue praising duty, gratitude, fidelity, love of England.

It is, thought Peter Walsh, beginning to keep step with them, a very fine training. But they did not look robust. They were weedy for the most part, boys of sixteen, who might, tomorrow, stand behind bowls of rice, cakes of soap on counters. Now they wore on them unmixed with sensual pleasure or daily preoccupations the solemnity of the wreath which they had fetched from Finsbury Pavement to the empty tomb. They had taken their vow. The traffic respected it; vans were stopped.

I can't keep up with them, Peter Walsh thought, as they marched up Whitehall, and sure enough, on they marched, past him, past every one, in their steady way, as if one will worked legs and arms uniformly, and life, with its varieties, its irreticences, had been laid under a pavement of monuments and wreaths and drugged into a stiff yet staring corpse by discipline. One had to respect it; one might laugh; but one had to respect it, he thought. There they go, thought Peter Walsh, pausing at the edge of the pavement; and all the exalted statues, Nelson, Gordon, Havelock, the black, the spectacular images of great soldiers stood looking ahead of them, as if they too had made the same renunciation (Peter Walsh felt he too had made it, the great renunciation), trampled under the same temptations, and achieved at length a marble stare. But the stare Peter Walsh did not want for himself in the least; though he could respect it in others. He could respect it in boys. They don't know the troubles of the flesh yet, he thought, as the marching boys disappeared in the direction of the Strand-all that I've been through, he thought, crossing the road, and standing under Gordon's statue, Gordon whom as a boy he had worshipped; Gordon standing lonely with one leg raised and his arms crossed,—poor Gordon, he thought.

And just because nobody yet knew he was in London, except Clarissa, and the earth, after the voyage, still seemed an island to him, the strangeness of standing alone, alive, unknown, at half-past eleven in Trafalgar Square overcame him. What is it? Where am I? And why, after all, does one do it? he thought, the divorce seeming all moonshine. And down his mind went flat as a marsh, and three great emotions bowled over him; understanding; a vast philanthropy;

and finally, as if the result of the others, an irrepressible, exquisite delight; as if inside his brain by another hand strings were pulled, shutters moved, and he, having nothing to do with it, yet stood at the opening of endless avenues, down which if he chose he might wander. He had not felt so young for years.

He had escaped! was utterly free-as happens in the downfall of habit when the mind, like an unguarded flame, bows and bends and seems about to blow from its holding. I haven't felt so young for years! thought Peter, escaping (only of course for an hour or so) from being precisely what he was, and feeling like a child who runs out of doors, and sees, as he runs, his old nurse waving at the wrong window. But she's extraordinarily attractive, he thought, as, walking across Trafalgar Square in the direction of the Haymarket, came a young woman who, as she passed Gordon's statue, seemed, Peter Walsh thought (susceptible as he was), to shed veil after veil, until she became the very woman he had always had in mind; young, but stately; merry, but discreet; black, but enchanting.

Straightening himself and stealthily fingering his pocket-knife he started after her to follow this woman, this excitement, which seemed even with its back turned to shed on him a light which connected them, which singled him out, as if the random uproar of the traffic had whispered through hollowed hands his name, not Peter, but his private name which he called himself in his own thoughts. "You," she said, only "you," saying it with her white gloves and her shoulders. Then the thin long cloak which the wind stirred as she walked past Dent's shop in Cockspur Street blew out with an enveloping kindness, a mournful tenderness, as of arms that would open and take the tired—

But she's not married; she's young; quite young, thought Peter, the red carnation he had seen her wear as she came across Trafalgar Square burning again in his eyes and making her lips red. But she waited at the kerbstone. There was a dignity about her. She was not worldly, like Clarissa; not rich, like Clarissa. Was she, he wondered as she moved, respectable? Witty, with a lizard's flickering tongue, he thought (for one must invent, must allow oneself a little diversion), a cool waiting wit, a darting wit; not noisy.

She moved; she crossed; he followed her. To embarrass her was the last thing he wished. Still if she stopped he would say "Come and have an ice," he would say, and she would answer, perfectly simply, "Oh yes."

But other people got between them in the street, obstructing him, blotting her out. He pursued; she changed. There was colour in her cheeks; mockery in her eyes; he was an adventurer, reckless, he thought, swift, daring, indeed (landed as he was last night from India) a romantic buccaneer, careless of all these damned proprieties, yellow dressing-gowns, pipes, fishing-rods, in the shop windows; and respectability and evening parties and spruce old men wearing white slips beneath their waistcoats. He was a buccaneer. On and on she went, across Piccadilly, and up Regent Street, ahead of him, her cloak, her gloves, her shoulders combining with the fringes and the laces and the feather boas in the windows to make the spirit of finery and whimsy which dwindled out of the shops on to the pavement, as the light of a lamp goes wavering at night over hedges in the darkness.

Laughing and delightful, she had crossed Oxford Street and Great Portland Street and turned down one of the little streets, and now, and now, the great moment was approaching, for now she slackened, opened her bag, and with one look in his direction, but not at him, one look that bade farewell, summed up the whole situation and dismissed it triumphantly, for ever, had fitted her key, opened the door, and gone! Clarissa's voice saying, Remember my party, Remember my party, sang in his ears. The house was one of those flat red houses with hanging flower-baskets of vague impropriety. It was over.

Well, I've had my fun; I've had it, he thought, looking up at the swinging baskets of pale geraniums. And it was smashed to atoms-his fun, for it was half made up, as he knew very well; invented, this escapade with the girl; made up, as one makes up the better part of life, he thought-making oneself up; making her up; creating an exquisite amusement, and something more. But odd it was, and quite true; all this one could never share-it smashed to atoms.

He turned; went up the street, thinking to find somewhere to sit, till it was time for Lincoln's Inn-for Messrs. Hooper and Grateley. Where should he go? No matter. Up the street, then, towards Regent's Park. His boots on the pavement struck out "no matter"; for it was early, still very early.

It was a splendid morning too. Like the pulse of a perfect heart, life struck straight through the streets. There was no fumbling-no hesitation. Sweeping and swerving, accurately, punctually, noiselessly, there, precisely at the right instant, the motor-car stopped at the door. The girl, silk-stockinged, feathered, evanescent, but not to him particularly attractive (for he had had his fling), alighted. Admirable butlers, tawny chow dogs, halls laid in black and white lozenges with white blinds blowing, Peter saw through the opened door and approved of. A splendid achievement in its own way, after all, London; the season; civilisation. Coming as he did from a respectable Anglo-Indian family which for at least three generations had administered the affairs of a continent (it's strange, he thought, what a sentiment I have about that, disliking India, and empire, and army as he did), there were moments when civilisation, even of this sort, seemed dear to him as a personal possession; moments of pride in England; in butlers; chow dogs; girls in their security. Ridiculous enough, still there it is, he thought. And the doctors and men of business and capable women all going about their business, punctual, alert, robust, seemed to him wholly admirable, good fellows, to whom one would entrust one's life, companions in the art of living, who would see one through. What with one thing and another, the show was really very tolerable; and he would sit down in the shade and smoke.

There was Regent's Park. Yes. As a child he had walked in Regent's Park-odd, he thought, how the thought of childhood keeps coming back to me-the result of seeing Clarissa, perhaps; for women live much more in the past than we do, he thought. They attach themselves to places; and their fathers—a woman's always proud of her father. Bourton was a nice place, a very nice place, but I could never get on with the old man, he thought. There was quite a scene one night-an argument about something or other, what, he could not remember. Politics presumably.

Yes, he remembered Regent's Park; the long straight walk; the little house where one bought air-balls to the left; an absurd statue with an inscription somewhere or other. He looked for an empty seat. He did not want to be bothered (feeling a little drowsy as he did) by people asking him the time. An elderly grey nurse, with a baby asleep in its perambulator-that was the best he could do for himself; sit down at the far end of the seat by that nurse.

She's a queer-looking girl, he thought, suddenly remembering Elizabeth as she came into the room and stood by her mother. Grown big; quite grown-up, not exactly pretty; handsome rather; and she can't be more than eighteen. Probably she doesn't get on with Clarissa. "There's my Elizabeth"—that sort of thing-why not "Here's Elizabeth" simply? —trying to make out, like most mothers, that things are what they're not. She trusts to her charm too much, he thought. She overdoes it.

The rich benignant cigar smoke eddied coolly down his throat; he puffed it out again in rings which breasted the air bravely for a moment; blue, circular—I shall try and get a word alone with Elizabeth tonight, he thought-then began to wobble into hour-glass shapes and taper away; odd shapes they take, he thought. Suddenly he closed his eyes, raised his hand with an effort, and threw away the heavy end of his cigar. A great brush swept smooth across his mind, sweeping across it moving branches, children's voices, the shuffle of feet, and people passing, and humming traffic, rising and falling traffic. Down, down he sank into the plumes and feathers of sleep, sank, and was muffled over.

The grey nurse resumed her knitting as Peter Walsh, on the hot seat beside her, began snoring. In her grey dress, moving her hands indefatigably yet quietly, she seemed like the champion of the rights of sleepers, like one of those spectral presences which rise in twilight in woods made of sky and branches. The solitary traveller, haunter of lanes, disturber of ferns, and devastator of great hemlock plants, looking up, suddenly sees the giant figure at the end of the ride.

By conviction an atheist perhaps, he is taken by surprise with moments of extraordinary exaltation. Nothing exists outside us except a state of mind, he thinks; a desire for solace, for relief, for something outside these miserable pigmies, these feeble, these ugly, these craven men and women. But if he can conceive of her, then in some sort she exists, he thinks, and advancing down the path with his eyes upon sky and branches he rapidly endows them with womanhood; sees with amazement how grave they become; how majestically, as the breeze stirs them, they dispense with a dark flutter of the leaves charity, comprehension, absolution, and then, flinging themselves suddenly aloft, confound the piety of their aspect with a wild carouse.

Such are the visions which proffer great cornucopias full of fruit to the solitary traveller, or murmur in his ear like sirens lolloping away on the green sea waves, or are dashed in his face like bunches of roses, or rise to the surface like pale faces which fishermen flounder through floods to embrace.

Such are the visions which ceaselessly float up, pace beside, put their faces in front of, the actual thing; often overpowering the solitary traveller and taking away from him the sense of the earth, the wish to return, and giving him for substitute a general peace, as if (so he thinks as he advances down the forest ride) all this fever of living were simplicity itself; and myriads of things merged in one thing; and this figure, made of sky and branches as it is, had risen from the troubled sea (he is elderly, past fifty now) as a shape might be sucked up out of the waves to shower down from her magnificent hands compassion, comprehension, absolution. So, he thinks, may I never go back to the lamplight; to the sitting-room; never finish my book; never knock out my pipe; never ring for Mrs. Turner to clear away; rather let me walk straight on to this great figure, who will, with a toss of her head, mount me on her streamers and let me blow to nothingness with the rest.

Such are the visions. The solitary traveller is soon beyond the wood; and there, coming to the door with shaded eyes, possibly to look for his return, with hands raised, with white apron blowing, is an elderly woman who seems (so powerful is this infirmity) to seek, over a desert, a lost son; to search for a rider destroyed; to be the figure of the mother whose sons have been killed in the battles of the world. So, as the solitary traveller advances down the village street where the women stand knitting and the men dig in the garden, the evening seems ominous; the figures still; as if some august fate, known to them, awaited without fear, were about to sweep them into complete annihilation.

Indoors among ordinary things, the cupboard, the table, the window-sill with its geraniums, suddenly the outline of the landlady, bending to remove the cloth, becomes soft with light, an adorable emblem which only the recollection of cold human contacts forbids us to embrace. She takes the marmalade; she shuts it in the cupboard.

"There is nothing more tonight, sir?"

But to whom does the solitary traveller make reply?

So the elderly nurse knitted over the sleeping baby in Regent's Park. So Peter Walsh snored. He woke with extreme suddenness, saying to himself, "The death of the soul."

"Lord, Lord!" he said to himself out loud, stretching and opening his eyes. "The death of the soul." The words attached themselves to some scene, to some room, to some past he had been dreaming of. It became clearer; the scene, the room, the past he had been dreaming of.

It was at Bourton that summer, early in the 'nineties, when he was so passionately in love with Clarissa. There were a great many people there, laughing and talking, sitting round a table after tea and the room was bathed in yellow light and full of cigarette smoke. They were talking about a man who had married his housemaid, one of the neighbouring squires, he had forgotten his name. He had married his housemaid, and she had been brought to Bourton to call-an awful visit it had been. She was absurdly over-dressed, "like a cockatoo," Clarissa had said, imitating her, and she never stopped talking. On and on she went, on and on. Clarissa imitated her. Then somebody said-Sally Seton it was-did it make any real difference to one's feelings to know that before they'd married she had had a baby? (In those days, in mixed company, it was a bold thing to say.) He could see Clarissa now, turning bright pink; somehow contracting; and saying, "Oh, I shall never be able to speak to her again!" Whereupon the whole party sitting round the tea-table seemed to wobble. It was very uncomfortable.

He hadn't blamed her for minding the fact, since in those days a girl brought up as she was, knew nothing, but it was her manner that annoyed him; timid; hard; something arrogant; unimaginative; prudish. "The death of the soul." He had said that instinctively, ticketing the moment as he used to do-the death of her soul.

Every one wobbled; every one seemed to bow, as she spoke, and then to stand up different. He could see Sally Seton, like a child who has been in mischief, leaning forward, rather flushed, wanting to talk, but afraid, and Clarissa did frighten people. (She was Clarissa's greatest friend, always about the place, totally unlike her, an attractive creature, handsome, dark, with the reputation in those days of great daring and he used to give her cigars, which she smoked in her bedroom. She had either been engaged to somebody or quarrelled with her family and old Parry disliked them both equally, which was a great bond.) Then Clarissa, still with an air of being offended with them all, got up, made some excuse, and went off, alone. As she opened the door, in came that great shaggy dog which ran after sheep. She flung herself upon him, went into raptures. It was as if she said to Peter-it was all aimed at him, he knew—"I know you thought me absurd about that woman just now; but see how extraordinarily sympathetic I am; see how I love my Rob!"

They had always this queer power of communicating without words. She knew directly he criticised her. Then she would do something quite obvious to defend herself, like this fuss with the dog-but it never took him in, he always saw through Clarissa. Not that he said anything, of course; just sat looking glum. It was the way their quarrels often began.

She shut the door. At once he became extremely depressed. It all seemed useless-going on being in love; going on quarrelling; going on making it up, and he wandered off alone, among outhouses, stables, looking at the horses. (The place was quite a humble one; the Parrys were never very well off; but there were always grooms and stable-boys about-Clarissa loved riding-and an old coachman-what was his name?—an old nurse, old Moody, old Goody, some such name they called her, whom one was taken to visit in a little room with lots of photographs, lots of bird-cages.)

It was an awful evening! He grew more and more gloomy, not about that only; about everything. And he couldn't see her; couldn't explain to her; couldn't have it out. There were always people about-she'd go on as if nothing had happened. That was the devilish part of her-this coldness, this woodenness, something very profound in her, which he had felt again this morning talking to her; an impenetrability. Yet Heaven knows he loved her. She had some queer power of fiddling on one's nerves, turning one's nerves to fiddle-strings, yes.

He had gone in to dinner rather late, from some idiotic idea of making himself felt, and had sat down by old Miss Parry-Aunt Helena-Mr. Parry's sister, who was supposed to preside. There she sat in her white Cashmere shawl, with her head against the window—a formidable old lady, but kind to him, for he had found her some rare flower, and she was a great botanist, marching off in thick boots with a black collecting-box slung between her shoulders. He sat down beside her, and couldn't speak. Everything seemed to race past him; he just sat there, eating. And then halfway through dinner he made himself look across at Clarissa for the first time. She was talking to a young man on her right. He had a sudden revelation. "She will marry that man," he said to himself. He didn't even know his name.

For of course it was that afternoon, that very afternoon, that Dalloway had come over; and Clarissa called him "Wickham"; that was the beginning of it all. Somebody had brought him over; and Clarissa got his name wrong. She introduced him to everybody as Wickham. At last he said "My name is Dalloway!"—that was his first view of Richard—a fair young man, rather awkward, sitting on a deck-chair, and blurting out "My name is Dalloway!" Sally got hold of it; always after that she called him "My name is Dalloway!"

He was a prey to revelations at that time. This one-that she would marry Dalloway-was blinding-overwhelming at the moment. There was a sort of-how could he put it? —a sort of ease in her manner to him; something maternal; something gentle. They were talking about politics. All through dinner he tried to hear what they were saying.

Afterwards he could remember standing by old Miss Parry's chair in the drawing-room. Clarissa came up, with her perfect manners, like a real hostess, and wanted to introduce him to some one-spoke as if they had never met before, which enraged him. Yet even then he admired her for it. He admired her courage; her social instinct; he admired her power of carrying things through. "The perfect hostess," he said to her, whereupon she winced all over. But he meant her to feel it. He would have done anything to hurt her after seeing her with Dalloway. So she left him. And he had a feeling that they were all gathered together in a conspiracy against him-laughing and talking-behind his back. There he stood by Miss Parry's chair as though he had been cut out of wood, he talking about wild flowers. Never, never had he suffered so infernally! He must have forgotten even to pretend to listen; at last he woke up; he saw Miss Parry looking rather disturbed, rather indignant, with her prominent eyes fixed. He almost cried out that he couldn't attend because he was in Hell! People began going out of the room. He heard them talking about fetching cloaks; about its being cold on the water, and so on. They were going boating on the lake by moonlight-one of Sally's mad ideas. He could hear her describing the moon. And they all went out. He was left quite alone.

"Don't you want to go with them?" said Aunt Helena-old Miss Parry! —she had guessed. And he turned round and there was Clarissa again. She had come back to fetch him. He was overcome by her generosity-her goodness.

"Come along," she said. "They're waiting." He had never felt so happy in the whole of his life! Without a word they made it up. They walked down to the lake. He had twenty minutes of perfect happiness. Her voice, her laugh, her dress (something floating, white, crimson), her spirit, her adventurousness; she made them all disembark and explore the island; she startled a hen; she laughed; she sang. And all the time, he knew perfectly well, Dalloway was falling in love with her; she was falling in love with Dalloway; but it didn't seem to matter. Nothing mattered. They sat on the ground and talked-he and Clarissa. They went in and out of each other's minds without any effort. And then in a second it was over. He said to himself as they were getting into the boat, "She will marry that man," dully, without any resentment; but it was an obvious thing. Dalloway would marry Clarissa.

Dalloway rowed them in. He said nothing. But somehow as they watched him start, jumping on to his bicycle to ride twenty miles through the woods, wobbling off down the drive, waving his hand and disappearing, he obviously did feel, instinctively, tremendously, strongly, all that; the night; the romance; Clarissa. He deserved to have her.

For himself, he was absurd. His demands upon Clarissa (he could see it now) were absurd. He asked impossible things. He made terrible scenes. She would have accepted him still, perhaps, if he had been less absurd. Sally thought so. She wrote him all that summer long letters; how they had talked of him; how she had praised him, how Clarissa burst into tears! It was an extraordinary summer-all letters, scenes, telegrams-arriving at Bourton early in the morning, hanging about till the servants were up; appalling *tête-à-têtes* with old Mr. Parry at breakfast; Aunt Helena formidable but kind; Sally sweeping him off for talks in the vegetable garden; Clarissa in bed with headaches.

The final scene, the terrible scene which he believed had mattered more than anything in the whole of his life (it might be an exaggeration-but still so it did seem now) happened at three o'clock in the afternoon of a very hot day. It was a trifle that led up to it-Sally at lunch saying something about Dalloway, and calling him "My name is Dalloway"; whereupon Clarissa suddenly stiffened, coloured, in a way she had, and rapped out sharply, "We've had enough of that feeble joke." That was all; but for him it was precisely as if she had said, "I'm only amusing myself with you; I've an understanding with Richard Dalloway." So he took it. He had not slept for nights. "It's got to be finished one way or the other," he said to himself. He sent a note to her by Sally asking her to meet him by the fountain at three. "Something very important has happened," he scribbled at the end of it.

The fountain was in the middle of a little shrubbery, far from the house, with shrubs and trees all round it. There she came, even before the time, and they stood with the fountain between them, the spout (it was broken) dribbling water incessantly. How sights fix themselves upon the mind! For example, the vivid green moss.

She did not move. "Tell me the truth, tell me the truth," he kept on saying. He felt as if his forehead would burst. She seemed contracted, petrified. She did not move. "Tell me the truth," he repeated, when suddenly that old man Breitkopf popped his head in carrying the *Times;* stared at them; gaped; and went away. They neither of them moved. "Tell me the truth," he repeated. He felt that he was grinding against something physically hard; she was unyielding. She was like iron, like flint, rigid up the backbone. And when she said, "It's no use. It's no use. This is the end" —after he had spoken for hours, it seemed, with the tears running down his cheeks-it was as if she had hit him in the face. She turned, she left him, went away.

"Clarissa!" he cried. "Clarissa!" But she never came back. It was over. He went away that night. He never saw her again.

It was awful, he cried, awful, awful!

Still, the sun was hot. Still, one got over things. Still, life had a way of adding day to day. Still, he thought, yawning and beginning to take notice-Regent's Park had changed very little since he was a boy, except for the squirrels-still, presumably there were compensations-when little Elise Mitchell, who had been picking up pebbles to add to the pebble collection which she and her brother were making on the nursery mantelpiece, plumped her handful down on the nurse's knee and scudded off again full tilt into a lady's legs. Peter Walsh laughed out.

But Lucrezia Warren Smith was saying to herself, It's wicked; why should I suffer? she was asking, as she walked down the broad path. No; I can't stand it any longer, she was saying, having left Septimus, who wasn't Septimus any longer, to say hard, cruel, wicked things, to talk to himself, to talk to a dead man, on the seat over there; when the child ran full tilt into her, fell flat, and burst out crying.

That was comforting rather. She stood her upright, dusted her frock, kissed her.

But for herself she had done nothing wrong; she had loved Septimus; she had been happy; she had had a beautiful home, and there her sisters lived still, making hats. Why should *she* suffer?

The child ran straight back to its nurse, and Rezia saw her scolded, comforted, taken up by the nurse who put down her knitting, and the kind-looking man gave her his watch to blow open to comfort her-but why should *she* be exposed? Why not left in Milan? Why tortured? Why?

Slightly waved by tears the broad path, the nurse, the man in grey, the perambulator, rose and fell before her eyes. To be rocked by this malignant torturer was her lot. But why? She was like a bird sheltering under the thin hollow of a leaf, who blinks at the sun when the leaf moves; starts at the crack of a dry twig. She was exposed; she was surrounded by the enormous trees, vast clouds of an indifferent world, exposed; tortured; and why should she suffer? Why?

She frowned; she stamped her foot. She must go back again to Septimus since it was almost time for them to be going to Sir William Bradshaw. She must go back and tell him, go back to him sitting there on the green chair under the tree, talking to himself, or to that dead man Evans, whom she had only seen once for a moment in the shop. He had seemed a nice quiet man; a great friend of Septimus's, and he had been killed in the War. But such things happen to every one. Every one has friends who were killed in the War. Every one gives up something when they marry. She had given up her home. She had come to live here, in this awful city. But Septimus let himself think about horrible things, as she could too, if she tried. He had grown stranger and stranger. He said people were talking behind the bedroom walls. Mrs. Filmer thought it odd. He saw things too-he had seen an old woman's head in the middle of a fern. Yet he could be happy when he chose. They went to Hampton Court on top of a bus, and they were perfectly happy. All the little red and yellow flowers were out on the grass, like floating lamps he said, and talked and chattered and laughed, making up stories. Suddenly he said, "Now we will kill ourselves," when they were standing by the river, and he looked at it with a look which she had seen in his eyes when a train went by, or an omnibus —a look as if something fascinated him; and she felt he was going from her and she caught him by the arm. But going home he was perfectly quiet-perfectly reasonable. He would argue with her about killing themselves; and explain how wicked people were; how he could see them making up lies as they passed in the street. He knew all their thoughts, he said; he knew everything. He knew the meaning of the world, he said.

Then when they got back he could hardly walk. He lay on the sofa and made her hold his hand to prevent him from falling down, down, he cried, into the flames! and saw faces laughing at him, calling him horrible disgusting names, from the walls, and hands pointing round the screen. Yet they were quite alone. But he began to talk aloud, answering people, arguing, laughing, crying, getting very excited and making her write things down. Perfect nonsense it was; about death; about Miss Isabel Pole. She could stand it no longer. She would go back.

She was close to him now, could see him staring at the sky, muttering, clasping his hands. Yet Dr. Holmes said there was nothing the matter with him. What then had happened-why had he gone, then, why, when she sat by him, did he start, frown at her, move away, and point at her hand, take her hand, look at it terrified?

Was it that she had taken off her wedding ring? "My hand has grown so thin," she said. "I have put it in my purse," she told him.

He dropped her hand. Their marriage was over, he thought, with agony, with relief. The rope was cut; he mounted; he was free, as it was decreed that he, Septimus, the lord of men, should be free; alone (since his wife had thrown away her wedding ring; since she had left him), he, Septimus, was alone, called forth in advance of the mass of men to hear the truth, to learn the meaning, which now at last, after all the toils of civilisation-Greeks, Romans, Shakespeare, Darwin, and now himself-was to be given whole to... . "To whom?" he asked aloud. "To the Prime Minister," the voices which rustled above his head replied. The supreme secret must be told to the Cabinet; first that trees are alive; next there is no crime; next love, universal love, he muttered, gasping, trembling, painfully drawing out these profound truths which needed, so deep were they, so difficult, an immense effort to speak out, but the world was entirely changed by them for ever.

No crime; love; he repeated, fumbling for his card and pencil, when a Skye terrier snuffed his trousers and he started in an agony of fear. It was turning into a man! He could not watch it happen! It was horrible, terrible to see a dog become a man! At once the dog trotted away.

Heaven was divinely merciful, infinitely benignant. It spared him, pardoned his weakness. But what was the scientific explanation (for one must be scientific above all things)? Why could he see through bodies, see into the future, when dogs will become men? It was the heat wave presumably, operating upon a brain made sensitive by eons of evolution. Scientifically speaking, the flesh was melted off the world. His body was macerated until only the nerve fibres were left. It was spread like a veil upon a rock.

He lay back in his chair, exhausted but upheld. He lay resting, waiting, before he again interpreted, with effort, with agony, to mankind. He lay very high, on the back of the world. The earth thrilled beneath him. Red flowers grew through his flesh; their stiff leaves rustled by his head. Music began clanging against the rocks up here. It is a motor horn down in the street, he muttered; but up here it cannoned from rock to rock, divided, met in shocks of sound which rose in smooth columns (that music should be visible was a discovery) and became an anthem, an anthem twined round now by a shepherd boy's piping (That's an old man playing a penny whistle by the public-house, he muttered) which, as the boy stood still came bubbling from his pipe, and then, as he climbed higher, made its exquisite plaint while the traffic passed beneath. This boy's elegy is played among the traffic, thought Septimus. Now he withdraws up into the snows, and roses hang about him-the thick red roses which grow on my bedroom wall, he reminded himself. The music stopped. He has his penny, he reasoned it out, and has gone on to the next public-house.

But he himself remained high on his rock, like a drowned sailor on a rock. I leant over the edge of the boat and fell down, he thought. I went under the sea. I have been dead, and yet am now alive, but let me rest still; he begged (he was talking to himself again-it was awful, awful!); and as, before waking, the voices of birds and the sound of wheels chime and chatter in a queer harmony, grow louder and louder and the sleeper feels himself drawing to the shores of life, so he felt himself drawing towards life, the sun growing hotter, cries sounding louder, something tremendous about to happen.

He had only to open his eyes; but a weight was on them; a fear. He strained; he pushed; he looked; he saw Regent's Park before him. Long streamers of sunlight fawned at his feet. The trees waved, brandished. We welcome, the world seemed to say; we accept; we create. Beauty, the world seemed to say. And as if to prove it (scientifically) wherever he looked at the houses, at the railings, at the antelopes stretching over the palings, beauty sprang instantly. To watch a leaf quivering in the rush of air was an exquisite joy. Up in the sky swallows swooping, swerving, flinging themselves in and out, round and round, yet always with perfect control as if elastics held them; and the flies rising and falling; and the sun spotting now this leaf, now that, in mockery, dazzling it with soft gold in pure good temper; and now and again some chime (it might be a motor horn) tinkling divinely on the grass stalks-all of this, calm and reasonable as it was, made out of ordinary things as it was, was the truth now; beauty, that was the truth now. Beauty was everywhere.

"It is time," said Rezia.

The word "time" split its husk; poured its riches over him; and from his lips fell like shells, like shavings from a plane, without his making them, hard, white, imperishable words, and flew to attach themselves to their places in an ode to Time; an immortal ode to Time. He sang. Evans answered from behind the tree. The dead were in Thessaly, Evans sang, among the orchids. There they waited till the War was over, and now the dead, now Evans himself—

"For God's sake don't come!" Septimus cried out. For he could not look upon the dead.

But the branches parted. A man in grey was actually walking towards them. It was Evans! But no mud was on him; no wounds; he was not changed. I must tell the whole world, Septimus cried, raising his hand (as the dead man in the grey suit came nearer), raising his hand like some colossal figure who has lamented the fate of man for ages in the desert alone with his hands pressed to his forehead, furrows of despair on his cheeks, and now sees light on the desert's edge which broadens and strikes the iron-black figure (and Septimus half rose from his chair), and with legions of men prostrate behind him he, the giant mourner, receives for one moment on his face the whole—

"But I am so unhappy, Septimus," said Rezia trying to make him sit down.

The millions lamented; for ages they had sorrowed. He would turn round, he would tell them in a few moments, only a few moments more, of this relief, of this joy, of this astonishing revelation—

"The time, Septimus," Rezia repeated. "What is the time?"

He was talking, he was starting, this man must notice him. He was looking at them.

"I will tell you the time," said Septimus, very slowly, very drowsily, smiling mysteriously. As he sat smiling at the dead man in the grey suit the quarter struck-the quarter to twelve.

And that is being young, Peter Walsh thought as he passed them. To be having an awful scene-the poor girl looked absolutely desperate-in the middle of the morning. But what was it about, he wondered, what had the young man in the overcoat been saying to her to make her look like that; what awful fix had they got themselves into, both to look so desperate as that on a fine summer morning? The amusing thing about coming back to England, after five years, was the way it made, anyhow the first days, things stand out as if one had never seen them before; lovers squabbling under a tree; the domestic family life of the parks. Never had he seen London look so enchanting-the softness of the distances; the richness; the greenness; the civilisation, after India, he thought, strolling across the grass.

This susceptibility to impressions had been his undoing no doubt. Still at his age he had, like a boy or a girl even, these alternations of mood; good days, bad days, for no reason whatever, happiness from a pretty face, downright misery at the sight of a frump. After India of course one fell in love with every woman one met. There was a freshness about them; even the poorest dressed better than five years ago surely; and to his eye the fashions had never been so becoming; the long black cloaks; the slimness; the elegance; and then the delicious and apparently universal habit of paint. Every woman, even the most respectable, had roses blooming under glass; lips cut with a knife; curls of Indian ink; there was design, art, everywhere; a change of some sort had undoubtedly taken place. What did the young people think about? Peter Walsh asked himself.

Those five years —1918 to 1923 —had been, he suspected, somehow very important. People looked different. Newspapers seemed different. Now for instance there was a man writing quite openly in one of the respectable weeklies about water-closets. That you couldn't have done ten years ago-written quite openly about water-closets in a respectable weekly. And then this taking out a stick of rouge, or a powder-puff and making up in public. On board ship coming home there were lots of young men and girls-Betty and Bertie he remembered in particular-carrying on quite openly; the old mother sitting and watching them with her knitting, cool as a cucumber. The girl would stand still and powder her nose in front of every one. And they weren't engaged; just having a good time; no feelings hurt on either side. As hard as nails she was-Betty What'shername —; but a thorough good sort. She would make a very good wife at thirty-she would marry when it suited her to marry; marry some rich man and live in a large house near Manchester.

Who was it now who had done that? Peter Walsh asked himself, turning into the Broad Walk, —married a rich man and lived in a large house near Manchester? Somebody who had written him a long, gushing letter quite lately about "blue hydrangeas." It was seeing blue hydrangeas that made her think of him and the old days-Sally Seton, of course! It was Sally Seton-the last person in the world one would have expected to marry a rich man and live in a large house near Manchester, the wild, the daring, the romantic Sally!

But of all that ancient lot, Clarissa's friends-Whitbreads, Kinderleys, Cunninghams, Kinloch-Jones's —Sally was probably the best. She tried to get hold of things by the right end anyhow. She saw through Hugh Whitbread anyhow-the admirable Hugh-when Clarissa and the rest were at his feet.

"The Whitbreads?" he could hear her saying. "Who are the Whitbreads? Coal merchants. Respectable tradespeople."

Hugh she detested for some reason. He thought of nothing but his own appearance, she said. He ought to have been a Duke. He would be certain to marry one of the Royal Princesses. And of course Hugh had the most extraordinary, the most natural, the most sublime respect for the British aristocracy of any human being he had ever come across. Even Clarissa had to own that. Oh, but he was such a dear, so unselfish, gave up shooting to please his old mother-remembered his aunts' birthdays, and so on.

Sally, to do her justice, saw through all that. One of the things he remembered best was an argument one Sunday morning at Bourton about women's rights (that antediluvian topic), when Sally suddenly lost her temper, flared up, and told Hugh that he represented all that was most detestable in British middle-class life. She told him that she considered him responsible for the state of "those poor girls in Piccadilly" —Hugh, the perfect gentleman, poor Hugh! —never did a man look more horrified! She did it on purpose she said afterwards (for they used to get together in the vegetable garden and compare notes). "He's read nothing, thought nothing, felt nothing," he could hear her saying in that very emphatic voice which carried so much farther than she knew. The stable boys had more life in them than Hugh, she said. He was a perfect specimen of the public school type, she said. No country but England could have produced him. She was really spiteful, for some reason; had some grudge against him. Something had happened-he forgot what-in the smoking-room. He had insulted her-kissed her? Incredible! Nobody believed a word against Hugh of course. Who could? Kissing Sally in the smoking-room! If it had been some Honourable Edith or Lady Violet, perhaps; but not that ragamuffin Sally without a penny to her name, and a father or a mother gambling at Monte Carlo. For of all the people he had ever met Hugh was the greatest snob-the most obsequious-no, he didn't cringe exactly. He was too much of a prig for that. A first-rate valet was the obvious comparison-somebody who walked behind carrying suit cases; could be trusted to send telegrams-indispensable to hostesses. And he'd found his job-married his Honourable Evelyn; got some little post at Court, looked after the King's cellars, polished the Imperial shoe-buckles, went about in knee-breeches and lace ruffles. How remorseless life is! A little job at Court!

He had married this lady, the Honourable Evelyn, and they lived hereabouts, so he thought (looking at the pompous houses overlooking the Park), for he had lunched there once in a house which had, like all Hugh's possessions, something that no other house could possibly have-linen cupboards it might have been. You had to go and look at them-you had to spend a great deal of time always admiring whatever it was-linen cupboards, pillow-cases, old oak furniture, pictures, which Hugh had picked up for an old song. But Mrs. Hugh sometimes gave the show away. She was one of those obscure mouse-like little women who admire big men. She was almost negligible. Then suddenly she would say something quite unexpected-something sharp. She had the relics of the grand manner perhaps. The steam coal was a little too strong for her-it made the atmosphere thick. And so there they lived, with their linen cupboards and their old masters and their pillow-cases fringed with real lace at the rate of five or ten thousand a year presumably, while he, who was two years older than Hugh, cadged for a job.

At fifty-three he had to come and ask them to put him into some secretary's office, to find him some usher's job teaching little boys Latin, at the beck and call of some mandarin in an office, something that brought in five hundred a year; for if he married Daisy, even with his pension, they could never do on less. Whitbread could do it presumably; or Dalloway. He didn't mind what he asked Dalloway. He was a thorough good sort; a bit limited; a bit thick in the head; yes; but a thorough good sort. Whatever he took up he did in the same matter-of-fact sensible way; without a touch of imagination, without a spark of brilliancy, but with the inexplicable niceness of his type. He ought to have been a country gentleman-he was wasted on politics. He was at his best out of doors, with horses and dogs-how good he was, for instance, when that great shaggy dog of Clarissa's got caught in a trap and had its paw half torn off, and Clarissa turned faint and Dalloway did the whole thing; bandaged, made splints; told Clarissa not to be a fool. That was what she liked him for perhaps-that was what she needed. "Now, my dear, don't be a fool. Hold this-fetch that," all the time talking to the dog as if it were a human being.

But how could she swallow all that stuff about poetry? How could she let him hold forth about Shakespeare? Seriously and solemnly Richard Dalloway got on his hind legs and said that no decent man ought to read Shakespeare's sonnets because it was like listening at keyholes (besides the relationship was not one that he approved). No decent man ought to let his wife visit a deceased wife's sister. Incredible! The only thing to do was to pelt him with sugared almonds-it was at dinner. But Clarissa sucked it all in; thought it so honest of him; so independent of him; Heaven knows if she didn't think him the most original mind she'd ever met!

That was one of the bonds between Sally and himself. There was a garden where they used to walk, a walled-in place, with rose-bushes and giant cauliflowers-he could remember Sally tearing off a rose, stopping to exclaim at the beauty of the cabbage leaves in the moonlight (it was extraordinary how vividly it all came back to him, things he hadn't thought of for years,) while she implored him, half laughing of course, to carry off Clarissa, to save her from the Hughs and the Dalloways and all the other "perfect gentlemen" who would "stifle her soul" (she wrote reams of poetry in those days), make a mere hostess of her, encourage her worldliness.

But one must do Clarissa justice. She wasn't going to marry Hugh anyhow. She had a perfectly clear notion of what she wanted. Her emotions were all on the surface. Beneath, she was very shrewd —a far better judge of character than Sally, for instance, and with it all, purely feminine; with that extraordinary gift, that woman's gift, of making a world of her own wherever she happened to be. She came into a room; she stood, as he had often seen her, in a doorway with lots of people round her. But it was Clarissa one remembered. Not that she was striking; not beautiful at all; there was nothing picturesque about her; she never said anything specially clever; there she was, however; there she was.

No, no, no! He was not in love with her any more! He only felt, after seeing her that morning, among her scissors and silks, making ready for the party, unable to get away from the thought of her; she kept coming back and back like a sleeper jolting against him in a railway carriage; which was not being in love, of course; it was thinking of her, criticising her, starting again, after thirty years, trying to explain her. The obvious thing to say of her was that she was worldly; cared too much for rank and society and getting on in the world-which was true in a sense; she had admitted it to him. (You could always get her to own up if you took the trouble; she was honest.) What she would say was that she hated frumps, fogies, failures, like himself presumably; thought people had no right to slouch about with their hands in their pockets; must do something, be something; and these great swells, these Duchesses, these hoary old Countesses one met in her drawing-room, unspeakably remote as he felt them to be from anything that mattered a straw, stood for something real to her. Lady Bexborough, she said once, held herself upright (so did Clarissa herself; she never lounged in any sense of the word; she was straight as a dart, a little rigid in fact). She said they had a kind of courage which the older she grew the more she respected. In all this there was a great deal of Dalloway, of course; a great deal of the public-spirited, British Empire, tariff-reform, governing-class spirit, which had grown on her, as it tends to do. With twice his wits, she had to see things through his eyes-one of the tragedies of married life. With a mind of her own, she must always be quoting Richard-as if one couldn't know to a tittle what Richard thought by reading the *Morning Post* of a morning! These parties for example were all for him, or for her idea of him (to do Richard justice he would have been happier farming in Norfolk). She made her drawing-room a sort of meeting-place; she had a genius for it. Over and over again he had seen her take some raw youth, twist him, turn him, wake him up; set him going. Infinite numbers of dull people conglomerated round her of course. But odd unexpected people turned up; an artist sometimes; sometimes a writer; queer fish in that atmosphere. And behind it all was that network of visiting, leaving cards, being kind to people; running about with bunches of flowers, little presents; So-and-so was going to France-must have an air-cushion; a real drain on her strength; all that interminable traffic that women of her sort keep up; but she did it genuinely, from a natural instinct.

Oddly enough, she was one of the most thoroughgoing sceptics he had ever met, and possibly (this was a theory he used to make up to account for her, so transparent in some ways, so inscrutable in others), possibly she said to herself, As we are a doomed race, chained to a sinking ship (her favourite reading as a girl was Huxley and Tyndall, and they were fond of these nautical metaphors), as the whole thing is a bad joke, let us, at any rate, do our part; mitigate the sufferings of our fellow-prisoners (Huxley again); decorate the dungeon with flowers and air-cushions; be as decent as we possibly can. Those ruffians, the Gods, shan't have it all their own way, —her notion being that the Gods, who never lost a chance of hurting, thwarting and spoiling human lives were seriously put out if, all the same, you behaved like a lady. That phase came directly after Sylvia's death-that horrible affair. To see your own sister killed by a falling tree (all Justin Parry's fault-all his carelessness) before your very eyes, a girl too on the verge of life, the most gifted of them, Clarissa always said, was enough to turn one bitter. Later she wasn't so positive perhaps; she thought there were no Gods; no one was to blame; and so she evolved this atheist's religion of doing good for the sake of goodness.

And of course she enjoyed life immensely. It was her nature to enjoy (though goodness only knows, she had her reserves; it was a mere sketch, he often felt, that even he, after all these years, could make of Clarissa). Anyhow there was no bitterness in her; none of that sense of moral virtue which is so repulsive in good women. She enjoyed practically everything. If you walked with her in Hyde Park now it was a bed of tulips, now a child in a perambulator, now some absurd little drama she made up on the spur of the moment. (Very likely, she would have talked to those lovers, if she had thought them unhappy.) She had a sense of comedy that was really exquisite, but she needed people, always people, to bring it out, with the inevitable result that she frittered her time away, lunching, dining, giving these incessant parties of hers, talking nonsense, sayings things she didn't mean, blunting the edge of her mind, losing her discrimination. There she would sit at the head of the table taking infinite pains with some old buffer who might be useful to Dalloway-they knew the most appalling bores in Europe-or in came Elizabeth and everything must give way to *her*. She was at a High School, at the inarticulate stage last time he was over, a round-eyed, pale-faced girl, with nothing of her mother in her, a silent stolid creature, who took it all as a matter of course, let her mother make a fuss of her, and then said "May I go now?" like a child of four; going off, Clarissa explained, with that mixture of amusement and pride which Dalloway himself seemed to rouse in her, to play hockey. And now Elizabeth was "out," presumably; thought him an old fogy, laughed at her mother's friends. Ah well, so be it. The compensation of growing old, Peter Walsh thought, coming out of Regent's Park, and holding his hat in hand, was simply this; that the passions remain as strong as ever, but one has gained-at last! —the power which adds the supreme flavour to existence, —the power of taking hold of experience, of turning it round, slowly, in the light.

A terrible confession it was (he put his hat on again), but now, at the age of fifty-three one scarcely needed people any more. Life itself, every moment of it, every drop of it, here, this instant, now, in the sun, in Regent's Park, was enough. Too much indeed. A whole lifetime was too short to bring out, now that one had acquired the power, the full flavour; to extract every ounce of pleasure, every shade of meaning; which both were so much more solid than they used to be, so much less personal. It was impossible that he should ever suffer again as Clarissa had made him suffer. For hours at a time (pray God that one might say these things without being overheard!), for hours and days he never thought of Daisy.

Could it be that he was in love with her then, remembering the misery, the torture, the extraordinary passion of those days? It was a different thing altogether —a much pleasanter thing-the truth being, of course, that now *she* was in love with *him*. And that perhaps was the reason why, when the ship actually sailed, he felt an extraordinary relief, wanted nothing so much as to be alone; was annoyed to find all her little attentions-cigars, notes, a rug for the voyage-in his cabin. Every one if they were honest would say the same; one doesn't want people after fifty; one doesn't want to go on telling women they are pretty; that's what most men of fifty would say, Peter Walsh thought, if they were honest.

But then these astonishing accesses of emotion-bursting into tears this morning, what was all that about? What could Clarissa have thought of him? thought him a fool presumably, not for the first time. It was jealousy that was at the bottom of it-jealousy which survives every other passion of mankind, Peter Walsh thought, holding his pocket-knife at arm's length. She had been meeting Major Orde, Daisy said in her last letter; said it on purpose he knew; said it to make him jealous; he could see her wrinkling her forehead as she wrote, wondering what she could say to hurt him; and yet it made no difference; he was furious! All this pother of coming to England and seeing lawyers wasn't to marry her, but to prevent her from marrying anybody else. That was what tortured him, that was what came over him when he saw Clarissa so calm, so cold, so intent on her dress or whatever it was; realising what she might have spared him, what she had reduced him to —a whimpering, snivelling old ass. But women, he thought, shutting his pocket-knife, don't know what passion is. They don't know the meaning of it to men. Clarissa was as cold as an icicle. There she would sit on the sofa by his side, let him take her hand, give him one kiss-Here he was at the crossing.

A sound interrupted him; a frail quivering sound, a voice bubbling up without direction, vigour, beginning or end, running weakly and shrilly and with an absence of all human meaning into

    ee um fah um so
    foo swee too eem oo —

the voice of no age or sex, the voice of an ancient spring spouting from the earth; which issued, just opposite Regent's Park Tube station from a tall quivering shape, like a funnel, like a rusty pump, like a wind-beaten tree for ever barren of leaves which lets the wind run up and down its branches singing

    ee um fah um so
    foo swee too eem oo

and rocks and creaks and moans in the eternal breeze.

Through all ages-when the pavement was grass, when it was swamp, through the age of tusk and mammoth, through the age of silent sunrise, the battered woman-for she wore a skirt-with her right hand exposed, her left clutching at her side, stood singing of love-love which has lasted a million years, she sang, love which prevails, and millions of years ago, her lover, who had been dead these centuries, had walked, she crooned, with her in May; but in the course of ages, long as summer days, and flaming, she remembered, with nothing but red asters, he had gone; death's enormous sickle had swept those tremendous hills, and when at last she laid her hoary and immensely aged head on the earth, now become a mere cinder of ice, she implored the Gods to lay by her side a bunch of purple-heather, there on her high burial place which the last rays of the last sun caressed; for then the pageant of the universe would be over.

As the ancient song bubbled up opposite Regent's Park Tube station still the earth seemed green and flowery; still, though it issued from so rude a mouth, a mere hole in the earth, muddy too, matted with root fibres and tangled grasses, still the old bubbling burbling song, soaking through the knotted roots of infinite ages, and skeletons and treasure, streamed away in rivulets over the pavement and all along the Marylebone Road, and down towards Euston, fertilising, leaving a damp stain.

Still remembering how once in some primeval May she had walked with her lover, this rusty pump, this battered old woman with one hand exposed for coppers the other clutching her side, would still be there in ten million years, remembering how once she had walked in May, where the sea flows now, with whom it did not matter-he was a man, oh yes, a man who had loved her. But the passage of ages had blurred the clarity of that ancient May day; the bright petalled flowers were hoar and silver frosted; and she no longer saw, when she implored him (as she did now quite clearly) "look in my eyes with thy sweet eyes intently," she no longer saw brown eyes, black whiskers or sunburnt face but only a looming shape, a shadow shape, to which, with the bird-like freshness of the very aged she still twittered "give me your hand and let me press it gently" (Peter Walsh couldn't help giving the poor creature a coin as he stepped into his taxi), "and if some one should see, what matter they?" she demanded; and her fist clutched at her side, and she smiled, pocketing her shilling, and all peering inquisitive eyes seemed blotted out, and the passing generations-the pavement was crowded with bustling middle-class people-vanished, like leaves, to be trodden under, to be soaked and steeped and made mould of by that eternal spring—

    ee um fah um so
    foo swee too eem oo

"Poor old woman," said Rezia Warren Smith, waiting to cross.
    Oh poor old wretch!

Suppose it was a wet night? Suppose one's father, or somebody who had known one in better days had happened to pass, and saw one standing there in the gutter? And where did she sleep at night?

Cheerfully, almost gaily, the invincible thread of sound wound up into the air like the smoke from a cottage chimney, winding up clean beech trees and issuing in a tuft of blue smoke among the topmost leaves. "And if some one should see, what matter they?"

Since she was so unhappy, for weeks and weeks now, Rezia had given meanings to things that happened, almost felt sometimes that she must stop people in the street, if they looked good, kind people, just to say to them "I am unhappy"; and this old woman singing in the street "if some one should see, what matter they?" made her suddenly quite sure that everything was going to be right. They were going to Sir William Bradshaw; she thought his name sounded nice; he would cure Septimus at once. And then there was a brewer's cart, and the grey horses had upright bristles of straw in their tails; there were newspaper placards. It was a silly, silly dream, being unhappy.

So they crossed, Mr. and Mrs. Septimus Warren Smith, and was there, after all, anything to draw attention to them, anything to make a passer-by suspect here is a young man who carries in him the greatest message in the world, and is, moreover, the happiest man in the world, and the most miserable? Perhaps they walked more slowly than other people, and there was something hesitating, trailing, in the man's walk, but what more natural for a clerk, who has not been in the West End on a weekday at this hour for years, than to keep looking at the sky, looking at this, that and the other, as if Portland Place were a room he had come into when the family are away, the chandeliers being hung in holland bags, and the caretaker, as she lets in long shafts of dusty light upon deserted, queer-looking armchairs, lifting one corner of the long blinds, explains to the visitors what a wonderful place it is; how wonderful, but at the same time, he thinks, as he looks at chairs and tables, how strange.

To look at, he might have been a clerk, but of the better sort; for he wore brown boots; his hands were educated; so, too, his profile-his angular, big-nosed, intelligent, sensitive profile; but not his lips altogether, for they were loose; and his eyes (as eyes tend to be), eyes merely; hazel, large; so that he was, on the whole, a border case, neither one thing nor the other, might end with a house at Purley and a motor car, or continue renting apartments in back streets all his life; one of those half-educated, self-educated men whose education is all learnt from books borrowed from public libraries, read in the evening after the day's work, on the advice of well-known authors consulted by letter.

As for the other experiences, the solitary ones, which people go through alone, in their bedrooms, in their offices, walking the fields and the streets of London, he had them; had left home, a mere boy, because of his mother; she lied; because he came down to tea for the fiftieth time with his hands unwashed; because he could see no future for a poet in Stroud; and so, making a confidant of his little sister, had gone to London leaving an absurd note behind him, such as great men have written, and the world has read later when the story of their struggles has become famous.

London has swallowed up many millions of young men called Smith; thought nothing of fantastic Christian names like Septimus with which their parents have thought to distinguish them. Lodging off the Euston Road, there were experiences, again experiences, such as change a face in two years from a pink innocent oval to a face lean, contracted, hostile. But of all this what could the most observant of friends have said except what a gardener says when he opens the conservatory door in the morning and finds a new blossom on his plant: —It has flowered; flowered from vanity, ambition, idealism, passion, loneliness, courage, laziness, the usual seeds, which all muddled up (in a room off the Euston Road), made him shy, and stammering, made him anxious to improve himself, made him fall in love with Miss Isabel Pole, lecturing in the Waterloo Road upon Shakespeare.

Was he not like Keats? she asked; and reflected how she might give him a taste of *Antony and Cleopatra* and the rest; lent him books; wrote him scraps of letters; and lit in him such a fire as burns only once in a lifetime, without heat, flickering a red gold flame infinitely ethereal and insubstantial over Miss Pole; *Antony and Cleopatra;* and the Waterloo Road. He thought her beautiful, believed her impeccably wise; dreamed of her, wrote poems to her, which, ignoring the subject, she corrected in red ink; he saw her, one summer evening, walking in a green dress in a square. "It has flowered," the gardener might have said, had he opened the door; had he come in, that is to say, any night about this time, and found him writing; found him tearing up his writing; found him finishing a masterpiece at three o'clock in the morning and running out to pace the streets, and visiting churches, and fasting one day, drinking another, devouring Shakespeare, Darwin, *The History of Civilisation,* and Bernard Shaw.

Something was up, Mr. Brewer knew; Mr. Brewer, managing clerk at Sibleys and Arrowsmiths, auctioneers, valuers, land and estate agents; something was up, he thought, and, being paternal with his young men, and thinking very highly of Smith's abilities, and prophesying that he would, in ten or fifteen years, succeed to the leather armchair in the inner room under the skylight with the deed-boxes round him, "if he keeps his health," said Mr. Brewer, and that was the danger-he looked weakly; advised football, invited him to supper and was seeing his way to consider recommending a rise of salary, when something happened which threw out many of Mr. Brewer's calculations, took away his ablest young fellows, and eventually, so prying and insidious were the fingers of the European War, smashed a plaster cast of Ceres, ploughed a hole in the geranium beds, and utterly ruined the cook's nerves at Mr. Brewer's establishment at Muswell Hill.

Septimus was one of the first to volunteer. He went to France to save an England which consisted almost entirely of Shakespeare's plays and Miss Isabel Pole in a green dress walking in a square. There in the trenches the change which Mr. Brewer desired when he advised football was produced instantly; he developed manliness; he was promoted; he drew the attention, indeed the affection of his officer, Evans by name. It was a case of two dogs playing on a hearth-rug; one worrying a paper screw, snarling, snapping, giving a pinch, now and then, at the old dog's ear; the other lying somnolent, blinking at the fire, raising a paw, turning and growling good-temperedly. They had to be together, share with each other, fight with each other, quarrel with each other. But when Evans (Rezia who had only seen him once called him "a quiet man," a sturdy red-haired man, undemonstrative in the company of women), when Evans was killed, just before the Armistice, in Italy, Septimus, far from showing any emotion or recognising that here was the end of a friendship, congratulated himself upon feeling very little and very reasonably. The War had taught him. It was sublime. He had gone through the whole show, friendship, European War, death, had won promotion, was still under thirty and was bound to survive. He was right there. The last shells missed him. He watched them explode with indifference. When peace came he was in Milan, billeted in the house of an innkeeper with a courtyard, flowers in tubs, little tables in the open, daughters making hats, and to Lucrezia, the younger daughter, he became engaged one evening when the panic was on him-that he could not feel.

For now that it was all over, truce signed, and the dead buried, he had, especially in the evening, these sudden thunder-claps of fear. He could not feel. As he opened the door of the room where the Italian girls sat making hats, he could see them; could hear them; they were rubbing wires among coloured beads in saucers; they were turning buckram shapes this way and that; the table was all strewn with feathers, spangles, silks, ribbons; scissors were rapping on the table; but something failed him; he could not feel. Still, scissors rapping, girls laughing, hats being made protected him; he was assured of safety; he had a refuge. But he could not sit there all night. There were moments of waking in the early morning. The bed was falling; he was falling. Oh for the scissors and the lamplight and the buckram shapes! He asked Lucrezia to marry him, the younger of the two, the gay, the frivolous, with those little artist's fingers that she would hold up and say "It is all in them." Silk, feathers, what not were alive to them.

"It is the hat that matters most," she would say, when they walked out together. Every hat that passed, she would examine; and the cloak and the dress and the way the woman held herself.

Ill-dressing, over-dressing she stigmatised, not savagely, rather with impatient movements of the hands, like those of a painter who puts from him some obvious well-meant glaring imposture; and then, generously, but always critically, she would welcome a shopgirl who had turned her little bit of stuff gallantly, or praise, wholly, with enthusiastic and professional understanding, a French lady descending from her carriage, in chinchilla, robes, pearls.

"Beautiful!" she would murmur, nudging Septimus, that he might see. But beauty was behind a pane of glass. Even taste (Rezia liked ices, chocolates, sweet things) had no relish to him. He put down his cup on the little marble table. He looked at people outside; happy they seemed, collecting in the middle of the street, shouting, laughing, squabbling over nothing. But he could not taste, he could not feel. In the tea-shop among the tables and the chattering waiters the appalling fear came over him-he could not feel. He could reason; he could read, Dante for example, quite easily ("Septimus, do put down your book," said Rezia, gently shutting the *Inferno)*, he could add up his bill; his brain was perfect; it must be the fault of the world then-that he could not feel.

"The English are so silent," Rezia said. She liked it, she said. She respected these Englishmen, and wanted to see London, and the English horses, and the tailor-made suits, and could remember hearing how wonderful the shops were, from an Aunt who had married and lived in Soho.

It might be possible, Septimus thought, looking at England from the train window, as they left Newhaven; it might be possible that the world itself is without meaning.

At the office they advanced him to a post of considerable responsibility. They were proud of him; he had won crosses. "You have done your duty; it is up to us —" began Mr. Brewer; and could not finish, so pleasurable was his emotion. They took admirable lodgings off the Tottenham Court Road.

Here he opened Shakespeare once more. That boy's business of the intoxication of language —*Antony and Cleopatra* —had shrivelled utterly. How Shakespeare loathed humanity-the putting on of clothes, the getting of children, the sordidity of the mouth and the belly! This was now revealed to Septimus; the message hidden in the beauty of words. The secret signal which one generation passes, under disguise, to the next is loathing, hatred, despair. Dante the same. Aeschylus (translated) the same. There Rezia sat at the table trimming hats. She trimmed hats for Mrs. Filmer's friends; she trimmed hats by the hour. She looked pale, mysterious, like a lily, drowned, under water, he thought.

"The English are so serious," she would say, putting her arms round Septimus, her cheek against his.

Love between man and woman was repulsive to Shakespeare. The business of copulation was filth to him before the end. But, Rezia said, she must have children. They had been married five years.

They went to the Tower together; to the Victoria and Albert Museum; stood in the crowd to see the King open Parliament. And there were the shops-hat shops, dress shops, shops with leather bags in the window, where she would stand staring. But she must have a boy.

She must have a son like Septimus, she said. But nobody could be like Septimus; so gentle; so serious; so clever. Could she not read Shakespeare too? Was Shakespeare a difficult author? she asked.

One cannot bring children into a world like this. One cannot perpetuate suffering, or increase the breed of these lustful animals, who have no lasting emotions, but only whims and vanities, eddying them now this way, now that.

He watched her snip, shape, as one watches a bird hop, flit in the grass, without daring to move a finger. For the truth is (let her ignore it) that human beings have neither kindness, nor faith, nor charity beyond what serves to increase the pleasure of the moment. They hunt in packs. Their packs scour the desert and vanish screaming into the wilderness. They desert the fallen. They are plastered over with grimaces. There was Brewer at the office, with his waxed moustache, coral tie-pin, white slip, and pleasurable emotions-all coldness and clamminess within, —his geraniums ruined in the War-his cook's nerves destroyed; or

Amelia What'shername, handing round cups of tea punctually at five — a leering, sneering obscene little harpy; and the Toms and Berties in their starched shirt fronts oozing thick drops of vice. They never saw him drawing pictures of them naked at their antics in his notebook. In the street, vans roared past him; brutality blared out on placards; men were trapped in mines; women burnt alive; and once a maimed file of lunatics being exercised or displayed for the diversion of the populace (who laughed aloud), ambled and nodded and grinned past him, in the Tottenham Court Road, each half apologetically, yet triumphantly, inflicting his hopeless woe. And would *he* go mad?

At tea Rezia told him that Mrs. Filmer's daughter was expecting a baby. *She* could not grow old and have no children! She was very lonely, she was very unhappy! She cried for the first time since they were married. Far away he heard her sobbing; he heard it accurately, he noticed it distinctly; he compared it to a piston thumping. But he felt nothing.

His wife was crying, and he felt nothing; only each time she sobbed in this profound, this silent, this hopeless way, he descended another step into the pit.

At last, with a melodramatic gesture which he assumed mechanically and with complete consciousness of its insincerity, he dropped his head on his hands. Now he had surrendered; now other people must help him. People must be sent for. He gave in.

Nothing could rouse him. Rezia put him to bed. She sent for a doctor-Mrs. Filmer's Dr. Holmes. Dr. Holmes examined him. There was nothing whatever the matter, said Dr. Holmes. Oh, what a relief! What a kind man, what a good man! thought Rezia. When he felt like that he went to the Music Hall, said Dr. Holmes. He took a day off with his wife and played golf. Why not try two tabloids of bromide dissolved in a glass of water at bedtime? These old Bloomsbury houses, said Dr. Holmes, tapping the wall, are often full of very fine panelling, which the landlords have the folly to paper over. Only the other day, visiting a patient, Sir Somebody Something in Bedford Square —

So there was no excuse; nothing whatever the matter, except the sin for which human nature had condemned him to death; that he did not feel. He had not cared when Evans was killed; that was worst; but all the other crimes raised their heads and shook their fingers and jeered and sneered over the rail of the bed in the early hours of the morning at the prostrate body which lay realising its degradation; how he had married his wife without loving her; had lied to her; seduced her; outraged Miss Isabel Pole, and was so pocked and marked with vice that women shuddered when they saw him in the street. The verdict of human nature on such a wretch was death.

Dr. Holmes came again. Large, fresh coloured, handsome, flicking his boots, looking in the glass, he brushed it all aside-headaches, sleeplessness, fears, dreams-nerve symptoms and nothing more, he said. If Dr. Holmes found himself even half a pound below eleven stone six, he asked his wife for another plate of porridge at breakfast. (Rezia would learn to cook porridge.) But, he continued, health is largely a matter in our own control. Throw yourself into outside interests; take up some hobby. He opened Shakespeare —*Antony and Cleopatra;* pushed Shakespeare aside. Some hobby, said Dr. Holmes, for did he not owe his own excellent health (and he worked as hard as any man in London) to the fact that he could always switch off from his patients on to old furniture? And what a very pretty comb, if he might say so, Mrs. Warren Smith was wearing!

When the damned fool came again, Septimus refused to see him. Did he indeed? said Dr. Holmes, smiling agreeably. Really he had to give that charming little lady, Mrs. Smith, a friendly push before he could get past her into her husband's bedroom.

"So you're in a funk," he said agreeably, sitting down by his patient's side. He had actually talked of killing himself to his wife, quite a girl, a foreigner, wasn't she? Didn't that give her a very odd idea of English husbands? Didn't one owe perhaps a duty to one's wife? Wouldn't it be better to do something instead of lying in bed? For he had had forty years' experience behind him; and Septimus could take Dr. Holmes's word for it-there was nothing whatever the matter with him. And next time Dr. Holmes came he hoped to find Smith out of bed and not making that charming little lady his wife anxious about him.

Human nature, in short, was on him-the repulsive brute, with the blood-red nostrils. Holmes was on him. Dr. Holmes came quite regularly every day. Once you stumble, Septimus wrote on the back of a postcard, human nature is on you. Holmes is on you. Their only chance was to escape, without letting Holmes know; to Italy-anywhere, anywhere, away from Dr. Holmes.

But Rezia could not understand him. Dr. Holmes was such a kind man. He was so interested in Septimus. He only wanted to help them, he said. He had four little children and he had asked her to tea, she told Septimus.

So he was deserted. The whole world was clamouring: Kill yourself, kill yourself, for our sakes. But why should he kill himself for their sakes? Food was pleasant; the sun hot; and this killing oneself, how does one set about it, with a table knife, uglily, with floods of blood,—by sucking a gaspipe? He was too weak; he could scarcely raise his hand. Besides, now that he was quite alone, condemned, deserted, as those who are about to die are alone, there was a luxury in it, an isolation full of sublimity; a freedom which the attached can never know. Holmes had won of course; the brute with the red nostrils had won. But even Holmes himself could not touch this last relic straying on the edge of the world, this outcast, who gazed back at the inhabited regions, who lay, like a drowned sailor, on the shore of the world.

It was at that moment (Rezia gone shopping) that the great revelation took place. A voice spoke from behind the screen. Evans was speaking. The dead were with him.

"Evans, Evans!" he cried.

Mr. Smith was talking aloud to himself, Agnes the servant girl cried to Mrs. Filmer in the kitchen. "Evans, Evans," he had said as she brought in the tray. She jumped, she did. She scuttled downstairs.

And Rezia came in, with her flowers, and walked across the room, and put the roses in a vase, upon which the sun struck directly, and it went laughing, leaping round the room.

She had had to buy the roses, Rezia said, from a poor man in the street. But they were almost dead already, she said, arranging the roses.

So there was a man outside; Evans presumably; and the roses, which Rezia said were half dead, had been picked by him in the fields of Greece. "Communication is health; communication is happiness, communication—" he muttered.

"What are you saying, Septimus?" Rezia asked, wild with terror, for he was talking to himself.

She sent Agnes running for Dr. Holmes. Her husband, she said, was mad. He scarcely knew her.

"You brute! You brute!" cried Septimus, seeing human nature, that is Dr. Holmes, enter the room.

"Now what's all this about?" said Dr. Holmes in the most amiable way in the world. "Talking nonsense to frighten your wife?" But he would give him something to make him sleep. And if they were rich people, said Dr. Holmes, looking ironically round the room, by all means let them go to Harley Street; if they had no confidence in him, said Dr. Holmes, looking not quite so kind.

It was precisely twelve o'clock; twelve by Big Ben; whose stroke was wafted over the northern part of London; blent with that of other clocks, mixed in a thin ethereal way with the clouds and wisps of smoke, and died up there among the seagulls-twelve o'clock struck as Clarissa Dalloway laid her green dress on her bed, and the Warren Smiths walked down Harley Street. Twelve was the hour of their appointment. Probably, Rezia thought, that was Sir William Bradshaw's house with the grey motor car in front of it. The leaden circles dissolved in the air.

Indeed it was-Sir William Bradshaw's motor car; low, powerful, grey with plain initials' interlocked on the panel, as if the pomps of heraldry were incongruous, this man being the ghostly helper, the priest of science; and, as the motor car was grey, so to match its sober suavity, grey furs, silver grey rugs were heaped in it, to keep her ladyship warm while she waited. For often Sir William would travel sixty miles or more down into the country to visit the rich, the afflicted, who could afford the very large fee which Sir William very properly charged for his advice. Her ladyship waited with the rugs about her knees an hour or more, leaning back, thinking sometimes of the patient, sometimes, excusably, of the wall of gold, mounting minute by minute while she waited; the wall of gold that was mounting between them and all shifts and anxieties (she had borne them bravely; they had had their struggles) until she felt wedged on a calm ocean, where only spice winds blow; respected, admired, envied, with scarcely anything left to wish for, though she regretted her stoutness; large dinner-parties every Thursday night to the profession; an occasional bazaar to be opened; Royalty greeted; too little time, alas, with her husband, whose work grew and grew; a boy doing well at Eton; she would have liked a daughter too; interests she had, however, in plenty; child welfare; the after-care of the epileptic, and photography, so that if there was a church building, or a church decaying, she bribed the sexton, got the key and took photographs, which were scarcely to be distinguished from the work of professionals, while she waited.

Sir William himself was no longer young. He had worked very hard; he had won his position by sheer ability (being the son of a shopkeeper); loved his profession; made a fine figurehead at ceremonies and spoke well-all of which had by the time he was knighted given him a heavy look, a weary look (the stream of patients being so incessant, the responsibilities and privileges of his profession so onerous), which weariness, together with his grey hairs, increased the extraordinary distinction of his presence and gave him the reputation (of the utmost importance in dealing with nerve cases) not merely of lightning skill, and almost infallible accuracy in diagnosis but of sympathy; tact; understanding of the human soul. He could see the first moment they came into the room (the Warren Smiths they were called); he was certain directly he saw the man; it was a case of extreme gravity. It was a case of complete breakdown-complete physical and nervous breakdown, with every symptom in an advanced stage, he ascertained in two or three minutes (writing answers to questions, murmured discreetly, on a pink card).

How long had Dr. Holmes been attending him?

Six weeks.

Prescribed a little bromide? Said there was nothing the matter? Ah yes (those general practitioners! thought Sir William. It took half his time to undo their blunders. Some were irreparable).

"You served with great distinction in the War?"

The patient repeated the word "war" interrogatively.

He was attaching meanings to words of a symbolical kind. A serious symptom, to be noted on the card.

"The War?" the patient asked. The European War-that little shindy of schoolboys with gunpowder? Had he served with distinction? He really forgot. In the War itself he had failed.

"Yes, he served with the greatest distinction," Rezia assured the doctor; "he was promoted."

"And they have the very highest opinion of you at your office?" Sir William murmured, glancing at Mr. Brewer's very generously worded letter. "So that you have nothing to worry you, no financial anxiety, nothing?"

He had committed an appalling crime and been condemned to death by human nature.

"I have —I have," he began, "committed a crime —"

"He has done nothing wrong whatever," Rezia assured the doctor. If Mr. Smith would wait, said Sir William, he would speak to Mrs. Smith in the next room. Her husband was very seriously ill, Sir William said. Did he threaten to kill himself?

Oh, he did, she cried. But he did not mean it, she said. Of course not. It was merely a question of rest, said Sir William; of rest, rest, rest; a long rest in bed. There was a delightful home down in the country where her husband would be perfectly looked after. Away from her? she asked. Unfortunately, yes; the people we care for most are not good for us when we are ill. But he was not mad, was he? Sir William said he never spoke of "madness"; he called it not having a sense of proportion. But her husband did not like doctors. He would refuse to go there.

Shortly and kindly Sir William explained to her the state of the case. He had threatened to kill himself. There was no alternative. It was a question of law. He would lie in bed in a beautiful house in the country. The nurses were admirable. Sir William would visit him once a week. If Mrs. Warren Smith was quite sure she had no more questions to ask-he never hurried his patients-they would return to her husband. She had nothing more to ask-not of Sir William.

So they returned to the most exalted of mankind; the criminal who faced his judges; the victim exposed on the heights; the fugitive; the drowned sailor; the poet of the immortal ode; the Lord who had gone from life to death; to Septimus Warren Smith, who sat in the armchair under the skylight staring at a photograph of Lady Bradshaw in Court dress, muttering messages about beauty.

"We have had our little talk," said Sir William.

"He says you are very, very ill," Rezia cried.

"We have been arranging that you should go into a home," said Sir William.

"One of Holmes's homes?" sneered Septimus.

The fellow made a distasteful impression. For there was in Sir William, whose father had been a tradesman, a natural respect for breeding and clothing, which shabbiness nettled; again, more profoundly, there was in Sir William, who had never had time for reading, a grudge, deeply buried, against cultivated people who came into his room and intimated that doctors, whose profession is a constant strain upon all the highest faculties, are not educated men.

"One of *my* homes, Mr. Warren Smith," he said, "where we will teach you to rest."

And there was just one thing more.

He was quite certain that when Mr. Warren Smith was well he was the last man in the world to frighten his wife. But he had talked of killing himself.

"We all have our moments of depression," said Sir William.

Once you fall, Septimus repeated to himself, human nature is on you. Holmes and Bradshaw are on you. They scour the desert. They fly screaming into the wilderness. The rack and the thumbscrew are applied. Human nature is remorseless.

"Impulses came upon him sometimes?" Sir William asked, with his pencil on a pink card.

That was his own affair, said Septimus.

"Nobody lives for himself alone," said Sir William, glancing at the photograph of his wife in Court dress.

"And you have a brilliant career before you," said Sir William. There was Mr. Brewer's letter on the table. "An exceptionally brilliant career."

But if he confessed? If he communicated? Would they let him off then, his torturers?

"I—I—" he stammered.

But what was his crime? He could not remember it.

"Yes?" Sir William encouraged him. (But it was growing late.)

Love, trees, there is no crime-what was his message?

He could not remember it.

"I—I—" Septimus stammered.

"Try to think as little about yourself as possible," said Sir William kindly. Really, he was not fit to be about.

Was there anything else they wished to ask him? Sir William would make all arrangements (he murmured to Rezia) and he would let her know between five and six that evening he murmured.

"Trust everything to me," he said, and dismissed them.

Never, never had Rezia felt such agony in her life! She had asked for help and been deserted! He had failed them! Sir William Bradshaw was not a nice man.

The upkeep of that motor car alone must cost him quite a lot, said Septimus, when they got out into the street.

She clung to his arm. They had been deserted.

But what more did she want?

To his patients he gave three-quarters of an hour; and if in this exacting science which has to do with what, after all, we know nothing about-the nervous system, the human brain—a doctor loses his sense of proportion, as a doctor he fails. Health we must have; and health is proportion; so that when a man comes into your room and says he is Christ (a common delusion), and has a message, as they mostly have, and threatens, as they often do, to kill himself, you invoke proportion; order rest in bed; rest in solitude; silence and rest; rest without friends, without books, without messages; six months' rest; until a man who went in weighing seven stone six comes out weighing twelve.

Proportion, divine proportion, Sir William's goddess, was acquired by Sir William walking hospitals, catching salmon, begetting one son in Harley Street by Lady Bradshaw, who caught salmon herself and took photographs scarcely to be distinguished from the work of professionals. Worshipping proportion, Sir William not only prospered himself but made England prosper, secluded her lunatics, forbade childbirth, penalised despair, made it impossible for the unfit to propagate their views until they, too, shared his sense of proportion-his, if they were men, Lady Bradshaw's if they were women (she embroidered, knitted, spent four nights out of seven at home with her son), so that not only did his colleagues respect him, his subordinates fear him, but the friends and relations of his patients felt for him the keenest gratitude for insisting that these prophetic Christs and Christesses, who prophesied the end of the world, or the advent of God, should drink milk in bed, as Sir William ordered; Sir William with his thirty years' experience of these kinds of cases, and his infallible instinct, this is madness, this sense; in fact, his sense of proportion.

But Proportion has a sister, less smiling, more formidable, a Goddess even now engaged-in the heat and sands of India, the mud and swamp of Africa, the purlieus of London, wherever in short the climate or the devil tempts men to fall from the true belief which is her own-is even now engaged in dashing down shrines, smashing idols, and setting up in their place her own stern countenance. Conversion is her name and she feasts on the wills of the weakly, loving to impress, to impose, adoring her own features stamped on the face of the populace. At Hyde Park Corner on a tub she stands preaching; shrouds herself in white and walks penitentially disguised as brotherly love through factories and parliaments; offers help, but desires power; smites out of her way roughly the dissentient, or dissatisfied; bestows her blessing on those who, looking upward, catch submissively from her eyes the light of their own. This lady too (Rezia Warren Smith divined it) had her dwelling in Sir William's heart, though concealed, as she mostly is, under some plausible disguise; some venerable name; love, duty, self sacrifice. How he would work-how toil to raise funds, propagate reforms, initiate institutions! But conversion, fastidious Goddess, loves blood better than brick, and feasts most subtly on the human will. For example, Lady Bradshaw. Fifteen years ago she had gone under. It was nothing you could put your finger on; there had been no scene, no snap; only the slow sinking, water-logged, of her will into his. Sweet was her smile, swift her submission; dinner in Harley Street, numbering eight or nine courses, feeding ten or fifteen guests of the professional classes, was smooth and urbane. Only as the evening wore on a very slight dulness, or uneasiness perhaps, a nervous twitch, fumble, stumble and confusion indicated, what it was really painful to believe-that the poor lady lied. Once, long ago, she had caught salmon freely: now, quick to minister to the craving which lit her husband's eye so oilily for dominion, for power, she cramped, squeezed, pared, pruned, drew back, peeped through; so that without knowing precisely what made the evening disagreeable, and caused this pressure on the top of the head (which might well be imputed to the professional conversation, or the fatigue of a great doctor whose life, Lady Bradshaw said, "is not his own but his patients'") disagreeable it was: so that guests, when the clock struck ten, breathed in the air of Harley Street even with rapture; which relief, however, was denied to his patients.

There in the grey room, with the pictures on the wall, and the valuable furniture, under the ground glass skylight, they learnt the extent of their transgressions; huddled up in armchairs, they watched him go through, for their benefit, a curious exercise with the arms, which he shot out, brought sharply back to his hip, to prove (if the patient was obstinate) that Sir William was master of his own actions, which the patient was not. There some weakly broke down; sobbed, submitted; others, inspired by Heaven knows what intemperate madness, called Sir William to his face a damnable humbug; questioned, even more impiously, life itself. Why live? they demanded. Sir William replied that life was good. Certainly Lady Bradshaw in ostrich feathers hung over the mantelpiece, and as for his income it was quite twelve thousand a year. But to us, they protested, life has given no such bounty. He acquiesced. They lacked a sense of proportion. And perhaps, after all, there is no God? He shrugged his shoulders. In short, this living or not living is an affair of our own? But there they were mistaken. Sir William had a friend in Surrey where they taught, what Sir William frankly admitted was a difficult art —a sense of proportion. There were, moreover, family affection; honour; courage; and a brilliant career. All of these had in Sir William a resolute champion. If they failed him, he had to support police and the good of society, which, he remarked very quietly, would take care, down in Surrey, that these unsocial impulses, bred more than anything by the lack of good blood, were held in control. And then stole out from her hiding-place and mounted her throne that Goddess whose lust is to override opposition, to stamp indelibly in the sanctuaries of others the image of herself. Naked, defenceless, the exhausted, the friendless received the impress of Sir William's will. He swooped; he devoured. He shut people up. It was this combination of decision and humanity that endeared Sir William so greatly to the relations of his victims.

But Rezia Warren Smith cried, walking down Harley Street, that she did not like that man.

Shredding and slicing, dividing and subdividing, the clocks of Harley Street nibbled at the June day, counselled submission, upheld authority, and pointed out in chorus the supreme advantages of a sense of proportion, until the mound of time was so far diminished that a commercial clock, suspended above a shop in Oxford Street, announced, genially and fraternally, as if it were a pleasure to Messrs. Rigby and Lowndes to give the information gratis, that it was half-past one.

Looking up, it appeared that each letter of their names stood for one of the hours; subconsciously one was grateful to Rigby and Lowndes for giving one time ratified by Greenwich; and this gratitude (so Hugh Whitbread ruminated, dallying there in front of the shop window), naturally took the form later of buying off Rigby and Lowndes socks or shoes. So he ruminated. It was his habit. He did not go deeply. He brushed surfaces; the dead languages, the living, life in Constantinople, Paris, Rome; riding, shooting, tennis, it had been once. The malicious asserted that he now kept guard at Buckingham Palace, dressed in silk stockings and knee-breeches, over what nobody knew. But he did it extremely efficiently. He had been afloat on the cream of English society for fifty-five years. He had known Prime Ministers. His affections were understood to be deep. And if it were true that he had not taken part in any of the great movements of the time or held important office, one or two humble reforms stood to his credit; an improvement in public shelters was one; the protection of owls in Norfolk another; servant girls had reason to be grateful to him; and his name at the end of letters to the *Times,* asking for funds, appealing to the public to protect, to preserve, to clear up litter, to abate smoke, and stamp out immorality in parks, commanded respect.

A magnificent figure he cut too, pausing for a moment (as the sound of the half hour died away) to look critically, magisterially, at socks and shoes; impeccable, substantial, as if he beheld the world from a certain eminence, and dressed to match; but realised the obligations which size, wealth, health, entail, and observed punctiliously even when not absolutely necessary, little courtesies, old-fashioned ceremonies which gave a quality to his manner, something to imitate, something to remember him by, for he would never lunch, for example, with Lady Bruton, whom he had known these twenty years, without bringing her in his outstretched hand a bunch of carnations and asking Miss Brush, Lady Bruton's secretary, after her brother in South Africa, which, for some reason, Miss Brush, deficient though she was in every attribute of female charm, so much resented that she said "Thank you, he's doing very well in South Africa," when, for half a dozen years, he had been doing badly in Portsmouth.

Lady Bruton herself preferred Richard Dalloway, who arrived at the next moment. Indeed they met on the doorstep.

Lady Bruton preferred Richard Dalloway of course. He was made of much finer material. But she wouldn't let them run down her poor dear Hugh. She could never forget his kindness-he had been really remarkably kind-she forgot precisely upon what occasion. But he had been-remarkably kind. Anyhow, the difference between one man and another does not amount to much. She had never seen the sense of cutting people up, as Clarissa Dalloway did-cutting them up and sticking them together again; not at any rate when one was sixty-two. She took Hugh's carnations with her angular grim smile. There was nobody else coming, she said. She had got them there on false pretences, to help her out of a difficulty—

"But let us eat first," she said.

And so there began a soundless and exquisite passing to and fro through swing doors of aproned white-capped maids, handmaidens not of necessity, but adepts in a mystery or grand deception practised by hostesses in Mayfair from one-thirty to two, when, with a wave of the hand, the traffic ceases, and there rises instead this profound illusion in the first place about the food-how it is not paid for; and then that the table spreads itself voluntarily with glass and silver, little mats, saucers of red fruit; films of brown cream mask turbot; in casseroles severed chickens swim; coloured, undomestic, the fire burns; and with the wine and the coffee (not paid for) rise jocund visions before musing eyes; gently speculative eyes; eyes to whom life appears musical, mysterious; eyes now kindled to observe genially the beauty of the red carnations which Lady Bruton (whose movements were always angular) had laid beside her plate, so that Hugh Whitbread, feeling at peace with the entire universe and at the same time completely sure of his standing, said, resting his fork,

"Wouldn't they look charming against your lace?"

Miss Brush resented this familiarity intensely. She thought him an underbred fellow. She made Lady Bruton laugh.

Lady Bruton raised the carnations, holding them rather stiffly with much the same attitude with which the General held the scroll in the picture behind her; she remained fixed, tranced. Which was she now, the General's great-grand-daughter? great-great-grand-daughter? Richard Dalloway asked himself. Sir Roderick, Sir Miles, Sir Talbot-that was it. It was remarkable how in that family the likeness persisted in the women. She should have been a general of dragoons herself. And Richard would have served under her, cheerfully; he had the greatest respect for her; he cherished these romantic views about well-set-up old women of pedigree, and would have liked, in his good-humoured way, to bring some young hot-heads of his acquaintance to lunch with her; as if a type like hers could be bred of amiable tea-drinking enthusiasts! He knew her country. He knew her people. There was a vine, still bearing, which either Lovelace or Herrick-she never read a word poetry of herself, but so the story ran-had sat under. Better wait to put before them the question that bothered her (about making an appeal to the public; if so, in what terms and so on), better wait until they have had their coffee, Lady Bruton thought; and so laid the carnations down beside her plate.

"How's Clarissa?" she asked abruptly.

Clarissa always said that Lady Bruton did not like her. Indeed, Lady Bruton had the reputation of being more interested in politics than people; of talking like a man; of having had a finger in some notorious intrigue of the eighties, which was now beginning to be mentioned in memoirs. Certainly there was an alcove in her drawing-room, and a table in that alcove, and a photograph upon that table of General Sir Talbot Moore, now deceased, who had written there (one evening in the eighties) in Lady Bruton's presence, with her cognisance, perhaps advice, a telegram ordering the British troops to advance upon an historical occasion. (She kept the pen and told the story.) Thus, when she said in her offhand way "How's Clarissa?" husbands had difficulty in persuading their wives and indeed, however devoted, were secretly doubtful themselves, of her interest in women who often got in their husbands' way, prevented them from accepting posts abroad, and had to be taken to the seaside in the middle of the session to recover from influenza. Nevertheless her inquiry, "How's Clarissa?" was known by women infallibly, to be a signal from a well-wisher, from an almost silent companion, whose utterances (half a dozen perhaps in the course of a lifetime) signified recognition of some feminine comradeship which went beneath masculine lunch parties and united Lady Bruton and Mrs. Dalloway, who seldom met, and appeared when they did meet indifferent and even hostile, in a singular bond.

"I met Clarissa in the Park this morning," said Hugh Whitbread, diving into the casserole, anxious to pay himself this little tribute, for he had only to come to London and he met everybody at once; but greedy, one of the greediest men she had ever known, Milly Brush thought, who observed men with unflinching rectitude, and was capable of everlasting devotion, to her own sex in particular, being knobbed, scraped, angular, and entirely without feminine charm.

"D'you know who's in town?" said Lady Bruton suddenly bethinking her. "Our old friend, Peter Walsh."

They all smiled. Peter Walsh! And Mr. Dalloway was genuinely glad, Milly Brush thought; and Mr. Whitbread thought only of his chicken.

Peter Walsh! All three, Lady Bruton, Hugh Whitbread, and Richard Dalloway, remembered the same thing-how passionately Peter had been in love; been rejected; gone to India; come a cropper; made a mess of things; and Richard Dalloway had a very great liking for the dear old fellow too. Milly Brush saw that; saw a depth in the brown of his eyes; saw him hesitate; consider; which interested her, as Mr. Dalloway always interested her, for what was he thinking, she wondered, about Peter Walsh?

That Peter Walsh had been in love with Clarissa; that he would go back directly after lunch and find Clarissa; that he would tell her, in so many words, that he loved her. Yes, he would say that.

Milly Brush once might almost have fallen in love with these silences; and Mr. Dalloway was always so dependable; such a gentleman too. Now, being forty, Lady Bruton had only to nod, or turn her head a little abruptly, and Milly Brush took the signal, however deeply she might be sunk in these reflections of a detached spirit, of an uncorrupted soul whom life could not bamboozle, because life had not offered her a trinket of the slightest value; not a curl, smile, lip, cheek, nose; nothing whatever; Lady Bruton had only to nod, and Perkins was instructed to quicken the coffee.

"Yes; Peter Walsh has come back," said Lady Bruton. It was vaguely flattering to them all. He had come back, battered, unsuccessful, to their secure shores. But to help him, they reflected, was impossible; there was some flaw in his character. Hugh Whitbread said one might of course mention his name to So-and-so. He wrinkled lugubriously, consequentially, at the thought of the letters he would write to the heads of Government offices about "my old friend, Peter Walsh," and so on. But it wouldn't lead to anything-not to anything permanent, because of his character.

"In trouble with some woman," said Lady Bruton. They had all guessed that *that* was at the bottom of it.

"However," said Lady Bruton, anxious to leave the subject, "we shall hear the whole story from Peter himself."

(The coffee was very slow in coming.)

"The address?" murmured Hugh Whitbread; and there was at once a ripple in the grey tide of service which washed round Lady Bruton day in, day out, collecting, intercepting, enveloping her in a fine tissue which broke concussions, mitigated interruptions, and spread round the house in Brook Street a fine net where things lodged and were picked out accurately, instantly, by grey-haired Perkins, who had been with Lady Bruton these thirty years and now wrote down the address; handed it to Mr. Whitbread, who took out his pocket-book, raised his eyebrows, and slipping it in among documents of the highest importance, said that he would get Evelyn to ask him to lunch.

(They were waiting to bring the coffee until Mr. Whitbread had finished.)

Hugh was very slow, Lady Bruton thought. He was getting fat, she noticed. Richard always kept himself in the pink of condition. She was getting impatient; the whole of her being was setting positively, undeniably, domineeringly brushing aside all this unnecessary trifling (Peter Walsh and his affairs) upon that subject which engaged her attention, and not merely her attention, but that fibre which was the ramrod of her soul, that essential part of her without which Millicent Bruton would not have been Millicent Bruton; that project for emigrating young people of both sexes born of respectable parents and setting them up with a fair prospect of doing well in Canada. She exaggerated. She had perhaps lost her sense of proportion. Emigration was not to others the obvious remedy, the sublime conception. It was not to them (not to Hugh, or Richard, or even to devoted Miss Brush) the liberator of the pent egotism, which a strong martial woman, well nourished, well descended, of direct impulses, downright feelings, and little introspective power (broad and simple-why could not every one be broad and simple? she asked) feels rise within her, once youth is past, and must eject upon some object-it may be Emigration, it may be Emancipation; but whatever it be, this object round which the essence of her soul is daily secreted, becomes inevitably prismatic, lustrous, half looking-glass, half precious stone; now carefully hidden in case people should sneer at it; now proudly displayed. Emigration had become, in short, largely Lady Bruton.

But she had to write. And one letter to the *Times,* she used to say to Miss Brush, cost her more than to organise an expedition to South Africa (which she had done in the war). After a morning's battle beginning, tearing up, beginning again, she used to feel the futility of her own womanhood as she felt it on no other occasion, and would turn gratefully to the thought of Hugh Whitbread who possessed-no one could doubt it-the art of writing letters to the *Times.*

A being so differently constituted from herself, with such a command of language; able to put things as editors like them put; had passions which one could not call simply greed. Lady Bruton often suspended judgement upon men in deference to the mysterious accord in which they, but no woman, stood to the laws of the universe; knew how to put things; knew what was said; so that if Richard advised her, and Hugh wrote for her, she was sure of being somehow right. So she let Hugh eat his soufflé; asked after poor Evelyn; waited until they were smoking, and then said,

"Milly, would you fetch the papers?"

And Miss Brush went out, came back; laid papers on the table; and Hugh produced his fountain pen; his silver fountain pen, which had done twenty years' service, he said, unscrewing the cap. It was still in perfect order; he had shown it to the makers; there was no reason, they said, why it should ever wear out; which was somehow to Hugh's credit, and to the credit of the sentiments which his pen expressed (so Richard Dalloway felt) as Hugh began carefully writing capital letters with rings round them in the margin, and thus marvellously reduced Lady Bruton's tangles to sense, to grammar such as the editor of the *Times,* Lady Bruton felt, watching the marvellous transformation, must respect. Hugh was slow. Hugh was pertinacious. Richard said one must take risks. Hugh proposed modifications in deference to people's feelings, which, he said rather tartly when Richard laughed, "had to be considered," and read out "how, therefore, we are of opinion that the times are ripe...the superfluous youth of our ever-increasing population...what we owe to the dead..." which Richard thought all stuffing and bunkum, but no harm in it, of course, and Hugh went on drafting sentiments in alphabetical order of the highest nobility, brushing the cigar ash from his waistcoat, and summing up now and then the progress they had made until, finally, he read out the draft of a letter which Lady Bruton felt certain was a masterpiece. Could her own meaning sound like that?

Hugh could not guarantee that the editor would put it in; but he would be meeting somebody at luncheon.

Whereupon Lady Bruton, who seldom did a graceful thing, stuffed all Hugh's carnations into the front of her dress, and flinging her hands out called him "My Prime Minister!" What she would have done without them both she did not know. They rose. And Richard Dalloway strolled off as usual to have a look at the General's portrait, because he meant, whenever he had a moment of leisure, to write a history of Lady Bruton's family.

And Millicent Bruton was very proud of her family. But they could wait, they could wait, she said, looking at the picture; meaning that her family, of military men, administrators, admirals, had been men of action, who had done their duty; and Richard's first duty was to his country, but it was a fine face, she said; and all the papers were ready for Richard down at Aldmixton whenever the time came; the Labour Government she meant. "Ah, the news from India!" she cried.

And then, as they stood in the hall taking yellow gloves from the bowl on the malachite table and Hugh was offering Miss Brush with quite unnecessary courtesy some discarded ticket or other compliment, which she loathed from the depths of her heart and blushed brick red, Richard turned to Lady Bruton, with his hat in his hand, and said,

"We shall see you at our party tonight?" whereupon Lady Bruton resumed the magnificence which letter-writing had shattered. She might come; or she might not come. Clarissa had wonderful energy. Parties terrified Lady Bruton. But then, she was getting old. So she intimated, standing at her doorway; handsome; very erect; while her chow stretched behind her, and Miss Brush disappeared into the background with her hands full of papers.

And Lady Bruton went ponderously, majestically, up to her room, lay, one arm extended, on the sofa. She sighed, she snored, not that she was asleep, only drowsy and heavy, drowsy and heavy, like a field of clover in the sunshine this hot June day, with the bees going round and about and the yellow butterflies. Always she went back to those fields down in Devonshire, where she had jumped the brooks on Patty, her pony, with Mortimer and Tom, her brothers. And there were the dogs; there were the rats; there were her father and mother on the lawn under the trees, with the tea-things out, and the beds of dahlias, the hollyhocks, the pampas grass; and they, little wretches, always up to some mischief! stealing back through the shrubbery, so as not to be seen, all bedraggled from some roguery. What old nurse used to say about her frocks!

Ah dear, she remembered—it was Wednesday in Brook Street. Those kind good fellows, Richard Dalloway, Hugh Whitbread, had gone this hot day through the streets whose growl came up to her lying on the sofa. Power was hers, position, income. She had lived in the forefront of her time. She had had good friends; known the ablest men of her day. Murmuring London flowed up to her, and her hand, lying on the sofa back, curled upon some imaginary baton such as her grandfathers might have held, holding which she seemed, drowsy and heavy, to be commanding battalions marching to Canada, and those good fellows walking across London, that territory of theirs, that little bit of carpet, Mayfair.

And they went further and further from her, being attached to her by a thin thread (since they had lunched with her) which would stretch and stretch, get thinner and thinner as they walked across London; as if one's friends were attached to one's body, after lunching with them, by a thin thread, which (as she dozed there) became hazy with the sound of bells, striking the hour or ringing to service, as a single spider's thread is blotted with rain-drops, and, burdened, sags down. So she slept.

And Richard Dalloway and Hugh Whitbread hesitated at the corner of Conduit Street at the very moment that Millicent Bruton, lying on the sofa, let the thread snap; snored. Contrary winds buffeted at the street corner. They looked in at a shop window; they did not wish to buy or to talk but to part, only with contrary winds buffeting the street corner, with some sort of lapse in the tides of the body, two forces meeting in a swirl, morning and afternoon, they paused. Some newspaper placard went up in the air, gallantly, like a kite at first, then paused, swooped, fluttered; and a lady's veil hung. Yellow awnings trembled. The speed of the morning traffic slackened, and single carts rattled carelessly down half-empty streets. In Norfolk, of which Richard Dalloway was half thinking, a soft warm wind blew back the petals; confused the waters; ruffled the flowering grasses. Haymakers, who had pitched beneath hedges to sleep away the morning toil, parted curtains of green blades; moved trembling globes of cow parsley to see the sky; the blue, the steadfast, the blazing summer sky.

Aware that he was looking at a silver two-handled Jacobean mug, and that Hugh Whitbread admired condescendingly with airs of connoisseurship a Spanish necklace which he thought of asking the price of in case Evelyn might like it-still Richard was torpid; could not think or move. Life had thrown up this wreckage; shop windows full of coloured paste, and one stood stark with the lethargy of the old, stiff with the rigidity of the old, looking in. Evelyn Whitbread might like to buy this Spanish necklace-so she might. Yawn he must. Hugh was going into the shop.

"Right you are!" said Richard, following.

Goodness knows he didn't want to go buying necklaces with Hugh. But there are tides in the body. Morning meets afternoon. Borne like a frail shallop on deep, deep floods, Lady Bruton's great-grandfather and his memoir and his campaigns in North America were whelmed and sunk. And Millicent Bruton too. She went under. Richard didn't care a straw what became of Emigration; about that letter, whether the editor put it in or not. The necklace hung stretched between Hugh's admirable fingers. Let him give it to a girl, if he must buy jewels-any girl, any girl in the street. For the worthlessness of this life did strike Richard pretty forcibly-buying necklaces for Evelyn. If he'd had a boy he'd have said, Work, work. But he had his Elizabeth; he adored his Elizabeth.

"I should like to see Mr. Dubonnet," said Hugh in his curt worldly way. It appeared that this Dubonnet had the measurements of Mrs. Whitbread's neck, or, more strangely still, knew her views upon Spanish jewellery and the extent of her possessions in that line (which Hugh could not remember). All of which seemed to Richard Dalloway awfully odd. For he never gave Clarissa presents, except a bracelet two or three years ago, which had not been a success. She never wore it. It pained him to remember that she never wore it. And as a single spider's thread after wavering here and there attaches itself to the point of a leaf, so Richard's mind, recovering from its lethargy, set now on his wife, Clarissa, whom Peter Walsh had loved so passionately; and Richard had had a sudden vision of her there at luncheon; of himself and Clarissa; of their life together; and he drew the tray of old jewels towards him, and taking up first this brooch then that ring, "How much is that?" he asked, but doubted his own taste. He wanted to open the drawing-room door and come in holding out something; a present for Clarissa. Only what? But Hugh was on his legs again. He was unspeakably pompous. Really, after dealing here for thirty-five years he was not going to be put off by a mere boy who did not know his business. For Dubonnet, it seemed, was out, and Hugh would not buy anything until Mr. Dubonnet chose to be in; at which the youth flushed and bowed his correct little bow. It was all perfectly correct. And yet Richard couldn't have said that to save his life! Why these people stood that damned insolence he could not conceive. Hugh was becoming an intolerable ass. Richard Dalloway could not stand more than an hour of his society. And, flicking his bowler hat by way of farewell, Richard turned at the corner of Conduit Street eager, yes, very eager, to travel that spider's thread of attachment between himself and Clarissa; he would go straight to her, in Westminster.

But he wanted to come in holding something. Flowers? Yes, flowers, since he did not trust his taste in gold; any number of flowers, roses, orchids, to celebrate what was, reckoning things as you will, an event; this feeling about her when they spoke of Peter Walsh at luncheon; and they never spoke of it; not for years had they spoken of it; which, he thought, grasping his red and white roses together (a vast bunch in tissue paper), is the greatest mistake in the world. The time comes when it can't be said; one's too shy to say it, he thought, pocketing his sixpence or two of change, setting off with his great bunch held against his body to Westminster to say straight out in so many words (whatever she might think of him), holding out his flowers, "I love you." Why not? Really it was a miracle thinking of the war, and thousands of poor chaps, with all their lives before them, shovelled together, already half forgotten; it was a miracle. Here he was walking across London to say to Clarissa in so many words that he loved her. Which one never does say, he thought. Partly one's lazy; partly one's shy. And Clarissa-it was difficult to think of her; except in starts, as at luncheon, when he saw her quite distinctly; their whole life.

He stopped at the crossing; and repeated-being simple by nature, and undebauched, because he had tramped, and shot; being pertinacious and dogged, having championed the down-trodden and followed his instincts in the House of Commons; being preserved in his simplicity yet at the same time grown rather speechless, rather stiff-he repeated that it was a miracle that he should have married Clarissa; a miracle-his life had been a miracle, he thought; hesitating to cross. But it did make his blood boil to see little creatures of five or six crossing Piccadilly alone. The police ought to have stopped the traffic at once. He had no illusions about the London police. Indeed, he was collecting evidence of their malpractices; and those costermongers, not allowed to stand their barrows in the streets; and prostitutes, good Lord, the fault wasn't in them, nor in young men either, but in our detestable social system and so forth; all of which he considered, could be seen considering, grey, dogged, dapper, clean, as he walked across the Park to tell his wife that he loved her.

For he would say it in so many words, when he came into the room. Because it is a thousand pities never to say what one feels, he thought, crossing the Green Park and observing with pleasure how in the shade of the trees whole families, poor families, were sprawling; children kicking up their legs; sucking milk; paper bags thrown about, which could easily be picked up (if people objected) by one of those fat gentlemen in livery; for he was of opinion that every park, and every square, during the summer months should be open to children (the grass of the park flushed and faded, lighting up the poor mothers of Westminster and their crawling babies, as if a yellow lamp were moved beneath). But what could be done for female vagrants like that poor creature, stretched on her elbow (as if she had flung herself on the earth, rid of all ties, to observe curiously, to speculate boldly, to consider the whys and the wherefores, impudent, loose-lipped, humorous), he did not know. Bearing his flowers like a weapon, Richard Dalloway approached her; intent he passed her; still there was time for a spark between them-she laughed at the sight of him, he smiled good-humouredly, considering the problem of the female vagrant; not that they would ever speak. But he would tell Clarissa that he loved her, in so many words. He had, once upon a time, been jealous of Peter Walsh; jealous of him and Clarissa. But she had often said to him that she had been right not to marry Peter Walsh; which, knowing Clarissa, was obviously true; she wanted support. Not that she was weak; but she wanted support.

As for Buckingham Palace (like an old prima donna facing the audience all in white) you can't deny it a certain dignity, he considered, nor despise what does, after all, stand to millions of people (a little crowd was waiting at the gate to see the King drive out) for a symbol, absurd though it is; a child with a box of bricks could have done better, he thought; looking at the memorial to Queen Victoria (whom he could remember in her horn spectacles driving through Kensington), its white mound, its billowing motherliness; but he liked being ruled by the descendant of Horsa; he liked continuity; and the sense of handing on the traditions of the past. It was a great age in which to have lived. Indeed, his own life was a miracle; let him make no mistake about it; here he was, in the prime of life, walking to his house in Westminster to tell Clarissa that he loved her. Happiness is this he thought.

It is this, he said, as he entered Dean's Yard. Big Ben was beginning to strike, first the warning, musical; then the hour, irrevocable. Lunch parties waste the entire afternoon, he thought, approaching his door.

The sound of Big Ben flooded Clarissa's drawing-room, where she sat, ever so annoyed, at her writing-table; worried; annoyed. It was perfectly true that she had not asked Ellie Henderson to her party; but she had done it on purpose. Now Mrs. Marsham wrote "she had told Ellie Henderson she would ask Clarissa-Ellie so much wanted to come."

But why should she invite all the dull women in London to her parties? Why should Mrs. Marsham interfere? And there was Elizabeth closeted all this time with Doris Kilman. Anything more nauseating she could not conceive. Prayer at this hour with that woman. And the sound of the bell flooded the room with its melancholy wave; which receded, and gathered itself together to fall once more, when she heard, distractingly, something fumbling, something scratching at the door. Who at this hour? Three, good Heavens! Three already! For with overpowering directness and dignity the clock struck three; and she heard nothing else; but the door handle slipped round and in came Richard! What a surprise! In came Richard, holding out flowers. She had failed him, once at Constantinople; and Lady Bruton, whose lunch parties were said to be extraordinarily amusing, had not asked her. He was holding out flowers-roses, red and white roses. (But he could not bring himself to say he loved her; not in so many words.)

But how lovely, she said, taking his flowers. She understood; she understood without his speaking; his Clarissa. She put them in vases on the mantelpiece. How lovely they looked! she said. And was it amusing, she asked? Had Lady Bruton asked after her? Peter Walsh was back. Mrs. Marsham had written. Must she ask Ellie Henderson? That woman Kilman was upstairs.

"But let us sit down for five minutes," said Richard.

It all looked so empty. All the chairs were against the wall. What had they been doing? Oh, it was for the party; no, he had not forgotten, the party. Peter Walsh was back. Oh yes; she had had him. And he was going to get a divorce; and he was in love with some woman out there. And he hadn't changed in the slightest. There she was, mending her dress....

"Thinking of Bourton," she said.

"Hugh was at lunch," said Richard. She had met him too! Well, he was getting absolutely intolerable. Buying Evelyn necklaces; fatter than ever; an intolerable ass.

"And it came over me 'I might have married you,'" she said, thinking of Peter sitting there in his little bow-tie; with that knife, opening it, shutting it. "Just as he always was, you know."

They were talking about him at lunch, said Richard. (But he could not tell her he loved her. He held her hand. Happiness is this, he thought.) They had been writing a letter to the *Times* for Millicent Bruton. That was about all Hugh was fit for.

"And our dear Miss Kilman?" he asked. Clarissa thought the roses absolutely lovely; first bunched together; now of their own accord starting apart.

"Kilman arrives just as we've done lunch," she said. "Elizabeth turns pink. They shut themselves up. I suppose they're praying."

Lord! He didn't like it; but these things pass over if you let them.

"In a mackintosh with an umbrella," said Clarissa.

He had not said "I love you"; but he held her hand. Happiness is this, is this, he thought.

"But why should I ask all the dull women in London to my parties?" said Clarissa. And if Mrs. Marsham gave a party, did *she* invite her guests?

"Poor Ellie Henderson," said Richard-it was a very odd thing how much Clarissa minded about her parties, he thought.

But Richard had no notion of the look of a room. However-what was he going to say?

If she worried about these parties he would not let her give them. Did she wish she had married Peter? But he must go.

He must be off, he said, getting up. But he stood for a moment as if he were about to say something; and she wondered what? Why? There were the roses.

"Some Committee?" she asked, as he opened the door.

"Armenians," he said; or perhaps it was "Albanians."

And there is a dignity in people; a solitude; even between husband and wife a gulf; and that one must respect, thought Clarissa, watching him open the door; for one would not part with it oneself, or take it, against his will, from one's husband, without losing one's independence, one's self-respect —something, after all, priceless.

He returned with a pillow and a quilt.

"An hour's complete rest after luncheon," he said. And he went.

How like him! He would go on saying "An hour's complete rest after luncheon" to the end of time, because a doctor had ordered it once. It was like him to take what doctors said literally; part of his adorable, divine simplicity, which no one had to the same extent; which made him go and do the thing while she and Peter frittered their time away bickering. He was already halfway to the House of Commons, to his Armenians, his Albanians, having settled her on the sofa, looking at his roses. And people would say, "Clarissa Dalloway is spoilt." She cared much more for her roses than for the Armenians. Hunted out of existence, maimed, frozen, the victims of cruelty and injustice (she had heard Richard say so over and over again) —no, she could feel nothing for the Albanians, or was it the Armenians? but she loved her roses (didn't that help the Armenians?) —the only flowers she could bear to see cut. But Richard was already at the House of Commons; at his Committee, having settled all her difficulties. But no; alas, that was not true. He did not see the reasons against asking Ellie Henderson. She would do it, of course, as he wished it. Since he had brought the pillows, she would lie down.... But-but-why did she suddenly feel, for no reason that she could discover, desperately unhappy? As a person who has dropped some grain of pearl or diamond into the grass and parts the tall blades very carefully, this way and that, and searches here and there vainly, and at last spies it there at the roots, so she went through one thing and another; no, it was not Sally Seton saying that Richard would never be in the Cabinet because he had a second-class brain (it came back to her); no, she did not mind that; nor was it to do with Elizabeth either and Doris Kilman; those were facts. It was a feeling, some unpleasant feeling, earlier in the day perhaps; something that Peter had said, combined with some depression of her own, in her bedroom, taking off her hat; and what Richard had said had added to it, but what had he said? There were his roses. Her parties! That was it! Her parties! Both of them criticised her very unfairly, laughed at her very unjustly, for her parties. That was it! That was it!

Well, how was she going to defend herself? Now that she knew what it was, she felt perfectly happy. They thought, or Peter at any rate thought, that she enjoyed imposing herself; liked to have famous people about her; great names; was simply a snob in short. Well, Peter might think so. Richard merely thought it foolish of her to like excitement when she knew it was bad for her heart. It was childish, he thought. And both were quite wrong. What she liked was simply life.

"That's what I do it for," she said, speaking aloud, to life.

Since she was lying on the sofa, cloistered, exempt, the presence of this thing which she felt to be so obvious became physically existent; with robes of sound from the street, sunny, with hot breath, whispering, blowing out the blinds. But suppose Peter said to her, "Yes, yes, but your parties-what's the sense of your parties?" all she could say was (and nobody could be expected to understand): They're an offering; which sounded horribly vague. But who was Peter to make out that life was all plain sailing? —Peter always in love, always in love with the wrong woman? What's your love? she might say to him. And she knew his answer; how it is the most important thing in the world and no woman possibly understood it. Very well. But could any man understand what she meant either? about life? She could not imagine Peter or Richard taking the trouble to give a party for no reason whatever.

But to go deeper, beneath what people said (and these judgements, how superficial, how fragmentary they are!) in her own mind now, what did it mean to her, this thing she called life? Oh, it was very queer. Here was So-and-so in South Kensington; some one up in Bayswater; and somebody else, say, in Mayfair. And she felt quite continuously a sense of their existence; and she felt what a waste; and she felt what a pity; and she felt if only they could be brought together; so she did it. And it was an offering; to combine, to create; but to whom?

An offering for the sake of offering, perhaps. Anyhow, it was her gift. Nothing else had she of the slightest importance; could not think, write, even play the piano. She muddled Armenians and Turks; loved success; hated discomfort; must be liked; talked oceans of nonsense: and to this day, ask her what the Equator was, and she did not know. All the same, that one day should follow another; Wednesday, Thursday, Friday, Saturday; that one should wake up in the morning; see the sky; walk in the park; meet Hugh Whitbread; then suddenly in came Peter; then these roses; it was enough. After that, how unbelievable death was! —that it must end; and no one in the whole world would know how she had loved it all; how, every instant...

The door opened. Elizabeth knew that her mother was resting. She came in very quietly. She stood perfectly still. Was it that some Mongol had been wrecked on the coast of Norfolk (as Mrs. Hilbery said), had mixed with the Dalloway ladies, perhaps, a hundred years ago? For the Dalloways, in general, were fair-haired; blue-eyed; Elizabeth, on the contrary, was dark; had Chinese eyes in a pale face; an Oriental mystery; was gentle, considerate, still. As a child, she had had a perfect sense of humour; but now at seventeen, why, Clarissa could not in the least understand, she had become very serious; like a hyacinth, sheathed in glossy green, with buds just tinted, a hyacinth which has had no sun.

She stood quite still and looked at her mother; but the door was ajar, and outside the door was Miss Kilman, as Clarissa knew; Miss Kilman in her mackintosh, listening to whatever they said.

Yes, Miss Kilman stood on the landing, and wore a mackintosh; but had her reasons. First, it was cheap; second, she was over forty; and did not, after all, dress to please. She was poor, moreover; degradingly poor. Otherwise she would not be taking jobs from people like the Dalloways; from rich people, who liked to be kind. Mr. Dalloway, to do him justice, had been kind. But Mrs. Dalloway had not. She had been merely condescending. She came from the most worthless of all classes-the rich, with a smattering of culture. They had expensive things everywhere; pictures, carpets, lots of servants. She considered that she had a perfect right to anything that the Dalloways did for her.

She had been cheated. Yes, the word was no exaggeration, for surely a girl has a right to some kind of happiness? And she had never been happy, what with being so clumsy and so poor. And then, just as she might have had a chance at Miss Dolby's school, the war came; and she had never been able to tell lies. Miss Dolby thought she would be happier with people who shared her views about the Germans. She had had to go. It was true that the family was of German origin; spelt the name Kiehlman in the eighteenth century; but her brother had been killed. They turned her out because she would not pretend that the Germans were all villains-when she had German friends, when the only happy days of her life had been spent in Germany! And after all, she could read history. She had had to take whatever she could get. Mr. Dalloway had come across her working for the Friends. He had allowed her (and that was really generous of him) to teach his daughter history. Also she did a little Extension lecturing and so on. Then Our Lord had come to her (and here she always bowed her head). She had seen the light two years and three months ago. Now she did not envy women like Clarissa Dalloway; she pitied them.

She pitied and despised them from the bottom of her heart, as she stood on the soft carpet, looking at the old engraving of a little girl with a muff. With all this luxury going on, what hope was there for a better state of things? Instead of lying on a sofa —"My mother is resting," Elizabeth had said-she should have been in a factory; behind a counter; Mrs. Dalloway and all the other fine ladies!

Bitter and burning, Miss Kilman had turned into a church two years three months ago. She had heard the Rev. Edward Whittaker preach; the boys sing; had seen the solemn lights descend, and whether it was the music, or the voices (she herself when alone in the evening found comfort in a violin; but the sound was excruciating; she had no ear), the hot and turbulent feelings which boiled and surged in her had been assuaged as she sat there, and she had wept copiously, and gone to call on Mr. Whittaker at his private house in Kensington. It was the hand of God, he said. The Lord had shown her the way. So now, whenever the hot and painful feelings boiled within her, this hatred of Mrs. Dalloway, this grudge against the world, she thought of God. She thought of Mr. Whittaker. Rage was succeeded by calm. A sweet savour filled her veins, her lips parted, and, standing formidable upon the landing in her mackintosh, she looked with steady and sinister serenity at Mrs. Dalloway, who came out with her daughter.

Elizabeth said she had forgotten her gloves. That was because Miss Kilman and her mother hated each other. She could not bear to see them together. She ran upstairs to find her gloves.

But Miss Kilman did not hate Mrs. Dalloway. Turning her large gooseberry-coloured eyes upon Clarissa, observing her small pink face, her delicate body, her air of freshness and fashion, Miss Kilman felt, Fool! Simpleton! You who have known neither sorrow nor pleasure; who have trifled your life away! And there rose in her an overmastering desire to overcome her; to unmask her. If she could have felled her it would have eased her. But it was not the body; it was the soul and its mockery that she wished to subdue; make feel her mastery. If only she could make her weep; could ruin her; humiliate her; bring her to her knees crying, You are right! But this was God's will, not Miss Kilman's. It was to be a religious victory. So she glared; so she glowered.

Clarissa was really shocked. This a Christian-this woman! This woman had taken her daughter from her! She in touch with invisible presences! Heavy, ugly, commonplace, without kindness or grace, she know the meaning of life!

"You are taking Elizabeth to the Stores?" Mrs. Dalloway said.

Miss Kilman said she was. They stood there. Miss Kilman was not going to make herself agreeable. She had always earned her living. Her knowledge of modern history was thorough in the extreme. She did out of her meagre income set aside so much for causes she believed in; whereas this woman did nothing, believed nothing; brought up her daughter-but here was Elizabeth, rather out of breath, the beautiful girl.

So they were going to the Stores. Odd it was, as Miss Kilman stood there (and stand she did, with the power and taciturnity of some prehistoric monster armoured for primeval warfare), how, second by second, the idea of her diminished, how hatred (which was for ideas, not people) crumbled, how she lost her malignity, her size, became second by second merely Miss Kilman, in a mackintosh, whom Heaven knows Clarissa would have liked to help.

At this dwindling of the monster, Clarissa laughed. Saying good-bye, she laughed.

Off they went together, Miss Kilman and Elizabeth, downstairs.

With a sudden impulse, with a violent anguish, for this woman was taking her daughter from her, Clarissa leant over the bannisters and cried out, "Remember the party! Remember our party tonight!"

But Elizabeth had already opened the front door; there was a van passing; she did not answer.

Love and religion! thought Clarissa, going back into the drawing-room, tingling all over. How detestable, how detestable they are! For now that the body of Miss Kilman was not before her, it overwhelmed her-the idea. The cruelest things in the world, she thought, seeing them clumsy, hot, domineering, hypocritical, eavesdropping, jealous, infinitely cruel and unscrupulous, dressed in a mackintosh coat, on the landing; love and religion. Had she ever tried to convert any one herself? Did she not wish everybody merely to be themselves? And she watched out of the window the old lady opposite climbing upstairs. Let her climb upstairs if she wanted to; let her stop; then let her, as Clarissa had often seen her, gain her bedroom, part her curtains, and disappear again into the background. Somehow one respected that-that old woman looking out of the window, quite unconscious that she was being watched. There was something solemn in it-but love and religion would destroy that, whatever it was, the privacy of the soul. The odious Kilman would destroy it. Yet it was a sight that made her want to cry.

Love destroyed too. Everything that was fine, everything that was true went. Take Peter Walsh now. There was a man, charming, clever, with ideas about everything. If you wanted to know about Pope, say, or Addison, or just to talk nonsense, what people were like, what things meant, Peter knew better than any one. It was Peter who had helped her; Peter who had lent her books. But look at the women he loved-vulgar, trivial, commonplace. Think of Peter in love-he came to see her after all these years, and what did he talk about? Himself. Horrible passion! she thought. Degrading passion! she thought, thinking of Kilman and her Elizabeth walking to the Army and Navy Stores.

Big Ben struck the half-hour.

How extraordinary it was, strange, yes, touching, to see the old lady (they had been neighbours ever so many years) move away from the window, as if she were attached to that sound, that string. Gigantic as it was, it had something to do with her. Down, down, into the midst of ordinary things the finger fell making the moment solemn. She was forced, so Clarissa imagined, by that sound, to move, to go-but where? Clarissa tried to follow her as she turned and disappeared, and could still just see her white cap moving at the back of the bedroom. She was still there moving about at the other end of the room. Why creeds and prayers and mackintoshes? when, thought Clarissa, that's the miracle, that's the mystery; that old lady, she meant, whom she could see going from chest of drawers to dressing-table. She could still see her. And the supreme mystery which Kilman might say she had solved, or Peter might say he had solved, but Clarissa didn't believe either of them had the ghost of an idea of solving, was simply this: here was one room; there another. Did religion solve that, or love?

Love-but here the other clock, the clock which always struck two minutes after Big Ben, came shuffling in with its lap full of odds and ends, which it dumped down as if Big Ben were all very well with his majesty laying down the law, so solemn, so just, but she must remember all sorts of little things besides-Mrs. Marsham, Ellie Henderson, glasses for ices-all sorts of little things came flooding and lapping and dancing in on the wake of that solemn stroke which lay flat like a bar of gold on the sea. Mrs. Marsham, Ellie Henderson, glasses for ices. She must telephone now at once.

Volubly, troublously, the late clock sounded, coming in on the wake of Big Ben, with its lap full of trifles. Beaten up, broken up by the assault of carriages, the brutality of vans, the eager advance of myriads of angular men, of flaunting women, the domes and spires of offices and hospitals, the last relics of this lap full of odds and ends seemed to break, like the spray of an exhausted wave, upon the body of Miss Kilman standing still in the street for a moment to mutter "It is the flesh."

It was the flesh that she must control. Clarissa Dalloway had insulted her. That she expected. But she had not triumphed; she had not mastered the flesh. Ugly, clumsy, Clarissa Dalloway had laughed at her for being that; and had revived the fleshly desires, for she minded looking as she did beside Clarissa. Nor could she talk as she did. But why wish to resemble her? Why? She despised Mrs. Dalloway from the bottom of her heart. She was not serious. She was not good. Her life was a tissue of vanity and deceit. Yet Doris Kilman had been overcome. She had, as a matter of fact, very nearly burst into tears when Clarissa Dalloway laughed at her. "It is the flesh, it is the flesh," she muttered (it being her habit to talk aloud) trying to subdue this turbulent and painful feeling as she walked down Victoria Street. She prayed to God. She could not help being ugly; she could not afford to buy pretty clothes. Clarissa Dalloway had laughed-but she would concentrate her mind upon something else until she had reached the pillar-box. At any rate she had got Elizabeth. But she would think of something else; she would think of Russia; until she reached the pillar-box.

How nice it must be, she said, in the country, struggling, as Mr. Whittaker had told her, with that violent grudge against the world which had scorned her, sneered at her, cast her off, beginning with this indignity-the infliction of her unlovable body which people could not bear to see. Do her hair as she might, her forehead remained like an egg, bald, white. No clothes suited her. She might buy anything. And for a woman, of course, that meant never meeting the opposite sex. Never would she come first with any one. Sometimes lately it had seemed to her that, except for Elizabeth, her food was all that she lived for; her comforts; her dinner, her tea; her hot-water bottle at night. But one must fight; vanquish; have faith in God. Mr. Whittaker had said she was there for a purpose. But no one knew the agony! He said, pointing to the crucifix, that God knew. But why should she have to suffer when other women, like Clarissa Dalloway, escaped? Knowledge comes through suffering, said Mr. Whittaker.

She had passed the pillar-box, and Elizabeth had turned into the cool brown tobacco department of the Army and Navy Stores while she was still muttering to herself what Mr. Whittaker had said about knowledge coming through suffering and the flesh. "The flesh," she muttered.

What department did she want? Elizabeth interrupted her.

"Petticoats," she said abruptly, and stalked straight on to the lift.

Up they went. Elizabeth guided her this way and that; guided her in her abstraction as if she had been a great child, an unwieldy battleship. There were the petticoats, brown, decorous, striped, frivolous, solid, flimsy; and she chose, in her abstraction, portentously, and the girl serving thought her mad.

Elizabeth rather wondered, as they did up the parcel, what Miss Kilman was thinking. They must have their tea, said Miss Kilman, rousing, collecting herself. They had their tea.

Elizabeth rather wondered whether Miss Kilman could be hungry. It was her way of eating, eating with intensity, then looking, again and again, at a plate of sugared cakes on the table next them; then, when a lady and a child sat down and the child took the cake, could Miss Kilman really mind it? Yes, Miss Kilman did mind it. She had wanted that cake-the pink one. The pleasure of eating was almost the only pure pleasure left her, and then to be baffled even in that!

When people are happy, they have a reserve, she had told Elizabeth, upon which to draw, whereas she was like a wheel without a tyre (she was fond of such metaphors), jolted by every pebble, so she would say staying on after the lesson standing by the fireplace with her bag of books, her "satchel," she called it, on a Tuesday morning, after the lesson was over. And she talked too about the war. After all, there were people who did not think the English invariably right. There were books. There were meetings. There were other points of view. Would Elizabeth like to come with her to listen to So-and-so (a most extraordinary looking old man)? Then Miss Kilman took her to some church in Kensington and they had tea with a clergyman. She had lent her books. Law, medicine, politics, all professions are open to women of your generation, said Miss Kilman. But for herself, her career was absolutely ruined and was it her fault? Good gracious, said Elizabeth, no.

And her mother would come calling to say that a hamper had come from Bourton and would Miss Kilman like some flowers? To Miss Kilman she was always very, very nice, but Miss Kilman squashed the flowers all in a bunch, and hadn't any small talk, and what interested Miss Kilman bored her mother, and Miss Kilman and she were terrible together; and Miss Kilman swelled and looked very plain. But then Miss Kilman was frightfully clever. Elizabeth had never thought about the poor. They lived with everything they wanted,—her mother had breakfast in bed every day; Lucy carried it up; and she liked old women because they were Duchesses, and being descended from some Lord. But Miss Kilman said (one of those Tuesday mornings when the lesson was over), "My grandfather kept an oil and colour shop in Kensington." Miss Kilman made one feel so small.

Miss Kilman took another cup of tea. Elizabeth, with her oriental bearing, her inscrutable mystery, sat perfectly upright; no, she did not want anything more. She looked for her gloves-her white gloves. They were under the table. Ah, but she must not go! Miss Kilman could not let her go! this youth, that was so beautiful, this girl, whom she genuinely loved! Her large hand opened and shut on the table.

But perhaps it was a little flat somehow, Elizabeth felt. And really she would like to go.

But said Miss Kilman, "I've not quite finished yet."

Of course, then, Elizabeth would wait. But it was rather stuffy in here.

"Are you going to the party tonight?" Miss Kilman said. Elizabeth supposed she was going; her mother wanted her to go. She must not let parties absorb her, Miss Kilman said, fingering the last two inches of a chocolate éclair.

She did not much like parties, Elizabeth said. Miss Kilman opened her mouth, slightly projected her chin, and swallowed down the last inches of the chocolate éclair, then wiped her fingers, and washed the tea round in her cup.

She was about to split asunder, she felt. The agony was so terrific. If she could grasp her, if she could clasp her, if she could make her hers absolutely and forever and then die; that was all she wanted. But to sit here, unable to think of anything to say; to see Elizabeth turning against her; to be felt repulsive even by her-it was too much; she could not stand it. The thick fingers curled inwards.

"I never go to parties," said Miss Kilman, just to keep Elizabeth from going. "People don't ask me to parties"—and she knew as she said it that it was this egotism that was her undoing; Mr. Whittaker had warned her; but she could not help it. She had suffered so horribly. "Why should they ask me?" she said. "I'm plain, I'm unhappy." She knew it was idiotic. But it was all those people passing-people with parcels who despised her, who made her say it. However,

437

she was Doris Kilman. She had her degree. She was a woman who had made her way in the world. Her knowledge of modern history was more than respectable.

"I don't pity myself," she said. "I pity"—she meant to say "your mother" but no, she could not, not to Elizabeth. "I pity other people," she said, "more."

Like some dumb creature who has been brought up to a gate for an unknown purpose, and stands there longing to gallop away, Elizabeth Dalloway sat silent. Was Miss Kilman going to say anything more?

"Don't quite forget me," said Doris Kilman; her voice quivered. Right away to the end of the field the dumb creature galloped in terror.

The great hand opened and shut.

Elizabeth turned her head. The waitress came. One had to pay at the desk, Elizabeth said, and went off, drawing out, so Miss Kilman felt, the very entrails in her body, stretching them as she crossed the room, and then, with a final twist, bowing her head very politely, she went.

She had gone. Miss Kilman sat at the marble table among the éclairs, stricken once, twice, thrice by shocks of suffering. She had gone. Mrs. Dalloway had triumphed. Elizabeth had gone. Beauty had gone, youth had gone.

So she sat. She got up, blundered off among the little tables, rocking slightly from side to side, and somebody came after her with her petticoat, and she lost her way, and was hemmed in by trunks specially prepared for taking to India; next got among the accouchement sets, and baby linen; through all the commodities of the world, perishable and permanent, hams, drugs, flowers, stationery, variously smelling, now sweet, now sour she lurched; saw herself thus lurching with her hat askew, very red in the face, full length in a looking-glass; and at last came out into the street.

The tower of Westminster Cathedral rose in front of her, the habitation of God. In the midst of the traffic, there was the habitation of God. Doggedly she set off with her parcel to that other sanctuary, the Abbey, where, raising her hands in a tent before her face, she sat beside those driven into shelter too; the variously assorted worshippers, now divested of social rank, almost of sex, as they raised their hands before their faces; but once they removed them, instantly reverent, middle class, English men and women, some of them desirous of seeing the wax works.

But Miss Kilman held her tent before her face. Now she was deserted; now rejoined. New worshippers came in from the street to replace the strollers, and still, as people gazed round and shuffled past the tomb of the Unknown Warrior, still she barred her eyes with her fingers and tried in this double darkness, for the light in the Abbey was bodiless, to aspire above the vanities, the desires, the commodities, to rid herself both of hatred and of love. Her hands twitched. She seemed to struggle. Yet to others God was accessible and the path to Him smooth. Mr. Fletcher, retired, of the Treasury, Mrs. Gorham, widow of the famous K.C., approached Him simply, and having done their praying, leant back, enjoyed the music (the organ pealed sweetly), and saw Miss Kilman at the end of the row, praying, praying, and, being still on the threshold of their underworld, thought of her sympathetically as a soul haunting the same territory; a soul cut out of immaterial substance; not a woman, a soul.

But Mr. Fletcher had to go. He had to pass her, and being himself neat as a new pin, could not help being a little distressed by the poor lady's disorder; her hair down; her parcel on the floor. She did not at once let him pass. But, as he stood gazing about him, at the white marbles, grey window panes, and accumulated treasures (for he was extremely proud of the Abbey), her largeness, robustness, and power as she sat there shifting her knees from time to time (it was so rough the approach to her God-so tough her desires) impressed him, as they had impressed Mrs. Dalloway (she could not get the thought of her out of her mind that afternoon), the Rev. Edward Whittaker, and Elizabeth too.

And Elizabeth waited in Victoria Street for an omnibus. It was so nice to be out of doors. She thought perhaps she need not go home just yet. It was so nice to be out in the air. So she would get on to an omnibus. And already, even as she stood there, in her very well cut clothes, it was beginning.... People were beginning to compare her to poplar trees, early dawn, hyacinths, fawns, running water, and garden lilies; and it made her life a burden to her, for she so much preferred being left alone to do what she liked in the country, but they would compare her to lilies, and she had to go to parties, and London was so dreary compared with being alone in the country with her father and the dogs.

Buses swooped, settled, were off-garish caravans, glistening with red and yellow varnish. But which should she get on to? She had no preferences. Of course, she would not push her way. She inclined to be passive. It was expression she needed, but her eyes were fine, Chinese, oriental, and, as her mother said, with such nice shoulders and holding herself so straight, she was always charming to look at; and lately, in the evening especially, when she was interested, for she never seemed excited, she looked almost beautiful, very stately, very serene. What could she be thinking? Every man fell in love with her, and she was really awfully bored. For it was beginning. Her mother could see that-the compliments were beginning. That she did not care more about it-for instance for her clothes-sometimes worried Clarissa, but perhaps it was as well with all those puppies and guinea pigs about having distemper, and it gave her a charm. And now there was this odd friendship with Miss Kilman. Well, thought Clarissa about three o'clock in the morning, reading Baron Marbot for she could not sleep, it proves she has a heart.

Suddenly Elizabeth stepped forward and most competently boarded the omnibus, in front of everybody. She took a seat on top. The impetuous creature —a pirate-started forward, sprang away; she had to hold the rail to steady herself, for a pirate it was, reckless, unscrupulous, bearing down ruthlessly, circumventing dangerously, boldly snatching a passenger, or ignoring a passenger, squeezing eel-like and arrogant in between, and then rushing insolently all sails spread up Whitehall. And did Elizabeth give one thought to poor Miss Kilman who loved her without jealousy, to whom she had been a fawn in the open, a moon in a glade? She was delighted to be free. The fresh air was so delicious. It had been so stuffy in the Army and Navy Stores. And now it was like riding, to be rushing up Whitehall; and to each movement of the omnibus the beautiful body in the fawn-coloured coat responded freely like a rider, like the figurehead of a ship, for the breeze slightly disarrayed her; the heat gave her cheeks the pallor of white painted wood; and her fine eyes, having no eyes to meet, gazed ahead, blank, bright, with the staring incredible innocence of sculpture.

It was always talking about her own sufferings that made Miss Kilman so difficult. And was she right? If it was being on committees and giving up hours and hours every day (she hardly ever saw him in London) that helped the poor, her father did that, goodness knows, —if that was what Miss Kilman meant about being a Christian; but it was so difficult to say. Oh, she would like to go a little further. Another penny was it to the Strand? Here was another penny then. She would go up the Strand.

She liked people who were ill. And every profession is open to the women of your generation, said Miss Kilman. So she might be a doctor. She might be a farmer. Animals are often ill. She might own a thousand acres and have people under her. She would go and see them in their cottages. This was Somerset House. One might be a very good farmer-and that, strangely enough though Miss Kilman had her share in it, was almost entirely due to Somerset House. It looked so splendid, so serious, that great grey building. And she liked the feeling of people working. She liked those churches, like shapes of grey paper, breasting the stream of the Strand. It was quite different here from Westminster, she thought, getting off at Chancery Lane. It was so serious; it was so busy. In short, she would like to have a profession. She would become a doctor, a farmer, possibly go into Parliament, if she found it necessary, all because of the Strand.

The feet of those people busy about their activities, hands putting stone to stone, minds eternally occupied not with trivial chatterings (comparing women to poplars-which was rather exciting, of course, but very silly), but with thoughts of ships, of business, of law, of administration, and with it all so stately (she was in the Temple), gay (there was the river), pious (there was the Church), made her quite determined, whatever her mother might say, to become either a farmer or a doctor. But she was, of course, rather lazy.

And it was much better to say nothing about it. It seemed so silly. It was the sort of thing that did sometimes happen, when one was alone-buildings without architects' names, crowds of people coming back from the city having more power than single clergymen in Kensington, than any of the books Miss Kilman had lent her, to stimulate what lay slumbrous, clumsy, and shy on the mind's sandy floor to break surface, as a child suddenly stretches its arms; it was just that, perhaps, a sigh, a stretch of the arms, an impulse, a revelation, which has its effects for ever, and then down again it went to the sandy floor. She must go home. She must dress for dinner. But what was the time? —where was a clock?

She looked up Fleet Street. She walked just a little way towards St. Paul's, shyly, like some one penetrating on tiptoe, exploring a strange house by night with a candle, on edge lest the owner should suddenly fling wide his bedroom door and ask her business, nor did she dare wander off into queer alleys, tempting bye-streets, any more than in a strange house open doors which might be bedroom doors, or sitting-room doors, or lead straight to the larder. For no Dalloways came down the Strand daily; she was a pioneer, a stray, venturing, trusting.

In many ways, her mother felt, she was extremely immature, like a child still, attached to dolls, to old slippers; a perfect baby; and that was charming. But then, of course, there was in the Dalloway family the tradition of public service. Abbesses, principals, head mistresses, dignitaries, in the republic of women-without being brilliant, any of them, they were that. She penetrated a little further in the direction of St. Paul's. She liked the geniality, sisterhood, motherhood, brotherhood of this uproar. It seemed to her good. The noise was tremendous; and suddenly there were trumpets (the unemployed) blaring, rattling about in the uproar; military music; as if people were marching; yet had they been dying-had some woman breathed her last and whoever was watching, opening the window of the room where she had just brought off that act of supreme dignity, looked down on Fleet Street, that uproar, that military music would have come triumphing up to him, consolatory, indifferent.

It was not conscious. There was no recognition in it of one fortune, or fate, and for that very reason even to those dazed with watching for the last shivers of consciousness on the faces of the dying, consoling. Forgetfulness in people might wound, their ingratitude corrode, but this voice, pouring endlessly, year in year out, would take whatever it might be; this vow; this van; this life; this procession, would wrap them all about and carry them on, as in the rough stream of a glacier the ice holds a splinter of bone, a blue petal, some oak trees, and rolls them on.

But it was later than she thought. Her mother would not like her to be wandering off alone like this. She turned back down the Strand.

A puff of wind (in spite of the heat, there was quite a wind) blew a thin black veil over the sun and over the Strand. The faces faded; the omnibuses suddenly lost their glow. For although the clouds were of mountainous white so that one could fancy hacking hard chips off with a hatchet, with broad golden slopes, lawns of celestial pleasure gardens, on their flanks, and had all the appearance of settled habitations assembled for the conference of gods above the world, there was a perpetual movement among them. Signs were interchanged, when, as if to fulfil some scheme arranged already, now a summit dwindled, now a whole block of pyramidal size which had kept its station inalterably advanced into the midst or gravely led the procession to fresh anchorage. Fixed though they seemed at their posts, at rest in perfect unanimity, nothing could be fresher, freer, more sensitive superficially than the snow-white or gold-kindled surface; to change, to go, to dismantle the solemn assemblage was immediately possible; and in spite of the grave fixity, the accumulated robustness and solidity, now they struck light to the earth, now darkness.

Calmly and competently, Elizabeth Dalloway mounted the Westminster omnibus.

Going and coming, beckoning, signalling, so the light and shadow which now made the wall grey, now the bananas bright yellow, now made the Strand grey, now made the omnibuses bright yellow, seemed to Septimus Warren Smith lying on the sofa in the sitting-room; watching the watery gold glow and fade with the astonishing sensibility of some live creature on the roses, on the wallpaper. Outside the trees dragged their leaves like nets through the depths of the air;

the sound of water was in the room and through the waves came the voices of birds singing. Every power poured its treasures on his head, and his hand lay there on the back of the sofa, as he had seen his hand lie when he was bathing, floating, on the top of the waves, while far away on shore he heard dogs barking and barking far away. Fear no more, says the heart in the body; fear no more.

He was not afraid. At every moment Nature signified by some laughing hint like that gold spot which went round the wall-there, there, there-her determination to show, by brandishing her plumes, shaking her tresses, flinging her mantle this way and that, beautifully, always beautifully, and standing close up to breathe through her hollowed hands Shakespeare's words, her meaning.

Rezia, sitting at the table twisting a hat in her hands, watched him; saw him smiling. He was happy then. But she could not bear to see him smiling. It was not marriage; it was not being one's husband to look strange like that, always to be starting, laughing, sitting hour after hour silent, or clutching her and telling her to write. The table drawer was full of those writings; about war; about Shakespeare; about great discoveries; how there is no death. Lately he had become excited suddenly for no reason (and both Dr. Holmes and Sir William Bradshaw said excitement was the worst thing for him), and waved his hands and cried out that he knew the truth! He knew everything! That man, his friend who was killed, Evans, had come, he said. He was singing behind the screen. She wrote it down just as he spoke it. Some things were very beautiful; others sheer nonsense. And he was always stopping in the middle, changing his mind; wanting to add something; hearing something new; listening with his hand up.

But she heard nothing.

And once they found the girl who did the room reading one of these papers in fits of laughter. It was a dreadful pity. For that made Septimus cry out about human cruelty-how they tear each other to pieces. The fallen, he said, they tear to pieces. "Holmes is on us," he would say, and he would invent stories about Holmes; Holmes eating porridge; Holmes reading Shakespeare-making himself roar with laughter or rage, for Dr. Holmes seemed to stand for something horrible to him. "Human nature," he called him. Then there were the visions. He was drowned, he used to say, and lying on a cliff with the gulls screaming over him. He would look over the edge of the sofa down into the sea. Or he was hearing music. Really it was only a barrel organ or some man crying in the street. But "Lovely!" he used to cry, and the tears would run down his cheeks, which was to her the most dreadful thing of all, to see a man like Septimus, who had fought, who was brave, crying. And he would lie listening until suddenly he would cry that he was falling down, down into the flames! Actually she would look for flames, it was so vivid. But there was nothing. They were alone in the room. It was a dream, she would tell him and so quiet him at last, but sometimes she was frightened too. She sighed as she sat sewing.

Her sigh was tender and enchanting, like the wind outside a wood in the evening. Now she put down her scissors; now she turned to take something from the table. A little stir, a little crinkling, a little tapping built up something on the table there, where she sat sewing. Through his eyelashes he could see her blurred outline; her little black body; her face and hands; her turning movements at the table, as she took up a reel, or looked (she was apt to lose things) for her silk. She was making a hat for Mrs. Filmer's married daughter, whose name was-he had forgotten her name.

"What is the name of Mrs. Filmer's married daughter?" he asked.

"Mrs. Peters," said Rezia. She was afraid it was too small, she said, holding it before her. Mrs. Peters was a big woman; but she did not like her. It was only because Mrs. Filmer had been so good to them. "She gave me grapes this morning," she said-that Rezia wanted to do something to show that they were grateful. She had come into the room the other evening and found Mrs. Peters, who thought they were out, playing the gramophone.

"Was it true?" he asked. She was playing the gramophone? Yes; she had told him about it at the time; she had found Mrs. Peters playing the gramophone.

He began, very cautiously, to open his eyes, to see whether a gramophone was really there. But real things-real things were too exciting. He must be cautious. He would not go mad. First he looked at the fashion papers on the lower shelf, then, gradually at the gramophone with the green trumpet. Nothing could be more exact. And so, gathering courage, he looked at the sideboard; the plate of bananas; the engraving of Queen Victoria and the Prince Consort; at the mantelpiece, with the jar of roses. None of these things moved. All were still; all were real.

"She is a woman with a spiteful tongue," said Rezia.

"What does Mr. Peters do?" Septimus asked.

"Ah," said Rezia, trying to remember. She thought Mrs. Filmer had said that he travelled for some company. "Just now he is in Hull," she said.

"Just now!" She said that with her Italian accent. She said that herself. He shaded his eyes so that he might see only a little of her face at a time, first the chin, then the nose, then the forehead, in case it were deformed, or had some terrible mark on it. But no, there she was, perfectly natural, sewing, with the pursed lips that women have, the set, the melancholy expression, when sewing. But there was nothing terrible about it, he assured himself, looking a second time, a third time at her face, her hands, for what was frightening or disgusting in her as she sat there in broad daylight, sewing? Mrs. Peters had a spiteful tongue. Mr. Peters was in Hull. Why then rage and prophesy? Why fly scourged and outcast? Why be made to tremble and sob by the clouds? Why seek truths and deliver messages when Rezia sat sticking pins into the front of her dress, and Mr. Peters was in Hull? Miracles, revelations, agonies, loneliness, falling through the sea, down, down into the flames, all were burnt out, for he had a sense, as he watched Rezia trimming the straw hat for Mrs. Peters, of a coverlet of flowers.

"It's too small for Mrs. Peters," said Septimus.

For the first time for days he was speaking as he used to do! Of course it was-absurdly small, she said. But Mrs. Peters had chosen it.

He took it out of her hands. He said it was an organ grinder's monkey's hat.

How it rejoiced her that! Not for weeks had they laughed like this together, poking fun privately like married people. What she meant was that if Mrs. Filmer had come in, or Mrs. Peters or anybody they would not have understood what she and Septimus were laughing at.

"There," she said, pinning a rose to one side of the hat. Never had she felt so happy! Never in her life!

But that was still more ridiculous, Septimus said. Now the poor woman looked like a pig at a fair. (Nobody ever made her laugh as Septimus did.)

What had she got in her work-box? She had ribbons and beads, tassels, artificial flowers. She tumbled them out on the table. He began putting odd colours together-for though he had no fingers, could not even do up a parcel, he had a wonderful eye, and often he was right, sometimes absurd, of course, but sometimes wonderfully right.

"She shall have a beautiful hat!" he murmured, taking up this and that, Rezia kneeling by his side, looking over his shoulder. Now it was finished-that is to say the design; she must stitch it together. But she must be very, very careful, he said, to keep it just as he had made it.

So she sewed. When she sewed, he thought, she made a sound like a kettle on the hob; bubbling, murmuring, always busy, her strong little pointed fingers pinching and poking; her needle flashing straight. The sun might go in and out, on the tassels, on the wallpaper, but he would wait, he thought, stretching out his feet, looking at his ringed sock at the end of the sofa; he would wait in this warm place, this pocket of still air, which one comes on at the edge of a wood sometimes in the evening, when, because of a fall in the ground, or some arrangement of the trees (one must be scientific above all, scientific), warmth lingers, and the air buffets the cheek like the wing of a bird.

"There it is," said Rezia, twirling Mrs. Peters' hat on the tips of her fingers. "That'll do for the moment. Later..." her sentence bubbled away drip, drip, drip, like a contented tap left running.

It was wonderful. Never had he done anything which made him feel so proud. It was so real, it was so substantial, Mrs. Peters' hat.

"Just look at it," he said.

Yes, it would always make her happy to see that hat. He had become himself then, he had laughed then. They had been alone together. Always she would like that hat.

He told her to try it on.

"But I must look so queer!" she cried, running over to the glass and looking first this side then that. Then she snatched it off again, for there was a tap at the door. Could it be Sir William Bradshaw? Had he sent already?

No! it was only the small girl with the evening paper.

What always happened, then happened—what happened every night of their lives. The small girl sucked her thumb at the door; Rezia went down on her knees; Rezia cooed and kissed; Rezia got a bag of sweets out of the table drawer. For so it always happened. First one thing, then another. So she built it up, first one thing and then another. Dancing, skipping, round and round the room they went. He took the paper. Surrey was all out, he read. There was a heat wave. Rezia repeated: Surrey was all out. There was a heat wave, making it part of the game she was playing with Mrs. Filmer's grandchild, both of them laughing, chattering at the same time, at their game. He was very tired. He was very happy. He would sleep. He shut his eyes. But directly he saw nothing the sounds of the game became fainter and stranger and sounded like the cries of people seeking and not finding, and passing further and further away. They had lost him!

He started up in terror. What did he see? The plate of bananas on the sideboard. Nobody was there (Rezia had taken the child to its mother. It was bedtime). That was it: to be alone forever. That was the doom pronounced in Milan when he came into the room and saw them cutting out buckram shapes with their scissors; to be alone forever.

He was alone with the sideboard and the bananas. He was alone, exposed on this bleak eminence, stretched out—but not on a hill-top; not on a crag; on Mrs. Filmer's sitting-room sofa. As for the visions, the faces, the voices of the dead, where were they? There was a screen in front of him, with black bulrushes and blue swallows. Where he had once seen mountains, where he had seen faces, where he had seen beauty, there was a screen.

"Evans!" he cried. There was no answer. A mouse had squeaked, or a curtain rustled. Those were the voices of the dead. The screen, the coalscuttle, the sideboard remained to him. Let him then face the screen, the coalscuttle and the sideboard... but Rezia burst into the room chattering.

Some letter had come. Everybody's plans were changed. Mrs. Filmer would not be able to go to Brighton after all. There was no time to let Mrs. Williams know, and really Rezia thought it very, very annoying, when she caught sight of the hat and thought... perhaps... she... might just make a little.... Her voice died out in contented melody.

"Ah, damn!" she cried (it was a joke of theirs, her swearing), the needle had broken. Hat, child, Brighton, needle. She built it up; first one thing, then another, she built it up, sewing.

She wanted him to say whether by moving the rose she had improved the hat. She sat on the end of the sofa.

They were perfectly happy now, she said, suddenly, putting the hat down. For she could say anything to him now. She could say whatever came into her head. That was almost the first thing she had felt about him, that night in the café when he had come in with his English friends. He had come in, rather shyly, looking round him, and his hat had fallen when he hung it up. That she could remember. She knew he was English, though not one of the large Englishmen her sister admired, for he was always thin; but he had a beautiful fresh colour; and with his big nose, his bright eyes, his way of sitting a little hunched made her think, she had often told him, of a young hawk, that first evening she saw him, when they were playing dominoes, and he had come in—of a young hawk; but with her he was always very gentle. She had never seen him wild or drunk, only suffering sometimes through this terrible war, but

443

even so, when she came in, he would put it all away. Anything, anything in the whole world, any little bother with her work, anything that struck her to say she would tell him, and he understood at once. Her own family even were not the same. Being older than she was and being so clever-how serious he was, wanting her to read Shakespeare before she could even read a child's story in English! —being so much more experienced, he could help her. And she too could help him.

But this hat now. And then (it was getting late) Sir William Bradshaw.

She held her hands to her head, waiting for him to say did he like the hat or not, and as she sat there, waiting, looking down, he could feel her mind, like a bird, falling from branch to branch, and always alighting, quite rightly; he could follow her mind, as she sat there in one of those loose lax poses that came to her naturally and, if he should say anything, at once she smiled, like a bird alighting with all its claws firm upon the bough.

But he remembered Bradshaw said, "The people we are most fond of are not good for us when we are ill." Bradshaw said, he must be taught to rest. Bradshaw said they must be separated.

"Must," "must," why "must"? What power had Bradshaw over him? "What right has Bradshaw to say 'must' to me?" he demanded.

"It is because you talked of killing yourself," said Rezia. (Mercifully, she could now say anything to Septimus.)

So he was in their power! Holmes and Bradshaw were on him! The brute with the red nostrils was snuffing into every secret place! "Must" it could say! Where were his papers? the things he had written?

She brought him his papers, the things he had written, things she had written for him. She tumbled them out on to the sofa. They looked at them together. Diagrams, designs, little men and women brandishing sticks for arms, with wings-were they? —on their backs; circles traced round shillings and sixpences-the suns and stars; zigzagging precipices with mountaineers ascending roped together, exactly like knives and forks; sea pieces with little faces laughing out of what might perhaps be waves: the map of the world. Burn them! he cried. Now for his writings; how the dead sing behind rhododendron bushes; odes to Time; conversations with Shakespeare; Evans, Evans, Evans-his messages from the dead; do not cut down trees; tell the Prime Minister. Universal love: the meaning of the world. Burn them! he cried.

But Rezia laid her hands on them. Some were very beautiful, she thought. She would tie them up (for she had no envelope) with a piece of silk.

Even if they took him, she said, she would go with him. They could not separate them against their wills, she said.

Shuffling the edges straight, she did up the papers, and tied the parcel almost without looking, sitting beside him, he thought, as if all her petals were about her. She was a flowering tree; and through her branches looked out the face of a lawgiver, who had reached a sanctuary where she feared no one; not Holmes; not Bradshaw; a miracle, a triumph, the last and greatest. Staggering he saw her mount the appalling staircase, laden with Holmes and Bradshaw, men who never weighed less than eleven stone six, who sent their wives to Court, men who made ten thousand a year and talked of proportion; who different in their verdicts (for Holmes said one thing, Bradshaw another), yet judges they were; who mixed the vision and the sideboard; saw nothing clear, yet ruled, yet inflicted. "Must" they said. Over them she triumphed.

"There!" she said. The papers were tied up. No one should get at them. She would put them away.

And, she said, nothing should separate them. She sat down beside him and called him by the name of that hawk or crow which being malicious and a great destroyer of crops was precisely like him. No one could separate them, she said.

Then she got up to go into the bedroom to pack their things, but hearing voices downstairs and thinking that Dr. Holmes had perhaps called, ran down to prevent him coming up.

Septimus could hear her talking to Holmes on the staircase.

"My dear lady, I have come as a friend," Holmes was saying.

"No. I will not allow you to see my husband," she said.

He could see her, like a little hen, with her wings spread barring his passage. But Holmes persevered.

"My dear lady, allow me..." Holmes said, putting her aside (Holmes was a powerfully built man).

Holmes was coming upstairs. Holmes would burst open the door. Holmes would say "In a funk, eh?" Holmes would get him. But no; not Holmes; not Bradshaw. Getting up rather unsteadily, hopping indeed from foot to foot, he considered Mrs. Filmer's nice clean bread knife with "Bread" carved on the handle. Ah, but one mustn't spoil that. The gas fire? But it was too late now. Holmes was coming. Razors he might have got, but Rezia, who always did that sort of thing, had packed them. There remained only the window, the large Bloomsbury-lodging house window, the tiresome, the troublesome, and rather melodramatic business of opening the window and throwing himself out. It was their idea of tragedy, not his or Rezia's (for she was with him). Holmes and Bradshaw like that sort of thing. (He sat on the sill.) But he would wait till the very last moment. He did not want to die. Life was good. The sun hot. Only human beings-what did *they* want? Coming down the staircase opposite an old man stopped and stared at him. Holmes was at the door. "I'll give it you!" he cried, and flung himself vigorously, violently down on to Mrs. Filmer's area railings.

"The coward!" cried Dr. Holmes, bursting the door open. Rezia ran to the window, she saw; she understood. Dr. Holmes and Mrs. Filmer collided with each other. Mrs. Filmer flapped her apron and made her hide her eyes in the bedroom. There was a great deal of running up and down stairs. Dr. Holmes came in-white as a sheet, shaking all over, with a glass in his hand. She must be brave and drink something, he said (What was it? Something sweet), for her husband was horribly mangled, would not recover consciousness, she must not see him, must be spared as much as possible, would have the inquest to go through, poor young woman. Who could have foretold it? A sudden impulse, no one was in the least to blame (he told Mrs. Filmer). And why the devil he did it, Dr. Holmes could not conceive.

It seemed to her as she drank the sweet stuff that she was opening long windows, stepping out into some garden. But where? The clock was striking-one, two, three: how sensible the sound was; compared with all this thumping and whispering; like Septimus himself. She was falling asleep. But the clock went on striking, four, five, six and Mrs. Filmer waving her apron (they wouldn't bring the body in here, would they?) seemed part of that garden; or a flag. She had once seen a flag slowly rippling out from a mast when she stayed with her aunt at Venice. Men killed in battle were thus saluted, and Septimus had been through the War. Of her memories, most were happy.

She put on her hat, and ran through cornfields-where could it have been? —on to some hill, somewhere near the sea, for there were ships, gulls, butterflies; they sat on a cliff. In London too, there they sat, and, half dreaming, came to her through the bedroom door, rain falling, whisperings, stirrings among dry corn, the caress of the sea, as it seemed to her, hollowing them in its arched shell and murmuring to her laid on shore, strewn she felt, like flying flowers over some tomb.

"He is dead," she said, smiling at the poor old woman who guarded her with her honest light-blue eyes fixed on the door. (They wouldn't bring him in here, would they?) But Mrs. Filmer pooh-poohed. Oh no, oh no! They were carrying him away now. Ought she not to be told? Married people ought to be together, Mrs. Filmer thought. But they must do as the doctor said.

"Let her sleep," said Dr. Holmes, feeling her pulse. She saw the large outline of his body standing dark against the window. So that was Dr. Holmes.

One of the triumphs of civilisation, Peter Walsh thought. It is one of the triumphs of civilisation, as the light high bell of the ambulance sounded. Swiftly, cleanly the ambulance sped to the hospital, having picked up instantly, humanely, some poor devil; some one hit on the head, struck down by disease, knocked over perhaps a minute or so ago at one of these crossings, as might happen to oneself. That was civilisation. It struck him coming back from the East-the efficiency, the organisation, the communal spirit of London. Every cart or carriage of its own accord drew aside to let the ambulance pass. Perhaps it was morbid; or was it not touching rather, the respect which they showed this ambulance with its victim inside-busy men hurrying home yet instantly bethinking them as it passed of some wife; or presumably how easily it might have been them there, stretched on a shelf with a doctor and a nurse.... Ah, but thinking became morbid, sentimental, directly one began conjuring up doctors, dead bodies; a little glow of pleasure, a sort of lust too over the visual impression warned one not to go on with that sort of thing any more-fatal to art, fatal to friendship. True. And yet, thought Peter Walsh, as the ambulance turned the corner though the light high bell could be heard down the next street and still farther as it crossed the Tottenham Court Road, chiming constantly, it is the privilege of loneliness; in privacy one may do as one chooses. One might weep if no one saw. It had been his undoing-this susceptibility-in Anglo-Indian society; not weeping at the right time, or laughing either. I have that in me, he thought standing by the pillar-box, which could now dissolve in tears. Why, Heaven knows. Beauty of some sort probably, and the weight of the day, which beginning with that visit to Clarissa had exhausted him with its heat, its intensity, and the drip, drip, of one impression after another down into that cellar where they stood, deep, dark, and no one would ever know. Partly for that reason, its secrecy, complete and inviolable, he had found life like an unknown garden, full of turns and corners, surprising, yes; really it took one's breath away, these moments; there coming to him by the pillar-box opposite the British Museum one of them, a moment, in which things came together; this ambulance; and life and death. It was as if he were sucked up to some very high roof by that rush of emotion and the rest of him, like a white shell-sprinkled beach, left bare. It had been his undoing in Anglo-Indian society-this susceptibility.

Clarissa once, going on top of an omnibus with him somewhere, Clarissa superficially at least, so easily moved, now in despair, now in the best of spirits, all aquiver in those days and such good company, spotting queer little scenes, names, people from the top of a bus, for they used to explore London and bring back bags full of treasures from the Caledonian market-Clarissa had a theory in those days-they had heaps of theories, always theories, as young people have. It was to explain the feeling they had of dissatisfaction; not knowing people; not being known. For how could they know each other? You met every day; then not for six months, or years. It was unsatisfactory, they agreed, how little one knew people. But she said, sitting on the bus going up Shaftesbury Avenue, she felt herself everywhere; not "here, here, here"; and she tapped the back of the seat; but everywhere. She waved her hand, going up Shaftesbury Avenue. She was all that. So that to know her, or any one, one must seek out the people who completed them; even the places. Odd affinities she had with people she had never spoken to, some woman in the street, some man behind a counter-even trees, or barns. It ended in a transcendental theory which, with her horror of death, allowed her to believe, or say that she believed (for all her scepticism), that since our apparitions, the part of us which appears, are so momentary compared with the other, the unseen part of us, which spreads wide, the unseen might survive, be recovered somehow attached to this person or that, or even haunting certain places after death... perhaps-perhaps.

Looking back over that long friendship of almost thirty years her theory worked to this extent. Brief, broken, often painful as their actual meetings had been what with his absences and interruptions (this morning, for instance, in came Elizabeth, like a long-legged colt, handsome, dumb, just as he was beginning to talk to Clarissa) the effect of them on his life was immeasurable. There was a mystery about it. You were given a sharp, acute, uncomfortable grain-the actual meeting; horribly painful as often as not; yet in absence, in the most unlikely places, it would flower out, open, shed its scent, let you touch, taste, look about you, get the whole feel of it and understanding, after years of lying lost. Thus she had come to him; on board ship; in the Himalayas; suggested by the oddest things (so Sally Seton, generous, enthusiastic goose! thought of *him* when she saw blue hydrangeas). She had influenced him more than any person he had ever known. And always in this way coming before him without his wishing it, cool, lady-like, critical; or ravishing, romantic, recalling some field or English harvest. He saw her most often in the country, not in London. One scene after another at Bourton....

He had reached his hotel. He crossed the hall, with its mounds of reddish chairs and sofas, its spike-leaved, withered-looking plants. He got his key off the hook. The young lady handed him some letters. He went upstairs-he saw her most often at Bourton, in the late summer, when he stayed there for a week, or fortnight even, as people did in those days. First on top of some hill there she would stand, hands clapped to her hair, her cloak blowing out, pointing, crying to them-she saw the Severn beneath. Or in a wood, making the kettle boil-very ineffective with her fingers; the smoke curtseying, blowing in their faces; her little pink face showing through; begging water from an old woman in a cottage, who came to the door to watch them go. They walked always; the others drove. She was bored driving, disliked all animals, except that dog. They tramped miles along roads. She would break off to get her bearings, pilot him back across country; and all the time they argued, discussed poetry, discussed people, discussed politics (she was a Radical then); never noticing a thing except when she stopped, cried out at a view or a tree, and made him look with her; and so on again, through stubble fields, she walking ahead, with a flower for her aunt, never tired of walking for all her delicacy; to drop down on Bourton in the dusk. Then, after dinner, old Breitkopf would open the piano and sing without any voice, and they would lie sunk in armchairs, trying not to laugh, but always breaking down and laughing, laughing-laughing at nothing. Breitkopf was supposed not to see. And then in the morning, flirting up and down like a wagtail in front of the house....

Oh it was a letter from her! This blue envelope; that was her hand. And he would have to read it. Here was another of those meetings, bound to be painful! To read her letter needed the devil of an effort. "How heavenly it was to see him. She must tell him that." That was all.

But it upset him. It annoyed him. He wished she hadn't written it. Coming on top of his thoughts, it was like a nudge in the ribs. Why couldn't she let him be? After all, she had married Dalloway, and lived with him in perfect happiness all these years.

These hotels are not consoling places. Far from it. Any number of people had hung up their hats on those pegs. Even the flies, if you thought of it, had settled on other people's noses. As for the cleanliness which hit him in the face, it wasn't cleanliness, so much as bareness, frigidity; a thing that had to be. Some arid matron made her rounds at dawn sniffing, peering, causing blue-nosed maids to scour, for all the world as if the next visitor were a joint of meat to be served on a perfectly clean platter. For sleep, one bed; for sitting in, one armchair; for cleaning one's teeth and shaving one's chin, one tumbler, one looking-glass. Books, letters, dressing-gown, slipped about on the impersonality of the horsehair like incongruous impertinences. And it was Clarissa's letter that made him see all this. "Heavenly to see you. She must say so!" He folded the paper; pushed it away; nothing would induce him to read it again!

To get that letter to him by six o'clock she must have sat down and written it directly he left her; stamped it; sent somebody to the post. It was, as people say, very like her. She was upset by his visit. She had felt a great deal; had for a moment, when she kissed his hand, regretted, envied him even, remembered possibly (for he saw her look it) something he had said-how they would change the world if she married him perhaps; whereas, it was this; it was middle age; it was mediocrity; then forced herself with her indomitable vitality to put all that aside, there being in her a thread of life which for toughness, endurance, power to overcome obstacles, and carry her triumphantly through he had never known the like of. Yes; but there would come a reaction directly he left the room. She would be frightfully sorry for him; she would think what in the world she could do to give him pleasure (short always of the one thing) and he could see her with the tears running down her cheeks going to her writing-table and dashing off that one line which he was to find greeting him.... "Heavenly to see you!" And she meant it.

Peter Walsh had now unlaced his boots.

But it would not have been a success, their marriage. The other thing, after all, came so much more naturally.

It was odd; it was true; lots of people felt it. Peter Walsh, who had done just respectably, filled the usual posts adequately, was liked, but thought a little cranky, gave himself airs-it was odd that *he* should have had, especially now that his hair was grey, a contented look; a look of having reserves. It was this that made him attractive to women who liked the sense that he was not altogether manly. There was something unusual about him, or something behind him. It might be that he was bookish-never came to see you without taking up the book on the table (he was now reading, with his bootlaces trailing on the floor); or that he was a gentleman, which showed itself in the way he knocked the ashes out of his pipe, and in his manners of course to women. For it was very charming and quite ridiculous how easily some girl without a grain of sense could twist him round her finger. But at her own risk. That is to say, though he might be ever so easy, and indeed with his gaiety and good-breeding fascinating to be with, it was only up to a point. She said something-no, no; he saw through that. He wouldn't stand that-no, no. Then he could shout and rock and hold his sides together over some joke with men. He was the best judge of cooking in India. He was a man. But not the sort of man one had to respect-which was a mercy; not like Major Simmons, for instance; not in the least like that, Daisy thought, when, in spite of her two small children, she used to compare them.

He pulled off his boots. He emptied his pockets. Out came with his pocket-knife a snapshot of Daisy on the verandah; Daisy all in white, with a fox-terrier on her knee; very charming, very dark; the best he had ever seen of her. It did come, after all so naturally; so much more naturally than Clarissa. No fuss. No bother. No finicking and fidgeting. All plain sailing. And the dark, adorably pretty girl on the verandah exclaimed (he could hear her). Of course, of course she would give him everything! she cried (she had no sense of discretion) everything he wanted! she cried, running to meet him, whoever might be looking. And she was only twenty-four. And she had two children. Well, well!

Well indeed he had got himself into a mess at his age. And it came over him when he woke in the night pretty forcibly. Suppose they did marry? For him it would be all very well, but what about her? Mrs. Burgess, a good sort and no chatterbox, in whom he had confided, thought this absence of his in England, ostensibly to see lawyers might serve to make Daisy reconsider, think what it meant. It was a question of her position, Mrs. Burgess said; the social barrier; giving up her children. She'd be a widow with a past one of these days, draggling about in the suburbs, or more likely, indiscriminate (you know, she said, what such women get like, with too much paint). But Peter Walsh pooh-poohed all that. He didn't mean to die yet. Anyhow she must settle for herself; judge for herself, he thought, padding about the room in his socks, smoothing out his dress-shirt, for he might go to Clarissa's party, or he might go to one of the Halls, or he might settle in and read an absorbing book written by a man he used to know at Oxford. And if he did retire, that's what he'd do-write books. He would go to Oxford and poke about in the Bodleian. Vainly the dark, adorably pretty girl ran to the end of the terrace; vainly waved her hand; vainly cried she didn't care a straw what people said. There he was, the man she thought the world of, the perfect gentleman, the fascinating, the distinguished (and his age made not the least difference to her), padding about a room in an hotel in Bloomsbury, shaving, washing, continuing, as he took up cans, put down razors, to poke about in the Bodleian, and get at the truth about one or two little matters that interested him. And he would have a chat with whoever it might be, and so come to disregard more and more precise hours for lunch, and miss engagements, and when Daisy asked him, as she would, for a kiss, a scene, fail to come up to the scratch (though he was genuinely devoted to her) —in short it might be happier, as Mrs. Burgess said, that she should forget him, or merely remember him as he was in August 1922, like a figure standing at the cross roads at dusk, which grows more and more remote as the dog-cart spins away, carrying her securely fastened to the back seat, though her arms are outstretched, and as she sees the figure dwindle and disappear still she cries out how she would do anything in the world, anything, anything, anything....

He never knew what people thought. It became more and more difficult for him to concentrate. He became absorbed; he became busied with his own concerns; now surly, now gay;

dependent on women, absent-minded, moody, less and less able (so he thought as he shaved) to understand why Clarissa couldn't simply find them a lodging and be nice to Daisy; introduce her. And then he could just-just do what? just haunt and hover (he was at the moment actually engaged in sorting out various keys, papers), swoop and taste, be alone, in short, sufficient to himself; and yet nobody of course was more dependent upon others (he buttoned his waistcoat); it had been his undoing. He could not keep out of smoking-rooms, liked colonels, liked golf, liked bridge, and above all women's society, and the fineness of their companionship, and their faithfulness and audacity and greatness in loving which though it had its drawbacks seemed to him (and the dark, adorably pretty face was on top of the envelopes) so wholly admirable, so splendid a flower to grow on the crest of human life, and yet he could not come up to the scratch, being always apt to see round things (Clarissa had sapped something in him permanently), and to tire very easily of mute devotion and to want variety in love, though it would make him furious if Daisy loved anybody else, furious! for he was jealous, uncontrollably jealous by temperament. He suffered tortures! But where was his knife; his watch; his seals, his note-case, and Clarissa's letter which he would not read again but liked to think of, and Daisy's photograph? And now for dinner.

They were eating.

Sitting at little tables round vases, dressed or not dressed, with their shawls and bags laid beside them, with their air of false composure, for they were not used to so many courses at dinner, and confidence, for they were able to pay for it, and strain, for they had been running about London all day shopping, sightseeing; and their natural curiosity, for they looked round and up as the nice-looking gentleman in horn-rimmed spectacles came in, and their good nature, for they would have been glad to do any little service, such as lend a time-table or impart useful information, and their desire, pulsing in them, tugging at them subterraneously, somehow to establish connections if it were only a birthplace (Liverpool, for example) in common or friends of the same name; with their furtive glances, odd silences, and sudden withdrawals into family jocularity and isolation; there they sat eating dinner when Mr. Walsh came in and took his seat at a little table by the curtain.

It was not that he said anything, for being solitary he could only address himself to the waiter; it was his way of looking at the menu, of pointing his forefinger to a particular wine, of hitching himself up to the table, of addressing himself seriously, not gluttonously to dinner, that won him their respect; which, having to remain unexpressed for the greater part of the meal, flared up at the table where the Morrises sat when Mr. Walsh was heard to say at the end of the meal, "Bartlett pears." Why he should have spoken so moderately yet firmly, with the air of a disciplinarian well within his rights which are founded upon justice, neither young Charles Morris, nor old Charles, neither Miss Elaine nor Mrs. Morris knew. But when he said, "Bartlett pears," sitting alone at his table, they felt that he counted on their support in some lawful demand; was champion of a cause which immediately became their own, so that their eyes met his eyes sympathetically, and when they all reached the smoking-room simultaneously, a little talk between them became inevitable.

It was not very profound-only to the effect that London was crowded; had changed in thirty years; that Mr. Morris preferred Liverpool; that Mrs. Morris had been to the Westminster flower-show, and that they had all seen the Prince of Wales. Yet, thought Peter Walsh, no family in the world can compare with the Morrises; none whatever; and their relations to each other are perfect, and they don't care a hang for the upper classes, and they like what they like, and Elaine is training for the family business, and the boy has won a scholarship at Leeds, and the old lady (who is about his own age) has three more children at home; and they have two motor cars, but Mr. Morris still mends the boots on Sunday: it is superb, it is absolutely superb, thought Peter Walsh, swaying a little backwards and forwards with his liqueur glass in his hand among the hairy red chairs and ash-trays, feeling very well pleased with himself, for the Morrises liked him. Yes, they liked a man who said, "Bartlett pears." They liked him, he felt.

He would go to Clarissa's party. (The Morrises moved off; but they would meet again.) He would go to Clarissa's party, because he wanted to ask Richard what they were doing in India-the conservative duffers. And what's being acted? And music.... Oh yes, and mere gossip.

For this is the truth about our soul, he thought, our self, who fish-like inhabits deep seas and plies among obscurities threading her way between the boles of giant weeds, over sun-flickered spaces and on and on into gloom, cold, deep, inscrutable; suddenly she shoots to the surface and sports on the wind-wrinkled waves; that is, has a positive need to brush, scrape, kindle herself, gossiping. What did the Government mean-Richard Dalloway would know-to do about India?

Since it was a very hot night and the paper boys went by with placards proclaiming in huge red letters that there was a heat-wave, wicker chairs were placed on the hotel steps and there, sipping, smoking, detached gentlemen sat. Peter Walsh sat there. One might fancy that day, the London day, was just beginning. Like a woman who had slipped off her print dress and white apron to array herself in blue and pearls, the day changed, put off stuff, took gauze, changed to evening, and with the same sigh of exhilaration that a woman breathes, tumbling petticoats on the floor, it too shed dust, heat, colour; the traffic thinned; motor cars, tinkling, darting, succeeded the lumber of vans; and here and there among the thick foliage of the squares an intense light hung. I resign, the evening seemed to say, as it paled and faded above the battlements and prominences, moulded, pointed, of hotel, flat, and block of shops, I fade, she was beginning, I disappear, but London would have none of it, and rushed her bayonets into the sky, pinioned her, constrained her to partnership in her revelry.

For the great revolution of Mr. Willett's summer time had taken place since Peter Walsh's last visit to England. The prolonged evening was new to him. It was inspiriting, rather. For as the young people went by with their despatch-boxes, awfully glad to be free, proud too, dumbly, of stepping this famous pavement, joy of a kind, cheap, tinselly, if you like, but all the same rapture, flushed their faces. They dressed well too; pink stockings; pretty shoes. They would now have two hours at the pictures. It sharpened, it refined them, the yellow-blue evening light; and on the leaves in the square shone lurid, livid-they looked as if dipped in sea water-the foliage of a submerged city. He was astonished by the beauty; it was encouraging too, for where the returned Anglo-Indian sat by rights (he knew crowds of them) in the Oriental Club biliously summing up the ruin of the world, here was he, as young as ever; envying young people their summer time and the rest of it, and more than suspecting from the words of a girl, from a housemaid's laughter-intangible things you couldn't lay your hands on-that shift in the whole pyramidal accumulation which in his youth had seemed immovable. On top of them it had pressed; weighed them down, the women especially, like those flowers Clarissa's Aunt Helena used to press between sheets of grey blotting-paper with Littré's dictionary on top, sitting under the lamp after dinner. She was dead now. He had heard of her, from Clarissa, losing the sight of one eye. It seemed so fitting-one of nature's masterpieces-that old Miss Parry should turn to glass. She would die like some bird in a frost gripping her perch. She belonged to a different age, but being so entire, so complete, would always stand up on the horizon, stone-white, eminent, like a lighthouse marking some past stage on this adventurous, long, long voyage, this interminable (he felt for a copper to buy a paper and read about Surrey and Yorkshire-he had held out that copper millions of times. Surrey was all out once more) —this interminable life. But cricket was no mere game. Cricket was important. He could never help reading about cricket. He read the scores in the stop press first, then how it was a hot day; then about a murder case. Having done things millions of times enriched them, though it might be said to take the surface off. The past enriched, and experience, and having cared for one or two people, and so having acquired the power which the young lack, of cutting short, doing what one likes, not caring a rap what people say and coming and going without any very great expectations (he left his paper on the table and moved off), which however (and he looked for his hat and coat) was not altogether true of him, not tonight, for here he was starting to go to a party, at his age, with the belief upon him that he was about to have an experience. But what?

450

Beauty anyhow. Not the crude beauty of the eye. It was not beauty pure and simple–Bedford Place leading into Russell Square. It was straightness and emptiness of course; the symmetry of a corridor; but it was also windows lit up, a piano, a gramophone sounding; a sense of pleasure-making hidden, but now and again emerging when, through the uncurtained window, the window left open, one saw parties sitting over tables, young people slowly circling, conversations between men and women, maids idly looking out (a strange comment theirs, when work was done), stockings drying on top ledges, a parrot, a few plants. Absorbing, mysterious, of infinite richness, this life. And in the large square where the cabs shot and swerved so quick, there were loitering couples, dallying, embracing, shrunk up under the shower of a tree; that was moving; so silent, so absorbed, that one passed, discreetly, timidly, as if in the presence of some sacred ceremony to interrupt which would have been impious. That was interesting. And so on into the flare and glare.

His light overcoat blew open, he stepped with indescribable idiosyncrasy, lent a little forward, tripped, with his hands behind his back and his eyes still a little hawklike; he tripped through London, towards Westminster, observing.

Was everybody dining out, then? Doors were being opened here by a footman to let issue a high-stepping old dame, in buckled shoes, with three purple ostrich feathers in her hair. Doors were being opened for ladies wrapped like mummies in shawls with bright flowers on them, ladies with bare heads. And in respectable quarters with stucco pillars through small front gardens lightly swathed with combs in their hair (having run up to see the children), women came; men waited for them, with their coats blowing open, and the motor started. Everybody was going out. What with these doors being opened, and the descent and the start, it seemed as if the whole of London were embarking in little boats moored to the bank, tossing on the waters, as if the whole place were floating off in carnival. And Whitehall was skated over, silver beaten as it was, skated over by spiders, and there was a sense of midges round the arc lamps; it was so hot that people stood about talking. And here in Westminster was a retired Judge, presumably, sitting four square at his house door dressed all in white. An Anglo-Indian presumably.

And here a shindy of brawling women, drunken women; here only a policeman and looming houses, high houses, domed houses, churches, parliaments, and the hoot of a steamer on the river, a hollow misty cry. But it was her street, this, Clarissa's; cabs were rushing round the corner, like water round the piers of a bridge, drawn together, it seemed to him because they bore people going to her party, Clarissa's party.

The cold stream of visual impressions failed him now as if the eye were a cup that overflowed and let the rest run down its china walls unrecorded. The brain must wake now. The body must contract now, entering the house, the lighted house, where the door stood open, where the motor cars were standing, and bright women descending: the soul must brave itself to endure. He opened the big blade of his pocket-knife.

Lucy came running full tilt downstairs, having just nipped in to the drawing-room to smooth a cover, to straighten a chair, to pause a moment and feel whoever came in must think how clean, how bright, how beautifully cared for, when they saw the beautiful silver, the brass fire-irons, the new chair-covers, and the curtains of yellow chintz: she appraised each; heard a roar of voices; people already coming up from dinner; she must fly!

The Prime Minister was coming, Agnes said: so she had heard them say in the dining-room, she said, coming in with a tray of glasses. Did it matter, did it matter in the least, one Prime Minister more or less? It made no difference at this hour of the night to Mrs. Walker among the plates, saucepans, cullenders, frying-pans, chicken in aspic, ice-cream freezers, pared crusts of bread, lemons, soup tureens, and pudding basins which, however hard they washed up in the scullery seemed to be all on top of her, on the kitchen table, on chairs, while the fire blared and roared, the electric lights glared, and still supper had to be laid. All she felt was, one Prime Minister more or less made not a scrap of difference to Mrs. Walker.

The ladies were going upstairs already, said Lucy; the ladies were going up, one by one, Mrs. Dalloway walking last and almost always sending back some message to the kitchen, "My love to Mrs. Walker," that was it one night. Next morning they would go over the dishes-the soup, the salmon; the salmon, Mrs. Walker knew, as usual underdone, for she always got nervous about the pudding and left it to Jenny; so it happened, the salmon was always underdone. But some lady with fair hair and silver ornaments had said, Lucy said, about the entrée, was it really made at home? But it was the salmon that bothered Mrs. Walker, as she spun the plates round and round, and pulled in dampers and pulled out dampers; and there came a burst of laughter from the dining-room; a voice speaking; then another burst of laughter-the gentlemen enjoying themselves when the ladies had gone. The tokay, said Lucy running in. Mr. Dalloway had sent for the tokay, from the Emperor's cellars, the Imperial Tokay.

It was borne through the kitchen. Over her shoulder Lucy reported how Miss Elizabeth looked quite lovely; she couldn't take her eyes off her; in her pink dress, wearing the necklace Mr. Dalloway had given her. Jenny must remember the dog, Miss Elizabeth's fox-terrier, which, since it bit, had to be shut up and might, Elizabeth thought, want something. Jenny must remember the dog. But Jenny was not going upstairs with all those people about. There was a motor at the door already! There was a ring at the bell-and the gentlemen still in the dining-room, drinking tokay!

There, they were going upstairs; that was the first to come, and now they would come faster and faster, so that Mrs. Parkinson (hired for parties) would leave the hall door ajar, and the hall would be full of gentlemen waiting (they stood waiting, sleeking down their hair) while the ladies took their cloaks off in the room along the passage; where Mrs. Barnet helped them, old Ellen Barnet, who had been with the family for forty years, and came every summer to help the ladies, and remembered mothers when they were girls, and though very unassuming did shake hands; said "milady" very respectfully, yet had a humorous way with her, looking at the young ladies, and ever so tactfully helping Lady Lovejoy, who had some trouble with her underbodice. And they could not help feeling, Lady Lovejoy and Miss Alice, that some little privilege in the matter of brush and comb, was awarded them having known Mrs. Barnet —"thirty years, milady," Mrs. Barnet supplied her. Young ladies did not use to rouge, said Lady Lovejoy, when they stayed at Bourton in the old days. And Miss Alice didn't need rouge, said Mrs. Barnet, looking at her fondly. There Mrs. Barnet would sit, in the cloakroom, patting down the furs, smoothing out the Spanish shawls, tidying the dressing-table, and knowing perfectly well, in spite of the furs and the embroideries, which were nice ladies, which were not. The dear old body, said Lady Lovejoy, mounting the stairs, Clarissa's old nurse.

And then Lady Lovejoy stiffened. "Lady and Miss Lovejoy," she said to Mr. Wilkins (hired for parties). He had an admirable manner, as he bent and straightened himself, bent and straightened himself and announced with perfect impartiality "Lady and Miss Lovejoy... Sir John and Lady Needham... Miss Weld... Mr. Walsh." His manner was admirable; his family life must be irreproachable, except that it seemed impossible that a being with greenish lips and shaven cheeks could ever have blundered into the nuisance of children.

"How delightful to see you!" said Clarissa. She said it to every one. How delightful to see you! She was at her worst-effusive, insincere. It was a great mistake to have come. He should have stayed at home and read his book, thought Peter Walsh; should have gone to a music hall; he should have stayed at home, for he knew no one.

Oh dear, it was going to be a failure; a complete failure, Clarissa felt it in her bones as dear old Lord Lexham stood there apologising for his wife who had caught cold at the Buckingham Palace garden party. She could see Peter out of the tail of her eye, criticising her, there, in that corner. Why, after all, did she do these things? Why seek pinnacles and stand drenched in fire? Might it consume her anyhow! Burn her to cinders! Better anything, better brandish one's torch and hurl it to earth than taper and dwindle away like some Ellie Henderson! It was extraordinary how Peter put her into these states just by coming and standing in a corner. He made her see herself; exaggerate. It was idiotic. But why did he come, then, merely to criticise? Why always take, never give? Why not risk one's one little point of view? There he was wandering off, and she must speak to him. But she would not get the chance. Life was that-humiliation, renunciation. What Lord Lexham was saying was that his wife would not wear her furs at the garden party because "my dear, you ladies are all alike" —Lady Lexham being seventy-five at least! It was delicious, how they petted each other, that old couple. She did like old Lord Lexham. She did think it mattered, her party, and it made her feel quite sick to know that it was all going wrong, all falling flat. Anything, any explosion, any horror was better than people wandering aimlessly, standing in a bunch at a corner like Ellie Henderson, not even caring to hold themselves upright.

Gently the yellow curtain with all the birds of Paradise blew out and it seemed as if there were a flight of wings into the room, right out, then sucked back. (For the windows were open.) Was it draughty, Ellie Henderson wondered? She was subject to chills. But it did not matter that she should come down sneezing tomorrow; it was the girls with their naked shoulders she thought of, being trained to think of others by an old father, an invalid, late vicar of Bourton, but he was dead now; and her chills never went to her chest, never. It was the girls she thought of, the young girls with their bare shoulders, she herself having always been a wisp of a creature, with her thin hair and meagre profile; though now, past fifty, there was beginning to shine through some mild beam, something purified into distinction by years of self-abnegation but obscured again, perpetually, by her distressing gentility, her panic fear, which arose from three hundred pounds' income, and her weaponless state (she could not earn a penny) and it made her timid, and more and more disqualified year by year to meet well-dressed people who did this sort of thing every night of the season, merely telling their maids "I'll wear so and so," whereas Ellie Henderson ran out nervously and bought cheap pink flowers, half a dozen, and then threw a shawl over her old black dress. For her invitation to Clarissa's party had come at the last moment. She was not quite happy about it. She had a sort of feeling that Clarissa had not meant to ask her this year.

Why should she? There was no reason really, except that they had always known each other. Indeed, they were cousins. But naturally they had rather drifted apart, Clarissa being so sought after. It was an event to her, going to a party. It was quite a treat just to see the lovely clothes. Wasn't that Elizabeth, grown up, with her hair done in the fashionable way, in the pink dress? Yet she could not be more than seventeen. She was very, very handsome. But girls when they first came out didn't seem to wear white as they used. (She must remember everything to tell Edith.) Girls wore straight frocks, perfectly tight, with skirts well above the ankles. It was not becoming, she thought.

So, with her weak eyesight, Ellie Henderson craned rather forward, and it wasn't so much she who minded not having any one to talk to (she hardly knew anybody there), for she felt that they were all such interesting people to watch; politicians presumably; Richard Dalloway's friends; but it was Richard himself who felt that he could not let the poor creature go on standing there all the evening by herself.

"Well, Ellie, and how's the world treating *you*?" he said in his genial way, and Ellie Henderson, getting nervous and flushing and feeling that it was extraordinarily nice of him to come and talk to her, said that many people really felt the heat more than the cold.

"Yes, they do," said Richard Dalloway. "Yes."

But what more did one say?

"Hullo, Richard," said somebody, taking him by the elbow, and, good Lord, there was old Peter, old Peter Walsh. He was delighted to see him-ever so pleased to see him! He hadn't changed a bit. And off they went together walking right across the room, giving each other little pats, as if they hadn't met for a long time, Ellie Henderson thought, watching them go, certain she knew that man's face. A tall man, middle aged, rather fine eyes, dark, wearing spectacles, with a look of John Burrows. Edith would be sure to know.

The curtain with its flight of birds of Paradise blew out again. And Clarissa saw-she saw Ralph Lyon beat it back, and go on talking. So it wasn't a failure after all! it was going to be all right now-her party. It had begun. It had started. But it was still touch and go. She must stand there for the present. People seemed to come in a rush.

453

Colonel and Mrs. Garrod...Mr. Hugh Whitbread...Mr. Bowley...Mrs. Hilbery...Lady Mary Maddox...Mr. Quin...intoned Wilkin. She had six or seven words with each, and they went on, they went into the rooms; into something now, not nothing, since Ralph Lyon had beat back the curtain.

And yet for her own part, it was too much of an effort. She was not enjoying it. It was too much like being-just anybody, standing there; anybody could do it; yet this anybody she did a little admire, couldn't help feeling that she had, anyhow, made this happen, that it marked a stage, this post that she felt herself to have become, for oddly enough she had quite forgotten what she looked like, but felt herself a stake driven in at the top of her stairs. Every time she gave a party she had this feeling of being something not herself, and that every one was unreal in one way; much more real in another. It was, she thought, partly their clothes, partly being taken out of their ordinary ways, partly the background, it was possible to say things you couldn't say anyhow else, things that needed an effort; possible to go much deeper. But not for her; not yet anyhow.

"How delightful to see you!" she said. Dear old Sir Harry! He would know every one.

And what was so odd about it was the sense one had as they came up the stairs one after another, Mrs. Mount and Celia, Herbert Ainsty, Mrs. Dakers-oh and Lady Bruton!

"How awfully good of you to come!" she said, and she meant it-it was odd how standing there one felt them going on, going on, some quite old, some...

What name? Lady Rosseter? But who on earth was Lady Rosseter?

"Clarissa!" That voice! It was Sally Seton! Sally Seton! after all these years! She loomed through a mist. For she hadn't looked like *that,* Sally Seton, when Clarissa grasped the hot water can, to think of her under this roof, under this roof! Not like that!

All on top of each other, embarrassed, laughing, words tumbled out-passing through London; heard from Clara Haydon; what a chance of seeing you! So I thrust myself in-without an invitation....

One might put down the hot water can quite composedly. The lustre had gone out of her. Yet it was extraordinary to see her again, older, happier, less lovely. They kissed each other, first this cheek then that, by the drawing-room door, and Clarissa turned, with Sally's hand in hers, and saw her rooms full, heard the roar of voices, saw the candlesticks, the blowing curtains, and the roses which Richard had given her.

"I have five enormous boys," said Sally.

She had the simplest egotism, the most open desire to be thought first always, and Clarissa loved her for being still like that. "I can't believe it!" she cried, kindling all over with pleasure at the thought of the past.

But alas, Wilkins; Wilkins wanted her; Wilkins was emitting in a voice of commanding authority as if the whole company must be admonished and the hostess reclaimed from frivolity, one name:

"The Prime Minister," said Peter Walsh.

The Prime Minister? Was it really? Ellie Henderson marvelled. What a thing to tell Edith!

One couldn't laugh at him. He looked so ordinary. You might have stood him behind a counter and bought biscuits-poor chap, all rigged up in gold lace. And to be fair, as he went his rounds, first with Clarissa then with Richard escorting him, he did it very well. He tried to look somebody. It was amusing to watch. Nobody looked at him. They just went on talking, yet it was perfectly plain that they all knew, felt to the marrow of their bones, this majesty passing; this symbol of what they all stood for, English society. Old Lady Bruton, and she looked very fine too, very stalwart in her lace, swam up, and they withdrew into a little room which at once became spied upon, guarded, and a sort of stir and rustle rippled through every one, openly: the Prime Minister!

Lord, lord, the snobbery of the English! thought Peter Walsh, standing in the corner. How they loved dressing up in gold lace and doing homage! There! That must be, by Jove it was,

Hugh Whitbread, snuffing round the precincts of the great, grown rather fatter, rather whiter, the admirable Hugh!

He looked always as if he were on duty, thought Peter, a privileged, but secretive being, hoarding secrets which he would die to defend, though it was only some little piece of tittle-tattle dropped by a court footman, which would be in all the papers tomorrow. Such were his rattles, his baubles, in playing with which he had grown white, come to the verge of old age, enjoying the respect and affection of all who had the privilege of knowing this type of the English public school man. Inevitably one made up things like that about Hugh; that was his style; the style of those admirable letters which Peter had read thousands of miles across the sea in the *Times,* and had thanked God he was out of that pernicious hubble-bubble if it were only to hear baboons chatter and coolies beat their wives. An olive-skinned youth from one of the Universities stood obsequiously by. Him he would patronise, initiate, teach how to get on. For he liked nothing better than doing kindnesses, making the hearts of old ladies palpitate with the joy of being thought of in their age, their affliction, thinking themselves quite forgotten, yet here was dear Hugh driving up and spending an hour talking of the past, remembering trifles, praising the home-made cake, though Hugh might eat cake with a Duchess any day of his life, and, to look at him, probably did spend a good deal of time in that agreeable occupation. The All-judging, the All-merciful, might excuse. Peter Walsh had no mercy. Villains there must be, and God knows the rascals who get hanged for battering the brains of a girl out in a train do less harm on the whole than Hugh Whitbread and his kindness. Look at him now, on tiptoe, dancing forward, bowing and scraping, as the Prime Minister and Lady Bruton emerged, intimating for all the world to see that he was privileged to say something, something private, to Lady Bruton as she passed. She stopped. She wagged her fine old head. She was thanking him presumably for some piece of servility. She had her toadies, minor officials in Government offices who ran about putting through little jobs on her behalf, in return for which she gave them luncheon. But she derived from the eighteenth century. She was all right.

And now Clarissa escorted her Prime Minister down the room, prancing, sparkling, with the stateliness of her grey hair. She wore ear-rings, and a silver-green mermaid's dress. Lolloping on the waves and braiding her tresses she seemed, having that gift still; to be; to exist; to sum it all up in the moment as she passed; turned, caught her scarf in some other woman's dress, unhitched it, laughed, all with the most perfect ease and air of a creature floating in its element. But age had brushed her; even as a mermaid might behold in her glass the setting sun on some very clear evening over the waves. There was a breath of tenderness; her severity, her prudery, her woodenness were all warmed through now, and she had about her as she said good-bye to the thick gold-laced man who was doing his best, and good luck to him, to look important, an inexpressible dignity; an exquisite cordiality; as if she wished the whole world well, and must now, being on the very verge and rim of things, take her leave. So she made him think. (But he was not in love.)

Indeed, Clarissa felt, the Prime Minister had been good to come. And, walking down the room with him, with Sally there and Peter there and Richard very pleased, with all those people rather inclined, perhaps, to envy, she had felt that intoxication of the moment, that dilatation of the nerves of the heart itself till it seemed to quiver, steeped, upright; —yes, but after all it was what other people felt, that; for, though she loved it and felt it tingle and sting, still these semblances, these triumphs (dear old Peter, for example, thinking her so brilliant), had a hollowness; at arm's length they were, not in the heart; and it might be that she was growing old but they satisfied her no longer as they used; and suddenly, as she saw the Prime Minister go down the stairs, the gilt rim of the Sir Joshua picture of the little girl with a muff brought back Kilman with a rush; Kilman her enemy. That was satisfying; that was real. Ah, how she hated her-hot, hypocritical, corrupt; with all that power; Elizabeth's seducer; the woman who had crept in to steal and defile (Richard would say, What nonsense!). She hated her: she loved her. It was enemies one wanted, not friends-not Mrs. Durrant and Clara, Sir William and

Lady Bradshaw, Miss Truelock and Eleanor Gibson (whom she saw coming upstairs). They must find her if they wanted her. She was for the party!

There was her old friend Sir Harry.

"Dear Sir Harry!" she said, going up to the fine old fellow who had produced more bad pictures than any other two Academicians in the whole of St. John's Wood (they were always of cattle, standing in sunset pools absorbing moisture, or signifying, for he had a certain range of gesture, by the raising of one foreleg and the toss of the antlers, "the Approach of the Stranger"—all his activities, dining out, racing, were founded on cattle standing absorbing moisture in sunset pools).

"What are you laughing at?" she asked him. For Willie Titcomb and Sir Harry and Herbert Ainsty were all laughing. But no. Sir Harry could not tell Clarissa Dalloway (much though he liked her; of her type he thought her perfect, and threatened to paint her) his stories of the music hall stage. He chaffed her about her party. He missed his brandy. These circles, he said, were above him. But he liked her; respected her, in spite of her damnable, difficult upper-class refinement, which made it impossible to ask Clarissa Dalloway to sit on his knee. And up came that wandering will-o'-the-wisp, that vagulous phosphorescence, old Mrs. Hilbery, stretching her hands to the blaze of his laughter (about the Duke and the Lady), which, as she heard it across the room, seemed to reassure her on a point which sometimes bothered her if she woke early in the morning and did not like to call her maid for a cup of tea; how it is certain we must die.

"They won't tell us their stories," said Clarissa.

"Dear Clarissa!" exclaimed Mrs. Hilbery. She looked tonight, she said, so like her mother as she first saw her walking in a garden in a grey hat.

And really Clarissa's eyes filled with tears. Her mother, walking in a garden! But alas, she must go.

For there was Professor Brierly, who lectured on Milton, talking to little Jim Hutton (who was unable even for a party like this to compass both tie and waistcoat or make his hair lie flat), and even at this distance they were quarrelling, she could see. For Professor Brierly was a very queer fish. With all those degrees, honours, lectureships between him and the scribblers he suspected instantly an atmosphere not favourable to his queer compound; his prodigious learning and timidity; his wintry charm without cordiality; his innocence blent with snobbery; he quivered if made conscious by a lady's unkempt hair, a youth's boots, of an underworld, very creditable doubtless, of rebels, of ardent young people; of would-be geniuses, and intimated with a little toss of the head, with a sniff—Humph!—the value of moderation; of some slight training in the classics in order to appreciate Milton. Professor Brierly (Clarissa could see) wasn't hitting it off with little Jim Hutton (who wore red socks, his black being at the laundry) about Milton. She interrupted.

She said she loved Bach. So did Hutton. That was the bond between them, and Hutton (a very bad poet) always felt that Mrs. Dalloway was far the best of the great ladies who took an interest in art. It was odd how strict she was. About music she was purely impersonal. She was rather a prig. But how charming to look at! She made her house so nice if it weren't for her Professors. Clarissa had half a mind to snatch him off and set him down at the piano in the back room. For he played divinely.

"But the noise!" she said. "The noise!"

"The sign of a successful party." Nodding urbanely, the Professor stepped delicately off.

"He knows everything in the whole world about Milton," said Clarissa.

"Does he indeed?" said Hutton, who would imitate the Professor throughout Hampstead; the Professor on Milton; the Professor on moderation; the Professor stepping delicately off.

But she must speak to that couple, said Clarissa, Lord Gayton and Nancy Blow.

Not that *they* added perceptibly to the noise of the party. They were not talking (perceptibly) as they stood side by side by the yellow curtains. They would soon be off elsewhere, together; and never had very much to say in any circumstances. They looked; that was all. That was

456

enough. They looked so clean, so sound, she with an apricot bloom of powder and paint, but he scrubbed, rinsed, with the eyes of a bird, so that no ball could pass him or stroke surprise him. He struck, he leapt, accurately, on the spot. Ponies' mouths quivered at the end of his reins. He had his honours, ancestral monuments, banners hanging in the church at home. He had his duties; his tenants; a mother and sisters; had been all day at Lords, and that was what they were talking about-cricket, cousins, the movies-when Mrs. Dalloway came up. Lord Gayton liked her most awfully. So did Miss Blow. She had such charming manners.

"It is angelic-it is delicious of you to have come!" she said. She loved Lords; she loved youth, and Nancy, dressed at enormous expense by the greatest artists in Paris, stood there looking as if her body had merely put forth, of its own accord, a green frill.

"I had meant to have dancing," said Clarissa.

For the young people could not talk. And why should they? Shout, embrace, swing, be up at dawn; carry sugar to ponies; kiss and caress the snouts of adorable chows; and then all tingling and streaming, plunge and swim. But the enormous resources of the English language, the power it bestows, after all, of communicating feelings (at their age, she and Peter would have been arguing all the evening), was not for them. They would solidify young. They would be good beyond measure to the people on the estate, but alone, perhaps, rather dull.

"What a pity!" she said. "I had hoped to have dancing."

It was so extraordinarily nice of them to have come! But talk of dancing! The rooms were packed.

There was old Aunt Helena in her shawl. Alas, she must leave them-Lord Gayton and Nancy Blow. There was old Miss Parry, her aunt.

For Miss Helena Parry was not dead: Miss Parry was alive. She was past eighty. She ascended staircases slowly with a stick. She was placed in a chair (Richard had seen to it). People who had known Burma in the 'seventies were always led up to her. Where had Peter got to? They used to be such friends. For at the mention of India, or even Ceylon, her eyes (only one was glass) slowly deepened, became blue, beheld, not human beings-she had no tender memories, no proud illusions about Viceroys, Generals, Mutinies-it was orchids she saw, and mountain passes and herself carried on the backs of coolies in the 'sixties over solitary peaks; or descending to uproot orchids (startling blossoms, never beheld before) which she painted in water-colour; an indomitable Englishwoman, fretful if disturbed by the War, say, which dropped a bomb at her very door, from her deep meditation over orchids and her own figure journeying in the 'sixties in India-but here was Peter.

"Come and talk to Aunt Helena about Burma," said Clarissa.

And yet he had not had a word with her all the evening!

"We will talk later," said Clarissa, leading him up to Aunt Helena, in her white shawl, with her stick.

"Peter Walsh," said Clarissa.

That meant nothing.

Clarissa had asked her. It was tiring; it was noisy; but Clarissa had asked her. So she had come. It was a pity that they lived in London-Richard and Clarissa. If only for Clarissa's health it would have been better to live in the country. But Clarissa had always been fond of society.

"He has been in Burma," said Clarissa.

Ah. She could not resist recalling what Charles Darwin had said about her little book on the orchids of Burma.

(Clarissa must speak to Lady Bruton.)

No doubt it was forgotten now, her book on the orchids of Burma, but it went into three editions before 1870, she told Peter. She remembered him now. He had been at Bourton (and he had left her, Peter Walsh remembered, without a word in the drawing-room that night when Clarissa had asked him to come boating).

"Richard so much enjoyed his lunch party," said Clarissa to Lady Bruton.

"Richard was the greatest possible help," Lady Bruton replied. "He helped me to write a letter. And how are you?"

"Oh, perfectly well!" said Clarissa. (Lady Bruton detested illness in the wives of politicians.)

"And there's Peter Walsh!" said Lady Bruton (for she could never think of anything to say to Clarissa; though she liked her. She had lots of fine qualities; but they had nothing in common—she and Clarissa. It might have been better if Richard had married a woman with less charm, who would have helped him more in his work. He had lost his chance of the Cabinet). "There's Peter Walsh!" she said, shaking hands with that agreeable sinner, that very able fellow who should have made a name for himself but hadn't (always in difficulties with women), and, of course, old Miss Parry. Wonderful old lady!

Lady Bruton stood by Miss Parry's chair, a spectral grenadier, draped in black, inviting Peter Walsh to lunch; cordial; but without small talk, remembering nothing whatever about the flora or fauna of India. She had been there, of course; had stayed with three Viceroys; thought some of the Indian civilians uncommonly fine fellows; but what a tragedy it was-the state of India! The Prime Minister had just been telling her (old Miss Parry huddled up in her shawl, did not care what the Prime Minister had just been telling her), and Lady Bruton would like to have Peter Walsh's opinion, he being fresh from the centre, and she would get Sir Sampson to meet him, for really it prevented her from sleeping at night, the folly of it, the wickedness she might say, being a soldier's daughter. She was an old woman now, not good for much. But her house, her servants, her good friend Milly Brush-did he remember her? —were all there only asking to be used if-if they could be of help, in short. For she never spoke of England, but this isle of men, this dear, dear land, was in her blood (without reading Shakespeare), and if ever a woman could have worn the helmet and shot the arrow, could have led troops to attack, ruled with indomitable justice barbarian hordes and lain under a shield noseless in a church, or made a green grass mound on some primeval hillside, that woman was Millicent Bruton. Debarred by her sex and some truancy, too, of the logical faculty (she found it impossible to write a letter to the *Times*), she had the thought of Empire always at hand, and had acquired from her association with that armoured goddess her ramrod bearing, her robustness of demeanour, so that one could not figure her even in death parted from the earth or roaming territories over which, in some spiritual shape, the Union Jack had ceased to fly. To be not English even among the dead-no, no! Impossible!

But was it Lady Bruton (whom she used to know)? Was it Peter Walsh grown grey? Lady Rosseter asked herself (who had been Sally Seton). It was old Miss Parry certainly-the old aunt who used to be so cross when she stayed at Bourton. Never should she forget running along the passage naked, and being sent for by Miss Parry! And Clarissa! oh Clarissa! Sally caught her by the arm.

Clarissa stopped beside them.

"But I can't stay," she said. "I shall come later. Wait," she said, looking at Peter and Sally. They must wait, she meant, until all these people had gone.

"I shall come back," she said, looking at her old friends, Sally and Peter, who were shaking hands, and Sally, remembering the past no doubt, was laughing.

But her voice was wrung of its old ravishing richness; her eyes not aglow as they used to be, when she smoked cigars, when she ran down the passage to fetch her sponge bag, without a stitch of clothing on her, and Ellen Atkins asked, What if the gentlemen had met her? But everybody forgave her. She stole a chicken from the larder because she was hungry in the night; she smoked cigars in her bedroom; she left a priceless book in the punt. But everybody adored her (except perhaps Papa). It was her warmth; her vitality-she would paint, she would write. Old women in the village never to this day forgot to ask after "your friend in the red cloak who seemed so bright." She accused Hugh Whitbread, of all people (and there he was, her old friend Hugh, talking to the Portuguese Ambassador), of kissing her in the smoking-room to punish her for saying that women should have votes. Vulgar men did, she said. And Clarissa remembered having to persuade her not to denounce him at family prayers-which she was capable of doing with her daring, her recklessness, her melodramatic love of being the centre of everything and creating scenes, and it was bound, Clarissa used to think, to end in some awful tragedy; her death; her martyrdom; instead of which she had married, quite unexpectedly, a bald man with a large buttonhole who owned, it was said, cotton mills at Manchester. And she had five boys!

She and Peter had settled down together. They were talking: it seemed so familiar-that they should be talking. They would discuss the past. With the two of them (more even than with Richard) she shared her past; the garden; the trees; old Joseph Breitkopf singing Brahms without any voice; the drawing-room wallpaper; the smell of the mats. A part of this Sally must always be; Peter must always be. But she must leave them. There were the Bradshaws, whom she disliked. She must go up to Lady Bradshaw (in grey and silver, balancing like a sealion at the edge of its tank, barking for invitations, Duchesses, the typical successful man's wife), she must go up to Lady Bradshaw and say...

But Lady Bradshaw anticipated her.

"We are shockingly late, dear Mrs. Dalloway, we hardly dared to come in," she said.

And Sir William, who looked very distinguished, with his grey hair and blue eyes, said yes; they had not been able to resist the temptation. He was talking to Richard about that Bill probably, which they wanted to get through the Commons. Why did the sight of him, talking to Richard, curl her up? He looked what he was, a great doctor. A man absolutely at the head of his profession, very powerful, rather worn. For think what cases came before him-people in the uttermost depths of misery; people on the verge of insanity; husbands and wives. He had to decide questions of appalling difficulty. Yet-what she felt was, one wouldn't like Sir William to see one unhappy. No; not that man.

"How is your son at Eton?" she asked Lady Bradshaw.

He had just missed his eleven, said Lady Bradshaw, because of the mumps. His father minded even more than he did, she thought "being," she said, "nothing but a great boy himself."

Clarissa looked at Sir William, talking to Richard. He did not look like a boy-not in the least like a boy. She had once gone with some one to ask his advice. He had been perfectly right; extremely sensible. But Heavens-what a relief to get out to the street again! There was some poor wretch sobbing, she remembered, in the waiting-room. But she did not know what it was-about Sir William; what exactly she disliked. Only Richard agreed with her, "didn't like his taste, didn't like his smell." But he was extraordinarily able. They were talking about this Bill. Some case, Sir William was mentioning, lowering his voice. It had its bearing upon what he was saying about the deferred effects of shell shock. There must be some provision in the Bill.

Sinking her voice, drawing Mrs. Dalloway into the shelter of a common femininity, a common pride in the illustrious qualities of husbands and their sad tendency to overwork, Lady Bradshaw (poor goose-one didn't dislike her) murmured how, "just as we were starting, my husband was called up on the telephone, a very sad case. A young man (that is what Sir William is telling Mr. Dalloway) had killed himself. He had been in the army." Oh! thought Clarissa, in the middle of my party, here's death, she thought.

She went on, into the little room where the Prime Minister had gone with Lady Bruton. Perhaps there was somebody there. But there was nobody. The chairs still kept the impress of the Prime Minister and Lady Bruton, she turned deferentially, he sitting four-square, authoritatively. They had been talking about India. There was nobody. The party's splendour fell to the floor, so strange it was to come in alone in her finery.

What business had the Bradshaws to talk of death at her party? A young man had killed himself. And they talked of it at her party-the Bradshaws, talked of death. He had killed himself-but how? Always her body went through it first, when she was told, suddenly, of an accident; her dress flamed, her body burnt. He had thrown himself from a window. Up had flashed the ground; through him, blundering, bruising, went the rusty spikes. There he lay with a thud, thud, thud in his brain, and then a suffocation of blackness. So she saw it. But why had he done it? And the Bradshaws talked of it at her party!

459

She had once thrown a shilling into the Serpentine, never anything more. But he had flung it away. They went on living (she would have to go back; the rooms were still crowded; people kept on coming). They (all day she had been thinking of Bourton, of Peter, of Sally), they would grow old. A thing there was that mattered; a thing, wreathed about with chatter, defaced, obscured in her own life, let drop every day in corruption, lies, chatter. This he had preserved. Death was defiance. Death was an attempt to communicate; people feeling the impossibility of reaching the centre which, mystically, evaded them; closeness drew apart; rapture faded, one was alone. There was an embrace in death.

But this young man who had killed himself-had he plunged holding his treasure? "If it were now to die, 'twere now to be most happy," she had said to herself once, coming down in white.

Or there were the poets and thinkers. Suppose he had had that passion, and had gone to Sir William Bradshaw, a great doctor yet to her obscurely evil, without sex or lust, extremely polite to women, but capable of some indescribable outrage-forcing your soul, that was it-if this young man had gone to him, and Sir William had impressed him, like that, with his power, might he not then have said (indeed she felt it now), Life is made intolerable; they make life intolerable, men like that?

Then (she had felt it only this morning) there was the terror; the overwhelming incapacity, one's parents giving it into one's hands, this life, to be lived to the end, to be walked with serenely; there was in the depths of her heart an awful fear. Even now, quite often if Richard had not been there reading the *Times,* so that she could crouch like a bird and gradually revive, send roaring up that immeasurable delight, rubbing stick to stick, one thing with another, she must have perished. But that young man had killed himself.

Somehow it was her disaster-her disgrace. It was her punishment to see sink and disappear here a man, there a woman, in this profound darkness, and she forced to stand here in her evening dress. She had schemed; she had pilfered. She was never wholly admirable. She had wanted success. Lady Bexborough and the rest of it. And once she had walked on the terrace at Bourton.

It was due to Richard; she had never been so happy. Nothing could be slow enough; nothing last too long. No pleasure could equal, she thought, straightening the chairs, pushing in one book on the shelf, this having done with the triumphs of youth, lost herself in the process of living, to find it, with a shock of delight, as the sun rose, as the day sank. Many a time had she gone, at Bourton when they were all talking, to look at the sky; or seen it between people's shoulders at dinner; seen it in London when she could not sleep. She walked to the window.

It held, foolish as the idea was, something of her own in it, this country sky, this sky above Westminster. She parted the curtains; she looked. Oh, but how surprising! —in the room opposite the old lady stared straight at her! She was going to bed. And the sky. It will be a solemn sky, she had thought, it will be a dusky sky, turning away its cheek in beauty. But there it was-ashen pale, raced over quickly by tapering vast clouds. It was new to her. The wind must have risen. She was going to bed, in the room opposite. It was fascinating to watch her, moving about, that old lady, crossing the room, coming to the window. Could she see her? It was fascinating, with people still laughing and shouting in the drawing-room, to watch that old woman, quite quietly, going to bed. She pulled the blind now. The clock began striking. The young man had killed himself; but she did not pity him; with the clock striking the hour, one, two, three, she did not pity him, with all this going on. There! the old lady had put out her light! the whole house was dark now with this going on, she repeated, and the words came to her, Fear no more the heat of the sun. She must go back to them. But what an extraordinary night! She felt somehow very like him-the young man who had killed himself. She felt glad that he had done it; thrown it away. The clock was striking. The leaden circles dissolved in the air. He made her feel the beauty; made her feel the fun. But she must go back. She must assemble. She must find Sally and Peter. And she came in from the little room.

"But where is Clarissa?" said Peter. He was sitting on the sofa with Sally. (After all these years he really could not call her "Lady Rosseter.") "Where's the woman gone to?" he asked. "Where's Clarissa?"

Sally supposed, and so did Peter for the matter of that, that there were people of importance, politicians, whom neither of them knew unless by sight in the picture papers, whom Clarissa had to be nice to, had to talk to. She was with them. Yet there was Richard Dalloway not in the Cabinet. He hadn't been a success, Sally supposed? For herself, she scarcely ever read the papers. She sometimes saw his name mentioned. But then-well, she lived a very solitary life, in the wilds, Clarissa would say, among great merchants, great manufacturers, men, after all, who did things. She had done things too!

"I have five sons!" she told him.

Lord, Lord, what a change had come over her! the softness of motherhood; its egotism too. Last time they met, Peter remembered, had been among the cauliflowers in the moonlight, the leaves "like rough bronze" she had said, with her literary turn; and she had picked a rose. She had marched him up and down that awful night, after the scene by the fountain; he was to catch the midnight train. Heavens, he had wept!

That was his old trick, opening a pocket-knife, thought Sally, always opening and shutting a knife when he got excited. They had been very, very intimate, she and Peter Walsh, when he was in love with Clarissa, and there was that dreadful, ridiculous scene over Richard Dalloway at lunch. She had called Richard "Wickham." Why not call Richard "Wickham"? Clarissa had flared up! and indeed they had never seen each other since, she and Clarissa, not more than half a dozen times perhaps in the last ten years. And Peter Walsh had gone off to India, and she had heard vaguely that he had made an unhappy marriage, and she didn't know whether he had any children, and she couldn't ask him, for he had changed. He was rather shrivelled-looking, but kinder, she felt, and she had a real affection for him, for he was connected with her youth, and she still had a little Emily Brontë he had given her, and he was to write, surely? In those days he was to write.

"Have you written?" she asked him, spreading her hand, her firm and shapely hand, on her knee in a way he recalled.

"Not a word!" said Peter Walsh, and she laughed.

She was still attractive, still a personage, Sally Seton. But who was this Rosseter? He wore two camellias on his wedding day-that was all Peter knew of him. "They have myriads of servants, miles of conservatories," Clarissa wrote; something like that. Sally owned it with a shout of laughter.

"Yes, I have ten thousand a year" —whether before the tax was paid or after, she couldn't remember, for her husband, "whom you must meet," she said, "whom you would like," she said, did all that for her.

And Sally used to be in rags and tatters. She had pawned her grandmother's ring which Marie Antoinette had given her great-grandfather to come to Bourton.

Oh yes, Sally remembered; she had it still, a ruby ring which Marie Antoinette had given her great-grandfather. She never had a penny to her name in those days, and going to Bourton always meant some frightful pinch. But going to Bourton had meant so much to her-had kept her sane, she believed, so unhappy had she been at home. But that was all a thing of the past-all over now, she said. And Mr. Parry was dead; and Miss Parry was still alive. Never had he had such a shock in his life! said Peter. He had been quite certain she was dead. And the marriage had been, Sally supposed, a success? And that very handsome, very self-possessed young woman was Elizabeth, over there, by the curtains, in red.

(She was like a poplar, she was like a river, she was like a hyacinth, Willie Titcomb was thinking. Oh how much nicer to be in the country and do what she liked! She could hear her poor dog howling, Elizabeth was certain.) She was not a bit like Clarissa, Peter Walsh said.

"Oh, Clarissa!" said Sally.

What Sally felt was simply this. She had owed Clarissa an enormous amount. They had been friends, not acquaintances, friends, and she still saw Clarissa all in white going about the house with her hands full of flowers-to this day tobacco plants made her think of Bourton. But-did Peter understand? —she lacked something. Lacked what was it? She had charm; she had extraordinary charm. But to be frank (and she felt that Peter was an old friend, a real friend-did absence matter? did distance matter? She had often wanted to write to him, but torn it up, yet felt he understood, for people understand without things being said, as one realises growing old, and old she was, had been that afternoon to see her sons at Eton, where they had the mumps), to be quite frank then, how could Clarissa have done it? —married Richard Dalloway? a sportsman, a man who cared only for dogs. Literally, when he came into the room he smelt of the stables. And then all this? She waved her hand.

Hugh Whitbread it was, strolling past in his white waistcoat, dim, fat, blind, past everything he looked, except self-esteem and comfort.

"He's not going to recognise *us*," said Sally, and really she hadn't the courage-so that was Hugh! the admirable Hugh!

"And what does he do?" she asked Peter.

He blacked the King's boots or counted bottles at Windsor, Peter told her. Peter kept his sharp tongue still! But Sally must be frank, Peter said. That kiss now, Hugh's.

On the lips, she assured him, in the smoking-room one evening. She went straight to Clarissa in a rage. Hugh didn't do such things! Clarissa said, the admirable Hugh! Hugh's socks were without exception the most beautiful she had ever seen-and now his evening dress. Perfect! And had he children?

"Everybody in the room has six sons at Eton," Peter told her, except himself. He, thank God, had none. No sons, no daughters, no wife. Well, he didn't seem to mind, said Sally. He looked younger, she thought, than any of them.

But it had been a silly thing to do, in many ways, Peter said, to marry like that; "a perfect goose she was," he said, but, he said, "we had a splendid time of it," but how could that be? Sally wondered; what did he mean? and how odd it was to know him and yet not know a single thing that had happened to him. And did he say it out of pride? Very likely, for after all it must be galling for him (though he was an oddity, a sort of sprite, not at all an ordinary man), it must be lonely at his age to have no home, nowhere to go to. But he must stay with them for weeks and weeks. Of course he would; he would love to stay with them, and that was how it came out. All these years the Dalloways had never been once. Time after time they had asked them. Clarissa (for it was Clarissa of course) would not come. For, said Sally, Clarissa was at heart a snob-one had to admit it, a snob. And it was that that was between them, she was convinced. Clarissa thought she had married beneath her, her husband being-she was proud of it—a miner's son. Every penny they had he had earned. As a little boy (her voice trembled) he had carried great sacks.

(And so she would go on, Peter felt, hour after hour; the miner's son; people thought she had married beneath her; her five sons; and what was the other thing-plants, hydrangeas, syringas, very, very rare hibiscus lilies that never grow north of the Suez Canal, but she, with one gardener in a suburb near Manchester, had beds of them, positively beds! Now all that Clarissa had escaped, unmaternal as she was.)

A snob was she? Yes, in many ways. Where was she, all this time? It was getting late.

"Yet," said Sally, "when I heard Clarissa was giving a party, I felt I couldn't *not* come-must see her again (and I'm staying in Victoria Street, practically next door). So I just came without an invitation. But," she whispered, "tell me, do. Who is this?"

It was Mrs. Hilbery, looking for the door. For how late it was getting! And, she murmured, as the night grew later, as people went, one found old friends; quiet nooks and corners; and the loveliest views. Did they know, she asked, that they were surrounded by an enchanted garden? Lights and trees and wonderful gleaming lakes and the sky. Just a few fairy lamps, Clarissa Dalloway had said, in the back garden! But she was a magician! It was a park.... And she didn't know their names, but friends she knew they were, friends without names, songs without words, always the best. But there were so many doors, such unexpected places, she could not find her way.

"Old Mrs. Hilbery," said Peter; but who was that? that lady standing by the curtain all the evening, without speaking? He knew her face; connected her with Bourton. Surely she used to cut up underclothes at the large table in the window? Davidson, was that her name?

"Oh, that is Ellie Henderson," said Sally. Clarissa was really very hard on her. She was a cousin, very poor. Clarissa *was* hard on people.

She was rather, said Peter. Yet, said Sally, in her emotional way, with a rush of that enthusiasm which Peter used to love her for, yet dreaded a little now, so effusive she might become-how generous to her friends Clarissa was! and what a rare quality one found it, and how sometimes at night or on Christmas Day, when she counted up her blessings, she put that friendship first. They were young; that was it. Clarissa was pure-hearted; that was it. Peter would think her sentimental. So she was. For she had come to feel that it was the only thing worth saying-what one felt. Cleverness was silly. One must say simply what one felt.

"But I do not know," said Peter Walsh, "what I feel."

Poor Peter, thought Sally. Why did not Clarissa come and talk to them? That was what he was longing for. She knew it. All the time he was thinking only of Clarissa, and was fidgeting with his knife.

He had not found life simple, Peter said. His relations with Clarissa had not been simple. It had spoilt his life, he said. (They had been so intimate-he and Sally Seton, it was absurd not to say it.) One could not be in love twice, he said. And what could she say? Still, it is better to have loved (but he would think her sentimental-he used to be so sharp). He must come and stay with them in Manchester. That is all very true, he said. All very true. He would love to come and stay with them, directly he had done what he had to do in London.

And Clarissa had cared for him more than she had ever cared for Richard. Sally was positive of that.

"No, no, no!" said Peter (Sally should not have said that-she went too far). That good fellow-there he was at the end of the room, holding forth, the same as ever, dear old Richard. Who was he talking to? Sally asked, that very distinguished-looking man? Living in the wilds as she did, she had an insatiable curiosity to know who people were. But Peter did not know. He did not like his looks, he said, probably a Cabinet Minister. Of them all, Richard seemed to him the best, he said-the most disinterested.

"But what has he done?" Sally asked. Public work, she supposed. And were they happy together? Sally asked (she herself was extremely happy); for, she admitted, she knew nothing about them, only jumped to conclusions, as one does, for what can one know even of the people one lives with every day? she asked. Are we not all prisoners? She had read a wonderful play about a man who scratched on the wall of his cell, and she had felt that was true of life-one scratched on the wall. Despairing of human relationships (people were so difficult), she often went into her garden and got from her flowers a peace which men and women never gave her. But no; he did not like cabbages; he preferred human beings, Peter said. Indeed, the young are beautiful, Sally said, watching Elizabeth cross the room. How unlike Clarissa at her age! Could he make anything of her? She would not open her lips. Not much, not yet, Peter admitted. She was like a lily, Sally said, a lily by the side of a pool. But Peter did not agree that we know nothing. We know everything, he said; at least he did.

But these two, Sally whispered, these two coming now (and really she must go, if Clarissa did not come soon), this distinguished-looking man and his rather common-looking wife who had been talking to Richard-what could one know about people like that?

"That they're damnable humbugs," said Peter, looking at them casually. He made Sally laugh.

But Sir William Bradshaw stopped at the door to look at a picture. He looked in the corner for the engraver's name. His wife looked too. Sir William Bradshaw was so interested in art.

When one was young, said Peter, one was too much excited to know people. Now that one was old, fifty-two to be precise (Sally was fifty-five, in body, she said, but her heart was like a girl's of twenty); now that one was mature then, said Peter, one could watch, one could understand, and one did not lose the power of feeling, he said. No, that is true, said Sally. She felt more deeply, more passionately, every year. It increased, he said, alas, perhaps, but one should be glad of it-it went on increasing in his experience. There was some one in India. He would like to tell Sally about her. He would like Sally to know her. She was married, he said. She had two small children. They must all come to Manchester, said Sally-he must promise before they left.

There's Elizabeth, he said, she feels not half what we feel, not yet. But, said Sally, watching Elizabeth go to her father, one can see they are devoted to each other. She could feel it by the way Elizabeth went to her father.

For her father had been looking at her, as he stood talking to the Bradshaws, and he had thought to himself, Who is that lovely girl? And suddenly he realised that it was his Elizabeth, and he had not recognised her, she looked so lovely in her pink frock! Elizabeth had felt him looking at her as she talked to Willie Titcomb. So she went to him and they stood together, now that the party was almost over, looking at the people going, and the rooms getting emptier and emptier, with things scattered on the floor. Even Ellie Henderson was going, nearly last of all, though no one had spoken to her, but she had wanted to see everything, to tell Edith. And Richard and Elizabeth were rather glad it was over, but Richard was proud of his daughter. And he had not meant to tell her, but he could not help telling her. He had looked at her, he said, and he had wondered, Who is that lovely girl? and it was his daughter! That did make her happy. But her poor dog was howling.

"Richard has improved. You are right," said Sally. "I shall go and talk to him. I shall say goodnight. What does the brain matter," said Lady Rosseter, getting up, "compared with the heart?"

"I will come," said Peter, but he sat on for a moment. What is this terror? what is this ecstasy? he thought to himself. What is it that fills me with extraordinary excitement?

It is Clarissa, he said.

For there she was.